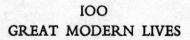

100
GREAT MODERN LIVES

100 GREAT MODERN LIVES

EDITED BY
JOHN CANNING

A Century Book

published by

SOUVENIR PRESS

Souvenir Press Edition 1972
Second Impression 1975
Second Edition 1977

ISBN 0 285 62041 X

Reproduced photolitho in Great Britain by
J. W. Arrowsmith Ltd., Bristol

Contents

CONTENTS

CONTENTS

Illustrations

9

ILLUSTRATIONS

Introduction

No NEWSPAPER STORY is thought to be properly slanted unless it deals in personalities. The most complex themes are stated in terms of particular people. Television reinforces the process by appearing to bring every kind of person, famous or unknown, right into the heart of the home.

At the same time so much happens in the twentieth century that even famous people quickly get forgotten. A new generation does not know what they looked like. Very often it has little incentive to know what they did. As long ago as 1906 a well-known writer complained that "history is made faster than it can be recorded". Given the greatly superior methods of recording, the remark remains true.

To understand the contemporary framework of reference, it is necessary to know about people from all parts of the world and about scientists and engineers as much as about writers and politicians. What is happening has to be placed in its context in space and time. Gandhi, Lenin and Sun Yat-sen are as "relevant" as any people nearer at home might be. Faraday, Edison and Rutherford influence our lives at least as much as any three politicians.

It is a more fascinating and certainly a more controversial task to select which hundred lives deserve special attention than to pick a test team or to choose the hundred best tunes. The selection in this volume is not mine, but it covers a remarkable diversity of talents and an immense store of experience. One man, Faraday, was born in the eighteenth century: a few are still alive. One man, Kennedy, might well have had a far bigger influence on the future than he had on the past. It is interesting to speculate on who will be included in the next "team"—which builders of new African states, for example, which physicists or, among one of the most creative groups of scientists, which biologists?

History is concerned not only with facts but with speculations of this kind and the debates surrounding them. There is still room for new interpretations of Darwin, new discoveries about Dickens, new assessments of Montgomery or Mountbatten. Just as we re-discover and in re-discovering re-mould the First World War, so we can breathe new life into the personalities of the past. Famous people may be quickly forgotten, but people who worked away from the limelight may become far more significant to other people after they are dead than when they were alive.

This book of great lives is for the general reader. At the same time it prompts a basic question for historians. For the most part modern history books are not like newspapers or television programmes. They deal less in personalities than in "themes", "tendencies" and "trends". Some of the complex changes of the twentieth century seem curiously impersonal: others carry with them a sense of inevitability. The growth of welfare states, for example, or the rise of African nationalism or the development of atomic weapons tend to be written about in terms of economic, political and scientific equations rather than in terms of people. When people are brought in, they are often people in the mass. One writer of science fiction, Isaac Asimov, has even suggested that in the future we may have what he calls "psycho-history", history that assumes that "the human conglomerate" being dealt with is sufficiently large for valid statistical treatment. Individual decisions become part of a pattern. The English historian Buckle had a somewhat similar idea in Victorian times. Another eminent Victorian, Goldwin Smith, agreed with him that the age of great men was past. With the American Civil War in mind, he wrote that "a Timon or an Attila towers unapproachably above his horde; but in the last great struggle which the world has seen the Cromwell was not a hero, but an intelligent and united nation".

It is never easy for the historian to separate individual biography from the social and cultural history in which it is enmeshed or to say confidently what would have happened if a particular individual had not appeared in the world at a particular time. The hundred lives described in this volume have all changed history, however, in different, often ambiguous and contradictory, ways. If they had not existed, we could not have invented them. Once they did exist, their influence moves in many different directions. Historians cannot escape the task of assessing individual motives and achievements. There is no other subject which is concerned in quite the same way with "judgments". Each brief biography in this volume, therefore, will best be appreciated if it is thought of not only as a work of reference but as an invitation to further reading and study.

ASA BRIGGS

Editor's Note

THE AIM of this book is simple: to give a view of our times through the lives of some of the people who have most influenced them.

However, what is simple is not necessarily easy, and the problem that has most exercised the editor has been the selection of a mere one hundred names from a huge and brilliant field. Often he has felt like an Olympics judge called upon to nominate a winner in a blanket-finish without recourse to photographs. Such a list is bound to reflect personal predilection, but given this necessary prerequisite he has tried to make it as broadly based as possible; to provide a spectrum of lives as wide as life itself.

He has taken as his criterion of a "modern" life one dealing with a modern theme and the productive part of which has fallen in significant measure, or wholly, in the period from 1850 to the present day. Thus, it may seem strange to see Abraham Lincoln in a list of moderns until it is remembered that the unity of the United States, the preservation of which was the culmination of his life's work, is still threatened today by the issue of racial segregation. Moreover, but for his untimely death he might still conceivably have been living at the turn of this century.

The use of the word "great" to describe these lives has no ethical connotation. It is used in its dictionary meaning of beyond the ordinary in size, scale and significance.

The arrangement of the lives is chronological, in order of the year of birth.

JOHN CANNING

Michael Faraday
1791-1867

MICHAEL FARADAY was born on 22 September, 1791, at Newington Butts on the Surrey side of the Thames—a village in those days, but sufficiently a part of the London "metropolis" to have attracted the blacksmith James Faraday and his young wife all the way down from the Yorkshire moors in search of employment. In this they somehow failed; their resources dwindled, they moved north of the river to a mews near Manchester Square, to Weymouth Street off Portland Square, into smaller and smaller lodgings. Work seemed harder and harder to come by and James's health deteriorated. He died when Michael was nineteen and working as a bookbinder.

Michael's employer, Mr Riebau, was a kindly man. He encouraged the youth to read, gave him time off to attend lectures on natural philosophy which appealed to him. His reading inclined him to science, but as he put it himself, years later:

> "Do not suppose that I was a very deep thinker, or was marked as a precocious person. I was a very lively, imaginative person, and could believe in the Arabian Nights as easily as in the Encyclopaedia, but facts were important to me and saved me. I could trust a fact, and always cross-examined an assertion."

The lectures he attended thrilled him: he made neat notes of everything that was said. In order to learn to draw well enough to illustrate them, he begged lessons from a French refugee artist, Masquerier, in return for which Faraday dusted his room, and blacked his boots. In 1812 he attended the lecture which altered the course of his life. A customer at the bookshop had given him tickets for four of the Royal Institution lectures of Sir Humphry Davy and from the first minute of the first lecture, there could no longer be any question of Michael Faraday remaining a bookbinder.

He wrote to Sir Humphry. The older man, flattered, wrote a gracious reply:

> "I am far from displeased with the proof you have given me of your confidence, which displays great zeal, power of memory, and attention —it would gratify me to be of any service to you; I wish it may be in my power."

As the letter was written on Christmas Eve, 1812, from Davy's study at the Royal Institution, we can assume that it made a welcome Christmas present to the twenty-one-year-old Faraday. He was invited to visit Sir Humphry, who was impressed with the youth and wondered how he could help him. Then came another stroke of good fortune, at least as good as the free tickets to the lecture. Sir Humphry's assistant at the Institution was dismissed for assaulting the instrument maker. Faraday, to his great joy, was offered the post at a salary of twenty-five shillings a week, and two rooms at the top of the house.

In October, 1814, a strange little party left England for France. The two countries were at war, but the Emperor Napoleon, patron of science, had asked Sir Humphry to lecture in France and travel wheresoever he would. Sir Humphry, Lady Davy, Lady Davy's maid and Michael Faraday, the "philosophical assistant", set sail from Plymouth. The party should have numbered five, but at the last moment Davy's valet refused to brave the terrors of France. The unfortunate Michael, to whom Lady Davy had taken an instant dislike, found himself more valet than philosopher. He continued to worship Sir Humphry, but relations with the wife grew daily worse.

Lady Davy disapproved of science (with reason, perhaps, as her husband had taken his chemical chest on their honeymoon) and disapproved of Michael's humble origins. Davy made not-too-energetic efforts to find himself a valet, and failed, but as Faraday admitted, "he required little done for him"; the post was a sop to Lady Davy's snobbery. He gradually got used to it and even found some of his two years of travel exciting and gay. He was present as "philosophical assistant" when Davy, in Paris, discovered the new element, iodine, in a mysterious substance given to him by Monsieur Ampère; he met the great man of electricity, Signor Volta; he found Sir Humphry "a mine inexhaustible of knowledge and improvement", even though the great man wasted too much time on sport. "Many a quail has been killed in the plains of Geneva, and many trout and grayling have been pulled out of the Rhône—"

On their return, Sir Humphry arranged his promotion to a salary of thirty shillings a week. He was free of Lady Davy, he was happy (he could give his mother in Weymouth Street a little money towards sending his sister to boarding school), he resolved to work hard. He was still doing menial laboratory work for Sir Humphry, but when the great man embarked on a second Continental trip, without him, he was able at last to get down to investigations and inquiries on his own behalf. Within a month Davy was writing regularly, hinting strongly that Faraday come out and join him, but Michael wisely refused. He was working hard on his first love, chemistry, isolating compounds of chlorine and carbon, making— without bothering to develop the idea—the first stainless steel.

In 1820, the Danish Professor Oersted noticed the peculiar behaviour of a compass needle when placed near a wire carrying electric current. Sir Humphry, back from the Continent, read of his researches, decided this was remarkable and dropped everything to investigate. Though he was only a little over forty, his powers of observation and deduction were waning, and his young assistant— who had put aside his chemistry to share Davy's research—made the greater progress. Slowly, jealousy grew, culminating some years later in Davy's hysterical attempts to prevent Faraday being elected a Fellow of the Royal Society. For the time being, Faraday was indispensable to Davy. When the former got married, in 1821, Sir Humphry, anxious not to lose him, persuaded the Royal Institution to let him bring his wife back there to live.

In September of that year, Faraday succeeded in making a wire carrying an electric current revolve round the pole of a magnet; if he then reversed the flow of current by reversing the connexions to his battery, the wire revolved in the opposite direction—a clear exposition of the electric motor. He was involved in chemical experiment for the next few years, and it was not until 1831 that he proved the converse, the principle of the dynamo, that an electric current can be produced by magnetism. This later discovery opened a number of doors, making possible not only the dynamo, but every transformer, electric motor or coupled circuit (without which radio and television would be impossible).

In 1830, his "professional business" brought him in more than £1,000. After years of poverty, he had discovered the secret of riches: by accepting a few of the offers from commercial firms that wanted him as adviser, analyst, expert witness, he could raise his income to any figure he chose. In 1831, he was well on the way to making £5,000 (a far larger sum those days than now), when he took his big decision. On 4 July, 1831, which has been rightly pointed out as Faraday's "Independence Day", he wrote the Secretary of the Royal Society in London that he no longer wished to continue the manufacture of optical glass: furthermore, he would give up his professional practice completely. From now on he would devote himself to pure research, to "philosophical inquiry".

In the following year, his earnings, over and above his small salary from the Royal Institution, were £155. They continued to dwindle, and from 1845 until his death twenty-two years later, they ceased to exist.

It has been argued that by cutting himself off from the world of commerce, Michael Faraday held up the techniques of electrical engineering by fifty years. As we have seen, he had invented the dynamo and the electric motor by the end of 1831, but it was a long, long time before anything practical was done with them. If he had remained in touch with the new Industrial Revolution, the age of steam might have yielded sooner to the age of electricity. On the other hand, many researches on the polarization of light and the effect of gravity on it (to be proved years later, by Einstein) might never have taken place.

By 1834 Faraday had further decided to "decline all dining out"; by 1838 he would "close the door for three days a week," see no one. His only contacts with ordinary people, non-scientists, were the lectures he gave at the Royal Institution. He had painstakingly developed a remarkable ability as lecturer, planting friends in the audience to give signals when he spoke too fast, too slow, or too long; some of his talks, taken down in shorthand, are an object lesson for speakers today. Perhaps his most successful lectures were the Christmas ones for young people, which he began at the Royal Institution in 1829. Their fame spread, and though Faraday insisted that children must make up the bulk of the audience, there were always plenty of adults.

Despite Sarah's considerable abilities as wife and housekeeper, the Faradays were extremely poor. He had refused to augment his salary by doing work for manufacturers and the like—it held up pure research—and his salary had stuck at £100 a year. He had discovered that two could not live as cheaply as one. The Prime Minister, Sir Robert Peel, to whose attention this was drawn (not by Faraday, who was shocked by such an approach) agreed that a pension should be granted from the Civil List. "I am sure," Peel said, "no man living has a better claim to consideration from the State." He was promptly defeated in the House of Commons and Lord Melbourne came to power. Faraday was requested to wait upon His Lordship, since for his wife's sake he had agreed to accept a pension, but he presented his case so badly—if he presented it at all—that Melbourne dismissed the suggestion as "humbug", refused to consider a pension. (Faraday, devout member of the small "Sandemanian" religious sect, was unwilling to note in his Journal the word that preceded "humbug", merely mentioning that it was "theological".) The scientist's friends refused to accept this refusal and made direct application to King William IV. William (in tears, it is said) overruled Melbourne and granted a pension of £300 a year.

A knighthood was offered, which Faraday refused: "I must remain plain Michael Faraday to the last." By now he was a man of substance, if not of wealth, having become head of the Royal Institution's laboratory when Davy retired. Though he refused to work commercially, he accepted a permanent appointment as scientific adviser to Trinity House, the body in charge of English lighthouses. He found his lighthouse-visiting a stimulus as well as relaxation and it drove him on to produce the first one lit by electricity.

At the age of fifty he suffered a severe nervous breakdown and for four years, until 1845, his researches stopped. Then he recovered his faculties. It was after an enforced rest in Switzerland (though Sarah wrote from that country, "he thinks nothing of walking 20 miles in a day; one day he walked 45, which I protested at his doing again—") that he turned his energies to the effect of magnetism on light, found that a beam of light would bend in a strong magnetic field. He also revealed that matter—all matter—was magnetically affected.

"It is curious to see such a list as this of bodies presenting on a sudden this remarkable property, and it is strange to find a piece of wood, or beef, or apple, obedient to or repelled by a magnet—"

Having proved that oxygen was "paramagnetic" or attracted by a magnet, he went on to present an elaborate memoir using this phenomenon to explain magnetic variation at different points on the earth's surface—a remarkable piece of reasoning and the only one of his theories which has been disproved: there are too many factors of which we know today, which Faraday was unable to take into consideration: cosmic rays, the Heaviside layer, sunspots. At the same time, he did important research on ionization, coining a whole new vocabulary of words like "anode", "cathode" and "ionization" itself, words now in common useage.

As he grew older, he continued his research, but became more famous for his lectures. As the British *Quarterly Review* put it, "to grey-headed wisdom he united wonderful juvenility of spirit—" There is a coloured lithograph of him at the Royal Institution, lecturing to a rapt audience which includes the Prince Consort with the Prince of Wales and Prince Alfred. So hypnotized was the young Prince of Wales, who sat down afterwards and wrote Faraday, "I hope to follow the advice you gave us—" that but for the distractions of monarchy he might have devoted his life to it.

Michael Faraday—still "plain Michael Faraday"—died peacefully in his study on 25 August, 1867. Perhaps the words in our own time of the physicist Sir William Bragg, best sum up his achievement: "Prometheus, they say, brought fire to the service of mankind; electricity we owe to Faraday."

Lord Shaftesbury
1801–1885

A BOY from the famous school was walking down Harrow hill when he was startled by shouts and yells coming from a side street. He stopped to see what was the matter, and there came round the corner a gang of men carrying between them a rough wooden coffin. One of the bearers slipped, the others staggered, and the coffin fell to the ground with a heavy thud. Whereupon the men broke out into the foulest curses.

The boy was appalled. "Can this sort of thing be permitted just because the man whose corpse they are carrying to the grave was poor and friendless?" Such was his horrified reflection, and he was never able to obliterate the incident from his memory. Nearly seventy years later, when that schoolboy had become an old man, he happened to be walking along that same street with the son of his former headmaster. "Can your lordship remember any particular incident or occasion which induced you to dedicate your life, as you have done, to the cause of the poor and wretched?" asked his friend. The reply was prompt and unhesitating: the decisive incident that had marked out his career had been the witnessing of that poor man's funeral. "Within ten yards of the spot where we are now standing I first resolved to make the cause of the poor my own." Let us take a closer look at the speaker, as boy and then as man.

Anthony Ashley Cooper was the eldest son of the 6th Earl of Shaftesbury, and was born on 28 April, 1801. In 1811, when his father succeeded to the earldom, he received the courtesy title of Lord Ashley, and by this title he was known until 1851, when on his father's death he became the 7th Earl. Thus he was born to a great and honourable name, to wealth and great possessions. But his early years were most miserable. His father was hard and cold to his children, harsh and sometimes cruel to his tenants, while his mother was devoted to the life of fashion and aristocratic society. Deprived of parental love and care, often neglected and always lonely, he found a friend in his old nurse who had become the housekeeper. This Maria Millis was a simple country-woman, of little education but of deep religious faith. She read to him the grand old Bible stories, and taught him his prayers. Alas, she died when he was away at school. She left him her gold watch—her one and only treasure—in her will. He wore it, and none other, to the day of his death. He used to show it proudly, and say: "That was given to me by the best friend I ever had in the world."

At the age of seven he was sent to boarding-school. It must have been a horrible place. He said it was very similar to Dotheboys Hall in *Nicholas Nickleby*, and to the end of his days he could never recall it without a shudder. After five years he was removed to Harrow, where things were ever so much better. Then to Oxford, where he did well, better than had been expected. After several years there he entered Parliament, as was the way then with the heirs to great titles, as M.P. for a "pocket borough". He sat as a Conservative. He was never what is called a good party-man. He was far too much of an individual for that, far too self-centred, far too convinced (after careful meditation and solitary prayer), that *his* way was right. Far above any question of party or political advantage he put his religion. He told Edwin Hodder when he was writing his life:

"My religious views are not very popular but they are the views that have sustained and comforted me all through my life. I think a man's religion, if it is worth anything, should enter into every sphere of life, and rule his conduct in every relation. I have always been—and, please God, always shall be—an Evangelical of the Evangelicals . . ."

As a member of Parliament he made a poor beginning. He spoke in so low a voice that the reporters complained that he was quite inaudible. But the occasion was significant. He was seconding a Bill to amend the Lunacy Laws. Thus his first effort was on behalf of what were then, and long remained, the most miserable and neglected and ill-treated of all the unfortunates of the British scene. He was downspirited by his poor showing, but some of his colleagues bade him cheer up—he would do better next time. Would there be a next time, he wondered; was he on the right road? Was he really cut out for this sort of thing? Why not keep quiet and let things run their course? That night he wrote in his diary, as was the custom with him for all his many years: "By God's blessing my first effort has been for the advancement of human happiness. May I improve hourly!"

The Bill he had supported became law, and soon after Ashley was appointed to the new body of Commissioners in Lunacy, and eventually became their chairman. He took his duties seriously. On more than one occasion he horrified the House with an account of the dreadful things he had witnessed on visits of inspection to the asylums.

He reported once:

"One of the first rooms we went into contained nearly a hundred and fifty patients, in every form of madness, a large proportion of them chained to the wall, some melancholy, some furious. We went into a court, where there were fifteen or twenty women, whose sole dress was a piece of red cloth, tied round the waist with a rope; many of them with long beards, covered with filth; they were crawling on their knees . . . I do not think I ever witnessed brute beasts in such a condition, and this had subsisted for years . . ."

Lunacy was an unpleasant subject, and most people were careful to avoid it. Everybody knew that lunatics existed, and perhaps such novelists as Wilkie Collins, in his *The Woman in White*, were right in maintaining that sane people sometimes got put away by relatives who had an eye on their property. But why worry? Ashley *did* worry. Time and again he rescued people from asylums who ought never to have been put there—and this was one of the very few pieces of business that he, a most confirmed Sabbatarian, was prepared to do if necessary on a Sunday. All through his life he laboured unceasingly to improve the conditions of the mentally afflicted. For *fifty years* he was a Commissioner in Lunacy, and he was still one when he died. In the records of British philanthropy there are some fine things to be discovered, but there is nothing to surpass, or even equal, *that*.

Not that it is his labours in this particular field that are most often remembered. One of the first of the social iniquities that he assailed was the employment of little children in the coalmines, where they worked for seldom less than twelve hours a day and were subjected to the most brutal treatment. Another was the employment in the mines underground of women, nearly as naked as the men beside whom they toiled. When at length, thanks very largely to Ashley's efforts, the Mines Act of 1842 was on the statute book, he turned his attention to the condition of the women and children working in the textile factories. For years he was the spokesman in Parliament of the movement aiming at the restriction of the hours of labour of factory operatives to ten hours a day, and although he was temporarily out of Parliament when the Bill was passed in 1847, his share in the tremendous struggle was generally acknowledged.

Another field of social advance in which he played a prominent and most honourable part was the public health movement. When after years of agitation the first Public Health Act was passed in 1848 Ashley was one of the members appointed to serve on the Central Board of Health, and he strove manfully to see that the ever-growing towns were supplied with drains and water supply and other necessities of civilized living.

Another of his long battles was on behalf of the chimney-sweep children. As long before as 1773 Jonas Hanway, inventor of the umbrella, had exposed the abominations resulting from the demand for small boys to sweep the chimneys of the houses of the well-to-do. An Act of 1788 had prohibited the employment for the purpose of boys below the age of eight, but it had soon become a dead letter. Little boys were still being apprenticed to brutal sweeps in 1837 when Dickens wrote *Oliver Twist*, and as late as 1863 Charles Kingsley made a climbing-boy the central figure of his *Water Babies*. Time after time Bills were introduced into Parliament to prohibit the practice, but most of them completely failed. Machines had been invented to do the work and builders had been urged to design chimneys that were easier to clean; but boys were cheaper than the machines—what matter if they *were* maltreated, were beaten mercilessly, became victims to a special form of skin cancer, and sometimes were suffocated and died? The years passed, and case after case of near-murder failed to shake public complacency. Ashley first championed the boy slaves in 1840. Thereafter in face of disappointment after disappointment, he kept up the fight. At last, but not until 1875, he was able to get this horrible evil banished from our life. "Had he done nothing else in the course of his long life," wrote J. L. and Barbara Hammond in their life of him, "he would have lived in history by this record alone."

Where now shall we follow him in his philanthropic exertions? Into the Ragged Schools? It is hard to believe that in 1843, little more than a century ago, there were haunts of utter misery and infamy in the greatest and wealthiest city in the world. One of the worst dens of the down-and-outs was in Field Lane, off Holborn, and here in 1841 some people associated with the London City Mission had started what came to be known, from the condition of the adults and children who were induced to attend it, as a Ragged School.

After it had been going for a couple of years those in charge put an advertisement in *The Times* appealing to the Christian public for support. Lord Ashley read the appeal, and at once offered his help. It was gladly accepted, and from that moment to the end of his life he threw himself heart and soul into the movement that had for its object the rescue and the restoration of the lowest of the low, the poorest and most downtrodden and hopeless, of the most vicious of London's population. In all his vast correspondence there were no letters he prized so greatly as those from men and women who had been rescued from a life of deprivation and destitution, and often crime, and had been enabled to emigrate to the Colonies where they had managed to make good.

Among members of his own rank and class, Shaftesbury was often ill at ease, and they often looked at him with suspicion, sometimes with dislike. He was a peer of the realm, a man who had been offered more than once a seat in the Cabinet, who had been spoken of as a possible leader of the Conservative Party—yet he mixed openly with social misfits and outcasts and sinners! Why, he seemed to prefer the company of the ragged waifs and strays of the London streets to that of the rich, powerful and cultured. He had been known to treat even a streetwalker with respect. He *would* interfere in what was surely none of his business; he *would* poke his nose into dark corners of society and haul out into the light of broad day things which were so ugly they had far better remain hidden. Then there was his religion: so uncompromising, so old-fashioned! Why, he believed every word of the Bible to be absolutely true and lived in constant hope of the Last Day! If it came soon, he had been heard to say, how much human misery might be spared!

Shaftesbury was not indifferent to the things that were said about him; on the contrary, he felt them deeply, for he was a most sensitive man. But he never swerved from what he believed was the right path. What if some people thought him a bit of a humbug? What if they sneered at his old-world views, criticized him for his cantankerousness, blamed him for being so difficult to work with? He knew his duty, and he did it to the very best of his ability.

Two things sustained him on his way. The first, and above all most important, was his religious faith, of which something has been said above. The second was his marriage. In 1830 he married Lady Emily Cowper, daughter of Earl Cowper and niece of Lord Melbourne, the famous Prime Minister of the early years of Queen Victoria's reign. Her family thought it a poor match. "What has poor Min done to deserve to be linked to such a fate, and in a family generally disliked, reputed mad, and of feelings, opinions, and connections directly the reverse of ours?" wrote one of her uncles when he heard of the proposed match. "The Girl has no fancy for him and what the Devil there is in its favour I am at a loss to perceive, except his being what you call in love with her and a Person as you think to be fallen in love with."

Ashley *was* in love with her, and, strange though it might appear to her worldly-minded relations, she was in love with him. For over forty years she was his constant companion, ever at hand to give him solace, help, advice, support. When she died in 1872 he confided to his diary that she had been "the purest, gentlest, kindest, sweetest, and most confiding spirit that ever lived".

One of the strangest consequences of his marriage was that it brought him into close contact with Lord Palmerston, who had married his wife's widowed mother. In almost everything Ashley and Palmerston were opposed, in politics, in attitude to religion and in way of life. Palmerston was something of a "gay dog" to the end of his long life, but he was a consummately able statesman, and he was quick to appreciate the excellent qualities of his stepson-in-law. For years he relied upon Ashley's advice in the choice of Church dignitaries and other important appointments he had to make as Prime Minister. Ashley for his part had a deep regard for the old man who in so many vital respects was his opposite.

So his years passed. From 1828 until his death on 1 October, 1885, there was never a time when he was not engaged in some worthy cause. In the Victorian scene there was no figure better known than the tall, slender, pale-faced, side-whiskered man in the braided frock-coat who seemed as indifferent to the cheering crowds that packed the halls to hear him speak as to the backbiting and worse of the members of his own class and order. One of his last expressed wishes was that he might "die in harness", and the wish was granted.

When his funeral procession passed through London to the service in Westminster Abbey it was accompanied by representatives of scores of societies and movements with which he had been most intimately connected. Vast crowds lined the streets to watch it go by, and to pay a last tribute of reverence and love. Even the poorest of the poor had somehow managed to procure some little piece of black to wear upon coat-sleeve or bonnet.

"Simply an old man who had endeavoured to do his duty in that state of life to which it has pleased God to call him:" that is how he described himself not long before his death. As a boy he had made a vow—and through seventy years he kept it.

Ralph Waldo Emerson
1803-1882

Young though America was in terms of nationhood in the middle decades of the nineteenth century, she was nevertheless producing men of great quality in almost every sphere of human activity. This was certainly true of the arts, and in the small band of giants, which included Whitman, Mark Twain and Longfellow, must be also included Ralph Waldo Emerson.

Emerson was a poet, essayist and philosopher, but it was as essayist that he excelled. His verse, often marked with penetrating thought and lofty conception, is for the most part lacking in beauty of form or music. His philosophy is that of the moment's consideration rather than of any fully developed scheme. His essays and lectures, on the other hand, place him at the head of American thinkers of his generation.

ON Election Day, 25 May, 1803, the Reverend William Emerson, minister of the First Church of Boston, Massachusetts, arrived home to be told the news that at a quarter past three in the afternoon, his fourth child, a son, had been born. Four days later, he recorded in the baptismal record of the parish the child's names—Ralph Waldo.

When Ralph was two weeks short of his eighth birthday, William died of a tumour of the stomach. Fortunately, the great qualities which their minister had brought to his work were so much appreciated by his congregation that they gave practical recognition of it by granting to his widow a stipend of five hundred dollars a year for seven years.

It was not much on which to bring up her surviving five children, but it stood between her and penury. And since they had also granted her the use of the parish house for a year or two, her immediate problems could be solved by well-planned housewifery.

On his ninth birthday Ralph entered the Boston Public Latin School, and joined, as a contemporary put it, "the most intractable and turbulent fellows, sixty or seventy in number, that ever met together to have Latin and Greek hammered into them".

The headmaster, William Biglow, followed teaching methods not unreminiscent of Mr Squeers's in Dotheboys Hall. Demanding a definition of an active verb, he would bring down his cane on a boy's haunches, exclaiming: "I'll tell you what it is. It expresses an action and necessarily an agent and an object which can be acted upon. As *castigo te*—I chastise thee. Do you understand now, boy?"

It would have been difficult for any but the least intelligent or pupils not to have gained some knowledge by these means, and Ralph was by no means unintelligent. He made good progress in learning the Classics, and equal progress in writing and cyphering under the tuition of Rufus Webb at the South Writing School. In his approach to learning and to the other aspects of life, he was a normal boy. Very often he played truant, and when caught took his punishment philosophically; if attacked, he fought back, and usually with such ferocity that he got the better of his opponent.

Though she might have stayed in the parish house longer had she wished, Mrs Emerson decided that life in the hurry and bustle of war-threatened Boston was too much for her, and in 1814 she took her family to Concord, where her husband's grandmother and step-grandfather offered her a home in the Old Manse. Concord at that time was a quiet village, and must have seemed a peaceful haven after the activity of the Massachusetts capital.

Ralph attended the grammar school, which was very different from the Boston Latin School. Here he continued to make progress, though, except in one particular, he does not seem to have been outstanding for a boy of his age. For some years he had been developing a love of poetry, and had already produced several poems of his own. Within the next six months his verses were to demonstrate that he had, at all events, mastered the metrical mechanics of the heroic couplet, even if the results were stiff and conventional in rhythm and diction:

> This morning I have come to bid adieu
> To you my schoolmates, and, Kind Sir, to you;
> For six short months my lot has here been cast,
> And oft I think how pleasantly they've past.

These lines open what he called *Valedictory Poem Spoken at Concord*, and they were written and spoken in March, 1815, on the day before the family returned to Boston, on the decision of Mrs Emerson, who found life at the Old Manse too restricting even for her.

The Latin School was now under a new headmaster, Benjamin Gould. He was very different from Biglow, and though he drove his pupils hard while they were at lessons, he also believed that time for relaxation was necessary "for the preservation of health and elasticity of mind".

Gould took a keen interest in Ralph, and was determined that the family's penury should not stand in the way of his going to college. To this end he visited the President of Harvard College, at Cambridge, a few miles from Boston, and persuaded him to accept the boy as his freshman, provided, of course, that Ralph successfully passed the entrance examination, of which there could be no doubt.

So in 1817, at the age of fourteen, Ralph Emerson became a student at "the oldest university on the American continent north of Mexico". Here he remained until 1821, at no time exhibiting any academic distinction. The fact is that he just reached the standard required for graduation.

Mrs Emerson was struggling, as she always seemed to be doing, to make sufficient money from taking paying guests to keep her family subsisting. So it was necessary that young Waldo should find a job quickly: in the circumstances there seemed only one profession open to him, and he approached Gould in the hope of obtaining an usher's post at the Latin School.

As there was no opening, he accepted an offer from his oldest brother William in the school which the latter had opened "for the education of Young Ladies".

By now he was insisting on being called Waldo instead of Ralph. (Of his family, only his mother could remember to do so.)

Waldo Emerson had no illusions about his efficiency as a teacher. He found that his female pupils were, quite unconsciously, a constant embarrassment. He made up his mind to escape "from our common Purgatory", and soon was planning to return to Harvard to study theology and to follow his father into the Church.

This he eventually achieved in 1825 and two years later he was admitted to the Congregational ministry. For two years he had no church of his own, but acted in the capacity of "supply preacher", going wherever a minister was needed owing to the temporary absence of a regular minister. In March, 1829, he was appointed Minister of the Second Church in Boston. Some time before, he had fallen in love with Ellen Tucker, and now that he could offer her a home, he asked her to marry him. For a little more than a year they lived a deeply satisfying, deeply happy life, which was violently disrupted, however, when Ellen contracted tuberculosis and died after a short illness on 8 February, 1832. She was nineteen.

The appointment to the Second Church had meant a fairly arduous régime for Emerson. Shortly after his arrival there, a new vestry had been completed, and the minister was required to give a series of thirty-six lectures on St Matthew's Gospel by way of inauguration. He found it a tedious undertaking, and it was in the preparation of these lectures that doubts as to the validity of some of the Christian precepts began to assail him. These doubts came to a head in the year following his wife's death, and soon he found himself in a position when he could not in honesty continue with his ministry. He would have liked to have devoted all his time to writing, but he was wise enough to realize that the money he would make from his literary work until he had established himself would not be sufficient to keep him.

Ellen Tucker's family were wealthy. Her father had died a year or two before her marriage, and when she came of age she stood to benefit from her father's estate to a quite sizable amount. Waldo approached the executors and Mr Tucker's widow and surviving children arguing that as Ellen Tucker's husband he was entitled to benefit from the estate as though his wife were still alive. Mrs Tucker was sympathetic, but the executors could not fall in with her or Emerson's wishes without legal sanction. So the matter was brought before the courts.

Before it was resolved, his religious doubts were doubts no longer. In June, 1832, he wrote to the committee of the church to inform them of "a change in my opinions concerning the ordinance of the Lord's Supper, and recommending some change in the mode of administering it". Exactly what change he wanted has never been made clear, but it is thought that he wished to be relieved of his own part in the rite as the Celebrant. Emerson was not the first Congregational Unitarian to have such doubts. His own father had been concerned on much the same points, and had once put forward a plan to liberalize its observance, but nothing came of it. Most Unitarians wished to keep the Sacrament as a sacred feast, but many were uneasy about the form of performance of the rite.

The committee reported to Emerson that after deep consideration of his proposals, they could not recommend that they should be adopted or any change be made, and on receiving their communication, he went off by himself to think over his personal situation, and to prepare an explanatory sermon for his congregation. Illness prevented his preaching the sermon until 9 September. In it he gave a simple but full exposition of his views, and concluded with the statement that though he would be content to let others observe the Lord's Supper until the end of the world, he could not personally continue to do so any longer. This statement could lead only to one thing. The church committee met on 28 October, and by a majority decided that their minister must leave them. He took formal leave of them three days before Christmas.

To recover his health he decided on a voyage to Europe, and for the next ten months he visited Italy, France and England returning to America in October, 1833. During his absence, the courts had decided in his favour, and he was to receive the two-thirds of the Tucker estate which would have come to his wife had she lived. Early in the following year he was financially secure.

It was, perhaps, a natural step to go from the pulpit to the lecture platform. So, late in December, 1833, he inaugurated his new career with a lecture *On the Relation of Man to the Globe*. This contained echoes of his foreign travel, and there were hints of a theory of evolution. This he followed with a series on natural history, and two lectures on Italy. At the same time he began writing his first essays, and was nearing the completion of his first book *Nature*. Though his popularity as a lecturer was immediate and of such a kind as to prompt him to continue with this way of making money, his literary work made slow progress towards recognition.

In 1835 he had settled in Concord, and had invested a good deal of the money he had received from the Tucker estate in property. It was to the house which was to be his home for the remainder of his life that, in the same year, he brought his second wife, Lydia Jackson.

By this time, Emerson and his circle of intellectual friends had become interested in the work and views of the German philosophers Kant, Fichte and Schelling, and under the influence of their teachings, they formed themselves into a group calling themselves the Transcendentalists. Put briefly, their beliefs—known as Transcendentalism—stated the dominance of intuition over reason. More particularly, Transcendentalism was a revolt against American Puritanism, and was to develop socially and economically into Socialism, and theologically into Unitarianism and mysticism, while at the same time strengthening the anti-slavery movement and literary romanticism.

Emerson became the leader of the group, which attracted large numbers of young men of progressive ideas and ideals, and as a result there was an almost ceaseless pilgrimage to Concord of such visitors eager to talk and argue with the chief exponent of Transcendentalism. Among them were Henry Thoreau, to become famous as a naturalist, and who was subsequently to make his home with the Emersons until his death in 1862; a friendship which was to play a great part in Emerson's life.

It was the writings and activities of the Transcendentalists which

were primarily responsible in bringing Emerson and his own ideas
and philosophy to national, and later, international prominence. In
1840 the group founded a journal, *The Dial*, through which to
propagate their ideas. From its inception, Emerson wrote extensively
for it, and when, in 1841, his *Dial* essays were collected into book-
form, they were to make him widely famous.

Between that date and 1847, when the first volume of his poems
was published, his reputation grew rapidly. In the autumn of the
latter year he revisited England and gave a series of lectures on
Representative Men, which, when published later as a book, added
to his fame. His ideas provoked much discussion among the intellectuals of most nations, and great, though not bitter, controversy
was always centred on him. In the controversy he took no part, but
was content to expound his thought with unremitting determination.

In his personal life, the death of his oldest son at the age of six was
a great blow to him, and the death of Thoreau twenty years later an
even greater blow. He tried to convince himself as he faced each of
the tragedies that he should not grieve, since this was contrary to his
belief that "life was optical, not practical"; but both had a considerable influence on his thought.

He suffered another blow of equal force when his home in
Concord was burned down in 1872. Though the house was rebuilt
and he was to live another ten years, he never recovered from the
shock. He continued his lecturing because he needed the money,
though as he put it in his poem *Terminus*, the "god of bounds" had
come to him and said:

> "No more!
> No farther shoot
> Thy broad ambitious branches, and thy root.
> Fancy departs: no more invent;
> Contract thy firmament
> To compass of a tent."

By degrees his powers faded, so that when he attended the funeral
of Longfellow in 1881, he did not know whose house he was in and
did not recognize the features of the man in the coffin, explaining,
"That gentleman was a sweet, beautiful soul, but I have entirely
forgotten his name."

His own end was now approaching. In the spring of 1882 he
contracted pneumonia, and four weeks before his seventy-ninth
birthday he died. On 30 April, 1882, he was buried in the cemetery
of Concord known as Sleepy Hollow.

Above: A contemporary picture (1871) shows a school-board inspector and a policeman apprehending London ragamuffins; another (*right*) shows Shaftesbury in a Black Country pit observing conditions at first hand. It was to banish this sort of squalor and degradation that Shaftesbury devoted his life.

Charles Dickens not only created one of the richest stores of "characters" in the English language, but was also instrumental through his writings in bringing about many improvements in the harsh conditions of nineteenth-century life. That he is as popular to-day as ever is witnessed by the musical adaption of his novels for the stage and the number of his works presented on television. Two musicals deriving from Dickens and that have recently enjoyed success on stage or film are *Pickwick*, the name part being played by Harry Secombe (*right*), and *Oliver* (*below:* Fagin and the Boys).

Giuseppe Garibaldi
1807-1882

ON the barren isle of Caprera, off the coast of Sardinia, an Italian soldier stands guard over a granite tomb. It is the tomb of a warrior, but not an unknown one for, hewn out of the granite, is a single word: *Garibaldi*. For all Italians that one word is enough because, more than any other name, Garibaldi symbolizes the making of their modern nation.

Yet the hero of a united Italy was born a French citizen and christened Joseph Marie; his birthplace was Nice and the date 4 July, 1807, so Garibaldi came into the world as a subject of Napoleon I. Since Nice reverted to the kingdom of Piedmont in 1815 and his parents were Italian, he not unnaturally regarded himself as having that nationality.

His father was a ship's captain and Giuseppe, as he soon called himself, went to sea as a cabin boy when he was sixteen and quickly showed great prowess as a sailor. It was in a Marseilles waterfront café that he first heard of an ideal that was to shape for him a glorious future—the ideal of a united Italy. He was twenty-six and in that year, 1833, the peninsula was still suffering from the aftermath of Napoleon. Under the Congress of Vienna in 1815, Austria had acquired domination of the Italian states, all of which were ruled by absolute monarchies which set about the ruthless extermination of revolutionary ideas about Liberty, Fraternity, Equality. It was in this explosive situation that the seeds of liberation through the idea of a united Italy were sown by another Giuseppe—Mazzini, who set about organizing his own secret society ("Young Italy") towards that goal. Garibaldi joined him and, when their revolutionary plot misfired, found himself sentenced by Piedmont—in his absence—to be "ignominiously executed".

Finding a ship about to sail for Rio de Janeiro, he prudently signed on as second mate and transferred himself from the old world to the new. He was not long in discovering a branch of "Young Italy" in Rio. His letters of that period show that he was fretting for action and, in May, 1837, he got it in the shape of a revolution in Brazil. Garibaldi was soon up to his neck on the side of the revolutionaries and it was while in command of one of the rebel ships that the first of a long procession of women entered his life, or, rather, he entered hers—forcibly.

She was Anita, the wife of a fisherman, and Garibaldi carried her off to sea with him. Whether or not he did this (as his autobiography seems to suggest) by force of arms, she turned out to be a worthy match for his buccaneering courage. She was, in fact, a virago of a woman fighting alongside him, carbine in hand, or loading cannon for his crew. Garibaldi called her his "Brazilian Amazon".

A fortnight after he had sailed off with his prize, the three ships under his command were sunk by the enemy and Garibaldi, with Anita and his co-revolutionaries, fled overland. When she gave birth to his first child, Menotti, on 16 September, 1840, Garibaldi was so hard up he could buy her nothing. At last it dawned on him that the revolutionary cause was irretrievably lost and that he had spent five dangerous and profitless years fighting for it. He made for Montevideo and had to take a job as a commercial traveller for spaghetti. Later he got a post in a school as a teacher of maths and history. In March, 1842, he went through a ceremony of marriage with Anita—thus being a party to bigamy.

Garibaldi settled in Uruguay and before long found himself plunged into a new war when the independence of that republic was threatened by its powerful neighbour, the Argentine. He got busy organizing an Italian Legion to defend Montevideo—its colours (a black flag with a volcano in the centre) and its uniform (the red shirt) were destined to become famous all over Europe two decades later.

The resistance of little Uruguay against her mightier aggressor captured the attention of Europe. Britain and France sent fleets and expeditionary forces. Montevideo, thanks to a victory by Garibaldi's Legion, was saved and a grateful country offered him promotion to general—a title he refused at that time, but made use of later on his return to the European scene.

In June, 1846, the death of the illiberal and much-hated Pope Gregory raised hopes in Italy that the era of liberty was at last dawning, especially when his successor, Pius IX ("Pio Nono") instituted a few trifling reforms. Garibaldi, now thoroughly disenchanted with South American politics, sent his wife, who had borne him three more children, to Europe to prepare the way for his return to Italy. In April, 1848, he sailed from Uruguay in the *Speranza*, taking with him sixty or so legionaires, some out-of-date weapons and a growing reputation as a gallant leader in adversity.

During the voyage exciting reports reached him of Europe in ferment, with revolts everywhere and especially in Italy. Several of the absolute monarchs were forced to grant their restless subjects constitutions. To his delight, he was given a hero's welcome by his old townspeople in Nice, now in the possession of Piedmont.

Recruits flocked to join his Legion and, after a week in Nice, he marched with 150 Legionaires to Genoa, bearing on high the two flags of Italy and Savoy. Soon Garibaldi learned that Charles Albert, the ruler of Piedmont, had taken on the Austrian Army, been defeated, and had accepted a humiliating armistice. Promptly he issued a proclamation in which he denounced the king as a traitor and declared that he and his volunteers would carry on the war against Austria. In the campaign that followed he proved himself a brilliant guerrilla leader. Although he had no chance of final victory over the Austrians, with a handful of men he successfully held up their advance and his reputation spread among all those who longed for the unification of the peninsula.

The problem was where to exercise his talents most effectively for the cause. Eventually he fixed his sights on Rome after the assassination of the Pope's strong man, Count Pellegrino Rossi, had scared the Pontiff into fleeing from the Holy City to Naples, and where, on 29 December, 1848, a junta, which had assumed power, ordered the election of a Constituent assembly on the basis of universal suffrage.

Rome had thus become the first city of Italy to achieve self-government and the Pope quickly appealed to France, Spain, Austria and Naples to suppress the new republic. Garibaldi offered his services to the provisional government but the politicians there, as everywhere else in Italy, were chary of his widespread popularity and were inclined to regard the penniless general and his ragged followers as "a plague of locusts". However he was given the rank of lieutenant-colonel in the Roman Army and authority to maintain a force of not more than 500 men.

Garibaldi, with the help of his volunteers, got himself elected as a deputy to the Constituent Assembly, forced the new War Ministry to raise the number of his troops to 1,000, stationed them fifty miles from the city and proceeded with the essential work of training and equipping them for action.

In March, 1849, Charles Albert of Piedmont denounced his armistice with the Austrians and led his troops to rescue Lombardy from their clutches. He was roundly defeated and abdicated in favour of his son, Victor Emmanuel II. This disaster meant that Rome could look for no allies among the Italian states. A triumvirate was formed to rule the city, with Mazzini the chief.

Louis Napoleon, later to become Napoleon III of France, was the first to answer the Pope's call to Rome. On 25 April, a French fleet anchored at Civita Vecchia and put 8,000 troops ashore. When the French columns marched on Rome, expecting to be welcomed as deliverers, they were met by a hail of grapeshot. Realizing that they would have to fight their way in, the French commander took the engagement a little more seriously, but not seriously enough. Garibaldi's ragged army put the French to flight.

As soon as he heard of the French defeat, King Ferdinand of Naples who was now sheltering the person of the Pope, sent 20,000 men to win Rome back for his guest. Garibaldi, with half that number, put the Neapolitan Army to rout.

He wanted to follow up his retreating enemy but was recalled to Rome by Mazzini. There he found a French diplomat, Ferdinand de Lesseps (later to become famous because of his plan for the Suez Canal) concluding an armistice under which the French forces would defend the Roman Republic from the Austrians who were approaching the city from the north.

Napoleon, however, had no intention of abiding by the armistice. His commander, General Oudinot, repudiated it in a brief note, then launched a surprise attack on the city. Despite the fantastic gallantry of Garibaldi and his men, the city fell and Garibaldi, with his wife, Anita, by his side, was on the run once more.

On 31 July, 1849, from the tiny Republic of San Marino he wrote his last Order of the Day to the remnants of his band:

"Soldiers, I release you from your duty to follow me. Return to your homes, but remember that Italy remains in slavery and shame. The Roman War for the independence of Italy has ended."

Disdaining safety for himself, he embarked with a couple of hundred men, to join the defence of Venice against the Austrians. By now his every movement was reported to the enemy and he was forced ashore; still with Anita, he fled inland. She was pregnant again and the long ordeal of retreat proved too much. She died as the Austrians were approaching the house in which her husband had taken refuge and he had to flee, asking the villagers to give her an honourable burial.

Garibaldi himself found final refuge in the house of the Sardinian consul at Tangier—he discarded his red shirt for black velvet, a symbol of mourning for his Anita and his Italy. He decided that, for the time being, the Italian states were too hot for him so, in June, 1850, he sailed for New York. He felt lonely and lost in America, even working as a labourer in a candle factory while he waited hopefully for someone to buy a ship he could command. At length he was put in charge of a 400-tonner, the *Carmen*, which he sailed to China.

By 1854 he felt he must return to Piedmont and on his way he spent a short time in London—long enough to become engaged to a wealthy English widow, Mrs Emma Roberts. However, her way of life soon bored him—footmen were available to attend to his every wish and dinner lasted three hours. So back he went to Nice to rejoin his children.

In 1855 his brother died and, with money inherited from the estate, he bought half the island of Caprera and took shares with Mrs Roberts in a ship, the *Emma*, which was soon wrecked off the Sardinian coast. Garibaldi tried to settle down as a farmer on Caprera. His engagement to Mrs Roberts petered out as a succession of women entered his life—first a fisherman's daughter, Battistina, whom he carried off from Nice to keep house for him on his island; next an English author whom he always called Speranza; and eventually there was a disastrous marriage with Giuseppina Raimondi, daughter of a marchese, whom he cast out within an hour of the wedding ceremony.

While Garibaldi was tilling the unrewarding soil of Caprera the plotters of Europe were busy. Count di Cavour was now Prime Minister of Piedmont and, with the connivance of his king, Victor Emmanuel, he arranged with the Emperor of France that France and Italy should make war on Austria in the spring of 1859. They even worked out the carve-up when the war had been won. This included the cession of Nice and the Savoy to France. These arrangements were destined to call Garibaldi away from the quiet life on Caprera.

In December a Piedmontese ship called to transport him from his island to Genoa where he had a secret interview with Cavour. As a result he burned for action, believing that the hour for uniting his country had struck. He set about the task of enrolling once more his faithful volunteers and even had a battle hymn written for them. For the first time he had a face-to-face interview with his king, Victor Emmanuel. On 26 April, the war with Austria began—strictly on Cavour's schedule.

The role assigned by Cavour to Garibaldi in this conflict was very different from what the general imagined. His value to the cause, the statesman had decided, was propagandist—to keep public morale high: he had no intention of allowing him to make any significant contribution to the action and thus enhance his glory.

By visiting Victor Emmanuel and receiving carte blanche to go where he liked with his volunteers, Garibaldi frustrated this design—and the result was a series of impressive victories over the Austrians. His progress through the country was marked with astonishing scenes of enthusiasm—Garibaldi was welcomed as a deliverer and major prophet. To the rejoicing crowds he gave this message: "Come, follow! I promise you weariness, hardship and suffering. We will conquer or die." His reputation had another effect: it caused the Austrians to abandon positions they might easily have held. He was summoned by his king to Milan where he received the Gold Medal for valour, the highest decoration Piedmont had to offer.

For him that was to be the high point of the war—the rest was anti-climax as the politicians saw to it that he was kept out of the limelight. There followed the spectacular French victory at Solferino, after which Napoleon III staggered the world by making peace with the Austrians. The result was that Italy could now become a confederation of states under the presidency of—the Pope.

The Treaty of Villafranca which followed the war gave Tuscany, the Romagna and Modena their independence and Garibaldi was made commander of their united army. He found the politics of that post frustrating and resigned after a few months. He launched a Million Rifles subscription fund with the slogan: "Let Italy arm herself and she will be free." The weapons bought with the money that poured in were stored in Milan for future use.

Soon the fire of revolt flared up in Sicily and gave Garibaldi the opportunity he had been praying for. His expedition to that island in two old steamers with 1,089 of his men aboard and their subsequent triumphs over the 20,000-strong Neapolitan Army—the best trained and equipped in the peninsula—are probably the highlights of his fantastic career.

They set out on 5 May, 1860, despite the unscrupulous opposition of Cavour and his government, and by the end of July Garibaldi was master of all Sicily and had freed the Straits of Messina for invasion of the Kingdom of Naples. Although Cavour redoubled his efforts to spike Garibaldi's guns—the foxy statesman had no wish for his country to be ruled by "adventurers and Communists" he lost that round, too, for by 7 September, the incredible general had won the city.

Garibaldi's final victory over the Neapolitans at the Battle of the Volturno river brought his king, Victor Emmanuel, post-haste to the scene, glittering in a uniform jingling with medals and at the head of his fresh Piedmontese Army. Garibaldi, in a sweat-stained red shirt, his poncho thrown loosely about him and a coloured kerchief binding his hair under a floppy hat, rode forward to meet him. Sweeping off his hat, the veteran of a hundred actions said: "Greetings to the first King of Italy."

It soon became plain that the king and his troops were there to steal Garibaldi's thunder—and the credit. The general was ordered to withdraw his volunteers from the line. Victor Emmanuel did not review the Redshirts or visit the wounded in hospital. He did, however, quickly occupy the throne so recently vacated by the King of Naples. He offered Garibaldi many honours—the princeship of Calatafimi, a castle, a dowry for his daughter, and a steam yacht. Garibaldi refused them all.

As soon as this Ruritanian comedy was over Garibaldi sailed sadly away to his island of Caprera, leaving his conquered territories to the none-too-tender mercies of Victor Emmanuel and Cavour. By this time he was crippled by arthritis and exhausted by his campaigns. For months he rarely left his peasant's cottage which had only three rooms and a kitchen. His bedroom furnishing consisted of an iron bedstead and a chest of drawers. It would be hard to find in history a hero who asked so little for himself.

Gathered around his humble home, however, were a number of faithful disciples who meant more to him than rich furnishings. And to that mosquito-plagued isle travelled the great ones of Europe as well as the little people of Italy—to do homage, or to urge high adventure upon him: including an emissary from America who wanted him to join the Army of the North in the Civil War. Indeed, the North's defeat at the battle of Bull Run on 21 July, 1861, provoked Abraham Lincoln to invite Garibaldi's services. He was ready to accept the invitation but only if there was a declaration for the abolition of slavery. Without it, he said, "it is only a civil war with which I have no sympathy".

Meanwhile his compatriots were pleading with him not to go to America but to complete the work of unifying Italy with a march on Rome. He was not to know that he had passed the zenith, the apogee of his career as a warrior and liberator. Other campaigns that lay ahead for him and his volunteers were all either ill-fated, or ill-advised—including a disastrous invasion of the Papal States to win Rome which was promptly crushed by Napoleon's forces, and a later intervention on the French side of the Franco-Prussian war once his arch-enemy Napoleon had been replaced by a Republican government. Garibaldi himself considered his French campaign to be his finest hour and, indeed, Victor Hugo told the French Assembly that Garibaldi was the only French general never to be defeated in that war.

When the tumult and the shouting that followed the Franco-Prussian conflict had died, back went Garibaldi to Caprera—to write his memoirs and his views on a score of controversies. In 1875 the Italian Assembly voted him a gift of a million lire and an annual pension of 50,000 but it took a year of hard persuasion before he accepted it. In 1880 the Civil Court of Appeal in Rome had at last granted an annulment of his 1860 marriage to the Marchesa Raimondi and he was married, in his seventy-third year, to Francesca who had arrived on Caprera as a wet nurse to his grandchild. After the ceremony he left his island only twice.

On 2 June, 1882, Garibaldi got Francesca to prop him up to see the evening sky from his window. Two birds landed on the sill. "Let them stay," he said (according to the version given by Francesca's daughter, Clelia). "Perhaps they are the spirits of my two dead children come to carry me away." A few minutes later the great warrior, glorious liberator of Italy, and old lion of Caprera breathed his last.

Abraham Lincoln
1809-1865

IT was Good Friday, 14 April, and a glorious spring day—sixth day of peace. Crowds still milled round the White House, hoping for a glimpse of the President who had led them safely through four years of civil war. He had appeared once today, smiling over his beard, a huge rugged giant of a man. People hoped he might wave the captured Confederate flag again, as he had done the day General Lee surrendered at Appomattox, but he had been in his office all morning. There had been a cabinet meeting at eleven and it was believed Lincoln had insisted on lenient treatment for the defeated South, and in particular for their army. Certainly he had signed pardons after lunch, one for a convicted Confederate spy, another for a Union deserter: "I think the boy can do us more good above ground than under . . ." Later he had been seen going for a drive with Mrs Lincoln, and, as many people knew their relations were strained, this, no less than the superb weather, was considered a good omen for the great man's second term of office, only just beginning.

The sun had set, the clear, bright evening had given way disappointingly to fog, as the Lincoln coach drew up outside Ford's Theatre, where Laura Keen was performing in *Our American Cousin*. It was half past eight as Charles Forbes, the White House coachman, drew rein. They were late, but it had been understood they would be, there had been so much business to be done, so many people to see. The play stopped, the audience cheered, as the party entered the theatre and were led by an usher to their flag-draped box. Major Rathbone and Miss Harris, the President's two young guests, were given front seats in the box; Mrs Lincoln sat a little behind them; and the President, exhausted, just able to smile, to wave at his ovation, slumped into a rocking chair at the back. By the third act, he had begun to enjoy the play: he was rested, relaxed. He leant forward and Mrs Lincoln smiled, touched his hand.

Someone approached Forbes the coachman, who was sitting on the aisle, outside the Presidential box, handed him a note. Forbes showed him in.

What followed was a confused dream, a nightmare: a shot was

41

heard, but muffled so that people argued later whether they had heard one or not; there were sounds of scuffling in the box; the play stopped. A small blue cloud of smoke drifted through the air and a young man leapt from the flag-hung parapet of the box and crashed down on the stage. People screamed. The man seemed to have broken his ankle—it was hardly surprising, few men would have attempted the leap—and he stood there for a moment nursing it, then waved his fist, shouted something, and was gone.

The President had been shot through the head. There was very little bleeding, he was still alive. Tenderly, he was carried out of the theatre across the street to the humble house of William Peterson, a tailor, and there placed diagonally on a bed—diagonally, because of his great height. Doctors were summoned, did their best: throughout the night he was given stimulants, but those around the bed could see it was hopeless. Mrs Lincoln wept in a front room, members of the Cabinet filed past her, shook their heads.

Dawn broke in the street outside, and at 07.22 on the morning of 15 April, 1865, Abraham Lincoln died.

John Wilkes Booth, supporter of the Confederate cause, but first and foremost a crank, frustrated actor, starved of the success he felt his looks, his voice, his athletic ability deserved, was run to earth and shot in a barn a few days later.

Lincoln had been born, 12 February, 1809, in a backwoods cabin three miles south of Hodgenville, Kentucky, the son of a small farmer, Thomas Lincoln, and his wife, Nancy. The family moved to Knob Creek, forty miles south of Louisville, when he was two, and he lived there for five years. The food was coarse, as were his clothes, which were cut out by his mother from the skins of animals his father shot, but the old Cumberland Trail from Louisville to Nashville passed the door of their home and young Abe watched fascinated as pioneers with covered waggons and livestock headed for the North-west. Now and then he saw and wondered at slaves, tied together, trudging behind a man on a horse.

School, too, was a joy, but a privilege granted only when Thomas Lincoln felt he could spare Abe or his elder sister from their chores— which was seldom.

When the boy was seven the Lincolns set out again, in search of new farmland. They travelled to Indiana on horseback, the four of them, fording the Ohio River to reach the Indiana shore. Here the country was wilder: grapevines laced the trees, the woods seemed almost solid. Thomas had to go ahead on foot hacking at vines and branches with his knife. The place abounded in animals: squirrels, raccoons, deer, wolves. Turkeys flew croaking from between the horses' feet—and there were huge, unkind, mosquitoes.

Sixteen miles from where they had forded the river, the Lincolns chose a site, and Thomas threw up a "half-faced camp", a shelter of logs, enclosed on only three of its sides, with a fire constantly burning on the fourth to keep warmth inside, animals out. For their first winter in their new home, the Lincoln family subsisted entirely on game, but they were gradually hacking out a clearing, preparing to stake a claim to land. Eventually Thomas laid claim, at the nearest government office, to a total of one hundred and sixty acres, and paid the first instalment of eighty dollars, a quarter of the purchase price.

The following year a disease, believed to be spread by cattle which ate a poisonous weed, a disease called "milk sick" spread over the expanding neighbourhood, killing many of the new settlers, including Mrs Lincoln. Abe had always been fond of her, but when Thomas went back to Kentucky in the winter of 1819 and got himself another wife, a widow, Sarah Johnston, with three young children of her own, he and his sister fell completely in love with her. She brought order out of the chaos, the dirt and poverty of the Lincoln home; took the motherless children to her heart; saw to it that all five children went to school.

The neighbourhood swelled as others moved in. Abe grew tall and angular, immensely strong, famed as athlete and clown, could mimic preachers and the itinerant politicians of the State with an accuracy that brought screams of laughter. He was believed to be lazy, everything seemed so effortless to him, but he was—and no one could deny it—a voracious reader, always ready with an apt quotation.

At seventeen, he got a job helping to operate a ferry at Anderson Creek. He was paid thirty-seven cents a day, a poor wage even in those days, but he loved to watch the pageant of riverboats go up and down the Ohio—stately steamboats with paddlewheels, scows, flatboats, comic rafts, laden with all sorts of people, all sorts of cargo. At nineteen he decided to investigate the river, left his underpaid work and contracted to take a cargo to New Orleans, a river journey on Ohio and Mississippi of over a thousand miles.

New Orleans, as he'd hoped it would be, was the most exciting place he had seen: there was wealth such as no man could dream of. People shouted in French, in Spanish, in Portuguese and other tongues—and all of them, Lincoln noted, seemed to be shouting at slaves—tired, patient black men, loading and unloading cargoes of cotton, tobacco, sugar. He returned, and, as was the custom, handed over the twenty-four dollars he had earned, to his father.

In 1830 the family moved again, to Illinois, and shortly after this Abe decided to cut loose. He was twenty-one, a man. He set off in a boat with two friends to deliver more cargo to New Orleans. On his return to Illinois he took a job as storekeeper in New Salem. It was here that he first found himself involved in politics: he was made clerk of the local election. By 1832 he had decided to enter politics himself—if politics would have him. He canvassed the neighbourhood as a candidate for the Illinois State Legislature and was heavily defeated. He returned to New Salem, became postmaster, then tried again in 1834 and was elected, top of the poll. By this time, the first and only real love of his life—according to his friends—had come and gone. He had fallen in love with Ann Rutledge. Though attracted by Lincoln, she had believed herself engaged to another man, and he had not pressed his suit. The man jilted her; she died—and Lincoln, friends said, never got over the loss.

He had been studying law in his spare time and he entered practice with a partner, but as both he and partner were more interested in politics than law, the business failed.

In 1842, after a long and tempestuous courtship, he married Mary Todd, an aristocratic girl from Kentucky. She was in many ways an unsuitable wife, though they were often happy in each other's company: she was vain, jealous, extravagant. A year after the marriage he entered into a successful law partnership with William H. Herndon, a man whom Mrs Lincoln—probably because her husband admired him—loathed from the outset. Despite this their friendship and their partnership lasted until Lincoln's death. In 1846 Mary, anxious to get out of Springfield, Illinois, drove Abe to stand for election as Congressman. He was elected, and in 1847 the Lincolns went to Washington to take his seat.

Ever since his first visit to New Orleans, the question of slavery had nagged at him. Now he introduced a bill with the modest intention of abolishing it within the tiny District of Columbia, but it was flatly rejected. At the end of the Congressional session he returned, discouraged, to Springfield, and was not too upset at not being re-elected. From now on he would be a good lawyer. He buckled down to the partnership, became a familiar sight in Springfield, dressed in black, wearing the high hat in which he crammed his legal documents. He became famous on the Illinois circuit, a brilliant speaker and an absolutely incorruptible man: he lost interest in politics.

In 1860 the new Republican party nominated him, while he continued his law work in Springfield, as their candidate for the Presidency. The Democrats had split on the question of slavery, the Republicans stood a good chance of winning. Lincoln was surprised and delighted; Mrs Lincoln was overjoyed. The distinguished Republican politicians forming the delegation that got off the train at Springfield to notify the nominee officially, were doubtful: he received them in his modest parlour and they were distressed at his ill-fitting clothes, sad, embarrassed look. When they had finished, Lincoln replied. The delegation was spellbound: he looked odd— but, my, how the man could speak! As they left the Lincoln home, Judge Kelley turned to another of his delegation and said:

"Well—we might have done a more brilliant thing—but we certainly couldn't have done a better thing."

It was during the campaign that followed, that Lincoln was invited—in order to "look more dignified"—to grow a beard. He objected, saying it would be a "piece of silly affectation", but was persuaded.

The scene was set for civil war. Extremist politicians in the South warned their voters that Republican victory would mean the plundering of the South for Yankee benefit—and the end of slavery. The South was angry, restless. It was not the question of economic loss if slaves were freed—after all, not many white people owned them—it was the spectre of black savages claiming equal rights with white men, ousting them from jobs, outvoting them. Slavery gave the poorest white a status: the black man was always below him.

Lincoln was elected on 6 November, 1860, and as they had threatened, the Southern States gave trouble. South Carolina seceded from the Union on 20 December, Mississippi, Florida, Alabama, Georgia and Louisiana followed suit. Texas left on 1 February, 1861, a month before Lincoln's inauguration—yet it seemed these seven might be the only ones: the other "slave states" might remain loyal. On 12 April, South Carolina bombarded Fort Sumter; war began and the remaining Southern States seceded. Lincoln, loath to join in, called for 75,000 volunteers: President Jefferson Davis of the newly declared Confederacy demanded 100,000 to oppose them.

The war went stubbornly on. The North, underrating its opponents, was trounced at the Battle of Bull Run, then settled down to serious fighting. Lincoln had trouble finding generals. Only one, Ulysses S. Grant, seemed to have any ability. When it was objected that Grant was a heavy whisky drinker, Lincoln retorted that he wished he could give the same whisky to his other generals. Six months before war ended, Lincoln won his second Presidential election, a huge victory, with 212 electoral college votes against 21 for his Democratic opponent. His second term began on 4 March, 1865, three weeks after his fifty-sixth birthday; and six weeks after that he was assassinated.

The whole nation, North and South, mourned his death with a deep, stunned, sense of loss. Now that he had gone, men realized his greatness; a figure unique in American history. Without formal education, he had revealed himself as one of the finest orators of his time and a great statesman; a man of infinite courage and patience, with a difficult, at times almost unbearable, private life, who yet managed to display a sense of humour, could see the other man's point of view, whether he were rich or poor, white or black. By his death he helped to heal the wounds between North and South, to ease the transition from slavery to the freedom for which he had worked.

Charles Darwin
1809-1882

No intellectual battle of the nineteenth century was fought upon so wide a front, nor stirred up so much bitterness and grief among individuals, as that which followed upon the publication of Charles Darwin's *Origin of Species* in 1859, in which he set out his theory of evolution. Few writers in any field have come under such attack or been made the subject of so much abuse as Darwin.

The main cause of the attacks was a general misunderstanding of his theory among laymen and churchmen, who believed that by rejecting the story of the Creation as set out in Genesis, he was denying the whole truth of Scripture. To confess to being a Darwinian was to confess to being an atheist, and all such converts were made objects of scorn by the opponents of the theory.

Happily, while the battle raged, more thoughtful people were studying the new philosophy more closely and were coming to the conclusion that despite the fact that it conflicted with many accepted theological dogmas, the evidence in its favour could not be denied.

Gradually, over the years, people began to see that the acceptance of evolution did not detract one whit from the previously held view of the Creator of Genesis, since creation by continuously operating laws was no less a wonderful demonstration of power than creation by one miraculous act.

It is true to say that no other nineteenth-century discovery had such widespread effect on men's thought as Darwin's theory of evolution.

ON a June day in 1858, a field naturalist called Charles Darwin received a letter from another field-naturalist, Alfred Wallace. Accompanying the letter was a copy of an essay by Wallace entitled "Essay on the Tendency of Varieties to depart indefinitely from the Original Type".

As Darwin read the essay he felt himself being more and more overcome with astonishment and disappointment, for it was as though he were reading an account of a theory of his own on which he had been working for the last twenty-one years.

He chided himself for not listening to his friends' advice which they had been proffering him these past half-dozen years or more, to publish his own theory. He had made excuses for not doing so, and now the warnings of his friends of what would happen had become fact—someone else had beaten him to the post.

His first reaction was to publish Wallace's essay, and accept failure. But for the insistence of his friends that he should do no such thing, it might have been Alfred Wallace who achieved fame as the originator of the theory of evolution. It was Wallace who accepted failure, and by one of the greatest acts of generosity known among scientists, almost entirely forgotten now, he withdrew his own theory and gave the field completely to Darwin.

Charles Darwin had been born at Shrewsbury on 12 February, 1809. His father was a successful doctor, but not a man of any great learning. He certainly had no interest in natural history beyond the plants in his own garden, and his interest in these sprang only from the fact that they gave pleasure to his eye.

Charles's grandfather, Erasmus Darwin, also a doctor, was, however, a naturalist, a poet and a philosopher. In his day he even put forward a theory of evolution—which his grandson was later to reject—and it seems clear that it was from his grandfather that Charles inherited his great interest in natural history.

This interest he first showed at the age of eight. He spent the greater part of his time collecting birds' eggs and plants, over which he spent hours of study to try to discover their names and their characteristics. At the same time he was exhibiting an almost equally keen interest in geology and added to his other collections one of stones and pebbles.

It was more or less taken for granted that he should follow the example of his father and elder brother and become a doctor. To this end after a very unsatisfactory seven years at Shrewsbury school he was sent to study medicine at Edinburgh. This second attempt to educate him also failed. It soon became clear that he was not destined to become a doctor. He continued, however, to increase his private study of natural history and his knowledge.

After two years at Edinburgh, his father bowed to the inevitable, and it was decided that Charles would become a clergyman. He did not object to the idea, for he realized that such work would give him the time to continue his pursuit of natural history.

Before he could be ordained, it was necessary for him to acquire a degree, and in 1828, he entered Christ's College, Cambridge. His failure at Shrewsbury to acquire any formal knowledge, particularly of the classics, became only too clearly apparent; though he did manage to leave the university with an ordinary degree in 1831, by this time his zeal for natural history had convinced him that he must devote all his time to its study. So all thought of ordination was put away.

Fortunately, a stroke of good fortune came his way. For some years past the Admirality had been surveying the coastline of South America, and the brig, H.M.S. *Beagle* was being fitted out to continue this work. Captain Fitzroy, in command of the new expedition, was in need of a young naturalist, and through a Cambridge friend, was put in touch with Darwin, who accepted with alacrity the proposal that he should join the *Beagle*; and against his father's wishes, he set out with Captain Fitzroy on 27 December, 1831. They did not return for four years.

When he had set out, Darwin had had no idea of what the opportunities offered would be. The discoveries he made were to amaze him; and it was certainly on this voyage that the problem of species developed in his mind. In La Plata he saw strange breeds of oxen; in another place he found the tooth of a fossilized horse; in Patagonia he made other fossil discoveries; in the Galapagos, he noted that every island had its own variety of bird.

On his return from the expedition, he settled in Cambridge, and since he knew that his share of his father's fortune would make it unnecessary for him to earn his living, he decided to devote his life to the study of science. His stay at Cambridge was, however, brief, and in 1837, he moved to London, and there wrote an account of his part in the voyage of the *Beagle*, which, on publication attracted no attention at all.

He now formed a friendship with Charles Lyell, who was later to become a noted geologist, and with him studied geology. The friendship was to be lifelong.

Within a short time, however, his health began to break up. The more than ordinarily robust young man who had served in the *Beagle* became a nervous wreck. It is thought that his illness sprang from psychological causes, for it was accompanied by a strange change in his character. He lost all his delight in poetry and music, and became a prey to an emotional instability.

Nevertheless, in January, 1839, he married his cousin, Emma Wedgwood, and for the first few years lived with her in London. Since his physical condition grew no better, in 1842 they moved to the secluded Kentish village of Down, where they were to live until Darwin's death.

Despite his health, however, he managed to perform an amazing amount of work. He wrote a number of geological studies and continued his own pursuit of the subject. By degrees he became more and more attracted to the problem of changing of species. In 1854 he decided to devote his whole mind to the study of this problem, and set himself the task of answering such highly important questions as: Had each species been created separately? Or were they connected with some common species? Or should each race be regarded as a separate species? What, in fact, is a species?

As he pored over all the facts that he had discovered for himself and had learned from other sources, by degrees he became convinced that there must be in nature a process similar to that which Malthus had put forward in his great essay *On Population*, in which he had asked the question, "Why do some men survive and others perish?" and had reached the conclusion that "The fittest survive".

Darwin called this process in Nature, Natural Selection; and he made it the foundation stone of his theory of evolution.

Put briefly, his theory was this. Many species of living creatures were not, as had been generally supposed, the result of special and individual acts of creation, but had developed from slight differences in individuals. These differences had quite often been brought about originally by the individual's special surroundings in which he found himself existing, and once formed, were perpetuated and indeed accentuated and increased in his descendants. This latter was brought about through the general struggle for existence, as a result of which struggle the fittest survived, this leading, in turn, to a natural selection in breeding.

When he explained his theory to scientist friends, he was able to convince them all that he had made not only an exciting discovery, but one of the most important scientific discoveries of all time. They urged him to publish his theory, but as we have seen, for one reason or another he delayed. Then came Wallace's essay.

The solution which his friends offered to his dilemma was that he should read Wallace's essay together with extracts from his own work to a learned society, called the Linnean Society. To this Wallace agreed, and then insisted that he should withdraw from the field, leaving it open to Darwin.

The reading to the Linnean Society, which took place on 1 July, 1858, met with lukewarm interest from its learned members. The views put forward were too novel and unexpected for any opposition to be raised immediately.

With the example of Wallace before him, Darwin realized that he must publish his work quickly lest he should be again forestalled, and some thirteen months later, in November, 1859, he published an abbreviated form of his theory entitled *The Origin of Species by means of Natural Selection, or the Preservation of Favoured Races in the Struggle for Life*, which became shortened to the *Origin of Species* or just *The Origin*.

If the members of the Linnean Society had been taken off their guard, the wider audiences of *The Origin* were not. It was quickly realized that here was a revolutionary idea of the first magnitude. The first edition was sold out on publication day; within a few years it had been translated into almost every civilized language.

Much of its success must be attributed to the fact that it was a highly controversial subject. The apparent attack on the validity of the Scriptures, written in a non-scientific language which the layman could understand, caused an uproar in Church circles, which merely made more people want to read the work.

It is difficult to appreciate in the mid-twentieth century the bitterness which the controversy provoked. While the opponents of the theory purported that it was the slur on the Creator which they most resented, what actually upset the vain, respectable Victorians was their mistaken view that Darwin was saying that they were descended from monkeys.

On all sides, Darwin was attacked by intelligent men who ought to have known better. The Press, seizing on the misunderstanding of Darwin's basic concept, added furious fuel to the fires of debate. Only the great scientists like T. H. Huxley and Charles Lyell were found in support, and they because they could evaluate the evidence which Darwin set out. Huxley was his chief champion. A powerful writer, a brilliant debater, a man possessing vast stores of zoological knowledge, he set about the critics with gusto, and it was largely owing to his efforts that sense was eventually brought to bear.

While the storm raged, Darwin remained silent, making no attempt to answer his detractors. In this he was wise, for besides lacking the physical resources which involvement in such controversy demands, he had not the gift of debate. He had, besides, faith in the rightness of his views, and seemed to appreciate that in time they would generally be accepted.

He continued with his work, and in 1868 published the full statement of his theory in *Variation of Animals and Plants*. In 1871 he tried to correct the mistaken views of the critics in a book called *Descent of Man*. The book aroused no further storm; all the fire had been applied to the earlier attacks, and only a few feeble rumbles were heard.

As the years passed, he made public the results of his further studies from his seclusion at Down. It is pleasant to be able to relate, that he lived to see his theories widely accepted, and to accept honours bestowed upon him by learned bodies, though no official recognition came from his Government. In 1881 his health deteriorated, and in December of that year he suffered a heart-attack while calling on a friend. Such attacks became more and more frequent, and he died on 19 April, 1882.

He had wished to be buried in Down churchyard, but at last the country made a gesture of recognition to his greatness, and he was buried in Westminster Abbey, just a few feet from that other great scientific discoverer, Isaac Newton.

Charles Dickens
1812-1870

THE blow fell on his twelfth birthday. Till then he had been certain that, somehow, he was destined for success. After all, he had read everything he could find on his father's extensive bookshelves, he had spent a wonderfully happy year soaking up knowledge like a sponge from Mr Giles's little school in Chatham, he had been acknowledged a clever lad, with a future. Now, on 7 February, 1824, when the family had come back to London and his father's fortunes had taken another of their sudden turns for the worse, he learnt he was being sent out to work. The family made light of it, behaved as if the job in the blacking factory was as good as a grammar school education, but young Charles found the blacking factory—where he had to seal the bottles and put labels on them—was overrun with rats which ran squealing over his feet while he worked. The factory was at the edge of the river, the rotten floor was slimy, the air cold and damp and permeated by nauseous smells. He was utterly miserable.

A fortnight after he had started work in this hateful establishment, the next blow fell. His father was arrested for a £40 debt and bundled off to the Marshalsea, the debtors' prison. Charles had to go before an appraiser and have the clothes on his back, the coppers in his pockets, his silver wrist watch, valued, for his father's total assets were appraised at just £10. However much the family tried, their possessions could not reach the sum of £40 and John Dickens was settled into his new home with every likelihood of a long stay. For a time his wife tried to carry on the household by pawning spoons, one by one, but eventually she gave up the struggle and moved into the Marshalsea with him.

Charles was in steady employment at Warren's Blacking Factory, and he did not enter the Marshalsea with the rest of his family: by his mother's arrangement, he lodged in Camden Town. Most of his wage—a shilling a day—went on this lodging. There was nothing over for transport and he had to walk daily from Camden Town to the river and back. On Sundays he would call for the only other member of his family who was not incarcerated, his sister Fanny at the Royal College of Music, and take her to spend the day in prison with their parents.

After three months, the family were able to pay their £40 debt and were released from the Marshalsea. John Dickens had dabbled in journalism and now, having mastered shorthand in prison, was able to indulge his whim of becoming a parliamentary reporter. The earnings from this enabled him to send Charles to school again, in London. The boy had been unfortunate, but now at the age of thirteen, he could make up for lost time. There was nothing remarkable about Mr Jones's Classical and Commercial Academy or Hampstead Road, parodied later by Charles as "Salem House", but it did enable him to recover some of what he had learnt from Mr Giles at Chatham. The sizable gap in his education kept him well behind boys of the same age, but as much like a sponge as ever, he picked up every bit of information that came his way, whether scholastic or not, and most of it appeared, sooner or later, in his books.

Charles Dickens had been born in 1812 in Portsmouth, his father John Dickens being a naval pay clerk who borrowed money from anyone rash enough to lend. There is no record of the debt which flung John into the Marshalsea when Charles was twelve, but his second visit, ten years later, was for a wine merchant's bill. There was never a moment in Charles's childhood when he was not painfully aware of his family's money problems, and the memory haunted him throughout his life, greatly influencing not only his writing but his general behaviour. He worked tirelessly, sometimes frantically, often engaged on several books at the same time and, towards the end of his life giving public readings of them, to earn more money, though by then he was a very rich man indeed.

When he left school in 1827, at the age of fifteen, Charles became office boy and then clerk to London solicitors. In his spare time he was busily learning shorthand from his father and after a few months he was able to hand in his notice and become a Court reporter. He enjoyed the work, though his ultimate intention was to follow his father into the Gallery of the House of Commons. He was able, however, to study and makes notes on the hundreds of varied eccentrics and malefactors who passed through the Courts, many of whom were subsequently to appear in his books. In the evenings he would spend his time at the theatre, with the idea of becoming, if other trades failed, a professional actor. It has been said that this is what he would have most liked to become. He would see a play, buy the script, memorize a part and practise it before a mirror; and this training, like everything Dickens did throughout his life, was made use of: the practice in projecting his voice, suggesting a mood, made his later public readings a huge financial success. Even the practice he gave himself before the mirror of entering a room and sitting down "tidily" stood him in good stead when literary fame opened the doors of the aristocracy and the London salons to the self-made man from the blacking factory.

In 1832 Dickens joined the staff of an evening paper and achieved his ambition of getting to the House of Commons as a reporter. He was so outstanding at his job that, as a journalist from a rival paper had to admit, "a more talented reporter never sat in the Gallery". Two years later, when Parliament burnt down—after two years in which the young Dickens had been increasingly angered by the reluctance of that august body to do anything about reform, either within their own House or outside, in the country—he was able to tell, with malicious pleasure, just how it happened. For ages, Dickens wrote, there had been a "savage method of keeping Exchequer accounts, Crusoe-like, on notched sticks, called tallies". Years of earnest consideration had at last resulted in the abolition of tallies—at last the new-fangled pen-and-ink might be used—and the piles of little wooden splints were carefully packed away. Eight years later, after more consideration, it was allowed that they might be destroyed "privately and confidentially". They were confidentially stuffed into a stove in the House of Lords and the sudden blaze of dried wood destroyed Parliament.

Between sessions Dickens was sent to various parts of the country to report political speeches and with his reports he was able to send his paper chatty columns setting the scene for the reported speech. These "sketches" were enthusiastically received and his salary was increased. Of course his family took advantage of that fact: he managed to prevent his father going to prison again by paying off a large debt, which nearly crippled him, and this was only the beginning. Throughout his life he was paying the debts of either his parents or his children. In order to make more money he tried submitting a non-political sketch to the new *Monthly Magazine* and was delighted when it was accepted. His delight was short-lived when the magazine's owner and editor, one Captain Holland, informed him that contributions were never paid for: it was an honour to be accepted.

Charles's interest in descriptive writing had been aroused and he soon had other sketches accepted by magazines which were prepared to pay for them. All these were well reviewed by the *Literary Gazette*.

which at the time was the absolute arbiter of literary and artistic fame, and it soon leaked out that "Boz", over whose name they appeared, was in reality the star reporter of the House of Commons Gallery. His fame spread. Harrison Ainsworth was the first professional writer to invite the young man to his house and Dickens was deeply touched and flattered. At the suggestion of Ainsworth he assembled his sketches into a book and was able, on his twenty-fourth birthday, to publish *Sketches by Boz, Illustrative of Every Day Life and Every Day People.* The reviews were extremely favourable and Dickens made up his mind to give up reporting and settle down to being a full-time author.

A few months later he married Kate Hogarth, the daughter of a Scottish colleague on his newspaper. George Hogarth had many daughters, but only one of a marriageable age and so it was to Kate that Charles paid court, although as he admitted freely, he "could love every one of them in turn". Kate was handsome, with a red, rosebud mouth, short, tip-tilted nose and fresh complexion, but her friends found her quiet and a little dull. At the time of their marriage, this hardly mattered, they were good friends, but later this friendship outlasted love: Kate was quite the wrong girl for a volatile, gregarious, brilliant man like Charles. Not only was she unimaginative, but she was easily hurt, so that three weeks before the wedding Charles was forced to be firm with her when she complained about not being taken to a dance. She must be, he complained to her

"incapable of understanding the claims of my profession; if one has not produced sufficient copy, one is not justified in going out. If the representations I have so often made to you be not sufficient to keep you in good humour, why then my dear, you must be out of humour and there is no help for it."

The courtship was a long one and the popular theory that Dickens repented at leisure after marrying in haste is questionable: Charles had thought it out most carefully, consulted all his friends and taken his time—but that he repented at leisure is probably true. They married in St Luke's, the vast new parish church of Chelsea, with a special licence which (as readers of "Pickwick" will know) had to be obtained from the Vicar-General. This allowed them to be married at any time or place without the formality of banns, thus avoiding a large and conspicuous wedding. (The same dispensation had earlier been claimed by Byron, and for the same reason, and no doubt this helped to make up the young author's mind.)

The first number of "Pickwick" was published at the end of

March, 1836, illustrated by Hablot Brown under his pseudonym of "Phiz", just two days before the wedding. It was a slim magazine, the first of a serial, and the first number was even better reviewed than the "Sketches". Now, with his mind made up to leave the Gallery of the House of Commons (though he had not yet done so), Dickens began to accept everything offered to him in the way of literary work, including a contract for a novel at £200, to be ready in six months, to be written concurrently with the one he was already working on, and a mass of other work.

He and Kate set up house in London and invited Kate's pretty sister Mary, aged sixteen, to live with them. The decision was seen by their friends as a mistake, but the household was a happy one until a year later when Mary died suddenly in her sleep. Charles had been much attracted to her and her totally unexpected death—a few hours before, she had been laughing and dancing—was a terrible shock to him. In an agony of sorrow he took a ring from her hand and slipped it on his own little finger where it remained until his death.

In an effort to make Mr and Mrs Dickens forget their sorrow, Hablot Brown persuaded them to venture on the Continent for a holiday. This was a revelation to Dickens: he found to his surprise that foreigners were human and that he liked them. Almost immediately he developed that craving for travel which was to lead him later on to live abroad for months on end.

Two years after his marriage Dickens was a successful full-time author turning out a prodigious amount of work on which the public fell with rapture, demanding more. He was producing his novels serially, each of them in twenty parts, at a great rate. Though most of them ran to some 350,000 words, he still found time for an active social life. Charles was not yet a rich man but he had inherited sufficient of his father's prodigality to want to do things lavishly. Some of the Dickens's new, aristocratic friends were bold enough to suggest that for a young man still climbing the ladder of success some of Kate's menus were a trifle lavish, but Charles was determined that while he had enough money to do so, he would "live like a gentleman". In a cookery book which Kate wrote, this is quoted as a simple meal for six guests—it was one she had served herself:

"carrot soup, turbot with shrimp sauce, lobster patties, stewed kidneys, roast saddle of lamb, boiled turkey, knuckle of ham, mashed and brown potatoes, stewed onions, cabinet pudding, blancmange and cream, macaroni."

With his love of luxury, good food, good wine, foppish clothes, Dickens was, throughout his life, obsessed with memories of poverty. Far from turning his back on it, he was determined to do what he could, as a writer, to improve the lot of the miserable poor of his day. *Oliver Twist* and *David Copperfield*—the latter a thinly disguised autobiography—brought home to Victorian readers the horrors going on around them.

His first major expedition abroad was to America. The idea had been at the back of his mind for years: here was a new, kingless country, where he would feel at home, escape from the English snobbery which not only enraged but alarmed him. By the time he and Kate had organized their trip, in 1842, Charles had completed the books with which he first conquered the world: *Sketches by Boz*, *The Pickwick Papers*, *Oliver Twist*, *Nicholas Nickleby*, *The Old Curiosity Shop* and *Barnaby Rudge*. His fame abroad was as great as at home. (*The Old Curiosity Shop* had, temporarily, a bad effect on his writing—he was flattered by letters about his over-sentimentalized Little Nell—but he recovered himself and in fact that book contains, with his worst writing, some of his best.)

On his arrival in Boston there was a huge welcome for this young and self-made man. Not only was he a great novelist but also he was a great moral force, and although Charles at first was flattered, he soon found the rôle of great reformer hard to sustain. In rebelling against it he managed to enrage some of his American public. At a banquet at which he was introduced in this way he responded with a few cordial phrases and then proceeded to lash his listeners with contempt for the way in which American publishers reprinted English books, ignoring their copyright. He, Charles Dickens, had been robbed of vast sums by this thieving. "There *must*", he ended, "be an international arrangement in this respect." After he sat down there was polite applause but from the next morning's newspapers he learnt he had given much offence, causing "huge dissonance where all else was triumphant unison".

From that moment Dickens became steadily more bitter about America, though he was still mobbed by her admiring crowds. When he left the country in June, 1842, after his six months' visit, he made the mistake of publishing a book of *American Notes* and following it up with a number of more or less offensive American character sketches in *Martin Chuzzlewit*. He was distressed to learn that Chuzzlewit was publicly burnt on the stage in New York.

Between his first return from America and his separation from Kate sixteen years later (after twenty-two years of marriage) came a second group of works which include *Martin Chuzzlewit, Dombey and Son, David Copperfield, Christmas Stories, Bleak House, Hard Times* and *Little Dorrit*. His keenly observant, satirical sketches gave way to more subjective, autobiographical, writing.

Two years after his return from America the whole family—Charles, Kate and five children—went to Italy for a year. He continued to write at the same tremendous rate. After Italy and a short stay back in England they moved to Switzerland, then to Paris. It was at this time that Dickens became attracted to another young sister-in-law, Georgina. She, like Mary, had moved in with them and now, at functions in Paris and in London which Kate was either too unwilling or too unwell to attend, "Georgie" became a willing and attractive partner.

At about this time Dickens did the first public reading of his work and was delighted to find that the little "theatrical" he so enjoyed putting on was profitable, for indeed the public made it plain that they would pay, in their hundreds, to see and to hear him. He obtained the services of an agent and soon it was only necessary for him to arrive at the correct place—London, Birmingham, Edinburgh —on the right day for him to be sure of his crowds of worshippers. At this time, when he was not only reading his own work but tinkering with the idea of writing and producing plays, he met and became infatuated with the young actress Ellen Ternan. He was already the father of ten children, but in his mind he was suddenly young again and this entanglement with Ellen brought about the collapse of his marriage to Kate. They separated in 1858 and there were many raised eyebrows when Georgie elected to stay on as his housekeeper. It is probable that Dickens encouraged this, at first, as a screen for his passing infatuation with Ellen Ternan. In any case, Georgie set out with a will to supplant her older sister, wrote letters to friends and acquaintances all over the world explaining what an unsuitable wife Kate had been. After Charles's death she even cut out from the collected edition of his letters all the references—and they were many—to his affection for her. The books written during this third, arbitrary, division of his life, after the separation, include *A Tale of Two Cities, Great Expectations, Our Mutual Friend* and the unfinished *Edwin Drood*.

He was still writing hard, but the rewards in money and satisfaction of reading his work in public seemed so much more attractive that he devoted more and more of his time to it. In 1867, he agreed with his agent that despite his unpleasant memories of an earlier visit, twenty-five years before, he would do a reading tour of

America. The decision, although it shortened his life, gave him the greatest possible pleasure and he left the States on such a wave of popularity that he was able to say on his last reading in New York:

> "I shall never regard you as a mere public audience, but rather as a host of personal friends, and ever with the greatest gratitude, tenderness and consideration. God bless you and God bless the land in which I leave you."

The arrangements for the visit had been clumsy—he was for ever having to travel back to one city or another where the inhabitants had failed to get into his readings, and he refused to disappoint an audience—so that his health failed. In 1870, after two years of ill health he died at his home near Rochester in Kent, with Georgie by his side. Earlier that day he had been working on his mystery story, *Edwin Drood*. This was to have been a new departure for him, something to keep his public guessing, but the premature death, at fifty-eight, of its idol, provided the public with as big a mystery. It was agreed that throughout his life he had burnt the candle at both ends, but as G. K. Chesterton remarked, it was a "great and glorious candle". He was buried in the Poet's Corner of Westminster Abbey.

Dickens had achieved much more than a purely literary success, though that was enormous. Thanks to him there was a wave of political and social reform—schools became better than those he depicted in *Nicholas Nickleby*, hospital nurses improved on Mrs Gamp, soon there was no imprisonment for debt—and this wave of reform swept away many of the old abuses. It is perhaps ironical that Dickens's work, which did so much to cure the evils of his time, is still held up in parts of the world as a mirror for the England of today.

Henry Bessemer
1813-1898

"IT IS", wrote Sir Henry Bessemer, near the close of his life, "an old man's privilege to look upon the past and compare it with the present. It is no less a privilege to do so when his thoughts turn to those subjects in which he himself has taken more or less conspicuous part—

"If we go back to the year 1861, we shall find Sheffield by far the largest producer of steel in the world, the greater portion of her annual make of 51,000 tons realizing from £50 to £60 a ton.

"For this purpose, the costly bar-iron of Sweden was chiefly employed as the raw material, costing from £15 to £20 per ton; the conversion of this expensive iron into crude steel occupied about ten days—that is, about two days and nights for the gradual heating of the furnace, in which the cold iron bars had been carefully packed in large stone boxes with a layer of charcoal powder between each bar: in these boxes the metal was retained for six days at white heat, two days more being required to cool down the furnace and get out the converted bars. The steel so produced was broken into small pieces and melted in crucibles holding not more than forty or fifty pounds each, and consuming from 2 to 3 tons of expensive oven coke for each ton of steel so melted. This steel was excellently adapted for the manufacture of knives, and for all other cutting instruments, but its hard and brittle character, as well as its excessively high price, absolutely precluded its use for the thousands of purposes to which steel is now universally applied.

"It was under such conditions of the steel trade that, thirty-three years ago, I endeavoured to introduce an entirely novel system of manufacture—so novel, in fact, and so antagonistic to the preconceived notions of practical men, that I was met on all sides with the most stolid incredulity and distrust. Perhaps I ought to make some allowance for this feeling, for I proposed to use as my raw material crude pig-iron costing £3 per ton, instead of the highly purified Swedish bar-iron then used, costing from £15 to £20 per ton. I proposed also to employ *no fuel whatever* in the converting process, which in my case, occupied only 25 *to* 30 *minutes*, instead of the ten days and nights required by the process then in use; and I further proposed to make five tons of steel at a single operation, instead of the small separate batches of 40 to 50 pounds, in which all the Sheffield cast steel was at that time made. What, however, appeared still more incredible was the fact that I proposed to make steel bars at £5 or £6 per ton, instead of £50 or £60 —the then ruling price of the trade."

Henry Bessemer was born on 19 January, 1813, in the village of Charlton, near Hitchin in Hertfordshire. His father, despite the family name which Henry admitted "does not sound like an English one", despite the fact that he spent many years in France, was an Englishman, born in the city of London. His parents had taken him to Holland, where they settled, and at twenty-one he went to France to work in the Paris Mint. At the age of twenty-six, Henry's father was made a member of the French Academy of Sciences for the improvement he had made in the microscope and went on to invent the "portrait lathe", for making medallion dies in steel from an enlarged model. He was living in Paris when the Revolution broke out and it was some time before he succeeded in getting home, with his wife, to England. When at last he arrived, having left almost everything he possessed behind, he put his skill to the manufacture of gold chains—chains which looked massive and were feather light, which immediately became popular with the jewellers. Soon the elder Bessemer had amassed enough money to retire to the small estate he purchased for himself in Hertfordshire. It was here that Henry was born.

The father could not stay idle, and though he had plenty of money, he decided to construct a type-foundry on the estate. Henry was interested in the work, and when he left school he asked his father's permission to stay at home to study practical engineering. His father agreed and bought him a lathe.

Village life was quiet but there was always excitement each time the big melting furnace was used to make type metal. Henry was forbidden to enter the melting house, but did so, almost invariably leaving it to be sick because of the powdered antimony which swirled about him. One thing he discovered in these clandestine visits was that his father's type lasted much longer than anyone else's for the simple reason that it contained both tin and copper.

By 1830, when Henry was seventeen, his father had become so involved in type-manufacture, the demand was so great, that he suddenly, almost overnight, moved his business to London. Henry was "overwhelmed with wonder and astonishment," spent the whole of his first week wandering about, drinking in the sights—getting home later and later each night. He soon realized that "here, amid the countless thousands, I stood alone, as much uncared for as the lamp-post beside me." Farm labourers no longer doffed caps, said "Good morning, Master Henry," schoolchildren no longer dropped him a curtsey. He made no bones about it, he was disappointed—and so he resolved, straight away, to make a name for himself, to take the place of the one he had lost. He took to making castings from flowers and vegetables, anything that caught his eye, reproducing them in metal. He found, to his disappointment, that delicate designs, the leaves of a rose, would smash when he took them from the mould.

He hit upon the idea of making the mould of limestone, Flanders brick and plaster of Paris. He would dip his rosebud in this mixture, let it dry, dip again, until he had built a stout shell around it. Then he would place it in the forge, allow it to become red-hot, and the rosebud inside would be consumed in the heat, leaving a hollow mould. Liquid metal could then be poured in through a hole at one end: when it had solidified, the mould could be washed away with a hose, leaving the delicate casting intact. He had not yet discovered a method of casting copper, but he soon found a way of plating his white metal castings with it, so that they gleamed like gold.

In the intervals of this, he experimented with a machine for stamping letters and documents, a version, in fact of the franking machine used today in offices. This would put an exact replica of the stamp on whatever document was inserted. He knew that the Government was losing thousands in revenue by people removing stamps from documents, using them a second time: with Henry Bessemer's stamp there would be no question of soaking it off, it was there for ever. The Government, if it adopted his machine, could never again be defrauded. There was of course the danger that unauthorized Bessemer stamp-machines would get into the wrong hands, but as Henry was confident only he could make them, this seemed no problem.

Sir Charles Presley, being astounded by the accuracy of Bessemer's stamp, remarked, "Young man, you treat this subject with a great deal of levity." He had all but agreed to adopt the Bessemer stamper when Henry's fiancée, hearing the details that evening, suggested it would be simpler, less likely to throw stamp-makers out of work, if he merely devised a method of printing the date on stamps, so they could not be re-used. This simple scheme (which gave an indication to the young Bessemer of how useful she would be as a wife) was made practical by Henry with a perforating machine which showed the date in little dots. It was adopted with delight and relief by the Stamp Office, but neither Henry nor his wife received a penny for an idea which was believed to save the Office £100,000 a year. Towards the end of his life, though he had remained silent for many years, he burst into angry correspondence with the Prime Minister, Lord Beaconsfield, a correspondence which had been precipitated by the Government's refusal to allow him to accept the Grand Cross of the French Legion of Honour. Enraged, Bessemer wrote Lord Beaconsfield on both subjects. The Prime Minister agreed that he had been unjustly treated and recommended to the Queen that she confer a knighthood. Bessemer accepted and his wife thus shared the honour. In this way, the greatest technologist of his time was honoured for a clever idea of his wife's, forty-six years before.

Bessemer as a young man went on to devise a cheaper method of making lead pencils and a quicker method of setting type, but as he was quite unversed in commerce, he made no money from his ideas. Then, quite by chance, came the opportunity for huge commercial success, which he used to the full. His sister had asked him, as he was "something of an expert in writing ornamental characters", to write "Studies of Flowers from Nature by Miss Bessemer" within a wreath of oak leaves on the cover of an album. Henry agreed, decided it would look well in gold lettering, and was then shocked to find the "gold powder" he bought cost him seven shillings an ounce. He took it home, tested whether in fact it was real gold or powdered brass—it was brass—then considered how brass at sixpence a pound retailed at five pounds twelve.

He found that the powder was made by a secret process in Nüremberg, found, too, that, however hard he tried to produce the same thing by grinding or cutting, it looked totally different, had no lustre. Eventually, under a microscope, he saw the reason: the German powder was in tiny flat sheets which reflected the light; his own were lumps, like sand. This brought him no nearer the secret of making it.

Eventually, as with every other problem, he produced an answer. The machines—for more than one process was involved—were complicated to build and had to be more or less automatic: an operator could be bribed to reveal their secrets. Bessemer had calculated his profit in selling "gold powder" at a price that undercut the German variety, and he was determined, this time, to get it. He leased factory premises in St Pancras, redesigned them so the engine

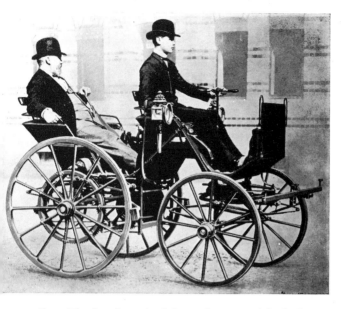

Above: The first four-wheeled Daimler automobile, built in 1886, was powered by a 1½ h.p. single-cylinder engine. In this photograph Herr Gottlieb Daimler himself is in the passenger seat. *Below:* One car shown at the Paris Exhibition of 1900 was remarkable both for "splendid performance" and as "a thing of breath-taking beauty". It was named after Daimler's daughter "Mercedes". Two of the latest models of this famous make shown are the Mercedes-Benz 350 SLC Coupé and the 280 SE 3·5 saloon.

Jamsetji Tata (*left*) was a Parsi of ambition and imagination; he set up a cotton mill with modern machinery which brought him wealth, and long dreamed of creating for India a steel industry. To-day the name of Tata is world famous and rests as much on its philanthropy as on its industrial connexions in steel and textiles. In the photograph *below* on the left is J. N. (Jamsetji) Tata; seated with him are his sons, Sir Ratan Tata and Sir Dorab Tata; standing is his cousin, R. D. Tata, whose son became chairman.

driver would be in a separate building, connected with the main factory only by the shafting from his 20 h.p. engine. The only people to work inside the factory would be his wife's three young brothers, who were eager, at the very high salary he offered, to oblige. The scheme worked perfectly.

Soon he was selling his product, the raw material of which cost sixpence, for eighty shillings a pound, found he could hardly make it fast enough. He was amused, a little later, to find one stolid London firm still buying their "gold paint" from Germany—paint which the Germans bought from Bessemer and "improved by twenty shillings a pound". He and his three young brothers-in-law managed to keep their secret for thirty years, at which point Bessemer gave them the factory and the right to market it themselves.

He always maintained that his powder was one of the most important factors in his career. The process was far more complicated than the steel manufacture on which his reputation now depends: it succeeded because it was undertaken when "my energy, endurance, faith in my powers, were at their highest". It provided funds for everything else.

His next invention was a press for sugar cane many times more efficient than anything known, for which he was awarded a gold medal by Prince Albert. Years later, looking back on this, Bessemer was to remark that he had an immense advantage over others in everything he undertook, simply because he had no fixed ideas.

"Indeed, the first bundle of canes I ever saw had not arrived from Madeira a week before I had settled in my own mind certain fundamental principles . . ."

Before being led into the investigation of steel manufacture, Bessemer interested himself in making optical and sheet glass, and in patenting a better method of silvering mirrors. He devised the first simultaneous braking system for a railway train, a brake that would stop all the carriages together, but it came before its time and was not accepted by the railway companies.

The Crimean War brought great interest in artillery, and Bessemer made improvements in gun design. This in turn brought up the question of iron and steel with which to make the guns, which led to the now universal "Bessemer Process" of conversion, which he describes at the beginning of this article, and which, although at first no manufacturer would believe it, made high quality steel worth over £50 a ton, out of pig iron costing £7, simply by forcing air through. The pig iron was either taken straight from the blast furnace, in liquid form, or melted in a retort near Bessemer's "Converter" into which it was then poured. Once in, it was kept molten by the combustion of its own impurities as a stream of air was blown through it. He set up his own factory for the process, in Sheffield. When private manufacturers took an interest, he licensed them to make steel by his process, at a royalty of £2 per ton. Within a year there were Bessemer convertors in many other countries, all of them under licence, all of his own design. It became a matter of pride with him that towns in America began to be named after him. By the time of his death there were thirteen of them, in states from Alabama to Wyoming.

He lived the last years of his life in a house at Denmark Hill, outside London, with large grounds on which he designed and built an observatory. Before he had completed the huge telescope his active mind got side-tracked on to the question of a "solar furnace", in which the sun's rays would melt metal. It worked—but its practical advantage was slight, and he scrapped it.

He died on 15 March, 1898, having made over a million pounds by the Bessemer Process alone—and heartbroken at the loss of his wife, who predeceased him by only a few months.

Richard Wagner
1813-1883

ANYONE dreaming in the streets of the beautiful old city of Leipzig in 1829 might well have been jolted out of his pleasant reverie by the caterwaulings of a violin, excruciatingly handled, issuing from the open window of a prosperous house. Looking up, he might have glimpsed the perpetrator of this musical mayhem, scraping away with an industry unrelieved by any grain of talent. He was a youth of sixteen, undersized, with a disproportionately large head, in which glowed a pair of immense and penetrating blue eyes. Of this youth his music-master was to despair, describing him in his report as his worst pupil. The name at the head of that report was "Richard Wagner".

Yet this lad was destined to revolutionize the future course of European music. So perhaps we should precede any consideration of his rather sordid life story by establishing why he ranks as one of the world's greatest composers. In its earlier stages, and as exemplified by the compositions of Schubert, Mendelssohn, Chopin, Weber, Schumann and Spohr, the music of the Romantic period took the form primarily of songs and short piano pieces. Wagner directed Romantic music into the field of dramatic story telling, so opening up the whole musical time-scale, and combining musical and dramatic ideas in a way that no previous composer had conceived possible. Indeed, perhaps his greatest achievement is that he succeeded in giving to music the same time-scale as that of the drama. In so doing he gave music a new direction and impetus which were to show their influence for all time.

In his hands the opera became an entirely new art-form in which musical, poetic and scenic elements were united. Wagner was his own librettist, and in every sense his operas are complex exercises in epoch-making stage-craft. The *leitmotiv* system, in which his work is framed, was in itself a revolutionary device. The term was invented by Hans von Wolzogen (1848–1938) the great Wagnerian analyst, to distinguish the use of the constantly recurring musical motives which play such an important rôle in Wagnerian opera, and the development of the whole field of post-Wagnerian opera-making.

Richard Wagner was born in Leipzig, on 22 May, 1813, the ninth child of Johanna, wife of Karl Friedrich Wagner. It is strongly suspected that the child's true father was not Johanna's husband but Ludwig Geyer, a playwright, painter and actor of partly Jewish blood, and an intimate family friend of the Wagners. In October, 1813, Napoleon's armies reached Leipzig, and following their ravages came an epidemic of typhus, to which Friedrich Wagner quickly succumbed. The widow, with seven surviving children and no income, was in desperate straits; however she was shortly relieved by Geyer, who married her in August, 1814. In February, 1815, she bore him a daughter; that same year the family moved to Dresden, where Geyer died in 1821, leaving Johanna in fairly prosperous circumstances. Wagner was later to describe Geyer as a "kind and affectionate step-father".

From 1822 to 1827, the boy attended the Dresden Kreutzschule, where he proved a good pupil, but showed little interest in music. In 1828 he enrolled at the Nicholaischule, Leipzig, where his musical passion was awakened by the discovery of the music of Beethoven. He writes: "In ecstatic dreams I met Beethoven and Shakespeare, and talked with them. I awoke bathed in tears." He began to compose music, and learned more by so doing than by studying books and rules. He also writes of the opera becoming "a deep-rooted, conscious passion. Life has only now begun to have true meaning."

In 1831 he went to Leipzig University, where he spent his time duelling, drinking and gambling. He worked only at music and actually had an overture performed at the Leipzig Theatre. It was almost laughed off by the audience. He persevered unabashed, and for one of his pieces he actually received £3 down.

In 1834 he was appointed conductor of the opera at Magdeburg. He now met an actress Minna Planer, three or four years his senior, who already had a six-year-old illegitimate daughter. Wagner pursued her, but she was wary of his advances. In 1836, the company with which Wagner had moved to Magdeburg went bankrupt, leaving him heavily in debt—a frequent embarrassment which he bore lightly enough.

Minna obtained an engagement at Königsberg, whither Wagner, mad with jealousy followed her. When Wagner coveted anything he was not to be denied, and throughout his life he was always able to convince himself that "my need is greater than thine". Wagner married Minna on 24 November, 1836.

At Königsberg he ran into further debt, and his concerts, where his overture "Rule Britannia" was probably first performed, made little profit. Desperate, Minna left him in May, 1837. There was a reconciliation but it was of short duration.

Wagner obtained the post of musical director of the Theatre in Riga, in the Russian province of Latvia. He held this post for two years and the repentant Minna rejoined him. Here he wrote most of *Rienzi,* which was to become his first successful work. In Riga, Wagner acted in real life the rôle of the unrecognized genius, dreaming in his shabby rooms of future triumphs. To him this was no fantasy—overweening egotist that he was he yet knew that his greatness was real and would eventually be acclaimed.

His debts mounted, and in March, 1839, he was hounded out of Riga by importunate creditors. With Minna, he crossed the border to East Prussia by stealth (their passports had been confiscated), in imminent danger of arrest or shooting by the frontier-guards. They dared not return to Königsberg for fear of their creditors, so managed to get themselves smuggled aboard an English ship at Pilau. They arrived in London on 13 August, after a protracted, stormy voyage which gave Wagner his first idea for *The Flying Dutchman.* On the 20th they set sail for Boulogne, en route for Paris. On board Wagner met some friends of Meyerbeer, the German-Jewish composer then the rage of Paris. He cadged a letter of introduction, which he presented to Meyerbeer, who fortunately happened to be in Boulogne. Meyerbeer heard part of *Rienzi*, with approval, and provided letters of introduction to influential personages in Paris. Despite this kindness, we find Wagner reviling him (anonymously) in a tirade against the Jewish influence on music, a few years later.

Wagner's three years in Paris were disastrous. His attempts to get his music performed failed everywhere, and he was reduced to writing scraps of criticism for musical periodicals, and taking in lodgers. He was twice jailed for debt, and almost starved; but with unquenchable resolution he finished *Rienzi*, which was presented by the Dresden Opera House. He wrote *The Flying Dutchman* entire in five months and it was performed at Berlin in February, 1842.

With borrowed money, the Wagners made their way to Dresden, where *Rienzi* was produced in October, 1842, with immediate and enormous success. He rejected a Berlin offer for the *Dutchman*, and it was put on in Dresden in January, 1843, but received only moderate approval. A month later he was made Conductor of the Dresden Royal Opera, at a modest but reasonable salary.

The rejection and humiliation which he suffered in Paris seem to have warped completely an already notably unattractive character. He was great enough to revolutionize opera, but at the same time he never blenched at any meanness, lie, infidelity or treachery that served his turn. Nor did he scruple to use his undoubted personal charm to achieve any expedient end.

Wagner had always been fascinated by ancient Teutonic legend, and henceforth it was the source from which his greatest masterpieces emanated. The first, *Tannhäuser*, was produced in Dresden in October, 1845, with doubtful success, caused by the failure of the singers to grasp the innovations of his style. His friend, the prima donna Schröder-Devrient, humorously complained that he was a genius who wrote such eccentric stuff that nobody could sing it!

He began work on *Lohengrin* and *The Mastersingers*, and seemed on the full tide of success, but once more he fell into debt to such an extent that his employers threatened dismissal unless he reformed. At the same time he became embroiled in Leftist politics through his friend August Röckel, a fervent socialist. The proclamation of the Second Republic in Paris set all Germany alight, and the disgruntled Wagner read a somewhat subversive paper to a large public meeting. He also met Bakunin, the Russian anarchist, and it has been suggested that Siegfried in the *Young Siegfried* (1851) was modelled on memories of Bakunin. In May, 1849, street-fighting broke out in Dresden. Röckel and Bakunin were arrested and condemned to death, though later reprieved. Wagner, in fear of his life, fled to Weimar, where a new acquaintance, the composer Liszt, engineered his escape to Zurich in Switzerland. Here he remained in exile for twelve years.

His political interests at this time were great; almost he renounced music in favour of writing provocative pamphlets on art and politics, such as "Judaism in Music", "Art and Revolution", and the enormous "Opera and Drama".

Lohengrin was put on by Liszt in Weimar in 1850, but Wagner composed nothing more till 1853, when he began *The Rheingold*. The unfortunate Minna, who was, at heart, a conventional German hausfrau, failed utterly to understand the clever "public relations" job that Wagner was doing. His controversial writings, together with his political firework display and his growing reputation as a composer, following the success of *Rienzi*, all combined to build up his public image as the most vivid in the world of German music. That did not prevent relations between Wagner and Minna steadily worsening.

In 1848, during the Dresden period, Wagner had met a young Englishwoman, Jessie Laussot, who seems instantly to have become infatuated with both the music and the man. Nothing dramatic seems to have occurred until 1850, when Wagner, at Minna's prompting, returned to Paris to try his luck again. Jessie Laussot invited him to stay with herself and her husband, a wealthy wine-merchant, at Bordeaux. Laussot, with the help of his mother-in-law, succeeded in turning his wife against the unscrupulous composer, who retaliated by charging her with childish weakness—"I can only regard her as pitiable."

He now began work on his master-project, *The Ring of the Nibelung*, which was to occupy him for twenty-nine years. The order of composition of his most important works is by no means clear, but runs approximately thus:

The Rheingold	1853–54
The Valkyrie	1854–56
Siegfried	1854–71
Tristan and Isolde	1857–59
The Mastersingers	1861–67
The Twilight of the Gods	1870–74
Parsifal	1876–82

About 1852 Wagner met Otto Wesendonck, a wealthy young businessman with a charming wife. To be wealthy, and to meet Wagner was a singularly unfortunate combination of circumstances, and Herr Wesendonck's first mistake was to finance a holiday for Wagner in Italy, where *The Rheingold* was conceived. At this time Wagner discovered the dolorous writings of the philosopher Schopenhauer, and read them with avidity; this doubtless has some bearing on the tragic mood of the *Ring*.

In personal relationships also a storm was brewing. In April, 1857, Wesendonck bought a delightful small house in Zurich, which he more or less presented to the Wagners—in point of fact he let it to them at a purely nominal rent. Wesendonck and his young wife, Mathilde, lived in a large new villa near by. Intrigue developed between Wagner and Mathilde; when Wesendonck and Minna discovered it the Wesendoncks departed abruptly for Italy, and Wagner—alone—for Venice. Even so, he contrived to maintain some sort of relations with Wesendonck, to the extent of even managing to borrow more money from him.

After more than a year's separation, Wagner and Minna were together again in Paris. Minna, by tireless efforts, obtained a political pardon for Wagner, whereby he was allowed to return to any part of Germany save Saxony itself.

Meanwhile *Tannhäuser* was disastrously produced in Paris in

March, 1861. On the opening night it was greeted with jeers and cat-calls, while at the fifth performance the audience signified their disapproval by blowing dog-whistles. Wagner departed for Germany, deep in debt as usual.

Once more Minna left him and went to Saxony. In November, 1862, Wagner was granted permission to enter Saxony, and so visited Minna for the last time, in Dresden; to his credit, he saw that she lacked for nothing till she died in 1866. Meantime Wagner himself was living in Berlin. Soon his debts compelled him to move, and in March, 1864, he had "pressing business" in Switzerland.

On his stealthy return came his most dramatic stroke of luck. Ludwig II of Bavaria (Mad Ludwig), eighteen years old and newly enthroned, decided to instal him at the Court in Munich. Before long Cosima von Bülow, a daughter of Liszt, and Wagner left together for Triebschen, near Lake Lucerne. She was divorced by von Bülow in July, 1870, and married Wagner within a month.

In Triebschen, Wagner met the philosopher Nietzsche, then a young Professor of Philology of the University of Basel. He was now at work on *The Twilight of the Gods*, the last part of *The Ring*. He had long dreamt of building a special opera-house, to be dedicated to the production of his gigantic work A huge sum of money was required. In raising it Nietzsche was of great assistance. He lent his name to the formation of Wagner Societies throughout Germany, for the gathering of subscriptions. In 1876 the dream became reality —the theatre was completed at Bayreuth. By now, however, Nietzsche had become disillusioned by Wagner's character, and turned away from him in disgust.

On 13 August, and during the ensuing four days, the entire "Ring" was given its first performance at Bayreuth, with fantastic success, the German Emperor and a glittering selection of royal personages and musical notabilities attending. This triumph was followed by a Wagner Festival in London. It was staged at the Royal Albert Hall with Wagner himself conducting. It was said in London that he did not do himself justice as a conductor, but this may have been owing to the fact that his health had begun to fail.

When *Parsifal* was produced at Bayreuth on 26 July, 1882, Wagner's heart was already weak, and the stress told on him. He spent the autumn of 1882 in Venice and appeared to be recovering his strength: but to the shock of his wife and friends he died of heart failure in the afternoon of 13 February, 1883.

Giuseppe Verdi
1813-1901

LE RONCOLE is merely a tiny group of farmhouses huddling around a little church in the midst of a huge and fertile plain watered by the river Po in Northern Italy. Here, in 1813, Carlo Verdi kept a wine and grocery store. He was also a frequent visitor at the local tavern where he spent much of his time in the company of idlers and vagabonds. As a result, the care of the little family store fell very largely upon the shoulders of his wife, Luigia Verdi, a tough, hard-working and uncomplaining woman. Her lot was hard. There is a legend that shortly before her son Giuseppe was born, a strolling player stopped at the little wineshop for refreshment. As he raised his glass he looked at Luigia and said: "When your boy is born I will bring my fellow minstrels and we will come and play beneath your window." Surely enough, as the stranger prophesied, the child was a boy, and the promised serenade took place. Thus the infant Verdi was welcomed into the world by "musical sounds of rejoicing, an omen of future glory".

Giuseppe was born on 10 October, 1813, and baptized in the parish church of Le Roncole. He grew up in his mother's loving care, often helping her in the little shop. His sister, Giuseppa, was a sad, feeble-minded little creature, destined to remain a helpless invalid. When he was seven, Giuseppe was sent to the parish priest to learn reading, writing, and arithmetic. He was a shy boy, quick to take offence, and subject to anger. Music alone had the power to charm and fascinate the little fellow. On one occasion while he was serving as an acolyte in the little church at Le Roncole he was so enraptured with the sound of the organ music that he failed to hear the priest's repeated calls for the water and the wine. So enraged was the good man that he gave young Giuseppe a sharp kick in the posterior that sent him hurtling down the altar steps. "God blast you!" shouted Giuseppe as he fled from the church in a storm of rage. Some years later, in September, 1828, the church was struck by lightning during a violent storm. Two priests were killed, one of them the man who had booted young Verdi down the altar steps.

Verdi's first encounter with the practical side of music-making was a battered old spinet that the village organist Pietro Baistrocchi used to let him play under his tuition. The teacher was astonished at the speed with which the boy learned to play this old instrument. Soon Baistrocchi could teach the brilliant youngster nothing more. Indeed, before Verdi was ten years old he substituted for his friend and teacher as the church organist.

In 1823 Giuseppe was sent to high school in the neighbouring town of Busseto, where he lived in the house of the local cobbler. Since his father was too poor to pay the full cost of his keep, Giuseppe travelled home to play the organ and so earn in part his expenses. Now began a strange and desperate struggle for the very soul of the young fellow. One of his teachers was determined that Giuseppe should enter the priesthood. The other was equally determined to make him a first-class musician. Eventually this latter teacher, by name Antonio Barezzi, persuaded Ferdinando Provesi, Director of the Music School and the choirmaster and organist of the local Cathedral, to accept Verdi as one of his regular pupils. This suited Giuseppe very well, he had no desire to don the cassock and devote his life to the priesthood. From this point on his destiny was settled. Music was to be his life, and Barezzi his lifelong friend.

During one of the Cathedral celebrations at Busseto the organist was taken ill and, jokingly, one of the officials turned to Giuseppe and suggested he should take the man's place. Verdi promptly agreed, and to the amazement of everyone played so brilliantly that he was afterwards given bits of operas, marches, and ballet music to compose for the musicians who studied under Provesi. Soon the young composer was helping the master with the teaching of his fellow pupils. Admiration for young Verdi spread through the town—for every Italian town loves a musician. He began to compose pieces for the flute, the clarinet, the bassoon, and the horn, complete with full orchestra accompaniment. Even at this stage of his career Verdi had to his credit a variety of religious compositions, including a Mass for full orchestra and four voices with a fugue. He was only fifteen years of age, but the signs of his unmistakable genius were already clearly apparent. The old Provesi referred to him with delight as "the rising genius who will soon be the finest ornament of our land".

It was obvious to Provesi and Barezzi, his first music-master, that there was no real future for Giuseppe in Busseto: not even in Parma. He must go to Milan, that great and glittering city of music, with its illustrious La Scala Theatre, and the Conservatory of Music. They recommended the award of a scholarship from the Council of the Sacred Monte do Pietà of Busseto, and in due course this was granted. However, the Conservatory at Milan refused admission to Verdi mainly on the grounds that he was the wrong age (he was 18 at the time) and also because he wanted to study composition, not the piano. It was all bitterly disappointing, both for Verdi and for his staunch friends. Giuseppe continued his studies privately with Vincenzo Lavigna, a well-known composer and a teacher at the Conservatory. At this time his devoted friend Antonio Barezzi helped to support him financially and Giuseppe vowed to repay his wonderful kindness in full as soon as he could. When the Conservatory rejected him Verdi was in despair and only Barezzi's faith and friendship kept him going. Since there was no denying his genius, Giuseppe attracted the notice of influential people. He began to conduct, and was commissioned by Count Renato Borromeo to write a cantata for voices and orchestra for the wedding celebrations of one of his family. Lavigna was more and more delighted with his pupil's progress.

In April, 1836, Verdi became engaged to Barezzi's beautiful daughter Margherita. They had long been in love and in May of that year they were married. Giuseppe was twenty-three, and his bride a year younger. Barezzi gave the young couple a house in Busseto where Verdi had just been appointed Master of Music for the Commune. Here they were to live for the next three years, during which time Margherita would present the young composer with two children: a daughter in 1837, and a son in 1838. There was sadness to follow these joys. On 12 August, 1838, a month after their second child was born, their daughter died. The tragedy greatly disturbed the young couple, and Verdi became determined to get away from Busseto.

Already he had written his first opera, *Oberto*—as yet unperformed —and with this as their only security the family set out for Milan. Here, through his friends and acquaintances, Verdi was able to arrange for the opera to be performed at La Scala. Before that happened the family was again bereaved. On 17 November, 1839, his son Icilio Romano, aged one year and four months, died. In the midst of all the preparations for the opera the blow was crushing. Only Margherita's love sustained Giuseppe. Their sorrow was overwhelming; but the opera was a success. Still more sorrow came to Verdi: only eight months later Margherita herself died at the age of twenty-seven. So Verdi's little family was wiped out. He was utterly alone.

In *Oberto*, one is already conscious of the distinctive style which was to mark all the later works of one of the greatest operatic composers of all time. A dramatic style, touched with melancholy mixed with powerful contrasts of violence and heart-rending sweetness. After the success of *Oberto*, Verdi was promptly offered a contract for three operas to be produced at La Scala, and at the Theatre in Vienna. *Un Giorno di Regno* was to be one of these. It was a failure. Not so the next. With *Nabucco*, as Verdi himself declared "my artistic career may truly be said to begin". *Nabucco* (Nebuchadnezzar) at once established his unique genius. Here at last he was free of the influences of his illustrious predecessors. He showed tor the first time his wonderful use of the chorus, a feature characteristic of all his greatest works. He was to be proclaimed "the father of the chorus".

The triumph of *Nabucco* marked the end of Donizetti's unchallenged supremacy in the field of dramatic music, a supremacy which he had held since the death of Bellini in 1835. In one great leap, Verdi, still not thirty years of age reached the very pinnacle of operatic fame. He had arrived as a great composer. Two years after the triumph of *Oberto* at La Scala, *Ernani* was lauded to the stars at Venice. The years that followed passed in work, and travels, and sickness too, for Verdi was subject to attacks of acute rheumatism which not infrequently laid him low. By the spring of 1847 *Macbeth* was being performed in all the principal theatres in Italy, and *I Masnadieri* was almost completed. Verdi was in Paris preparing to set out for London, which he did in June.

London gave the young composer a warm welcome, and in July, *Masnadieri* was presented at Covent Garden by command of H.M. The Queen. The first performance was a roaring success. The Theatre was besieged by enthusiasts clamouring for seats to see and hear the first opera ever written by an Italian composer specially for London. Said Verdi; "London is a marvellous city, the surroundings are beautiful, but the climate is horrible!"

On his way home to Italy, again via Paris, Verdi was besieged by the Directors of the Opéra who were eager to show what *they* could do with the music of the Italian maestro. On 26 November, 1847, *Jerusalem* was presented at the Paris Opéra, but was coolly received. Verdi fell sick again, and listened gravely to the news from Italy that there was fighting between his countrymen and the Austrians. Soon, not only Italy, but all Europe was in an uproar of revolts and fighting.

In February, 1848, the Paris mobs overthrew Louis Philippe and proclaimed the republic. Berlin and Vienna at once revolted, as also did Palermo, Milan, Rome and Venice. On 18 March, the Milanese drove the Austrians out, and Verdi hurried home to Italy.

The tragic struggles of the Italian people were drowned in a welter of blood. They had no leaders, and collapsed. So Italy remained divided between Austria, the Pope, and the Kingdoms of Sardinia and Naples. This was the atmosphere of turmoil and blood to which Verdi returned after the abortive revolts of 1848.

Verdi met and fell in love with the great operatic singer Giuseppina Strepponi, but it was not until 1859 that he made her his wife. The date of the marriage was 29 April, the very day that Victor Emmanuel II summoned the Italian people to the struggle for independence. Meanwhile, the years passed in a long series of triumphs. Every capital in Europe thrilled to the operas of Verdi. In 1851 came *Rigoletto;* in 1853, *Il Trovatore;* also in 1853 *La Traviata. Don Carlos* was presented in 1867, and *Aïda* in 1871.

On 25 October, 1880, an honour was accorded the great man that was not altogether to his liking. On that day statues of Bellini and Verdi were unveiled in the entrance hall of La Scala, where they joined those of Rossini and Donizetti. Verdi was not present for this celebration, and when he was congratulated by the Countess Maffei he retorted: "Do you know what this means? It means I am an old man!"

Verdi was at work on his next opera, *Otello.* It took a long while to mature. Not until 5 February, 1887, was it presented at La Scala. It was received with tremendous enthusiasm, and on 7 February, the City Council of Milan conferred the status of honorary citizenship upon Giuseppe Verdi. With *Otello,* Verdi established his concept of "lyrical drama", in which the singers are required to make their voices into unique and personal instruments. This by way of contrast with the objectives of Richard Wagner, the other great operatic composer of the nineteenth century, who demanded a complete subordination of the singers to his own consuming will. Whereas Wagner held the chorus in chains, Verdi set it free to soar on the wings of song almost of its own free will. He held the reins, of course, but not too tightly. Verdi also revolutionized the writing of sacred music. His *Requiem* broke all the existing rules of musical grammar, as well as establishing the theatrical treatment of sacred subjects.

After the success of *Otello,* Verdi retreated for a time into the country to his own farm at Sant' Agata. For a while he busied himself only with farm affairs. So great a musician could not be allowed to vegetate indefinitely. His journeying began again: to Milan, to Genoa, to Venice. He was working on a new opera—*Falstaff.* On 9 February, 1893, the curtain went up on the new work. Everyone, critics and public alike marvelled at the genius of the grand old man.

At eighty years of age the flame of his genius was burning brightly. In 1893, Verdi received a congratulatory telegram from King Umberto who had received him in Rome a few months earlier:

> "On this day when you attain the eightieth year of a glorious and stainless career, I join the nation's wishes that you may continue to serve the musical art which has won you honour and admiration throughout the civilized world."

The next three years passed in work, and travel, and success after success. Verdi was a man of considerable wealth, but he remained, always, an intensely modest and unassuming person, ever reluctant to accept honours. The year 1897 was to see the passing of his beloved wife Giuseppina Strepponi. She had long been ill, and we have a picture of the aged lovers left by Corrado Ricci, a close friend who saw them often, right up to the time of Giuseppina's death. He wrote in his diary at this time:

> "Giuseppina Strepponi hobbles along all bent over, on his arm, although something about her still bears witness to her past beauty. The Maestro on the other hand is still vigorous for his eighty-four years. He has a cloud of white hair which, joined to his beard, forms a sort of aureole around him. He holds himself erect, walks briskly, displays an excellent memory for dates and names, and sets forth his ideas about art clearly. . . ."

On 16 November, a cold winter's day, Giuseppina died peacefully, and Giuseppe was left alone. He stayed on at the Sant' Agata farm over the Christmas of that year, and early in January, 1898, went to Milan to stay with his cousin. He was in poor health himself. Although he still travelled whenever he could, he was unable to go to Paris, as he had hoped, for the performance of his *Sacred Music*. Most of his time was spent quietly revising his various works. On the morning of 21 January, 1901, Verdi suffered a cerebral hæmorrhage which paralysed the whole of his right side. Five days later, on 26 January, he died. The whole of Italy was plunged into mourning for this most illustrious son, one of the greatest operatic composers of all time.

Otto Von Bismarck
1815-1898

RATHER less than a hundred years ago, that part of Europe known before the last war as Germany was a collection of thirty-nine sovereign States, some of them only a few square miles in area, ruled by kings (Prussia, Bavaria, Saxony, Würtemburg, for example) Grand Dukes, or Margraves, all of whom claimed divine right. These states were loosely allied in a German Confederation which met in a Diet, at Frankfurt, created by the Congress of Vienna which remade Europe after the Napoleonic wars. The Diet was the scene of rivalry between Protestant Prussia, a poor country but with an excellent army and administration, and Catholic Austria: for the Austrian empire of the Hapsburgs (the majority of whose inhabitants were not German but Italians, Croats, Slavs or Magyars) was also a member of the Confederation. The southern German States leant towards Austria on the whole, the rest towards Prussia. Since the thirty-nine princes were above all anxious to preserve their privileges and independence, the Frankfurt Diet, which had the nominal function of seeing that all member States evolved a constitution which gave some voice to the people, accomplished little either in unifying Germany or in political evolution.

There was, of course, a strong desire among the Germans for some kind of unity, but "the liberals", mostly middle-class professional men and professors at the many German universities, scattered among the various German States, had little organization. Moreover, the mass of the German people were apathetic and, a fundamental German trait, intensely respectful of authority.

In 1848, when the French people chased Louis Philippe off the throne and founded the Second Republic, there was some stirring in Germany. A German Parliament met, also at Frankfurt, and offered the crown of a unified Germany to the King of Prussia, who refused it out of solidarity with his fellow-rulers. There were riots in many cities, including Berlin and Vienna; but the liberals were firmly put in their places and, after 1848, Germany seemed likely to go on indefinitely as a collection of States and as a basically feudal area.

Yet by the end of the century Germany was a powerful country, perhaps the most powerful on the European continent. In 1880 indeed all the nations of Europe, including Britain, assembled in Berlin to discuss the Balkans and the Eastern question under German chairmanship. There was an overseas German empire. German industry was the most modern in the world and the workers were the best housed in the world and incidentally the first to be covered by social insurance. The making of Germany was very largely the work of one man, Otto von Bismarck.

Bismarck was by birth a Prussian Junker, a member of the land-owning class in Prussia. This class was intensely conservative, hating new ideas, devoted to its rights and privileges and sending its younger sons into the Prussian Army or the administration. Bismarck looked a typical Prussian squire. Ungainly, huge in stature, stern in expression, he had an appetite to match his appearance and once said that before a man died he should have smoked 100,000 cigars and drunk 5,000 bottles of champagne.

The first king he served, Frederick William IV, noted of him "a reactionary, smells of blood, only to be used once the bayonet rules". Yet it was Bismarck who made the Germany the liberals wanted, made it against the princes and called successfully on the liberals to help him. His most celebrated remark was "Germany will not be made by talk but by blood and iron". It was his policy of blood and iron which engineered the war which drove Austria out of the German Confederation in 1866 and that with France in 1870 which resulted in all Germany accepting the King of Prussia as Emperor; it was a policy which had the support of the rising forces of the nation.

Bismarck ruled Germany from 1862 to 1890 and left his imprint on all corporate German life. Germany at the end of the nineteenth century with its excellent administration and its well-planned industry, its respect for learning and science was Bismarck's Germany. So too were the defects of that Germany.

Otto von Bismarck was born in 1815, the year of Waterloo. His father's family was well connected but not particularly rich or conspicuous for talent.

His mother, whom Otto never liked, was the daughter of a high Prussian official and came from the more liberal environment of the Hamburg merchant families. From her and not from his Junker ancestry, Bismarck inherited his small hands and feet, his intelligence and quick perception, which lifted him well above the dull members of his class and the rather limited Prussian officials. He had immense charm. It was Bismarck's mother who insisted that Otto and his brothers should be educated in Berlin and whilst there introduced Bismarck into the Hohenzollern circle, a fact of great importance, for Bismarck owed his beginnings to Royal favour. Yet his mother died in 1839 without seeing any fruits of her care for her son.

Bismarck went into the civil service after leaving the University, left his job to chase after an English heiress, went to Leicester and then to Scotland. He thought of enlisting in the British Army in India. He did not do so because, he said, he couldn't think what harm the Indians had ever done him. He got out of his difficulties with the Prussian administration by doing his military service—which was undistinguished.

He retired to his estates which he managed, with his brother, after his father's death. He spent his time eating and drinking enormously and indulging in every sort of country pleasure including that of seducing young peasant girls. He used to ride about the woods at night giving a "View-hallo", and he once released a fox out of the bag in a drawing-room. He became widely known as "the mad Junker".

Bismarck was called to Berlin as part of an assembly of Prussian land-owners gathered to advise King Frederick William IV how to handle the Prussian liberals and the new middle classes demanding more say in government. He made his mark in 1848 as a fanatical defender of the King's privileges. In 1851 he was rewarded by being made Prussian representative at the Diet of Frankfurt, a very important job for a young man of thirty-six totally inexperienced in politics or diplomacy.

Just before this appointment, Bismarck had married Joanna von Puttkamez, a very devout Lutheran. The cynical Bismarck of that period wrote, with a backhand reference to his mother, "I like piety in women and have a horror of female cleverness." His wife certainly was not clever. His marriage, however, unified his character and confirmed his ambition, for the fundamental impulse in Bismarck was never political idealism but rather a desire to work and accomplish things for the benefit first of his family and then of his King.

When at an advanced age he was asked what in his life he was proudest of, he answered the fact that "God has not taken away any one of my children". His wife totally consented to play the rôle of a focus. She never complained of his infidelities which seemed to have been emotional rather than sexual. It is said that, as a result of his marriage, Bismarck became a religious man: it is rather that religion was brought into his life as a result of his family. As an old man he once said to one of his few intimate friends, Count

Keyersling, that now that his sexual desires had abated he found that his belief in God and in the tenets of Lutheranism had declined too.

From Frankfurt, Bismarck bombarded the King and the Foreign Minister with his advice and his advice was always the same; try to isolate Austria from the rest of the world, let Prussia take the lead in German affairs, if necessary make an alliance with France. The young reactionary who had smelt of blood now told the King that whilst he was loyal to the King of Prussia with the last drop of his blood, Prussia should call an all-German Parliament and end the "Sovereignty swindle" of the small German powers.

King Frederick William IV died. The new King, his brother, was reported to be very much less intelligent, but for all that he was stiff and lacking in imagination he was a man capable of recognizing exceptional qualities in his advisers. A government with liberal tendencies was formed in Prussia and this meant the end of Bismarck's career in Frankfurt. He was sent as Minister to St Petersburg where he stayed for three years. The new King couldn't get Bismarck out of his mind for two reasons. One, it was clear that Bismarck was a royalist and a man of extreme determination who would shrink at nothing, a pillar therefore against dangerous subversive trends; and, secondly, the King felt that Bismarck talked more sense about the future than any of his Ministers.

Early in 1862 when there was a crisis between the King and the Prussian Parliament, the King asked Bismarck to be Prime Minister. He refused because he was not to be given power over foreign policy. Bismarck was then made Minister in Paris to be near at hand. Troubles in Prussia grew worse.

Bismarck, in France, disliked Paris, spent most of his time in Biarritz where he fell in love with the wife of the Russian Ambassador, Kathi Orlov. He did not hide this from his wife who wrote "my soul has no room for jealousy and I rejoice greatly that my husband has found this charming woman. Without her he would never have known peace for so long or become as well as he boasts of being in every letter." Partly because of Kathi Orlov, Bismarck never replied to letters from Berlin in which Ministers told him that the King wanted him and thought he was the only man who could save the monarchy. He returned to Berlin in September, 1862, perhaps because Kathi Orlov had gone back to Paris.

The King of Prussia was desperate; he dared not dismiss Parliament, he could not persuade it, he would not give way. He had his act of abdication in his pocket. He appointed Bismarck Prime Minister as well as Minister of Foreign Affairs and gave him a free hand to settle all issues. So at forty-seven Bismarck reached supreme power which he was to exercise for the next twenty-seven years.

Bismarck alternately bullied and cajoled Parliament. Germany could only be able to devise an up-to-date constitution, he told the liberals, when Germany became unified—that was the task ahead. He made a clever compromise about the law of military service which had caused the crisis. He knew how to handle the King; once when the King said to him that his policies would lead him (the King) to the scaffold like Charles I, Bismarck answered, "Better that than surrender." According to Bismarck, the King drew himself up like an officer answering the command of a superior.

In 1864, Bismarck took the masterly step of allying Prussia and Austria in a war against Denmark over the possession of Schleswig-Holstein. It was a quick war and it left Austria and Prussia something to quarrel over other than abstract principles about German unity.

In 1865, Prussia made an alliance with Italy and in 1866, when Austria protested to the Frankfurt Diet that Prussian troops had compelled the Austrians to withdraw from Schleswig, Prussia left the Diet, proclaimed that the German Confederation no longer existed, announced a new constitution which excluded Austria and included the election of a federal parliament by popular vote. In June, 1866, Prussian forces entered various German States which supported Austria, crossed the Bohemian frontier and, with the King of Prussia on the battlefield, won the great victory of Sadowa. After two other minor engagements, the Prussian Army threatened Vienna and Austria capitulated.

During the Battle of Sadowa, the King of Prussia exposed himself to danger from gunshot and refused to withdraw in spite of military advice. It is said that Bismarck, who had remained silent during the arguments, gave the King's horse a sharp unnoticed kick in the flank which caused the horse to turn round and move quickly backwards. As A. J. P. Taylor states, this was a parable of Bismarck's relations with the King—outward obedience, secret kicks.

Bismarck had his way with Austria. Against the wishes of the King and the Prussian generals, Bismarck made a very lenient peace ensuring, in fact, that once Austria was out of Germany, she would be an ally.

France was alarmed at Prussian predominance in Germany. War with France was not inevitable but likely, for France was ruled by an adventurer, the Emperor Napoleon III, and Bismarck knew that war could seal German unity around Prussia. The Prussian generals, of whom the most eminent was von Moltke, knew that if war came

Prussia would win. Bismarck managed to turn a quarrel over the candidature of a German Prince to the Spanish throne—a quarrel which would not have enlisted the support of other German States for Prussia—into a situation in which Prussia and Germany were being humiliated by France. By cutting certain words and conciliatory phrases out of a telegram from the King to the French Emperor, Bismarck made war inevitable. Once again, the German Army easily triumphed. And once again Bismarck modified the peace demands of the General Staff. He would have preferred even more leniency and didn't really want to annex Alsace Lorraine. In 1871, King William I was crowned German Emperor in the Great Hall of Mirrors in the Palace of Versailles. A united Germany was born and Bismarck became Imperial Chancellor.

Bismarck was made a prince for his part in German reunification. His task was only beginning and rarely has any statesman exercised a more undisputed sway than he did. It was he who settled all the complicated dynastic difficulties of Germany and made a great centralized State. He controlled the Reichstag, at first with the help of the liberals, later with conservatives, but always skilfully playing one against the other and both against the King. He introduced legislation in favour of the workers, in part to spite and in part to steal the thunder of the increasingly powerful Social Democrats.

He and Disraeli liked each other: indeed they could both be called "reactionary progressives". Bismarck, however, wielded absolute power, whilst Disraeli had to manoeuvre in a real parliamentary system. Bismarck ensured that the German political system should remain based on absolute power: though whether the absolute power was that of the Chancellor or the Emperor was a matter for the future to decide.

In foreign policy, Bismarck, from 1870 to 1890, strove to maintain peace in Europe, realizing that Austria-Hungary, as it was now called, and Russia must be kept from fighting each other. Germany, Bismarck made it appear, was the friend and ally of both. He built up a German empire in Africa without greatly offending the British: not for him the foolish policy of attempting to dispute the control of the seas with Britannia.

He isolated France. He helped the Third Republic to survive against the French royalists because he considered that the Republic was the most inefficient form of government and likely to keep France weak. Later, he encouraged the French to build an empire overseas to distract them from a war of revenge and to encourage them to quarrel with Britain.

His foreign policy was peace at all costs because he considered that war was too great a risk.

Neither in domestic nor foreign politics had Bismarck any moral or political principles whatever; indeed his only principle was to keep himself in power because he believed that he alone was capable of guiding Germany and Europe and because, no doubt, he had an unquenchable appetite for exerting power.

So long as his master, King William I lived, Bismarck's power was never questioned. The relations between Bismarck and the King remained much as they began—Bismarck being outwardly respectful but always getting his way in the long run.

The idea of Bismarck as the Iron Chancellor is really quite an erroneous one; if he had been a man of blood and iron he would have hardly have been so skilled a diplomat. In fact, he was a highly emotional man and both he and the King were accustomed to shout at each other and even sob during their many disagreements. Once after an unusually painful argument with the King, Bismarck pulled off the door handle as he left the room so great was his tension and dashed a vase in the ante-room against the wall. "There are white men, there are black men and there are monarchs," he was to say. The King would remark more equably, "It is not easy to be the Emperor under such a Chancellor."

By 1883 or so Bismarck's health began to give way; his huge appetite had made him bloated. He lost his temper easily. He complained bitterly the King never asked him how he slept but always spoke of his own bad nights. He met a Dr Schweninger who said he could help him. Bismarck said all right, but don't ask me a lot of questions. "Then you had better get a vet", was the answer. Bismarck submitted himself; he started keeping regular hours and for many months lived on a diet of herrings. He took up horse riding again. By 1885 he had made a complete recovery, he appeared renewed, completely master of himself and obviously capable of living a long time. His eldest son Herbert whom he had bullied all his life, whose marriage he had prevented, was now Secretary of State and Bismarck felt his control over everything was secure.

In 1888 King William I died, to be succeeded by the Crown Prince who had been brought up in the shadow of Bismarck even though the two men did not see eye to eye. Frederick III died of cancer three months after coming to the throne and was succeeded by William II a young man of the generation which considered that the Bismarck era was over. William II had no respect for the

Chancellor particularly as, at that moment, the Reichstag was fairly solidly against Bismarck. The Monarch not the Chancellor was the ruler, William II considered.

In 1890 William forced Bismarck to resign over a quarrel about the right of Ministers to advise the Emperor. Bismarck bowed unwillingly to fate, campaigned against the government, and made no secret of his feelings for the new Emperor. It is said that he invariably put down his money with the German eagle uppermost, not being able to bear to look at the false face on the other side. People respected Bismarck still but, out of power and fulminating against the Kaiser and his new advisers, he seemed, now he was no longer Germany's hidden ruler, simply like an old man surviving too long from another period.

There were of course Germans who heeded Bismarck's warnings and saw that under "the All Highest," as the new Emperor liked to be called, the world was lurching towards war. The Kaiser abandoned Bismarck's foreign policy, alienated Russia, quarrelled with England: by 1904, the Triple Entente of Russia, France and Britain faced the Triple Alliance of Germany, Austria and Italy.

"Twenty years after my departure," said Bismarck, "Germany will crash to ruin". He warned the Kaiser in a last conversation—for the two men had a sort of public reconciliation before Bismarck died—that whilst the Kaiser had a corps of Prussian officers around him, his power would be undisturbed; but if that corps was shattered, so would be the monarchy. About twenty years after, when Germany was defeated in a world war and her army was broken, the Kaiser fled, a discredited and unregretted fugitive, to Holland and the rule of the Hohenzollerns was over.

Bismarck's Germany had been a stable and moderate force in world politics because Bismarck had been a wise man. Had Bismarck been a wiser statesman still, he might have seen that what Germany needed was a living political democracy which could check the manias of great men and keep adventurers in their places. Bismarck and his régime represented all that was best in Germany. It was the Germany of the learned professors who were the admiration of the world: a well and honestly administered country, with a large section of the population who took an intelligent interest in science and the arts. But this Germany was politically highly autocratic and Bismarck made it so, determined that it should remain so, while, at least, he was there.

Before his death, the once monarchical reactionary spoke in favour of a Republican form of government. Kings, he said, even good ones, were dangerous if they had power. Bismarck cannot escape some responsibility for what happened after 1914. Indeed, when Germany tried democracy in 1920 there was nothing to build on. Thereafter Germany went through the terrible experience of Hitler. Bismarck's great error was to despise democratic institutions. He had united the Germans but not given them liberty. That perhaps was even more a fault of the Germans themselves.

Karl Marx
1818-1883

In all history, there are very few men whose thought and theories have had the effect of splitting the world into two camps. One such man however, is Karl Marx. It was his theory of the materialist conception of history which attracted the leaders of the Russian Revolutionary Movement, when they were formulating policies with which they hoped to replace the corrupt, out-of-date policies of the Tsarist régime when the time came, and they took it to form the basis of Marxist Communism. Though the Communism as practised in Russia today has departed somewhat from pure Marxist theory, it cannot be denied that the strength of Communism derives very largely from the fact that by the adoption of Marxist ideas in the very early days their ideology was given a firm foundation which it might otherwise have lacked. Without this foundation, whatever ideology the Socialists of Russia might have developed, Russian Communism might well not have acquired the force it has today, and the sharp divisions which separate the two ideological halves of the world, might not exist, might never have existed.

ALMOST every advanced political movement in early nineteenth-century Germany had its home on the banks of the Rhine, a fact which was established by the prosperity of the Rhineland provinces which far outstripped that of old Prussia, which, while the western provinces formed part of the modern world, still retained the medieval tradition.

One small and not very important sign of the liberalism of the Rhineland was that whereas in the rest of Germany the Jews still retained the ghetto tradition, here they did not, but were permitted to achieve professional status and were granted a measure of social recognition. Among the Rhineland Jews in the second decade of the nineteenth century were Hirschel and Henriette Marx who lived in Trier, where Hirschel practised as a lawyer. They were members of the solid, respectable middle class, and as such were treated as equals by their Aryan German fellow citizens.

At two o'clock in the morning of 5 May, 1818, Henriette gave birth to her second child and eldest son, whom she named Karl. Six years after the birth of Karl, the Marxes—never the holders of strong religious convictions—were converted to Christianity. The motives for the change, whatever they may have been, were certainly not religious, for they never became any better Christians than they had been Jews. Neither religion nor race was ever to have much significance for Karl Marx, who, when he visited Ramsgate in his old age at the height of the season, could describe it as being "full of fleas and Jews".

At the age of twelve, Karl entered Trier High School, and remained there for five years. When he left, the certificate granted to him stated among other things:

"He has good abilities, and has shown in ancient languages, in German and in history very satisfactory, in mathematics satisfactory, and in French only moderate application. It is to be hoped that he will fulfil the favourable expectations which are justified by his abilities."

In October, 1835, Marx entered Bonn University to study law. After a year there he moved to Berlin University. Here, besides applying himself to his studies with moderate zeal, he formed a great liking for poetry and fell in love for the first and only time in his life. The object of his love was Jenny von Westphalen, the companion of his elder sister Sophie, and the daughter of an official in the Prussian administration at Trier. She was four years older than he, but as deeply in love. He poured out his feelings for her in numerous poems which are not without merit. Her parents thought sufficiently of the young man to give permission for their engagement.

From Berlin, Marx moved to the University of Jena, and there in 1841 presented his dissertation for his doctorate in philosophy. The subject he chose was "The Differences between the Natural Philosophy of Democritus and of Epicurus". He defended his arguments so skilfully that his examiners were satisfied.

By this time he had given up the idea of practising law and was planning to adopt an academic career. His father had died in 1838, but his mother and his fiancée still lived in Trier. He visited them on his way to join his friend Bruno Bauer, then a lecturer at Bonn.

After some months in Bonn, he gave up the idea of university teaching and was asked to accept the editorship of a new newspaper, the *Rheinische Zeitung*, which had been founded by a group of young disciples of the philosopher Hegel to counteract the influence of the reactionary *Kölnische Zeitung*. So, at the beginning of May, 1842, he settled in Cologne. In his articles for the paper—which were mostly attacks on the Prussian Government of the day—he displayed a fearlessness and a ruthlessness which made a striking impression on readers accustomed to frightened and compliant journalism. Indeed, they earned for Marx the reputation of being the first German journalist of note.

He fought the censorship, the Prussian Government and his more cautious friends. His interest in philosophy was replaced by a deep and far-ranging interest in practical politics, and he devoted his outstanding literary powers to pressing for the reform of many Prussian laws which, in his view, were outmoded. His work on the *Rheinische Zeitung* did much more than change his interests or make of him a figure in the German world. During the period that he was with the paper, he began to formulate the ideas which were to achieve a measure of immortality for him.

In June, 1843, after a seven-year engagement, he and Jenny von Westphalen were at last married. Three months before this the paper had been suppressed by the censor and he had formed a plan for continuing his attacks on the Government in a paper published abroad. Which country should be accorded the honour he had not yet decided, but a friend, who had been making a reconnaissance on his behalf, persuaded him that Paris would be the most suitable place. So in November, 1843, Marx and his wife arrived in Paris. Except for a few months during the German revolutionary outbreaks of 1848–9, he was to be a permanent exile from his homeland.

The fifteen months he was to stay in Paris was the key-period for the ripening and clarification of his thought. Almost of equal importance, however, was his meeting with Friedrich Engels, with whom he formed a life-long friendship and who was to become his partner in the founding of the Communist Party.

From Paris, Marx moved to Brussels. While there he paid a visit to England, where he was received by various working-men's organizations in Manchester and London. This visit was to play a vital part in his development. Until that time he had been content with literary attacks on all he believed to be wrong with the social order, and had kept aloof from the Socialist associations which were, in fact, not only thinking along the same lines as himself but actively working for the achievement of Socialist ideas in practice.

On his return to Brussels, he devoted himself for the next two years to setting up machinery which would provide a means by which the Socialist groups, now termed Communist groups, in all countries might collaborate. He also travelled abroad to meet as many of the active groups as he could. As a result, he reached the conclusion that Communists wherever they might be, should have a common central organization, and after discussions, an international Communist League was formed. The first congress of the League did little more than formulate a constitution and draft statutes. A "confession of faith" was to be drawn up and submitted to a second congress later in the year.

When this congress met in London in December, 1847, Marx presented to it a *Communist Manifesto*, which he and Engels, who was working closely with him, had drawn up together. In it he had set out in popular form the main points of his doctrine and the way in which the more practical parts of his teaching might be applied. Having defined the principles of Communism, it advocated a series of immediate reforms, all of which appeared to the *bourgeoisie* of 1848 the very peak of revolutionary madness. The *Manifesto* had not yet been printed and distributed when the second French Revolution broke out in February, 1848, spreading over western Europe a wave of revolution which reached Germany.

Immediately he heard the news, Marx and Engels hurried home, but before they could make an effective contribution, the revolution petered out. The fact that they had tried to assist brought repercussions. The Belgian authorities listed them as "dangerous persons", and they were given twenty-four hours to leave the country.

Owing to administrative muddles, Marx was arrested, and a few hours later his wife was seized. After a night in gaol they were brought before a magistrate, who warned them that they must not stay another night on Belgian soil. In a few hours, the Marxes and their three young children were on their way to London, where they were to live for the rest of their lives.

From this point, Marx devoted all his energies to promoting Communism. He made frequent visits to members abroad, but his most fruitful activity was the part he played in the foundation of the International Working Men's Association, whose affairs he directed until it was wound up in 1873.

At the same time he was developing his thought and working on the formulation of the theory for which he will surely ever be known. To support himself and his family, he returned to journalism, and contributed articles in newspapers and periodicals all over the world.

In 1867 he published the first volume of his great work *Capital* (two further volumes were to be published after his death) in which he set out his doctrine in full. Since western Communism has, in its development, diverged somewhat from the principles of pure

Marxist doctrine, it will not be out of place here to set out very briefly what Marx taught.

By the materialist conception of history he expressed the belief that the basis of historical development is to be found in economic considerations above everything else. On the purely economic side, he held the theory, not generally accepted, that the value of any article or product depends upon the amount of labour expended on it, as measured by time.

Labour, he taught, produced far more than it consumed and this surplus value, as he termed it, was inevitably appropriated by the capitalist, who allowed the labourer in wages only enough to provide for a bare subsistence and to enable him to raise children. From this it followed that there could be nothing in common between the employers and the employed, the proletariat. The latter must recognize this by developing a class-consciousness which, when sufficiently developed, would result in a class war, in which the whole of the capitalist system would be overthrown.

The International Working Men's Association, or as it was much better known, the First International, was undermined by internal disagreements, which began as criticisms and ended as quarrels, followed by manoeuvres by each faction to discredit the other. In these manoeuvres Marx played an active part. Though he succeeded in destroying his enemies he equally alienated his friends by the methods he used. In his efforts to keep the Communists to the tracks of his own doctrine, he committed political suicide, and by 1873 the First International had ceased to exist.

He was still in middle-age, only fifty-six, and up to this time had been robust and healthy, but now he fell ill and the doctors diagnosed an enlargment of the liver, a complaint which made him very irritable. He was sent on a round of the spas, but none gave him much relief. In the summer of 1878 he was told that he could no longer visit Germany, and he tried in turn the English spas—Malvern, the south-coast resorts and the Channel Islands.

He was, by this time, something of a hypochondriac, but he did not die of his liver. Jenny Marx died first, of cancer of the breast, on 2 December, 1881. Though she had been a sick woman for some time, her death left Marx, as he put it, "a moral cripple". The whole of 1882 he wandered in search of health. In January he was in the Isle of Wight, in February in Algiers, in June in Monte Carlo, in July at Enghien, near Paris, and in Switzerland.

In January, 1883, his eldest daughter died, and this deepened the wound made by his wife's death. He returned to London. He was suffering from chronic lung trouble, and he knew that he himself had not long to live. He lingered on for two months, and died quietly, but rather unexpectedly, on 14 March, 1883, a few weeks before his sixty-sixth birthday.

Three days later he was buried beside his wife in Highgate Cemetery, London, with fewer than a dozen mourners to bid him farewell.

Queen Victoria
1819-1901

WHEN Queen Victoria died in 1901, the vast majority of her subjects had little idea of what England had been like in 1837, when, at the age of eighteen, she had come to the throne. Her reign seemed to have begun right outside what was thought of as the contemporary world. The Queen's capacity for survival was a major factor evoking the admiration of her subjects.

At the time of her accession, the country was seething with discontent. Already, thanks to the use of steam power in industry, Britain was a rich country, but her new industrial proletariat lived in filthy slums and in extreme poverty. The average life of a middle-class person was fifty-five and that of a worker twenty-five. England's formerly prosperous peasants and yeoman farmers were losing their rights to common land and becoming underpaid landless labourers under the enclosure Bills, measures necessary perhaps for producing food for the towns but which embittered and degraded the people who had once been the backbone of the nation. Parliament was dominated by the aristocracy and the squires and, though the first Reform Bill of 1832 had abolished "rotten" boroughs and given the middle classes some representation in the House of Commons, there was a general fear of revolution and, from the governing classes, an increasingly stern resistance to change.

From the viewpoint of comfort, sanitation and communications, England still belonged to the eighteenth century. The development of railways and of electricity had barely begun; in 1830 the Duke of Wellington had opened the first railway between Liverpool and Manchester and in that same year Faraday had discovered the way in which an electric current could be generated.

By the end of the century, Britain was the most prosperous country in the world with an admirably functioning Parliamentary democracy. If the standard of living and housing of the working classes still left much to be desired, the working classes themselves believed that progress would come about inevitably with the spread of science and the development of education.

Britain had been involved between 1837 and 1901 in many small wars and colonial struggles—the Crimean War fought in 1854; the Indian Mutiny of 1857; continual fighting on the borders of India and Afghanistan; and the Boer War, which was in its last stages when Queen Victoria died. But basically it had been an era of peace ever since 1815 when Napoleon had been finally defeated. Europe had avoided major conflicts and good sense had prevented the war between Austria and Prussia (1866) and the Franco-Prussian war (1870) from becoming general.

There was indeed a widespread belief among European intellectuals that the growing industrial prosperity, accompanied as it was by the satisfaction of nationalist aspirations (Germany and Italy were nations, Greece and most of the Balkans had been freed from Turkish rule) meant the beginning of universal peace. The British believed that their Empire would last for a long time and the White Man's Burden was to awaken Asiatics and Africans to the benefits of civilization and Christianity. The Victorian age was the age of confidence, particularly so in Britain. Einstein and Freud, though born in the Victorian era, had yet to undo this superb confidence. There were many rebels, of course—there was Carlyle, Ruskin, William Morris, Matthew Arnold; all these attacked Victorian complacency and philistinism without, however, seriously disturbing it.

It was not only because she happened to be the British monarch during nearly all the long and significant period which came to an end with the First World War that Queen Victoria gave her name to it. It was also because with her powerful, optimistic character, her serious, confident even if limited views and her sense of duty she was almost *the* typical Victorian.

In 1830, King George IV, once known as the First Gentleman of Europe, immensely fat, gouty and selfish died and, leaving no heir of his body, was succeeded by his brother, The Duke of Clarence, known as William IV, a testy, elderly gentleman of no great intelligence, of no tact whatever, but with good intentions. None of King George IV's other brothers had produced suitable issue except the Duke of Kent who, on the death of George IV's daughter Charlotte had hastily abandoned the mistress with whom he had lived for nearly twenty-seven years and had taken to wife a German Princess of Saxe-Coburg. He confidently expected a child and a large bounty from Parliament to pay off his debts. He got the former, but the latter was grossly insufficient in his view. He died shortly after having produced Victoria. His widow and the baby were left in rather straitened circumstances. During William IV's reign, the young

Princess and her mother were popular among the people and the aristocracy as well, if only because everyone dreaded the coming to the throne of another of the brothers of George IV and particularly of the Duke of Cumberland. The Duchess of Kent instilled into her daughter a dislike of the lax moral standards of her uncles and a firm sense of duty. Victoria was, up to a point, a responsive daughter; but the duchess was over-insistent and Victoria's first act, after her coronation, was to remove her bed from her mother's room.

The new influence in her life was the Prime Minister, Lord Melbourne, a man of great charm, broadness of mind and intellectual vigour. Lord Melbourne felt, on his side, the charm of being the confidant of the young Queen who with her bold, slightly protruding eyes, her retreating chin and good figure was attractive and, as monarch, the object of respect. As Prime Minister he never sat down during their long sessions of State business; as her friend he felt he mattered to her more than anyone else.

The relations of Crown and Parliament were as yet unfixed and, when the Whigs were overthrown in the House of Commons, Victoria for a while refused to call a Tory ministry because the Tories insisted on changing the Women of her Bedchamber. In 1840 she married Prince Albert of Saxe-Coburg, her favourite cousin. She did not altogether want to marry, but when Albert came on a visit, she was overcome by his beauty as well as his intellect: she was always extremely frank and even unguarded and in her diary she wrote of "His exquisite nose . . . the delicate moustachios . . . the beautiful figure broad in the shoulder and the fine waist".

At first Albert was not encouraged to take an interest in politics. Little by little, her love for him growing, she perceived that, like her, he was animated by a sense of duty and of the importance of the Crown; moreover that he had a better and clearer mind.

There is the story that once, after Albert had retired to his room in Windsor slightly annoyed at the Queen's late hours (she loved dancing until the dawn and he liked going to bed early) the Queen knocked at the door. "Who is there?" asked the Prince. "The Queen of England," was the answer. There was no reply. The knocking, the question, the answer and the silence were repeated. A third time and the door was opened when the answer was "Your wife, Albert".

The Prince Consort gradually dominated his wife. He was intensely industrious, a man who wrote endless memoranda and whose advice could not be ignored because it was so painstaking and often so sensible. In 1851 the Great Exhibition in Hyde Park marked the triumph of Albert's work on behalf of industry.

Victoria and Albert had nine children. They stayed when they could at Osborne, which they built in the Isle of Wight, and at Balmoral where Albert designed a medieval castle in place of a small lodge. They were extremely popular because their happy domestic life was the image of royalty which the middle classes desired. As Lytton Strachey[1] has written:

"They liked a love match; they liked too a household which combined the advantages of royalty and virtue, and in which they seemed to see reflected as in some resplendent looking-glass, the ideal image of the very lives they lived themselves. Their own existences, less exalted, but so soothingly similar, acquired an added excellence, an added succulence, from the early hours, the regularity, the plain tuckers, the round games, the roast beef and Yorkshire pudding of Osborne. It was indeed a model court. Not only with its central personages the patterns of propriety, but no breath of scandal, no shadow of indecorum, might approach its utmost boundaries."

Albert was not as happy as Victoria. He felt, and this was true, that he was not liked even though he was increasingly respected by the court and by the aristocracy. He drove himself hard. He was a man who could not relax; his health suffered; the once beautiful young Hussar grew into a sallow, tired-looking man, bald on the top of his head. Beside Victoria he made a pitiful contrast. She too was stout, "but it was with the plumpness of a vigorous matron and an eager vitality was everywhere visible—in her energetic bearing, her protruding, inquiring glances, her small fat, capable and commanding hands".[2]

Albert contracted an illness which began with a journey to Cambridge where he had gone to admonish his eldest son, Berty, afterwards Edward VII, against laziness and dissipation. He died some weeks later and his illness was diagnosed—too late, and not by the Queen's physician—as typhoid. Victoria's grief was terrible and long lasting. Every day, for the next forty years, in the Prince Consort's suite at Windsor his evening clothes were laid afresh on his bed and water was poured into a wash basin. Victoria's affection for John Brown, Albert's gillie at Balmoral, was a reflection of her love for her husband. Only in the last years of her reign when she was the head of an immense family of British and German Princes and the Empress of India did the memory of Albert begin to fade.

[1] Lytton Strachey: *Queen Victoria*, Chatto and Windus, 1921.
[2] See Lytton Strachey.

For some years after Albert's death so rigid was her mourning that, though she still carried out her State business with exactitude and tenacity, she had no time for public appearances. The monarchy for a time knew once more a period of unpopularity, the civil list was cavilled at, and she was attacked even in the House of Lords.

Victoria was a woman of immense vitality and, revived by her friendship with Benjamin Disraeli, she became once more an attractive figure for her people. Disraeli first won his way into her affection by his tributes to the late Prince Consort. Both aroused in the other a strong romantic streak. Victoria sent her beloved Prime Minister primroses from the woods of Osborne: he responded with extravagant flattery in which he was, strangely enough, sincere. The Queen though exhilarated by contact with this unusual and un-English genius, had nonetheless her feet on the ground. She signed her letters to him "Yours Aff 'ly Victoria Regina et Imperatrix". No more than Lord Melbourne did Disraeli sit during business sessions.

Until the death of Albert it could be said that imperceptibly the power of the Crown had increased as compared with that of the Cabinet. This was owing, in part, to the extraordinary industry of both the Queen and the Prince Consort as well as to Albert's good sense. His last act, indeed, had been to draft a memorandum criticizing a despatch of the Prime Minister, Lord John Russell, to the northern States of America which might have led to Britain being drawn into the American Civil War. His criticism of this was accepted.

It is true the Crown only warned and advised; but it did so with so much insistence and regularity that, with a weak Prime Minister, the King or Queen could easily have stepped out of the category of advisers. After Albert's death, the Queen abated no jot of her right to be consulted on everything, but she never attempted to force her will on the Prime Minister and behaved with complete fairness even to Mr Gladstone whom she disliked (saying of him that he insisted on addressing her as though she were a public meeting).

As the social leader of Britain Victoria's influence remained, as it had always been, in favour of the rather narrow domestic virtues. The slightest ribaldry or misplaced allusion could and did draw down the terrifying remark, with the lively eyes turned suddenly expressionless, "We are not amused." Her tastes (Landseer in painting, Tennyson in poetry and the more sentimental novelists of the period) and her manners were those approved of by the majority of her subjects. In her old age there was added an additional majesty. The last years of her life were those of the new imperialism when the Empire became a sort of religious obsession with the British people. Victoria was the symbol of England's new imperial destiny. So the Crown whose political influence had diminished, acquired a new significance.

The Queen still loved Balmoral, her donkey carriage and her plain clothes; she still took a lively interest in the gossip of her household; she still reproved the tastes of society for luxury and dissipation, tastes which her eldest son shared. She was nonetheless fully aware of the new *mystique* which surrounded her. Indian servants attended her in the Great State processions which increased in number and magnificence. Her work also grew in volume. In 1900 she decided that instead of taking her holiday in the South of France she was going to Dublin on account of the large numbers of Irishmen serving in the Boer War. She died in harness, having kept her faculties almost to the last except for some incipient cataract and some stiffness of the joints.

To some it may appear strange to include Queen Victoria in a work devoted to the makers of the twentieth century. She was, it could be said, the symbol of another age and an age as different as possible from our own troubled, war-ridden one, in which confidence in European civilization, not to mention the specific Victorian interpretations of its values, has been shaken to the point at which it seems scarcely to survive. This great difference cannot be denied and our age has horrors as well as virtues which never entered the mind of Queen Victoria. Yet it remains true that the twentieth century cannot be understood without some knowledge of the history out of which it grew and of the values it rejected.

Victoria played an important rôle in the history of that time. Around her matronly form, the British nineteenth-century values crystallized. She has even a more direct importance. It was thanks to her that the British monarchy survived, that it came to have the importance it has today in the modern world. It may not necessarily last for ever, but it has played, after Victoria's death, an extremely important part in moulding the new Commonwealth and in acting as an efficient part of the well-oiled machine of British government. Thanks to this, Britain has remained a country of order in which the constitution is respected by the vast majority of the nation.

Queen Victoria made a greater contribution to the political solidarity of the British people than any other single individual, and it is for this reason that she can properly be described as one of the makers of the twentieth century.

Gustave Flaubert
1821-1880

Over a hundred years ago a book was published in France which became established throughout the world as a classic. It is the greatest French novel of the nineteenth century and some people have even called it the greatest in French literature. An eminent French critic has said that its characters were more real to him than Shakespeare's and he called it "the most complete portrait of a woman in all literature". The lesser characters, the style, the realism, have also come in for the highest praise, and not only from Frenchmen. The English critic George Saintsbury wrote of its author: "I do not think that Europe at large has ever had a greater since the death of Thackeray." The book has, of course, been translated into English and still sells well. In our own time it has been filmed and adapted for TV. Few people have not heard of Gustave Flaubert's *Madame Bovary*.

Madame Bovary is a longish novel; it took five years to write. When you have finished it you feel you have had an experience which has enlarged your understanding of life. While you were reading the book you were living with greater intensity than you normally do. This surely is the test of all great books. Yet the story is not at all sensational. The setting is a sleepy French village in the 1830s. The villagers, not excluding the Catholic priest and the local apothecary who boasts of his enlightened views, are extraordinarily limited in their intelligence and outlook. Nothing much goes on in the place except gossip between the housewives, the moo of cows, the ringing of the angelus bell and the steady procession of birth, life and death.

To this puddle of routine and boredom come Madame Bovary— "Emma"—and her doctor husband. Even before they get there we know that the atmosphere will prove lethal to her. For Emma is an intelligent young woman whose imagination is perpetually at war with reality. She is a farmer's daughter, an only child whose parents left her very much to herself and it so happened that not one single thing to do with chickens, dung-heaps, muck or milking appealed to her. Instead, as soon as she could read she plunged into an orgy of romantic stuff about dying swans, ruins and pale-faced cavaliers kissing frail hands beside blue lakes mirroring snow-clad mountains. To her, visions of medieval splendour or idyllic life on far-off tropic shores were a kind of super-reality. She never asked herself whether life as portrayed by romantic writers had in fact ever existed. Its spell was powerful, therefore it must be true and somewhere, she felt sure, she would find it. Emma Bovary was, in short, an escapist, and in her teens at the farm the only hope which gave meaning to her life was that one day *her* cavalier would turn up with the key to eternal bliss in his hand.

So far, you may say, not very different from some teenagers today. No. But Emma was lonely. Her mother was dead, her father talked of nothing but crops and cattle, and her education amid the prayer and incense of a convent had carried her even further from life. So she never made firm contact with reality at any point. Romanticism became the perpetual climate of her mind, a pink cloud that she took with her everywhere.

When the widowed Doctor Bovary turned up one day to set the farmer's broken leg it was this cloud which prevented Emma from seeing him clearly. Charles Bovary was, in fact, a plump, stupid young man without an ounce of imagination. More from habit than anything else, because he was used to a wife, he eventually asked Emma's father for her hand and the old man consented.

So Charles and Emma got married. Their first home was in the depths of the country and for Emma it soon became a prison. She was bored all day when Charles was out tending his patients and even more bored at night because she could not love him and his own placid contentment exasperated her. Finally, after a ball at a big house had given her a tantalizing glimpse of cultured life, she could bear the monotony no longer and she persuaded Charles to get a practice in the little village of Yonville.

Life at Yonville was just as dreary. Soon Emma began to see that Charles would never change. The daughter that was born to her was ugly and left her indifferent. The local people were stupid beyond redemption. No faintest whiff here of romance, excitement or culture. Nothing but drab reality, the monotonous passage of time, growing old without hope or reason for living. There was one gleam—a young notary's clerk with a certain natural elegance and refinement. He and Emma talked literature and music together. It was a sentimental friendship which stirred them both and left both unsatisfied. Yet for a while the young Léon was the focus of all her dreams. When he left for study in Rouen the sluggish routine flooded back: the church bell ringing for vespers, dogs barking in the distance, horses led morning and evening to drink in the village pond.

To Emma some distraction was now a necessity. It had to come—and it came in the shape of Rodolphe, a country gentleman who proceeded to seduce her with the calm of an experienced general conducting a military campaign. Of course, he said the right things and for a time he was passionate. At heart, though, he was cynical and selfish. Emma saw nothing of that. "I have a lover! A lover!" she exclaimed—but not, you will notice, "I am in love."

As Rodolphe's passion cooled Emma became more demanding until at last she implored him to elope with her and weakly he agreed, planning everything for a certain Sunday. He never came. Instead, he sent her a letter full of lofty sentiments, pretending it was in her interest that they should never meet again. After that Emma was very ill and nearly died. Charles was still devoted and made no protest when she squandered money on fine clothes and furniture for the house. Soon she was deep in debt and happiness was further away than ever. When would it come? Was Léon the answer? A chance meeting, and she believed he might be. They became lovers, hired a room in Rouen and met every Thursday. Emma showered gifts on him and to pay for them began borrowing and signing IOU's. She even stole part of her husband's earnings to pay her creditors. She was reckless because even this affair with Léon failed to satisfy her. It became a habit and as such just as boring as her marriage.

Disaster came. Reality, which she had always despised, took its revenge. She had already been threatened with the seizure of her furniture unless she paid her debts. She asked Léon for money. He made excuses and when she went home she found the bailiffs at the door. Now she faced exposure, the final shattering of her dreams. Her husband, the whole village would know her story. In desperation, abandoning the last vestige of self-respect, she ran to Rodolphe, the man who had jilted her, clung to him, implored his help. Rodolphe refused.

There was no hope left. The cold grim fact that life, with its iron chain of cause and effect, cannot be twisted to suit romantic notions, remained. So Emma left it. She took poison and Charles, tears streaming down his face, loving her to the end, watched her die. . . . Some months later, he found letters which Léon had written to her and a miniature of Rodolphe. Then the whole tragedy of his life with Emma burst upon him. He did not blame her or anyone, it was "fate", he said. A few days later, his daughter found him dead in the garden, dead, as they say, of a broken heart.

This novel brought Flaubert immediate fame and I have told its story first because his life lies in his books. To him, writing *was* life. He had no other ambition or interest. Born in 1821, the son of a famous surgeon of Rouen, he was improvising plays even before he could read. He grew up in Rouen, living at the hospital where his father worked. He became, according to a woman who knew him then, a handsome youth:

"like a young Greek—tall, slender, graceful as an athlete, unconscious of the gifts he possessed, careless of the impression he made and entirely indifferent to convention."

School did not please him and law studies in Paris at the age of nineteen he found equally boring. He had yet to find his place in life and he declared he had made at least one good resolution: not to pursue any profession at all, "for I despise men too much to wish to do them good or evil".

Flaubert was disgusted with life which he compared to a "nauseating smell of cooking escaping through a ventilator". At this early age he was in fact, going through a romantic crisis; throughout his life it was never entirely resolved. On the one hand was the world of reality—drudgery, squalor, ugly faces and petty minds; on the other, ecstatic visions called up by his intensely imaginative mind. Soon the strain produced the first signs of a nervous ailment which became chronic. The stupendous toil he later devoted to his books may have been the only way to keep it under control.

In 1846 his father died and he abandoned the law for ever. Three months later, after the death of his sister, he went to live in Croisset near Rouen where his mother joined him. The long low house set in a delightful garden was close to the Seine and from its windows could be seen the busy traffic on the river. Here Flaubert lived until his death, except for one stay in Brittany, another longer visit to the Mediterranean and irregular trips to Paris.

His first book, which was not published till many years later, was a dream-novel about the temptations of Saint Anthony, magnificent in style, powerful and at times terrifying in content. In 1850, he began to draft the plot of *Madame Bovary* and here his Herculean labours began. This was to be no product of overheated imagination, but a down-to-earth, scrupulously-documented study of one woman's fate and the setting in which she lived.

For every character in the book—and there are many excellent ones which I have had no space to mention—Flaubert worked out an entire life story, though only a small part of it appeared in the novel. He produced several long synopses of the plot, adding some incidents, altering others till the whole dovetailed together with an iron logic. Then at last he began to write, and this was the most laborious part of all because Flaubert had a theory which he stuck to all his life. There was, he believed, only one perfect way of telling a story, only one perfect succession of words. The difficulty was to achieve this perfection. Paragraphs were altered again and again, phrases were changed, for hours at a time he chewed over a single word, spoke it aloud, considered it in its context, sometimes asked the opinion of friends. After writing and rewriting till the pages were black with ink, he slowly, in five years, produced his masterpiece. When it was published and selling in thousands he said he wished he had enough money to buy up every copy and burn the lot!

Discerning readers, however, noticed certain things about this book which made it truly revolutionary: Its realism, first and foremost. By supreme art Flaubert had condensed into its pages the illusion of real life. Secondly, every single incident, indeed every word in the book was relevant to the main theme. Thirdly, the prose was superb—taut, rhythmic and perpetually alive. Lastly, and most important of all, like the *Iliad* or Shakespeare's plays, *Madame Bovary* told you nothing about its author. He had effaced himself, remained impassive, feeling with all his characters, but siding with none of them. Consequently the impact of the book was direct. It contained no sentimentality, no moralizing. There was no "explanation" of the tragedy. It was sharp, brutal and as inexplicable as life itself.

Flaubert wrote other novels after this—*Salammbo*, *L'Education Sentimentale*, the unfinished *Bouvard et Pécuchet*, alternating between realism and romanticism. He also wrote stories and plays and into all these books went the same intense application, the same dedicated aim to reach perfection as he understood it. He died of a heart-attack in 1880, "Tired," as he said, "to the marrow of my bones." He had slaved for thirty-four years and today, when the inexhaustible demands of true art are sometimes forgotten, it is good to remember Flaubert, the dedicated writer who in *Madame Bovary* made the story of one foolish woman into immortal literature. So let us take leave of him as Guy de Maupassant, a close friend and ardent admirer saw him at work:

"Crouched in an oak, high-backed chair, head sunk between his broad shoulders, he scrutinized the paper, the small pupils of his blue eyes seeming like black dots in continual movement. A silk skullcap,

like those worn by ecclesiastics, covered the top of his head, leaving
long locks of hair curled at the ends to fall over his back. A huge
dressing-gown of brown cloth enveloped him completely, and his red
face, with its white trailing moustache, was congested by a violent rush
of blood. Beneath dark heavy eyebrows his eyes traversed the lines,
rummaging the words, shunting the phrases, studying the appearance
of the assembled letters, gauging the effect like a hunter stalking his
prey.

"Then he began to write, slowly, stopping continually, striking out,
writing between the lines, filling up the margins, adding words slant-
wise, blackening twenty pages to complete one, groaning under the
laborious effort of his thought like a galley-slave.

"Sometimes, throwing his pen into a big Oriental dish full of carefully trimmed goose quills, he would pick up the sheet of paper, raise
it to his eyes and, leaning on one elbow, declaim a passage in a sharp,
high-pitched voice. He listened to the rhythm of his prose, stopped as
though to catch some elusive resonance, adjust the sounds, removed
unintentional rhymes, spaced the commas scientifically like pauses on
a lengthy road.

"At the same time a thousand other considerations preoccupied and
obsessed him and always this harassing certainty remained fixed in his
mind. 'Among all these phrases, these forms, these turns of speech there
is only one phrase, one form, one turn of speech to express perfectly
what I want to say.' So, red of face, tensing his muscles like an
athlete, he fought furiously with ideas and words, seizing on to them,
coupling them up, holding them together by the power of his will.

"No one cherished a greater respect and love for his art than Gustave
Flaubert or a greater feeling for the dignity of literature. Finally, one
day, he fell, struck down at the foot of his desk, killed by literature,
killed like all those great and ardent people whom their passion
devours."

Mary Baker Eddy
1821–1910

On a winter's day in 1866 a middle-aged lady was walking along the icy pavements of a small town in Massachusetts when she slipped and fell. Unconscious and obviously badly injured, she was carried into the nearest house. A doctor was summoned. He found her injuries to be internal and said she should not be moved. The following day, however, she insisted on being taken to her home, and this was done.

This was on the Friday, and on Sunday morning they thought she was dying. The doctor wore a gloomy face. A clergyman was sent for, and while they were waiting for his coming the woman asked to be left alone with her Bible. She opened it at St Matthew's Gospel, and read Chapter 9, which relates the story of the man who was brought to Jesus with a palsy and was told to be of good cheer, take up his bed and go to his house, for his sins had been forgiven him. She had read the words over so many times before, but now they seemed to have a fresh meaning. She took them as a message given directly to herself. Getting out of bed she dressed herself and left her sickroom. To the friends who gathered round in shocked surprise she declared that she had been cured, cured instantaneously, of the affliction that had carried her so near to the gates of death.

From that room where tears had been so suddenly overtaken by rejoicing, she moved out to establish a religion which ere long had its adherents in all the countries of the civilized globe. Forty-four years of life were left to her, and when at length she died in 1910, at the age of eighty-nine, she was mourned as few other women have been mourned.

Mrs Mary Patterson was her name when she was picked up from where she had fallen on that day of bitter cold and treacherous ice. She had been born forty-five years earlier (16 July, 1821) as Mary Baker, the youngest of the seven children of a thriving farmer in the insignificant township of Bow, New Hampshire, U.S.A. He was a man of strong character, sharp-tempered and very devout, a deacon of the local Congregationalist church. He held in its extreme form the Calvinist doctrine of the eternal damnation of by far the greater proportion of the human race, from which the love of a serene and comparatively cultured wife failed to detach him.

Mary was a delicate child from the first, subject to fits of hysteria and much given to melancholy reflections. She took after her mother far more than after her father, however, and at length she revolted against his crude and fierce theology. The resulting arguments were so distressing that she was reduced to a bed of sickness. When the village physician failed to effect a cure she listened with eagerness to her mother, who bade her remember that God was after all a God of Love. The girl prayed, and with the lifting of the horrid burden of dogma she felt infinitely better in body and mind and spirit.

For a girl of that period and environment she was reasonably well educated, although we may perhaps doubt the statements made by some of her enthusiastic biographers, that she was well grounded in natural philosophy, moral science, logic, and the Greek and Hebrew tongues. As a girl in her teens she started writing in prose and verse for the local papers and magazines. She developed a style which though by no means to everybody's taste was peculiarly her own.

This delicate young lady was destined to be three times married. Her first husband was George Washington Glover, a builder and contractor who had been in business locally but was established at Charleston, in South Carolina. They were married just before Christmas, 1843, and he died six months later, from yellow fever, at Wilmington, where he had gone in pursuit of business. His young wife was pregnant, and she bore a son, her only child as it turned out, three months after her husband's decease. She did not take at all kindly to motherhood, and before long the care of the boy was transferred to people less likely to be exhausted by his noisy ways.

After nine years of widowhood, spent more or less as an invalid but with interesting excursions into spiritualism (then all the rage in the States), mesmerism, and the movement for the abolition of Negro slavery—Mr Glover had owned slaves, and she hadn't liked it—Mrs Glover became Mrs Patterson. Dr Daniel Patterson was a dentist who practised homoeopathy as a sideline. He was big and handsome and rather flashy, with a way with women. He found the still young widow—so cultured and talented, pleasant in her appearance and displaying a nice sense in dress—very much to his taste. The marriage was in 1853, and it was a most unfortunate one for her. Dr Patterson was a wayward spirit; the course of his wanderings took him on a sightseeing trip to the battlefield of Bull Run; he was taken prisoner by the Southerners and had to spend the remaining two years of the American Civil War in gaol.

For the second time Mary was deprived of her husband, and this at a time when her health had once again become a matter of the most pressing concern. Doctors could find nothing seriously wrong with her, and yet she never felt really well. She tried all sorts of "cures", but was no better at the end of any of them. Then she had recourse to a healer of somewhat dubious reputation, one Phineas P. Quimby, whose name had been given to her by her husband. The son of a blacksmith and in his early days a watchmaker, Quimby had discovered that he possessed considerable mesmeric powers. Now he was a man of sixty, carrying on a practice of unorthodox medicine in Portland, Maine.

At their first consultation, the healer diagnosed spinal disease, rubbed Mrs Patterson's head vigorously with his hands, and then sent her into a hypnotic sleep. When she awoke, she felt better. The treatment was resumed, again with the most satisfactory results. She was delighted, and at once set about preaching the Quimby system by word and pen. As for Quimby, he may well have been embarrassed by the enthusiasm of his disciple, but the situation was resolved when he died in 1866 of a stomach ulcer that had proved resistant to clairvoyance, mesmerism, mind-cure and the rest.

Meanwhile Dr Patterson had reappeared in his wife's life, and they established a home in the small town of Lynn, outside Boston. He was as restless as ever, and set out on a long lecturing tour of the southern states, describing in colourful detail his experiences as a prisoner-of-war. Then came the tidings that he had run off with the daughter of a wealthy patient. His wife never saw him again. In 1873 she obtained a divorce, on the grounds of desertion and adultery.

After his departure, she was in poor circumstances, but she proved once more that she was quite capable of standing on her own feet. She continued her studies in mental phenomena, and probably engaged in a little healing on her own account. Quimby was dead, but he had left behind him some of his lecture notes, and (so some of her critics have alleged) she found these of considerable use in the formation of her own teaching. So we come to the day of the accident, followed by the recovery that was so sudden and so complete that she looked upon it as occasioned by a miracle.

Years afterwards she was to write that:

"in the year 1866 I discovered the Christ Science, or Divine Laws of Life, Truth, and Love, and named my discovery Christian Science".

About a year later she started a school of Christian Science Mind-healing, with only one student, in Lynn. Much more important was her venture into authorship. As early as 1862 (she tells us) she had begun to write down and give to friends the results of her Scriptural study, "but these compositions were crude—the first steps of a child in the newly discovered world of Spirit". Now as always, "the Bible was her sole teacher".

This period in her career has always been something of a mystery to her biographers. She seems to have moved from place to place, lodging-house to lodging-house, teaching, practising healing work, studying her Bible, and putting her thoughts and discoveries on paper. The first of her pamphlets was published in 1870, in a very limited edition, but in 1875 she emerged as the author of a book that was destined to become a most remarkable best-seller. It was called *Science and Health*. Some years later chapters on the interpretation of Scripture were included, and the book was known henceforth as *Science and Health with Key to the Scriptures*.

As a work of literature the book has little to commend it. It is long, running to over 600 pages; it lacks arrangement, there is in it no sense of style, the English is awkward, there is no poetry, no sense of humour, no force of sustained argument. But it has something which many much better-written books altogether lack: it has power. Innumerable readers throughout the world in more than one generation have found it convincing through its sheer assertiveness, have found in it the answer to their deepest needs. By the end of the century its circulation was nearing 270,000, and by now it runs into millions. As the textbook of Christian Science it stands beside the Bible, and passages from both books are read as a regular feature of worship in Christian Science churches everywhere.

From time to time the book was revised under the author's direction, to give, as she put it, a fuller and clearer expression of her teaching. Each edition was carefully copyrighted, for she was an excellent business woman, and each volume bears a facsimile of her signature and a reproduction of the design of the Cross and Crown which had been registered as a trademark.

While it is impossible to reduce her doctrine to a few words and sentences, it may be stated here that she summarized the "fundamental propositions of divine metaphysics" in what to her were four "*self-evident* propositions," namely: (1) God is All-in-All. (2) God is good. Good is Mind. (3) God, Spirit, being all, nothing is matter. (4) Life, God, omnipotent good, deny death, evil, sin, disease. "Even if reversed," she wrote, "these propositions will be found to agree in statement and proof, showing mathematically their exact relation to Truth."

From these propositions it is deduced that since there is no such thing as matter, and sickness is one of the things "denied" by God, sickness does not really exist. We *think* we are ill, when what is really wrong with us is a false belief. To quote an actual illustration from the pages of *Science and Health*;

"You say a boil is painful; but that is impossible, for matter without mind is not painful. The boil simply manifests, through inflammation and swelling, a belief in pain, and this belief is called a boil."

How, then, is it to be cured? To quote further;

"Now administer mentally to your patient a high attenuation of truth, and it will soon cure the boil. The fact that pain cannot exist where there is no mortal mind to feel it is a proof that this so-called mind makes its own pain—that is, its own *belief* in pain."

As a consequence of this conviction, Christian Science repudiated not only spiritualists, mesmerists, mind-cures, and the ordinary run of faith-healers, but the whole body of practitioners of orthodox medicine. In their place there developed a special class of Christian Science healers, who are selected, trained, registered and licensed as strictly as are the members of our colleges of physicians and surgeons.

One of the first—perhaps the first—of this special corps was the man whom Mrs Glover (she had returned to this style after Mr Patterson's desertion) took for her third, and last, husband. His name was Asa Gilbert Eddy, and he had a job in Boston as agent for a firm of sewing-machine manufacturers. When he was introduced to her by a mutual friend he was very much out of sorts, and she cured him of his nervous complaint. He proposed marriage, was accepted, and they were united on New Year's Day, 1877. So she became Mrs Eddy, the name by which she became universally known.

Mr Eddy was a mild-mannered, unassuming little man, but he had a sound business sense, and much of the success of the struggling new movement was attributable to him. His wife was grateful. Dr Eddy, as she called him, was the first of her students to announce himself publicly as a Christian Scientist; he organized the first Christian Science Sunday school, and taught a special Bible class; he also lectured so ably that "clergymen of other denominations listened to him with deep interest. He was remarkably successful in mind-healing, and untiring in his chosen work." What was more to the point, perhaps, was that he attended very competently to the business side of *Science and Health*, securing its copyright and proper promotion. Furthermore, as a Boston businessman he was able to arrange for his wife to open a missionary campaign in this centre of American cultural life. He died unfortunately in 1882, and the "Reverend Mother" as she was now styled, felt it incumbent upon her to apologize publicly for being so entirely absorbed in the business of the movement that she had been unable to give to his case the personal attention it deserved.

By this time she was well on the road to becoming not only famous but rich. Her book was selling in thousands, at three dollars a copy. She was running courses of instruction in spiritual healing for which the charge was a hundred dollars or more. She had founded the Massachusetts Metaphysical College, which was attended by over four thousand students in seven years. She had launched a monthly magazine, the *Christian Science Journal*, which had a wide circulation. Already she had founded, in 1879, the Church of Christ, Scientist, in Boston, and in 1892 she reorganized it under the name of The First Church of Christ, Scientist. (Note the "The" in the title: it was Mrs Eddy's particular wish that it should be used in the title of this, the Mother Church of the whole Christian Science communion.)

Although as old age grew upon her, she tried to withdraw more and more from the public eye, her energy was unabated, her spirit unresting. Then very near the end of her long life she launched, in 1908, something that had long been her cherished ambition, an international daily newspaper which should not only uphold Christian Science principles but be a model to the world of enlightened journalism. The *Christian Science Monitor* is among the most notable and most worthy contributions of Christian Science to our modern world.

After living a number of years in a pleasant house in Concord, within sight of her birthplace, she moved to a mansion in one of the best suburbs of Boston, where she was most tenderly watched over by a staff of secretaries, domestics, and other helpers. There at length she died. She had been out for a drive on a bitterly cold winter's day, and returned home chilled to the bone and weary. A few days later, on 3 December, 1910, she succumbed to an attack of pneumonia. Shortly before her end she called for a writing tablet, and on it was able to write in pencil the words, "God is my life".

From the beginning she had directed the affairs of the Christian Science movement with so firm a hand and in so highly individual a fashion that it was expected by some of its critics that it would not long survive her. In fact, while there does not seem to have been any spectacular advance, Christian Science has improved its position in the land of its birth and has offshoots in most countries today. When

Mrs Eddy died there were about 1,200 Christian Science churches and societies in the U.S.A., and the number at present is in excess of 2,300. For the British Isles the figure is given as 324; while some of these are only small groups, others have congregations of several hundred members.

For the rest, Christian Science is as its founder left it, and that was what she intended and desired. She left the most strict instructions, and backed them up with the strongest legal sanctions that could be devised, that there should be no changes in Christian Science doctrine, forms of worship, organization, and of course in its text-book *Science and Health*, without the written consent of Mary Baker Eddy. For more than half a century Mary Baker Eddy has been dead, but in Christian Science as we know it today she is still very much alive.

Feodor Dostoievsky
1821-1881

Of the three great Russian writers who flourished in the latter half of the nineteenth century and who are best known in the West—Tolstoy, Chekov and Dostoievsky—it is the latter who has had the most direct effect on the literary development of the West. A rebel, embittered, morbid, incurably suspicious of everything, an inveterate gambler, he was, nevertheless, a literary genius of a quality rarely encountered.

The full flowering of this genius can be seen in the series of novels which began with *Crime and Punishment*, in 1866, and ended with *The Brothers Karamazov*, in 1880.

In these he attempted to justify the ways of God with man, and in the novels mentioned he achieves a power of expression which some critics think has never been equalled by any other novelist. With his vivid characterization and deep insight into the psychology of the emotions, he inaugurated a new school of writing.

ON a December day in 1849, twenty-one political prisoners stood in two lines in Semyonovsky Square, in St Petersburg, the capital of Russia. In the middle of the square a scaffold had been erected, and on it stood the sheriff holding a paper in his hand from which he read the names of the men in the two lines below him, and after each the words: "Sentenced to be shot."

As he finished and stepped down from the scaffold, the sun suddenly broke through the December gloom, and one of the men whispered to his companion, "It's impossible. They can't mean to kill us!" For answer, the companion silently pointed to a line of coffins which stood near the scaffold covered with a large cloth.

The first three men were led to the scaffold, tied to the posts and blindfolded with a bag enveloping their heads.

The young man who had whispered to his companion felt that his last hope had vanished. Perhaps he might have five minutes more to live. He stared at a church with a gilt dome which reflected the sunbeams, and suddenly felt as if these beams came from a region where he himself was to be in a few moments.

There was a pause, longer than was usual or necessary on these occasions, before the firing-squad were given their orders. The young man, who was short-sighted, could not see what was happening, until suddenly an officer on horse-back, waving a white handkerchief, galloped at break-neck speed into the square.

"I have an order from the Tsar. The death sentences are commuted to four years' penal servitude in Siberia, with the exception of one, who is to receive a full pardon. That is Palm."

The young man was never to forget those twenty minutes during which he had waited, in 20 degrees of frost clothed only in his shirt, to take his place at the posts in the second batch. His name was Feodor Dostoievsky. He had already made his mark on the Russian literary scene, though only twenty-eight, and was destined to become one of the greatest Russian novelists of all time.

In 1821, there was on the staff of St Mary's hospital in Moscow, a certain Army surgeon named Mikhail Andreyvitch Dostoievsky. With his wife, a pretty, gentle creature, he lived in a small flat attached to the hospital. Here, on 30 October, there was born his second son whom he named Feodor Mikhailovitch.

The doctor was a strange man. His great weakness was drink, and he ruled his family with strict discipline. Even when they were young ladies, he would never allow his daughters to go out alone, but always accompanied them when they visited friends and neighbours. He treated his four sons with a harshness which would have been approved of only by a psychopathic sergeant-major. His temper was exceedingly short, and when he lost it, which was often, his children had good cause to fear him. Only the frail and pretty woman who was his wife had any control over him. She checked his drinking to excess, and could calm him as no one else could. While she was there to intervene between him and the children, she could save them from the worst of his rages.

Another trait was his extreme meanness. Until the boys were sixteen or seventeen, he allowed them no pocket-money at all. Yet he was well enough off to buy a small estate near Tula, when Feodor was nine years old, and he chose good schools for his sons. On the estate, Mme Dostoievsky and the children spent the summer months; and it was here that Feodor grew to be attached to the serfs, the simple peasants, who worked for his father. This experience was to make a deep mark on the boy's future life.

Early in 1837 the mother died, and in the same year Feodor and his elder brother presented themselves for entry to the School of Engineering. To the family's surprise, Feodor was accepted, while his more robust brother was rejected.

After his wife's death, the doctor went to pieces altogether. He developed into a chronic drinker, and his temper became even more savage. He could no longer concentrate on his work, he resigned his appointment and retired to his estate. Here he treated his serfs with such savagery, that eventually he drove them to murder him.

In 1843 Feodor finished the course at the School of Engineering and entered the army with a commission as a Designer in the Department of Engineering. He embarked on an existence which, by all accounts, was completely meaningless. He attached himself to Bohemian circles. Despite the fact that he received from his official salary and his allowance from his guardian a total of 5,000 roubles a year, he was always hard up. He had developed a passion for billiards, at which he always lost. He was to remain extravagant throughout his entire life, and except during the last few years, when his great novels had brought him fame, he was always plagued by penury.

Amidst this strange, uncontrolled behaviour something was happening to him which was to transform his life. He developed a strong interest in literature, and began to translate Balzac's *Eugénie Grandet*. He quickly tired of Army life, and he wrote to his brother Mikhail towards the end of 1843, "The Service disgusts me like potatoes." By the end of the following year he could stand it no longer, and resigned.

Writing to his brother to tell him of his decision, he said: "I have no regrets. I have a hope. I am in the act of finishing a novel. It is rather original."

He had hoped to place it in the *Otechestvennia Zapiski*, a leading literary journal, but a year later still he was giving signs of being in great distress by the refusal of the journal to print his work unless he made vast alterations.

Rather than change it, however, he decided to publish it at his own expense. He told Mikhail:

"If the work is good, not only will it not be lost, it will also deliver me from my troubles and my debts . . . If the affair does not succeed, I may have to hang myself."

Though it meant involving himself even more deeply in debt, Dostoievsky kept his resolve. In 1846 he published *Poor Folk*. On reading the book, the foremost critic of the day sent for him and said:

"You have delved to the very essence of things and at a stroke have revealed a great truth. Value your gift, I beg of you, and remain ever true to it. Thus will you become a great writer."

Nor was Bielinsky the only critic to praise the work, and overnight Dostoievsky found himself famous and sought after. "I am received everywhere as a marvel," he told his brother.

The manner in which he met this fame, however, was unfortunate. He became arrogant and attacked his admirers and would-be helpers in a most cruel way. The inevitable happened. Whom did this young puppy from the provinces think he was? People began to retaliate in the only way they knew—they mocked him and every word he spoke. This affected him so much that there is little doubt that at this time he suffered from a mild form of persecution mania. This isolated him all the more, for he saw insult where none was intended.

The success of *Poor Folk* was followed by a period of failure. His driving force was to get rid of his burden of debt, but it seemed that his first triumph was never to be repeated. The scorn of the literary world increased.

Shut out by one circle, it was inevitable that Dostoievsky should turn to another. The circle he chose was one which was devoted to the preaching of reform, and which, at the time of Dostoievsky's joining it, was debating the iniquitous censorship imposed on all freedom of speech by the Government, and the freedom of the peasants from serfdom. Both affected him deeply, the first, as a writer, the second, on account of his experiences on his father's estate at Tula.

The authorities were always on guard against such groups, and the secret police were able to penetrate them almost at will, so naïve were their members in the ways of the autocratic world. As a result of an unguarded moment, in which Dostoievsky had been trapped by his genuine compassion for the serfs into seeming to advocate revolution, he was arrested on 23 April, 1849, while still in bed. At the same time twenty others of the circle were arrested also, and on 22 December they were led for execution into the Semyonovsky Square.

It was Christmas Eve when the reprieved men set out for their imprisonment at Omsk. The terrible experiences which Dostoievsky suffered during four years there he has recorded in *The House of the Dead*, which was published in 1861. The prison sentence was to be followed by a further period of exile, and this he had to pass in the town of Semipalatinsk.

To support himself, Dostoievsky rejoined the Army as a private. (He had been stripped of his military rank and his title of nobility on being sent to prison.) With the permission of his captain, he was able to live in private quarters, and he was befriended by the District

Attorney to Siberia, Baron Wrangel, a friendship which did much to relieve the hardships of exile. He began to write *The House of the Dead*; he also fell in love with Mme Maria Issayev, the wife of an officer, and she with him. When, in 1857, Mme Issayev became a widow, they married.

In 1858, his period of exile was ended, and he was permitted to return to St Petersburg. Here he finished *The House of the Dead*, which was published in the review *Vremya* before appearing in book form.

His wife had become very ill with tuberculosis and had returned to live in Tver, in Siberia. So it was that he came to make his first visit abroad, in 1862, going to Paris, London and Geneva, and in 1863 to Rome. Thence he went to Germany and Denmark.

As ever, Dostoievsky was troubled about money. His wife had no means and relied on him to support her in her illness. There was also her son, Pasha, by her first husband, who had to be looked after. In an attempt to increase his literary earnings, he turned once more to gambling, this time at roulette. While at Wiesbaden he believed he had invented a foolproof system for winning, for when he put it into practice, he won 10,000 francs at once. The next evening, he won another 3,000; but on the day after, he lost all but 5,000.

The following year, 1864, brought the deaths of his wife, of his brother Mikhail, and of his friend and collaborator on the *Vremya*, Apollon Grigoriev. He had planned to put his past unhappy marriage behind him by marrying his friend Pauline Suslov, whom he had met in Moscow, and who had accompanied him on his visits to Europe in 1862 and 1863. She, however, broke off their association shortly after the death of Mme Dostoievsky. He had been working hard on his new novel *Crime and Punishment*, and had gone to Wiesbaden to be free of distraction. It was his desertion of her that Mlle Suslov gave as her reason for breaking with him.

While he was in Wiesbaden, his *Letters from the Underworld* were published. In this period of desperate unhappiness, almost despair, the new genius which was revealed in the *Letters* attracted the serious notice of the critics and seemed to hold out a hope for the future.

His brother Mikhail had died leaving large debts. Though he was always confronted with money troubles of his own, Feodor undertook to meet Mikhail's debts also, though no court would have compelled him to do so. Thus he added to the burdens which were weighing him down.

In 1866 *Crime and Punishment* appeared as a serial. On the proceeds of it, had he been clear of debts, he might have found financial relief, but instead, he was as badly off as he had ever been. The book had a mixed reception. The psychological probings were new and either not understood or misunderstood, though the genius that lay behind could not be denied. This did not bring in the roubles which were so badly needed.

Crime and Punishment was published as Dostoievsky wrote it instalment by instalment. Before he had completed it, he interrupted his work on it to write a new story, *The Gamblers*.

He seemed to be possessed with the urge to write, and as a consequence his eyes began to suffer under the strain. To help him, he employed a young stenographer to act as his amanuensis. Her name was Anna Snitkin. They met for the first time on 4 October, 1866, and on 8 November became engaged. Shortly before Easter 1867, they married, and departed to Europe on their honeymoon. They had planned to be away two or three months at the outside, but they did not return to Russia until four years had passed.

His marriage to Anna was the best thing that could have happened to him. Though at first she was unable through inexperience to cope with his chaotic way of life, with his clinging relatives, with his pressing creditors, gradually she learned. In time she began to arrange the practical aspects of his life for him. She met and dealt with publishers who were out to make the best bargain for themselves that they could, she arranged with creditors the paying off of the debts; she freed him from as much worry as she could.

During the four years abroad, Dostoievsky wrote three of the five great novels on which his reputation rests—*The Idiot*, *The Eternal Husband* and *The Possessed*.

Little by little, thanks to Anna Dostoievsky's skilful management, at last all the debts were paid and there was money enough to make life pleasant, even if it had to be modest. For the first time in his life the novelist was happy, and in his happiness he could afford the time to propagate in journalism his ideas on the future to which Russia should address herself. It was his own special kind of patriotism, admittedly, but he found enthusiastic listeners in the students of the University of Moscow.

Happiness was also tinged with some anxiety caused by Dostoievsky's increasingly bad health. From childhood he had suffered from epileptic fits, and from early manhood had been plagued by a disease which recurred at intervals. Now both the epilepsy and the disease were increasing. It was under the pressure of this ill-health, that in 1879 he began work on his last great book, which some say is his greatest, *The Brothers Karamazov*. It began to appear in instalments in *Russky Weistnik* towards the end of that year, and ran throughout the following year.

On 8 November 1880 he sent the last instalment to the editor, saying in a letter that accompanied it:

> "Let me not say goodbye to you. I intend to go on living and writing for another twenty years."

On 25 January, 1881, he was taken ill again. Next day a specialist was summoned. He told the family that the coming night would see the crisis. Dostoievsky passed a restless night, and in the morning on waking realized that he had not long to live. He asked his wife to read to him the parable of the Prodigal Son, and for a priest to give him the last Sacrament. Conscious to the last, he died at half past eight in the evening.

Only on the day before his last illness he had written to his editor: "I now need money badly. Please send me four thousand roubles." After his death, his works were published in edition after quick edition, each of which brought to his heirs 75,000 roubles.

Joseph Lister
1827–1912

At the beginning of the nineteenth century, surgeons frankly admitted that a man admitted to a surgical ward was exposed "to more chances of death than the soldier fighting on any of the world's great battlefields." Periodically, gangrene swept through the surgical side of a hospital, bringing death, or at best life-long invalidism to all patients. These epidemics were so repetitive that they were regarded as inevitable concomitants of surgery, which, in a way, was true. Nevertheless, the sepsis death-rate in hospitals was so appalling that it stood in the way of the development of surgery. This was particularly galling, because the discovery of anaesthetics had given the surgeon time to operate in cases which previously had been inoperable. But what was the good of technical advance if the patient was to die of blood-poisoning? The man who ended the dilemma was Joseph Lister, who, with the discoverers of anaesthetics, must be regarded as the father of modern surgery.

SHORTLY after Joseph Lister began his surgical studies at University College Hospital, he witnessed the first operation in Great Britain carried out under anaesthesia. The year was 1846; the surgeon was the great Robert Liston. The following description, by Dr F. William Cork, who was present, illustrates, even to the layman who knows only the rudiments of anti-sepsis hygiene, why the risks from blood-poisoning were so great.

"The well of the theatre is now almost full; it is 2.15 p.m. A firm footstep is heard, and Robert Liston enters. . . . He nods quietly to Squire, and turning round to the packed crowd of onlookers, students, colleagues, old students, and many of the neighbouring practitioners, says dryly; 'We are going to try a Yankee dodge today, gentlemen, for making men insensible.'

"He then takes from a long, narrow case one of the straight amputating knives of his own invention. It is evidently a favourite instrument, for on the handle are little notches showing the number of times he had used it before. His house-surgeon, Ransome, puts the saw, two or three tenacula, and the artery forceps, named after the operator, on to the chair close by, and covers them with a towel, then threads a whisp of well-waxed hemp ligatures through his own button-hole. 'Ready Mr Ransome?' 'Yes, sir.' 'Then have him brought in.'

"The patient (he was a butler named Frederick Churchill) is carried in on a stretcher and laid on the table. The tube is put into his mouth, William Squire holds it and the patient's nostrils. A couple of dressers stand by to hold the patient if necessary, but he never moves. . . . Liston stands by, trying the edge of his knife against his thumb-nail, and the tension increases. . . . William Squire looks at Liston and says, 'I think he'll do, sir.' 'Take the artery, Mr Cadge,' cries Liston. 'Now gentlemen, time me,' says Liston to the students.

"The huge left hand grasps the thigh, a thrust of the long straight knife, two or three rapid sawing movements, and the upper flap is made; under go his fingers and the flap is held back; another thrust, and the knife comes out in the angle of the upper flap; two or three more lightning movements, and the lower flap is cut; under goes the great thumb and holds it back also.

"A touch or two of the point, and the dresser, holding the saw by its end, hands it to the surgeon, and takes the knife in return; half a dozen strokes, and Ransome places the limb in the sawdust. . . . 'Twenty-five seconds, sir,' says proud Edward Palmer, the dresser, to his surgeon, who smiles in reply.

"The femoral artery is taken up on a tenaculum and tied with two stout ligatures from Mr Ransome's button-hole, and five or six more vessels with the bow forceps and a single thread, a strip of wet lint put between the flaps and the stump is raised.

"Then the handkerchief is removed from the patient's face, and trying to raise himself, he says 'When are you going to begin? Take me back; I can't have it done.' He is shown the elevated stump, drops back and weeps a little; then the porters come in and he is carried back to bed.

"As he goes out, Liston turns again to his audience, so excited that he almost stammers and hesitates, and exclaims: 'This Yankee dodge, gentlemen, beats mesmerism hollow.' "

Not even the first principles of surgical hygiene had been observed. The surgeon wore no sterilized gown or gloves; the instruments were handled freely; the wound was tied with ligatures taken from the button-hole of the assisting surgeon.

All this the young spectator, Joseph Lister, was destined to change.

Joseph Jackson Lister, the father of Joseph Lister, was a remarkable man. Sprung from an old Quaker family, he inherited from his father a flourishing wine business in London. He had one great interest outside business—he was attracted by the study of optics, and learned to grind lenses himself. This interest, which started as a hobby, eventually led him to an invention, the importance of which was acknowledged by his election to a Fellowship of the Royal Society.

He had married the younger daughter of another famous Quaker, Mrs Harris, the superintendent of the Quaker School at Ackworth, near Pontefract. Before her marriage, Mrs Lister had taught elocution and reading in her mother's school, and her literary interests offset the scientific learnings of her husband, bringing into the home a diffuse culture.

A year before Joseph Lister was born, his father had decided that as his wine business was prospering and the suburb of Stoke Newington, in which they were living, was not the most suitable place in which to rear a growing family, to buy a Queen Anne mansion near Upton in Essex. Though Upton was isolated there were other Quaker families living in the neighbourhood; Samuel Gurney, the banker, the Barclays, the Dimsdales and the Buxtons, while Elizabeth Fry, the prison reformer, was an occasional guest.

It was in a comfortable, cultured home atmosphere, amid beautiful surroundings, therefore, that Joseph Lister grew up. A close relationship grew up between father and son, for not only did they share a love of nature and an interest in science, but they possessed similar temperaments. This relationship was to last into manhood, and Lister would always go to his father whenever he found himself in difficulties.

Lister was not yet in his teens when he made known his intention of becoming a doctor. Since there had never been a doctor in the Lister family, at first Lister senior tried to discourage his son, but he soon appreciated that the boy's determination was firm, and set about doing all he could to help him.

After a moderately distinguished career at Grove School, Tottenham, Lister prepared for the realization of his ambition. Since he was a Quaker, the universities of Oxford and Cambridge were closed to him, since all their members were required to be communicants of the Church of England. University College, London, had no such requirement, and when he applied for entrance he was accepted.

His father insisted that before he began to specialize in medicine, his son should acquire an all-round education. So, for his first two years, Lister studied for his Bachelor of Arts degree. He found it very hard work, however, and with the additional strain of a mild attack of small-pox, he was compelled to stop his studies for the time and take a long holiday in Ireland. He made a full recovery, successfully passed his degree examinations and entered University College Hospital.

Lister took his Bachelor of Medicine degree in 1852, and shortly afterwards passed, though with no high distinction, the examinations for a Fellowship of the Royal College of Surgeons. This he followed with a period of research into the musculature of the iris. By his experiments, Lister was able to demonstrate, what had not been realized before, that the iris possesses two muscles which dilate and contract the pupil. He published the result in a learned journal, and at once attracted attention to himself.

Next he embarked on a research of the involuntary muscles of the skin, the muscles responsible for raising "Goose-flesh". His experiments in this field also attracted much attention, and these, together with his work on the iris, set him apart, in medical circles, from the rest of his contemporaries.

He had always been more attracted to surgery than to medicine, and had been encouraged to specialize in this field by the famous surgeon Erichsen, to whom he became house-surgeon for a time. It was, however, on the advice of another great friend, Professor Sharpey, of University College, that he decided to approach the Edinburgh Medical School, then one of the leading schools of surgery in Europe, with a request that he might study there for a month. His request was granted, and he became the pupil of the leading Edinburgh surgeon of the day, Professor James Symes. The two men quickly became firm friends. The original month prolonged itself into several months, and when Symes's house-surgeon, for private reasons, resigned his post, at the Professor's suggestion Lister accepted the appointment.

They had not been working together long, however, when yet another stroke of good fortune came Lister's way. The surgeon to the Royal Infirmary and lecturer in surgery to the Edinburgh College of Surgeons was called to the Crimea, where war was raging; there he died of cholera within a short time. On Symes's advice, Lister applied for the vacant post and was appointed.

He was by now so completely absorbed in his work, that he devoted himself utterly to it. In the spring of 1856, however, he married Agnes Symes, though, since she was not a Quaker, it meant his leaving the Society of Friends. They spent their honeymoon visiting Continental hospitals and clinics, a tour which took them to France, Germany, Austria and Italy.

In addition to his work at the Royal Infirmary and his lecturing, Lister undertook further research, this time into the causes of the clotting of the blood. The work was so complicated, however, that he finally came to the conclusion he would never be able to explain his results satisfactorily.

Within three years of his marriage, fortune again favoured him.

He was invited to become Professor of Surgery at Glasgow. He was in some personal doubt whether to accept and as on all occasions like this, he wrote to his father for advice. His father replied that if he felt he could fulfil the requirements of the post to his own satisfaction, then he ought to accept. So it was that in 1860 the Listers moved to Glasgow, and it was here, in his rounds of his own wards, that he became impressed by the problem of post-operative gangrene and determined to do something about it if he could.

At first Lister subscribed to the view of many of his fellow surgeons that the incidence of septicaemia, or blood-poisoning, after operations was owing to germs in the polluted atmosphere of the wards, that these germs were carried from one patient to another. As a first experiment, therefore, he instructed that more space should be left between the beds. When this produced no more favourable results, he told himself that there must be another cause. Though he continued searching and making experiments in the dressing of wounds, it was not until a chance remark of a colleague about the work of the famous French chemist, Louis Pasteur, on the natural processes of fermentation and putrefaction, and his subsequent study of Pasteur's findings, that he believed that he might be on the track of "this other unknown cause".

As a beginning, Lister decided to repeat all Pasteur's experiments for himself so that he might have practical experience. When these experiments confirmed Pasteur's findings that the tiny organisms responsible for decomposition were spread by the air, it occurred to him that the same might be true for the organisms which caused wound infection. He, therefore, determined to carry out a surgical test. He would choose a particular kind of wound and he would make every effort to prevent dust and air-carried germs from entering it. The wound he chose was a compound fracture complicated by an open wound. The question was, how was he to prevent dust and germs from attacking it?

Pasteur had shown that germs could be destroyed in three ways: by filtration, by heat and by the use of antiseptics. Clearly, only the third method could be used in this experiment.

In the operation, then, he cleansed the area of skin surrounding the wound with carbolic acid, and when he had completed the operation, he swabbed out the wound with the same disinfectant. Though no poisoning set in, the use of the crude carbolic acid gave rise to severe irritation of the skin, and Lister set about finding another disinfectant which would not react so severely and yet be sufficiently strong to kill the septicaemia germs.

It was slow work, but Lister persisted, and in 1867 he felt able to publish an account of his first experiments in antiseptic surgery. This he did in *The Lancet*, the journal of the profession. His articles caused a great deal of interest, but also a great deal of opposition. Fierce attacks were made on him, notably by Sir James Simpson, the discoverer of chloroform.

Lister resisted the attacks and carried on with his work of improving antiseptic surgery. It was to require a long, and at times heart-breaking crusade to get his theories and his practices widely accepted by the profession. Gradually, however, opposition was worn down. The moment of triumph came when in 1879 most of the London hospitals—now run by younger men than the older generation who had so strenuously opposed him—adopted his antiseptic techniques. Almost within a twinkling of an eye, the situation in the surgical wards changed. In a remarkably short period the man who had been looked upon by many as a crank found himself loaded with honours. The universities conferred high degrees upon him; he was made a baronet by the Queen; foreign governments gave him the highest honours in their gift.

In 1893 his wife died while they were on the first holiday they had taken for many years. Their marriage had meant much to him, so that his loss affected his whole life. Though he was to introduce no other great surgical innovation, what he had done already was increasingly appreciated. He was one of the first members of The Order of Merit, and on his eightieth birthday was granted the Freedom of the City of London.

He died on 10 February, 1912, at the age of eighty-five.

Leo Tolstoy
1828–1910

Say Count Leo Tolstoy's name, and you and your hearers will immediately think of two great books—*War and Peace* and *Anna Karenina*. Russia, which has produced many literary geniuses, has few, if any, greater than he. His two great masterpieces, and most of his other writings, were written, however, against a background of fierce inner struggle as he searched for what he hoped would be revealed as the true meaning of life. In middle age, he believed he had found the answer. "The Kingdom of God is within you. God is love." For the next thirty years by his writings and by the example of his personal life, he tried to bring his message to all.

COUNT LEO TOLSTOY was born at Yasnaya Polyana, the great family estate, in the province of Tula in Russia, on 28 August, 1828. He was the most remarkable member of a very remarkable family. One of his ancestors, Count Peter, had been the highly successful, if unscrupulous, minister of Tsar Peter the Great. One of his cousins, Count Alexei Constantinovits Tolstoy, was a poet and dramatist who achieved fame with his trilogy of plays, the best known of which is *The Death of Ivan the Terrible*. On his mother's side, his grandfather, Prince Nicolai Volkonsky, had been Commander-in-Chief of Catherine the Great's armies.

Born to great wealth and social position, one of a large family of boys and girls, at his birth it would have seemed that a pleasant and comfortable life lay ahead of him. As lord of great estates he had the power of life and death over the hundreds of peasants who worked for him; he had access to the gaiety and sophisticated entertainment of the Court and the cream of Russian society in the brilliant capital of St Petersburg.

Yet from an early age, strange conflicting qualities warred within his nature. Before he was six his mother died, and, when he was nine, his father. Thereafter he and his brothers and sisters were brought up by relatives, all of whom were indulgent. Among them was an aunt, Tatiana, a deeply pious woman, who was to have, by her influence in these early days, a lasting effect on her young charge's whole life.

There is an early photograph of Tolstoy taken with his sister, Marie, who is dressed as a nun, which gives an indication of the strange mixture of which his character was composed. For in the eyes and in the features of the young boy are clearly visible the deep religious feelings of the near fanatic coupled with a joyful, great vitality, and the impression of strong virility. From early youth he was to be a seeker after truth with one side of his nature, and with the other a searcher for the supposedly "good things", the frivolous trivialities, of life.

Nor was this the only evidence of the paradoxes which had come together to produce what was eventually to prove one of the greatest Russian geniuses of all time. Though he had been born a great aristocrat, instead of the finely chiselled features that more often than not go with high birth, as he himself said: "My face was that of an ordinary peasant."

From his youth, Tolstoy was conscious of how unpleasing his looks were. He once asked:

"How can a man with so broad a nose, such thick lips and little grey eyes like mine, ever find happiness on earth?"

To disguise the coarseness, as soon as his beard was strong enough to spring from his chin, he let it grow until it covered as much of his face as possible. There are many who think that by doing so, he made himself look more like a Russian peasant than ever. His appearance was, in fact, to be a disappointment not only to himself, but, when his writings and his teaching had become famous throughout Russia and Europe, to his would-be admirers and disciples, too. They often came great distances to see him, would sit in his drawing-room waiting for the master, expecting to see, when he came to them, a mighty and majestic man, with a patriarch's flowing beard, a man of great dignity, a giant, a genius.

When he came to them, what did they see?

As one such visitor described him:

"A short, thick-set man, who moved so quickly that his beard wagged, who advanced rather at a run than a walk. When he spoke, it was cheerfully, but he seemed to prattle his welcome."

As the visitor gazed upon the great man with feelings that were a mixture of wonder and disappointment, all of a sudden, from beneath the bushy jungle of his eyebrows, the grey eyes flashed, and a piercing glance would be concentrated upon the guest. It was like a knife-thrust, hard as steel. One could not evade it. Hypnotized, one had to endure its probings. It lasted only for a second, then the eyes softened in a gentle and kindly smile. It was the eyes that saved the peasant face from ordinariness. Through them, and them alone, Tolstoy expressed his every emotion. Few men have possessed such expressive eyes. As a fellow-writer, also a genius, Maxim Gorky, described them, "In his eyes, Tolstoy had a hundred eyes."

Though given as a youth to serious thoughts about life and its meaning—thoughts which were to multiply and eventually to dominate his existence as he grew older—they were but infrequent incidents so far. It was the less serious side of his nature that was predominant.

At Kazan University he joined in all the frivolous activities of the young men of his age and class, experimenting always to discover new physical experiences, pandering to the promptings of a healthy vitality and an overstrong virility, happy only in the enjoyment of the creature comforts that riches and wealthy companionship could provide. So, too, in the capital, St Petersburg, he frittered away the days in meaningless and unproductive social activities. He spent hours playing cards, seeking the company of women, drinking hard, and now and again surrendering to a craze for sport.

At the same time, however, he would have moments of truth in which he would realize how he was wasting his time and his talents; at such moments he would resolve to cut away from it all. Then he would draw up programmes for himself of a life of study and social usefulness, programmes which he never followed. He desired nothing more than to become morally perfect, yet somehow he could not bring himself to make a break with the happy-go-lucky life of the Russian aristocrat in the capital.

At twenty-two he had to face the first real decision of his life. As his time at the University drew to a close in 1851, the Tolstoy family expected him to return to Yasnaya Polyana, to take over the direction of the estates which he had inherited from his father. The alternative was to hand these over to a brother, and for himself to enter the Government service. He could not bring himself to make the choice.

When he did, quite suddenly, come to a decision, it was neither of the alternatives. Instead, he returned with his brother Nicolai, who was an officer in the army, to the Caucasus where the Tsar's forces were trying to subdue rebellious Tartar tribes. As a volunteer, he went with the troops on their raids on the mountain villages, and the following year he wrote about these experiences in *A Raid*. Even in his early writing the acuteness and wide range of his observation, and his great gifts for poetic description are striking.

A Raid was not his first literary venture. He had already published in a St Petersburg magazine an autobiographical piece called *Childhood*, which had made a tremendous impression both on the reading public and the leading writers for the great promise which it displayed. *A Raid* was even more enthusiastically received, and, having decided to enter the army himself, in his leisure moments he began to work on his first full-length novel, *The Cossacks*, which was not published, however, until 1863. Before *The Cossacks* appeared he had further increased his reputation as a writer with his impressions of the siege of Sebastopol, which drew from the great Turgenev himself the remark: "This young writer will eclipse us all. One might as well give up writing."

Tolstoy was not happy as a soldier. His experiences had given him a strong dislike of war, the horrors of which seemed to him to destroy the dignity of man. These experiences had also caused him to take stock of himself once more, and to a degree extraordinary in so young a man; though in his youth, amidst the pleasures of the social life he was leading, he had often paused to ponder the real meaning of life.

When he was only twenty-six and some months, he had a sudden moment of inspiration. In his diary on 5 March, 1855, he wrote:

"I have had a great, a stupendous idea . . . the foundation of a new religion corresponding to the development of mankind; the religion of Jesus Christ . . . a practical religion, not promising bliss in the future, but giving happiness on earth . . . To work consciously for the union of mankind by religion. . . ."

Though twenty-four years were to pass before he was to begin to work unremittingly to achieve this aim, during the quarter of a century which separated the "idea" from the fulfilment, he was working his way forward all the time to this end.

Unhappy in the army, he resigned his commission, and settled for a time in St Petersburg where, despite what he had written in his diary, he returned to his old life of dissipation, spurning the welcome given to him by the literary giants of the day because he did not agree with their views. All the time he had moments of disquiet and dissatisfaction on account of his own moral behaviour.

In 1851 he embarked on a tour of Europe. In Lucerne there happened an incident which plainly showed the direction in which he was going. A wandering singer arrived at the hotel where he was staying, and asked permission to entertain the rich guests. They made fun of him and told him to go away, whereupon Tolstoy went after him, brought him back to the hotel, sat him down at his own table and shared a meal with him.

Early in 1858, he returned to Russia, to Yasnaya Polyana, where, in the intervals of looking after his estates, he led the life of a country gentleman. He also began to make a study of the peasants' way of life.

Two years later he went abroad again, this time to study educational methods, and on his return, he set up a school at Yasnaya Polyana, of which he took charge himself and into which he introduced an entirely revolutionary method of teaching. There were no compulsory lessons, no orders, rewards or punishment, "the children came as they liked, sat where they liked, and listened or not as it pleased them".

Unfortunately, ill-health caused him to abandon the experiment after a year. While he was away taking a cure, the police arrived and ransacked his house and the school in search of revolutionary documents—of which none was found, because there were none.

Although his unorthodox actions and teaching brought him into constant conflict with the authorities, by now he was a very famous author, and this, added to the fact that he came of a great aristocratic family, gave him a certain protection against serious persecution.

Tolstoy found the management of his estates a great inspiration, and he devoted all his time and energies to it and to his writing. The middle period of his life, 1862 to 1876, saw him at his calmest and happiest. Early in 1862 he married Sophia Behrs, the daughter of an old family friend. In those days of arranged marriages, this was a marriage of love. From the very beginning the young couple were blissfully happy. Soon after marrying, Tolstoy began to write *War and Peace*. This epic novel is built round the family fortunes of two aristocratic households, whose private lives are interwoven with the chain of historical events. Tolstoy drew for his material on the Tolstoy family records, and those of his mother's family, the Volkonskys. In this great work, which many critics believe to be the greatest novel ever written, Tolstoy's full genius is seen.

In March, 1873, he began his second great novel, *Anna Karenina*. His personal life while he was engaged upon it was much troubled. His beloved aunt Tatiana died, his wife fell ill, two of his children died and his educational plans were obstructed by the authorities. Despite all this, however, *Anna Karenina* is an undoubted masterpiece. In it Tolstoy reveals his great understanding of the nature of men and women to a degree almost unequalled by any other writer except Shakespeare.

Tolstoy was beginning to be greatly worried by attacks of spiritual fear and bewilderment. Between 1876 and 1879 his anxiety on this account brought him near to killing himself and he had consciously to resist strong suicidal desires. He was saved from being overwhelmed by these desires by another moment of inspiration, when the idea he had had twenty-four years previously was suddenly crystallized into a greater clarity, and he was determined to act upon it.

From this time on until he died in 1910, he worked only to bring about "the union of mankind through religion". His writings—among the most remarkable being *The Power of Darkness*, a study of peasant life, *The Kreutzer Sonata*, in which he attacked the worldly women for whose pleasure nine-tenths of the factories and shops existed, and the extremely important *Resurrection*, in which he expressed his gospel of the brotherhood of men, were all devoted to teaching his ideas. He tried his utmost to model his life on his teaching, to make it simple and to adjust it to the life of the peasant.

In the last year of his life he decided to carry out his dream of abandoning his home and possessions, and disappearing among the peasants. His wish to do this had caused a rift between him and his wife for several years, and their first great love wore itself out. In the train that was taking him away, he fell ill, and after a week he died, aged 82. His books live on, but his ideas are still ideals.

Lewis Carroll
1832-1898

To many of the people who encountered Lewis Carroll during his lifetime he must have seemed almost as odd as some of his fanciful literary creations—as crazy as The Mad Hatter, as dreamy as The Dormouse, as flustered as The White Rabbit, as droll as Tweedle-dum or Tweedle-dee and as petulant, on occasion, as The Duchess. Yet his was a split personality. As Lewis Carroll, gentle creator of the immortal "Alice", he was literally capable of thinking of "six impossible things before breakfast"; as Charles Lutwidge Dodgson (his real name) he was, if not a mathematical genius, at least a considerable master of such subjects as logic and geometry.

Born in 1832, at Daresbury, near Warrington, Lancashire, he followed the famous "Tom Brown", going first to Rugby and then to Oxford. He distinguished himself as an undergraduate for, when only twenty-three, he became a mathematical lecturer at Christ Church.

As a young man he was serious and reserved with thoughts of the Church as a career. In 1861 he took Deacon's orders; but in spite of his leaning, his shyness, accentuated by a tendency to stammer, prevented him from seeking a priesthood. Nevertheless he continued to lecture and in addition devoted himself to serious mathematical works on formal logic and Euclidean geometry. Though they are recognized as valuable in their way these works may be said to lack the immortal quality evinced in his lighter excursions into realms of inspired nonsense.

Alice's Adventures in Wonderland, and the sequel, *Through the Looking Glass*, were written in the first place solely to amuse a young friend, Alice Liddell, daughter of the Dean of Christ Church. This charming girl was a prime favourite among the many young people with whom the shy scholar was on friendly terms. She has, as it happens, given her own simple account of the circumstances in which the first spark of inspiration was kindled:

> Most of Mr Dodgson's stories were told to us on river expeditions to Nuneham or Godstow, near Oxford. My eldest sister was Prima, I was Secunda and Tertia was my sister Edith. I believe the beginning of

Alice was told one summer afternoon when the sun was so burning that we had landed in the meadows down the river, deserting the boat and taking refuge in the only bit of shade to be found, which was under a new-made hayrick. Here from all three came the old petition of "Tell us a story!" and so began the ever-delightful tale.

Lewis Carroll (it seems quite senseless to call him by his real name when his nom-de-plume is so much more famous) was thirty-three when Alice first made her bow in book form. He was especially fortunate in having Sir John Tenniel as his illustrator for, as a leading *Punch* artist of his day, Tenniel had just the right flair for interpreting the shy young author's sublime sense of the ludicrous and for adding his own inspired touches to underline the quaint whimsy and humour of it all.

Just a year before the official publication of *Alice's Adventures in Wonderland*, the author had gone to great pains to prepare a special version of the story in his own meticulous handwriting and with his own pleasing illustrations in line which, in fact, served as an additional guide for Sir John Tenniel.

Carroll had this manuscript volume bound and he presented it to Alice Liddell as a surprise for Christmas, 1864. The rapturous joy that it must have given to its favoured recipient may easily be imagined. This version was, to all intents and purposes, the story as originally told to Alice and her sisters on that hot, lazy afternoon of 4 July, 1862, in the hayrick's shade, but it bears the title *Alice's Adventures Under Ground*, and, though the tale is very much the same as the familiar "Alice" known and loved in every part of the modern world, the printed version, first published in 1865, is nearly twice as long. The exquisite manuscript volume may be seen by anyone at the British Museum, having been presented to the nation in 1948 by "A Group of well-wishers in the United States of America".

Carroll once applied his skilful penmanship to the task of concocting a supposed invitation to a Royal Garden Party. He signed it Victoria R.I. and used the spurious document to impress and amuse some of his young friends who readily swallowed his grave assurances that it had come from the great Queen Victoria herself. It could so easily have been true, for the Queen was certainly among the countless celebrities who fell under the spell of the entrancing "Alice". There is even a story to the effect that Her Majesty gave royal instructions for someone to make sure that she received this clever author's next work. Alas! for Royal patronage. The next work, as it happened, was a formidable mathematical tome! What Her Gracious Majesty made of that does not seem to be on record.

In any case, "Alice" engaged a great deal of her shy creator's attention, and he was to become a great trial to the editorial staff of his publisher, Macmillan. He rejected the first printing and sent parcels to various children's hospitals. Thereafter his visits to the publisher's office usually meant trouble for someone. He developed the habit of subjecting copies of his books to intensive scrutiny in an endeavour to discover faults, however trifling they might be. He became unreasonably exacting on the finer points of printing and binding. Such was his insistence on perfectionism that he would "fault" a copy if he found that the type on two facing pages chanced to be even slightly out of alignment. No doubt his obsession with logic and mathematics and geometry had something to do with this punctiliousness; but he also found other ways in which to plague the life of his long-suffering publishers.

He liked to place an order for special presentation copies and would tax their patience with the most exacting demands for so many copies to be printed and bound in a stipulated style and so many copies in another, always supplying the most detailed instructions as to the kind of paper he desired and the colour of the cloth to be used in binding. Needless to say, his scrutiny of these special copies was even more critical and exacting so that in one way or another he contrived to lead his publishers a merry dance.

His love of perfection was evidenced in other ways. His special hobby was photography and in this, as in nearly everything else he tackled, he was never content with half measures. He was also something of a pioneer for, at a time when the majority of amateur photographic efforts were decidedly crude, he attained some truly commendable results.

He bought his camera in London for £15, which did not include the additional paraphernalia—the flash powder, the trays, bowls, glazing boards, rollers, clips, red lamp and chemicals then essential for anyone who was obliged to do all his own developing and fixing and printing. Photography remained a consuming interest for most of his life.

Another of his loves was the theatre. When in his twenties he went to the Princess's Theatre, in Oxford Street, London, where he saw Charles Kean and the young Ellen Terry in *Henry VIII*, voting this "the greatest theatrical treat I ever had or expect to have". Some ten years later Ellen Terry was to grant the amateur photographer a special sitting, and a first-class portrait study resulted.

Carroll also photographed an undergraduate actor in the character of the Artful Dodger, from *Oliver Twist*. Another costume study he made is of a niece of Mrs Tennyson, wife of the Poet Laureate, dressed up as Little Red Riding Hood. Among his many fine photographic studies which survive today is a charming portrait of the redoubtable "Alice" at the age of six.

Carroll was also a master of the art of parody, and though nearly everyone remembers "You Are Old Father William", based on Southey's poem, fewer may know of an amusing experiment in this field entitled "Hiawatha's Photographing". It is included in a miscellany first published in 1883 (when he was fifty-one) under the title *Rhyme? and Reason?* In a characteristic introduction to the parody he disclaims any particular virtue "for this slight attempt at doing what is known to be easy." This introduction itself, though set out as prose, is in the Hiawatha metre:

"Any fairly practised writer, with the slightest ear for rhythm, could compose for hours together, in the easy running metre of the 'Song of Hiawatha'. Having, then, distinctly stated that I challenge no attention in the following little poem to its merely verbal jingle, I must beg the candid reader to confine his criticism to its treatment of the subject."

The poem itself tells of Hiawatha's attempts to photograph each member of a family in turn—the father, the mother, two daughters, the elder son and the youngest. In each attempt his efforts are thwarted by the subjects' lack of co-operation, their failure to keep still (a prime requisite in early photographic days) or by their stubborn insistence upon adopting poses of their own devising. Thus, the youngest son, a schoolboy, spoiled his portrait by being "very fidgety in manner".

Each picture proves a failure until, in sheer despair, the photographer takes one more picture—a family group.

> Finally my Hiawatha
> Tumbled all the tribe together
> ('Grouped' is not the right expression),
> And, as happy chance would have it
> Did at last obtain a picture
> Where the faces all succeeded:
> Each came out a perfect likeness.
>
> Then they joined and all abused it,
> Unrestrainedly abused it,
> As the worst and ugliest picture
> They could possibly have dreamed of.
> 'Giving us such strange expressions—

Sullen, stupid, pert expressions.
Really anyone would take us
(Anyone who did not know us)
For the most unpleasant people!'
(Hiawatha seemed to think so,
Seemed to think it not unlikely).

The parody closes with the disgruntled Hiawatha hurriedly packing up all his photographic paraphernalia and making a bee line for the railway station leaving his impossible sitters behind him. No doubt the enthusiastic Carroll did encounter some difficult subjects, and certainly the exasperation and impatience shown by his imaginary photographer were characteristic. He himself was far from being the most patient of men. When Sir John Tenniel fell behind schedule with his illustrations for "Alice", the author fretted and fumed at the prospect of any delay and pointed out that his young friends had a distressing habit of growing up at an astonishing rate.

Yet with his youthful admirers he showed infinite patience. He never tired of their company, and if earlier friends grew up there were always younger ones coming into his circle. One of these was Greville Macdonald, son of a popular novelist and poet who was also a great preacher. Carroll himself never married, but his love of young people never waned.

Both the "Alice" books were published during his long academic career at Christ Church, the first when he was thirty-three, and Through The Looking Glass seven years later. Nor did his post as a mathematical lecturer prevent him from indulging in further literary experiments for it was during this period that he published two volumes of comic verse and parodies—Phantasmagoria and The Hunting of the Snark which he later included in the miscellany Rhyme? and Reason? already mentioned.

When he left Christ Church, in 1881, he made a further attempt to write for the juvenile market and created two new characters, "Sylvie and Bruno". He published two books about them, one when he was fifty-seven, the second when he was sixty-one. Nearly a quarter of a century had elapsed since he had given "Alice" to the world, and the old magic was not to be recaptured.

There were solid mathematical studies, but nothing could add to Carroll's fame. When he died at Guildford, in Surrey, aged sixty-six, from pneumonia, following influenza, it was as the author of "Alice" that he was mourned.

"Alice" is immortal. The shy, quiet lecturer's masterpiece has been translated into most languages—German, Dutch, French,

Italian and the rest. A dramatized version was presented in her creator's lifetime, in 1886. Her adventures in Wonderland have been filmed repeatedly in silent and talking versions; they have given delight on radio and television and, in a multiplicity of editions, the book itself remains a constant seller.

Lewis Carroll will always be sure of a following among admirers young and old in every part of the world. But what of Charles Lutwidge Dodgson? Does anyone read *his* masterpiece, *Curiosa Mathematica*, today? It is one of life's ironies that he is remembered more for his fantasies than for his serious work; but who of the millions who adore "Alice" would have it otherwise?

Alfred Nobel
1833-1896

IT would be hard to imagine a greater contradiction than was summed up in the life of this insignificant-looking Swede who yearned for world peace—and became a millionaire by selling the merchandise of death to each and every country who would pay his price for it; who died working to invent a force of total destruction—and whose last Will and Testament laid down the terms of an imaginative effort to end all wars: the Nobel Peace Prize.

Alfred Nobel was, in fact, a mass of contradictions. He was small in stature, inconspicuous, self-effacing, colourless. He was a cynical idealist, a brilliant conversationalist who preferred his own company (he never married), a lover of poetry who made pathetic attempts to write. Yet he was the inventor of dynamite and many other high explosives, amassed a considerable fortune in ten years from his mighty international munitions business, and earnestly desired that his wealth should be used "for the purpose of promoting friendship between nations and bringing about whole or partial disarmament". Today his reputation rests, not on his inventive genius, but on the international awards which bear his name.

He was born in a grey backyard house at 9 Normansgatan, Stockholm, in 1833—the year of his father's bankruptcy. So sickly and weak was he as a child that he owed his survival to his mother's devoted nursing and ceaseless care. His father, Immanuel, left his three sons to their mother and went off to Finland to build himself a new career. The parting was to last four years and it was during that period that bonds of affection were woven between the mother and the three sons which were to remain unbroken for the rest of Alfred's life.

Suddenly Immanuel announced to his family that he was back in the money with the invention of an explosive mine which had captured the interest of the Tsar of Russia and, on 18 October, 1842, the Nobel family set off from Stockholm for St Petersburg. There Immanuel was determined to make up for the gap in their lives and lavished the best on his wife and three sons, even engaging a Swedish tutor. Alfred learned Russian, English, French and German. Perhaps because of his wretched health and total dependence on his mother his father showed a certain resentment of Alfred, once rating the talents of his sons thus: "Ludwig has most genius, Alfred most industry, Robert most courage."

Immanuel prospered in Russia. His mines were a success and thereafter he poured out inventions which he marketed with profit. He became a member of St Petersburg's first Merchants' Guild and he was even presented at court, receiving the Imperial Gold Medal from the Tsar. When Robert was twenty, Ludwig eighteen and Alfred sixteen their father decided that they had now sufficient education and he took them into his business, Alfred being sent abroad "to have a look at the world". Alfred's travels took him to most countries of Europe and to New York. After two years of it, he returned to find his father involved in vast projects. The onset of the Crimean War of 1854 brought orders pouring into the Nobel factories. After that war, disastrous for Russia, the new Tsar, Alexander II, cancelled all contracts given to private enterprises. A fire at the main Nobel factory completed Immanuel's ruin and he had no option but to endure his second bankruptcy.

The sons went out on their own. Ludwig was appointed liquidator of his father's business and then rented a small factory near St Petersburg; Robert opened a lamp business in Finland and Alfred experimented with a new liquid which he had studied during the Crimean War—nitro-glycerine, discovered in 1847 by an Italian chemist, Ascanio Sobrero. Finally Alfred returned to Stockholm with his father and mother and they carried out dozens of experiments in their search for a new explosive.

On 14 October, 1863, Alfred Nobel was granted his first patent for his nitro-glycerine product. Meanwhile a general principle was forming in his mind, that of using a small amount of one explosive to produce the shock which would blow up a large volume of another explosive. This principle, known as the primary charge, became the foundation of high explosives and has been described as the greatest advance in that field since the discovery of gunpowder.

Alfred went to work on this principle in his laboratory, assisted by his youngest brother, Oscar Emil, who was a student at Stockholm University. One day, when Alfred was in town discussing finance with a wealthy banker, Mr J. W. Smitt, an explosion wrecked his laboratory and killed four people. One of them was his brother, Oscar Emil. Alfred was distraught—but he felt no moral guilt. The making of explosives was a dangerous occupation which would be for the ultimate benefit of humanity, he felt, and those who worked in it must risk their lives. A police inquiry into the explosion led to a ban on the manufacture of nitro-glycerine within the city limits but the Nobels escaped prosecution.

Alfred refused to be deterred by this tragic set-back and, indeed, the force of the explosion impressed financiers who formed a company to exploit Alfred's patent in Sweden. This company was to make Sweden the pioneer country in the high explosives industry.

Robert was given the power to apply for the Finnish patent in Alfred's name and to exploit it for his own benefit. Father Immanuel was stricken by the explosion which killed his youngest son and the ordeal of the police inquiry. A month after the accident he suffered a stroke and Alfred sold his patent rights in Norway for cash so that he could send his parents to a spa—this was the only instance in which he did not hold on to any part of the rights to one of his patents.

Immanuel regained his strength but not his enthusiasm for explosives. His inventive mind would not retire—he occupied himself with trying to think of some raw material inexpensive enough to manufacture new articles of great public utility. He came up with the idea—wood shavings—and, in 1870, published a little pamphlet with the title: "An attempt to create employment in order to check the emigration fever now caused by the lack of it." In it he pointed out that the scrap from sawmills was being burned "to no other end than of getting rid of the stuff" and he proposed to have these shavings glued together by special machinery to make a new fabric. In short, old Nobel invented plywood.

He even worked out detailed plans for prefabricating plywood houses and transporting them where needed all ready to be set up. Before he could take his idea—probably the most important of his lifetime—any further, Immanuel died on 3 September, 1872—the eighth anniversary of the explosion which killed his youngest son.

Meanwhile Alfred was travelling Europe extending his nitro-glycerine business and the countries with mining industries and rail-and-road-building programmes were eager to buy this powerful new explosive. The transporting of nitro-glycerine all over the world was marked by sensation after sensation when careless handling and leakages caused gigantic explosions until its very name spelled terror —in fact, the Nobels changed it to the more innocuous-sounding "glonion oil".

Alfred, fearing that the widespread panic caused by the serious accidents would bring a ban on the manufacture of nitro-glycerine in many countries, set to work feverishly to devise a safer mixture. He appreciated that in a global business it would be impossible to avoid careless handling of the explosive liquid. The answer was to solidify it and he tried a variety of absorbents, including powdered charcoal, sawdust, brick-dust, even cement.

When the brainwave came, it was by accident. For one shipment someone had changed the sawdust stuffing of the nitro-glycerine crated for a sort of clay prevalent in northern Germany called *kieselguhr*. One can in this crate leaked and Alfred Nobel noticed that the *kieselguhr* had soaked up all the nitro-glycerine and remained granular. He tested it in the lab. and found the *kieselguhr* reacted to heat and shock as did nitro-glycerine. He detonated it with the percussion cap and found it worked better than the oil. Thus was the world given dynamite. Nobel patented his new mixture under two names: "Dynamite" and "Nobel's Safety Powder".

This *kieselguhr* which had done the trick for Alfred Nobel was scientifically known as distomaceous earth, or diatomite, formed by fossils pressed together in huge deposits over millions of years. In 1867 Nobel and Co. started shipping dynamite in quantity. Thus was a munitions king set on his way to the throne. His dynamite was to spread—like wildfire—over the face of the earth. In 1868 Alfred Nobel, who had a sincere contempt for honours and awards, received the one which gave him most satisfaction: a gold medal from the Swedish Academy of Science "for outstanding original work in the realm of art, literature and science, or for important discoveries of practical value for mankind".

While his factories mushroomed all over Europe, he found business methods in the United States too full of double dealing for him and, after a bout of cut-throat competition there, he lost interest and never set foot in America after 1885, leaving the Du Pont Empire to become the giant company in his field over there. Although France refused to admit nitro-glycerine, Nobel made his residence in Paris, then in the twilight of the second Empire. Britain also resisted his deadly liquid at first but gave way to dynamite and Nobel chose Ardder, near Ardrossan in Ayrshire, as his site for the greatest dynamite factory in the world.

By this time the money was cascading on him and he was surrounded by business associates who were eager to help him to make plenty more—and cash in themselves. He wrote to an acquaintance:

"Where are they, my numerous friends? They are stuck fast in the morass of lost illusions, or in the bogs of money-making. I assure you that numerous friends are to be found only among dogs whom we feed with the flesh of others, and among those whom we feed with our own."

Because he was now rich, he distrusted everyone's motives. He liked to talk intelligently with men and gallantly with women. But even his most enterprising biographers could not trace a love affair until he was well into his forties.[1] Perhaps that was because of affection for his mother—and his platonic association with a remarkable woman, Bertha von Suttner. She became his secretary in Paris when he was forty-three—she was thirty-three, spoke four languages, had the beauty and poise of a perfect lady, as, indeed, she was, being the Countess Bertha Kinsky von Chinic und Tettau.

Her mother having gone through all the family fortune at roulette, Bertha had taken the post of governess in the baronial house of Suttner in Vienna—and proceeded to fall deeply in love with the son, Arthur. She, therefore, felt it discreet to take Nobel's post when it was advertised. Her beauty, wit, intelligence and integrity captivated the eerie and lonely millionaire. He took her completely into his confidence—unprecedented for him—and rebuilt a wing of his house in Paris for her, only to find that her heart was still in Vienna. When Alfred Nobel was summoned to Stockholm to meet his King, Oscar II, Bertha received a terse telegram which sent her racing off to Vienna. It was from her beloved Arthur and simply said: "Cannot live without you."

The new wing of the Dynamite King's Palace remained empty from then on.

Bertha and Arthur were married in Austria in June, 1876, and the name Bertha von Suttner was to become famous throughout western Europe as the nineteenth century's most inspired propagandist for peace—much later the world was to learn that her greatest inspiration was: the Nobel Peace Prize.

The von Suttners went off to the Caucasus for a honeymoon, and stayed there for ten years. She had to wait even longer before Alfred Nobel completely forgave her—they did not exchange a dozen letters in eleven years.

Bertha and her husband spent much of their time in the Caucasus writing travel books which sold so well that they decided to return to the civilizations of Vienna and Paris. They met Nobel, who played host to the couple and got them invitations to some of the famous literary salons. The talk was almost all of war so Bertha

[1] Alfred Nobel's only serious love affair, with Sofie Hess, a Viennese shop-girl, lasted from 1876 (when he was forty-three) for eighteen years, but it did not really come to light until 1950 when the Nobel Institute in Stockholm disclosed the existence of 216 letters written to her by Alfred. The affair ended after she had an illegitimate child by a Hungarian cavalry officer whom she later married.

decided to fight for peace, with a novel. It was a work which swept Europe: *Die Waffen Nieder!* ("Lay Down Arms!").

She was soon sought out by peace societies everywhere and attended the Third World Peace Congress as chairman of the Austrian delegation. And she went seriously to work on Alfred Nobel, even persuading him to attend the Fourth Congress in Berne, which he did incognito. There they spent a week together arguing, exchanging and dissecting ideas. If she did not convert him to her methods for ending the scourge of war, she at least managed to shatter his pet theory—that, by inventing a weapon "of such horrible capacity for mass annihilation", wars would become impossible.

When he parted from her in Switzerland he had committed himself to do something great for the movement. On 7 January, 1893 he wrote to her:

> "I should like to allot part of my fortune to the formation of a prize fund to be distributed in every period of five years. . . . this prize would be awarded to the man or woman who had done most to advance the idea of general peace in Europe. . . .".

It was the first reference to the Peace Prize. Two years later, in November, 1895, he signed his final will in which he took the aim of the prize a stage further. This decreed that the Prize should go to

> "the person who has done the most effective work to promote friendship between nations, and to secure the elimination or reduction of standing armies, as well as for the formation and popularization of peace congresses."

This was the formula which became official after his death.

The year of his final will he had moved back to Sweden where he struggled to write a play—so bad that no one would produce or publish it. He had it printed in Paris. Before it came off the press his old butler, who was alone in the house with him, found his millionaire master dead at his desk. That was on 10 December, 1896. Inside the desk, beneath a pile of designs for a new war weapon, lay his Last Will and Testament of Peace.

This directed that his capital should constitute a fund, the annual interest of which was to be split into five equal parts and used to award prizes to the persons adjudged to have made the most important discovery or invention in the fields of physics, chemistry, physiology or medicine; the person who has produced the outstanding work of literature, "idealistic in character"; and to the person who "has done the most or best work for the brotherhood of nations,

the abolition of standing armies as well as the formation or popular-
ization of peace congresses".

Owing to an unseemly squabble over the administration of the
will, the first Nobel prizes were not awarded until five years after his
death, on 10 December, 1901. Then the Peace Award was divided
between Henri Dunant of Switzerland (the founder of the Red Cross)
and Frederic Passy, a veteran French pacifist. Bertha von Suttner,
whom Nobel had clearly wished to have the first Peace Prize, was
passed over. However, justice was done to her in 1905 when she was
the first woman to win it.

In succeeding years the awards rarely failed to stir controversy,
even bitterness. Among those who were chagrined not to win it were
Kaiser Wilhelm—and Adolf Hitler. The most courageous award of
all was the decision in 1935 to give the Peace Prize to Carl von
Ossietsky, a distinguished German editor and fighter for peace,
when he was a prisoner in one of Hitler's concentration camps.
Despite every kind of inducement to him by the Nazis, he insisted
on claiming it. By doing that, he signed his own death warrant. For
the first time in the history of the Prize, no one turned up in Oslo to
receive it. The following year, 1937, Goering declared that henceforth no German would accept a Nobel Prize. On 4 May, 1938,
Ossietsky died in Berlin as a result of his brutal treatment at the
hands of the Nazis. It was the last year until 1944 that the prize
was awarded—and it went to the International Red Cross in Geneva.

Now that scientists have discovered the weapon for which Alfred
Nobel was searching—the weapon of total annihilation—the world
shares his hope that, more than all his peace prizes put together, it
will indeed offer the final solution—and make war impossible.

Johannes Brahms
1833-1897

IN 1853 in his mansion at Weimar, the great composer Liszt, the idol of all the younger forward-looking musicians in Germany, was holding court like a king. Among his guests that evening was a promising young student from Hamburg, Johannes Brahms. The youngster was cordially invited to play some of his own compositions for Liszt was more affable and generous to struggling young unknowns than most men who wield power and influence; but the raw, awkward young provincial gracelessly refused the honour, whereupon the great Liszt took the boy's music to the piano, and himself played it with matchless fluency, to the delight of the company in general, and Brahms in particular.

Having congratulated the young composer, Liszt went on to play one of his own pieces. Glancing up at Brahms, doubtless with the intention of conveying the sense of immortal kinship which only great artists can feel for one another, he was mortified and furious to behold the brash youth fast asleep. Liszt closed the piano and stalked from the room without a word, leaving his other guests to awaken Brahms and appraise him of his intolerable solecism.

Nevertheless, next day, the magnanimous Liszt forbore to mention the incident, pressed Brahms to remain his guest, and on his eventual departure, even made him a gift of a handsome cigar case; but Brahms never forgave him.

Of all the great composers, Brahms is the least interesting as a personality. Most biographers content themselves with eulogizing his achievements in music, and treating his colourless private life as an itinerary of places he visited and of people with whom he did business. Certainly by comparison with his contemporaries Wagner and Liszt, Brahms is a dull dog. Yet, if not on the surface spectacular, he was, in his way, a complex and contradictory man, whose personal life is puzzling for the very reason that his rather prosaic unpleasantness fits so ill with the nobility of his music.

Sometimes called the last of the great classical masters, Brahms' great contribution to music was the broadening perspective he imparted to the classical tradition as exemplified by Beethoven. In an age dominated on the operatic side by the romanticism of Wagner, Brahms stands for a continuation of the formal disciplines of the classical manner. He positively extended the forms which had sufficed for Beethoven, and his practice in latter life of welding the "working-out" and the "recapitulation" sections of his symphonic movements in a closer union than ever before, was a profound creative contribution to the patterns of European music. It was his wonderful power to handle recognized classical elements in such a way as to make them appear absolutely new, which stamps him as the greatest creative architect of formal music since Beethoven. He was also of course a famed pianist and conductor of his own music.

The composer was born on 7 May, 1833, in the great North German port of Hamburg, to humble parents, his father being a double-bass player in an orchestra—not too good a player, according to his own account. At school, Johannes was a dull pupil, and the tortures which he endured in trying to learn French engendered in him a life-long detestation of that nation. However, he was no dunce at music, and rapidly became an accomplished pianist. He received a thorough grounding in the classics from the then famous Edward Marxsen, whom he later, in his inimitably boorish way, described as the most inartistic musician in Hamburg!

As a youth, Brahms earned a living playing the piano in dance halls, cafés and taverns, and said in later life that he learned his uncouth manners from the sailors and general riff-raff of Hamburg with whom he mixed at that time. At the age of twenty, he fell in with a Hungarian-Jewish violinist, Remenyi. Together they set out on tour, mostly walking, and playing in the various towns on their wandering route. At Hanover, Remenyi, who knew the German composer Joseph Joachim, introduced Brahms, and Joachim was sufficiently impressed by the young man's performance as a pianist to recommend him to Liszt and promise a letter of introduction to Schumann.

Liszt was then leader of a party calling itself "The New Germans" at Weimar, which was made up of young *avant-garde* musicians who, like most young artists, despised the great achievements of the past, and wanted to "modernize" German music. He welcomed Brahms and Remenyi, and duly enrolled them in the ranks of the New Germans. In point of fact, Brahms was something of a traditionalist, the heir of Beethoven, and in due course he withdrew from the Liszt circle and published a letter, signed also by Joachim and two other musicians, Grimm and Scholz, protesting against "the so-called

Music of the Future". The patrician Liszt forgave him this gesture, as he had previously done in the notorious instance of Brahms' nap during his performance, but Brahms chose henceforth to regard him as an enemy—it seems to have been one of the peculiarities of Brahms' nature that he could never forgive anyone whom he himself had ill-used.

It is possible that Liszt's generosity, *savoir-faire*, and cosmopolitan ease of manner gave the raw Brahms an inferiority complex; certainly his experience at Weimar made him reluctant to meet Schumann. However, he did eventually find the courage to visit the Schumann household at Düsseldorf, where he was warmly welcomed by the great composer and his wife, Clara. Schumann asked Brahms to play, admired his work tremendously, and declared him "the heir of the great German tradition". A happy relationship developed between the two, terminated only by the tragic onset of the madness which overtook Schumann a few months later. Clara Schumann was perhaps the one great friend of his life. He remained in correspondence with her until her death, which was to precede his own by only a short stretch of time.

In the matter of his career, Brahms' friendship with the Schumanns was immensely fortunate. It began in September, 1853, and an article on Brahms written by Schumann the next month secured Brahms' position to the extent that four of his works—a book of songs, a scherzo and two piano sonatas—were published. Also he made the acquaintance of eminent musicians, including Berlioz and Peter Cornelius. Thus, in the nine short months after his departure from Hamburg with Remenyi, as an unknown student, he had become an accepted member of the highest musical circles in Germany.

Curiously, his native Hamburg was lukewarm in its recognition of his success, and eventually he accepted the post of director of music to a German prince at Detmold. He was there for three months during which time the respect which his work gained him was offset by his none-too-well-concealed contempt for the nobility of the Court. About this time, his capacious ill-humour began to include England, which he had never visited, and his attitude seems to have been nothing more than the conventional prejudice of an ignorant man against "foreigners". Once, when in company with an Englishman and a German, he proffered the latter only his cigar case, then pocketed it with the curt affirmation that "Englishmen do not smoke".

On leaving Detmold, Brahms journeyed, via Hamburg, to Göttingen, and it was there that he seems, for the only time in his life, to have roused his sluggish spirits sufficiently to fall genuinely in love. The object of this passion was a certain Agathe von Siebold, in whose honour he composed various songs and a sextet in G major. Yet, though he was confident that she returned his feelings, he never declared himself to her. He let her go out of his life with little more than a few expressions of polite regret. This curious episode has been variously explained, but it seems at least possible that, outside of his music, Brahms was incapable of scaling any great heights of emotion. True, he could show a certain affection, particularly for children, and he had a definite streak of spleen and boorish irritability, but he could never match the sheer blackguardism of Wagner, nor the princely generosity of which Liszt was capable.

The proposition that Brahms was an artist of the highest genius, and at the same time, a commonplace, petty individual, is reinforced by the evidence that he was a poor hand at assessing the comparative merits of either his own works or those of other composers. He preferred Schumann to Beethoven, and saw nothing in Tchaikovsky; on the other hand, he thought Joachim a greater composer than himself, and leaned constantly upon him for advice and support. One is inevitably drawn to the conclusion that Brahms the musician and Brahms the man were two utterly separate and totally different entities who had no knowledge whatever of each other.

In the case of the piano concerto in D minor, Brahms was afraid to place it before the public until Joachim insisted. It was first tried at Hanover, Brahms playing the solo part, while Joachim conducted. It was given an enthusiastic reception, but at the subsequent performance in Leipzig, it was a failure—some authorities suggesting that this was owing to the machinations of Brahms' enemies in the "New German" party. The piece was next tried at the composer's native Hamburg, where in contradiction to previous coolness, it received warm applause; but Hamburg was not yet wholly won, for when Brahms applied for the post then vacant, of conductor of the Philharmonic concerts, he was passed over in favour of his friend Stockhausen, a singer and a man of inferior ability and experience.

Disappointed but phlegmatic, he pressed on with his work, making sketches for the German Requiem and the first symphony, and completing two piano quartets (A major and G minor), armed with which he made up his mind to try his luck in Vienna—a momentous decision as it turned out. A warm welcome awaited him there, and he was at once given two concerts which were received as almost unqualified successes. He enjoyed life in the Austrian capital and attended concerts, notably by Wagner, at which it is said that he cautioned a friend, who was applauding too vigorously for his taste, not to wear out his gloves.

He returned to Hamburg, but was shortly offered, and accepted, the post of conductor of the Vienna Singacademie. He was not, however, a great success as a conductor, and resigned the post in July, 1863. On returning to Hamburg, he found his mother dying, almost destitute, having been deserted by his father. She died in February, 1864, and Brahms, in sombre mood, set to work once more on the German Requiem. Part of it was performed in Vienna in 1867, with indifferent success, but in 1868 it was acclaimed in Bremen as a masterpiece.

In Vienna, life was pleasant for Brahms. His reputation was such that his bad manners were accepted as the eccentricity of genius. The indulgent, easy-going ways of the Viennese suited him. His somewhat spiteful wit earned him numerous enemies. One singer complained that Brahms, who was accompanying him, played so loudly that he could not hear himself sing: "You lucky man!" came the instant riposte. He insulted a Jewish composer for writing music for Protestant Psalms, and never gave any of his students a word of praise. He even quarrelled fatally with his old friend and helper, Joachim.

The quarrel with Joachim originated with Brahms' desire to have his Requiem played at the Bonn commemoration of Schubert. The request was refused, and he blamed Joachim. The two composers met again after an estrangement of two years, and the quarrel was more or less patched up, but they were never again intimate friends; later Brahms submitted a double concerto to Joachim, who played it, but openly declared that he considered it below Brahms' best standard. Among others, Brahms also earned the enmity of Wagner —but then, who did not?

Whatever his shortcomings as a man, Brahms went from strength to strength as a composer. His four symphonies, published in 1877, 1878, 1884 and 1886 respectively, mark the height of his fame. There are many other major works, too numerous to list here, and most critics agree that their outstanding characteristic is their even standard of excellence. Schumann correctly forecast that the young Brahms was fully equipped from the start, and that experience had little to offer him.

The last years of Brahms' life were happy. He was well-off financially, enjoyed a great and justified reputation, and travelled to play or conduct his music as he pleased. With Vienna as his centre, he often spent the spring in Italy and the summer in the mountains.

One by one, his friends died, but he seemed little affected until the death of Clara Schumann. Early in 1896 she became ill and depressed, and her lifelong correspondence with Brahms dwindled to perfunctory notes. On 7 May, Brahms' birthday, she sent him her last note—a few feebly scrawled words of greeting. On 20 May, she died; he had been kept informed of the progress of her illness, and walked at the head of the funeral cortège. Her death seems to have sounded a knell in his own heart. Hers was the one friendship that endured throughout, and with her passing, Brahms seems to have been too frightened of death to find consolation in the deep religious feelings that inspired the German Requiem. He fell ill, eventually taking to his bed, and the best that his doctor could do was to relieve him of pain. He died of cancer of the liver on 3 April, 1897, less than a year after his beloved friend.

Gottlieb Daimler
1834-1900

THE peace of years was shattered rudely and for ever in Stuttgart, in the suburb of Cannstadt, much less than a hundred years ago. On that day in 1885, the upright, dignified figure of Herr Gottlieb Daimler could be observed getting on his bicycle at the top of the road which slopes gently to the Neckar. Bicycles were fairly common in Cannstadt, but they were expensive, and this particular one looked more expensive than most. A crowd, quite a big crowd, had gathered round Herr Daimler; men and women with apparently nothing better to do than watch a middle-aged gentleman try out a new bicycle; there was the usual preponderance of small boys, and a large Schnauzer dog which sniffed at the machine and had to be dragged off by its small owner.

Suddenly, Herr Daimler was off. With considerable agility for a man of over fifty, he ran a few paces with the bicycle, holding it by the handlebars, and as it began to nose over the hill, hopped on board and began to pedal. Then the small boys could see him lean down to fiddle with the "engine" he had bolted to the frame. At the same time, he stopped pedalling.

With the noise of a hundred firecrackers and an eruption of deep blue smoke which all but obliterated machine and rider, the engine began to work. There was a confused cheer from the crowd—confused because no one was sure what was happening. The bicycle had started off downhill, propelled by gravity and pedals: it was still going downhill, in the middle of its private cloud, but to the accompaniment of a truly frightening noise and at a frightening speed. It was rather, someone remarked, as if the Lord had leant down and embraced Gottlieb (and why should He not, with a name like Gottlieb, God's Love?) and was taking him away, in a roar of smoke and noise. On the other hand, Herr Daimler was indisputably going down, and fast: perhaps the Devil had reached up to claim his own. A minute later Daimler was returning, he was ascending the slope from the Neckar and his feet—as the crowd excitedly noticed—were stationary on their pedals. Gottlieb Daimler, the world's first motor-cyclist, ancestor of a generation of young men in black leather

151

jackets, had gone down to the river and up again, on his own motor-bike.

If this were Daimler's only contribution to history he might not have earned a place in this book—but he did more, far more than invent the motor-cycle. He is the inventor of the high-speed internal combustion engine, without which the motor-cycle, the motor-boat and above all the motor-car, would not exist. He has given his name to many of the finest engines ever made, one of the finest makes of motor-car, and had he not died a few years before the Wright Brothers proved the possibility of powered flight, he would almost certainly have developed this astonishing new dimension with the enthusiasm that characterized everything he did. As it is, aircraft engines developed by men like Benz to whom he sold his patents were used throughout the Second World War.

Gottlieb Daimler was born in 1834, in the small south-west German town of Schorndorf, not far from Stuttgart. His parents were well-to-do. After a few years at the Stuttgart Polytechnic he was able to go on with his training as a mechanical engineer in Germany and in England—where he worked for a while with the firm of Whitworth's in Manchester, the engineering centre, men said, of the world.

For years the idea of a "horseless carriage" had fascinated men, and Manchester buzzed with ideas on the subject. There had been strange contraptions on the Continent as far back as the sixteenth century—things that worked, but not for long, with coiled springs and even sails—and in the early years of the seventeenth century, Ramsay and Wildgoose, in England, had patented their own horseless carriage. Probably the first vehicle to approach our own ideas of what a motor-car should be was a French steam carriage of 1770 which carried its two passengers on three wheels at a speed of four miles an hour. At this point France was ahead of the world, but the Revolution postponed any further effort and soon it was England which had taken the lead.

All the vehicles used steam, which had many disadvantages, including the major one that, like a tea-kettle, a car was useless until its water boiled. This took a considerable time, quite apart from the lighting of the fire in the first place. Attempts were made to keep a small fire permanently alight and then fan it rapidly to great heat, to keep water just off the boil in padded tanks, but they came to nothing. Then in 1872, when Daimler's compatriot Nicholas Otto was working on the recently invented but highly unsatisfactory "internal combustion engine", Daimler joined him in Cologne. Already

Gottlieb Daimler had seen that the new principle would come to nothing unless the machinery could be made lighter, could move more quickly. When Otto's big breakthrough came, with his invention of the four-stroke, or "Otto" Cycle, it was Daimler's design of the actual engine, with unbelievably light but strong components, moving at undreamed of speeds, that made the new engine a practical venture. The internal combustion engine dates, historically, from the discovery of Otto's Cycle, but it was Daimler's efforts that made it work.

Before Nicholas Otto, the internal combustion engine had been a curiosity, a bulky metal cylinder in which something was exploded to drive a "piston" with great force from one end to the other. An explosion on the other side of the piston would then drive it back, and this movement, violent and uncontrolled though it was, could be used, like the leg of a bicyclist, to turn a wheel—though the problem of fuelling the cylinder before each explosion made the process absurdly cumbersome.

In Dr Otto's Cycle—which is still the principle on which the majority of motor-car engines function—a piston sliding up and down in a cylinder, would suck in an explosive mixture of air and gas from opened valves at the top. Then, when the piston, moved by hand with a crank, had reached the bottom of its stroke, and the cylinder was full of mixture, the valves would be closed and the piston would compress it in an ascending second stroke. At the top of this stroke, with the mixture under pressure, a flame would be introduced through another valve, and the resultant explosion would drive the piston down again, to the bottom of its stroke. The fourth stroke, the piston's return to the top, with valve again opened, would drive out exhaust gases, making room for the whole four-stroke cycle to repeat itself, sucking in more mixture. Though only one of the four strokes delivered power, a heavy flywheel could be connected to the "pedalling" action of the piston and tide it over the three non-productive strokes with the energy from the fourth. If two or more cylinders, as Daimler arranged them, could be connected to the same flywheel in such a way that their power strokes were spaced out, the internal combustion engine would not only deliver great power, but do so smoothly and immediately, a moment after the process had been set in motion by hand.

After Daimler had lightened the machine and made it practical, both Otto and Daimler saw that the next major improvement would be in the supply of fuel. After noting and rejecting the earlier, historic, experiments with gunpowder and the like, Otto had developed his machine using gas and air. The two were mixed, under pressure, and introduced through a valve. Although the machine fired satisfactorily, the fuel was awkward to handle. It could be kept under pressure, only in a heavy, reinforced container; moreover, it was not always convenient to obtain. Daimler realized that a fuel which could be introduced into the engine as a liquid would be a great improvement and he experimented with various early "carburetters" for vaporizing spirits. At last he was able, in 1883, to patent his light-weight, high-speed engine using liquid fuel; the improbable idea of a motor-bicycle became accomplished fact.

While using and improving on Otto's four-stroke cycle of operations, Daimler made much study of a two-stroke cycle. In this, the piston travels past an ingenious arrangement of ports in the cylinder and is able to recharge itself with mixture during its power stroke, while the incoming vapour drives out the exhaust gas. With a power stroke in every two rather than every four, it was lighter for each horsepower developed than the four-stroke "Otto" version: as such it was ideal for the early motor-cycles. Daimler brought the two-stroke engine to a peak of efficiency, though he soon appreciated that the heavier, smoother-running, multi-cylinder four-stroke was the solution to most problems of locomotion. His first multi-cylinder engine was produced in 1889, with two cylinders set in a "V"—the ancestor of the modern "V8", "V12" and bigger engines.

By 1895 the Paris-Bordeaux race of 735 miles had been won at the considerable average speed of just under fifteen miles an hour, with one of Daimler's engines—and the feat brought a huge upsurge of interest in "motoring" and "automobiles". The Automobile Club of France was founded almost immediately, and a year or two later another followed in Britain. By the end of the nineteenth century, motoring had come to stay.

In the meantime Daimler had perfected his motor-cycle and his motor-boat—the latter doing its first noisy trip up the Rhine in 1887. In a way, he found marine engines more satisfying to work with. One of the problems of the internal combustion engine had always been that the temperature developed during the explosion —the "internal combustion"—reached anything up to 2,000 degrees Centigrade, enough to melt the iron of which piston and cylinder were made. To avoid having the engine dissolve like a chocolate toy, various systems of cooling were developed, with air, water, oil and other things circulating around the cylinder block, taking away excess heat. In a marine engine, the problem of water supply was straightforward; there was no need for a "radiator" to cool the water before it could be used again: there was an unlimited supply available, under the boat. The company which Daimler founded sold its patents all over the world, then turned its energies to marine engines.

A quiet unassuming man who loved his own Baden-Württemburg, he preferred to stroll through on foot rather than roar through on his motor-bicycle, Daimler's name has been forgotten in many of the places where his engines, manufactured under licence, are most used. Certainly his contribution to the development of the motor-car must take precedence over even that of William Royce (who cheerfully admitted that one of the finest Rolls-Royce engines he ever made was an "improved copy" of one of Daimler's, impounded in England at the start of the First World War, with its Mercedes racing car). Henry Ford, too, who developed mass-production to give a good cheap car to the man in the street, would have had his conveyor belts full of coal-bunkers and water-tanks for a steam carriage, without Daimler's work on internal combustion.

Having sold his patents to men like Panhard, Levassor and Benz, Daimler allowed his name almost to vanish from the industry he had created. One exception is the handsome Daimler car made in England. Another, delightful, way his family is remembered is through a famous make of German car. It was first shown at the Paris Exhibition in 1900, where people agreed that, quite apart from its "splendid performance", it was a "thing of breath-taking beauty". Taking these points into consideration, Wilhelm Maybach, manager of the Daimler factory in Cannstadt, said, "Obviously, Herr Daimler, there can be but one name—" and the dark-eyed daughter of the founder, Fraulein Mercedes Daimler, gave her name to one of the world's most beautiful cars.

The twentieth century has been called the century of the internal combustion engine, but Gottlieb Daimler, who did so much to make it so, survived only its first two months. He died in Bad Cannstadt, on 6 March, 1900.

Mark Twain
1835-1910

It is rare that the humour of one nation is appreciated by the people of
another. Only when the humour has stamped upon it the universal
truths, can this happen. The humour of Mark Twain possesses these
qualities. Truth hates sham; and sham was the pet hatred of Mark
Twain.

DURING his lifetime, Samuel Langhorne Clemens, better known
by his pen-name of Mark Twain, used to joke, "I came into the world
with Halley's comet, and I reckon I'll go out with it." He had been
born on 30 November, 1835, the day on which the famous comet
made its nineteenth-century appearance. He died on 21 April, 1910,
two days after its next appearance.

Samuel's father was John Marshall Clemens, who kept a general
store in Florida, a small village in Missouri. When business fell off
he stood outside the shop's door two barrels, one of which contained
brown sugar; when a housewife left, she could help herself to a
handful of it provided she had made a purchase. If a man made a
purchase, he could help himself from the other barrel, which contained whisky.

When Samuel was four, the Clemens family moved to Hannibal,
on the banks of the Mississippi, and with his brothers and sister, there
he grew up. Here, too, he made friends with the original of Becky
Thatcher, a girl named Laura Hawkins, who, when questioned
later about some of the incidents in *Tom Sawyer*, confirmed that they
had actually happened to her and Samuel. She remembered him as a
boy and as a man:

> "He hadn't changed much. He had the same slow way of drawling
> out his words as he had when we played together, and like the boy he
> saw the joke in everything quicker than a hound-dog sees a rabbit."

It was from his mother that Samuel inherited his sense of humour
and love of fun; he inherited also her absent-mindedness. Once she
was asked if she was not afraid that her son would be killed or
drowned, since he was always up to some trick or other. She replied
in the slow drawl which she had also passed on:

"He is such a perpetual nuisance that I am only afraid that he will *not* be drowned or killed."

The boys of Hannibal swam in Bear Creek, and it was here that Samuel at length mastered the art. It was only his persistence that made him keep at it, for while he was learning two of his play-fellows were drowned and twice he himself was dragged out just in time to save him from drowning.

It was in Hannibal, too, that Samuel met Huck Finn. His real name was Tom Blankensap; his father was the town drunkard. The family made a precarious living fishing and hunting.

One day while out with Tom Blankensap, Samuel caught a raccoon. The boys skinned it and Sam was delegated to sell it to the local dealer, from whom he received, much to his disgust, only ten cents. As he was leaving the shop, however, he noticed that the man threw the skin into a back room, the window of which was open. He crept round to the window, climbed in, retrieved the skin. Later he entered the front door once more, to come out with a second ten cents. This was repeated many times, until the storekeeper happened to look into the back room to see how many skins he had bought and found just the one.

Samuel first attended the dame school in Hannibal, and from there passed on to a small establishment kept by a dour, elderly man named Cross. This was to be the sum total of his formal education.

When Sam was twelve, his father died, and he was so filled with remorse for all his disobedience to his parent in the past that the day after the funeral his mother began to be worried on his account. At last she coaxed out of him what was troubling him. When she heard what it was, she begged him to forget the past, concentrate on being good in the future and to go on making a success of his life.

Like many other great American writers—Walt Whitman, Artemus Ward and Bret Harte among them—Clemens took his first step into adult life as a printer's apprentice. When he had worked out his apprenticeship he took various posts on other Hannibal journals, until a quarrel with his beloved brother Orion, over a very trivial matter, determined him to go to St Louis and find work.

His sister Pamela lived in St Louis, and he went to stay with her while he worked as a compositor on the *St Louis Evening News*. For the first time in his life he began to save money, intending as soon as he had enough, to go to New York. This he achieved in 1853, when he was eighteen. There he got a job at four dollars a week in a printing firm and lodged in a mechanics' boarding-house.

New York came as a great surprise to him. He was thrilled by the buses, but most of all by discovering that no one in the city had to pump water, and that under the streets there were sewers so large that men could walk in them.

After a comparatively short stay in New York he moved on to Philadelphia, where he worked for a year on *The Inquirer*. By now he was a very skilful and swift compositor, able to set ten thousand ems a day. As he was paid by piece-work, he was earning a good salary, but he never had any money put by; what was left over after he had paid for his board and lodging was spent on seeing life.

Tired of the east after a year with *The Inquirer*, Clemens returned to St Louis and worked again for the *Evening News*. He could not settle, and moved on to various other printing jobs in other towns, until he met Captain Horace Bixby and asked him to teach him the river. This was in April, 1857; Clemens was just twenty-two. Bixby was one of the most famous pilots on the Mississippi, and he agreed to teach the young printer the river in his boat the *Paul Jones* for five hundred dollars, payable in instalments. In 1859 Clemens took his pilot's licence, and for the next two years he worked as a co-pilot.

On the outbreak of the Civil War in 1861, Clemens returned to Hannibal, and there joined the Marion Rangers, a cavalry company that was being formed for the defence of the State. He was too late to be allotted a horse, and had to be content with a mule called Paintbrush. He and the mule served with the Confederate Army until July, when he was invalided out suffering from exhaustion.

He went to be a private secretary to his brother Orion, who had recently been appointed secretary of the Nevada Territory, and together they went to Carson City. Clemens found that there was neither work nor pay attached to his appointment, so, for a time, he tried gold mining. He failed to find any rich deposit, however, and during odd moments when he was not prospecting, wrote a number of articles which, when published in the *Virginia City Enterprise* attracted considerable attention, especially a burlesque report of a Fourth of July oration.

A few days after this last appeared, he received from the editor of the *Enterprise* the offer of a job as a reporter at twenty-five dollars a week. As, by this time, he was penniless he accepted, and walked the seventy miles to Virginia City to take up the post. He covered the distance in four days. When he had proved himself as a reporter, the editor assigned him to reporting the debates of the Territorial Legislature. These reports also attracted great attention. The editor suggested that he should use a pen-name for them.

While he was pondering the choice of name, he heard that an old acquaintance called Isaiah Sellers, who had written articles under the name of Mark Twain, had just died, and it at once struck him that here was a pen-name that was original and striking, and he decided to use it himself. He signed Mark Twain for the first time on a report from Carson City dated 2 February, 1863. As he had hoped, the name caught on very quickly. In a short time everyone was calling him Mark, and his own name was forgotten.

While he was on a visit to Virginia City in 1863, Artemus Ward, the outstanding American humorous writer of this period, who had taken up lecturing on the failure of the New York *Vanity Fair*, came to the town to give a lecture, and made the *Enterprise* offices his headquarters. The two men met and became friends.

It was still customary in certain quarters for attacks on personal honour to be defended by duels, and Mark Twain became involved in one with the editor of the rival newspaper, the *Chronicle*. Twain chose as his second the reputedly best shot in Nevada, one Steve Gillis. Twain, who was quite helpless with a gun of any sort, was given some instruction by Gillis, but he was unable to hit a barn door only a few feet from him.

Gillis and Twain went to the appointed place before the time arranged, and while they were waiting Gillis took a shot at a bird and brought it down. The rival editor happened to appear just at that moment, but thought that it was Twain who had made the shot. Remarking, "I won't fight that devil Twain; it would be sheer suicide," he threw his weapon away.

Governor Nye of Nevada Territory was determined to stamp out duelling, and had given orders that any participant should be arrested. Though he had escaped certain injury by his rival's capitulation, Twain learned that a warrant had been issued against him. Before the sheriff could reach him, he escaped over the border into California.

In San Francisco, Twain worked at one or two reporting jobs, and met and became friends with Bret Harte, the novelist and poet. This friendship lasted for some time, but eventually broke up when they quarrelled over the failure of a play in the writing of which they had collaborated.

Unable to settle down, and never able to keep for long any of the money he earned, Twain wandered from job to job. In 1866 he heard that an expedition was going to Hawaii, and persuaded the *Sacramento Union* to appoint him their correspondent. Twain was greatly impressed by the trip.

On his return, not knowing what to do, at the suggestion of a friend, he embarked on a lecture tour, his subject being the Hawaiian Islands. His lectures were successful from the start. He made 1,400 dollars from his first, which was a fortune to one previously able to think only in tens of dollars. At last he believed he had found his real métier. On the proceeds of the first tour, he made a visit to Europe, travelling as far east as Odessa. On his way home a shipboard acquaintance showed him a photograph of his sister, and Twain immediately fell in love with her. On arrival in New York, the friend's parents and his lovely sister were at the dock to meet him, and so Twain met Olivia Langdon in the flesh and found her even more beautiful than her picture had suggested.

They were married in February, 1870.

Shortly before marrying, Twain had bought a part-interest in the *Buffalo Express* and became one of its editors. He hated being tied down to one place and one job. So a year later he sold his interest at a loss of 10,000 dollars. Fortunately, he was able to stand losing this sum, for his first book, *Innocents Abroad*, which he had published immediately on his return from Europe, had become such a hit with the American reading public, that even after two years, it was still bringing him 1,000 dollars a month in royalties. There has probably never been such a distinctively personal travel book as this.

In 1872 the Twains moved to Hartford, where their next-door neighbour was Mrs Harriet Beecher Stowe, author of *Uncle Tom's Cabin*. When Twain went to call on her for the first time, he forgot to put on his collar and tie, and when his wife drew his attention to it, he ran upstairs, came down with a collar and tie, and sent them round to Mrs Stowe with the note, "Dear Mrs Stowe, Herewith receive a visit from the rest of me."

In this same year Twain visited England to arrange for the English publication of his *Innocents Abroad* in a copyright edition. The book had already been pirated in London and had become as popular in England as it was in America. Its author had become a household name.

He now devoted his time to writing books. *Roughing It* and *The Gilded Age* further enhanced his reputation as a humorist. His fourth book was *Tom Sawyer*, which he began as a play. As he got into the story, however, he realized that he was using the wrong form, and changed the story into a novel. He wrote every morning and afternoon, not pausing for lunch, until dinner. After dinner he read what he had written to Mrs Twain, listened to her criticisms and, where he agreed, made alterations. He worked very quickly, covering an

Above: Aix: Paysage Rocheux by Paul Cézanne. Though for a time closely associated with the Impressionists, Cézanne broke from that school to develop his own approach, to "treat nature by the cylinder, the sphere and the cone". His search for the inherent geometry of nature provided the flashpoint for Cubism.

Below: Landscape with Cypress Trees by Vincent Van Gogh. Though in the end Van Gogh's mind failed, he has had great influence. Much of his work belongs to the post-Impressionist school and he used violent colour with paint very thickly applied. His style is a base from which stems modern Expressionism.

Drawing was Auguste Rodin's first love. Usually he drew swiftly and fluently, often tinting the drawing with pale washes in delicate colour. His *Recumbent Nude* is masterly in its economy of line.

Auguste Rodin was one of the greatest sculptors of all time. The immense realism of his figures (such as in *The Kiss*, pictured *right*) is so astounding that some critics, probably from jealousy, contended that he had used casts!

average of fifty pages a day. He had written it as a story for boys, but from the first day of its appearance when it was hailed as a humorous masterpiece, it was read by more adults than children.

Huckleberry Finn, the companion volume to *Tom Sawyer*, did not appear until nine years later, by which time Mark Twain had become an international figure. The success of Huck Finn helped him to liquidate the considerable losses which he incurred when the publishing house of Charles L. Webster and to which he was connected, failed in 1894. It took him five hard years of lecturing before he was free from all his debts.

Of his many other books, *A Yankee at the Court of King Arthur* is probably best known. It was his most successful venture into satire, and displayed qualities which rank him with Swift.

In 1907 Oxford University honoured him by conferring on him an honorary doctorate in Letters; the first purely humorous writer to be so honoured by a great university.

He has never lost his hold on the reading public, and today *Tom Sawyer* and *Huckleberry Finn* have established themselves as classics in the English language. These two books have probably brought more joy and more laughter to people of all nationalities than any others with a comparable circulation.

Jamsetji Tata
1839-1904

THE PARSIS came to India from Persia in the eighth century. They were followers of Zoroaster, and they settled on the coast of Gujurat, Bombay being the centre of their community. Some have names which to Western ears are like any other Indian names, but others are called, for example, "Mr Engineer", "Mr Doctor", and "Mr Bottlewallah". These are names which their families adopted long ago when the English ruled India. They are names, not titles; Mr Engineer may well be a professional cricketer, and Mr Bottle-wallah a surgeon. Their names mean no more than the English Smith, Shepherd and Hunter. In their religion, customs and way of life, they are to an extent distinctive, but they are singled out more signally for their intelligence and industry.

They were the first indians to move into city flats. They realized that the traditional house was expensive and hard to run; that in a crowded city centre, for the ordinary man, the flat was cheaper, more suitable, more comfortable. They are held in respect not only by India but all over the world and the name of one Parsi in particular has for many years been famous from London to New York and Tokyo. That name is "TATA".

Jamsetji Tata was born in the town of Navsari, Baroda State, in 1839. The son of well-to-do Parsi parents, he was sent to Elphinstone College in Bombay for his education. His father ran a prosperous trading firm and Jamsetji joined it, as the family had planned, when he was twenty. Already the family and friends had noticed his ambition and imagination. Soon it was pretty obvious that young Jamsetji would not be content to remain a merchant. Within a few years he had set up a cotton mill of the most modern sort in the town of Nagpur, and another in Bombay. Because of their advanced design, with machinery from England and innovations which Jamsetji, travelling indefatigably all over the world, had studied, they were a huge commercial success from the outset—and he found himself a very rich man in early middle age.

For a long time he had dreamed of an Indian steel industry. There was iron ore available in many parts of the continent, though early

162

attempts to smelt it with charcoal had not been a commercial success. Increasing quantities of Indian coal were being discovered, and this looked to Jamsetji like a possible solution: for years in England ore had been smelted by coal. For years in India iron had been fashioned, but in very small quantities. Tata had read that the Chinese were the first workers in iron, no doubt they had taught the people of India how to smelt and forge it. After all, the famous iron column at Kutab Minar, near Delhi, was believed to be three thousand years old, and the method by which it had been produced and erected was a mystery as great as that of the pyramids. For Tata there was no question of an Indian iron and steel industry being impossible: progress had stopped at a certain point, the villager had gone on smelting tiny quantities with a wooden bellows, just as his ancestors has done when Alexander the Great invaded the country; there was no reason why India could not go on from there.

It seemed, the more Jamsetji thought of it, that British rule had held up the development more than anything else: the British had introduced railways, by which cheap, imported steel was being carried all over the sub-continent; no local manufacturer would have been able to compete.

Tata chanced in 1882 to see a paper which had been issued by the Government of India. It was a report by the German expert, Ritter von Schwartz, who had been invited to survey the prospects for an iron and steel industry. He was enthusiastic about an enormous deposit of ore at Lohara—there was a "hill of iron" he wrote, "three-eighths of a mile long, two hundred yards broad and between one and two hundred feet high. Unfortunately," he added, "the only nearby coal, at Warora, was no good for smelting." Tata was excited by this, refused to accept that the coal was no good, and offered a large reward for anyone devising a method of smelting Lohara ore with Warora coal or coke. Although no entirely adequate answer emerged, he got a sufficient number of helpful suggestions to justify dividing the prize among several competitors. (These suggestions were of great value to Jamsetji's son, years later, who carried on his father's plan.)

Jamsetji approached the Government of India for a licence to prospect. He would form an iron and steel company to smelt and manufacture; even though the coal was unsatisfactory, he would do it somehow, it was a challenge. He asked that a convenient branch railway be placed under the control of his proposed company, for transporting coal to the ore. The Government, which had always considered railways in the sub-continent as strategic affairs, refused to hand one over to private enterprise. They also invoked absurd regulations for prospectors, whereby if a valuable seam of ore was found, the Government could demand to take it over, without compensation—regulations designed, in fact, to prevent development of heavy industry: India was to remain, as long as possible, a source of raw material, a market for manufactured goods. No one—except possibly Indians—wanted Indian steel to compete with the English sort. Nothing further could be done about Tata's plan for the best part of twenty years, but he never abandoned it, keipt albums of newspaper cuttings into which he pasted any ment on however small or apparently trivial, of Indian minerals, Indian mining.

In 1899—by which time Jamsetji Tata was sixty—a new Viceroy, Lord Curzon, swept away the archaic restrictions and it seemed as if Tata's hour had come. He approached the Secretary of State for India during a visit to London (a visit in which he handsomely endowed a number of British institutions) and was told to press on immediately with his scheme. By now this had become entirely a matter of patriotism for Tata, an opportunity to advance the welfare of his country. He had enough wealth and to spare for himself. It seemed all important that some sort of huge, self-supporting industry, financed if at all possible by Indian money, be started—and be started quickly.

In the next five years he travelled, nursing his dream, all over the world, seeking advice, expert help. He was still concerned with his other enterprises: the new Taj Mahal Hotel which he had built in Bombay was the finest hotel in Asia. For its electric lighting plant Tata had travelled to Germany. He still owned huge cotton mills on behalf of which he spent months investigating developments in the southern states of the U.S.A. During these travels he was able to study iron and steel plants in Pittsburgh, in Cleveland, all over the world, assiduously noting anything which could be of use for his own dream. He decided that American prospecting engineers were the sort he needed; he brought one back.

In April, 1903, when the goal seemed in sight—there was so much iron ore, so much coal; Jamsetji had devised the finest plant in the world, all that was needed was the best possible site on which to erect it—his health began to fail. He realized that his own days were numbered, that if he wanted to get the scheme to work he would have to pass it on to his sons: after all, everything they did had been a family matter; their concern was Tata Sons and Company.

Dorab Tata was forty-four when his father handed on the work to him. He embarked, for love of father and ambition for India, on a period of wildly adventurous prospecting with the indefatigable American expert, C. M. Weld. They investigated districts which were the delight of hunters because tigers were so numerous, which for that reason were highly unpleasant to prospectors; they operated far from roads and railways, in great discomfort in the hottest part of the year; they found nothing of interest and were badgered incessantly by the Government of India which, years too late, had woken to the possibility of such an enterprise and wanted to know what was being done.

Jamsetji's original scheme at Lohara had been abandoned; during the twenty years' delay the nearby coal had been exhausted. Now Dorab was dashing from place to place with Mr Weld, driven by crumbs of information, specks of rumour. By much the same chance as had displayed the German report to his father, he came across an old geological map of the central Provinces with a large area shaded to indicate "deposits of iron ore".

Tata and his expert wasted no time, rushed to the district and were shown the local curiosity, a hill three hundred feet high, on which men's footsteps rang. Frantically they applied for another licence, began to take samples. With each sample, their spirits rose. There appeared to be no coal available, but with this extraordinary find of what they now estimated to be two and a half million tons of high-grade ore, it was worth while bringing the fuel in from any distance. In the course of their investigations they had communicated with the Geological Survey which produced the map and were told that it had been annotated fifteen years before by a Bengali, P. N. Bose, who had found iron and had not bothered to investigate further. Tata's plans were beginning to crystallize when Mr Bose himself wrote to say that he knew of a vastly better deposit, in Bihar, with more ore, with coal nearby, and only a short run to the port of Calcutta.

Dorab and Weld were understandably puzzled, but they duly investigated. All was as Bose had said. The "iron hills" in Bihar were seven hundred feet high, the coal was next door. Like good businessmen, they abandoned their earlier, second-best, plan, managed to convey their enthusiasm to the Government of India and persuaded them not only to build a short branch railway line from the siding at Kalimati to the village of Sakchi where they proposed to build their works, but to buy, as they became available, 20,000 tons of steel rails a year.

Dorab decided to see whether his father's hope had been justified: would the ordinary people of India invest in such an enterprise?

They did. The only sadness for Dorab was that Jamsetji, who had died three years earlier, in 1904, had never lived to see it. From early morning to late at night the Tata offices were besieged by Indians, young and old, rich and poor, driven as much by patriotism as by desire for personal gain, rushing to offer their mite. At the end of three weeks the capital required—£1,630,000—had been raised, entirely from Indians.

The village of Sakchi, the wayside station of Kalimati, grew enormously. (Within a few years, as the steel empire grew, the names of these two villages, rapidly becoming towns, then one large city, were changed to Jamshetpur and Tatanagar.) There was ample land around Sakchi and it was near to the ore at Gurumaishi and the coal at Jherria. Only 152 miles of railway separated Kalimati from Calcutta. Construction began in the autumn of 1908 and the first iron was produced at the end of 1911. By this time the population of Sakchi, soon to be Jamshetpur, had risen from a few hundred to 5,672. (Forty years later, it was to be 218,000.)

The Tata fortune, already huge, grew vaster, but the family's fame rests as much on its philanthropy as its industry. They have set up cotton mills, an iron and steel plant, hydro-electric supply for Bombay, an airline; their interests include textiles, locomotives and rolling stock, chemicals, cement, and a host of other things; but 83 per cent of the capital of the parent company, Tata Sons, Private, Ltd., is held by charitable trusts endowed by the family. They have endowed a department of social science and administration at the London School of Economics, as well as helping other British universities, they have established a trust for international research into leukaemia, endowed a Cancer Research Hospital in Bombay, the Indian Institute of Science in Bangalore, all in addition to most comprehensive welfare schemes for the thousands of their employees.

Probably no other family has ever contributed as much in the way of wise guidance, industrial development and advancing philanthropy to any country as the Tatas have to India, both before and since independence.

Paul Cézanne
1839-1906

PAUL CÉZANNE won fame as one of the first great painters to develop
the style known as Impressionist, yet it is not for that only that he is
remembered. Had Cézanne been content with Impressionism he
would still have been great; Renoir, Monet and Pissarro also painted
in the Impressionist manner and Cézanne's work in this style ranks at
least with theirs. Cézanne, however, did more, very much more. He
it was who broke away from the limiting formlessness of Impressionism. He argued that the basis of nature is structure, that structure
basically is an organization of simple geometric elements. "Treat
nature by the cylinders, the sphere and the cone" was his dictum. He
might have added "by the square and the rectangle as well", but
that did not happen until 1907, a year after his death, when Picasso,
then a man in his twenties, raised that cry and led the way to Cubism,
a movement which has affected the future course of much in painting,
the applied arts, in architecture and industrial design. In fact much of
the simplification of form in evidence around us springs more or less
directly from the later work of Cézanne and the painting of Picasso.

Cézanne was born on 19 January, 1839, in Aix-en-Provence. His
father, Louis-Auguste Cézanne, began life as a hat manufacturer.
His mother was a girl who worked in that business. Louis-Auguste
prospered; in 1847 he was able to set up as a banker.

In 1849 Paul was sent as a day-boarder to the Pensionnat St Joseph,
from which in 1852 he entered as a boarder the Collège Bourbon.
Both institutions were in Aix. He appears to have been an industrious
scholar, winning prizes in Greek, Latin, history and mathematics,
but these successes were achieved more by hard study than by any
special natural aptitude.

Most of Cézanne's life was shadowed by the fear of his father, who
was a man of powerful, overbearing personality, and there was a
prolonged, sometimes agonizing struggle between them. His early
letters, and accounts by friends of his youth, show him as unsociable,
moody, passionate and given to alternating bouts of violence and
despair. During this period, however, he had two close friends, one
the orphan, Emile Zola (later to become the famous "Realist"

novelist), and the other a lad named Baptistin Baille, who became an engineer. The three youths spent their holidays in the beautiful countryside around Aix, mountaineering, swimming and hunting. They also indulged freely in the ardent, romantic dreams of youth, of poetry, of painting and the glamour of the bohemian life.

Some of the letters written by the young Paul during this time have been preserved, and he reveals himself both in a vein of self-disgust at his own inadequacy, and in a fulsome, poetic mood on the beauties of nature. Many of these writings are in verse and illustrated by the author. In one, he imagines a family seated at dinner, partaking of a severed human head, carved and proffered by the father. In another fantasy he is alone in a storm, trapped in a dark forest, and besieged by devils. A coach and horses draws up and the devils flee. In the coach sits a beautiful girl. He enters and embraces her, whereupon she changes into a skeleton. Such macabre fancies suggest the effect upon the youth of his ceaseless struggle against his domineering and hated father.

It is thought that his long series of paintings of still life—simple, domestic objects arranged upon a table—is an unconscious psychological effort to restore peace and order to the dining-table, the setting of so many of his battles with his father. Nevertheless, he was very like his father in one respect, the possession of an iron will. Indeed he managed to persuade his father to indulge his passion for painting to the extent of allowing him to study for two years (1856-8) at the Aix School of Drawing, under one, Gilbert.

Louis-Auguste bought a grand new house, the Jas De Bouffan in 1859, and allowed Paul to decorate it with mural paintings which he signed with the name of the famous painter "Ingres".

Eventually the father lost patience and packed his son off to study at the Law School at Aix. However, Paul's stubbornness exceeded his father's and the old man grudgingly agreed in April, 1861, to allow his son to go to Paris, on a meagre allowance, to study painting. Paris was then, as now, the centre of the world of art, the magnet which drew young "genius" with dreams of wealth and fame. Cézanne enrolled at the Académie Suisse, a kind of art school, but after six months of failure and discouragement, he gave up and returned to his father's business in Aix. This he found unbearable and, after a period of vacillation, he returned to Paris and the Académie Suisse in November, 1862. He applied for admission to the school of Fine Arts, but was not accepted. However, he made friends with many other young painters of future eminence, including Camille Pissarro, who later influenced him greatly.

Contemporary witnesses have it that it was impossible for Cézanne to draw directly from the living female nude, because his erotic impulses were too strong for him to concentrate on the work. Be that as it may, his paintings in this early phase were certainly passionate and violent.

Some time before 1860, Cézanne formed an irregular union with a young woman named Hortense Fiquet, a model, and a reputed beauty; she became the mother of his son, Paul, on 4 January, 1862. As ever, he greatly feared the wrath of his father, should the latter discover that he was keeping a mistress, and was hard pressed to support her and the child on the miserly pittance which the old man doled out to him. Other than this liaison with Hortense Fiquet, Cézanne's love-life was, notwithstanding his eroticisms in paint and poetry, insignificant; in his sex-life, as in every other aspect, two men lived and warred eternally within Cézanne.

Beneath a rough, brow-beating manner Paul was in fact painfully timid and sensitive. While he would bluster and sneer, his shrinking sensibilities manifested themselves in an extreme fear of physical contact with other human beings, to the extent that it was really repugnant to him to shake hands even with a friend. The only person whom he unstintingly adored was his mother; to her he poured forth his troubles and his dreams; she it was who often stood as a buffer between him and his formidable father.

The only way this timorous, outwardly roaring bully could find peace or come to terms at all with life was in his painting. He could not bear to be overlooked while he was at work, and it is related that, one day, as he sat painting his beloved southern landscape, a busybody discovered him, and after regarding the sonorous magnificence of his colour with a fussily disapproving eye, patronizingly suggested that, as a former pupil of the painter Corot, he would, out of the goodness of his heart, give a free demonstration by knocking Cézanne's painting into shape. Ironically Cézanne stood aside while the nonentity took the brushes and busily "corrected" the jewel-like colours with a mixture of muddy greys, then stood back, confidently awaiting this bumpkin's open-mouthed admiration. Cézanne took a palette-knife, went to the canvas and thoroughly scraped the idiot's efforts from it. Then he sat down, and noisily breaking wind, remarked: "What a relief."

Of himself, Cézanne said: "Isolation is all I'm good for. Then, at least, no one will get his hooks into me." In this phrase he puts his own character in a nutshell—the coarse, rustic, deliberately uncouth manner is a shield with which he protects himself from his fellows because he fears them. Fear and anxiety drive him deeper and deeper into himself until he cannot even bear them within touching distance. Despite assumption of boorishness and contempt for the conventions, Cézanne always secretly coveted official recognition. In this respect he differed markedly from many other revolutionary artists of his acquaintance, who sought fame by exhibiting independently, and genuinely scorned "Establishment" art and artists.

He offered his work repeatedly to the Salon—a large annual exhibition in Paris, corresponding to some extent to the Royal Academy in England; but until almost the end of his life he received nothing but derisive abuse from the critics. Typically, when rejected by the Salon of 1866, he despatched an irate letter of protest to the Director of Fine Arts. Only once did he ever get a painting accepted, and this by the "back-door". The Salon had a rule whereby any member of the jury (who selected the pictures for the exhibition) was allowed to enter a work by one of his pupils. In 1882, Guillemet, a juror and friend of Cézanne, got one of his paintings into the exhibition by this means.

Cézanne was not alone in this discontent with the Salon; in 1863 so many artists protested against the prejudice and favouritism of the jury that the Emperor ordered a public exhibition of all the rejected works—the Salon des Refusés. Cézanne is said to have shown at this gigantic hotch-potch, which proved a complete fiasco.

On 19 July, 1870, France declared war on Prussia. One might well imagine that Cézanne, the fire-eater, with his passionate temper and savage tongue, would have rushed hotfoot to defend the soil of France (outside of which he ventured only once, when he travelled to Switzerland and the Jura in 1890). In fact he fled post-haste in the opposite direction to L'Estaque, a small seaside place on the Mediterranean, near Marseilles. There he remained until the autumn of the following year, when, the victorious Prussians having departed, and the ensuing disturbances of the Commune having died down, he returned to Paris.

During his sojourns in Paris, Cézanne revealed another facet of his strange and complex nature with its irrational fear and suspicion of men. He was constantly changing his lodgings. On one occasion he encountered in the street a friend whom he had not seen for a long time. "Where are you living now?" asked the friend, naturally enough. "Oh—I live in a house—in a street—a long way off," stammered Cézanne, and turning in his heel, walked off as fast as his legs could carry him.

In 1872 Cézanne joined his old friend of the Académie Suisse days

Pissarro in Pontoise, a small country town, charmingly situated on the banks of the River Oise. He admired Pissarro, whom he described as "humble and gigantic", and was much influenced by him. Under this influence, Cézanne began to move away from the violently dramatic style of painting of his early days, and to paint landscape in the open fields. This was a turning-point in his career, and henceforward he began to produce the great series of landscape, still life and portrait paintings on which his reputation rests. However, his greatness was not yet recognized; his work continued to be greeted with howls of derision. He painted extremely slowly and one reads of an old peasant, who, having watched Cézanne and Pissarro at work for some time, remarked to Pissarro, "Well, sir, you have an assistant there who does absolutely nothing!"

Pissarro was a member of the then revolutionary group of painters known as "the Impressionists" and under his patronage Cézanne exhibited at the first Impressionist Exhibition (1874) with three canvasses, and the third (1877) with seventeen, but in both cases his work was utterly derided, one writer even suggesting that he suffered from delirium tremens.

Thereafter, Cézanne moved restlessly between Paris and the south, but tended increasingly to live the life of a recluse in the country. 1886 was a memorable year from him. His father died, leaving him the Jas de Bouffan, and a substantial fortune so that at last he was able to cease worrying about money. In this year also he quarrelled mortally with his friend Emile Zola, who, in his book *L'Oeuvre*, based one of his characters, an unsuccessful painter, only too obviously on Cézanne. Characteristically, Cézanne suffered great remorse at Zola's death sixteen years later.

Henceforward, the tide began to turn, though slowly, in Cézanne's favour as an artist, although, unhappily, his health began to fail—in 1891 he had his first attack of diabetes. In 1895 Ambrose Vollard, a pioneer art-dealer of Paris, gave him his first one-man show in his gallery. Although it was ignored or abused by the public, it was praised highly by artists and connoisseurs. Vollard had his portrait painted by Cézanne in 1899. As ever, the painter worked incredibly slowly, and poor Vollard sometimes fell asleep, whereupon Cézanne would huffily admonish him: "You should sit like an apple; an apple does not move." After a couple of hundred sittings or so, Cézanne remarked of the portrait: "I am not displeased with the shirt front."

Cézanne's paintings were exhibited in Brussels in 1887 and 1901, and more notably at the big Central Exhibition in Paris in 1900. On this latter occasion, the National-Galerie of Berlin purchased one of his pictures. His greatest triumph, however, was in 1904, when his paintings filled an entire room at the Salon D'Automne in Paris.

That Cézanne was aware of his own stature, at a time when, far from receiving acclamation he was constantly subjected to ridicule, is evidenced by his remark to his sister: "I am the greatest living painter." On the other hand, he seemed curiously blind to the genius of two of his greatest contemporaries, who with him, laid the foundations of modern art. On seeing some paintings by van Gogh, he simply said: "He is mad." Of Gauguin he spitefully remarked: "He is a maker of Chinese images."

Cézanne died on 22 October, 1906, at the age of sixty-seven. The circumstances of his death are as bizarre as any in his life. From 1900 he had lived almost entirely in Aix: it was his custom when painting landscape, to hire a cab to transport him and his painting gear to the site. On the last occasion the cabby asked for a slight increase in fare, whereat Cézanne, with typical peasant closeness, abruptly dismissed him and set out on foot, carrying his weighty painting apparatus.

On arrival at his goal he was drenched in a rainstorm and collapsed in a fainting fit, as a result of over-exertion. Eventually he was discovered and brought home in the back of a laundry-van. He died of congestion of the liver, caused by a chill. He is buried in Aix-en-Provence cemetery.

John D. Rockefeller
1839-1937

"WELL, look, Bill—it's like this. I just gotta have fifty dollars. I'll pay seven per cent on it—I just gotta have it, that's all, for the farm . . ."

"Yeah. I see your problem. Only, can't help you. Haven't got fifty."

"Nope. Didn't think you would have, Bill. Just thought I'd tell you my little difficulty, that's all, Bill . . ."

"Yeah."

The little boy came round the corner of the open door where he had been listening. "Hullo," he said.

"Why, hullo, Johnny," said the visitor. "Thought you'd be in bed by now."

"No, sir. Excuse me, sir . . ."

"Yes, son?"

"What does seven per cent mean?"

The older Rockefeller suddenly roared with laughter. "*That's* my boy!" he shouted. "*He's* got his head screwed on that, that kid . . ."

"But *what*," Johnnie repeated, "does *seven per cent* mean?"

"Well, son, it's like this," said the visitor. "I'd like to borrow fifty dollars and I would be willing to pay seven per cent—seven hundredths—of that fifty dollars, every single year, just as a little thank you for being able to have the borrow of it. That's three dollars fifty a year—just for doing nothing—to the fellow who lets me have it—"

"Three fifty a year. Every year?"

"Until I pay him back the money."

"When do you pay this—this interest?"

The visitor laughed at the inquisitive ten-year-old in the blue sailor suit. "Why, son, if you was to loan me that fifty now, why, I'd pay three fifty exactly one year from today. I'd pay Johnny Rockefeller three dollars and fifty cents on—let's see—the twenty-third of June, 1850 . . ."

"All right, sir. I'll lend you that fifty dollars."

"You'll what? Where d'*you* get fifty dollars?"

"Earned it, sir. Every penny."

"That's right," said his father. "Johnny's been putting coins in that blue bowl of his for three years or more, ever since I gave him fifty cents for cleaning away a lot of stones. Every odd job the boys do, me or the wife, we give 'em a quarter or fifty cents. And Johnny don't spend much—do you, Johnny boy?"

The solemn little boy shook his head. "You want that fifty dollars then, sir? 'Cos I got it upstairs."

"You bet I want it," said the visitor. "Thanks a lot, Johnny . . ."

Johnny Rockefeller had earned his first money three years before, at the age of seven; now, at ten, he invested it. As he said later, "From that time on, I decided to make money work for me."

John Davison Rockefeller had been born in the village of Richford, 125 miles outside New York, on 8 July, 1839. The family, the Rockenfellers of Hagendorf, was of German descent, they had settled in America a hundred years before. John's father, William Rockefeller, was a good-looking, plausible, thoroughly unreliable man who inspired little confidence among his neighbours, partly because his source of income was unknown in Richford. He claimed to be a "salesman" but refused to divulge what he sold or where, and it was a suspicion that the man was up to no good which made John Davison of Richford refuse the hand of his daughter Eliza when William asked to marry her. Overwhelmed by her suitor's good looks and charm, Eliza promptly ran away with him and then repented sufficiently of the snub to her father to call her first son after him.

Every three or four months William Rockefeller would kiss his young wife goodbye, hand her a small parcel of notes and tell her he'd be back before the family had spent it. He seldom was and the family would be on short commons when suddenly, without warning, he would gallop into Richford, smartly dressed in new clothes, laughing and joking with the villagers while they greeted him with wonder and suspicion. It was several years before a neighbour, on a visit to the neighbouring state of Ohio, discovered "Doc" William Rockefeller selling, by the hundred, his bottles of "Rockefeller's Patent Cancer Cure—a guaranteed cure unless the case is too far gone, and then it helps a lot".

Eliza was shocked and upset to learn her husband was a quack doctor, making a living from the misfortunes of others, but as he returned a few weeks after this unmasking, with new clothes for all the family, he was forgiven. No mention was ever made in the family circle of Father's unorthodox way of earning a living. The neighbours however, disapproved and showed it: so shortly afterwards the Rockefeller family found themselves on the move. They made several moves while John, older sister Lucy, and younger brother Bill, were still children. By 1853, when John was fourteen, they had moved into Ohio, to the village of Strongville. John, because he showed some academic promise, was sent on to Cleveland to lodge and attend the Central High School.

At this time a man called Kier began to market his "American Oil", a substance which he scraped off the surface of streams in Pennsylvania, selling it in half-pint bottles as an embrocation "for tired limbs". The oil was well known already; it could be found in small quantities in many parts of eastern America, usually as an unpleasant-smelling film on the surface of certain streams, and it had been called variously fossil oil, rock oil, Seneca oil—from the tribe of Indians in whose territory it was first noticed—and even "petroleum". At the time that Kier's sales of oil were mounting—people had discovered that, apart from its dubious value as an embrocation, it made a good substitute for the candles with which most houses were lit—John D. Rockefeller took his first job, at the age of sixteen, as a clerk on four dollars a week.

Two years later the senior Rockefellers, having chosen to move again, made what was to be their last move to the bustling city of Cleveland and joined their son. William Rockefeller was just in time to lend John the thousand dollars he had promised him on reaching the age of twenty-one. The boy, having considered the advantages of not only lending but of borrowing, if good reason arose, cheerfully agreed to pay interest for the three years until he attained the age of twenty-one.

With it and his own savings he set up in partnership with a young Englishman, Maurice Clark, styling themselves Clark & Rockefeller, Produce and Commission, 32 River Street, Cleveland. They were tired of working for other people; they would experiment, dabble in every aspect of merchandizing, selling farm implements, fertilizers, household goods, and marketing the farm produce. Within a year they had made a sizable profit.

By now the people who sold oil in small bottles had discovered it could be refined and made into a very superior fuel. The only trouble lay in getting sufficient of the stuff. They reasoned that as it was on the surface of the streams it had probably seeped through the earth and could be dug for: to this end they mounted an expedition to Titusville, Pennsylvania, where most of the oil had been collected and put it in charge of a retired railwayman, Edwin Drake, on whom, to lend a certain dignity, they conferred the title of "Colonel". Drake made exhaustive inquiries around the neighbourhood, examined the sources of several streams, took samples of the oil he saw and eventually—more or less by instinct, as he knew nothing of geology and had been chosen entirely for his commanding personality—began to drill a hole. The equipment was primitive and it took several days to reach a depth of sixty-nine and a half feet, at which, suddenly, black oil gushed forth.

"Colonel" Drake was satisfied, but not elated. He had found the source of oil, fulfilled the hopes of his backers. He accepted his fee and retired gracefully, confident that he, Drake, had hit upon the only source of oil in the United States, that it would enrich his backers for a few years and then peter out. Years later, when the men who had sent him on the expedition were rich—some of them millionaires—he was discovered in Brooklyn, old, sick, destitute and disillusioned. One of the original team of backers conferred a small annuity on him.

At first none of this impressed the young firm of Clark and Rockefeller. John had been able to study the situation at first hand when he was selected—at the age of twenty—to go as representative of the businessmen of Cleveland to the "oil regions" and consider whether the city wished to become involved. His decision was, "Not now—wait and see."

In 1862 Samuel Andrews developed a better, cheaper method of refining this crude petroleum and Clark and Rockefeller joined forces with him in a new firm, Clark and Andrews. Already Rockefeller was learning the virtues of anonymity. Two years later, at the age of twenty-five, he married. He and his wife lived quietly, devoutly, and every Wednesday evening John, with his wife's blessing, taught a Bible class at the Erie Street Baptist Church in Cleveland. The next year he persuaded Maurice Clark to sell his share in Clark and Andrews and to buy up his own share of Clark and Rockefeller, so that oil would be his sole interest and enterprise. He emerged briefly into the open as Rockefeller and Andrews, oil refiners of Cleveland, but shortly afterwards the vastly expanded firm was simply Standard Oil of Ohio.

Rockefeller considered the possibility of a monopoly. He approached the railway company which was charging him forty cents a barrel for bringing the crude petroleum from the oil wells to his Cleveland refineries and two dollars a barrel to move the refined product to New York, suggesting that if they reduced these rates to thirty-five cents and a dollar thirty—and to him alone—he would guarantee sixty car-loads a day. The railway company agreed, the cost of production of Standard Oil dropped, and within a year four of his thirty competitors were out of business. Many others were seriously feeling the competition and these he was able to buy at low rates. One operator whose refinery had just been valued at twelve thousand dollars was so alarmed by the Rockefeller threat to drive all but Standard out of the market that he accepted an offer of three thousand. The story spread: "It's no use competing with Standard Oil—sell out while you can," and many firms did. Rockefeller was surprised and distressed, as a devout churchman, to read in the newspaper that many of his compatriots considered him a rogue, a "shrewd operator". An article in the *Cleveland Plain Dealer* in 1872 was the first adverse comment that had appeared in print, but other papers took up the witch hunt and, with only brief pauses, kept it up for forty-two years, until 1914, when his huge donations to war charities and the "Victory Loan" made Rockefeller respectable.

Nothing if not single-minded, Rockefeller refused to allow the Press campaign to divert him from his intention of monopolizing not only the oil refining of Cleveland but the refining, transporting and marketing of all oil in the United States. In this he was largely successful, though desperate efforts were made to thwart him and there was at one time an embargo by many producers on selling oil to him, until they realized that without Standard Oil there was practically no one to whom they could sell the stuff. Even if they were prepared to mark time, stop drilling, the farmers and small-holders on whose land the oil rigs had been erected were paid on a royalty basis and these demanded, brandishing axes, shovels and ploughshares, that the drilling be kept up.

By 1890 Rockefeller had bought out Samuel Andrews for the sum of a million dollars and Standard Oil had swollen into an immense "Trust", a monopoly which could fix its own prices and terms of business because it had no competitors. Shortly afterwards, the Anti-Trust Law was passed, making such a monopoly illegal, and Standard Oil split up into a number of ostensibly separate firms —Standard Oil of Ohio, Standard Oil of New York, and so on. The change made very little difference to the overall, vast, profits.

Rockefeller, a multi-millionaire, began to organize a system of philanthropy. The invention of the internal combustion engine had enormously added to Standard's profits, and the time seemed ripe for him to start unloading some of them. As the Press campaign was still at its height, he found that though charities eagerly accepted his generosity, they then apologized for doing so: his money was "tainted". He remained the hated philanthropist until the outbreak of war. By this time he had been retired for nearly twenty years and between his retirement in 1896 and his death in 1937 he gave away three times as much as he had taken into retirement: the money, wisely invested, "just grew". He was, in fact, quite unable to get rid of it. By 1928 the official estimate of John D. Rockefeller's donations to various causes stood at 508,921,123-dollars-and-one-cent and he was still a multi-millionaire. He had set up the Rockefeller Foundation (to administer his various charities) the General Education Board (to provide scholarships to schools and universities); the Rockefeller Institute of Medical Research, and had endowed each of them with many millions. As a sideline he made a series of gifts to the University of Chicago totalling twenty-three million dollars.

By the time of his death in Florida on 23 May, 1937, he had completely rehabilitated himself in the eyes of the American public. From having been an "octopus", an "anaconda", he became a popular national figure, whose every birthday was a field day for the Press. Sargent painted a portrait of him and reported that he felt himself "in the company of a sort of medieval saint, a Francis of Assisi". On the rare occasions that he appeared in public people would applaud and he would delight them by giving dimes to the children—a ten-cent piece for each one. He was mourned throughout the country, not only as America's first "billionaire" but as a great and generous man.

Auguste Rodin
1840-1917

THE winter of 1917 was particularly bitter. Europe was locked in a bloody and consuming war. Food and fuel were short throughout France. In the Villa des Brillants, on the hill of Meudon, not far from Paris, a curious wedding ceremony took place between the greatest sculptor since Michelangelo and an elderly woman named Rose Beuret, who had been his faithful companion for more than fifty years. Auguste Rodin was seventy-seven years of age, and his bride only a little younger. The two old people sat shivering with cold as the formalities of their marriage were hurried through. The date was 29 January. Scarcely a month later Madame Rodin died, and on 16 November, 1917, Rodin himself followed his beloved wife. There seems little doubt that their deaths were hastened by the intolerable conditions of that icy winter.

Everyone can call to mind some of Rodin's masterpieces. They are household words. "The Thinker", "The Burghers of Calais", "The Kiss" (a marble edition of which is in the Tate Gallery, London), are known and revered throughout the world. Yet, in his lifetime, Rodin's work was often the subject of bitter controversy, for he was, like all the greatest of creative geniuses, an innovator; a breaker of conventions; a maker of new images, using new conceptions of the meaning and purpose of sculpture to establish his place as one of the greatest sculptors of all time, not even excepting Michelangelo. This meant of course that he inevitably fell foul of the Academies and the Academicians. The moribund officials of the academic world became his mortal enemies. They were jealous of his genius, and did all they could to injure his reputation.

Auguste Rodin was above all a humanist; passionately concerned with human condition, and above all, with the relationship between the sexes. Many of his greatest works deal with the love of man for woman, a subject which so often is misunderstood when it is dealt with by the artist, whether he be novelist, poet, painter or sculptor. One such work was "*Le Baiser*" (The Kiss), which in 1914 was loaned to the town of Lewes, in Sussex, by its owner, Mr Edward Warren, a local inhabitant. Some little while before he had commissioned a copy direct from Rodin, and felt that the citizens of Lewes should have the opportunity of seeing and enjoying this superb piece of sculpture. It was put on show in the local Town Hall, where it at once gave rise to such a storm of abuse from the local Grundies that the Council was obliged to shroud the offending statue with a tarpaulin, until such time as it could be returned to its owner. Today this very piece graces the sculpture halls of the Tate Gallery. But in 1914 it was called an "obscene and corrupting influence on the young" by one local hypocrite. An official of the Town Council, who had not supported the Corporation's acceptance of Mr Warren's generous offer, attacked it on the grounds that "we have soldiers billeted in the town, and young people flock to look at it. It is dreadful. It must go!" A leading Lewes matron and champion of Grundyism described this superb work as "a monstrous and disgraceful statue!" Today, those bigoted nobodies are forgotten, but Rodin's "Kiss", based on the story of Paolo and Francesca the immortal lovers of Dante's *Divine Comedy*, remains as one of the world's most beautiful and moving portrayals of man's love for woman.

Rodin came under fire also for his portraiture. It was natural enough that his genius in this field should arouse the enmity of lesser artists, for there is money in portraiture—big money, and the artists of the academies and salons look out for any threat to their dominance in securing commissions. The two portraits which aroused the greatest hostility among Rodin's contemporaries were his studies of the novelists Victor Hugo and Honoré de Balzac. In 1886 he completed the Victor Hugo monument, which had been commissioned by the State in 1883. The result was a devastating blow at all the conventions regarding official portraiture. Hugo was depicted stark naked! The sculptor was at once charged with obscenity. When in later years he was asked to explain this scandalous conception, Rodin replied with a shattering argument:

"Why should I clothe M. Hugo in the ridiculous masculine fashions of his time? There is nothing more banal than those statues of recent notabilities masquerading as tailor's dummies of their ugly period. On the other hand man's naked form belongs to no particular moment in history; it is eternal and can be looked upon with joy by the people of all ages."

When this argument was countered with the observation that the Roman Emperors and heroes were represented in the dress of their time, Rodin replied:

"True; but Roman dress did not mar the beauty of the human body. That is why I did not strip Balzac, because as you know, his habit of working in a sort of dressing-gown gave me the opportunity of putting him into a loose, flowing robe that supplied me with good lines that did not date the statue as belonging simply to our own ugly period . . ."

The Balzac statue (1898), an immensely free, vigorous conception, was also received with great disfavour. The *Société des Gens de Lettres* which had commissioned the work refused to accept the artist's sketch model, and the commission was forthwith passed to an inferior sculptor. So Rodin's statue of Balzac found its way back to the sculptor's studio where it remained until his death. Even today it has lost nothing of its originality and power to astound.

Auguste Rodin was born on 14 November, 1840, at No. 3 rue de l'Arbalète, in the Mouffetard quarter of Paris. His father, Jean Baptiste Rodin, was a clerk in the offices of the Prefecture of the Seine. His parents being poor, Auguste was obliged to leave school at the age of fourteen. But by this time his taste for art, and his love for drawing were so well developed that he was permitted, reluctantly, to join a free drawing school. His father did not wish the lad to become an artist, holding the view that "artists are idlers and good for nothings". Young Rodin was determined to become an artist, and he worked at his drawing, supplementing his studies with visits to the Louvre and the Imperial Library where he examined and copied the work of the old masters. To earn his bread—for it was necessary to eat—Auguste was obliged to combine his studies with work at the premises of an ornament maker, where he helped to prepare models for purposes of interior decoration. Although at first he despised this work and considered it a gross prostitution of his gifts, there is no doubt that it led directly to his growing interest in modelling and sculpture. During his years at the drawing school Rodin made many friends, among them the sculptor Dalou and the painter Legros, both of whom were themselves to achieve a modest distinction in later years.

Three years after entering the drawing school, Rodin sought admission to the *École des Beaux Arts*, the French national school of art. He was refused entry. He tried again, and yet again, and each time he was turned down. This was his first, bitter encounter with the official field of art. It was not a pleasant experience. The bitterness with which in later years he spoke of the pontiffs of the art world can be traced to these early disappointments.

In 1863 Rodin lost his dearly loved sister Clotilde, his senior by two years. He loved her deeply and felt her loss severely. So profoundly did it affect him that he all but went out of his mind with grief. His reason was saved only by the care of a priest of the Catholic Church, and for a while afterwards Rodin seriously considered the possibility of taking Holy Orders. In 1865, when he was twenty-five years of age, he met the young woman who was destined to become his life partner. Rose Beuret hailed from the district of Champagne and found work in Paris as a needlewoman. It was during her employment in this capacity that she met Rodin. At the time of this meeting Auguste was working on some decorations for the *Théâtre des Gobelins*, and it was there that the two young people met and instantly fell passionately in love. Soon afterwards they took up residence together. Although throughout the years ahead Rose would be known to all as "Madame Rodin" it was not until 1917 that officially they became man and wife.

It was about the time that Rodin met Rose Beuret that he gave up his employment with the ornament maker to become the assistant of the then popular and celebrated Carrier-Belleuse, sculptor. For six years he assisted his new master, all the time gaining invaluable experience as a sculptor. He could not develop his own style freely because the greater part of his work consisted of completing the rough sketches that Carrier-Belleuse passed over to him. His own creative personality was not involved. He was released from this thankless work by the outbreak of the Franco-Prussian War which led to a spell of service in the National Guard. The rôle of soldier was utterly hateful to Rodin, and he fled to Brussels before the beginning of the Commune, leaving behind, temporarily, Rose and their baby son, while he sought a more auspicious future in the Belgian capital. Luckily, he was soon engaged on architectural projects for two of the most important public buildings in Brussels; the Bourse, and the Palais des Académies. So Rose and young Auguste joined Rodin in Brussels, where they lived a simple and happy life in a little cottage on the outskirts of the city. Rodin was now at work on one of his most famous works, "The Age of Bronze", and beginning to make a sizable income as a sculptor.

In 1875 he visited Italy and made a thorough study of the art of the Renaissance, and in particular the work of Michelangelo. "The Age of Bronze" was exhibited at the Brussels *Cercle Artistique* in 1877, and so astounding was the extreme realism of this magnificent work, that certain members of the exhibition committee insisted that it could not have been created by the sculptors' unaided hand. Both in Brussels, and later in France, the Academicians were adamant in their opinion of this masterpiece; Rodin had taken casts direct from life they argued, and from there pieced together his figure. Rodin at once replied to these charges with an indignant letter, flatly refuting such malicious charges. But it was only after intervention by Edmond Turquet, Under Secretary of State for Fine Arts, and as a result of support from many distinguished artists and friends that at last Rodin was cleared of the slander upon his name. Turquet, delighted at the outcome of the issue, promptly awarded Rodin a medal, and purchased "The Age of Bronze" for the State. It's an ill wind, as the saying goes, and although "The Age of Bronze" controversy left Rodin with an even deeper hatred than ever of the official world of art, it did win him many new and influential friends.

In 1880 he began "The Gates of Hell", the great work that was to occupy him on and off for the rest of his life. An official commission for the *Palais des Arts Décoratifs*, it was also undertaken partly as a challenge to his adversaries in the Salon.

"Having been accused of casting from the life, I shall execute this order by making a number of bas-reliefs on a small scale so that no one can say I have cheated! And I will take my subject matter from Dante."

Rodin paid his first visit to England in 1881. He met the writers Henley and Stevenson, both of whom were to become his friends. Later Henley was to provide the subject for one of his most famous portrait busts. As a portrait sculptor Rodin was without equal in any age. In 1884 he received a commission from the town of Calais for "The Burghers of Calais", one of his greatest and best-known masterpieces. When the group was exhibited at the International Exhibition in Paris in 1889, Rodin was once again the target of the philistines and reactionaries. The extreme unconventionality of the way in which he grouped the figures, and his harrowing depiction of their abject misery, set all Paris talking, and arguing. However, in the end, all the adverse criticisms were drowned in the unstinting praise that was voiced throughout the city. The work obviously was an original achievement, yet the authorities at Calais refused to place the monument in the ancient market-place, the site it was originally intended to occupy, and placed it instead on a low pedestal in the Place de la Poste. There were compensations. In 1888 Rodin had been made a Chevalier of the Legion of Honour; his work was beginning to be known far beyond the boundaries of France. At forty-eight, Auguste Rodin was a world-famous sculptor.

All his life Rodin continued to practise his first love—the art of drawing, and is especially famous for his wonderfully spirited, fluent drawings of the female nude. Legend has it that in order to capture the maximum feeling of life, and action, Rodin frequently worked from two or three models simultaneously. They moved slowly around the studio while Rodin made rapid sketches.

As the years passed, the hostility and lack of understanding became less widespread and of no account. At the Great Exhibition of 1900 in Paris, the Rodin Pavilion showed the genius of the sculptor to the world. Adverse criticism was muted; so evidently was he the most original sculptor of his day. In 1902 Rodin visited London again, this time to celebrate the presentation of his "St John the Baptist" to the South Kensington Museum (now the Victoria and Albert Museum). He was given a wildly enthusiastic welcome; art students from the South Kensington and Slade Schools unharnessed the horses from his carriage, and themselves drew it through the streets of Kensington. Soon after this event, and following the death of Whistler, President of the International Society of Painters, Sculptors and Engravers, a delegation of British artists went to Paris to invite Rodin to accept the nomination for the vacant Presidency. He at once accepted, and in 1904, again journeyed to London for the International Society's opening ceremony and banquet at the Café Royal. 1904 also saw the first public showing of the "Thinker", the massive, powerful, and brooding figure in which the sculptor endeavoured to capture the very essence and quality of human thought.

Rodin was living at the Villa des Brillants where he was engaged mainly on portrait busts of wealthy and well-known people who came from every corner of the earth to sit for him. The famous clamoured, even begged, to be immortalized by him. Although in his middle sixties, he was still superbly robust and healthy. Though more limited as regards output, his power as a sculptor had in no way declined. He employed a large staff to do routine carving and casting for him. In 1911 for instance, when he was seventy-one, he produced his wonderful portrait of M. Clemenceau. In 1908 King Edward VII visited him at Meudon, and in the following year a special gallery containing only works by Rodin was opened in his honour at the Metropolitan Museum, in New York. So the closing years of his life were crowned with fame and glory. During the last years of his life Rodin acquired a beautiful old mansion in Paris, known as the Hôtel Biron, which was to become his studio. War, with all its agonies and privations, was near. Soon France, and Europe, were engulfed in the holocaust. In 1916 Rodin made his will, in which he left all his original work to the State, and the formal handing over ceremony took place on 13 September, 1916, in the presence of representatives of the French Government. It was his wish that all these works, together with his personal possessions should be collected in the Hôtel Biron, which was to become, after his death, the Rodin Museum. In due course this came to pass, with the State paying Rodin's son a small annuity by way of compensation for his lost inheritance. So we come to the closing moments of this great sculptor's life which were described in the opening paragraph.

Friedrich Nietzsche
1844-1900

THROUGHOUT life human beings have a sense of belonging, of doing a useful job, of having a place in the community. As for the values, cultural, religious and political, which that community observes and expects us to observe we never doubt that they are sound. We are, in the modern phrase, "with it"—and glad to be with it. Not to be with it would feel both dangerous and sinful.

Sometimes, though, we have a sensation of impotence, of being devitalized—yet we hardly know why. At any rate, we are too timid and conditioned to the herd mentality to think of challenging the accepted standards and striking out for some form of personal fulfilment which hovers at the back of our minds. No. Safety first! Let's not look too closely at reality or we might become permanently dissatisfied and that would be painful and pointless.

Yet the reality of our comparative impotence as individuals is still there and one of the few men who has had the courage to face the fact and its reasons was the German, Friedrich Nietzsche (1844–1900). He was convinced that all existing religious and political creeds were harmful to the free development of human beings and so he did his best to destroy them. There was no tradition, no convention, no established doctrine in any sphere of life that he held to be sacred or even worthy of respect and he attacked them all in powerful prose with the vigour of an Old Testament prophet.

Nietzsche firmly believed he was a prophet, a leader unique in history destined to blaze the trail to a new and glorious future for mankind. One can really call him a "digger for reality" and his first concern was to get at the reality of human beings. Was Man basically a social creature, a worshipping creature, a being who by his nature sought the good and the beautiful? No, he was none of these things. The basic instinct in all men, said Nietzsche, was the *will to power*. In the case of the lower men, the herd, this meant the will to dominate, to dictate the conditions of life for the sake of their own security, but with the higher men, the men of outstanding gifts, the will to power was the urge to realize all potential abilities, to be free, bound to nothing and no one in the most literal sense.

These "Supermen" (it was Nietzsche who invented the word) were in his opinion the true masters of life, but before considering their qualities he examined existing society. Why was it that great leaders like Napoleon were destroyed? Because society was designed for slaves and could not tolerate them. Society arose to protect the herd, not to foster genius; its religious and political institutions, its culture were established by the will to power of "the impotent, the humble, the feeble, the subjected, the peace-loving". Christianity was popular with the masses because it gave them souls, supplied them with hopes of a future life and held up the poor and needy as worthy objects, better men indeed than their masters. Moreover, by making man conscious of sin Christianity set him against himself, weakened his will to action and subjected him to a priesthood whose own will to power was thus satisfied at his expense.

Christianity and all religion was a shackle which Nietzsche utterly rejected. He condemned the modern state as the "cold monster" which gave power where it did not belong, to the herd. He despised modern culture because it drew a veil over uncomfortable truths. Democracy and socialism he saw as the great levellers which would indefinitely postpone the rise of the Supermen. Morality was another shackle invented by the underdogs to fetter the natural leaders. There was, according to Nietzsche, no absolute moral law. Morals were relative. What was good for one type of man was not necessarily good for another. The whole basis of modern life was not only false, but harmful to the development of human beings.

When we remember how much easier it is to accept the rules or life as we find them we can see that Nietzsche possessed great courage. He was like a man who finds himself in a house and says: "I don't like this building"—then proceeds to pull the roof over his head. Nietzsche considered this process of clearance merely as a prelude to building his own house, in other words to the positive side of his philosophy. His destructive criticism was expressed in a series of books published between 1876 and 1883: *Thoughts out of Season, Human All-too Human, The Dawn of Day* and *The Joyful Wisdom*. They brought him abuse, but little recognition.

Nietzsche spoke a vehement "no" to life as it was, but an equally emphatic "yes" to life as it might be. In later books—*Thus Spake Zarathustra, Beyond Good and Evil, The Genealogy of Morals, The Antichrist, Ecce Homo* and *The Twilight of the Idols*—he supplied his vision of the future in which ordinary people would continue to live by the traditional standards, but the whole of existence would be modelled to give absolute freedom to the Supermen. He wrote:

"Not mankind, but Superman is the goal . . . My desire is to bring forth creatures which stand sublimely above the whole species."

What were these Supermen, apart from Nietzsche himself? What were they like? They were to be tough in body and mind, egoistic in the pursuit of their highest interests, pitiless because pity is a weakening emotion. He visualized them as the lords of life, but not as mere exuberant savages. They were to be the true "yes-sayers", proud, free, joyful and creative, hard on themselves and—though this may sound a paradox—not self-indulgent. They were to live "beyond good and evil", or rather they would set up new standards of good and evil directly related to themselves. Everything that increased their power, reduced their limitations and gave them more scope for action was good. Everything that made them dependent on forces outside themselves, whether established ideas of God, morality or law, was bad. There was no God, said Nietzsche, but he would make new gods out of men.

Now to realize the positive value of this vision we must remember all the countless pressures in life which tend to weaken our personalities and canalize them in directions not of our choosing. All that Nietzsche was preaching was the necessity of putting man's centre of gravity back inside himself, so making him truly free, creative and happy. He also set an example of ruthless intellectual courage which dared to dissect and examine the whole basis of modern life. Few people are able or willing to do this because the process is highly disturbing to themselves and even fewer can bring to the task Nietzsche's brilliant analytical mind. But no progress is possible in human affairs unless men can be found who will challenge accepted beliefs and either reject them or positively, through conviction, make them truly their own.

All the same, Nietzsche's thought brought tragedy for himself and, as part of a wider process, near-disaster for mankind. His books became popular with young people in Germany at the beginning of this century, but, as always when a great thinker is seized on by the mob, his ideas immediately assumed a cruder form. People took from him what they wanted—and ignored the rest. Of course, the Superman was immediately attractive, especially by contrast with the rigid, semi-medieval life in Imperial Germany. As for morals, many people were only too glad to be rid of them. The result among teenagers was an undercurrent of petty rebelliousness and the feeling that what they chose to do, unfettered by authority, was automatically good.

After the First World War, when Germany was humiliated, starving and governed by weak parliamentary majorities, disgust with life as it was seemed only too justified. The feeling arose that something completely new in the way of values and political organization was needed and years before Hitler appeared on the scene the soil so drastically ploughed up by Nietzsche was bearing dangerous fruit: a cult of irrationalism which set instinct above reason, a worship of power, contempt for democracy and a belief that vitality and action were their own rewards, no matter how they were applied. Nietzsche's picture of a world serving the interests of the Superman contained the seeds of totalitarianism and nourished the thirst for a Leader already present among the dejected and despairing Germans. Nietzsche's vision was a poet's dream and when applied to real life it assumed an ugly form which he had never intended. The Superman who said "yes" to life became Hitler with his ungovernable appetite for destruction. The cult of freedom for the natural leaders resulted in the enslavement of the German people. Nietzsche's attack on existing values loosened the whole structure of civilization and in the cracks grew the odious weed "Might is Right". Moreover, the cult of the Superman standing in splendid isolation as the Lord of Life is a cold vision, dangerously unreal. Isolation is not splendid. We do and must have links with our fellow-men and beyond them with spiritual reality, which indeed corresponds to our deepest need. In trying to break these links Nietzsche himself went mad.

Nietzsche was born in 1844, the eldest child of a country clergyman in Saxony. Both his father and mother came from a long line of Protestant pastors and the atmosphere of the home was quiet, cultivated and rigidly orthodox. The young Friedrich was a very bright, but rather prim child who obeyed authority eagerly and to the letter. There is a story of him walking sedately home from school one day in pouring rain. Told by his mother to hurry up, he replied that regulations forbade the boys to jump or run when returning from school.

At this time his mother was already a widow and the family, increased by a baby girl, had transferred to a neighbouring town where the boy lived as the only male in a household of women (mother, grandmother and aunts), attending the local school until he was fourteen. Though timid in outward behaviour, he possessed an original and imaginative mind. He wrote poetry, composed music and at the age of twelve he had, as he said later, "a vision of God in His glory". Meanwhile, he had solved the problem of evil for himself by redefining the Trinity as God the Father, God the Son and God the Devil. How his mother would have been scandalized!

This was, in fact, the first step in a revolt against the beliefs he had learnt at home. For the next six years he attended a boarding school run on the strictest lines where the boys were taught self-sacrifice to the community and their minds were sharpened by intensive studies in Greek, Latin and philology. The plunge from homely cotton wool to monastic iron must have been extremely upsetting for the young man, while the enforced development of his mental powers made him more conscious of his individuality and more not less anxious for independence. So the second stage in his revolt was prepared: but it was slow to develop.

In 1864 he went to Bonn University, studied philology, and went on, convinced now that the pursuit not of happiness but of truth—"however evil and terrible it may be"—would be his life's task, to Leipzig where he completed his studies and then obtained, at the early age of twenty-four, an appointment as Professor of Philology at Basel University in Switzerland.

At Basel, Nietzsche's revolt against the accepted values of his time burst into the open and he wrote the first three of his books. At the same time he became conscious of increasing spiritual isolation. Few people understood his ideas and those that did were not enthusiastic. Though passionately anxious for friendship, he made few lasting friends and, indeed, could find no intellectual equals. Adoration for Wagner turned to disgust with his music and dislike of the man. Service as a medical orderly in the Franco-Prussian War left him ill and horrified by his brief contact with crude reality. After ten years at Basel a severe illness affecting his eyes and brain made it necessary for him to resign his professorship.

In the years that followed, when he expounded his positive philosophy, the gulf between Nietzsche as he was and Nietzsche as he wanted to be became wider and wider. The violence of his ideas contrasted pathetically with the meek suitor for a lady's hand who got a friend to propose for him—and was turned down. Far from freeing himself from accepted standards, he could not, in real life, escape the influence of his mother and sister. Far from killing pity in his heart, as he preached in his books, he was a man of the most exquisite tact, terrified of being a stumbling block to sincere Christians. Yet he persevered, ruthless for the truth as he saw it, a man whose heart was perpetually at war with his brain.

With his extreme sensitivity and intelligence this perpetual conflict was bound to be intense and in the long run unendurable. The collapse came on 3 January, 1889. In the previous month there had been signs that his wits were turning. He had written letters full of chaotic violence, stating in one of them that he intended to shoot the young Kaiser and signing others "The Crucified". Then on that day in the street he saw a cab-horse being maltreated by its driver. He flung his arms round the animal's neck—one sufferer embracing another—then burst into tears and fell unconscious to the ground.

It is impossible to interpret this incident accurately, but it may have represented a final breakthrough of part of himself which Nietzsche, the tough "Superman", had always tried to repress. At any rate, the collapse was absolute. He never recovered full sanity. He wrote no more books. For nineteen months he lived the life of an invalid, showing a touching patience and consideration for others, under the care of his mother and sister. He died of pneumonia in August, 1900, and joined his Christian forefathers in the church-yard of the village where he had been born. Perhaps, after all, he felt happiest with them.

Thomas Alva Edison
1847-1931

SLOWLY, noisily, the train puffed into the snowbound station. Most of those on board were friends and there was an air of expectancy from one rattling, sooty end to the other. Tom Edison's parties were always fun, always memorable (he usually produced some new and startling invention to entertain his guests) but an additional draw—and it had needed one to get all these people twenty-five miles out of New York on New Year's Eve—was that the party was actually being held in Edison's new laboratory, in the beauty spot of Menlo Park. Happy, laughing, expectant, the guests jumped down from the train and, by the smoky light of kerosene lamps, climbed into the horse-drawn buggies which awaited them.

Suddenly, the night and its moon, its few stars, disappeared, and the snow on the ground lit up like a million diamonds. The guests stared at each other, at the party clothes they hadn't really noticed before, and gasped.

They made their way up the short road from station to laboratory and now they could see the whole way lit by little incandescent pears that hung, hundred upon hundred of them, in a line from a wire just over their heads.

Outside the laboratory, Edison was laughing. "Like it?"

"Yes—yes, of course! But what—what *is* it?"

"Electric light. Glad you like it."

The startled guests went on into the brightly lit laboratory and the party began. In a few hours time it would be 1880, there was dancing and music and wine and light to be enjoyed.

Edison had just produced the world's first incandescent light. Half a century earlier Humphry Davy in England had made light electrically by passing a current through two sticks of charcoal. It had burnt dazzlingly, glaringly, painfully to the eyes, then burnt itself out in a few minutes. No one had been surprised: it was against the laws of nature for there to be "electric light"; it was a contradiction in terms, it was blasphemy, it was nonsense.

It needed only this to start Tom Edison in his search for a way of proving these opinions wrong. He was convinced it could be done,

The service shown *above* was held in Salisbury, Rhodesia, to mark the 61st anniversary of the death of Cecil Rhodes, a man of indomitable courage who dreamed a dream and in a life of adventure tried to convert that dream into reality. His statue (of which the front view is shown on the *right*) is by Mr John Tweed. His grave (*below*) is in the Matoppo Hills, near Bulawayo, overlooking a vista that he himself called "World's View".

Right: In 1913 the Home Secretary said in the House of Commons: "We have to deal with a phenomenon which I believe is absolutely without precedent in our history." He referred to the Suffragettes, women who were demanding the right to vote. Their leader was Mrs Emmeline Pankhurst, seen (*right*) being arrested on 30 May, 1914. The picture *below*, also taken in 1914, shows a Suffragette demonstration outside Buckingham Palace. The First World War ended agitation by the Suffragettes, and women in a wide variety of war jobs proceeded to demonstrate equality instead of demanding it. In February, 1918, a Bill to give women the vote received the Royal Assent.

that he would do it. And yet he was modest: he knew only too well that what the public was now beginning to call his "genius", was "ninety-eight per cent perspiration, two per cent inspiration". He didn't mind being "The Wizard of Menlo Park", that amused him—but "genius", no.

Although he undoubtedly was a genius, Edison worked hard. He inherited his determination: his great-grandfather had been condemned to death as a British sympathizer in the War of Independence but had escaped to Nova Scotia; the next generation had migrated from Nova Scotia to Canada. Edison's father, Samuel, had been in a plot to overthrow the Canadian government and replace it by one more like that of the United States. His plot was discovered but he managed to escape—back to the United States. Through the help of a barge captain, Alva Bradley, Samuel was able to smuggle out his wife and six children, to Milan, Ohio, and it was here, on 11 February, 1847, that his seventh was born and named, in honour of the captain, Thomas Alva Edison.

When Thomas was seven, the family moved to Port Huron, Michigan, and it was there that Tom Edison went to his first and only school—for three months. After that—well, he was "addled", the teacher said, and, anyway, he was bottom of the class. His mother was forced to undertake his education and this, apart from the huge amounts he taught himself, ended at the age of twelve. He was going to be an inventor, inventors needed money for their experiments, and the only way he could get it was by getting a job. A new railway line had just opened from Port Huron to Detroit and here was his opportunity. His parents agreed to let him go: after all, his experiments about the house were a bit of a nuisance; he'd sat on eggs to hatch them, given a playmate Seidlitz powders to blow him up like a balloon so he could fly, had even fed worms—suitably disguised—to the servant girl to make her fly, too.

The railway agreed to let him sell papers and sweets on board, without pay, and keep what profit he made. It seemed an ideal arrangement for a young inventor. The company allowed him to convert a part of the baggage car into a laboratory, and, as the train sat each day in Detroit for six and a half hours, what time he didn't spend in his lab he devoted to studying chemistry and physics in the Detroit library. Then, each afternoon at four-thirty, he began the return trip, selling things, experimenting, selling more things, until he arrived home at Port Huron at ten.

Then he started, in the same baggage car, his own paper, printing it on a second-hand press. It was one sheet, the size of a handkerchief, and it always contained red-hot news which his telegraph operator friends passed to him before the stuff got into the country papers. His profits rose and he might well have concentrated on journalism had not an experiment with phosphorus set the baggage car on fire. Edison, his press and his lab., went out at the next stop.

Right after this disaster, he was able to save the small son of the Mount Clemens stationmaster from an oncoming train, and the man promised to make him "the best telegraph man in the country" and get him a job.

He kept his word and Edison did in fact become one of the best telegraphists in the country. Unfortunately, his first successful experiment got him the sack from his first job. He signed on in Stratford, Ontario, as operator, and on learning that he was expected to send the letter "A" each hour of the night to prove he was awake, he found it only too easy to make an attachment to the clock which would send the signal for him and let him sleep. But when the chief operator in Toronto decided to reply and got no response, he rode down to Stratford, saw the device and its sleeping inventor, and sacked Edison.

For months after this he was a vagabond. Always untidy, he now became a scarecrow and succeeded in getting a job with Western Union Telegraph in Boston only by asserting that, despite his appearance, he was a better operator than their best. They arranged, tongue in cheek, for their best man, in New York, to send him a thousand words at several times the normal speed. The Boston operators crowded round for a laugh, but it was soon obvious that the New York man's speed was inferior to Edison's. Halfway through the message, seeing the looks on the operators' faces, realizing what they'd hoped for, Edison opened his key and tapped out a peremptory "Hurry" to his opponent. He was hired.

It was while he was with Western Union that Edison patented his first invention—a vote-recorder. It was a marvel of ingenuity, but nothing could have appealed less to the politicians of the day, so he set himself to producing other inventions more likely to meet with approval. He invented a duplex telegraph system in which two messages could be sent, in opposite directions, over the same wire, and while he perfected it he was simultaneously working on quadruplex telegraphy and a ticker-tape machine.

Bored with Boston, he moved to New York. He arrived, now twenty-two and quite penniless. For the first three days he found no one interested in him or his inventions. A friend arranged for him to sleep in the cellar of a company which ran a ticker-tape service

over New York for stockbrokers, and it was his good fortune to
have the system break down while he was on the premises. Messenger
boys rushed in from subscribers, screaming for service, engineers
tore from one installation to another. Amid the resulting confusion
Edison quietly offered his services to the President of the company,
who was almost tearing his hair in the centre of the room.

Edison had no trouble in finding the broken spring in the transmitter and within a minute the whole system was working. A
grateful management made him foreman on the spot, with the
comparatively huge salary of three hundred dollars a month.
Edison was rich.

A year later, in 1870, when he was twenty-three, he resigned,
having saved the money to open a workshop, and went into partnership with an electrical engineer, Franklin Pope. He began to manufacture his own ticker-tape machines in a workshop in Newark.
Business was brisk, the shop needed little supervision, and Edison
was able—by averaging only four hours' sleep a night—to devote
more time to experiment. Between 1870 and 1876 he received
patents for 122 inventions.

He married in 1871, and his devoted Mary must have seen very
little of him, but they were idyllically happy. They had two children
—nicknamed Dot and Dash—by the time his widowed father came
to live with them in Newark, and the first thing Edison did with the
old man was send him into the country to find a site for a bigger,
better laboratory. Within a few days, Samuel Edison had found the
village of Menlo Park in New Jersey. Here the young man set up his
first big laboratory, which was, within a few years, to earn him an
international reputation as "The Wizard of Menlo Park".

It was at Menlo that most of his major discoveries were made:
his "phonograph" or gramophone, which was a logical development
of his earlier morse-recording machine; the electric light, the electric
tram; a practical telephone; to name only a few. In many ways
Edison, who was a perfectionist, improved on the ideas of others, as
in the telephone, for which he designed the carbon transmitter that
increased the range and clarity of the instrument Bell had invented
and made it unnecessary to keep bobbing the device up and down
between mouth and ear. (Bell's electromagnet-and-diaphragm had
been both transmitter and receiver, and had done neither job very
efficiently.) But one discovery he left for others to develop: the
"Edison Effect", the emission of electrons from a hot filament, led
to the development by others of the thermionic valve on which
were to depend radio telephony, the long-distance telephone, and

talking pictures. With the thermionic valve small electrical currents could be amplified.

His phonograph performed faithfully for friends in 1877, repeating the rhyme, "Mary had a little lamb . . ." but so much work was required to make it into the instrument Edison dreamed of that he shelved it and went on to invent the light bulb. This, too, required months of work, even after the spectacular demonstration of New Year's Eve, 1879, before he was satisfied. He experimented with twelve hundred different varieties of bamboo before finding the ideal for the filament, and only then did he market the lamp.

In 1884 Mary died of typhoid. He was heartbroken but he dug himself yet deeper into his work, scarcely sleeping, pressing on with his schemes, opening a big plant in Schenectady. In 1885, as he watched the countryside go by from a moving train, he hit on the idea of moving pictures: at once he began drawings of his kinetograph and kinetoscope, the forerunners of today's motion picture camera and projector. He might at this point have worked himself to death, but for the timely arrival of the beautiful Mina Miller, eighteen years his junior, whom he married in 1886. He was then thirty-nine, with a name famous throughout the world. For Mina and the three children by Mary he built a large house in West Orange, and the next year, in order to be near them, he moved his laboratory there, from Menlo Park.

Mina bore him another three children and here she and Tom lived happily until his death, over forty years later. During much of this time he worked to perfect his moving pictures, but in the First World War he devoted his energies to synthesizing the chemicals which in peacetime had come from Germany. He designed a plant for making carbolic acid and was told it would take nine months to build: he went out and built it with his own hands and those of his chemical workers in seventeen days and produced seven hundred pounds of synthetic carbolic acid on the eighteenth.

Before his death at West Orange on 18 October, 1931—he was eighty-four—he had patented 1,300 inventions. Shortly before he died, American newspapers conducted polls to determine the ten greatest living Americans: there was considerable difference of opinion over the lists, but each poll agreed that the greatest of all was Thomas Alva Edison.

Vincent Van Gogh
1853-1890

ONE evening, two days before Christmas, in the year 1888, the painter Paul Gauguin was quietly crossing the Place Lamartine in the little southern French town of Arles when he heard the sound of hurried footsteps behind him. Turning, he saw a man coming for him wearing a look of intense hostility and holding in his raised hand an open razor. The two men came to a halt, only a few feet separating them. In a firm, strong, and compelling tone Gauguin said: "Go back home, Vincent." The hand holding the razor dropped slowly to the other's side. Then in a moment or so, he turned away without any struggle, and ran back to the little yellow house which he was then sharing with Gauguin. The fit of madness was not yet over; inside the house, the artist stood before the mirror he had so often used for painting his frequent self-portraits and in a frenzy of madness hacked away part of his left ear. He tied a scarf tightly around his mutilated head, wrapped the severed portion of ear in paper, put it in an envelope and walked out of the house. The route he took led to a brothel in the town, which he often frequented. He walked in, gave the envelope to one of the girls he knew, and waited as she opened the little packet. On discovering the contents she promptly fainted, and in a moment the establishment was in an uproar, at the centre of which stood Vincent van Gogh, a ghastly swaying figure with blood pouring down the side of his face from the injury beneath the soaked scarf. The incident was the culmination of a precarious friendship between the two painters, and the first real sign of the insanity which would soon overtake one of the greatest painters of the nineteenth century.

On 30 March, 1852, Anna, wife of Theodorus van Gogh, a Calvinist preacher in the little Dutch village of Groot-Zundert, gave birth to a baby boy, who was named Vincent. A few weeks after his birth, the infant died. Exactly a year later, on 30 March, 1853, another boy was born. He was given the same name as his dead brother. Red-haired, with blue-green eyes, and a freckled complexion, Vincent, even in his early childhood displayed a temper of such uncontrollable fury that it must have suggested some mental instability. The basis of this early instability, and perhaps of Vincent's future madness, can be sought to a large extent in the fact that the child was brought up in the full knowledge that in the eyes of his mother he was but a shadowy substitute for that other Vincent who had died. He felt unwanted. Throughout his life he sought, in all his mainly sordid associations with women, a mother; a woman who would love him always, for himself alone, and whom he, in turn, could adore. Alas, he was to find little happiness in this direction.

Vincent found little real love within his own family. With his three sisters he had nothing in common. But he loved his younger brother Theo; a love that was returned, and that endured through the whole of Vincent's tragic life.

In 1864 when Vincent was eleven years old his parents, unable to understand or cope with the difficult temperament of their eldest son, sent him to a school far away at Zevenbergen, where he was to spend the next five years. They were not happy years and, in July, 1869, young Vincent went to work at the Goupil Art Gallery, in the Hague, in which his rich Uncle Vincent had a substantial interest. So, at the age of sixteen, the young man was introduced to the world of art. In 1873 Vincent was transferred from the Hague to the London branch of the Goupil business in Southampton Street. He was an earnest young man who had developed a passionate interest in pictures and painting. His work brought him in touch with the work of the great masters, and gradually he began to evolve the idea that was to obsess him throughout the rest of his life: that art should have a moral purpose. He placed Rembrandt and Millet among his favourite painters.

Shortly after his arrival in London, the young man took lodgings with Mrs Loyer a Frenchwoman. She and her daughter Ursula ran a small school for boys. For the first and the last time in his life Vincent was to know the happiness of being fully received as one of a family. The Loyers were kind and understanding people. He was very happy. But it was not to last. Vincent fell deeply and passionately in love with Ursula; but she was not in love with him. When the young man at last declared the love he could no longer keep pent up within himself, mother and daughter were greatly distressed. They explained as kindly and as gently as they could that Ursula was secretly engaged to a young man who had lodged in their house before Vincent's arrival. Vincent refused to accept the situation. To her protestations that she did not love him, he opposed the argument that it was enough that he loved her! His love was so great he pleaded, it would suffice for them both! And anyway, in the end, would not such a gigantic passion inevitably stir love in herself? Ursula did not see it that way at all. She was adamant—nothing of this sort could ever exist between Vincent and herself. He pestered her. There were angry scenes.

At last Vincent realized the hopelessness of his love. He lost confidence. He began to hate himself, and everyone about him. In the depths of utter despair and loneliness, he packed his things and left for Holland. In desperation he resorted to the one type of woman who would not reject him—the prostitute. For the rest of his life, he would frequently resort to her kind.

After his grief had somewhat moderated, Vincent moved for a time between London and Paris, still working for his uncle. All he wanted now was to do good in the world; he wanted to live unselfishly. He would devote his life to the cause of suffering humantiy. He began to lecture prospective customers, and generally to introduce a moralizing line of argument into his business dealings. The general manager of Goupil dismissed him.

Van Gogh took low-grade teaching jobs in England and began studying the Bible in earnest. He developed a desire to enter the Church; to be a preacher. Returning to Holland he set off for the mining village of Paturages in the Borinage, and began work as a lay preacher living among the miners of the locality. He moved among the lowest and the humblest of these hard-working men, preaching and helping them and their families in every way he could. To this demonstration of practical Christianity the elders of the Church reacted angrily and he was forced to abandon this way of life. This was August 1880.

He had begun to make drawings, many, many drawings of the miners of the Borinage. Vincent had found his real vocation. His brother Theo was overjoyed. Many letters passed between the two men. Theo, who held an important post at Goupil, began sending money to Vincent, who was desperately in need of finance for materials, for models, for food and for shelter.

In a little while Vincent moved to the Hague, and wrote to Theo: "For the last month or two I've been sleeping with a prostitute. I want to live with her, I'm going to marry her." His brother was appalled: what in heaven's name was Vincent thinking of to ruin his prospects by such an association and in the Hague of all places, where the van Gogh family was well known. Vincent had met the woman soon after settling in the Hague and, touched by her wretchedness, for she was pregnant, with a young daughter and a mother to support, vowed to help her. Her name was Sien; she was foul mouthed, vile tempered, and riddled with disease. Poor Vincent was cruelly deceived by his ideals. They quarrelled, and lived in intolerable squalor, but Vincent refused to leave her and the baby, in whom he took great pleasure. All the time he was drawing and painting, helped continuously with gifts of money by Theo. He could not have survived otherwise. At length the relationship became intolerable even for the patient van Gogh. He left Sien and took up residence in Drenthe, a town in the north Netherlands. Here he had been told a painter could live cheaply.

Drenthe was a country town where the peasants reminded Vincent of the miners of the Borinage. He worked, and struggled, but he could not settle. In 1883 he returned home to Nuenen. He attacked his work with new vigour. His father's parsonage stood among weavers' cottages, and he painted the good, simple folk of Nuenen with passion and insight. In the house next door to the parsonage lived a family named Begemann. The father was an elder in the parson's church. Almost at once Vincent fell in love with Margot, Begemann's youngest sister, a woman much older than himself. This time his love was returned; but the idyll had a short life, and a dramatic ending. Margot's family met the couple's plans to marry with derision and anger. "You are too old for that kind of thing," they screamed. "Besides the fellow is a disreputable good-for-nothing artist." She at first faced the onslaught bravely. Then, driven to distraction by the continued abuses of her family, the poor woman made an unsuccessful attempt at suicide by taking poison. Vincent never saw her again. After her recovery she was kept permanently inside the house. Vincent, maddened by grief, hurled his curses at the Begemann family; at the bigoted people who had ruined their two lives. His sole surviving link with the human love he craved was his brother Theo. Relations with others of his family worsened. He quarrelled with his parents.

In 1885 Vincent's father collapsed outside the door of his parsonage and died suddenly. Soon after the funeral Vincent moved to Antwerp. He threw himself into a frenzy of painting. He was tormented by the thought of wasted years; he was thirty-three and in his six grinding years of drawing and painting he had not sold a single picture. He grudged every moment of sleep, every fall of darkness, for he felt he had no time to lose. Life was hard in the city of Antwerp and expensive. If he wanted models he had to pay for them; there were no peasants to sit for him free of charge. Vincent wrote letter after letter to Theo; he must have more money; his little allowance from the family simply was not enough. Theo began to grow tired of the continuous demands. Why not return to Nuenen he suggested. "Never!" replied Vincent. Theo must find the money.

His brother was now in Paris. Suddenly, Vincent decided to visit the long-suffering Theo. Leaving his canvasses as payment for arrears of rent, he boarded a train for the capital. The same day Theo received a scrawled message in his gallery. It said simply: "Meet me in the Louvre, Vincent." Theo found him staring enraptured at a Rembrandt, and although at first he was consumed with anger, his annoyance disappeared when he saw how ill and worn out his brother looked. His teeth were decayed and broken; he was appallingly thin. The first essential, thought the good brother, was to restore Vincent to health. During the weeks that followed, Vincent shared Theo's flat where he drew and painted furiously and wandered around the great galleries of Paris to study the work of the masters. He began to study also the work of contemporary painters; the Impressionists in particular. Impressionism was by this time firmly established; the painters of light and atmosphere had pushed the once revolutionary movement as far as it could go. By this time, life had turned Vincent into a fierce rebel. The Impressionists for all their qualities were bourgeois! They had become respectable. It was time for a new school to develop out of Impressionism! This ought to be a school of individualists—for did not all the Impressionists paint alike? You could hardly tell the work of one from that of another. What was needed were artists with a unique, personal vision. Only one painter really matched his dream of what a painter should be, and that was Paul Gauguin, a group of whose pictures he had first seen in a Paris exhibition.

His ambition became to meet the man who had given up his family and a lucrative job on the Paris Bourse, to paint. At last he met his hero in Theo's gallery, a swaggering, romantically attired figure, already famous for his intensely original style of painting. Gauguin was not an easy man to get to know. Sarcastic and violent, he was something of a terror to everyone. But in 1888, Vincent tentatively suggested to Gauguin that they should head for the South of France together to settle and found a new school. Gauguin cruelly laughed off the suggestion. When he went to the south he retorted, it would be to the real south—the South Seas! For the moment he would content himself with Brittany where he was working at Port-Aven.

In despair, Vincent headed alone for the south; for Arles, where so many of his most famous pictures were to be painted. In this sun-drenched locality he found inspiration for the wonderful use of yellow which distinguishes his work from that of any other master. Here among others he painted the famous picture of his little bedroom, of the sun-flowers and the self portrait with bandage, after the mutilation episode.

In 1888 Gauguin agreed to set up house in Arles with his worshipper. From the outset, the two men argued and quarrelled. Gauguin, in every way the stronger of the two, sought to dominate Vincent. After many quarrels, and the incident with the razor, Gauguin departed and Vincent once more was on his own. He worked like a madman; painting, painting, painting—always in a frenzy. But his mind now was definitely unhinged. There followed a series of incarcerations in the local asylum, arranged of course by his brother Theo.

Not far from Arles at St Remy, was the old monastery of St Paul, which had been turned into a private asylum, and it was here that he was sent. Vincent wrote to Theo: "I should like to be shut up for a while as much for my peace of mind as for others." However, he was still free to come and go, more or less as he pleased. In between his attacks of madness, he painted desperately, wandering around the countryside with his canvasses and equipment, a strange figure with a tortured mind. He knew there was no cure for him; no hope of recovery.

In March, 1890, he took up residence in Auvers under the watchful eye of a specialist, Dr Gachet, a man who sympathized with, and understood the tragedy of the artist's life, and insanity. In the first week he painted that portrait of Dr Gachet which is one of his most celebrated works. A few weeks later he shot himself in the stomach. His heartbroken brother hurried from Paris to Auvers to be with the dying man. "Who could imagine that life would be so sad," said Vincent, "I wish I could die." A few minutes later the great painter was dead. He was buried in the churchyard at Auvers. During his lifetime Vincent van Gogh never sold one single picture. Today his works fetch thousands, even hundreds of thousands of pounds. He was a great and lonely genius who introduced a new, and personal, note into European painting.

Cecil Rhodes
1853-1902

ACROSS the South African veld, yellow and purple in the blazing sun, moved with ponderous tread sixteen oxen, dragging behind them a light, two-wheeled cart in which sat an eighteen-year-old Englishman. Here and there across the plain he spied villages of mushroom-shaped huts, white walled and black roofed, in which the natives dwelt. He knew very little of them as yet. Everything was strange, but at the same time deeply interesting, even exciting.

Cecil John Rhodes was the young fellow's name. He was born on 5 July, 1853, at Bishop's Stortford, in Hertfordshire, where his father was vicar. For eight years, from when he was eight until he was sixteen, he was at the local grammar school and did fairly well there, although he never shone as a scholar. He was particularly good at history and geography, and once won a prize for elocution. When he left school there were the usual family discussions about what career he should adopt. His father wanted him to go to a university and become a clergyman, but it did not appear that the youth had any vocation for preaching.

Then his health broke down. Doctors diagnosed possible tuberculosis. It was essential that he should go to live in a warm climate, and what better place than South Africa, where one of his older brothers was a cotton planter? So to South Africa he went. For some time he helped his brother Herbert on his farm in Natal. He liked the life, and made friends among the farmers of the district. He also got on well with the native labourers; they in their turn came to respect him and even to like him. In the evenings the two brothers would get out their schoolbooks, and try to "keep up their classics", for they both had the intention of returning to England one day and of going to Oxford as students.

This was their dream, but for the present they had their livings to get, and the farm demanded their constant attention. They heard a rumour that diamonds had been discovered in the Orange Free State, far up country; fortunes were being made there almost overnight by those who were prepared to rough it and take their chances in the rough and tumble of the diggings. Herbert was the first to go, leaving Cecil to dispose of the stock on the farm and wind up their affairs in Natal. At length in October, 1871, he too set off, in the ox-drawn cart. Underneath the seat were a pick and a couple of spades, and somewhere in the back was a box containing his precious books, Greek and Latin classics, and a great fat volume of a Greek dictionary.

Hardly had he arrived at Kimberley, in the centre of the diamond diggings, when he was once again left on his own, for Herbert went off back to England for a time. Cecil was happy enough. The "claim" was not a rich one, but it paid its way. The climate was bracing and just what was needed to restore his health. After a couple of years it was his turn to go back to England for a spell, and he seized the opportunity to go to Oxford. He matriculated at Oriel in 1873, but early in the new year he caught a chill while out rowing and the bad old symptoms came back. The specialist who examined him kept his diagnosis to himself, but in his casebook he noted, "Not six months to live."

So Cecil Rhodes returned to South Africa. For the next eight years he divided his time between Oxford and Kimberley. By dogged application he at length obtained his B.A. in 1881. Meanwhile his career had been taking shape in Africa. Herbert went off on a shooting and exploring expedition, from which he never returned, for he lost his life by accident in what is now Malawi. Cecil formed a partnership with some other young Englishmen and built up a powerful interest in one of the two great mines in Kimberley, the one that was called De Beers after the Dutch farmer who had originally owned the land. The enterprise proved to be immensely profitable, and in 1880 the Rhodes group were able to float the De Beers Mining Company with a capital of £200,000.

Rhodes was still under thirty, and looked even younger than he was. He was over six feet, very broad and deep chested, with a huge head and massive brow, deep-blue eyes and light-brown, wavy hair. One of the men who worked most closely with him at De Beers described him at this time as

"a tall, gaunt youth, roughly dressed, coated with dust, sitting moodily on a bucket, deaf to the clatter and rattle about him, his blue eyes fixed intently on his work, or on some fabric in his brain".

That phrase, "fabric in his brain", is a richly suggestive one; it gives the key to the man's subsequent development, and indeed to much that had gone before. For this young man, who was such a "sticker", who found a challenge in difficulties that made other men leave the diggings in despair and pushed others into bankruptcy, who

had such a way with managing men, of white skins and of black—
this hard-headed, hard-as-nails adventurer was a man of vision. He
had dreamed a dream, and he spent his life in trying to convert the
dream into the actual.

That dream was centred on a map, the map of South Africa. He
was never tired of looking at it, he could not get it out of his mind.
There in the south were the British colonies of the Cape and Natal,
and there, far up country, were the two Boer republics of the Orange
Free State and the Transvaal. That took you to the Orange River and
the Limpopo. Beyond these two rivers, what was there? An immense
territory, beautiful, potentially rich, sparsely peopled by native tribes
in a state of barbarism, a country with no history worth speaking of,
but beyond any doubt assured of a tremendous future! Yet only if
the White Man could somehow obtain possession of it, and develop
it with his brains, energy and capital. The question arose, *which*
White Man? The Boer, who was essentially a farmer, living in an
old-world age—or the Briton, who had behind him all the resources
of science, political organization and industrial technique?

Rhodes had no doubt in his own mind which it ought to be,
which indeed it *must* be. In his first will, made in 1877 at the age of
twenty-four, he disposed of the fortune that he had yet to make, in
the establishment of a secret society the aim and object of which
should be the extension of British rule throughout the world, the
perfecting of a system of emigration from the United Kingdom and
of the colonization by British subjects of all lands where the means
of livelihood were attainable by energy, labour, and enterprise, also
especially the occupation by British settlers of the entire continent
of Africa—not to mention the Holy Land, Cyprus, the whole of
South America, the islands of the Pacific, the Malay Archipelago, the
seaboard of China and Japan, and the "ultimate recovery of the
United States of America as an integral part of the British Empire"
—and finally, the foundation of so great a power as would render
wars impossible and promote the best interests of humanity.

This was the programme he set himself, at an age when most
young men of his class and station were just completing their education. What is more, he never really abandoned it. He would have
deeply resented being called a Jingo. He believed as he believed in
nothing else in the colonizing mission of the British Empire, and he
devoted his life to its accomplishment. South Africa was the jumping-
off ground, as it were. There is a story told of him that one day,
when he had become a member of the local parliament at Cape
Town, he took a friend aside and asked him to look at the map of

Africa. Then he put his hand on that vast region in the middle of what was still the Dark Continent, a region that as yet had been appropriated by none of the great Powers of Europe. "That is my dream," he declared solemnly; "that—all British!" To other friends and associates he confessed that among his chief aims was the construction of a railway from the Cape to Cairo in Egypt (which had recently come under British control) as an essential step in the creation of a vast new British Empire in Africa.

Some of those he tackled were not at all keen on the idea; they advised him to stick to money-making, at which he had proved himself so extraordinarily successful. Some pooh-poohed, some sneered, some openly opposed, for fear of arousing Boer hostility. Even the British Government in London were half-hearted and gave him next to no encouragement. The Empire was big enough already, too big indeed, they urged.

Before long Rhodes had to acknowledge to himself that if his dream were ever to be realized it would have to be through his efforts and the efforts of those whom he could induce by promises of wealth or power or prestige to join him in what must prove to be a tremendous adventure. The British Government were not prepared to run the risks involved? So be it; he would be left with a free hand, *he* would dare and venture, and succeed! Backed by the enormous wealth he had acquired in his mining activities, he took the lead in forming a chartered company—one after the model of the old East India Company that had played so large a part in the establishment of British rule in the East—and this British South Africa Company was granted in 1889 control over the territory that lay to the north of the Boer Republics and Bechuanaland (part of Cape Colony) and extended vaguely as far as the Zambesi.

Speed was essential, for Germany had already occupied what became South-west Africa; the Boers in the Transvaal were reaching out to the west and north. Rhodes decided that the first step should be the establishment of British supremacy in Matabeleland and Mashonaland, and in 1890 he sent Dr Jameson, one of his most trusted subordinates, to negotiate with the formidable Lobengula, king of the Matebele tribesfolk. Lobengula was hard to convince that he would be better off under the Chartered Company than as an independent chieftain, but at length terms were settled. On 11 September, 1890, Dr Jameson hoisted the Union Jack where eventually the great city of Salisbury was to stand.

Three years later, however, there was a Matabele rising, and even after their complete defeat—the savage warriors proved no match at all for the white men's machine-guns—they were still restive. There was a famous occasion when Rhodes himself went to their stronghold in the Matoppo Hills to see if he could persuade them to come to terms and settle down under British rule. It was a most daring thing to do, but Rhodes knew that the Matabele, being brave men themselves, would appreciate courage in others. Surrounded by hordes of spearmen he never turned a hair, but sat down and offered to talk. Once the chiefs were so menacing that the men with Rhodes advised him that they should mount their horses and attempt a quick get-away. Rhodes stood up and shouted to the advancing Matabele, "Go back, I tell you!" Staggered at his calm, they stopped dead. Then he continued, "Is it peace, or is it war?" They answered with one voice, "It is peace." As he rode off, Rhodes was heard to say, "These are the things that make life worth while."

At such a moment it must have seemed that his dream was taking shape. In 1890 he had become Prime Minister of Cape Colony, while retaining his directorship of the British South Africa Company, which was now extending British rule throughout what was already being called Rhodesia in his honour. He was the most powerful figure in South Africa, the undisputed ruler of almost the whole of the vast territory between the Cape and the Zambesi. Only the two Boer republics stood aloof. Rhodes must have thought that the time must soon come when they should be brought to heel. Trouble was brewing particularly in the Transvaal, where President Kruger harshly refused to make any political concessions to the Uitlanders ("foreigners"), men from Britain, America and many other countries, who had flocked to the Rand to make their fortunes in the goldmines. Naturally enough, these men looked to Rhodes for support. In a rash moment he agreed to countenance a rising in the Transvaal to be led by Dr Jameson.

The result was disaster. The "Jameson Raid" of 1 January, 1896, was a fiasco. Jameson and all his men were taken prisoner, Kruger was triumphant, and such was the storm of public opinion against him, Rhodes was forced to resign his premiership. Three years later war broke out between Boer and Briton and peace was not concluded until 1902. The Boers were worsted and lost their independence—for a time—and there was engendered between the two races a spirit of hostility that even now is not dissipated.

At the outbreak of the war Rhodes was in Kimberley and he remained there throughout the four months of siege, organizing the defences and encouraging the people by his example. The hardships he endured severely affected his health, and he took very much to heart the failure of his policy, the collapse of all his plans for the establishment of a union of South African states under the British flag. Stricken with a most painful illness, he sought relief in reading the *Meditations of Marcus Aurelius*, a book which had been his companion and frequent solace since his schooldays. As he lay dying he murmured to Dr Jameson, in faithful attendance at his bedside, "So little done—so much to do!" He died on 26 March, 1902, a little short of his forty-ninth birthday.

Rhodes was buried where he had willed it, in a grave cut out of the granite in the Matoppo Hills at a place where, in the time of the Matabele troubles, he had often sat and mused and which he had named "World's View".

When his will was read it was found that he had left a great part of his fortune of six millions to found a hundred and sixty scholarships at Oxford, to be held by young men from the British colonies, the United States, and Germany; and it was characteristic of him that he laid it down that they should be chosen not only on the strength of their scholastic attainments but also because of their athletic capacity and their moral force.

Where, now, does Cecil Rhodes stand in the retrospect of history? At first glance, he may seem to present all the signs of the grand imperialist who failed. Winds of change have been blowing across the length and breadth of the African continent, and nowhere more fiercely than in those parts that constituted his stage. If Rhodes could see the present-day map he might well be saddened and dismayed, what with South Africa a republic largely under the control of the Afrikaner, or Boer, element, and those vast territories to which his own name was given divided into a Zambia that is an extension of Black Africa and a Rhodesia that in 1965 made a unilateral declaration of independence.

But while the political arrangements that Rhodes devised and strove to advance have been swept into limbo, we should recognize (if we would do him something like justice) that it was his initial enterprise that has led to the transformation of much that, when he first went there, was part of "Darkest Africa", into lands of far-spreading agriculture, thrusting industries and rapidly expanding towns and cities. But this is not all. There is also the man himself, in all his grit and resolution, his indomitable courage, and his profound belief in the manifold virtues of a broadly based and soundly framed civilization.

Flinders Petrie
1853-1942

WHEN the small boy heard of the discovery of the Roman villa in the Isle of Wight he was thrilled. For more than fifteen hundred years its remains had lain beneath the ground, and now it was being dug up and restored to the light of day. As the story developed, his feelings changed. Men had been put to work with shovels and told to dig and keep on digging, and see what should be found. No preliminary investigation of the site had been made, no drawings prepared, no records had been kept of what had been found just below the surface, a few inches down, a foot down. Now it was too late!

Many years later he described his reactions.

"I was horrified at hearing of the rough shovelling out of the contents and protested that the earth ought to be pared away inch by inch, to see all that was in it and how it lay. All that I have done since was there to begin with, so true is it that we can only develop what is born in the mind. I was already in archaeology by nature."

Flinders Petrie was the boy's name, and he was born on 3 June, 1853, at Charlton, in Kent. He was fortunate in his parents. His father, William Petrie, was a man of varied tastes and pursuits, a civil engineer and surveyor by profession and interested in chemistry and ancient history and many other things. His mother was Anne Flinders before her marriage, and she was the daughter of the famous English navigator and explorer Matthew Flinders who, when a captain in the Royal Navy, was responsible for the discovery and mapping of a great part of the Australian coastline. As the daughter of so remarkable a man she took a great interest in scientific discoveries and in such things as fossils and minerals, and she was able to arouse in her son—he was the only child—a similar interest. Her collection of rock specimens was one of his earliest playthings, and soon he was able to distinguish a hundred different sorts.

Minerals led on to chemistry, and the boy was never so happy as when he was messing about with dozens of pots and bottles, conducting simple experiments. Almost as soon as he had learnt to read he was turning the pages of books on mineralogy and chemistry and trying to make out the diagrams. When he was fifteen he came across a copy of Euclid, and he was absolutely delighted with it; he took the book into the garden and feasted on it—so he tells us—for a whole day, a day that was filled with "full delight".

Another of the interests that he owed to his mother's stimulation was in ancient coins. She collected them, and let him play with them. They fascinated him. He studied the designs on them and wondered who the people were and what the designs meant. He weighed them in his hand and learnt what they were made of. He even tried to make out the inscriptions on them. When he was thirteen he was walking with his mother about Blackheath when they saw in a shop window a large tray of Greek coins, priced at twopence each. His mother went into the shop with him to see them, and in this way he got to know the owner, who turned out to be a most interesting character. Seeing that Mrs Petrie and her boy were fascinated with the coins spread out before them on the counter, and could not make up their minds as to which they wanted to buy, the man fetched a bag, poured the whole lot into it, without bothering to count them, and told them—entire strangers though they were—to take them home, pick out what they required, and return the rest to him later.

Petrie never forgot the incident, or the man. His shop was piled with old instruments, books, furniture, pictures and antiquities, while at the back was a tempting workshop with a lathe. The boy was given the run of the premises, and he revelled in the permission.

Soon after this time, Petrie paid his first visits to the British Museum. Before long he knew all the collections that were open to him, almost by heart. He also started going to Sotheby's salerooms in London, and made a careful note of the prices that were paid for old coins and antiquities. Since he was always short of pocket-money he thought that perhaps here was an opportunity of making a little extra. He was introduced to the keeper of the coin rooms in the British Museum, and was told that any coins he might come across in second-hand shops and the like would be carefully considered and perhaps purchased for the Museum. In this way he became a "jackal" for the coin room, scouring the suburbs for Greek coins, Roman coins, Byzantine, ancient Egyptian, Mesopotamian. Once he had made a goodly haul of copper coins and the Museum gave him five pounds for them, much to his satisfaction. With hardly any pocket-money to rely on, he tells us, he yet managed to round up a couple of thousand representative coins of all countries, which were interpreted by the kindly authorities in the coin room, and the miscellaneous observation learnt in this way was of great help to him later.

Proper schooling he had none. When we learn that he lived to be nearly ninety it is strange to be told that as a boy he was considered to be too delicate to be sent to school. He owed his education to what he could pick up by himself and from what his parents taught him, in a rather haphazard fashion. In this way he acquired an immense amount of information on a number of subjects, but he was never a scholar, in the strict sense of the term. His strength lay elsewhere, in practical work, "in the field" as an archaeological discoverer, and still more, as the pioneer in the development of archaeology as a science.

With his father's encouragement he found work as a practical surveyor in southern England. In 1880 he made an excellent detailed examination of Stonehenge, that served as a basis for all later discoveries on that ancient site. His father was greatly pleased, for he looked upon this as a deliberate preparation for a visit to Egypt, in which the young man should make a careful study of the Pyramids and confirm the theories of those who (like Mr Petrie himself) held that these monstrous masses of stone piled upon stone comprised in their planning and construction the key to all subsequent history. Mr Petrie had hoped to accompany his son on his quest, but in the end Flinders Petrie went alone. This was in 1880, and for the next forty-six years Egypt saw him nearly every year.

To begin with, he was nothing more than an amateur; he had no official backing; his funds were of the slenderest, since he had to pay his way entirely out of his own pocket. He liked it best this way. He proved to be an excellent manager, but while he was good at giving orders, since he knew full well what was to be done and the proper way to do it, he was not at all keen on receiving them. As a rule he insisted on being and remaining his own master, and the result justified his determination.

At first he was not allowed to do any digging, but he established himself in a tomb beside the Pyramids of Gizeh and spent days and weeks in making the most careful measurements of these most impressive of ancient monuments. Then he ventured into the interiors, and worked for hours on end, mostly in the dark and, since there was hardly a current of air and the heat was intense, with next to no clothes on. For work outside he wore vest and pants, and preferred them to be pink, since tourists, seeing a creature so strangely garbed, thought it best to give him a wide berth. At dusk he returned to his tomb, cooked his evening meal on a paraffin stove, and sat up late into the night writing up his notes on what the day's work had disclosed. In 1883 he published his conclusions in a book entitled *The Pyramids and Temples of Gizeh*, and perhaps his father received his copy with mixed feelings. For Petrie had found not the slightest evidence to support the fanciful theories that had filled the old man's head: on the contrary, they were "fantastic", he asserted, and should be left to believers in a flat earth and suchlike absurdities.

He had discovered much else, of the greatest interest and importance, and as the years passed he was increasingly recognized as the creator of the new science of Egyptology. His methods were quite different from those adopted by the earlier discoverers on Egyptian sites. Where they had dug almost indiscriminately in the hope of turning up some remarkable object, he put his workpeople to dig slowly and carefully. Each shovelful of soil was examined, turned over, passed through a sieve, and a systematic record was made of everything that was found, however small and apparently insignificant.

At first he had great difficulty in getting his diggers to work the way he wanted. He once wrote:

"An Arab's notion of digging is to sink a circular pit and lay about him with his pick hither and thither, and I have some trouble to make them run straight, narrow trenches."

Some of his best workers were young girls, notwithstanding some of them would insist on singing and clapping in the middle of work. There was one specially boisterous damsel, who used to slang the old man she worked with, and even banged him about the head with her basket, until at length Petrie had to threaten to set her to work with another old fellow in some out of the way part of the diggings, "and as old Aly Basha is about the oldest and dullest old fellow on the premises, the threat was serious". Another girl was so poor that she came to work in a garment full of holes and developing more splits every day, so that Petrie made her the "munificent offer of an old pair of trousers—they came out of packing three years ago and the moths have lived in them since".

However strange they thought him, his workers respected and even loved him. How pleased he was one day when on the march he was passed by a party of girls who, as soon as they recognized him, ran back and one by one kissed his hand in greeting! He commented:

"A nice instance of native manners; when you have got the confidence of the shyest part of a company, you have won the whole."

There were many people at home who failed to understand just what he was trying to do. He wrote to Dr Spurrell, one of his most intimate friends:

"You seem to take for granted that as I am not working for money I must therefore be working for fame of some sort. But this is not my mainspring. I work because I can do what I am doing better than I can do anything else. The work ought to be done, and I may fairly say I believe that at present there is no one else who will do what I am now doing; hence I delight in doing it. I believe that I should do just the same in quantity and quality if all that I did was published in someone else's name . . ."

On the face of it, there was nothing very spectacular to show for his lifetime of digging in Egypt—scraping, would be the better word perhaps, for most of his time was occupied in the most painstaking examination of the Egyptian soil for what it might contain of the life of the peoples of long, long ago. He never discovered a rich treasure such as Schliemann unearthed at Mycenae; he never discovered an entirely, or almost entirely, unknown civilization such as Evans dug up at Knossos in the island of Crete; he never had the extraordinary good fortune to penetrate to the hitherto untouched tomb of some great Egyptian pharaoh—although the finding of Tutankhamen's Tomb at Thebes in 1923 was made by Howard Carter, who was one of his disciples, a man trained in his technique.

He had his moments of triumph nonetheless. One of the first was his excavation of the ancient Greek trading-city of Naucratis in the Egyptian Delta; no building had survived, but there were piles of broken pottery which, when properly studied, provided the basis for an Egyptian chronology far more accurate than any that had been devised before. Not for nothing did his Arab workers nickname him "the father of pots". Then there were the Egyptian graves that he disinterred in an ancient cemetry at Hawara; he writes almost lovingly of the children's toys that he found, the knitted woollen socks with separate great toes, in order to allow for the sandal strap, and the mummies of two little girls "quite too splendaciously got up; all head, bust, and arms and feet of moulded stucco, gilt all over, all sorts of jewellery moulded in relief on neck and arms and hands, and inlaid with actual stones".

Even more remarkable was the fresco from Akhenaten's palace at Tell el Amarna showing two charming little princesses seated together on big cushions. What Bible students throughout the world came to consider his greatest and most important "find" was the triumphal inscription of the Pharaoh Merenptah at Thebes, for this contained the first mention of the Israelites to be given on an Egyptian monument.

From time to time Petrie went back to England, where as the years passed and the extent of his achievement became increasingly appreciated he was made much of. From 1892 to 1933 he was Professor of Egyptology at University College, London. He was given a number of honorary degrees—he, a man who had not even been to school! He was elected a fellow of the Royal Society. He wrote many books. He directed for years the British School of Archaeology in Egypt which had been established to promote and popularize his work. In 1897 he was at last in a position to marry, his bride being Miss Hilda Urlin; when he came to write his *Seventy Years in Archaeology* he dedicated it to "My Wife, on whose toil most of my work has depended".

Generally he was glad to get back to his work in Egypt, or in his latter years, in Palestine. What he called the merciless rush, the turmoil of strife for money, in England, distressed him. He wrote to Dr Spurrell from Egypt in 1890:

"Here am I once more in peace in this land, and the relief of getting back here I never felt so much before. The real tranquillity and room for quiet thought in this sort of life is refreshing. I here *live*. In a narrow tomb, with the figure of Nefermat standing on each side of me—as he has stood through all that we know as human history—I have just room for my bed and a row of good reading in which I can take my pleasure when I retire to the blankets after dinner. Behind me is that Great Peace, the Desert . . ."

After 1926 political conditions in Egypt made archaeological work there increasingly difficult and Sir Flinders Petrie—he had been knighted in 1923—transferred his activities to the Holy Land. His health was failing; at last old age had overtaken him; but he was still digging, still watching his workmen as they upturned the soil, still sifting and scraping with his own hands the precious relics of peoples and civilizations that had grown up and flourished and passed away long before written history began. In Jerusalem, on 28 July, 1942, he died—the man who, above all others, had by his genius in discovering the vastly important in the apparently insignificant, raised Archaeology from the pastime of curio-seeking amateurs into one of the most exact and most rewarding of sciences.

Woodrow Wilson
1856-1924

IN February, 1906, a dinner was held in New York, at the Lotos Club. As usual, it was a good dinner, quietly, unostentatiously served, a dinner befitting a gathering of rich and powerful men, representatives of many financial and industrial interests throughout the country—with, as make-weight, a sprinkling of rather less wealthy intellectuals. At the end came speeches and as usual the best was expected and received from Colonel Harvey, the eminent political journalist. Surprisingly, he produced, at the end of it, a forecast that the future President of the United States—and in the not too distant future—would be one of the guests in front of him.

He waved his hand at the slender, middle-aged academician who was sitting at the far end of one of the tables. "There he is," Harvey said, "the future President of the United States!"

On the face of it, this was absurd. Woodrow Wilson was not even in politics, he was a Doctor of Philosophy, who after twelve years as Professor of Jurisprudence at the starchily Presbyterian "College of New Jersey", had been made its President—at about the time it changed its name to Princeton. It was true that he had been a campus reformer, anxious to "democratize" the College, improve the conditions as well as the standards of its work, but first and foremost he was an academician. Moreover, the ebullient "Teddy" Roosevelt still had another three years of his second term left. Should he choose to flaunt the convention that no President serves three terms, he would probably be returned a third time and by a thumping majority.

Yet Colonel Harvey had his reasons and he was right. As an astute journalist and a rich man with Wall Street friends, his forecast was a combination of sagacity and wishful thinking. Wilson was renowned as a brilliant speaker—so brilliant a speaker that he might easily be elected if sincerely and in silver tones he offered some permutation of "government by the people". Once safely inside the White House he would find it impossible—and this, in the minds of practically everyone present at the Lotos Club dinner was all important. He would find it impossible to prevent big business running the country. This, the guests reasoned over their port and cigars, was as it should be: business had made America what it was, business should keep it that way.

That, in their eyes, was the trouble with Roosevelt. The man had just announced that "there must be an increase in the supervision exercised by the Government over business enterprises". If this was the way of a Republican President—and Republican Presidents had the reputation of favouring big business, not cramping it— then the only answer for business was a Democratic President who would be elected on an even more vote-catching platform of Fair Shares For All, etcetera, etcetera—and could then be kept as an amiable figurehead. He would be allowed to pass one or two un-important and popular laws, and then—then he would be kept under control. In that, Colonel Harvey was wrong. Woodrow Wilson was not cut out for a figurehead: he was, behind the stern pince-nez, a man of action.

Thomas Woodrow Wilson was born on 28 December, 1856, at Staunton, Virginia, in the valley where Stonewall Jackson, half a dozen years later, was to distinguish himself. His father, Joseph Wilson, was of Irish descent and the Presbyterian minister, and his mother, whose maiden name was Woodrow, was Scots.

The family moved just before the Civil War to Augusta, Georgia, spent the war there and moved again, in 1870, to Columbus, South Carolina, where Dr Wilson had been appointed to a theological seminary. The family was not well off, but at last his mother got a small legacy and was able to send Tom in 1873 to Davidson College, North Carolina, and after that to the College of New Jersey (Princeton) where he took his B.A. The College had been founded by ascetic, God-fearing Presbyterians, was the fourth oldest in the U.S.A. and, many said, the best. Dr Wilson was delighted when his son received his B.A. though Tom had to admit there were no honours attached, he had been an indifferent pupil.

It was at Princeton that he had drafted his first Constitution— one for the "Liberal Debating Club" which he founded. These "rules of conduct" fascinated him and from then on he wrote dozens, for every sort of organization, but his friends found to their annoy-ance that Tom Wilson took his Constitutions seriously, his rules were there to be obeyed to the letter and anyone who infringed them was morally wrong—"deformed" was his word to cover the situation. He was developing his interest in politics, but from an entirely moral standpoint. Though he became politically more astute as he learnt, he seldom, throughout his life differentiated between the two, morals and politics. If a thing was right and good, it was necessary—the question of feasibility never arose.

After Princeton he went on to the University of Virginia to study law and in 1882 he joined a classmate in Atlanta to form the law business of "Rennick and Wilson". Unhappily for the new firm, there was still, in the ebb tide of post-Civil War litigation, one lawyer to every 270 people in Atlanta; the new firm lasted under a year.

At this point Woodrow (he had decided he preferred his middle name) joined the Graduate School of Johns Hopkins University in Baltimore, to study politics and government. He took his Ph.D. in 1886, but after ten years of College, there was an urgent need to start earning a living, so he taught, first at the Women's College of Bryn Mawr, then at Wesleyan College, Connecticut—where in the afternoons he became football coach. At the same time he published in book form the thesis he was writing for his doctorate, a scholarly work under the forbidding title *Congressional Government* which turned out to be eminently readable.

At the age of thirty he was appointed to Princeton as Professor of Jurisprudence. He was now married to his first wife, a remarkable woman who cared for him, looked after him with both strength and devotion—he was self-willed, often arrogant—and nursed him through those terrible sloughs of despond which followed the failure of any of his attempts to push through reform. They were happy at Princeton, the scholastic level was high, the moral tone sound, the faculty intelligent and friendly. The University still had its strong Presbyterian tradition, it was still an old-fashioned, rich man's college and it stoutly refused to lower its sights.

As a professor, Wilson was a huge success. His long face with its firm jaw and the pince-nez that seemed almost a physical part of it concealed the delightful fact that he was a born mimic with a re-markable sense of humour. He was accessible to everyone and year after year he was elected "Most Popular Professor"; year after year he was invited to address, as only he could, gatherings all over the eastern states, on any subject that interested him.

In 1902, when he was forty-five, he was nominated by the out-going President of Princeton as his successor. Wilson was a staunch Presbyterian, he would keep up traditions, better perhaps than an older man. But Professor Patton was wrong. Wilson had definite ideas of his own, he would make the University more attainable to the less wealthy, would abolish the expensive and snobbish club life which flourished on and around the campus and introduce "quad-rangles" on the English pattern where undergraduates and lecturers would be in closer personal contact. By the date of the dinner, four years later, when as we have seen, he was suggested as future President of the United States, he had run into tough opposition from the Trustees of the University. He had already, trusting to his silver oratory, taken a trip across the country addressing alumni to win them over to his reforms, but without much success. His discouragement grew and by 1910 he might well have resigned. Then, out of the blue, came the offer of Democratic nomination for Governor of New Jersey. He accepted, was elected, and was able to resign honourably from the University in order to serve his country.

The motives behind the choice of Wilson for Governor were much like those which had been in Colonel Harvey's mind when he forecast him for President. The Democratic Party bosses believed they had a figurehead who would win votes but become impotent on attaining office, would condone the corruption on which they thrived. In this they were wrong: Wilson became the absolute master of his party, a zealous, reforming and at times fanatical leader. His fame spread and by 1912—now a nationwide public figure—he was nominated Democratic candidate for the Presidency. The Republican Party had just ended a disastrous convention of their own, in which they failed to agree on a candidate. Their National Committee, which had originally urged Theodore Roosevelt to "throw his hat in the ring again", changed its mind and nominated Taft, while the enraged Roosevelt became a candidate on a "Progressive Party" ticket. The Republican vote was split: Wilson romped in.

His platform—which had not differed much from those of his two main opponents—the spirit of reform was in the air—had been based on anti-trust legislation which would give organized labour its charter of freedom, the repeal of the Panama Canal Toll Act to allow American coastwise shipping to pass through the canal free, and a graduated Federal Income Tax. This and much more legislation was forced through, in the most remarkable programme of national legislation for half a century. In international affairs, Wilson was less fortunate. His experience of Europe was of two short visits to Britain: far from adequate for the rôle he was called on to fill. He was able to say complacently, in his first Annual Message to Congress, in December, 1913, "Many happy manifestations multiply around us of a growing cordiality and sense of unity among the nations, foreshadowing an era of settled peace and goodwill . . ."

The war which began eight months later took him by surprise. His first reaction was one of profound irritation at this interruption in his programme of domestic reform, but there was much else on his mind at the time: his wife's long illness was drawing to an end and on 6 August, two days after war began, she died. He carried out his duties conscientiously, but there is no doubt that this personal tragedy blunted the sharpness of his reaction to what was happening overseas.

He proclaimed American neutrality. He had seen the wreckage left behind by the Civil War, he was convinced war could settle nothing. He urged his countrymen to be "impartial in thought as well as in action"—a pious hope, with Americans drawn for the most part from countries now at war, and one obviously impossible of achievement Yet he pursued this policy with stubborn determination and in 1916, under the Democratic slogan "He kept us out of war", he was re-elected.

Wilson's "peace without victory" address on 22 January, 1917—an unfortunate phrase capable of much misinterpretation, was a last attempt to bring the war to an end by peaceful means. In April he reluctantly asked Congress to declare war.

With America in the war against Germany he still maintained his hope of a lasting settlement under a world government. As far back as 1915 he had spoken of his idea of a "League of Nations"—though even then the idea was not a new one—and in January, 1918, he incorporated it in his famous "Fourteen Points", his ideas for a fair settlement.

When the war ended, he announced that he would lead the United States delegation to the Peace Conference himself. He did so, but was forced to compromise his ideals in order to reach any sort of accommodation with the other Allied representatives. They had made agreements with each other, granting each other special privileges, they were ruthless and bent on vengeance. They jockeyed him into conferences of two or three men, knowing his inability to deal with people in small numbers, the concomitant of his ability as an orator, and defeated, one by one, his most cherished plans. The Treaty of Versailles may not have been the wicked document it has been called, but it was not the treaty Wilson wanted—even though he managed to have his League incorporated into it.

He came home to present both Treaty and League to Congress and, to his dismay, was repudiated. Tired of international responsibility, Congress refused to ratify the Treaty or accept United States membership of the League. In a last, despairing mood, Wilson decided to appeal to the people over the heads of their Congress and to this end he undertook—as he had at Princeton—a nation-wide tour. On 3 September, 1919, twenty years to the day before the second catastrophic war which his advice was intended to prevent, he set off to address the people. In twenty-two days he delivered forty addresses, some of them the best he ever gave, but the strain was too great: on 26 September he collapsed with a stroke.

From now on he was a cripple, remaining in office with the help of his devoted second wife and his staff, unable to perform many of its duties, until the next election a year later, when he did not stand and the Democratic candidate Cox was overwhelmingly defeated by Harding. One major consolation to him was the award of the Nobel Peace Prize in 1919.

The failure, in his eyes, of the Peace Treaty destroyed Wilson. He died, still a cripple, in 1924, having slipped from the international summit even more rapidly than he had attained it. He had been repudiated at home and his reputation in the world as a peacemaker collapsed from his failure to achieve the "peace without victory" he had pledged himself to and from his failure to persuade his own country to accept even the inferior peace which he eventually did secure.

Perhaps General Smuts was right, after the Peace Conference: "It was not Wilson who failed at Paris—it was humanity." Wilson's place in history is secure, though many of his actions are still topics of controversy. He lacked the robustness and vitality which endeared his opponent "Teddy" Roosevelt to the public, but he was intensely aware of the fears and sufferings of men and women; he was intensely concerned with what was right. Surprisingly, for one who had travelled so little, he showed ability to see beyond the boundaries of his own country and its own immediate problems. He failed, but his failure was only partial and he left many monuments, including the short-lived League of Nations which was the precursor of the present United Nations. He was a great man, but not enough of a politician to realize that politics is the art of the possible.

Sigmund Freud
1856-1939

WHEN Sigmund Freud embarked upon his researches into human behaviour, he found psychology still a branch of philosophy, its experimental side concerned either with the borderland between psychology and physiology, or carried out by introspection. He left it a connected whole, with the main features of the geography of the human mind, including the hitherto hardly suspected preconscious and the unconscious, at the least comprehended.

He traced several aspects of the growth of the individual from infancy to maturity, and in this field probably his most important contribution was his account of how conscience is formed of primitive fears. Of equal value was his work on human instinct and the formation of character.

Anyone working to discover the causes of a man's behaviour, work which presupposes delving into the operation of the mind, must inevitably lay himself open to criticism; for the mind, being invisible and intangible, cannot have its working diagnosed with the same sureness as the physician can diagnose and the surgeon confirm, a defect in a physical organ of the body. Freud's discoveries were so unexpected and so far-reaching, that the criticism—and the abuse—with which much of his work was met, was in excess of that which was encountered by other outstanding pioneers in this field. This was particularly true of his theories regarding the development of sexual life and his thesis that all friendly, social impulses depend upon the healthy development of the individual's sexual life. Many even of his followers were unable to accept completely his doctrines in this sphere; and his general theory of instinct is widely unacceptable still. Nevertheless, his work and his teaching made an impact on psychology which will last so long as man studies human behaviour.

It is for this work that Freud is largely remembered. It is not generally appreciated, except by the specialists, that his researches, experiments and theories changed the whole approach to the study of mental illness. For the first time, its causes were uncovered and its symptoms given meaning. It is very largely due to Freud that insanity is no longer regarded as a social stigma, and that its victims are looked upon as sick people, no different from the victims of bronchitis or cancer, and as much to be pitied.

When Sigmund Freud was born on 6 May, 1856, at 117, Schlossergasse in the little Austrian town of Freiburg, his mother was twenty-one and his father, the owner of a small cloth-mill, forty-one.

Though Sigmund was Amalia Freud's first child, he was Jacob Freud's fifth son. In fact, only a house or two away, there was already living a nephew and a niece for Sigmund, John aged one, and Pauline aged a few months, the children of Emmanuel Freud, the oldest of Jacob's sons by his first wife.

From the moment of his birth, his mother was convinced that Sigmund had been born to fulfil a high destiny. This conviction remained with her all her life, and it coloured her relationship with her first-born to an extraordinary degree. Everything that Sigmund wanted he must have. Once, while in his early teens, he complained that his sister Anna's piano-practising disturbed his studies, and threatened that if the piano did not go, he would. The piano went.

Sigmund, as he grew up, was fully aware of this special relationship with his mother, and of the effect that it had on his own development. At the time when he was achieving fame, he wrote:

"A man who has been the undisputed favourite of his mother throughout all his life has the feelings of a conqueror, and has such confidence of success that actual success is often induced by it."

The cloth-weaving industry in Austria was one of those most affected by the changes introduced by the industrial revolution which had reached that country in the 1840s. The little man was unable to compete with the new machines which the larger mill-owners could afford to install. Jacob Freud was already fighting a losing battle when his fifth son was born, and four years later he decided that he could no longer carry on. So he moved his family to Vienna and set up as a cloth merchant.

The Freuds were Jews, and at this time, despite the fact that many Jews were prominent in all the professions, there was a good deal of anti-Semitic feeling among Austrians, who took no trouble to disguise how they felt. Like his father in his younger days, the young Sigmund was often the object of Aryan spite, which engendered in him a determination to prove his superiority.

But it was within the family circle that he was most conscious of his Jewishness. Jacob Freud was a traditional Jewish head of family.

He demanded obedience, and though he tempered his strictness with justice, the relationship which developed between him and his son, arising out of the discipline he enforced, was one of an irreconcilable mixture of love and fear. It was totally different from the mother-son relationship, and just as this was to have an effect upon his development, so, in its own way, was his relationship with his father to colour his way of life.

Until he was eight, Sigmund's father was his teacher. He proved an eager and clever pupil, developing an increasing fondness for books until they completely dominated his whole existence. He had no interest in sport or outdoor activities except walking. When he was eight, he entered the Sperl High School, in Vienna. At the end of his first semester he was the top of his class, and he maintained this position for the next eight years as he moved up the school.

He was scarcely in his teens when he became completely captivated by German literature and the writing of Shakespeare. In the family apartment there were three bedrooms to accommodate parents and six children. Leading off the hallway was a small room which his mother allocated to Sigmund so that he might have the privacy he demanded. In this tiny room he lived and worked until he became an intern.

The friends he made at school he did not choose for their out-of-school activities, but because they were serious students like himself, with whom he could discuss the subjects and problems that interested him, first, literature, and then philosophy; for when he was fourteen he discovered Kant, and was led from Kant to the works of Fichte, Hegel and Schopenhauer, the great German philosophers.

For a time he toyed with the idea of becoming a philosopher, and then developed a secret wish to become a second Goethe; but he was practical enough to realize that his financial situation was one which would not permit him to follow any calling, either in philosophy or literature, which would not provide for his wants. So he suppressed these desires.

When the time came for him to leave school, he made up his mind to study medicine. This choice arose out of the deep interest he had developed for natural science through the discoveries and theories of Darwin, which had just burst on the world. Medicine would provide both opportunity of study and money.

His father made no objections despite his own somewhat straitened financial circumstances which would make it difficult for him to support a son during a long university course. So in the autumn of 1873, Freud entered the University of Vienna.

His first days at the University were disappointing. The anti-Semitism which had caused him frequent unhappiness at school pursued him here. His fellow students expected him to feel himself inferior because he was a Jew, and he flatly refused to comply. Why should he be ashamed of his race and his descent?

For the first two years of his University career he floundered. Unable to find a particular branch of natural science which would completely engage his interest, he wandered from department to department. He might have continued these wanderings indefinitely had not his father sent him on a visit to England—as a reward for his brilliant school career—to see his oldest half-brother, Emmanuel, who had emigrated to Manchester when the parents had moved to Vienna. Emmanuel's son, John, Sigmund's nephew and his childhood playmate, was now twenty, and Sigmund was happy that he could renew acquaintance with father and son on terms of equal manhood. He himself was nineteen.

The most impressive of his new experiences in England was that for the very first time, he was living in an atmosphere entirely different from any he had previously known. For the first time he was not a Jew among German-speaking people, and the experience was strangely revealing.

He returned to the university in 1876 revitalized it seemed, and he had not been back long when he discovered at last the branch of science which he had been hoping to find but was beginning to believe he never would.

Ernst Brücke taught physiology. An elderly venerable man, he was a disciple of Robert Mayer, the eminent physicist, whose discoveries concerning the conservation of energy had caused almost as great a sensation in scientific circles as Darwin's theories. Brücke was one of the great investigators of his time, and in his laboratory the young Freud believed that he had found what he had been searching for for so long. For the next six years he carried out researches set him by Brücke.

Freud was so immersed in these researches that he paid little attention to the rest of his medical studies, and though a medical student usually graduated at the end of five years, Freud did not qualify as a doctor of medicine until the end of his eighth year; and he might not have done so even then if Brücke had not told him bluntly one day that he had no intention of making Freud his assistant, as the young man had hoped and expected he would.

During the previous year, 1881, Freud had become engaged to his sister Anna's sister-in-law, Martha Bernays, and he realized that he would never be able to marry until he could earn sufficient to support a family. So he left Brücke's laboratory to become an intern at the Vienna General Hospital, and within a short time a junior resident physician.

Under Brücke, Freud had made a study of the nervous system of fish. In the hospital he came under the influence of one of the leading psychiatrists of the day, Theodore Meynert. Under Meynert he studied the central nervous system of the human being.

This, however, was not likely to lead him to a lucrative post, so after six months he decided to study nervous diseases. There were few specialists in this branch of medicine in Vienna, and such as there were did not appeal to Freud, so he reached the conclusion that he must save enough money to enable him to go to Paris to study under Jean Charcot, then the greatest living specialist in nervous disorders. He applied for, and was appointed to, the Lecture-ship in Neuropathology at the hospital. He had been in this post only a few months when he was awarded a travelling fellowship which made study under Charcot possible at once.

Freud stayed in Paris from the autumn of 1885 to the spring of 1886. But he was longing to marry the patient young woman who had already waited four years for him, and he decided to return to Vienna. Within a few weeks of his return, he and Martha Bernays were married. Freud set himself up in practice as a specialist in nervous diseases.

In his early days of independent practice, Freud met nothing but opposition and trouble. The Vienna Medical Society poured scorn on the new ideas he had developed under Charcot's guidance, and his old teacher Meynert took exception to Freud's use of hypnosis in treatment and banned him from his Institute of Cerebral Anatomy. In the face of this opposition, Freud was compelled to withdraw from all academic activity and devote himself entirely to his practice.

Although the medical experts shut him out of their ranks, his work among his patients soon began to attract wide attention; within a short time his consulting rooms were filled to overflowing with neurotics of all kinds. It was in the course of treating these patients that he began the experiments which were to lead him to his discoveries and theories. His first study was into the causes of hysteria, and at the end of ten years, in 1895, he published the results of his work.

Studies in Hysteria was a landmark in the history of medical psychology, for it revealed that there existed an unconscious mind wherein lay the root of nervous illness. The treatment of nervous illness on this basis introduced a new medical discipline—psycho-analysis. The whole concept was so new that it was bound to give rise to medical controversy. Freud was convinced that he was right; despite all opposition, he continued to advance his studies of the causes of neurotic diseases and their treatment. In these studies, it was logical that he should try to discover the nature of the mind. Soon he had developed theories which were even more startling and controversial than his earlier ones.

These latest theories gave a meaning to dreams and explained the unconscious forces which find expression in the customs of savages, in wit and humour, literature and art, and in many of the acts performed and opinions held in everyday life. His *Interpretation of Dreams*, published in 1900, brought him an international reputation, and the controversy which had raged about him in Vienna now raged throughout the whole world. He let it rage, continued with his work, and at intervals added fuel to its flames with further theories—*The Psychopathology of Everyday Life* (1904), *Wit and Its Relation to the Unconscious*, and *Three Contributions to the Theory of Sexuality* (both 1905), and in 1913, *Totem and Tabu*, which many consider to be the finest of his investigations of religion.

Despite the fierce arguments which his work provoked (even leading to splits among his disciples, the most famous of whom, Adler and Jung, set up rival theories of their own) psychoanalysis as a method of treating neurotic disorders had been established in principle, and though it may still be in what may be called its adolescence, this is undoubtedly Freud's supreme achievement, for it has led to great efforts being made to understand the functioning of the mind and the treatment and cure of mental illness.

Storms raged about him all his life. When the Nazis came to power in Germany, they condemned his writings as "Jewish pornography" and burned his books publicly. When the take-over of Austria by Hitler seemed imminent in 1937, Freud's friends, fearful for his safety, urged him to leave Vienna. He was eighty-two, and had had cancer of the jaw for the last fifteen years, but he refused to leave. When the Anschluss did take place, he was forbidden to continue his work, all his money and property were seized and his passport confiscated.

Friends and admirers abroad went to work on his behalf. They persuaded him to move to England, and when the Nazis demanded roughly £20,000 as the price of their permission, Princess George of Greece paid them the whole of this sum.

Freud arrived in London on 4 June, 1938. Fifteen months later, on 24 September, 1939, he died.

George Bernard Shaw
1856-1950

"You bet He didn't make us for nothing; and He wouldn't have made us at all if He could have done His work without us. . . . He made me because He had a job for me. He let me run loose till the job was ready; and then I had to come along and do it, hanging or no hanging," says Blanco in Shaw's one-act play *The Shewing up of Blanco Posnet*.

In these words is the essence of Shaw's religious theory; that God is an Imperfect Being seeking to make Himself perfect and using for His purpose any instrument that will serve His purpose. It is this theory which suffuses all Shaw's plays. He was, in the strictest sense of the word a writer of religious plays. His wit and intellectual verve and a kind of moral fury which he possessed, enabled him to pass off on audiences a great quantity of argument and doctrinal statement, which they would probably never have accepted from anyone else.

That these opinions were sound, especially when he attacked the current morality, and the fact that he restored dramatic subject-matter to its classical universality, place him, in English literature, the playwright next after Shakespeare.

GEORGE BERNARD SHAW was born on 26 July, 1856, at 3 Upper Synge Street, Dublin. He was the third child—two sisters had preceded him—of George Carr Shaw and his young wife, the former Lucinda Gurly. George Carr Shaw was a gentleman, but he had no money. He carried on business as a retail corn-merchant, but knowing nothing about the commodities which he bought and sold, his profits were scarcely discernible. Nevertheless, his family did not live in too great discomfort.

The Shaw parents were not greatly attracted towards their children, and kept out of their way as much as they could. Their place was taken by a series of governesses and nurses.

When George Bernard was ten, he went to his first school, the Wesleyan Connexional School in Dublin. He remained here for a short time, and left, with a completely undistinguished record, for two or three more schools, at which he failed to make any kind of mark whatsoever. All in all, as a schoolboy he was a failure. He disliked games; and was too lazy to qualify as a scholar. Yet he had more than the ordinary boy's curiosity, and would never accept anything he was told without trying to prove the truth of it.

Perhaps the great love of his schooldays was literature. He had learned to read very early, and at an age when most children are grappling with their alphabet he was reading such books as *A Day's Ride* by Charles Lever, and Dickens's *Great Expectations*. As he remarked later, "I was saturated with the Bible and with Shakespeare before I was ten years old."

Mrs Shaw was musical and had a pleasant singing voice, which was trained by a somewhat unorthodox teacher, a near-neighbour of and later a lodger with the Shaws, George Lee. Lee passed on the secrets of his method, which was very successful though much criticized by the orthodox, to Mrs Shaw. This turned out to be useful, for when she abandoned her husband and settled with her daughters in London, she supported herself and them by teaching singing by Lee's method, though he himself had abandoned it.

In his middle teens Shaw was apprenticed to a firm of land agents. He had become the irrepressible talker that he was to remain for the rest of his life; he was also an atheist, and he relieved the tedium of his work by constant discussions on atheism with his colleagues, until the senior partner in the firm got to hear about it and forbade the discussion of religion during office hours.

Mrs Shaw was not the only musical member of the Shaw family. The Shaw clan was a large one and most of them lived in Dublin or within easy reach. They were always visiting one another's houses, where they passed the time music-making in one form or another. When Mrs Shaw sold up the furniture and departed for London, she left behind the family piano. In the evenings, after a dull, drab day at the office, Shaw attempted to teach himself to play the instrument, characteristically beginning, not with exercises, but the overture from *Don Giovanni*.

In March, 1876, he could bear his work no longer, and left, making his way to London, where he planted himself upon his mother.

For the past two or three years, he had been experimenting with writing. Now he sat down and wrote in succession over the next four years, five novels, all of which were rejected "by every publisher in London". During this time his mother supported him. Though he was not successful as a novelist, the time and energy he spent on his novels was not lost. They taught him how to write. When at a later period, after he had made a reputation as a dramatist, they were published, one of them, *Cashel Byron's Profession*, became a best-seller. Shaw always declared that he was ashamed of those novels.

As a young man in his early twenties, Shaw became a vegetarian. As he never drank and never smoked, the vitality with which his frugal habits seemed to endow him had to find an outlet somewhere. He was nervous and shy by nature, so what that outlet was to be it was difficult to decide. In 1884 he read Karl Marx, was converted to Socialism and joined the Fabian Society. Then he found the outlet he was searching for in public speaking, but he had first to overcome his nervousness, which he forced himself to do.

Soon he had won fame as a first-class speaker and debater, first at open-air meetings and among the working classes of the East End of London, and finally as a star attraction to well-paying audiences in fashionable halls.

In 1885 Shaw began to earn his own living again. He became book critic for the *Pall Mall Gazette*, and art critic for the *World;* but it was as *Corno di Bassetto*, music critic of the *Star* and later of the *World*, that he established his reputation as a music writer. His musical criticisms annoyed the orthodox intensely, but delighted the ordinary reader.

In all his critical work (from 1895 to 1898 he was dramatic critic for the *Saturday Review*) he worked from a classical basis. It was his irreverence for many of the popular idols of the day, whom he knocked from their eminences to set up others of his own choice, that attracted the attention of readers of all kinds. All his criticism came from a sound knowledge. He would not pronounce until he was certain of his facts, and when he did so, he poked fun in a way which very often disguised, except from the most sensitively perceptive, the worth of his most considered judgments. Slap-dash work he hated, and when he came upon it, he attacked it savagely. By doing so, he undoubtedly raised the standard of musical and dramatic performance in London, since conductors, performers and producers sought to avoid the lash of his pen.

While he was engaged in his critical work, he had himself been experimenting with play-writing. The first of these to be produced was a tragi-comedy dealing with slum-landlords, called *Widowers' Houses*. When staged at the Independent Theatre on 9 December, 1892, it had a very mixed reception.

His second play was not produced for several years, while his third, *Mrs Warren's Profession*, dealing with prostitution, was banned by the censor. This play, however, did silence those of Shaw's critics, who believed that they saw in him the theoretical reformer who would have been better employed turning out pamphlets, for as a play it contained few flaws. The ban on it was not lifted until 1924. Nowadays we should call it a moral play, and find it difficult to understand how it could be said by intelligent men and women to be "conscientiously immoral".

These three plays, both critics and public thought to be nasty. Seizing on this Shaw immediately dubbed them Plays Unpleasant.

So far he had made not a penny out of drama, and he turned to what he has himself called his Plays Pleasant. The first of these was *Arms and the Man*, written in 1894. To help a producer friend who had been left in a difficult position by the failure of a play, Shaw completed his play in a hurry. The rehearsals also were hurried. On the first night the actors, who could not understand what the play was really about, played it with a seriousness which Shaw had deliberately insisted upon. Apparently the first-night audience also did not understand what it was all about and tried to obtain relief from their bewilderment with inordinate laughter. At the end they acclaimed it as a great success. Unhappily, the actors, misinterpreting the cause of the audience's laughter, believed they were actually playing a farce and at future performances treated it as such. Shaw had planned each laugh, and knew that they could be achieved only if the play were acted with earnest sincerity. As soon as the performance became comic, all the effect was lost. The first-night success was never repeated during the remainder of its eleven-week run.

Other Pleasant Plays followed—*Candida, You Never Can Tell*, and *The Devil's Disciple*. The last was the nearest Shaw was ever to come to pure melodrama. It had a tremendous success in New York when produced there in 1897, bringing Shaw about £3,000. For the first time in his life he was relieved of financial worry, and on the strength of it he married a wealthy young woman of Irish descent, Charlotte Payne Townshend, with strongly socialistic ideas.

Shortly after his marriage he suffered a breakdown in health, but during this time he wrote one of his greatest plays, *Caesar and Cleopatra*. With this play, which treats an historical subject naturally and humorously, Shaw greatly influenced the subsequent writing of historical drama and biography.

Between 1897 and 1903 Shaw was deeply involved with the Fabians and in the local politics of St Pancras, where he was elected a borough councillor. He was embroiled in a number of controversies, which, combined with the novelty of his plays and their pungent setting forth of his message, made him one of the most talked about men in England. In Germany, also, his plays were very popular, for their social message applied equally to the Kaiser's Reich as it did to England.

However, it was the performance of his plays at the Court Theatre, London, under the management of J. E. Vedrenne and Granville Barker between 1904 and 1907, which really established him as a dramatist. At the Court during this period *John Bull's Other Island, Man and Superman* (in which he set out in clear terms his faith as an evolutionist), *Major Barbara, The Doctor's Dilemma, Captain Brassbound's Conversion* were first staged, and the earlier plays revived.

West End managers competed strenuously with one another for his work. *Pygmalion* and *Fanny's First Play* were tremendous successes in the commercial theatre. He insisted on producing all his own plays whenever he could; he would allow no cuts or alterations to be made when others produced them. He revealed himself also to be a superb businessman. On the proceeds of these first successes he laid the foundations of what was to become a large fortune of over half a million pounds before he died.

During the First World War his outspoken views of British responsibility for the conflict made him unpopular for a time, but as the war dragged on and became a test of every man's patriotism, it was quietly recognized that he had not been so wrong after all.

During the war he wrote *Heartbreak House*, and his play cycle *Back to Methuselah*. The latter was his testament to the human race, as Wells conceived his *Outline of History* to be his.

The peak of his career as a dramatist was reached, however, with *St Joan*, which was first produced in 1924. Whatever he said or did after this date was received with respect, and by many with awe, so greatly did it add to his prestige. Every word he spoke, every silly joke he made, every activity in which he indulged was treated by the world's Press as though their author were some fabulous film-star. There are some who maintain that he was too clear-sighted, too level-headed to allow this to affect him in any way. Others, however, find it very difficult not to believe that it trans-formed him into a poseur. He had always been an egotist; he had never deliberately suppressed the caustic wit which hurt for the soft answer which could have had an equal effect without inflicting wounds. Yet the public delighted in his vaunting, and greeted his most outrageous gestures with glee.

St Joan was chiefly responsible for his being awarded the Nobel Prize for Literature in 1925, and the British Government, also wishing to do honour to the man who, whatever one may feel or think of him, had established himself a firm favourite for the Valhalla of British literary giants by his great work, offered him a peerage, which he refused.

He was then offered what many regard as the supreme mark of distinction, the Order of Merit. This he also turned down with the comment: "It would be superfluous, as I have already conferred this order on myself."

Of his later plays, *The Apple Cart*, which inaugurated the annual Malvern Festival arranged by Sir Barry Jackson in his honour in 1929, but discontinued since 1949, is the most successful.

Besides his plays and his early novels, he produced several prose works. The Prefaces to the printed versions of his plays are as famous as the plays themselves, but outstanding among the rest are *The Adventures of a Black Girl in Her Search for God*, and *The Intelligent Woman's Guide to Socialism*, in which he brought together into a cohesive whole the statement of his economic doctrine.

He lived to the great age of ninety-four, revered to the last for his indisputably great achievement. Whatever one may think of him, one thing is undeniable; of all British writers, he, with H. G. Wells, more greatly influenced the development of British political thought in the first half of the twentieth century than any other.

The centre of so much controversy during much of his lifetime, with his death he created a problem the seeds of which are as controversial as anything which involved him in life. He left the bulk of his fortune for establishing "a fit alphabet containing at least forty-two letters, and thereby capable of noting with sufficient accuracy for recognition all the sounds of spoken English without having to use more than one letter for each sound".

Lord Baden-Powell
1857-1941

In 1907 twenty-five boys, half from Eton and Harrow, and the other half from the poorer classes, went camping on Brownsea Island, in Poole Harbour, under the watchful eye of Major-General Baden-Powell. It was an experiment, but was so successful that its organizer decided to launch a movement for boys based on open-air life, on scouting and observation, and the study of nature. This he did in the following year.

From this small beginning on Brownsea, the Scout Movement became a world-wide organization, which, in half a century, numbered five and a half million boys, with another three million girls in its sister Movement, the Girl Guides.

IN 1845 Professor the Reverend Thomas Baden-Powell married Henrietta Smyth, daughter of Admiral Smyth, as his third wife. By his second wife he had had three children; within twelve years of their marriage his third wife had presented him with five sons, the youngest of whom, born on 22 February, 1857, at 6 Stanhope Street, London, was named Robert Stephenson Smyth Baden-Powell. Robert did not remain the baby for long; a year later he was joined by a sister, Agnes, and in 1860 by another brother, Baden Fletcher. Within a month of the latter's birth, the Professor died.

The Baden-Powell parents were somewhat in advance of their times in the relationship which they tried to promote with their children. They were gay, happy people, and they did all they could to make the family home a happy and gay place for their children. No matter what they were doing, they were always accessible to the boys and Agnes. When they were asked questions, no matter what the subject was, they did their best to give honest and straightforward answers.

It was some slight relief that her step-children had already grown-up when their father died, for Mrs Baden-Powell found the task of supporting her own brood of seven on her small income no easy one; but it was lightened by the children's happy natures, their keen interest in all that went on about them, their ability to fend for themselves, and their thought for and kindness towards others.

It soon became evident, that intelligent and gifted as her other children were, the young Robert had been endowed with the greater talents. As a small boy of five, his drawing and painting impressed Ruskin; while his intelligence made him the intellectual equal of his older brothers.

Professor Baden-Powell had been a keen nature-lover, and one of his greatest joys was to take the boys on country rambles and explain to them about plant life and animals. He had made a fine collection of plants, flowers, butterflies and birds' eggs; he encouraged his children to emulate him. When he died, their mother realized how much they would miss him. Though she had little time for much outside the work of the home, as often as she could she took them on expeditions to Epping Forest and other woods and fields around the capital. Carrying on with the Professor's methods of training the boys, she encouraged them to be observant, to notice the small things that escape most people's attention. This she extended from the realms of nature to people, places and all the things about them. She would not be satisfied until they could remember the smallest detail. It was all a great game, for the mother was a woman of high spirits, who enjoyed living and was determined that her children should share her enjoyment.

"The whole secret of my getting on lay with my mother," Robert was to write much later in life. "She trained me as a boy, and she watched every step of my work as a man."

On holidays at their grandfather Smyth's house at Tunbridge Wells, this training continued. Here each boy had his own garden which he was expected to keep in good trim; here the brothers were taught to have no fear of animals and were made to ride their ponies bare-back. When the oldest, Warrington, who was training for a career at sea in the *Conway*, was able to join them, he showed his younger brothers how to climb the tallest trees and how to make shelters of branches and hay. He organized expeditions, on which they took with them only bread and butter, and showed them how to add to these basic provisions wild fruits and berries found on the way, or a fish or rabbit caught and cooked over a rough fire.

Robert's first experience of school was at a private establishment for boys and girls near his home. At eleven, he was sent to Rosehill School, at Tunbridge Wells, where, at the end of two years, he won scholarships to two public schools. One of them was Charterhouse. As it was in London it was decided that he should go to that school. He gained some distinction in the academic side, though there were certain lacunae. Science, for example, he did not like; and his

French master complained that he appeared to go to sleep as soon as the lesson began. He excelled, however, in English and in art.

He took a wide interest in all other school activities. He enjoyed theatricals. Though his ideas of football were somewhat unorthodox he enjoyed the game. Much of his spare time he spent in The Copse practising woodcraft, which, he would assure his friends, held the secret of life. When he was not setting traps, or building smokeless fires, he was watching the habits of birds and other animals and making meticulous drawings of them. "Without knowing it," he said, "I was gaining an education that was to be of infinite value to me later."

During the holidays from Charterhouse, with his brothers he indulged his love for outdoor life. Almost invariably they would go off on rambling expeditions which would last for days. At night they would make themselves shelters, or if it were wet, would find a farmer willing to let them sleep in a barn or shed.

Though he made no particular friends at Charterhouse, he was universally popular, and as he moved up the school he played an ever-increasing part in its life. He sat on all House and sports committees, he joined the Cadet Corps, and was appointed a Monitor of the Sixth Form. His quality as a leader impressed itself deeply on all his masters. It was intended that he should follow his brothers George and Frank to Balliol College, Oxford, but he was set against reading for an Honours Degree, so Balliol would not have him, and Christchurch similarly rejected him. While he was wondering what he should do, his brother Warrington remarked to him one day, "Since you're so keen on travel and adventure, why don't you try the Army?"

The idea appealed to Baden-Powell, but he doubted whether he would pass the entrance examinations to Sandhurst. Nevertheless, he started to study on his own. To his great surprise, when the results were announced, he found that he had gained second place. Because of his experience in the school cadet corps and his high position in the lists, he was exempted from passing through Sandhurst, and was immediately commissioned as a junior subaltern in the 13th Hussars, then stationed in India.

His pay as a junior subaltern was £120 a year. On arrival in Lucknow, he discovered, to his horror, that most of his fellow officers found that they could not live on this sum and relied on allowances from home. As it was impossible for his mother to provide him with any money, he decided that he would make do on his pay, and to this end did not smoke or drink.

After a time it occurred to him that perhaps he might be able to earn a little extra by writing and illustrating articles for English newspapers. His first article was accepted by the *Daily Graphic*, which, to his delight, paid him six guineas for it. Thereafter he made useful sums for himself in this way.

He worked hard, played hard, and made a great impression on his men. But he overdid it, and within two years was so emaciated by recurrent bouts of fever that he was ordered home.

After a protracted leave, he returned to India, where his regiment was now commanded by a soldier of advanced views. Colonel Sir Baker Russell firmly believed that drills and parades were carried to extremes, that too much time was spent uselessly cleaning uniforms and polishing buttons, and that the men had the right to be taken into the confidence of their officers. As these views coincided exactly with Baden-Powell's, the Colonel and the subaltern found they had a good deal in common. The young officer's scouting tactics and skill in surveying greatly impressed the Colonel. Together they set about reorganizing the training of the regiment.

In 1884, the 13th Hussars were ordered home. Because of a threat of trouble from the Boers of the Transvaal and Orange Free State, they were diverted to Durban.

Among his early discoveries here, Sir Baker Russell found that there were no adequate maps of the area between Natal and the Boer frontier. This was particularly true of the smaller passes through the Drakensburg Mountains, which would be of great importance should war break out. He, therefore, summoned Baden-Powell and asked him if he would be willing to supply the need.

Disguising himself as a settler, Baden-Powell set out on a six-hundred-mile trek. Within thirty days he was back with a complete set of maps for the area.

War on this occasion was avoided, and the Hussars sailed for England. From 1885 to 1887 Baden-Powell served with his regiment in England, with one short break, when with his brother Baden, he went to Herzegovina to collect information about the Austro-Hungarian defences. In other words, for a time he operated as a spy.

In 1887 his uncle, General Smyth, was appointed General Officer Commanding, South Africa, and asked Baden-Powell if he would like to accompany him as his aide-de-camp. Baden-Powell, delightedly accepted.

They had been in South Africa only a few months when Dinuzulu, the Zulu chief, rebelled. On receiving the news, General Smyth and his A.D.C. at once set out for Eshowe, and almost immediately Baden-Powell was sent to relieve a fort some fifty miles away; this he did successfully. He remained on active service for the remainder of the campaign.

When, in 1889, General Smyth was appointed Governor of Malta, Baden-Powell accompanied him, but he was not really happy performing the dog's-body work that is the A.D.C.'s normal lot. His uncle, realizing this, obtained for him the post of Intelligence Officer for the Mediterranean. He remained in this post until 1893, very often carrying out espionage missions personally.

In 1893, on his uncle's advice, he rejoined his regiment. Two years later, when the British Government decided that the infamous ruler of Ashanti must be deposed, the task was entrusted to Baden-Powell. For his success, he was promoted to lieutenant-colonel, at the age of thirty-six.

He had no sooner returned home, when he was sent back once more to Africa, to take part in the war against the Matabele. It was in this campaign that for the first time he appreciated the lessons which his mother and father had taught him in observation; it was in this campaign, too, that he learned the native art of tracking, which he was to incorporate later into scouting. For his great services on this expedition he was promoted to colonel.

In April, 1896, he was appointed to command the 5th Dragoon Guards, then stationed in India. After two years with his regiment, which he transformed, according to the C.-in-C., India, into the best regiment in the country, he was asked by the Commander-in-Chief of the British Army if he would be willing to return to Africa, where the first uneasy rumblings, which were later to break out into the Boer War, were beginning to be heard. He agreed with alacrity. It was this return to Africa which was to bring him world-wide fame.

He had not long been in his new post, when the Boers declared war. Baden-Powell took over the defence of Mafeking, which became the first objective of the Boer attack. He held off the initial assaults of the enemy, but the Boers laid siege to the town. The siege lasted for 217 days, during which time the stubborn resistance of its defenders won the admiration of the world. When at last Mafeking was relieved, England, at all events, went mad with joy. The defence of Mafeking had been a vital factor in the eventual success of British arms, and for the great part he played in it, Baden-Powell was promoted to major-general.

Between the relief of Mafeking and his retirement in 1907, Baden-Powell organized the South African Constabulary. From 1903 to 1907 he served as Inspector General of Cavalry.

On his retirement from the Army, Baden-Powell was fifty years old. Several years before he had written a little book called *Aids to Scouting,* which he now discovered was being used by Charlotte Mason, an outstanding educationalist, in her Training College for Governesses. In the preceding two or three years he had been pressed by several friends, interested in the welfare of youth, to adapt the book so that it could be used in the training of boys.

These two events gave Baden-Powell the initial inspiration which was eventually to lead him to found the Scout Movement. He realized, however, that what had been interesting to himself and his brothers might not appeal to other boys. To attempt to clarify his ideas the experimental camp on Brownsea Island was held. The success of this camp encouraged Baden-Powell to make a country-wide approach to those who had the welfare of boys at heart and to boys themselves. He did this by publishing an account of the organization he had in mind and the lines on which it should be run, in a book called *Scouting For Boys*. This was to become the handbook of the Movement.

The extraordinary demand for *Scouting For Boys* made the founding of the Movement inevitable, and within a short time scout troops had been organized throughout the country. The Movement rapidly spread, and soon had been taken up in most of the countries of the Commonwealth. Then other countries were attracted to the ideals which the Movement taught. Within four years of its founding, Baden-Powell, Chief Scout of All the World, set out on his first world tour.

It was on this tour that he met and became engaged to Miss Olive Soames. Within six months they were married, and spent their honeymoon camping.

The development of the Scout Movement is too well known to need description here. After the First World War it grew from strength to strength, and became such a moral force that the totalitarian rulers banned it in their countries. Its companion Movement, the Girl Guides, in whose formation Mrs Baden-Powell played a large part, made similar strides, though numerically it was never so strong as the boys' Movement.

Baden-Powell retained active leadership of the Movement until he attained the age of eighty, in 1937. He then retired and with Lady Baden-Powell—he had been made a baronet in 1921 and raised to the peerage in 1929 on the coming-of-age of the Movement—to a small home in the highlands of Kenya.

There he died on 8 January, 1941. He was buried near Mount Kenya.

No one has done so much in the service of youth as Robert Baden-Powell; no one is ever likely to excel him.

Emmeline Pankhurst
1858-1928

ONE of the things we most often take for granted in our British way of life is democracy—Parliamentary government based on universal adult "suffrage" (the right to vote in political elections). This is, we feel, one of our best and longest—established traditions, rooted in history, giving us superiority over many other less-fortunate countries which do not have such a background.

Yet it is in fact only a little over fifty years ago that people in our own country were being imprisoned in their thousands for demanding the right to vote, and were subjected to brutality and violence in attempts to break their spirit and crush the reforming movement to which they belonged. These people were regarded as second-class citizens who could have no say in their own government: they belonged to an inferior class: they were women.

The great Liberal statesman and Prime Minister William Ewart Gladstone (1809-98) had a longer and more successful record of practical reforms than any other British politician, but the one idea he would never consider was that of giving the vote to women. He successfully opposed every attempt at legislation towards it during the second half of the nineteenth century. Yet, ardent social reformer that he was, he had said once in a political speech:

> "I am sorry to say that if no instructions had ever been addressed in political crises to the people of this country, except to remember to hate violence, to love order, and to exercise patience—the liberties of this country would never have been attained."

Ten years after his death, his own words were being quoted in court, as justification for action which had caused extensive civil disturbance, by the woman who was leading a growing campaign to make the Government give women the right to vote. She was Mrs Emmeline Pankhurst, founder of the Women's Social and Political Union, better known as "The Suffragettes"—a name given them by a contemporary newspaper, which had written that not only did the "suffragists" of the W.S.P.U. *want* female suffrage but they meant to *get* it.

Emmeline was born in Manchester in 1858. She was the eldest of ten children whose father, Robert Goulden, was a prosperous director of a Lancashire cotton-printing company, and a man of liberal and progressive ideas. Manchester was then already the centre of the movement for emancipation of women, and had an active Suffrage Committee to which Robert Goulden belonged. In 1866 John Stuart Mill presented to Parliament his historic petition for women's citizenship and a Bill to secure votes for women—which had been drafted for him by another member of the Manchester Suffrage Committee, Dr Richard Marsden Pankhurst. Then aged nine, Emmeline Goulden could hardly have guessed how closely her future life was to be linked with that of her father's friend.

Growing up as she did in a household where ideas of social reform were constantly under discussion, and with all her father's large library of books to read whenever she wished, it is not surprising that she became interested, very early in her life, in progressive ideas. When she was fourteen her father took her to France and placed her at the École Normale in Paris, one of the pioneer institutions for higher education for girls. By the time she returned five years later she was, in the words of a friend:

"A graceful and elegant young lady, speaking fluent French, wearing her clothes and carrying herself like a Parisienne; slender, with raven-black hair, a delicate olive complexion, and beautiful eyes of a deep violet-blue."

Dr Richard Pankhurst, twenty years her senior but still unmarried, had become by then even more respected and prominent in Manchester radical circles. He wrote soon after her return:

"Dear Miss Goulden, there is as you know now in action an important movement for the higher education of women. As one of the party of progress you must be interested in this. . . ."

Emmeline saw in him the perfect leader and the perfect man. Immediately they fell deeply in love, and only a fortnight after this first letter he was beginning another to her with the words "My dearest Treasure . . ."

They were married in 1879, and had four children within six years—Christabel, Sylvia, Frank and Adela. In two local Parliamentary by-elections Dr Pankhurst stood as an Independent Radical, and Emmeline enthusiastically worked with him in his electoral campaigns. He was unsuccessful on both occasions, and continued his practice as a barrister in Manchester and London.

Because she wanted financial independence, Emmeline opened a small-furnishings shop in Hampstead and moved her family to live there. When the four-year-old Frank died of diphtheria she was convinced this was because the drainage of the house and shop was defective and inadequate. She moved the business to other premises near Oxford Street, and the family to a bigger house in Russell Square. A year later another son, Harry, was born.

In 1893 the family moved back to Manchester, where Dr Pankhurst was again unsuccessful as a candidate in another election, this time standing on behalf of Keir Hardie's Independent Labour Party. This did not stop his own and Emmeline's work to help the poor. The following year they formed a Relief Committee to give practical help to the many unemployed. During the winter they collected food given by the stall-holders in Shudehill Market, and distributed it each day to the queue of two thousand or more cold and starving people waiting in Stevenson Square. When hunger and unemployment were at their worst, Emmeline was elected to the Board of Poor Law Guardians and began to agitate, at both public and private meetings, for extensive reform of the workhouses where the poor were fed mainly on bread, and treated like criminals. So great was the feeling she aroused that the Manchester City Council tried to prohibit her from speaking in any of the public parks by passing a restrictive by-law. She retaliated by persuading a number of members of Parliament to bring pressure on the Home Secretary. The City Council was forced to rescind its decision.

When her eldest daughter Christabel was eighteen, Emmeline decided to take her to Switzerland for a year's stay with one of the friends she herself had been at school with in Paris. Soon after they reached Geneva there was a telegram from her husband: "Please come home. I am not well." Immediately she began the long journey back, by train across France, by boat across the Channel, and by train again from London to Manchester. At one of the intermediate stations on the last stage of her journey a passenger got into her compartment carrying an evening newspaper, and she saw its headline: "Dr Pankhurst Dead."

Though her partner was gone, Emmeline knew that all he believed in and worked for must be carried on. He had never been rich, and now she had four children to support on her own. The house was sold and the family moved into a smaller one. With the help of influential friends she obtained the post of local Registrar of Births and Deaths. This was secure employment, it brought her a small but regular income, and held the prospect of a pension when she retired; but for someone as active as Emmeline, it was not enough to occupy her time fully. With a basic stock of a few dozen cushion-covers, she opened another small shop.

Nothing could change her deep interest in social problems and her fiery concern for the poor. Moreover her work as Registrar began to bring experiences which formed in her mind a sure conviction where the greatest need of all for reform lay. There were desperate mothers of large families who came to record the birth of yet another child, yet another mouth to feed; women who came to register the death of a husband and now faced even greater poverty; wives with children whose husbands had deserted them; young unmarried girls with babies which they had to face bringing-up on their own. . . . Emmeline Pankhurst saw with increasing clarity and indignation, that of the many contemporary social injustices, the most important by far was the total lack of rights for women.

As she herself had been influenced when she was a child by the radical ideas which were discussed in her father's house, so too were her children. Christabel, returned from Switzerland, was twenty-three; Sylvia was twenty-one; and Adela eighteen. They and their mother, and a few women members of the Independent Labour Party, founded the Women's Social and Political Union on 10 October, 1903, at their small house in Manchester. They took as their slogan the simple one of "Votes For Women", and their intention was to achieve it by bringing pressure to bear on members of Parliament. The movement spread rapidly. At political meetings throughout the country speakers, both Liberal and Conservative, began to find themselves faced at question-time with women constantly asking the same thing—"If returned to power at the next election, will your Party give us the vote?" At first it was treated by all politicians as a joke.

In 1905 after persistent lobbying of M.P.'s, at last one of them, Bamford Slack, agreed to introduce a Bill in Parliament, and the whole Women's Suffrage movement was afire. The Bill was set down for debate on 12 May, and on that day the lobbies of the House of Commons and the streets outside were packed with women, impatiently awaiting the moment when Slack would be able to rise and speak. It never came. Discussion on the previous matter before the House went on and on; one after another Members rose to speak, other M.P.'s laughing uproariously at the absurd devices they were using to prolong the debate until there was no time left for Slack to introduce his Bill.

It was as a result of this, said Sylvia Pankhurst many years later, that Emmeline and her daughters realized that if ever "Votes For Women" were to be achieved, it would not be by leaving the matter indefinitely to men. Action, militant action, would be needed.

Six months later the Conservative Government was about to fall, and the Liberal Sir Edward Grey came to speak at a meeting in the Free Trade Hall in Manchester, to outline the policy of his party if it came to power. Christabel and one of her friends, Annie Kenney, rose to question him. "Will the Liberal Party give women the vote?" Sir Edward refused to answer and the girls were ejected shouting from the hall. Outside they began to address the assembled crowds and were arrested for causing a disturbance. Taken to court they were offered the alternative of a small fine or imprisonment—seven days for Christabel, three for Annie. Both refused to pay.

Emmeline hurried to the jail. "You have carried it far enough," she said to Christabel. "Now I think you ought to let me pay your fines and take you home."

"If you pay my fine," said her daughter grimly, "I shall never go home again." So Mrs Pankhurst went back home alone, concerned for her daughter and unhappy; yet also full of admiration and pride.

In December the Conservative Government resigned, and the Liberals under Campbell-Bannerman came into power. They announced a General Election to confirm their position. Again at meetings up and down the country election candidates found themselves under persistent questioning from women in their audiences: "Will you give us the vote?" There were disturbances, fights, arrests, fines, refusals to pay, and imprisonments. Men in the audience turned on the women and hit them, or pelted them with bad eggs and tomatoes when they tried to speak outside the halls.

In the election the Liberals were returned to power, and the new Parliament met on 16 February, 1906, to hear the King's Speech outlining the coming programme. In the nearby Caxton Hall Emmeline Pankhurst organized a meeting of the Suffragettes and to it was brought, almost as it was being spoken, news of what the Speech contained. "The promise of a Bill for Electoral Reform, to democratize the franchise . . ." (their hopes rose) ". . . by abolishing plural voting." That was all. On the subject of votes for women, there was not a word. There were angry scenes in Parliament Square, to which Mrs Pankhurst led a protest deputation from the meeting. Police on horseback charged into the crowds of women, men attacked them, and there was the usual quota of arrests.

It was useless, Mrs Pankhurst knew, to maintain the headquarters of the W.S.P.U. in Manchester any longer. They must be in London.

With the aid of the wealthy lawyer Frederick Pethick-Lawrence and his wife (also called Emmeline), who had long been enthusiastic supporters of the movement, new headquarters were opened in Clements Inn, Strand. Mrs Pankhurst spent more and more of her time on the work, travelling round the country addressing meetings, writing handbills and petitions, bombarding members of Parliament and prominent people with letters. She said in one of her speeches:

> "We shall never rest or falter until the long, weary struggle for enfranchisement is won. For the vote, we are prepared to give life itself—or, what is perhaps even harder, the means by which we live."

They were not idle words. She had to give up her shop in Manchester because she had no time to look after it, and was officially rebuked for her frequent absences from her post as Registrar; soon afterwards she was made to resign.

The generous Pethick-Lawrences came to her help, by making it possible for the W.S.P.U. to appoint her full-time paid organizer of the movement, and Emmeline flung herself even more determinedly into the work. There were increasingly frequent demonstrations in and near the House of Commons, mass-meetings and protest marches, interruptions at political gatherings, and a "Women's Parliament" which met regularly at Caxton Hall.

The number of arrests mounted. Her daughters and many other women went regularly to prison for refusing to pay their fines, and Emmeline knew that she herself was responsible for what was happening to them. She felt strongly that she should suffer by their side, even though this would leave the movement without its leader. Her chance came in October, 1908, after yet another demonstration in Parliament Square, when she was among those arrested and taken to Bow Street. Convicted, she took the opportunity of addressing the magistrate from the dock.

She said:

> "I am here to take upon myself the full responsibility for this agitation. I want to make you realize that if you bind us over, we shall not sign any undertaking. We are determined to go on with the agitation. I do not come here as an ordinary law-breaker—and in this I speak for all other women who in the same cause have come before you and other magistrates. If you had power to send us to prison not for six months but for six years, for ten years, or for the whole of our lives, the Government must not think they can stop this agitation. We are here not because we are law-breakers—we are here in our efforts to become law-makers!"

She was sent to prison for three months; and immediately on release was back at work on the campaign. As the agitation for women's suffrage increased, still the Government obstructed any attempt to allow it, and, using every device possible, prevented discussion of any private Member's Bill. The Prime Minister, Asquith, steadfastly refused even to discuss the matter with Mrs Pankhurst or her supporters in Parliament. Tricks, evasions, and increasing harshness in the treatment of women imprisoned for demonstrating—these were the weapons the Government used to try to stem the tide.

Mrs Pankhurst and her followers could not be intimidated. She said at one meeting:

> "I believe that the sacrifice of personal liberty always has been and always will be the most powerful appeal to the sympathy and imagination of the great mass of human beings."

Whenever she herself was reimprisoned, as she now frequently was, there was an empty chair on the platform at W.S.P.U. meetings, and on it a placard: "Mrs Pankhurst's Chair."

The Suffragettes became more violent in their anger and frustration. They threw stones through the windows of 10 Downing Street, smashed windows in the large stores, and slashed pictures in public art-galleries, in wild attempts to draw attention to their cause. This lost them some public sympathy, and the Government continued as implacably opposed as ever to consideration of their arguments. Militant suffragettes demanded to be treated in prison as political prisoners rather than common law-breakers. When this was refused, they began hunger-strikes. They were forcibly fed. One of them, Lady Constance Lytton, was not subjected to this indignity in Holloway when she refused food: instead, she was immediately released after examination by the prison doctor on the grounds that she had a weak heart. Lady Lytton suspected her title had more to do with her release than her medical condition. She went up to Liverpool and when arrested in a demonstration there gave her name as "Jane Warton". Again refusing to eat in prison, she was forcibly fed, this time without any prior medical examination.

Refused admission now to any political meeting, the Suffragettes hid themselves on roofs and let themselves down on ropes into halls where the meetings were in progress. They chained themselves to railings in Westminster. One of them threw herself in front of the King's horse at the Derby and was killed.

In 1912 Emmeline Pankhurst and the Pethick-Lawrences were

tried at the Old Bailey for conspiracy, the Attorney-General himself appearing for the prosecution. There could be no other verdict than guilty, but the jury added a rider expressing the hope that the accused would be treated with clemency. Mrs Pankhurst was sentenced to nine months' imprisonment. Demanding treatment as a political prisoner, she refused to eat when it was not granted. After five days, she was released on medical grounds.

The following year, 1913, she received the heavy sentence of three years' imprisonment. Again she went on hunger-strike, and again the prison authorities dared not try to feed her by force. Instead the Home Secretary, McKenna, rushed through Parliament "The Prisoners' Temporary Discharge for Health Act"—which became known, as its effects were seen, as "The Cat And Mouse Act". It allowed the authorities to release a prisoner temporarily "on medical grounds" and then take her back to prison to continue the sentence as soon as she showed signs of recovering from the effects of a hunger-strike. It was used against Mrs Pankhurst in this fashion a total of eight times.

Every time she was released, she immediately attended whatever meetings of the W.S.P.U. were being held, and spoke from the platform. Once she was so weak she had to be wheeled into the hall in an invalid chair; on another occasion she was taken on a stretcher in an ambulance to a meeting, but was rearrested by the police before she reached the hall.

Home Secretary McKenna said in the House of Commons:

"We have to deal with a phenomenon which I believe is absolutely without precedent in our history. There are four alternative ways of dealing with it. The first is to let these women die in prison; the second is to deport them; the third to treat them as lunatics; and the fourth to give them the vote."

He was not prepared to adopt the last.

What might have happened, what would have happened, had the battle continued any longer, can never be known—for in August, 1914, the First World War began. The Government, the Suffragettes, the whole people of Britain, were caught up in another and larger struggle which brought far greater problems and difficulties for them all.

Mrs Pankhurst called on her followers to stop the fight and unite behind the Government. It is often said that during the four years which followed, women ceased to demand equality and demonstrated it instead, by their work to support the war effort in factories, in hospitals, and even as ambulance-drivers on the battlefields. Before the end of the war a Bill to give them the vote was passed through Parliament, and received the Royal Assent in February, 1918.

Yet still the franchise was not universal for all women, and after the war was over Emmeline continued to work to extend it. The main battle had been won. The principle of "Votes For Women" had been accepted; it was only a matter of time before it spread universally to all adults, male and female, of voting age. Emmeline secured a definite promise from the Government that it would come.

It did. The final Bill went through the Commons and was passed eventually too by the House of Lords—in June, 1928, on the very day that Emmeline Pankhurst, the determined, fiery, autocratic leader of the campaign which achieved it died peacefully at the age of seventy-one in a Hampstead nursing home. It was the Prime Minister of Britain himself, Stanley Baldwin, who eighteen months later unveiled the statue of her which stands in Victoria Tower Gardens. "After all," she had said as she was dying, "I have had a wonderful life!"

Theodore Roosevelt
1858-1919

"I was a sickly, delicate boy, suffered much from asthma, and frequently had to be taken away on trips to find a place where I could breathe. One of my memories is of my father walking up and down the room with me in his arms at night, when I was a very small person, and of sitting up in bed gasping, with my father and mother trying to help me . . ."

"A shabby individual in a broad hat with a cocked gun in each hand was walking up and down the floor talking with strident profanity. He had evidently been shooting at the clock, which had two or three holes in its face. As soon as he saw me he hailed me as 'Four Eyes' in reference to my spectacles and said, 'Four Eyes is going to treat'. He stood leaning over me, a gun in each hand, using very foul language. He was foolish to stand so near, and moreover his heels were close together, so that his position was unstable. As I rose, I struck quick and hard with my right just to one side of the point of his jaw, hitting with my left as I straightened out, and then again with my right. He fired the guns, but I do not know whether this was merely a convulsive action of his hands or whether he was trying to shoot at me. When he went down he struck the corner of the bar with his head. I took away his guns . . ."

"It is important to a city to have a businessman's mayor, but more important to have a working man's mayor. It is an excellent thing to have rapid transit, but it is a good deal more important to have ample playgrounds in the poorer quarters of the city and to take the children off the streets so as to prevent them growing up toughs. It is an admirable thing to have clean streets; indeed, it is an essential thing to have them; but it would be a better thing to have our schools large enough to give ample accommodation to all who should be pupils and to provide them with proper playgrounds . . ."

THESE three short excerpts from Theodore Roosevelt's autobiography suggest clearly the man he was. He was born—the son of a wealthy aristocratic family of Dutch descent (from that same ancestor, Claes Van Roosevelt, who had arrived in New Amsterdam in 1644 and been the forbear of his distant cousin Franklin

Roosevelt), in New York City on 27 October, 1858. His father had been Collector of the Port of New York and was prominent as a merchant, a patriot and a righteous, stern and honest man. Young "Teddy" was a disappointment to him, being a sickly child, but the boy made up his mind that he would rise above his disabilities and achieve a strong physique. To this end, he undertook a daily régime of exercises that might well have discouraged or even crippled a lesser man. In the intervals of his political life he spent months, sometimes years, testing himself against the lawlessness of his own Wild West, the climate and wild life of Africa, the diseases of the Amazon jungle. Always he came back to politics. He was a man with a missionary zeal, inherited from his father, bent on stamping out all forms of corruption, in business, the services, the police force, the government.

In 1876 he went to Harvard and because of—rather than despite— his poor physique, he boxed, rode, shot and lifted weights with a fervour not far short of obsession: by the time he graduated, four years later at the age of twenty-two, he had achieved the physique he wanted, coupled with remarkable stamina. He also had boundless, restless, energy, so that he was quite incapable of sitting still, doing nothing. Before graduation he had written part of his *History of the Naval War of 1812* and a month later it was complete. It was a well-written, scholarly work, of which he remarked that it was "so dry it would make a dictionary light reading". He had undertaken the work, not because the subject particularly interested him—natural history was his obsession—but because he found American history books biased and "unfair to the enemy".

He had studied law, but the next year, when he was twenty-three, he was elected to the Assembly of the State of New York. His family had long been Republicans, and this was the party he joined, but on a personal, independent platform of anti-corruption. Already he had been shocked by some of the excesses of the politicians he had met, from both major parties.

In 1884 his mother and his first wife, Alice, died within hours of each other and this double tragedy, coupled with his distress at his party's tactics in nominating as candidate for the Presidency a man he deplored and distrusted, James Blaine, made him give up politics and retire to the—then—very wild West, as a cattleman for two years during which the shooting incident mentioned earlier took place. He returned in 1886, married a second time, to Edith Carow, and accepted his party's nomination for Mayor of New York. He was then defeated by the party panicking over the unexpected entry of a "United Labour" candidate and voting *en bloc* for the Democrat candidate rather than split the vote against a hated Labour supporter by backing the comparatively unknown Roosevelt. The Democrat was returned and both the United Labour and Republican candidates returned to the political wilderness.

Three years later, at the age of thirty-one, Roosevelt attended in a private capacity the National Conference of Civil Service Reformers in Baltimore. His contributions to the meeting were so impressive that President Harrison invited him to become a member of the Civil Service Commission. This, though it might well have signalled the end of a political career—a good Civil Servant had to offend too many politicians—Roosevelt accepted with pride. He held the post for five years, becoming the scourge of crooked politicians and one of the most unpopular men in political circles. He joked happily about the end of his career and then quite suddenly resigned to become Police Commissioner for New York. He had worried about the increasing corruption of the Force, its brutality and ineffectiveness, and here at last was a chance to do something about it.

He cleaned up the Force after a long and, as he put it, "grimy struggle", leaving it a model for police forces all over the country. He was then invited to become Assistant Secretary of the Navy. By the time the Spanish-American war broke out his reorganization and modernization of the United States Navy ensured that it gave a good and decisive account of itself—but "Teddy" was not there to see: he had resigned to become lieutenant-colonel in a volunteer cavalry unit, the "Rough Riders".

He served with great distinction and resigned when the war ended and the unit was disbanded. Back in politics, he became Republican candidate for the Governorship of New York. He owed his nomination to party bosses who hated and feared him, but who realized he was the only possible Republican contender and were determined not to be put out of office by the election of a Democrat. He was elected and almost immediately the bosses realized their mistake. Every racket, every enterprise, every doubtful business ethic, all were investigated and dealt with. At last, in a desperate move to get him out of State politics, the party bosses forced his nomination for Vice President of the United States at the National Convention in 1900. The post was regarded as a sinecure, its holder politically impotent. He was returned to office and in September of the following year President McKinley was murdered. The man big business and the party bosses had tried to kick upstairs into obscurity became the first executive of his country.

A history of Theodore Roosevelt's presidency would be a history of the country for seven and a half hugely important years. (He was elected by a vast majority for four years, in 1904, after the expiry of the unfortunate McKinley's elected term, and he announced at the time that he would not stand for election in 1908. Despite a nation-wide clamour to draft him into a third term, he kept his word: he went big-game hunting in Africa, leaving the country to find his successor.) Among a great many achievements he was responsible for the building of the Panama Canal, which was opened a year after his death, for the ending of the Russo-Japanese War by more or less compelling the contestants to send delegates to the U.S.A. and discuss a treaty—for which he received the Nobel Peace Prize in 1906—for the wholesale cleaning up of politics, the services and police in his own country, the defeat of big business monopolies or "trusts" designed to beat the consumer to his knees, the settlement of a long and crippling coal strike. He was also the first American President to do anything about the conservation of the country's vast but dwindling natural resources.

After these achievements and after his two years of self-imposed exile in Africa, he returned to find that Taft, the President he had helped elect, believing him the most suitable candidate, was a failure; he was urged by his party to "throw his hat in the ring" again. Reluctantly, he did so, in 1912. Then the bosses, remembering suddenly what life under Roosevelt had been, how no racket could flourish, changed their minds and nominated Taft. At this, Roosevelt became angry and let his hat remain in the ring by standing for a new "Progressive," "Bull Moose" Party. This splitting of the Republican vote resulted in the humiliating defeat of Taft, who carried only two small states, and allowed the Democratic nominee, Woodrow Wilson, to gain the Presidency.

Once again Roosevelt set sail for foreign parts, this time—in October, 1913—for the wilderness of upper Brazil. He was struck down by illness and urged the rest of his expedition to leave him to die in the jungle, but recovered and got home in May of the next year. His self-made stamina and endurance had vanished; he was an old, sick man. A year later Europe was at war and Roosevelt loudly and passionately opposed Wilson's policy of "watchful waiting" and "too proud to fight". War, he was convinced, was not only righteous but inevitable and it was vital for the country's preservation that preparation be made. None was, and so in 1916, in order to bring about Wilson's downfall, he refused to stand again as a "Bull Moose" (thereby virtually destroying that party) in the hope that the Republican candidate would defeat Wilson. Unfortunately, the Republican candidate was a very poor one and in 1916 Wilson was elected for a further four years.

That Wilson was compelled to break with Germany the next year was an agreeable surprise to Roosevelt who flung himself into the prosecution of the war, raised a division of volunteers and asked permission to serve with it. He was refused, by the President himself, on the simple but ungenerous grounds that a Teddy Roosevelt returning heroically from war would be too dangerous a candidate in a Presidential election. This was a bitter pill for Roosevelt to swallow, but he did so, at the same time keeping up his continual sniping at the President's attitude to the war, convinced, and with reason, that Wilson wanted "Peace Without Victory".

Forbidden to fight himself, he encouraged his sons and all four served: one was killed in action, two others wounded. His health was steadily failing, but he drove himself with the same old energy; at midnight on 5 January, 1919, he dictated a final fiery memo to the Chairman of the Republican National Committee on the paramount issue of getting rid of Wilson, and died four hours later, in his sleep.

Roosevelt's services to politics and public life were only a part of his activities. He was a voluminous writer, with books to his credit like *Winning of the West, Hunting Trips of a Ranchman, African Game Trails, Through the Brazilian Wilderness* and *The Rough Riders*, as well as many biographies, including his own. He was an accepted authority on natural history and had his own private museum. His boundless enthusiasm and courage, his determination to do what he knew was right, even if he were alone in doing it, coupled with his striking appearance—half comic, half fierce, with the thick spectacles and walrus moustache—endeared him to a public which was world wide.

Pierre 1859-1906 and
Marie Curie 1867-1934

"Now, Bronya, I ask you for a definite answer. Decide if you can really take me in at your house, for I can come now. I have enough to pay all my expenses. If, therefore, without depriving yourself of a great deal, you could give me food—write to me and say so. It would be a great happiness, as that would restore me spiritually after the cruel trials I have been through this summer. Since you are expecting a child, perhaps I might be of use to you . . ."

So wrote Manya Sklodovska from Poland to her elder sister Bronya, married and living in Paris. The sisters were children of a Warsaw professor whose refusal to teach in the Russian—the oppressor's—language had resulted in his dismissal. The family was a proud one, and happy. Their mother and the oldest sister had died when Manya was a small girl; those remaining had taken jobs as soon as they were old enough to sustain themselves and their father. Manya, the youngest, became a children's governess at eighteen, working for a wealthy country family, landowners with the address, strange to English eyes and ears, of "Szczuki, near Przasnysz": Manya's daughter, who, many years later, wrote her mother's biography, forbore to give their name. Here Manya managed to save a small sum each month and send it to Bronya, studying medicine in Paris.

When Bronya married a young, exiled Pole, she no longer needed Manya's help. Manya, baby of the family, decided she too must go to Paris and study. From childhood she had been fascinated by science, partly because it was one of the "higher studies" the Russians forbade Poles to engage in, one that people studied in cellars: now she was anxious to go to the only place in Europe where the subject was taught properly, the Sorbonne. Her decision was hastened by an unhappy love affair. A month after joining the family at Szczuki she had fallen in love with the son. The parents had seemed devoted to her, had treated her as an equal—which in all but money she was—but when young Casimir asked their permission to marry, they were horrified. As Manya's daughter says, in her biography:

"The fact that the girl was of good family, that she was cultivated, brilliant and of irreproachable reputation, the fact that her father was honourably known in Warsaw—none of this counted against six implacable little words; one does not marry a governess."

Bronya was overjoyed at the prospect of being joined by her "little 'sister". She and her husband (also a Casimir, Dr Casimir Dluski) were not rich, but if Manya would bring bedclothes, towels, mattress, stout shoes and both her hats, they would happily look after her; she would be warm, well-fed, and loved—and this, at the moment, was what Manya wanted as much as anything else in the world, affection and a chance to get down to study, to make something of herself.

She was not disappointed; the Dluskis treated her like a daughter, fussed over her, showed her how to enrol at the Sorbonne, entertained her. The house was never still, she was never lonely. Dluski would play the piano far into the night. Sometimes he would be joined by a friend, a young Polish pianist with a technique far superior to his own, whose name was Ignace Paderewski and who one day would become not only a world-famous musician but prime minister of a new, free, Poland.

Manya flung herself into the science course at the Sorbonne, though at first she was too shy to mix with the French students, would talk only to the Poles. She was disappointed in her command of the French language; she had hoped it was up to the demands of this new study, but she found herself misunderstanding or failing to comprehend whole sentences in the lectures. She found that, apart from homework in science, she had to devote precious time to mastering the language in which it was taught, and now, sadly, she realized that she would have to leave Bronya's household: the social life was too much, she could not take part in it and have any hope of passing her exams. She was constantly being interrupted by music, by well-intentioned conversation, by the sound of patients bursting into the surgery at all hours. Moreover she never heard a word of French.

The Dluskis were upset, not a little offended, but they arranged for her to move to lodgings, gave her presents to take with her, to brighten up the bleak room she had chosen, kissed her farewell.

This move, which in many ways had been as big a step as the journey from Poland, marked a step in the young girl's life. From now on she was alone, without any sort of human entanglement; she would devote her life to study: furthermore, she would now be "Marie" Sklodovska, writing her name in the French style. It was simpler, would avoid foolish questions: Later, there would be time for nationalism; now all that mattered was study.

Marie had set her heart on two Masters' degrees, in physics and in mathematics, and in a very short time she had them. Shortly afterwards she was awarded a scholarship which would let her stay a little longer in Paris and she was overjoyed. She paid a quick visit to her father in Warsaw, then returned, intending to find research work which would provide the money to lengthen her stay indefinitely.

Shortly afterwards, the Society for Encouragement of National Industry ordered a study from her on the magnetic properties of various steels. She was delighted at being offered the work, but it required cumbersome equipment, far larger than she could fit into her own small laboratory. She was told to contact a young French scientist, Pierre Curie, who was doing very advanced work in his well-equipped laboratory: he, perhaps, might be able to find room for her. She was shy of this approach, and so a friend asked them both to tea. As their daughter, Eve, was to write, many years later:

> "how strange it was, the physicist thought, to talk to a woman of the work one loves, using technical terms, complicated formulae, and to see that woman, charming and young, become animated, understand . . ."

Marie was twenty-seven, Pierre thirty-five. He had been born in Paris, 15 May, 1859, the son of a doctor. He had never been to school because the father, deciding his mind was too unorthodox for school life, had educated him at home with the aid of a remarkable tutor. At sixteen the boy had become a Bachelor of Science. Three years later he was appointed Laboratory Assistant at the Sorbonne. With his brother Jacques he announced the discovery of Piezo-electricity, which was to open up new fields in the accurate measurement of electricity and, later, in its use for the transmission of sounds. This was the man who fell in love with Marie Sklodovska—but her reply disappointed him. No, she would never marry a Frenchman, it would mean leaving her family for ever, abandoning Poland; it was unthinkable. But, says their daughter, "Pierre Curie gradually made a human being out of the young hermit." She changed her mind and in 1895 they were married.

In 1897 they had their first daughter, Irene, a beautiful child who, like her parents, was destined one day to be a winner of the Nobel Prize.

For some time the scientist Henri Becquerel had been experimenting with the element uranium. He had discovered that a

As a soldier Baden-Powell distinguished himself particularly by the defence of Mafeking during the Boer War. After he had left the Army two little books, *Aids to Scouting* and *Scouting for Boys*, led to the founding of the Boy Scout Movement which made him world famous. On the *left* Lord Baden-Powell is seen in Scout uniform; *below* he is in the centre of a group of leaders at the Scouts' World Jamboree in Arrowe Park, Birkenhead, in 1929. On the Chief Scout's left stands H.R.H. The Prince of Wales, now the Duke of Windsor.

Above: A 40-50 h.p. Rolls-Royce chassis transformed into an ambulance which did valuable work in the First World War.

Left: The first 15 h.p. Rolls-Royce Landaulette which was exhibited at the Paris Salon in 1904.

Below: Very few of the characteristics of Royce's first car were new, but in that one machine were combined the best features of many other cars. Royce might borrow ideas, but always he improved on them. After Royce joined forces with Rolls, experiments produced a 20-h.p., four-cylinder car which in 1906 won the Isle of Man Tourist Trophy Race. C. S. Rolls is at the wheel.

compound of it placed on a photographic plate made an impression, even through a sheet of black paper. He decided that the element emitted a form of radiation, not unlike X-rays, which could penetrate where light would not go. Both Pierre and Marie Curie were fascinated by this phenomenon and Marie, using equipment invented by her husband and his brother, set out to measure its extent. Step by step she catalogued the peculiarities of the radiation, decided it must be some "atomic" property, found that it could be observed in compounds of another element, thorium. Because this peculiar property for convenience had to have its own special name she christened it, "radioactivity". In search of other substances which might have the same property, she selected, with Pierre, samples from the mineral collection at the School of Physics. Here came a dramatic discovery. When she found radioactivity it was a great deal stronger than with either uranium or thorium. It must therefore be some other element—but Marie Curie had examined every one known.

The answer was clear to her: she was on the track of a new element. Pierre decided to interrupt his own research to help her isolate it. In the spring of 1898 there began a collaboration which lasted eight years. They began by investigating an ore of uranium, pitch-blende, even though its composition had been known for years. They reasoned that the new element would be in it; they calculated, with what they hoped was pessimism, that it would be present to a maximum quantity of one per cent. (In fact it was a millionth part.) Within a month of the start of their collaboration they were able to isolate a radioactive element, which in honour of Marie's country they called "polonium", but this was not the powerful substance they were seeking. Slowly though, they were beginning to isolate that substance and by the end of 1898 they were able to christen it "radium". Yet the fact remained that no one had seen it, nobody knew its atomic weight. To prove its existence, Pierre and Marie were to work for another four years. The pitch-blende, found in Austria and used in the manufacture of glass, was expensive, impossibly expensive, but they reasoned that the residue after glass manufacture would be suitable for their purpose. They persuaded the Austrian Government to allow them a ton of the stuff, if they would pay for its transport to Paris. There was a long delay. Then one morning a horse-drawn waggon drew up and delivered a load of sacks, full of the dull brown ore, still mixed with the pine needles of Bohemia.

Painfully over the weeks they discovered that their guess of one per cent had been ludicrously wrong. The radiation was so powerful that only the tiniest quantity of radium was needed to produce amazing phenomena—but they seemed no nearer to isolating it. "Pierre," Marie said one day, "what form do you imagine it will take?"

"I don't know. But I'd like it to have a very beautiful colour."

By now Pierre would cheerfully have abandoned the task of preparing pure radium. What did it matter? Surely the meaning of the phenomenon was more interesting than its material reality? He urged Marie to give up, but he was unable to shake her determination.

Forty-five months after the day on which they had announced the probable existence of radium, Marie was successful. She prepared a tenth of a gram of pure radium, measured its atomic weight. At last the element existed officially. It was more beautiful even than Pierre's "beautiful colour": it shone by itself, like a glow-worm.

Radium had been isolated, but there was much to do; because they had devoted four years to the task when Pierre might have been advancing himself in more profitable research, they were desperately poor. They refused an offer to work as a team at the University of Geneva, as this would have interrupted their researches on radium, which was almost impossible to transport. In order to keep body and soul together, Pierre accepted a junior position teaching children.

Life was bleak, almost hopeless it seemed, until the exciting discovery that radium destroyed human cells. It could thus, under proper conditions, be used to destroy diseased ones; it might cure growths, even cancer. At last—and the Press was quick to take up the tale—the new element could be shown to be useful. A French industrialist founded a factory to make it, gave the Curies a handsome laboratory. Then a personal problem arose: now that radium would soon be manufactured on a larger scale, perhaps all over the world, they ought—it was simple common sense, their friends said—they ought to patent the process. In this way they would become rich.

The Curies refused to take out a patent. Radium, they declared, belonged to the world; no one had any right to demand a profit from it.

Though they were not rich, honours poured in on them. In 1903 they shared the Nobel Prize for Physics with Henri Becquerel and from then on their life seemed a series of prize-givings. A sudden demand sprang up for radium; journalists descended on them, discovered or invented details of their private life, hazarded wild guesses as to the availability and curative properties of the new element and succeeded in arousing impatience and anger among the public: why was the new panacea not available, to all, what were the Curies doing? Once again, life became difficult, brightened only by the birth of a second daughter, Eve, when Marie was thirty-seven.

Tragedy struck in 1906. Pierre was run down by a cart in the street and killed. He was by this time director of the physics laboratory at the Sorbonne and in that post Marie succeeded him, the first woman ever to be appointed. Her researches continued. In 1911 she received her second Nobel Prize, for Chemistry.

Throughout the First World War Marie Curie, refusing to flee from Paris, organized and equipped X-ray stations and X-ray care for the wounded. Famed as the discoverer of radium, she also knew more than anyone else about the application of the X-ray, and she put her knowledge, selflessly, to use. Thousands of wounded passed through her hands. Governments sent representatives to her "Radium Institute" to learn the uses of X-rays, of radium therapy. At the end of the war she had the double satisfaction of peace and a free Poland. Her native land, slave for a century and a half, became free again.

Marie Curie was the first known victim of radioactivity. The disease from which she had suffered for so long had been variously diagnosed as bronchitis, cancer and tuberculosis: eventually it was proved to be "pernicious anaemia, caused by the destruction of bone marrow after a long accumulation of radiations". Marie Curie had died in July, 1934, in the service of mankind.

Ignace Jan Paderewski
1860-1941

Disraeli was Prime Minister and novelist, Winston Churchill was Prime Minister and historian, Paul Claudel was French Ambassador to Tokyo, Washington and Brussels as well as a poet and dramatist of note. These are but three examples from a long list of statesmen who have been outstanding in the literary arts. There is, however, one who is unique. He is Ignace Paderewski, renowned as a concert pianist, in the significant opinion of Bernard Shaw, the outstanding pianist of all time, who, at the height of his artistic career, was elected President and Prime Minister of his country, Poland.

In his memoirs Paderewski describes his father as being a member of the "smaller nobility", but does not explain what he means by this term. Maybe he meant to imply that his family came from the upper middle classes, for his father managed the estates of a noble family near Kwrylowka, in what was then Russian Poland. Jan Paderewski had chosen for his wife the daughter of a professor of Vilno University, and this, too, seems to place him in the upper middle class rather than among the nobility. They were married in 1857. A year later a daughter Antonina was born, and in 1860 a son, on 18 November, whom they christened Ignace Jan.

Within a few months of the boy's birth, the mother died. Since the father did not marry again, the children were brought up by women servants, though there were occasional long visits to various aunts.

Madame Paderewski had been very musical—the father, too, played the violin a little—and there was a piano in the house. The instrument attracted the small boy's attention before he was three, and nothing pleased him more than to sit strumming at it for hours on end, not the uncontrolled strumming of a child little more than a baby, but attempts to pick out tunes and simple harmonies.

Of all the eastern European countries, Poland had had the most unhappy history. It had fallen under the suzerainty of foreigners, it had been a kingdom and a republic several times over, and three times within a short period—in 1772, 1793 and 1815—it had been partitioned between the Central Powers (Prussia and Austria) and

Russia. Russia treated her Polish subjects harshly, and the proud Poles were in a constant state of ferment against the Tsarist rule. In 1830 this came to a head in a popular uprising, which was suppressed; and for the next thirty years the rumblings of unrest, though frequently audible, were muted. In 1863 rebellion broke out once again. This time the rebels were better organized, and it took the Russian forces a year to suppress them.

It would appear that Jan Paderewski's sympathies lay with the rebels, for in 1864 a party of Cossacks arrived at his house, and in the presence of his two small children, dragged him away to prison. During the eighteen months which he spent in Siberia, Antonina and Ignace were cared for by an aunt, but as soon as he was released he took his children into his own care again.

By this time the small boy's musical leanings had been noticed, and probably because he himself played the violin, the father arranged for him to be taught that instrument. He made little progress, however, and eventually persuaded his father to let him have piano lessons. His piano teacher was an old man who failed to recognize the talent in the small pupil. Paderewski has said:

"I learned nothing from him; but that did not stop me from making some progress. I taught myself to improvise."

He was, in fact, forced into learning improvisation by the absence of music from which to study. His father knowing nothing about the instrument, did not appreciate that his son was making no progress in technique and that he was "making up" the pieces that he played hour after hour. The boy's playing, however, began to attract the attention of his father's employers, the Count and Countess Chodkicqiez, and after his first public appearance—at a charity concert at the age of twelve, when his programme consisted entirely of improvisations—they took him to Kiev, where he heard his first concert.

Convinced of the boy's talents by his reactions in Kiev, the Count persuaded Jan Paderewski that his son had remarkable musical powers which ought to be developed, and he agreed with their suggestion that Ignace should be sent to study at the Warsaw Conservatoire. In Warsaw the twelve-year-old lived with a family called Kerntopf, who sold musical instruments and who also recognized his outstanding musical qualities. Especially was he encouraged by one of the sons, Edward.

Paderewski's first teacher at the Conservatoire told him that he would never be a pianist, as "he hadn't the hands for it", and recommended that he should be a composer. A second teacher, however, told him exactly the opposite, but before he could make much progress, this teacher left the Conservatoire.

The young student now turned to a number of other instruments, while making composition his main study and at the same time working at the piano by himself. Towards the end of his second year, shortly before he was due to take his examinations in composition, he was required to perform in the Conservatoire orchestra. Since he felt that rehearsals would interfere with his work for his examinations, he refused, and was expelled by the Director. News of what had happened reached the newspapers, and the Director was sharply attacked in public, with the result that Paderewski was reinstated. Once more he was told to abandon the piano; once more he struggled on by himself.

During his third year he made such strides in his study of the piano that he decided to enter for his diploma in it rather than in composition. He chose the Grieg Concerto as his test-piece, and his performance surprised and astounded his examiners, who granted him his diploma with honours.

He continued his studies at the Conservatoire for a further three years, devoting the greater part of his time to composition and to learning other instruments. Then in 1878 he was offered a teaching post at the Conservatoire.

In 1880 he married Antonina Korsak, a student at the Conservatoire. A year later she died giving birth to a son, who, tragically, was to be an invalid all his life, until he died in 1902, at the age of twenty-one. For a time after his wife's death, Paderewski continued to teach at the Conservatoire, but his wife had a little money of her own which he had inherited, so at the age of twenty-one he decided to go to Berlin to study composition under Friedrich Kiel. Though he showed great talent as a composer, he still harboured the ambition to make the piano his career. In this he was encouraged by one of the famous contemporary Polish actresses, Madame Modjeska, who insisted that he should study in Vienna under the great teacher, Theodore Leschetizky.

Leschetizky, however, was one of those who believed that Paderewski had a greater future as a composer than as a pianist, and though the two men worked together for a time, when Leschetizky was asked to recommend a Professor of Harmony and Counterpoint for Strasbourg Conservatoire, he urged Paderewski to take the post.

Paderewski was unhappy in Strasbourg; for by now his desire to devote his time and energies to the piano was almost overwhelming.

He continued to study the piano by himself, developing his own technique, and after a year Edward Kerntopf persuaded Leschetizky to take him back, guaranteeing the master's fees himself.

Leschetizky now had a change of heart, but there was little he could teach his pupil, and in 1887 he urged Paderewski to give his first performance as a concert pianist. Vienna was chosen for the occasion and the concert was such an outstanding success that in March of the following year it was decided that he should appear in Paris. Here his success was sensational, and he was urged to give a second concert. So far, however, he had worked on only one programme. Therefore for eight weeks he worked furiously at preparing a second programme. His second concert was an even greater success than the first.

His Paris appearances had launched him on what was to be one of the most successful careers ever achieved by a pianist on the concert platform. A series of forty concerts given in the old St James's Hall, in London—which brought him the acclaim of Bernard Shaw, then in his hey-day as a music critic—was followed by an extensive tour of Germany, and by an American tour in 1891. From then on he travelled the world, hailed as the great piano virtuoso wherever he went. His programme always contained two or three of his own compositions. His orchestral works, among them the B minor Symphony, were included in the repertoires of most of the leading orchestras. While he was touring he continued to compose, and in 1899 he began work on an opera, *Manru*, which was given its first performance on 29 May, 1901, and was an immediate success.

The success was overshadowed by the death of his son. During the last few years of his life the young man had been cared for by a Madame Gorska, with whom Paderewski had fallen in love, and she with him. Seeing what had happened, Gorska suggested a divorce, and when the formalities were completed, Mme Gorska and Paderewski married. Between 1901 and 1904, the Paderewskis toured Australia and New Zealand, and when they returned to Europe, Paderewski was suddenly afflicted with what he has termed "a revolt against the piano". He could no longer bring himself to go near the instrument.

His friends tried to convince him that this was but a temporary aversion, and suggested that he should farm for a time. This he did, but after two years the need for money sent him back to the concert stage, and he toured America.

The history of their country has induced in all Poles a fierce patriotism. Paderewski was no exception, and when Poland was overrun by Russia at the beginning of the First World War, he threw himself into charitable work for the relief of Polish refugees. Not only did he devote the proceeds of his concerts to this cause, but he lectured on Polish history in America, and when that country entered the war, he organized the training of Poles in Canada.

The Poles saw in the confusion of the Russian revolution an opportunity to regain their independence, and they rose under the militant leadership of Josef Pilsudski. At this time, though he had a long revolutionary career behind him, Pilsudski was more of a military leader than a politician. Not only that, but Poland could never hope to achieve a successful independence unless she received the support of the Allies.

Of all Poles at this time, the most internationally famous was Paderewski, and he was asked to undertake the task of winning the support of the Allies. Fortunately, he had interested himself deeply in politics during his remarkable concert career, and in every country in which he played he made a point of getting to know on intimate terms all the leading politicians, with whom he had discussed the future of his country. He accepted the rôle which the leaders of his people asked him to undertake. His success in it was as great as had been his personal success as a pianist; and it also revealed that he possessed considerable political insight. Not only that but his personal honesty and integrity made a great impression on Western statesmen.

His chief success at this time was his persuasion of President Wilson to include Polish self-determination in his Fourteen Points, which the American leader put forward as a solution to war-stricken Europe's problems. After the war he was appointed Poland's delegate at the Peace Conference.

In their attempts to fashion their newly independent country, there sprang up deep disagreements among the Polish leaders. Pilsudski, who had become the first President, was in favour of a comparatively extreme socialist form of government: in this he was opposed by the moderates. Pilsudski's ideas did not please the Western democratic Powers, and, since their assistance was needed to set Poland upon a firm economic basis, they were able to bring influence to bear on Poland's politics. The outcome was that Pilsudski resigned.

The Poles now needed a leader who had the confidence of the Western Powers. No one was better fitted for this rôle than Paderewski, even if he was to be only a figurehead. So he was invited to become President. He accepted. It soon became clear, however, that he was not going to be content with being a mere figurehead. He displayed tremendous energy and great qualities of leadership; and this just at the time when Poland was in desperate need of a leader.

So as well as being President, Paderewski was elected Prime Minister. For four years he led his country and under his leadership Poland made considerable strides towards economic stability and a position of repute on the international scene.

Pilsudski, however, was not content to see all his ideas and ideals rejected, and in 1924 he organized a revolt against the government of Paderewski. Pilsudski's action brought about the fall of the Paderewski Government, and the pianist retired from politics into self-imposed exile, settling first in Switzerland and later in California. He returned to the concert platform, and in 1925 and 1933 gave a series of concerts in England.

During the immediate post-war years he had rendered great services to the British Legion, giving concerts, of which the proceeds were devoted to its cause. In 1926 he was knighted for these services, but he never used the title.

In 1936 he appeared in a film, *Moonlight Sonata*.

When Poland was attacked and overrun by the Nazis in 1939, a Polish Government-in-Exile was set up in Paris. Of this Paderewski was appointed President. His work, however, was unhappily cut short by his death in New York on 29 June, 1941.

His great art as a pianist was a reflection of his highly emotional temperament, but his brilliant technique, which was entirely original, prevented it from being merely spectacular. Few, if any, concert pianists before or since have achieved the world-wide reputation and acclaim which were accorded him.

In the political field the influence which he was able to exert on his country's affairs during his short-lived period of leadership had a greater effect than might have been expected. Many of his measures were incorporated into his own policies by Pilsudski, and there are indications that his liberality in the political field is still bearing fruit in the changed Poland of modern times.

Frederick Royce
1863-1933

FOR three months in 1940, the fate not of Britain only but of the world seemed to hang in the balance. Hitler's avowed object was to end the war before the close of 1940; to do this, an invasion of Britain was essential, and it could be attempted only if Britain's air power were destroyed. On 8 August and for the next ten days huge attacks were made by German bombers, escorted by large numbers of fighters. The attacks at first were on shipping and south-coast ports. Their failure was so complete that the enemy changed his tactics, began to attack fighter aerodromes. The British fighters, Hurricanes and Spitfires, were more—far more—than he had bargained for, his losses in aircraft and pilots enormously greater than he had anticipated. Change tactics as he might, the battle was lost. Daylight bombing of England petered away to nothing. The invasion of Britain never took place.

A large part of the credit for this must go to a modest Englishman who had died seven years before the Battle of Britain began, a man whose "Merlin" engine, which powered both Spitfire and Hurricane, played a decisive rôle. It is probable that the Spitfire and the Hurricane were the two finest fighters then built; probable that British pilots were better than their German counterparts, but certain that the Rolls-Royce Merlin engine was the finest in the sky, giving reserves of power at enormous altitudes, fool-proof in operation, easy of maintenance, as nearly perfect a piece of machinery as had been developed.

The man who made the Merlin, Frederick Henry Royce, has a statue standing in Derby, and people have suggested that another should be standing on the cliffs of Dover.

He was born in the village of Alwalton, near Peterborough, the son of a miller who died when Frederick was nine. The family moved to London and young Fred sold newspapers until he was accepted as a telegraph boy messenger. Already he had shown interest in engineering and, after a few months with the Post Office, he managed to persuade an aunt to send him back to Peterborough where he could be apprenticed to the Great Northern Railway. The apprenticeship lasted a year before the aunt died and funds dried up. Rather than return to London, Royce set out and walked to Leeds. Here he found a job with a firm of toolmakers; but it was uninteresting, routine· work and he decided electricity, of which he had read so much, was his real bent. He took himself back to London, to his mother's delight, got a job with the Electric Light and Power Company.

The work fascinated him; he tucked into the back of his mind every fact and process of this new science, even found time to attend night classes, not only in electrical engineering—a very new subject indeed—but in a variety of other studies. On his free afternoon he would conduct "experiments" in the little tool shed belonging to his landlord.

Before long, the collapse of the subsidiary firm he was working for put him out of work again. He had long toyed with the idea of starting a firm of his own, and now, by a stroke of luck, he met, during a visit to Manchester, a man called A. E. Claremont who had £50, was willing to put it into the electrical business Royce was planning. They set up the business in Cook Street, Manchester; in 1884, for the first time, the name so soon to be famous went up on the door. F. H. Royce & Co. were in business. Royce and Claremont lived over the factory, making simple electrical devices like bells and buzzers, from which they progressed to making small dynamos. Like everything Royce made, the dynamo was a great improvement on anything of the sort made before, and soon the firm had become prosperous, selling to cotton mills, shipyards, factories. So prosperous, in fact, that both partners decided to get married.

Settled back into business after this interlude, they changed the name to Royce Ltd., went on to make much larger dynamos, then electric cranes. These too were a huge success, not only in Britain—but after a while they were driven off the market by an influx of cheaper ones from the United States and Germany. As Royce's guiding principle was to remain, throughout his life, the manufacture of the best possible machine, irrespective of price, it was impossible for him to cheapen his product in competition with his rivals.

Fortunately, there was no need. He bought himself a second-hand French Decauville car, drove it happily about Manchester, and decided, as he had done with bells, buzzers, dynamos, that it should be improved. He drove it home, took it to bits, put it back, with modifications which made it go a great deal faster. This was not enough: he settled down to make a completely new car. The first car he achieved had a two-cylinder vertical water-cooled engine of ten horsepower, and with overhead valves. It ran almost silently, an innovation which was to be the main characteristic of all his subsequent models.

At this point Frederick Royce met the Hon. Charles Rolls, a wealthy young man with enthusiasm for anything new. He had had a brilliant scholastic career at Eton and Cambridge and was clever enough, rich enough, to try anything he wanted. Motor racing, ballooning, gliding, everything he put his hand to went well, and he was running, at a considerable profit, a business which sold cars under the name of C. S. Rolls & Co. He tried the new Royce car, was fascinated by it, determined to have the sole selling rights —so much so that he abandoned the sale of all other makes. Within a few months he had united with its designer as Rolls-Royce Ltd.

Very few of the characteristics of a Royce car, apart from its silence, were new: the innovation lay in having them all in the car at once. Some manufacturers had overhead valves; some had bevel-driven rear axles instead of the more familiar chain drive; some had balanced crankshafts: the Royce car had all these and more. Now Royce and Rolls turned with Claremont, and Rolls's earlier partner, Johnson, both of whom had joined the new firm, to bigger cars. Royce experimented with several models of widely different type, settled on the one he preferred, decided that he would have to make his own components, the carburettor, coil, and distributor particularly, if he wanted the best. He placed his distributor behind the dashboard, so the driver could adjust it without leaving his seat. The steering was balanced to be finger light, and a four-speed gearbox was built, with an overdrive: direct drive from the engine went, not to top gear, but to third.

After a few years Royce had decided that his best model was a twenty-horsepower, four-cylinder type, and the turning point in the firm's history was when their unknown car was entered for the Tourist Trophy Race on the Isle of Man. It came second. Orders poured in, and Royce tried a car of thirty horsepower; with six cylinders—the design to which he remained attached all his life, steadily perfecting it through the years. This "Silver Cloud" was entered for the Scottish Reliability Trials and amazed the judges by losing no marks. Immediately after the trial, in a test observed by the Royal Automobile Club, it was driven almost nonstop for 15,000 miles (a petrol tap was accidentally turned off, resulting in a stop of one minute), and at the end of this the entire vehicle was dismantled to the last bolt. Any part showing wear was replaced, still under the surveillance of the R.A.C. The total cost of replacement came to £2. 2s. 7d.

So great was this second boost to Rolls-Royce reputation that the firm settled down to a one-car policy. The car would be improved, year by year, but in essentials it would remain the same—a decision taken, later and at a different price level, by the German Volkswagen Company, with equal success. (Volkswagen have more recently diversified with a sports model and a water-cooled model.)

By now the Manchester factory was too small and Derby was chosen as a new site. Royce planned the factory to the smallest detail, it was his child. After it was running he could be seen there most days of the week, keeping an eye on techniques, ever ready to fling off his jacket, give a demonstration of the right way to turn a casting or drill a hole. As there were complicated parts in the car, for which no tool had been invented, Royce sat down and invented them himself—tools which drilled curved holes, ground camshafts of a shape never before seen. The firm, in order to keep up their standards, tried to limit output; but as the demand for the car was over four times the limit they had proposed, they abandoned the limit.

The firm's first setback was the refusal of a Rolls-Royce to climb the long, one-in-four gradient of the 1912 Austrian Alpine Trial. This was an embarrassing lesson, but a valuable one, taken to heart. Frederick Royce had done little travelling, had assumed no hill could be more taxing than those in Derbyshire. He was proved wrong, and immediately he sent observers to the Austrian Alps to bring back details of these extraordinary conditions. They were very different indeed. Slowly, painstakingly, he redesigned his Rolls-Royce car, with different suspension, bigger radiator.

As he was, through his life, absolutely unwilling—unable, some said—to delegate anything to anyone, his work strained him to the limit. He was getting little sleep, missing meals, wearing himself out, and shortly before the First World War, he had a serious physical breakdown, from which he never entirely recovered.

On the outbreak of war, in 1914, every one of the firm's orders was cancelled, and for a time it looked as if the Rolls-Royce firm was finished. Then, with the Army commandeering any vehicle capable of movement, orders began to pour in for cars, and for chassis to be made into scout cars, armoured cars, staff cars.

Royce, who excelled at improving the ideas of others, now had a golden opportunity. Mercedes cars had taken the first three places in the 1914 Grand Prix near Lyons, and the Mercedes Company proudly sent one of them over from Germany to England. It was well known that the Mercedes racing engine was a variant of the same firm's aircraft engine. When war broke out the car could not be returned to Germany, it was hastily hidden by the firm's London representatives. Found later, in a cellar, it was sent to Frederick Royce at Derby, and the result of his analysis was the seventy-five-horsepower "Hawk" aero engine, superior to any other, British or German.

Though cars were the mainstay of his business, Royce devoted more and more time to aircraft engines. After the "Hawk" came the liquid cooled, twelve-cylinder, "Eagle". This in its earlier models developed 225 horsepower, then 360, and by the time two of them powered Alcock and Brown in their flight across the Atlantic, in 1919, the power had been boosted to 375 horsepower.

It became necessary to go back on the decision to stick to one car. In 1920 world conditions compelled the production of a smaller, cheaper model of 20 h.p. In 1925 came the "Phantom" rather larger again; then, in 1929, the "Phantom II" and in 1935, two years after Royce's death, his last design, the "Phantom III".

Royce made many painstaking improvements to his engines: for example he took his "Buzzard" engine, a bigger version of the "Eagle", increased its power by 21 per cent for a weight increase of only 6 per cent. Before his death that engine had won for Britain the Schneider Trophy Race and shortly afterwards a world record air speed of 383 m.p.h. This "R" engine was unequalled, went on to gain records on land and sea as well as in the air.

The British nation came to realize the debt it owed to Frederick Royce, and in 1930 he was made a baronet. For the last three years of his life his time was taken up with the development of the Merlin aircraft engine, which, as we have seen, won the Battle of Britain. His health was failing, he knew he could not live long, and he carefully handed over all his designs to colleagues, so that when he did die, on 12 April, 1933, the Merlin's development was able to go forward without any check.

Yet even after Royce's death the standards of design and workmanship for which he stood remained unchanged, thanks to the team he had built up and left behind him, under the redoubtable E. W. Hives, later Lord Hives. Emphasis then changed, and in the air, the piston engine gave pride of place to the jet. Totally different in design and principle to anything previous, it was snapped up by the firm, developed from Air Commodore Whittle's original into a range of jet engines finer than those of any rival. If ever the self-effacing Frederick Royce had needed any monument, this would be it: Rolls-Royce engines on passenger airliners, on bombers, on fighters, humming their way through the air, twenty-four hours a day, every day of the year.

But in 1971 disaster struck Rolls-Royce. Three years previously the firm had won an order to supply the American aircraft firm of Lockheed with engines for its giant Tri-Star airbus. It was the biggest order in the company's history, but because Rolls were determined to out-do their rivals, they committed themselves to producing an engine more than twice as big as anything they had made before, in half the time. By 1971 they found themselves unable to afford the vast expenses of development. On 22 January the company informed the Ministry of Aviation Supply that it would be unable to deliver the RB211 engines on time to the Lockheed Company.

After three months of hectic negotiation during which it often seemed the troubles of the RB211 engine would bankrupt both Rolls-Royce and Lockheed, a satisfactory arrangement was made, with financial help from both British and American governments. This ensured that Rolls-Royce would be able to deliver the engine and remain in business to keep up both supply and maintenance throughout its life. And by a separate arrangement, a new motor firm was formed as "Rolls-Royce Motors Ltd", to keep up the skilled, and highly profitable, work of making superlative cars.

David Lloyd George
1863-1945

IT was by-election day in a remote Welsh constituency. The Conservative squire was being challenged by a young Liberal solicitor whom he had known as a village lad. The contest was close, but the count went to the squire. "Demand a recount!" urged the Liberal agent. The recount gave the young lawyer a majority of eighteen. By that slender margin, David Lloyd George was launched into a political career.

Born twenty-seven years before this, on 17 January, 1863, he was by ancestry and upbringing a Welsh peasant, cultured and Nonconformist. His father, who died prematurely when David was seventeen months old, was a schoolmaster, coming from a line of small Pembrokeshire farmers. His mother's family in Caernarvonshire were leaders in Welsh literary culture. His uncle, Richard Lloyd, who adopted and brought up the orphaned family, was a bootmaker and unpaid pastor of the Campbellite Baptist church in Criccieth. Nonconformity, Welsh Nationalism and hostility to the Anglicized, game-preserving landowners, were in the air he breathed in his boyhood. His pugnacious temperament was channelled early into heading poaching enterprises in woodland and salmon river, and rebellion against teaching of the Church catechism in the local national school.

His mental brilliance marked him out for a professional career. The Church was of course barred. For Medicine the course was costlier than his uncle could well afford, and was in any case repugnant to him, for he recoiled from disease and his unskilful hands would have been useless for surgery. There remained the Law. Helped by his indomitable uncle, who himself took up the study of Latin and French to coach him, he passed his preliminary law examination and was articled to a firm of solicitors in Portmadoc. At the age of twenty-one he was admitted as a solicitor, and set up his own office in Criccieth.

His gifts as an orator soon made him a well-known figure. His activities sprang from his early background, the influence of which persisted through his life. A Welsh Nationalist, a champion of the small nation, of the poor peasant, the under-dog, the Nonconformist, he soon gained a reputation for successful defence of poachers and for defiant exchanges with the justices, for organizing the local Anti-Tithe League and for securing the election of Liberals to the County Council, newly set up in 1889, in which he was made an Alderman. He was a formidable fighter because, while a spell-binding orator, he was never a wind-bag. He always made sure of his facts and of the law. This habit of basing his efforts on knowledge, not wishful thinking, persisted all through his later career.

When the by-election sent him to Westminster in 1890, his chief interest was still mainly with the issues that had stirred his youth: Welsh Disestablishment, Welsh Home Rule, the overthrow of landlord dominance, temperance reform. Before long these drew him on to concern with allied problems: with the lot of the aged, the unemployed, the sick. These were eventually to produce his greatest achievements of statesmanship.

The South African War of 1899-1902 raised him to national notoriety. He was no pacifist, but his whole instinct was to rally to the defence of a small nation against a big one. He detested the slaughter and waste of what he held to be a needless conflict. Defying the leaders of the Liberal Party, he became the foremost spokesman of the opponents of the war, who were dubbed "Pro-Boers". He remained unmoved by the fact that he was opposed by the mass of the nation, lost most of his legal practice, narrowly held his seat in the 1900 Election, and barely escaped with his life when he held a meeting in Birmingham, where Joseph Chamberlain, the Colonial Secretary, was the local deity. By the time the war was over, he had become a figure whom none could ignore.

He opposed Balfour's Education Bill in 1902 because he held it to be unjust to Nonconformists. In Parliament his attack, though brilliant, was unsuccessful. In Wales it was devastating, for he taught the County Councils to apply the letter of the law in a way that defeated its operation. Then Chamberlain tried, in 1904, to revive the fading strength of the Tory Party by the policy of Tariff Reform. Lloyd George saw this as an attack on the poor man's loaf. He was no economist, but he amassed facts and statistics about British industry and trade with which to shatter the plea that it needed protection. Travelling up and down the country he became a most pungent and effective Free Trade orator.

The Conservatives were themselves deeply divided about Tariff Reform. At the end of 1905 the unstable Government resigned, and the election in 1906 swept the Liberals into power with an over-whelming majority. With their allies, the Labour and Irish Nation-alist members, they held 512 of the 670 seats. Their programme included Welsh Disestablishment, Irish Home Rule, Licensing Reform, Education and a wide range of social reforms. Lloyd George, an inevitable member of the Liberal Cabinet, was given the prosaic job of the Board of Trade.

It ceased to be prosaic. Essentially constructive, and with an unrivalled gift for conciliation, he summoned the numerous jangling interests concerned with the Port of London into conference, and worked the miracle of getting them to unite in a Port of London Authority which brought smooth working into that vital com-mercial area. He called together ship-owners and marine workers and, with their agreement, carried the Merchant Shipping Act, 1907, a sorely needed charter to protect the food, wages and medical care of seamen. With his passion for accurate information as a guide for statesmanship, he initiated the Census of Production. In the Cabinet he tirelessly pressed for immediate action on a big pro-gramme of social reforms such as school meals, workmen's com-pensation, the Children's Charter, factory inspection, and a scheme for Old Age Pensions—a measure in which he had long taken an active interest.

The Prime Minister, Campbell-Bannerman, died in 1908 and Asquith took his place. Lloyd George, the most vigorous figure in a Cabinet of distinguished men, was Asquith's obvious successor as Chancellor of the Exchequer. His first task was to carry the Old Age Pensions Act, so long advocated by him and already drafted by his predecessor. His Development and Road Improvement Funds Act set up the Development Commissioners to restore agriculture, and the Road Fund to renew and extend the country's roads, which the growing new motor traffic had reduced to channels of dust and mud.

The Liberal Government's major legislation for Education, Licensing Reform, Irish Home Rule, Welsh Disestablishment, though carried in the Commons, had meanwhile battered vainly against the stone wall of the Tory House of Lords. Lloyd George saw that the veto of these reactionary land-owners must be broken, and seized the tool lying ready to his hand in the constitutional authority of the Commons over taxation. Money was needed for Pensions and for further measures of social welfare he was planning, so in his 1909 Budget he set out to raise it by levying taxes on land values.

This, as he foresaw, loosed a tempest. The Tory peers, furious at such sacrilege, responded by the reckless and unconstitutional step of throwing out the Budget. Open war w˙s joined. Lloyd George stumped the country, castigating the peers with witty and wounding oratory. His attack on slum landlords at Limehouse even drew a pained protest from King Edward VII. The Liberal Government successfully appealed twice to the country in 1910. After the first Election, they passed the rejected Budget; after the second, the Parliament Act of 1911, which limited the veto powers of the House of Lords.

Lloyd George's Land Campaign was not only a political victory. It was a hardly realized social revolution, ending the lingering feudalism which had made land ownership the one qualification for social status and political authority.

In 1911 followed Lloyd George's greatest constructive feat of statesmanship: the National Insurance Act, providing sickness benefit, maternity benefit, unemployment relief, contributory pensions and funeral grants. So well was it framed that it has continued to be the basis of all further extensions, expanding to the fullness of today's Welfare State.

The outbreak of the First World War broke off the tedious march of Irish Home Rule and Welsh Disestablishment Bills back and forth between Lords and Commons under Parliament Act procedure. Although no pacifist, Lloyd George resented the waste and suffering and the interruption of domestic reform which joining in a European conflict would involve; but when the Germans invaded Belgium, his hesitations vanished. A small nation was being bullied, and we had to fight the bully. Into the task he threw his whole energy and fertility of resource. His prompt moratorium saved the City from financial panic, and won its adoring gratitude. Vainly he urged the adoption of an intelligent strategy that would attack the enemy's vulnerable flank. When news exploded of the shell shortage in our army, he gave up his important post as Chancellor to create a Ministry of Munitions through which to supply the troops, and disdaining War Office objections, poured forth guns, machine-guns and ammunition in an ever-swelling flood.

His Cabinet colleagues were gifted, cultured men, but apart from Winston Churchill, who was cast out in May, 1915, when a Coalition Government was formed, none was temperamentally a fighter. They could debate and criticize, but not decide and act. By the autumn of 1916, they were aimlessly drifting into national disaster. Lloyd George demanded a Cabinet reconstruction with himself in charge of a small executive responsible for directing the war effort. Asquith refused and resigned. Lloyd George formed a new Cabinet and took charge.

With the same kind of thrust and drive as he had exerted in the Ministry of Munitions, Lloyd George swiftly rallied the nation's resources to deal with its desperate situation. He compelled the reluctant Admiralty to adopt a convoy system to protect the shipping importing our vital supplies. He set up the Ministries of Shipping, Food, Pensions, Air, Labour and National Service. When in April, 1917, the United States, stung by Germany's ruthless submarine attacks, declared war on her, Lloyd George arranged for the transport of American troops to France and supplied them with heavy artillery. He persuaded the stubborn British generals and their Allies to accept unity of command under General Foch when, in the spring of 1918, the Allied front was near collapse. The tide of battle turned. By the autumn the enemy were suing for peace, and on 11 November the Armistice was signed and the war was over.

Everyone recognized to whom the credit for the victory was due, and her Allies joined with Britain in hailing Lloyd George as "The Man Who Won The War".

In the long-overdue election that followed, the Lloyd George candidates swept the country. Most of them were Conservatives. By displacing Asquith in 1916, Lloyd George had saved the country and the cause of world freedom, but at the cost of wrecking the Liberal Party. Split into bitterly acrimonious factions, it crumbled down and was replaced by Labour as the alternative to Toryism.

At the Peace Conference in Paris, Lloyd George together with Wilson of America, Clemenceau of France and Orlando of Italy set up a League of Nations to safeguard world peace. They redrew the map of Europe, giving national freedom to Poland, Czechoslovakia, Jugoslavia and the Baltic States. In the teeth of attacks from the Tory wing of his supporters and of pressure by France, Lloyd George refused to insert in the Peace Treaty some impossibly high figure for German Reparations, but left this open for later settlement. Historians now acknowledge that as finally framed, the Peace Treaty was a surprisingly generous one.

One war remained. Lloyd George returned from Paris to find a bitter guerilla struggle being waged in Ireland between the Irish Republican Army and the Crown forces. He put forth at full stretch all his powers of persuasion, cajolery and statecraft to secure a peace treaty with the leaders of Sinn Fein. Somehow he succeeded, and the page seemed at last to be turned on eight centuries of strife and tyranny, neglect and exploitation.

On the Home Front, Lloyd George's premiership saw great legislative and administrative reforms. Welsh Disestablishment was carried through; Women's Suffrage was passed; the Fisher Education Act extended secondary and higher education, and the Electricity Commission was created to develop and co-ordinate the nation's electrical supplies. The Ministries of Health and Transport were set up; the scope of Unemployment Insurance extended and an Unemployment (Relief Works) Act passed to provide remedies for post-war unemployment. A Forestry Commission was appointed. The Government of India Act laid the basis for the ultimate grant of independence to that vast sub-continent.

Many of the Tories among his Coalition supporters sullenly disapproved of all this radicalism. Revolt was triggered by the crisis in a war between Greece and Turkey, where, betrayed by his Allies, France and Italy, Lloyd George narrowly succeeded in checking the Turks from advancing into Thrace and massacring its inhabitants. A Carlton Club meeting, engineered by Baldwin and Beaverbrook (who had long been tirelessly intriguing for Lloyd George's overthrow) broke up the Coalition, and on 21 October, 1922, he resigned.

He never held office again. But his achievements during the fifteen years he had been a Minister of The Crown had changed the face of Britain, and his restless creative energy, often in the teeth of reluctance or opposition from his colleagues, had placed on the Statute Book and established in the Administration a body of reform measures unrivalled before or since in our history. Every aspect of our national life is in his debt: roads, ports, harbours, the merchant seamen, Air Force, electricity supply, housing, health, pensions, national insurance, medical, industrial and agricultural research, town planning, afforestation—the list is interminable. On a wider stage, his decisive personal triumph in the conduct of the First World War, his work of reshaping Europe in a fair peace settlement, and in bringing to a conclusion the age-old problem of Ireland, will set his name high in world history.

Though out of office, he continued tirelessly to devise, in consultation with a number of the best experts, schemes for the control of coal and power, of agriculture and housing, and the ending of national unemployment. His proposals for a broad programme of national development, in 1934, to provide work for the millions unemployed through the depression were rejected by the National Government (because of Ramsay Macdonald's jealousy and Neville Chamberlain's personal animosity), though they are now recognized to have been the right policy. In vain he urged a firm stand against

Mussolini and Hitler when they embarked on their campaigns of aggression.

The outbreak of the Second World War found him a spent force, though his scathing onslaught on Chamberlain in May, 1940, helped to force that disastrous Premier's resignation and Winston Churchill's rise to leadership. Wisely he refused further office, and retired to his Surrey orchards and thence to his home village of Llanystumdwy in Caernarvonshire. In January, 1945, the King created him Earl Lloyd-George of Dwyfor. On 26 March he passed away.

His grave beside the River Dwyfor at Llanystumdwy has become a place of pilgrimage. Uncrowned king of the Welsh, and at his zenith the world's most honoured figure, he has for his finest monument the British Welfare State which he spent himself to establish.

Henry Ford
1863-1947

THE name of Henry Ford raises two major controversies of our times—much exploited by school and university debating societies: Is the internal combustion engine a blessing or a curse? Does mass production make men slaves? Whatever the individual's answer to these questions, Ford is assured of a permanent place in any history of twentieth-century civilization as the first American to realize the potential of the petrol-driven engine and, perhaps even more important, to appreciate that the motor-car would become almost as important to mankind as feet.

As a result of his vision this brilliant engineer built up an industrial empire on which the sun never sets and, in doing so, posed questions of labour and road conditions which, in 1964, we are still struggling desperately to solve.

He was born in 1863, the year of Gettysburg, of farming stock in Greenfield Township, near Dearborn, on the Detroit River which winds through Michigan and divides the United States from Canada. On the day of his birth, 30 July, the fate of the Civil War was still in the balance and the stage was set for the March through Georgia. The telephone, the typewriter, the electric dynamo and, of course, the motor-car were still unknown.

When he was nearly eight Henry went to school in the Scotch Settlement and sat next to a boy named Edsel Ruddiman. He named his first-born Edsel after him. He showed an early facility for repairing clocks and watches but at home on the farm he had to take his share of the inevitable chores, chopping wood, milking cows, learning to harness a team of horses. When he was twelve he was ploughing and doing a man-sized job on the farm. He had no education in science—he got his considerable mechanical knowledge from experience. Engines fascinated him and, after experimenting in a boyish way with water-wheels and boilers, he came upon a traction engine chugging along a road near Detroit. That old tractor was destined to change the course of industrial history. While the driver and his mate were resting by the side of the road, young Henry studied the mechanism—it was his first sight of a self-propelled vehicle apart from a railway locomotive. The power unit of the tractor's steam engine was connected to the rear wheels by a chain and there was a belt to transmit the power to a sawmill.

He asked the driver how fast his engine could run and was told: "Two hundred turns a minute." That reply, Ford was to say much later, put him into the motor-car business.

His mother, who was originally Dutch, died when Henry was thirteen and three years later he decided to leave the farm and seek work in Detroit. The future multi-millionaire's first steady job was repairing watches for a few dollars a week. During this period he read in a magazine, *World of Science*, that a German, Dr Nicolaus Otto, had invented an internal combustion engine, which had just been patented for manufacture in the United States. The description of this invention so excited him that he joined the Dry Dock Engine Company at lower pay to learn every aspect of the machinist's trade.

Now nineteen, he began to join in the social life of his village, Greenfield, and met a farmer's daughter, Clara Bryant, three years younger than himself. Ford was later quoted as saying that half an hour after he met her, he knew she was the one for him. When in April, 1888, they were married, Henry's father gave him a lot of forty acres on which the young couple built a storey-and-a-half house, with a lean-to for Henry's tools. There he experimented with a farm locomotive and a steam road carriage. This decided him that steam was not the best propellant force for a passenger road vehicle. One day in Detroit he saw an engine for filling lemonade bottles which had been made on the principle of Otto's gas internal combustion engine. "I've been on the wrong track," he told his wife later. "What I'm after is to make an engine that will run by petrol and get it to do the work of a horse."

To do that meant leaving their comfortable home in the country for the chancy life of Detroit, but the couple didn't hesitate—on 25 September, 1891, their hay waggon rolled east, with Henry bound for a job as a steam engineer with the Edison Company of Detroit. In 1893, when he was aged thirty, he visited the World Fair in Chicago and there he studied the exhibit of a small petrol engine to be used for pumping water. He went home and resumed work on his plans to apply a petrol engine to "a horseless carriage".

Within the year he became chief engineer at the Edison plant at a salary of 100 dollars a month and the Fords took a larger house at 58 Bagley Avenue, Detroit, to live nearer his work. At the back of this house was a brick shed for storing fuel, half for the Fords and the other half for their next-door neighbours.

On his side Ford set up his tools and got down to his work on the petrol engine. A length of one-inch gas pipe served him as a cylinder and in it he fitted a piston with rings. This he attached to a crankshaft by a rod and a hand-wheel from an old lathe served as the fly-wheel. A gearing arrangement operated a cam, opening the exhaust valve and timing the spark with a piece of fibre wired through the centre to do duty as a plug. Contact was made with another wire at the end of the piston and when this contact was broken, a spark leaped across, exploding the petrol. He completed this engine within a week, tested it in his kitchen, made sure it would work, then at once got down to the business of making a two-cylinder outfit.

For the next two years he laboured to apply his two-cylinder engine to propel a bicycle, using the drive wheel of the bicycle as a fly-wheel. He could not get it to work as it always proved too powerful for the wheels. At length he abandoned that idea in favour of a more ambitious one—to make his engine drive a four-wheel carriage. He had taken his first step into the automobile business. The world's No. 1 Ford car was built in the little brick shed at the back of his house in Bagley Avenue.

As it began to take shape his next-door neighbour, Mr Felix Julien, decently gave up his half of the shed and would sit there for hours watching "The Thing" emerge. Parts were made from scrap metal, machined on the lathe and worked on with the tools. The cylinders were bored and fitted in sections of a steam engine's exhaust pipe, the crankshaft was forged at the Dry Docks Works where Ford had once had a job, and a friend produced two intake valves. Ford used four 28-in. bicycle wheels and attached a tiller to the front wheels for steering. The seat was a bicycle saddle. He arranged two belts to offer a choice of speed—10 or 20 m.p.h. There was no reverse—and no brakes.

This veritable "Tin Lizzie", as the later mass-produced Fords came to be called, had its first trial in May, 1896—and its maker overlooked the fact that it was too wide to get it out of his doorway. He just couldn't wait to test it on a road, so he grabbed an axe and smashed down the back wall. After a minor mishap, he drove it once round the block—and the first Ford had made its bow in the city that is now the motor-car capital of the world.

Henry Ford carried on with his job at the Edison plant while he set about designing and building his second car, but the time inevitably came when he was confronted with the choice by his bosses: "You can work on your car or you can work for us—but not both." Meanwhile several prominent Detroit businessmen discussed a project to manufacture Ford's cars and eventually they formed a company offering him a 10,000-dollar advance, enough to pay for the building of ten cars. Their condition was that he resign his job at Edison's and become chief engineer for the new company, using his design for the cars. By August, 1899, he was out of Edison's and launched on his new career. He was determined that the first car to bear his name and hall-mark would be as near perfect as he could make it and he insisted on improving the carburation system. The ten thousand dollars melted away and his backers began to show their impatience. After 86,000 dollars had been spent they decided to part—and the company's name was changed to "Cadillac Automobile Company".

Ford determined to establish himself so completely with the public that he would find other backers who would set up a company more in accord with his ideas. So he built a racing car and entered it against the most daring driver of the day, Alexander Winton. At the Grosse Pointe Blue Ribbon Track in Detroit, he won an event styled "the first big race in the west" over Winton by almost a mile. Now track champion of the U.S., he had no trouble in finding backers to launch, on 23 November, 1901, the Henry Ford Company with 6,000 shares at a par value of ten dollars each.

By this time there were many others manufacturing high-priced vehicles. Again Ford suffered from production delays, again there was friction with the stockholders and again they and Ford parted. Before he made his third try, he wisely consulted Detroit's successful businessmen and from them learned the know-how of running a sound and prosperous company.

Back he went to the drawing-board to design two powerful racing cars. One called "The Arrow" was wrecked in a race, the other named the "999" after a famous train of that day became the greatest racing car up till then. Its first big win persuaded a Scots coal dealer in Detroit, Alexander Malcolmson, to put his money down on Henry Ford's future. He it was who persuaded an important Detroit figure, Albert Strelow, to provide a factory for Ford and subscribe 5,000 dollars cash for a new venture.

Malcolmson launched with enthusiasm into the task of finding investors for Ford's third—and final—try. Eventually in June, 1903, there were twelve stockholders who between them had raised 28,000 dollars in cash to float the company which is to this day one of the wonders of the world. One of them, James Couzens, who was to be secretary and business manager of the new concern, borrowed 100 dollars from his sister, Miss Rosetta V. Couzens, who was later entered on the books as a stockholder with one share. That 100-dollar loan was eventually to bring her 355,000 dollars.

The infant company struck a snag at the outset. Because of a petrol engine patent granted in 1895 to George Selden, of Rochester, all car manufacturers were required to pay royalties to the lessee of the patent—and there were already a score of tough competitors in the field. To protect themselves these manufacturers had formed an association and had arranged with the lessee of the patent, the Electric Vehicle Company, of Connecticut, to control the industry. Ford refused to knuckle under and was threatened with prosecution hardly a month after he had started in business. His answer was to challenge the validity of the patent. By the time the court's decision upholding the Selden patent was handed down, it was 1910, Ford's profits had topped the million-dollar mark for the first time and his company had put the Model T—perhaps the most remarkable motor-car in the history of the industry—on the popular market.

The verdict could well have put Ford out of business. Instead, absolutely convinced that he was in the right, he immediately appealed to a higher court. The association warned him that it would be "war to the death" if he did not join. His reply:

> "It is said that everyone has his price, but I can assure you that, while I am head of the Ford Motor Company there will be no price that would induce me to add my name to the association."

For nearly two years he had been spending around 2,000 dollars a week defending himself against these manufacturers. Now he was served with an injunction ordering him to stop infringing the patent and his dealers were warned not to offer his "unlicensed cars" for sale. Ford went right ahead building Model Ts. Then the U.S. Court of Appeals gave out its verdict completely upholding all Henry Ford's contentions with regard to the patent. It was an outright victory and even his rivals tumbled over one another to congratulate him on his unyielding fight.

The stage was set for the great leap forward—and it came. Look at the figures of production: 1909—10,600 cars; 1910—18,660; 1911—34,520; 1912—78,440; 1913—168,220; 1914—248,300. Profits soared from 3,000,000 dollars in 1909 to 25,000,000 dollars in 1914. Fantastic as these bounding figures seem, by 1925 Ford was producing 10,000 cars every 24 hours. And, by 1927, when he abandoned the Model T, he had made 15,000,000 of them.

In 1914 Ford exploded a twin sensation—he doubled wages and cut hours to eight a day. It was the beginning of a profit-sharing policy which, the following year, he even extended to all buyers of new Fords, and the apparently unlimited expansion of his organization was halted only by the First World War.

Henry Ford opposed America's entry and he even financed a Peace Ship to carry delegates to a conference of neutrals for "continuous mediation" in the hope of bringing the war to an end. This exercise in practical idealism cost him 400,000 dollars and was the subject of scoffing and ridicule all over the U.S.A. He turned to promoting welfare schemes for his employees, including the Henry Ford Trade School for boys who would otherwise have had no chance of a high-school education.

By the time he could be convinced that motorists were ready for variety and comfort, he had lost the leadership of the industry to General Motors. In 1927 he shut down his vast plant to retool for the Model A and again in 1932 to produce the V-8.

As in the First World War—which he opposed as a pacifist—so in the Second World War—which he also opposed until Pearl Harbour was attacked—he turned over his vast production resources to his country. In the First World War his contribution was in the form of Eagle boats and Liberty motor-cars; in 1941 he laid out a huge bomber factory at Willow Run which eventually produced one complete Liberator bomber every hour and by March, 1945, had achieved the fantastic total of 8,000 of these four-engined warplanes. In the midst of this gigantic war effort his only son, Edsel, died, in the spring of 1943—25 years after his father had handed over to him the presidency of the world's greatest one-man industrial organization. Although his eightieth birthday was only two months off, Henry Ford announced that he himself would take over the presidency again.

When his own time at last came—at Dearborn on 7 April, 1947, in his eighty-fourth year—Ford left his mighty empire intact. He left, too, the largest trust fund in the world, now known as the Ford Foundation, which is dedicated to the welfare of all mankind.

It is not difficult to summarize his industrial philosophy, which was to cut the price of the product, step up the volume of sales, improve the production efficiency and increase output to sell at still lower prices—and so *ad infinitum*.

It is much more difficult to summarize his controversial genius— so outstandingly brilliant in the mechanics of his age and so woefully naïve in national, international—and trade union—politics. Perhaps it is kinder to give him an uncomplicated seven-word epitaph: The Man Who Thought With His Hands.

Edith Cavell
1865-1915

IT was Tuesday the twelfth of October and dawn was rising. It was cooler than in England at this time of year, but in many ways the two towns, Brussels and London, were similar. There was the same greyness, the same smell of smoke, the same October tang. But there was a difference. Brussels was a town under occupation, a repressed, silent, grieving town, full of hated Germans. Two long black cars with spike-helmeted guards inside caused hardly a stir. The cars drove across Brussels to the rifle range, the Tir National, in the suburb of Schaerbeek, and there each vehicle unloaded its prisoner and escort. One was a thirty-five-year-old Belgian architect, Philippe Baucq; the other a forty-nine-year-old English hospital nurse, Edith Cavell.

The two were led away through the administrative building of the Tir National to the range, and there, with the dawn mounting fast, they were blindfolded and made fast with leather arm and leg straps to two posts. Just before she was blindfolded, the English-woman bent down and produced the three large pins she had requested from the Commandant. Carefully, she pinned the long skirt tight around her ankles. She would be modest, even in death.

Five yards apart the two died simultaneously at the crack of the rifles of the firing squads.

Edith Louisa Cavell had been born forty-nine years before, on 4 December, 1865, in the village of Swardeston in Norfolk, the daughter of its vicar, the Reverend Frederick Cavell. It was a prosperous village in a peaceful, prosperous era: the Crimean War was over, and so was the one in America; good Queen Victoria was steering Britain through an unprecedented prosperity—at least, for many of its inhabitants—and the Empire was a major power in the world. The vicar, a modest man, had restricted most of his large family to a few years' private tuition with himself, but Edith, who seemed to show more promise, more diligence than the rest, was sent to a good school, and she repaid her parents' effort. She did brilliantly in all her subjects, including French though she was never, throughout her life, able to master its accent. She loved the language, and when she left Laurel Court School in Peterborough, she was thrilled to be accepted as governess to the children of a lawyer in Brussels. Here, at last, was a chance to see some of the world, escape from village life, speak languages.

She arrived in Belgium breathless with excitement and found at once that it was all she had hoped for. The François family for whom she was to work were delightful; the gay, cosmopolitan life of Brussels was both a challenge and a delight. To the children of the grateful family François she gave an affection and imparted a learning which, in nineteenth-century Brussels, could not be bought. She taught them—and they remembered and spoke in hushed voices of it later—her "veritable horror of lying", her refusal to tell an untruth, whatever the temptation.

After a few years with the family she returned home in 1895 to take care of her ailing father. Her mother was still living, but frail, and Edith took complete charge. Her touch seemed to work wonders: within a few months the old man had quite recovered and she was able to leave. She decided to give up teaching children and take up the profession she now knew she loved. Though already thirty, she joined the London Hospital in Whitechapel Road as a student nurse, a "probationer", where she did well, qualified and was almost immediately put in charge of the nurses dealing with a typhoid epidemic in Maidstone. From this she progressed and became, very quickly, a matron at a London hospital. Somehow, the qualities of this quiet, determined, little mouse-haired woman were apparent to everyone who met her. As one of her colleagues put it: "Next to Miss Cavell, other women seem so weak, so thin . . ."

The ties Edith had established as a governess brought her back, in 1907, to Brussels. She was a woman of forty-two, an experienced nurse. The Belgian surgeon, Antoine Depage, had invited her to join his clinic at 149 Rue de la Culture. He had been shocked by the shortage in his country of good nurses—or even bad ones—he had heard of Edith Cavell, he believed English nurses were the best in the world, and invited her to join him in training others.

Within hours of her arrival she was established in the "Clinique", training the young nurses and at the same time caring for their patients. Her fame spread and soon she gathered around her a staff of graduate nurses from England, Holland, France, Switzerland and Germany to help train the younger ones. Later, she was ready to admit that without their devoted help she would never have been able to train so many giggling, semi-educated juveniles. Many were only seventeen, with an annual pay of less than ten pounds, but the new Matron of the Clinique inspired them with a love of their work and they stayed; while more flocked to join. One thing which did much to win their affection was her insistence on the girls' social status: if a nurse did private work in a household, as many did, she was to be treated as a member of it, must sit with the family for meals, not be relegated to the sickroom and the kitchen. In the Clinique itself, even the youngest nurse was to be treated with respect by doctors and patients. At the same time she insisted that a nurse see a case through, however disagreeable or unreasonable the patient.

Although the pupils and staff admired and trusted her, many of the younger ones found her solemn and difficult to know. She thought of nothing but her work, of the standard of nursing and teaching at her Clinique, how it could be improved. She worked herself, and her staff, hard and then, in the evening when lectures were over, she would do a final round of all the patients before sitting down at her out-of-tune upright piano to play softly to herself. It was her only relaxation.

By 1914 she was, in addition to her teaching, doing a great deal of practical nursing. She was much in demand as Surgeon's Assistant in the Brussels hospitals and indeed on more than one occasion she was asked to become a specialist in this branch of nursing, but she refused to specialize, maintaining that nursing must embrace all illness, that no nurse should pour all her talent, her compassion, her skill, into just one aspect of it, and to this end she cared for, and made her nurses care for, every case, from drug-addiction to maternity. There was so much in the work she had raised to the dignity of a profession, one must participate in it as much as one's strength would allow.

In July she went back—a tired prematurely old woman of forty-eight—to pay what turned out to be a final visit to her family in England. Three weeks later England was at war with Germany. As a citizen of England, Edith Cavell might well have stayed at home, nursing in an English hospital or—if she wished—with one in the field, where her rights as a non-combatant under the Geneva Convention would be recognized. However, without hesitation she decided to return to her work in Brussels: her nurses needed her, there was no question of deserting them. Those nurses were delighted and relieved to see her. One of her first duties was to escort a party of the German girls who had been working with her to the railway station. She was sad to see them go, sorry for them, innocent girls caught suddenly in an alien city where they were hated, feared and despised. They bade each other farewell, promised to meet "when this fearful thing is over".

On 12 August, a week after war had been declared, she wrote to *The Times* offering the services of her hospital for wounded British soldiers and begging subscriptions from the British public to make it capable of looking after more of them. Money poured in from all over the world, and the staff worked round the clock to expand the hospital's facilities. No sooner was the hospital ready for use on a large scale than Brussels fell to the Germans—and that within a month of the war's outbreak. Edith Cavell and the other English nurses were offered safe conduct to Holland. She refused, as did most of the others: their work was for humanity, whether it be Belgian, British, French or German, and they would stay where they were. By mid-September the staff was nursing Germans.

War rushed on; Brussels became a rear area. The Kaiser had planned to complete his conquest by winter, he was keeping to his timetable, the gunfire was fading away into the west.

Then suddenly at the Marne the advance was stopped. The generals had miscalculated. The German Army withdrew a few miles and the war settled down into a muddy, bloody, stalemate. Casualties mounted, new crosses sprang up in old cemeteries: English crosses, French ones, German ones, each with its own inscription—each marking its own personal tragedy. The Germans, thwarted in their master plan, resorted to atrocity. The university town of Louvain, twenty miles from Brussels, was burned and its inhabitants shot. The world was appalled, and none more than Edith Cavell. "I can only ask myself," she wrote in a letter, "why, oh why, should these innocent people be made to suffer . . ." When warned that she was being imprudent, she answered: "In times like these, when terror makes might seem right, there is a higher duty than prudence."

There were no longer any wounded to look after: the Germans were being sent back to their own country, the Allies never came, and the hospital's patients were almost entirely Belgian civilians. A rule laid down by the German Military Governor stated that all male patients over eighteen years of age would report on discharge from hospital to the Military Police. This would mean internment or forced labour. Edith Cavell resolved to thwart the order and she hit upon the idea of ordering each discharged patient to "go to the Military Police, if you can find them, or to the house of Madame X". She could thus, in her weekly reports, say truthfully that she

Above: Carved from a mooring pile of Cookham Lock in the River Thames by David Weeks, this statue of Robert Falcon Scott was unveiled at the Church of St Mark's, Ford, Plymouth, in 1958.

Below: "Patriotism is not enough, I must have no hatred or bitterness for anyone" are the words at the foot of the statue to Edith Cavell in London.

A still from the film *The War of the Worlds*, based on the book of that title written by Herbert George Wells in 1896. Even before the nineteenth century was out, Wells had brilliantly evoked in a range of scientific and futuristic fantasies the new worlds (and challenges) which mankind was opening up for himself through his scientific knowledge.

had ordered her patients to the Military Police Headquarters—though it was surprising how many of them seemed to lose their way.

Meanwhile, on the French border near Mons, the Belgian Princess de Croÿ had converted her chateau to a hospital. At first, most of its patients were German soldiers; then, as the war stabilized eastward along the Marne, they were French and English. With the aid of a young schoolteacher, Louise Thuliez, she worked out a scheme to smuggle some of these Allied soldiers right across the country into Holland, whence they could make their way to England. It was dangerous work, carrying a heavy penalty, and they soon found they needed a staging point. The Princess decided to approach Nurse Cavell. If she, in Brussels, could help by harbouring the men for a few days, they could be led from Brussels in parties of four or five towards Turnhout on the Dutch border, with a good chance of being able to cross at that point. Without hesitation, Edith Cavell agreed—though at first a few of her nurses were shocked that she should so wantonly involve them in what had become a capital offence.

The scheme worked well, the men spent a day or two, sometimes weeks, in the hospital before being led away, often by Edith herself, to one of several rendezvous in the town where guides would take them on to Turnhout. By May of the following year Edith Cavell was "certain"—a tragic certainty that was not justified—that the Germans knew Allied soldiers were being sheltered in her hospital: However, she made up her mind to do the job, and she would stick to it, relying on her own ability to hide the men if the Germans came. As if to warn her, they set up a Secret Police Headquarters in Brussels and boasted of having in their pay a total of six thousand spies, spies who were everywhere, in every public place and in most private ones, in every firm, every factory, every hospital. The Germans had in fact begun to wonder what was going on at 149 rue de la Culture, but as yet they had nothing on which to nourish their suspicion.

On 5 August, 1915, Edith Cavell was, as she had anticipated, arrested, together with her assistant, Sister Wilkins. A foolish letter of thanks from a returned soldier in England had been found in the hospital during a police search.

"You may as well admit it," said the officer in charge of the Secret Police. "Two of the men you tried to smuggle have given us a complete report . . ." The women were questioned separately and Sister Wilkins, who denied everything, was—to her amazement—

released. Edith Cavell, perhaps because she made so little attempt to deny her guilt, was held.

Meanwhile, throughout Belgium, Secret Police completed their arrests, on the basis of reports from spies they had planted among escaping Allied soldiers and also, it must be admitted, from information given by Edith Cavell herself in her astonishing confession. For, believing the others had told everything, she made a complete admission, almost an abject admission of her part in the affair. She ended by adding:

> "My statements, which have just been read over to me, translated into French, conform to the truth at every point. They are perfectly intelligible to me in every detail and I will repeat them before the tribunal. Signed and Witnessed, Edith Cavell."

It was a confession of proud resignation, rather than despair, but as her appointed lawyer remarked when the Court-Martial was over, "she rendered her defence impossible".

The final list of prisoners, arranged for a mass trial, included, with Edith Cavell, the Princess de Croÿ and Louise Thuliez, together with a young Belgian architect, Philippe Baucq, who was accused not only of the general charge of conveying soldiers to the enemy, but of "circulating seditious pamphlets". The list totalled thirty-five names.

The trial took place on 7 October, and a day or two later, when the verdict was known, the American Minister in Brussels wrote his Ambassador in London,

> "... the German prosecutor has asked for sentence of death against her and eight other persons implicated by her testimony—I have some hope that the Court may decline to pass the rigorous sentence ..."

He was wrong. Eight of the thirty-five were acquitted, twenty-five received long prison sentences and Philippe Baucq and Edith Cavell were sentenced to be shot.

Despite pleas from the American Minister and from many others (though few people could believe the sentence when they learnt of it—surely no enemy, however cruel, could shoot a woman, a nurse, and one not even accused of spying, only of helping soldiers to get home?) yet as we have seen, the sentence was carried out in the early morning of 12 October. Just before she requested the large pins to hold her skirt, Edith Cavell paused in the long corridor of the Tir National, the rifle range on which she was about to die, to make a last entry in the margin of her Prayer Book. "Died at 7 a.m. on 12 October, 1915. With love to my mother, E. Cavell."

Edith Cavell's martyrdom, though to many it seemed unnecessary —*why* did she confess so completely?—had one unexpected but all-important result. As the American author Owen Wister put it, referring to the possibility that America might never have entered the war: "That possibility was killed for ever when Edith Cavell died for England". American public opinion was appalled and enraged and although President Wilson did much to delay the plunge, the country came into war on the side of the Allies. By doing so, it made victory certain.

Arguments have raged as to why this brave woman, who showed not a flicker of concern at her death sentence, nor at its execution, should have made her abject confession. Perhaps Jacqueline Van Til, one of her nurses, was right when she said later:

> "How better could Edith Cavell summon attention to the terrible conditions in nursing? How could she better serve and dramatize the needs and difficulties than by her own execution? In death her goal would be achieved—the service of humanity, through the service of nursing."

Alfred Harmsworth
1865-1922

THE small boy was entranced. He watched the printers picking up
the tiny pieces of type with forefinger and thumb and putting them
in a strange contrivance that they told him was called a setting-stick.
He gazed open-eyed and open-mouthed as they transferred the lines
of type to a sort of frame, and wondered why the words looked as
though they were the wrong way round. Then he moved across to
where rollers were being covered with the thickest and blackest of
ink. Handles were pulled, cranks rattled, wheels turned, the rollers
gobbled up the white sheets and—extraordinary thing, this!—the
sheets emerged with printing on them, words that you could read!

He liked the noise, the clatter and banging, the rough humour of
the men. He must have liked the smell too—the smell of printer's
ink. He never got that smell out of his nostrils. In course of time it
became as the breath of life to him.

So obviously thrilled was he by what he heard and saw in that
small newspaper printing-works that the kindly proprietor gave him
a toy printing-set for his birthday, his eighth. "And that," confessed
nearly fifty years later the man who had been that small boy, "that
was how I came to know printers and their ways."

A few years later that same small boy was a pupil at a private
school in St John's Wood, in the north-west of London. It was not a
very good school, and he did not learn very much there. He always
did badly in his arithmetic exams, but he excelled in spelling and
English composition. He was also a great reader; he knew his
Dickens and Daniel Defoe and was making a start on Thackeray.
For these reasons the headmaster gladly agreed when the boy asked
him if he might start a school magazine. The first number appeared
in March, 1881; the *Henley House School Magazine* it was called, and
underneath the name were the words: Edited by Alfred C. Harmsworth.

That was the boy's name. The C stood for Charles and he was
also christened William, but he was always known as Alfred
Harmsworth. Always, that is, until he won his place in the history
books as Lord Northcliffe. He was born on 15 July, 1865, at

Chapelizod, Dublin, where his father was a teacher on the staff of the Royal Hibernian Military Academy. This was the only Irish thing about him, however, for he came of country folk in Hampshire. Alfred's mother was Geraldine Maffett, and came of a family of Scottish descent settled in Ireland who were much better off than the Harmsworths. She was a remarkable woman, a *materfamilias* in the best and truest sense of that old Latin term. She was twenty-six when she married Alfred Harmsworth, senior, in 1864, and he was a year older; before she was forty-eight she had borne fourteen children, of whom eleven survived. Alfred was the eldest, and throughout his life he was absolutely devoted to her. Years after Northcliffe had fought his way to the top in Fleet Street, when his name had become almost a synonym for ruthless determination in the struggle for wealth and power, J. L. Garvin, one of his most famous editors, said that Northcliffe's devotion to his mother was "exquisite, the most beautiful thing . . . a better son never lived".

Mrs Harmsworth certainly had need of all the courage and resolution that she could muster. Realizing that he would never be a success as a schoolmaster, she pushed and prodded her husband into becoming a barrister. They moved to London, and at length Mr Harmsworth duly qualified and practised in the courts. He was an excellent speaker and won many friends, but he was too fond of the bottle. All through their married life Mrs Harmsworth had to fight a constant battle with genteel poverty, that form of poverty that is perhaps the worst to bear. The Harmsworth children knew what it was to go short, not only of luxuries but of the necessities of life.

One story of those days of desperate striving to keep up appearances on a meagre income, or sometimes no income at all, has come down to us because it provided the basis for a famous joke in *Punch*. Alfred and Harold, his next younger brother (the future Lord Rothermere) had gone to tea at a neighbour's, and Harold was silent at table. Whereupon Alfred suddenly spoke up. "I know what he's thinking about," he said; "he's thinking about cake—he's always thinking about cake." The remark came to the ears of George du Maurier, a contributor to *Punch* who lived near by, and he used it beneath one of his drawings.

Since money was so short in the Harmsworth household, "Sunny" Harmsworth, as Alfred was called on account of his generally cheerful disposition, did not go to school until he was eight, and then only to a small establishment next door. When he was eleven his father somehow managed to get him into Stamford Grammar School, and he was there for two years—years which he declared afterwards were the unhappiest he had ever spent. The headmaster was a brute, who "picked on" him at every opportunity and thrashed him on the average three times a week.

Then he went to Henley House, where if he was a hopeless duffer at doing sums he made his mark as an "editor". He haunted the small printing-works where the school magazine was printed, and made himself a thorough nuisance with his innumerable questions and suggestions. But the proprietor of the works, George Jealous, was so impressed by the sixteen-year-old boy's eagerness and ability that he gave him reporting jobs to do in his holidays on the local newspaper that he also owned.

The lad's father was not at all impressed. He gave Alfred not the least encouragement in his ambition to become a journalist, and when the boy left school a few months later he had to seek his own openings. He started writing short articles for newspapers and periodicals, and although he got plenty of rejection slips he never lost heart. By the time he was eighteen he was making £3 a week by his pen, and for a time he was editor of a paper called *Youth* at a salary of £2 a week.

He moved to Coventry where he got a job with the firm of Iliffe as editor of *Bicycling News*, a job for which he was well suited since he had owned a half-share in a bicycle as a schoolboy and was a keen cyclist. The paper was in low water when he took it over, but it soon responded to what came to be known as the Harmsworth touch. Cycling was still a novelty, and women cyclists were considered a bad joke: sometimes lady cyclists were stoned by people who thought they were acting in a most unladylike manner. Alfred was convinced that women on bicycles had come to stay, and moreover, that cycling would play a great part in the emancipation of their sex from the trammels of Victorian decorum. In this he was a pioneer, just as years later he was the pioneer in the encouragement of the motor-car and then of the aeroplane.

"The yellow-headed worm" as some of his colleagues styled him when he had slashed their "copy" with his editorial blue pencil, was not content with the editorship of a small trade paper in the Iliffe "stable". He had big ideas, and among them was the launching of an entirely new paper of his own. He suggested that it should be called *Answers to Correspondents*, and he was not in the least deterred by the scornful comments of those who were jealous of him as a young man in too much of a hurry. "What an absurd title!" they scoffed, but he was convinced that it was a most excellent one. After all, people were curious—he was judging them by himself—they wanted to know about all the tremendously interesting, important, exciting things that were going on around them.

"Somehow I knew from the first just what people wanted to read," he said some years later, when he had proved beyond any doubt that he was right. Since the passing of the first great Education Act in 1870 a vast new reading public had grown up, people who had learned to read if not to think. They wanted information, but it must be presented in an interesting way, a way which they could understand. Young Harmsworth was convinced that most newspapers and periodicals of the time took far too much for granted. They appealed to the educated—and the great majority of men and women were uneducated, or at best had received only such a smattering as he himself had been given. In his own writing he worked out a series of rules, which he insisted should be followed by his contributors and later his editors. Simple language, no showing off in the shape of foreign quotations; short sentences and short paragraphs, and each paragraph should contain at least one *interesting* fact.

Not that he was the first to make these discoveries. As early as 1881 George Newnes had started *Tit Bits* and was making a great success of it. Harmsworth thought he could produce something even better, something that would be not just a collection of interesting little articles but a carefully-thought-out presentation of all the subjects on which ordinary people wanted to be informed, with the answers prepared by experts under the guidance and supervision of the most experienced journalists such as himself. The Iliffes were impressed, but thought the proposition too risky. Whereupon Harmsworth, now twenty-two, resigned from their employ and set off to London with the full and firm determination to have his own publishing company, his own publications, and above all, his own way.

Capital was the first requisite. He had none. Fortunately, however, a friend of his mother's was about to marry a man with £1,500 to invest. This sum was borrowed to launch the first of the many companies with which Harmsworth was to be associated—and, it should be said, most profitably, for others as well as for himself. The plans for the publication of *Answers to Correspondents* were pushed on with as fast as possible, and on the strength of future prospects Harmsworth got married. The bride was Mary Milner, the eldest daughter of a city merchant in by no means prosperous circumstances, and the wedding was in April, 1888. Mr Jealous's newspaper reported the event, but the reporter missed what was surely worthy of note: the bridegroom and his best man each had a dummy copy of *Answers to Correspondents* sticking out of their jacket pocket.

Less than two months later the first issue of the new weekly appeared; 60,000 copies were said to have been printed, and only 12,000 copies were sold. The circulation dropped to 8,000, and then rose slowly to 30,000 a week. This was nothing like good enough: a boost was demanded, and Alfred and his brother Harold promptly supplied it. They were walking along the Thames Embankment one evening when an obviously down-and-out man begged the price of a meal. They chatted with him, as was their way with any chance encounter; he asked them what they did for a living, and one of them mentioned something about prize competitions. "There's only one prize *I* want," rejoined the man, "a pound a week for life."

To Alfred that remark was an inspiration. Very shortly *Answers* (the rest of the title had been soon dropped) was offering to its readers the chance of winning a pound a week for life: all you had to do was to guess correctly the exact amount of gold coinage in the Banking Department of the Bank of England at close of business on 4 December, 1889. Replies on a postcard please: each entry to be accompanied by the names and addresses of five witnesses. The "greatest ever" competition was an unqualified success; 718,218 postcards were received, and the prize was won by a military sapper at Southampton, whose guess was within £2 of the correct figure. He lived to receive his £1 a week only for eight years, when he died of consumption; Alfred sent his widow a cheque for £50 in final settlement.

The result of the competition was announced in the Christmas number of *Answers*, 1889, and 205,000 copies of the issue were sold. For the possible expenditure of £1,100, Harmsworth noted with glee, "I managed to excite the interest of nearly five millions of people."

This was the beginning of an almost uninterrupted success story. For years new publications streamed from the Harmsworth Press as it was called. *Comic Cuts*—"100 laughs for ½d."—was the first of a long list of "juveniles" which at least showed a considerable advance on the "penny dreadfuls" of the age; *Sunday Companion* appealed to the religious public who were interested in Evangelicalism and not in denominational differences; *Home Chat* answered the needs of a great new army of women readers whose existence had passed unnoticed until the Harmsworths realized the potential market waiting to be explored; in its wake came dozens of weeklies and monthlies which carried their generally good advice on the problems of motherhood and the home and women's interests into practically every home in the land. *The Children's Newspaper*, edited by Arthur Mee, set a fresh and high standard in periodicals for the younger generation, and *Harmsworth's Self Educator* and the *Harmsworth Encyclopaedia* went a very long way to answering the needs of hosts of information-hungry but indifferently educated young men and women of the class to which Harmsworth himself belonged. All these publications and many more were brought under the umbrella of the Amalgamated Press Ltd., in whose fine new building, Fleetway House in Farringdon Street, "The Chief" had his room.

When *Answers* was launched in 1888 Harmsworth would have been hard put to it to produce a hundred pounds out of his own pocket. Only a couple of years later he was able to buy a substantial house at St Peter's, between Broadstairs and Margate, for some £4,000, and at the same time to buy his mother a house in London and provide her with a carriage-and-pair. By the time he was in his early forties his income was estimated at £200,000 a year. He died a millionaire, but he was no money-grubber, and showed no pride in his wealth: it was not money he valued, but the power that money could give. After he became Lord Northcliffe, in 1905, it was to the acquisition of power to be used in the ways which he thought were to the advantage of Britain and her Empire that his efforts were mainly directed. By this time he was a Press Lord, the greatest of them indeed, for in 1896 he had launched the *Daily Mail*, the first London newspaper to be sold for $\frac{1}{2}d$. but to give as much for $\frac{1}{2}d$. as other newspapers provided for $1d$. It is a commonplace of newspaper history to say that the coming of the *Daily Mail* revolutionized Fleet Street, and this is true even though the *Daily Mail* of 4 May, 1896, looks stodgy and uninteresting and old-fashioned compared with any of our newspapers of today. That, perhaps, is a measure of the revolution it started.

Even before the launching of the *Daily Mail*, Harmsworth had bought the London *Evening News*, when it was on its last legs, and shortly transformed it into a most profitable concern. Then in 1903 appeared the *Daily Mirror*, intended originally to be largely written by women for women. It was a disaster. Heads wagged in Fleet Street. The paper was losing thousands of pounds a week and the circulation was dropping abysmally. Harmsworth drastically reshaped it into a daily picture paper. It had cost him £100,000, but he said that the experience gained had been worth it.

Still he had not finished. In 1908 he reached the summit of his ambition as a newspaper proprietor by securing a controlling interest in *The Times*. Very shortly he must have regretted his purchase, for it proved an immensely difficult and wearying task to restore the then decrepit old newspaper to a position of eminence such as it had formerly enjoyed.

In the First World War Northcliffe played an increasingly influential part. He flung all his newspapers into the struggle against Germany, and was not afraid of incurring hostility and odium when he decided that he was right. When he exposed the shortage of shells on the Western Front, his *Daily Mail* was burnt in execration on the London Stock Exchange, but soon it was proved that the British armies *were* short of shells and were suffering enormous casualties as a result. Northcliffe supported Lloyd George as Premier against Asquith, and fell out with him later. He was offered a place in the Cabinet, and became an outstandingly successful director of propaganda against Germany. He was even spoken of as a possible Prime Minister, and no doubt he thought in his heart of hearts that he would make an excellent choice. Towards the end of his life he became increasingly domineering—what he might have preferred to style, Napoleonic—and when he died it was openly said that his megalomania had developed into real madness. He died on 14 August, 1922, when he was still only fifty-seven. His last message to *The Times*, shortly before his death, was: "I should like a page reviewing my life-work by someone who really knows and a leading article by the best man available on the night." The Napoleon of Fleet Street was a good newspaper-man to the last.

Rudyard Kipling
1865-1936

Whatever the modern critic may think of Rudyard Kipling, he cannot deny that in his day his success was extraordinary and fascinating. In fact, Kipling's success was equalled, neither in its immediate achievement, nor in the period over which it was sustained, by no other of his contemporary writers. (Wells and Maugham, whose success most nearly approached Kipling's both in point of arrival and in the period of survival, belong to the next generation.)

Kipling's success was due to three things: first, to his skill as a story-teller, which he acquired from the outset; second, he came upon the English literary scene in the middle of a pause between the end of the period of the great Victorian novel and the flowering of the next outstanding phase in the development of the English novel—the Wells, Conrad, Bennett, Galsworthy era—and third, because he wrote in a vein which appealed to a public proud of Britain's great imperial power, which was at its zenith when Kipling published his first work.

He was scorned by many critics of his day, just as he is by almost all critics of today, yet his contemporaries bought his books in their hundreds of thousands; even more strange, today more than a quarter of a century after his death and in times when all he stood for are anathema to the great majority, his books still sell in large number.

On 18 March, 1865, a bitterly cold day, all the lions of literary and artistic London attended a wedding reception. Dante Gabriel Rossetti was there with his sister Christina; so was Swinburne the poet, Burne-Jones the artist, his fellow artist, Ford Madox Brown, and several others. The only important people missing were the bride and bridegroom, John Lockwood Kipling and his very new wife, Alice Macdonald. While their guests enjoyed themselves, they were boarding a liner at Tilbury which was to take them to India.

John Kipling was the son of a Methodist minister, the Reverend Joseph Kipling; Alice Kipling the daughter of another Methodist minister, the Reverend George Macdonald. Her sister Louisa, a year or two later, married the wealthy iron-master, Alfred Baldwin of Bewdley, and became the mother of a future Prime Minister, Stanley, Earl Baldwin of Bewdley.

John Kipling was an artist and an architect. Shortly before his marriage he had been offered and accepted the post of principal of a new art school just set up in Bombay, and it was to that new commercial city, then enjoying a wave of prosperity, that he was taking his bride. A kindly man, keenly interested in all that went on around him, a true artist, a good, refreshing talker, John Kipling soon made a deep impression on all who came into contact with him. His influence on the development of modern Indian art was, in time, to be tremendous.

Mrs Kipling was already pregnant when she and her husband arrived in Bombay, and on 30 December, 1865, her first child was born. A boy, he was named Rudyard, after the place where his parents had first met, and Joseph, after his grandfather Kipling. Two years later he was joined by a sister, christened Alice, but known as Trix, to distinguish her from her mother.

The children of English parents, born in India, were invariably sent home to be educated, usually at the age of eight or nine. Mrs Kipling, however, during the early years of her marriage, suffered ill-health, and for this reason, when Rudyard was only five and his sister three, she brought them to England, and left them, as paying guests, with a retired naval officer and his wife, at Southsea.

Here they remained, Rudyard for the next five years, Trix for a year or two longer. They were years of deepening misery for the small boy. "Aunty Rosa", the officer's wife, jealous for her own son Harry, some five or six years older then Rudyard, apparently treated her small charge in something of the manner of the cruel stepmother of fiction. In her opinion, Rudyard particularly had been spoiled by over-indulgent parents. At six he could not read or write, but he knew a great deal more than boys of six usually do and liked to parade his knowledge. On the other hand, she looked after their bodily comforts, and when their grandmother visited them in 1872, she found them to all outward appearances, thriving.

The five years at Southsea made upon Rudyard's spirit scars that were never to heal so long as he lived.

In 1877 he fell ill. The doctor diagnosed the trouble as a neglected defect in his eyesight, which would have to be remedied by glasses. Hearing of this, Mrs Kipling hurried to England and took the children from Southsea to a farm near Loughton, where they spent a wonderful summer in the company of their cousin Stanley Baldwin, a year or two younger than Rudyard.

Mrs Kipling had decided that Rudyard should return with her to India, and with the threat of the miserable existence at Southsea removed, he recovered his spirits. Though he was to wear spectacles for the rest of his life, his eyesight also rapidly improved.

Rudyard stayed only a few months in India, for he was now twelve, and his serious education must begin. A friend of the Kiplings, Cormell Price, had just been appointed headmaster of a new Public School, founded by a group of Army officers to provide their sons with a cheap education, and it was to the United Services College that Rudyard was sent.

In those days the College was housed in a row of converted villas at Westward Ho!, in Bideford Bay, north Devon. It differed from most mid-Victorian Public Schools chiefly in its secular tone; there was no school chapel. As it had to be run as cheaply as possible, practically all comforts were non-existent. A number of the senior boys had come from Haileybury. They were not the best specimens which that famous school turned out; the masters, too, because of the necessity for keeping costs down, were not outstanding members of their profession.

It was a rough experience for the boys, and could have been particularly so for Kipling, who thrived most in the happy atmosphere of family affection. Now, however, he was stronger, he liked the company of boys, and his approach to life made him generally liked in return. One of his school-friends, George Beresford, has left this impression of him:

> "Kipling was rather short for his age of just twelve years, but he took it out in extra width. He was not noticeably muscular or sinewy, and was accordingly ineffectual at fisticuffs, for which, in any case, his exceedingly short sight unfitted him. He preferred to side-track physical violence by his tact and friendliness and by not quarrelling with any boy unless he had allies. He was always noticeable for his caution, and for his habit of 'getting there' by diplomatic means."

Kipling was most influenced during his stay at the College by William Crofts, his enthusiastic teacher of English literature. A deep bond of sympathy was quickly established between the boy and the man. Crofts recognized the talents that lay in Kipling, and spared no effort to draw them out and develop them. He, more than anyone else—though the headmaster Cormell Price must also share some of the credit—imparted to him a deep love of English literature, and guided him through a course of reading which included most of the great English classics. Price helped by giving the boy the run of his extensive private library.

Even before he came to the College, Kipling had experimented with writing verses. These were of such quality for so young a boy, that in 1881 his mother persuaded his father to have a collection of them privately printed. Many examples of his prose and verse appeared in the *College Chronicle*, of which Kipling was the editor for several years. One poem, written for the *Chronicle* in 1882, entitled *Ave Imperatrix*, was of such quality that when T. S. Eliot came to make his selection of Kipling's verse many years later, he included it.

After four years at the College, Kipling returned to India. For the past seven years his father and mother had been living in Lahore, where Lockwood Kipling was Principal of the Mayo School of Art and Curator of the Lahore Museum. It was a much pleasanter place to live in than Bombay. It was a military station, with a small colony of British residents living in the civilian lines.

A job had already been procured for Kipling, with his consent, as an assistant editor on the provincial newspaper, the *Civil and Military Gazette*. He took up the post in November, 1882. A month later, owing to an accident to the editor, he found himself in temporary charge of the paper. Kipling very quickly impressed his employers with his talents, and within a remarkably short time, he was taken from the humdrum business of reading news telegrams and writing up items from them, and given reporting. In this work he exhibited so individual a style and such deep interest in and love for the people and places he was writing about, that his "pieces" rapidly gained for him a local fame.

Lockwood Kipling and his wife were much loved by all who had contact with them. Both were highly talented, both interesting and intelligent in conversation. Lockwood was becoming known throughout India for the great work he was doing in the field of art. Though comfortably off, they were by no means rich, and most others in their position would have had to be content with the acquaintance of people their financial equals. Their acquaintance was sought, however, by the leading lights of Anglo-Indian society, and when they moved to Simla, this included the Viceroy, Lord Dufferin, whose heir, Lord Clandeboye, for a time paid court to Trix.

The young Kipling profited from the movement of his parents in these circles. When his talents became plain for all to see, he was provided with a body of influential admirers who were in a position, by their approval, to set him on the road to success.

Besides his reporting, Kipling wrote verses, sometimes signed, sometimes not, for his newspaper. These, dealing with various facets of the life of the British in India, were also much appreciated, and added to his reputation as a writer. In 1886 he decided to collect the best of these verses and publish them in book-form. They appeared under the title of *Departmental Ditties*, and reached a far wider public, which greeted them with delight.

The following year he left the *Gazette* and joined the staff of the *Pioneer*, a more important paper owned by the proprietors of the *Gazette*, who, recognizing their young genius, felt that it would offer him greater scope for his talents. He decided to collect the best of his *Gazette* articles into a book, and the publishers Thacker Spink and Co., of Calcutta, undertook to produce it. The book appeared in January, 1888, under the title of *Plain Tales from the Hills*.

Plain Tales had an immediate success throughout India. (The thousand copies sent to English booksellers remained unsold on the shelves.) Apart from their competence, versatility, cocksureness and frequent brilliance, it is in them that Kipling revealed first his power as a story-teller. Taking the merest trifle—a confidence whispered at a ball, a scrap of gossip, a yarn told by a half-drunk soldier—he could work them up into stories which reminded many of the stories of Maupassant.

Many people could not understand why a man of such obvious talents should be content to employ them in the service of an Indian provincial newspaper. When the question was put to him, Kipling replied that he considered himself to be bound in duty to serve the newspaper which had given him his start for at least seven years. More by coincidence than design, in his seventh year of working for the paper, 1889, he decided that journalism no longer gave him sufficient scope. *Plain Tales* had provided him with a useful sum of money, which, together with an advance of £200 which he had received for a series of stories he had written for the Indian Railway Library, was enough to make him plan to take a long leave in America and England.

The editor of the *Pioneer* encouraged him in this project, and commissioned him to write accounts of his travels for the paper. So he set out in March, 1889, going by way of Singapore, Hong Kong and Japan, to the United States. He spent several exciting and interesting months there, and eventually arrived in London in October. This was his first visit home for seven years. He had left a precocious boy; he returned as a travel-experienced young man.

By this time, something of his reputation as a writer had reached literary circles in London, and he was befriended by a small number of writers.

The following year was Kipling's *annus mirabilis*. Sampson Low, the publisher, arranged to reissue the six volumes in the *Indian Railway Library*, and the first volume, *Soldiers Three*, came out early in the spring and was enthusiastically received. This brought him commissions from magazines. But it was a poem, *The Ballad of East and West*, which at once raised him to the front rank of contemporary writers. Simultaneously, an article in *The Times*, which reviewed all his former work for the Indian papers, swept him to fame. Overnight he became the most sought-after writer in London.

Kipling enjoyed every moment of the limelight which fame brought him, but he did not allow the clatter of the social round to deflect him from his work. Besides his output of stories and verses, he worked on a novel, *The Light That Failed*. The older generation of literary men, who were not of the same mind as the younger generation, or the society which acclaimed him, were confirmed in their view of the limitations of his genius, by the appearance of this novel. Taken from any point of view, it was a failure. No one recognized this better than Kipling; he never again attempted a full-length novel. On the other hand he did not allow the failure to depress him or put him off his stroke, and he justified the faith of his younger admirers by the quality of the verses he proceeded to pour out. Indeed, within a short time, it was as though *The Light That Failed* had never been.

From this time, he carried his success to yearly higher limits; and not only in England, but in America, and in countries abroad where his work began to appear in translation. It was not merely his literary talent which made him so popular at home. He revealed in his stories and poems the greatness of England in her empire, and by reflection, the greatness of the English at home. The sentiments of both poems and stories, especially of the former, suited to a nicety the imperialistic mood of the hour. He achieved the peak of his popularity in 1897, the year of the Queen's Diamond Jubilee, with the poem *Recessional*. Only a lapse which displeased the Queen—*The Ballad of the Widow of Windsor*—prevented his being appointed Poet Laureate.

During the Boer War he edited a newspaper for the troops in South Africa and his imperialistic sentiments rose to a new peak in poems written during this time.

In 1901, with the publication of *Kim*, he said farewell to India. Gradually he discovered a new theme based on a deep love of England and one of the English soil. This was already evident in his children's book, *Just-so Stories*, published in 1902, but it reached full development in *Puck of Pook's Hill* (1906) and its companion volume, *Rewards and Fairies* (1910).

After the Boer War, he settled with his American wife, whom he had married in 1892, in Sussex, and after the death of his only son, John, at the battle of Loos in 1915, the pace of his output became slower. Though new stories and verses appeared occasionally in magazines, their collection into volumes became rare literary events. In the post-First World War years there grew up a generation to whom his name meant little.

Kipling received many honours. In 1907 he was awarded the Nobel Prize for Literature; the universities of Oxford, Cambridge, Durham, Edinburgh, McGill, Paris, Strasbourg and Athens conferred honorary degrees upon him; in 1926, he received the Gold Medal of the Royal Society of Literature, an honour previously given only to Walter Scott, George Meredith and Thomas Hardy. He was offered the Order of Merit, but declined it.

He died on 18 January, 1936, and was buried in the Poets' Corner in Westminster Abbey.

No matter on which side one may be in a consideration of his work, about one thing at least there can be no difference of opinion. From first to last he was a superb literary craftsman, with a prose style so individual and so consistent, that apart from choice of subject matter, there is little to distinguish a story written in 1890 from one written in 1930. Yet the authorship of both is unmistakable. This, perhaps, is one of the secrets of his present "hidden" popularity, for no matter how undiscerning a reader may be, he is readily seduced by a good story superbly told.

Sun Yat-sen
1866-1925

THE man who freed China from its 4,000-year-old servitude to absolute monarchy and whose ruling principle was "The Earth and the Universe belong to everyone" was born the son of a poor farmer on 2 November, 1866, in a village near the island of Macao. If the event of which he was the main architect—the Chinese Revolution of 1911—was not necessarily "the greatest event since Waterloo", as his second wife was to describe it, he certainly brought his country out of the fifteenth century into the twentieth by his idealism and integrity.

His father had been a convert to Christianity and Sun Yat-sen, or Sun Wen, as he is known in China, always claimed to be a Christian. In fact, just before his death in 1925, he gave instructions that he was to have a Christian burial. He was the youngest of three sons and, as he played in his boyhood around the mud hut which was his home, he drank in soldiers' stories of a strange revolutionary army of Taipings who fought the Chinese warlords under the banner of Christ, advocated monogamy, sought to abolish slavery, and believed in redistribution of the land.

Life in his village offered him nothing and, at the age of 14, he seized the chance to join an elder brother who owned a farm and a store in Hawaii. This brother, Ah Mei, sent him to a Church of England school where he studied the Bible—strange training for a successful revolutionary in China in those days. He proved so adept at learning the English language and customs that Ah Mei, fearing his younger brother was becoming "Westernized", shipped him back to China.

Home again, young Sun was soon in trouble for his rebellion against ancient customs of ancestor worship and idolatry. He mocked at village superstitions and committed an act of sacrilege by insulting a wooden god. He was promptly banished to Hong Kong. There he became a Bible student and a proselytizer for the Christian Church. He was now eighteen and, as was customary, his family arranged a marriage for him to a farmer's daughter from a nearby village. He went home for his wedding but immediately returned to Hong

Kong, leaving his bride with his mother. It was touch-and-go at this stage whether the future Father of the Republic would become a Christian missionary. But he became more and more appalled by his country's slave system under which families sold their daughters for prostitution and their sons into bondage.

It was at this critical point in Sun Yat-sen's development in 1887 that Dr James Cantlie, who was to remain a life-long friend, opened a new hospital in Hong Kong. Sun Yat-sen decided to launch himself into a medical career and was the first pupil to enrol under Dr Cantlie. He was also among the first graduates five years later. As a student he had joined a secret revolutionary society and now, as Dr Sun, he organized his first terrorist group, called the "Dare to Die", and worked on a revolutionary plot, which was betrayed to the authorities; his co-plotters were arrested and executed; Dr Sun got away. He began a long exile, during which he worked and planned towards fomenting revolution from abroad. He travelled to Hawaii, Britain and America, trying to raise funds to carry on his campaign to overthrow the imperialists then in power in his homeland.

The Manchu Government put a price of £100,000 on his head, and in 1896 he was kidnapped in London and held prisoner in the Chinese Legation but a message was smuggled out to his friend, Sir James Cantlie, who made such a fuss about the incident that Lord Salisbury had to take up the case and, as a result, the British Government forced his release.

Two years later Dr Sun adopted three fundamental principles for his revolutionary programme: Nationalism, Democracy, and Socialism; and he proposed to apply these principles in the spheres of executive government, the legislature and the judiciary, the civil service, the censorship, and in the impartial supervision of officialdom and of all public concerns. After the Boxer Rising of 1900 he tried to establish a democratic government to replace the Manchu régime but his propaganda was too sudden to be effective at that time and the revolution-in-exile proved abortive.

He decided that he had better do much more spade work before he could hope for success. The result was the formation of the Chinese Revolutionary League in Europe and Japan. Through this instrument Sun Yat-sen was able to recruit the support of a large number of his countrymen outside China. Meantime he worked out his programme for reform in much greater detail and raised large sums of money to propagate his ideas inside China through a network of secret agencies.

One of his do-or-die supporters in this vital field of disseminating the reform programme was Charlie Soong, the American-educated industrialist who was brought up as a Methodist. Soong became Sun Yat-sen's right-hand man, acting as his secretary, assistant and distributor of propaganda. He ran a publishing firm ostensibly to turn out religious literature but its main purpose was to print revolutionary tracts and pamphlets written by Dr Sun.

Charlie Soong had three beautiful daughters—and each one married a famous man. Chingling, the second of them, had admired Sun Yat-sen—who was around the same age as her father—since childhood. When she became a student at a Wesleyan co-educational college in Macon, Georgia, her feelings for the doctor-reformer were just this side of idolatry. She determined to marry him, despite the age difference—she was twenty, he was fifty—and despite the fact that he was already married. What the Soong sisters wanted, the Soong sisters invariably got. Since both Chingling and Sun Yat-sen were Christians, a marriage between them would be bigamous, but no amount of family pressure could diminish her resolve—she pleaded and protested, she begged and coaxed, she threatened and, when these tactics failed to win over her family, she ran away and married him.

When the revolution inside China became an accomplished fact— a bomb explosion in Hankow in September, 1911, touched it off— Sun Yat-sen was in the United States. The news reached him in Colorado, with the important additional item that one of his devoted supporters, Chiang Kai-shek, had been appointed Chief-of-Staff in Hanchow. He was on his way across America when he read in a newspaper that he himself had been nominated first President of the new Chinese Republic. He got back to China in January, 1912, and took the oath as provisional president of the national convention at Nanking. The news, of course, electrified the world but nowhere was there more excitement than in the Soong household. All three sisters were to prove a major force in establishing libertarian doctrines in their country. The youngest was later to marry Chiang Kai-shek, and the eldest the banker, H. H. Kung.

On 12 February an imperial edict announced the abdication of the Emperor and the substitution of republican for monarchical government. This historic *volte face* had been made possible by Sun Yat-sen's tireless preparations behind the scenes—his creation of the Kuomintang, or Republican Party, and its efficient organization inside China had turned the anti-Manchu factions into a real force.

The new Republic rested on extremely shaky foundations—

sincere republican feeling existed only among small groups of students who had been educated in Europe or by Europeans in China and among the traders who formed the bulk of the middle classes. The three main anti-Manchu groups were welded together only by their desire to be rid of the hated dynasty. These were: the Left Wing of the Kuomintang mainly composed of intellectuals and manual workers whose aims were vaguely Socialist; the Liberals who wanted a Chinese democracy on the American style; and the Nationalists who simply wanted to be rid of the Manchus to seize power for themselves. They all, however, gave unreserved allegiance to Sun Yat-sen who had succeeded in mobilizing enthusiasm for action not only because of the integrity of his aims but also because he was able to present the new Socialist ideology in an alluring form.

The struggle for power within the Kuomintang began at once and, no sooner had Sun Yat-sen formed his first cabinet than he realized it was impossible to unite the country under his presidency. Besides he had no training as an administrator—his great asset was as a propagandist for his cause. He believed that the infant Republic needed a president the people knew well and could trust. He therefore resigned in favour of Yuan Shih-K'ai, a Liberal statesman and reformer. The Father of the Republic declared in a speech of resignation: "North and South are brought together by the abdication of the Emperor. Yuan promises to support the Republic. He is experienced in affairs of state, and a loyal believer in that democracy for which we have struggled for so long."

Yuan turned out to be more of a dictator than a democrat. He has been called by Sun Yat-sen's biographers "a Chinese Judas, an opportunistic traitor, a murderer and tyrannical monster opposing the advance of the people". They accuse him of tricking the hero out of the presidency.

Certainly within a year Sun Yat-sen and Yuan led armies against one another—the doctor lost that round, being forced to take flight after a battle at Nanking. He went to Japan this time where he heard the news that Yuan had declared himself Emperor in December, 1915. Yuan's triumph was short-lived. The country was plunged into anarchy, chaos and terror. Whole provinces were in revolt and uprisings were put down with a bestial savagery. At the height of the confusion, however, Yuan died and Dr Sun returned to resume his constitutional government.

North and South were again divided so Sun Yat-sen spearheaded a movement for an independent republic of South China and became its President.

Once more he found it impossible to co-operate with the army leaders in Canton, and once more he resigned A military dictatorship followed but was overthrown in 1921 when Sun was called in again. He was destined not to enjoy much peace because he soon quarrelled with the General Ch'en Ch'iung-ming who had restored him to power and was driven yet again from his native province, taking refuge this time in Shanghai. Chingling, who was now with him, had to escape disguised as an old peasant woman.

China was being broken up by a mass of warring factions. There were flare-ups in the North, in Peking, in the Yangtse valley. All manner of new alignments were hastily patched together—and just as swiftly fell apart. However, Sun Yat-sen was loyally and ably supported by Chiang Kai-shek and he managed to gather an army from Kwangsi and Yunnan which defeated General Ch'en. From then on Sun was the acknowledged leader of his native Kwang-Tung Province although his rule did not extend much further than Canton. He, too, was guilty of conniving at violence in his domain which led to the burning and looting of the City of Canton in 1924. This cost him a good deal of support from Chinese overseas but his Socialist views kept the working classes in the main faithful to the Kuomintang.

When anarchy threatened to ruin the young republic, Sun was invited at a People's Conference in Peking to join leaders of other factions—many of them his enemies. He was doubtful of the value of such a congress and he was a sick man, but he went. He had just reached Peking, in January, 1925, when he was struck down by a raging fever. Cancer was diagnosed and an operation was performed, but the disease had gained too firm a hold. He was moved to the house of Dr Wellington Koo, where he died at the age of fifty-nine on 12 March, 1925, still talking of freedom and unity for China.

China's civil war raged on long after the death of Sun Yat-sen until, in 1946, a National Government was formed and headed by Chiang Kai-shek but that, too, had a short life and was overthrown by the Communists in 1949. In October of that year the People's Republic of China was proclaimed, with Mao Tse-tung as its head.

Now a world whose future lies in the shadow of the hydrogen bomb looks uneasily towards the great new Power being welded in the East. Even her mighty neighbour, Soviet Russia, has become apprehensive about China's emerging strength. The end of the chapter has not yet been written. Yet it is safe to say that, but for Sun Yat-sen there would have been no new beginning.

H. G. Wells
1866-1946

The prophets who have been able to foretell the scientific and political future have been very few, especially among those who have commanded respect for their other qualities. Among the small number who do come to mind, however, are Jules Verne, who foretold the advent of the submarine, Aldous Huxley, who in his *Brave New World*, described the influence which automation would have on man's individual behaviour, a prophecy which seems to be imminent of fulfilment, and H. G. Wells, whose *The War of the Worlds*, *The First Men in the Moon* and *The War in the Air*, foretold the Space Age in which we are now living.

Wells, like all the great novelists, was a man with a message. He believed that by scientific education, with the emphasis on biology, mankind could be brought to a consciousness that society too can be established upon a biological basis, as a single living organism, in which no member is more important than another, because all are complementary.

At first he was content to symbolize his emotional reaction to the evils of society through a gallery of characters in the Dickens tradition, all of whom were struggling to get out of the rut, to look around on the mess which the machine age was making of the world of nature.

He joined in the struggle, and like Tolstoy took his mission seriously. His writings make him, with Shaw, one of the most powerful influences of his time.

HERBERT GEORGE WELLS was born at Bromley, in Kent, on 21 September, 1866. His father was a professional cricketer who kept a retail china shop, and his mother had been, and was to be again, a domestic servant.

The family was poor, and Mrs Wells had a succession of children. She dreaded each new pregnancy, not because of the physical risk of giving birth, but because another child meant another mouth to feed. She prayed earnestly and aloud to God to protect her from the consequences of her husband's love; again and again her prayers went unanswered.

Her small boy would hear her praying, and he knew enough of the facts of life to realize when her prayers had not found favour.

This failure to hear his mother's pleas was sufficient to make him in later life reject God altogether. This was one influence from his early life which was to leave its mark upon him for as long as he lived. Another was the legacy of an accident.

One day, before he was in his teens, the son of the landlord of The Bell at Bromley, picked him up and threw him into the air, shouting, "Whose kid are you?" Unfortunately, in his interest to learn the answer to his question, he forgot to catch the weakly Herbert, with the result that the boy hit the ground with a hard thud which broke a tibia.

Carried home, he was placed upon the sofa, and there he remained for several days, the centre of attention. His maimer's mother sent him delicacies unheard of in the Wells household—brawn, jellies and fruits—and with them all kinds of books. Never had the boy had access to so many and so varied books, and they opened for him a new world. He was to say in later life that but for his broken leg and these books he would have remained a draper's shop assistant all his life.

That was what he started out to be on leaving school at fourteen. He was employed by a local firm to operate their cash till, with a chance to learn the business. He found the work dull and boring, and there came a time when he began to wonder how he could extricate himself from this drab meaningless existence. He thought up all sorts of schemes; should he hit Mr Denyer over the head with a roll of cloth, or insult a difficult customer, or kiss a pretty girl in full view of both the partners . . .?

Before he could decide which it should be, his employers themselves took action. The till had been short time and time again, and they practically accused Herbert George of pilfering. He had not, but where the missing money had gone he was never to discover while he lived. Just as he thought he was about to be freed, Rodgers and Denyer said they would give him another chance. Whether it was the shock of what he had missed, or some entirely inexplicable reaction, he got into a brawl with the porter and they came to blows outside the shop. This was too much! He must go! And quickly. Before they could change their minds, he fled to freedom.

His father had become an invalid some time before this and his mother had returned to domestic service as housekeeper at Up Park, owned by a Miss Featherstonehaugh. It was there that he went to stay until it should be decided what he would do next. He met an entirely unbelievable world, and here he first made the acquaintance of Plato's *Republic*, from which he learned that society is not changed by minor adjustments but by bold and wide sweeps of a vivid imagination.

It had been his mother who had chosen drapery, ."because it was safe". Now, for the same reason, she chose pharmacy, and Herbert George departed for Cowap's chemist's shop in Church Street, Midhurst, Sussex. It did not take him or his employer long to discover that he was not cut out to be a chemist, but the brief encounter with Midhurst was to have a great and lasting effect on his life.

As he had no Latin, Mr Cowap had arranged for him to receive lessons in the subject from Mr Byatt, headmaster of Midhurst Grammar School. Wells amazed Byatt with the speed with which he learned, and when he heard that Wells and Mr Cowap were to part company, he persuaded Mrs Wells to allow her son to go to his school as a boarder for a time.

After seven weeks Mrs Wells was once more seized by her passion to see her son safely settled. Though his contact with more advanced education had been brief, it had been sufficient for him to realize what learning was about.

Mrs Wells had returned to drapery as the safest means by which her son could earn his living, and this time he was apprenticed for four years to Hyde's Drapery Store in Southsea, near Hythe. He tried to do his mother's bidding for two weary, galling years, and then decided that he could stand it no longer. One August Sunday morning in 1883—he was sixteen—he ran away, walked seventeen miles to Up Park, and told his mother that he would rather drown himself than return to Messrs Hyde.

Byatt now offered him a job at Midhurst Grammar School as a pupil teacher at £20 a year. He was not a good, though he was a sympathetic, teacher, but this second contact with education confirmed him in the belief that it was education he must have if he was to get on in the world, and he conceived a daring idea by which he was to achieve his ambition. He sat for a scholarship as a teacher-trainer at the Normal School of Science in South Kensington, and was successful.

The scholarship entitled him to free tuition and a guinea a week. On this sum he tried to support himself while he studied and taught. It was difficult; it meant privation; and these experiences, together with his home background almost inevitably compelled Wells to be a Socialist.

The Normal School did not achieve for him all he had hoped it would. He was brilliant only in zoology; in all other subjects scarcely passable; but it did one thing for him—it brought him for a time under the influence of the great biologist, T. H. Huxley, who had already been his hero before he had joined the School.

Presently leaving the School, he took a post as master in an Academy on the borders of Wales, which proved to be almost a Dotheboys Hall. Within a few weeks, he realized that when he had completed his first six months he would have to find another job. It was during these months, in an effort to distract himself from his unpleasant surroundings that he began to write, and found it easy and exciting.

A deliberately inflicted injury on the football field, which seriously damaged one kidney, brought his stay at the Academy to an earlier close than he had intended, and he went to live at Up Park with his mother while he was recovering. He used his enforced leisure to read greedily and to write. He tried to sell what he wrote, but with little success. In one year he sold one short story for £1. But he refused to be discouraged.

In 1888, more or less recovered, he returned to London with £5 in his pocket and no idea of what he was going to do. Presently he found a job with the University Correspondence College as a tutor. He stayed with them for the next six years. During this time he married his cousin Isabel, and moved to Sevenoaks to live without her, for the marriage quickly turned out to have been a great mistake. When he was not working for the College, he was writing, and by 1893 was making two or three hundred pounds a year from stories and articles with a scientific background which magazines like *The Saturday Review* and the *Pall Mall Gazette* bought from him.

His first real success came in 1894, by which time he had taken a B.Sc. degree at London University, when the *Pall Mall Gazette* bought *The Time Machine* for £100. Besides the material reward which this sum represented, the reception which the story was given provoked Wells to a frenzy of inspiration. He had something to say, and he had found a way of saying it which attracted people. It seemed that he knew exactly how to reveal the excitements and the worlds of imagination which lay beneath dull scientific facts. He appreciated that there were bounds beyond which he must not go in the fantasies his brain conceived, and he avoided doing so by creating characters who looked upon life from their own strange stand-point with entirely authentic emotional reactions, so that they were credible and acceptable.

The speed with which he worked can be judged by his output for 1895 to 1897. *The Stolen Bacillus* had followed quickly on the heels of *The Time Machine* in 1895; early in 1896 *The Island of Dr Moreau* appeared, while *The War of the Worlds* and *The Invisible Man* were completed, *When the Sleeper Wakes* was begun, *Love and Mr Lewisham* was in the planning stage, and four brilliant short stories were finished, all before the end of 1897.

The Time Machine had attracted the attention of several of the leading critics—it had drawn from W. T. Stead the comment, "H. G. Wells is a man of genius"—and the succeeding books established him upon the English literary scene. He knew and spent some time in the company of the great literary figures of the day—Conrad, Henry James, Ford Madox Ford, Chesterton, Shaw and Arnold Bennett among them. At thirty he was himself an outstanding author, in a class of his own making.

There was to be no stopping him; the breadth of his vision, the broad sweep of his imagination, his deep involvement with life, his emotional reactions to the evils of society, all kept him at a fever-heat of enthusiasm. In what would today be termed his "science fiction" books he had tried to warn mankind of the dangers that lay ahead if science and industry were not controlled. As dear to his heart was the present lot of the man in the street in his environment of the monstrously growing industrial society.

Though his science fiction will always be remembered, it is for his books in which he made his hero the meek, mild, obstinate little "common man"—Bert Smallways, Kipps, Mr Polly, Mr Lewisham —that he is most likely to be remembered. It is such books as *Love and Mr Lewisham*, *Kipps*, *Tono-Bungay* (considered by many to be his most characteristic and most mature novel) *Ann Veronica*, *The History of Mr Polly*, *The Passionate Friends* and *Joan and Peter*—all written between 1900 and 1918, which represents the core of his work. In these he identified himself with his heroes' struggles to get out of the rut in which the machine age was confining mankind. He used his novels as a stamping ground on which his ideas fought with his indignation.

If his background, his upbringing and his views of the world inevitably made a Socialist (though not an orthodox one) of him, his deep concern with sociology just as inevitably was to bring him into contact with that cradle of intellectual Socialism, the Fabian Society.

His ideas, however, proved too revolutionary even for the Fabians, and his stormy contact with them came to a head in 1906, when he read to the Society a paper entitled *The Faults of the Fabians*. This brought down the full wrath of the leaders of the Society, Shaw,

Sidney and Beatrice Webb, Hubert Bland and Lord Olivier. His ideas for the reform of the Society were defeated, but not Wells. In the years up to 1918 he took on all opponents, no matter who or what they were.

He made enemies. They called him a snob, they called him vain, they called him an exhibitionist, they asked one another who this little man thought he was, they exercised their cruel satiric wit on his private life. This last had become complicated not long after his first marriage by his interpreting the need to satisfy his physical demands by behaviour which, at the time, and even now, was and is regarded as outrageous. Even in this sphere he took no notice of the reactions of the society whose conventions he so blatantly flouted. "Your cheek," Henry James once said to him in another context, "is the very essence of your genius."

During the First World War he adopted a pro-war attitude, and used his gifts for thinly veiled propaganda. The outstanding book of this period is *Mr Britling Sees it Through*, in which he recorded the day-by-day reaction of one Englishman to the war. The book became a best-seller even among Wells's best-sellers, and strangely it was because he made many thousands of pounds by it that he was able to write what is surely his monumental work, *The Outline of History*.

In this great book—which albeit contains several flaws; it was hastily written, and did not contain half the story of mankind—he cut away the mumbo-jumbo of the professors, presented a new view of history by insisting that biology was an essential part of its study, and related the story of Man in language which ordinary people could understand at once. It surprised the experts, for all its faults, and it took the reading public by storm. Over two million of them bought the book.

He followed this work with a number of books which were variations on different aspects of his main theme. He still produced novels, which he used to present what appeared to him to be urgent social problems. None of these later stories, however, is so memorable as any one of his first group, written before the war.

Until his death in August, 1946, he remained one of the most prolific writers ever to appear on the English literary stage. In his last years, though tired and ill, and almost having lost all hope in mankind, he still tried to push the human race along the road which he believed would lead to its salvation.

Wilbur 1867-1912
and
Orville Wright 1871-1948

"After running the motor a few minutes to heat it up, I released the wire that held the machine to the track, and the machine started forward into the wind. Wilbur ran at the side of the machine, holding the wing to balance it on the track—Wilbur was able to stay with it till it lifted from the track after a forty-foot run . . .

"This flight lasted only twelve seconds, but it was nevertheless the first—in which a machine carrying a man had raised itself by its own power into the air in full flight, had sailed forward without reduction of speed, and had finally landed at a point as high as that from which it started . . ."

So, on the morning of 17 December, 1903, at Kitty Hawk, North Carolina, the Wright brothers made the world's first powered flight. Orville, from whose subsequent account the above extract is taken, made the first and third of four; Wilbur, the second and fourth. There were five witnesses, apart from the brothers themselves: three of them members of the Kill Devil life-saving station who had come in from their homes in response to a prearranged signal raised when the wind became suitable for take-off. The longest of the flights lasted fifty-nine seconds. Delighted with their success, the brothers telegraphed their father, the Bishop, at home in Dayton, Ohio, suggesting he inform the local Press. Bishop Wright did so. In the meantime each of the five witnesses told his friends. Such was the incredulity—even hostility—with which these reports were received that the United States Army, to whom the invention was offered, refused even to see a demonstration until 1908.

At last, on 3 September of that year, 1908, while Wilbur was in France demonstrating to the French Government (both French and British Governments had shown interest after the first "incredible" reports, but had done little else) Orville Wright took off from a field near Washington before a small, apathetic crowd of officers and civilians. According to Theodore Roosevelt, Junior, who was there to give a report to his father:

317

"When the plane rose, the crowd's gasp of astonishment was not only at the wonder of it, but because it was unexpected. I'll never forget the impression the sound from the crowd made on me. It was a sound of complete surprise."

When Orville descended, a minute and eleven seconds later, he was met—to *his* surprise—by reporters with tears pouring down their cheeks. By now there was no reason at all for tears or surprise. Even if those present had ignored every rumour and report for four and a half years, there were well-authenticated reports of Wilbur's demonstration flights in France, which had been taking place for a month even though the Press paid little attention. On 9 August, the day after Wilbur's Le Mans flight of a minute and forty-five seconds (dressed as usual in grey business suit and high stiff collar) a flight which electrified his French audience, the *New York Times* gave front page coverage to a balloon flight in Ohio, made no mention of Wilbur.

On 12 September, still demonstrating at Fort Myer, outside Washington, Orville circled the field seventy-one times in an hour and fifteen minutes, reached a height of 300 feet. Still the Press played it down; it was a freak, a phoney, and even if reporters on the spot wired ecstatic stories, these would be edited down to a small paragraph for the back page. On 17 September Orville and his Army passenger had an accident. The passenger died of a fractured skull and Orville went to hospital with broken leg, hip and ribs. At last, the Press took notice. The Wrights became front page news in America: thanks to Wilbur's demonstration flights on the Continent, they were already a household word in Europe. Companies were being organized in France and Germany to manufacture Wright aeroplanes and the Wright team—though half of it lay in plaster of Paris in hospital—was in "aviation business" at last.

They had been born four years apart: Wilbur in 1867, Orville in 1871, sons of the Rev. Milton Wright, in Dayton, Ohio, and they were eleven and seven years old when their father, back from a trip on Church business, threw them a "present" which rose to the ceiling, fluttered there, before dropping to the floor. They rushed at the toy flying machine, a fragile French thing of cork, paper and rubber bands, wound it up again, watched in wonder as it repeated the trick—and never forgot the lesson.

Their father became a Bishop, they moved from place to place, and eventually returned to Dayton when the boys were seventeen and thirteen. They decided to improve the old house. They built themselves a lathe, with it turned posts for a new front porch.

When they had carried out every possible improvement and repair, they busied themselves reconditioning an old printing press, started a newspaper.

Shortly afterwards, though they continued printing as a hobby for many years, the brothers went into the cycle business. They began by selling and repairing well-known makes but by 1895 (at much the time that William Morris, later Lord Nuffield, was doing the same, in England) they went over to making their own model. They did this upstairs, when business was slack, and contrived an ingenious means of knowing whether a caller wanted to make a purchase or only wanted to borrow their pump. By fitting a two-tone bell to the door and an upstairs pointer to the hook on which the pump hung, they were able to tell whether the visitor was customer or not, whether he merited a walk downstairs.

This same year they were much impressed by a magazine article on the German, Otto Lilienthal, who had been gliding in a home-made machine. A year later, in 1896, Lilienthal was killed in a crash, but this only served to whet the brothers' appetite. They read everything available about Lilienthal, considered their own designs, hit upon the idea of a wing with variable inclination which would enable the pilot to keep his balance by adjusting the lift of one wing against the other. Practical means of making such a wing strong enough seemed to be eluding them when Wilbur had an idea. A customer had bought an inner tube for his cycle tyre and while they chatted, Wilbur fiddled with its flat square box. Suddenly he realized that, as he twisted it, the sides stayed vertical while top and bottom were forced into different angles to the horizontal at opposite ends. This was the answer to gliding: a wing like a long, flat box, which could be warped from one end to the other.

The brothers immediately built a kite to test the theory and found that it worked. Having, they believed, solved the problem of stability, they devoted themselves to designing a kite big enough to carry a man. The main difficulty became that of finding a place with suitable winds, and after much inquiry, they chose a site on the Atlantic coast of North Carolina—many miles from Dayton—with the pleasing name of Kitty Hawk. In September, 1900, Wilbur set out, leaving Orville to look after the shop while he got settled.

It took longer than he'd expected. The strip of sandy beach which contained Kitty Hawk proved, on inspection, to be an island, with no bridge to the mainland. Apart from the hamlet of Kitty Hawk, it contained two life-saving stations and a Government weather bureau. It was approached by a weekly boat—which had sailed the day before. He managed to book passage on a fishing boat and got there, exhausted from a two-day trip without food (everything on the filthy vessel horrified him, he made wild excuses for not eating) and was taken in by hospitable residents, the Tate family. He got to work, assembled the "kite", and sent a message to Orville, who shut up shop and came to join him. Five days after Orville joined his elder brother, they moved from the hospitable Tates, set up camp under canvas. Here they were studiously avoided by the locals: they used a petrol stove for cooking, they were obviously dangerous, as well as mad.

The glider weighed fifty-two pounds, had a total span of seventeen and a half feet and possessed two features never before tried: a front rudder, and an arrangement for warping the wings. By hauling the machine four miles to a suitable eminence, Kill Devil Hill, they managed to make a dozen successful glides on their first day. The control of the machine was better than they had dared expect. When the weather grew wintry, they returned to the cycle shop in Dayton. Mrs Tate, to whom they gave the glider, used the covering to make dresses for her small daughters.

The following summer Wilbur and Orville returned to Kitty Hawk with a bigger glider. By the time they left, at the end of August, they had satisfied themselves that it was as easy to control a big one as a small. When they got back to Dayton they made a wind-tunnel to test their calculation, an open-ended wooden box sixteen inches square by six feet long, and during the winter tested two hundred types of wing and compiled tables. Even today, the results from elaborate instruments in huge wind-tunnels hardly differ from those obtained by the Wrights.

In their third, 1902, season at Kitty Hawk, the machine's most obvious difference from its predecessors lay in a tail of fixed vertical vanes. With this glider they made trips of over six hundred feet, were able to soar over one spot without descending, stay up for over a minute. As a result of these experiments they decided to reduce the tail to one vertical "rudder" which they could control from the same wires as warped the wings. They also decided to build a machine with an engine.

On their return to Dayton, they wrote to car manufacturers, asking if they could furnish a motor developing 8-brake horsepower, weighing under 200 pounds. Such was the prejudice against ideas of human flight that no manufacturer would become involved. Eventually Wilbur and Orville made their own. It took time and hard work and not before September, 1903, were they able to set out again for Kitty Hawk. Here they were beset by difficulties: a backfire from the motor twisted a propeller shaft; a sudden storm nearly removed the entire camp. It was not until 12 December that the machine, with new, reinforced, propeller shafts (it had one engine but two propellers, chain-driven) was ready to fly. Then the wind vanished, and the test was postponed.

On the 14th, the machine stalled after three seconds in the air and damaged itself on hitting the ground. As this "flight" had demonstrated that their new method of take-off, from a wood and metal track on the sand, really worked, they were, according to Orville, "much pleased". They spent two days on repairs and on the morning of 17 December the four flights were made, in wind velocities of between 24 and 27 m.p.h. Ten years later Orville wrote:

> "I would hardly think today of making my first flight in a strange machine in a 27-mile wind, even if I knew that the machine had already flown and was safe—yet faith in our calculations and the design of the first machine, based on our tables of air pressures, had convinced me . . ."

As we have seen, it was years before a hostile Press took notice, years during which Wilbur and Orville flew many miles, at Dayton as well as at Kitty Hawk, improving their designs. Wilbur died of typhoid in 1912, before the full potentialities of their invention had been realized, but messages of sympathy poured in from all over the world.

Owing largely to delay in having the invention taken up by any government or manufacturer, Orville Wright found, when he and it became famous, that there were plenty of people prepared to steal his patents. For a while much of his time was devoted to the prosecution of patent suits; and although he won them all, it was a very different matter collecting royalties: he was swindled out of thousands, possibly millions, of dollars.

The final and most extraordinary injustice was the insistence of the Smithsonian Institution in Washington that its one-time director, Dr Samuel Langley, who had given up his own unsuccessful attempts after repeatedly falling into the Potomac River, had invented the "first man-carrying machine capable of powered flight". He himself had never claimed this during his lifetime, but the Smithsonian elected to exhibit side by side, as working aircraft, Langley's small *model* plane which had worked in 1903 and a small model of a 1908 Wright plane, suggesting thereby that Langley had been five years ahead of the Wrights with a full-size machine (which he never achieved). After remonstrating with the Smithsonian, to no avail, Orville allowed the Science Museum in London to have the first powered machine, in 1928.

The reason for the Smithsonian's behaviour seemed to be that they had allowed a Wright competitor, Glenn Curtis, to borrow a full-size, unworkable, Langley plane, in 1914. Curtis, anxious to prove that Wright patents were not patents at all, that it had all been done before, quietly fitted new engine parts and wing supports and flew the plane. The Smithsonian was delighted to learn that their director's aircraft had been capable, all along, of powered flight; proudly gave it pride of place. However, at long last, in 1942, the Smithsonian Institute published a long statement with diagrams of the Langley plane as it had been in 1903 and again in 1914. This proved without doubt that the original model could never have flown, and Orville was at last satisfied. After his death in 1948, the Wright machine—the first one to fly, *and* the first one capable of so doing—was returned to America and given its rightful place in the Institute.

Arturo Toscanini
1867-1957

THE Opera House in Rio de Janeiro was in an uproar. The singers
on the stage were trembling behind the curtain which none of the
stagehands dared raise on the performance of *Aïda* due to begin. In
the orchestra pit, the musicians cowered behind their music-stands,
horrified at the sight they had just seen, of their conductor being
dragged off the rostrum and thrown out into the street by spectators
from the front rows of the stalls. "Down with the Italians, down
with the Italians!" the audience was yelling, angrily whistling and
jeering and stamping their feet.

Who could possibly face them, control them, quieten them now
into listening to the performance by the visiting company from Italy?
There were frantic consultations between the singers on the stage
and the musicians in the orchestra. Then someone said suddenly:
"Toscanini! He's the only one who could save us! Where is he?"

"But he is only one of the 'cellists!" said someone else. "What
does he know about conducting? And besides, he isn't in the
orchestra tonight—he sent word he couldn't come because he was
ill."

"I know where he is," said one of the other players in the orchestra.
"He's staying in the hotel down the street. And he *can* conduct. I
don't think he's very ill, either—he might come if we asked him."

Two or three members of the company slipped out of a side door
in the theatre. They ran down the street, into the hotel and up to
one of the rooms, and started to bang on the door.

"What is it?" called a female voice from inside the room. Then a
male voice: "Go away, can't you, leave me alone. I'm entertaining a
friend."

"Please, Arturo!" called the musicians. "Please come to the
theatre and conduct tonight's performance. The audience are going
mad, they'll attack the whole company if you don't!"

They had good reason to be afraid. That week the orchestra had
refused to play under Brazil's most famous conductor, Leopoldo
Miguez, because they thought he was incompetent: during rehearsals
they would not co-operate, and deliberately made mistakes. Miguez

walked out in a fury, and the next day published a letter in the news-papers saying the only reason they would not accept his direction was because he was Brazilian. Now on the night of the actual perform-ance, the citizens of Rio were retaliating by jeering the whole company and attacking Superti, the Italian reserve-conductor who was appearing in Miguez's place.

Grumbling, Toscanini opened the door of his hotel room to argue with his fellow musicians. They must be mad, he told them. Was he not, like Superti, also an Italian? And how could he, a nineteen-year-old 'cellist, be expected to conduct the entire performance? It was impossible, ridiculous, it simply could not be done. . . . He was dragged, still protesting, to the theatre and pushed out in front of the orchestra.

The audience had either tired of demonstrating, or else were so surprised by the appearance of a small slight youth on the rostrum, that they suddenly fell silent. Giving them no time to recover, Toscanini abruptly rapped on the music stand with his baton to call the orchestra to attention, and started to conduct.

After the first few opening bars he ignored the score lying open in front of him and relied on his own memory. By the entry of the first chorus he was completely immersed in the performance, and the orchestra and singers were responding absolutely to his direction. As he continued the audience gradually forgot their anger and allowed themselves to be caught up in the music. With each scene and each act they became more and more enthusiastic in their appreciation—until, by the end of the opera, they were on their feet cheering and clapping, and giving the young and unknown con-ductor prolonged and tumultuous applause.

Toscanini laid down the baton, turned, made a slight bow to the audience, got down from the rostrum and disappeared back stage. Members of the company rushed to find him, applauding him them-selves and begging him to go back in front of the orchestra to acknowledge the ovation the audience were still giving. But he shook his head. "It was bad" he said mournfully. "I made two mistakes." He left the theatre, still shaking his head sadly, and went back to his hotel.

Even at nineteen, nothing less than perfection of performance would satisfy him.

Arturo Toscanini, the greatest conductor the world has ever known, was born on 25 March, 1867, in Parma in northern Italy. His father, Claudio, had fought with Garibaldi and was a tailor—

when he worked, which was not often, for he much preferred to sit all day in cafés with his friends, talking of politics and battles. His wife Paola worked as a seamstress to try to earn money to feed her children, and Arturo recalled in later life how he had never once eaten meat as a child. Living as they did on bread, soup and cheese, the family were often hungry. Once when Arturo ate a big meal at his aunt's house, his mother whipped him when she found out, for she was a proud woman and did not want her relatives to know her children went hungry because their father would not work.

Neither Claudio nor Paola was musical, and it was only by chance that a local teacher of music, Señora Vernoni, noticed one day that the eight-year-old Arturo Toscanini who lived near by could pick out on her piano the notes of tunes he had heard only once before. She persuaded his parents to scrape together enough money to send him, the next year, to the Parma Conservatory of Music, where not long afterwards he won a scholarship which paid for the rest of his education there.

At the Conservatory all the students wore uniforms, lived in small and sparsely furnished rooms, and had to obey a discipline that was almost military in its strictness. Yet Arturo was happy. His only interest in life now was music. The Conservatory had a huge library of scores, and he spent every spare moment from classes in it. He was so engrossed in his studies that he asked for, and was given, permission to stay at the Conservatory even during the holidays. In addition to his main study, which was the 'cello, he taught himself to play the piano, and also to conduct, persuading some of his fellow students to form an orchestra he could practise with. At first the Conservatory authorities tried to prevent him dividing his interests, but he was so good a student that they eventually relented, even allowing him after a time also to take occasional work as a 'cellist in the orchestra at the local opera house. Here he played in the first performance of *Lohengrin* ever given in Parma, of which experience he said many years afterwards, "I had then the first true, great, sublime revelation of Wagner's genius." His admiration for the German composer was to remain with him throughout the rest of his life.

So too was one other profound influence which also began in Parma. Like many others in Italy that city was passionately devoted to opera, and its audiences always responded to performances in a way that was both violent and direct. The famous singer Frances Alda describes in her autobiography how she was once appearing there in *Lorelei* when another singer in the company could not reach a note: immediately the whole audience of the Parma Teatro Regio began to sing the aria absolutely correctly, and the singer had to leave the stage to a barrage of whistles and jeers. The Parma audiences were so devoted to music, and so knowledgable about it, that they were almost ready to attack physically any singer who displeased them by an inept performance. Equally, a triumphantly exact high note or a beautifully sustained trill would bring forth thunderous applause. Growing up as he did in this atmosphere, and knowing no other way of reacting to faults in performers, it is perhaps not surprising that Toscanini should have raged and cursed at musicians who did not come up to the standard he required. When he stormed and shouted abuse—as he very frequently did—he was behaving only as a true citizen of Parma.

At the age of eighteen he finished his course of studies at the Conservatory, and passed the final Diploma Examination with 160 marks out of a possible 160 for the 'cello; 50 out of 50 for composition; and 50 out of 50 for the piano, which he had to persuade the examiners to allow him to attempt, since he was not officially studying it. His first job afterwards was as 'cellist and assistant chorus-master with a company going to Brazil, and it was on this tour that the incident occurred which gave him his first chance to conduct in public.

Despite that success, he returned quietly at the end of the tour to Parma, and soon afterwards went to Genoa as a teacher of singing. He knew he was not yet ready to devote himself entirely to conducting, and also he had to find regular work so he could send money to his parents and family, for by now his father Claudio was hardly working at all. Arturo was earning at this time between 800 and 1,000 lire (about £90–£110) for a season with an orchestra as a 'cellist, and about the same amount again as a teacher of singing.

Between 1887 and 1893 he moved from one northern Italian city to another, taking whatever work he could get, and still studying in every spare moment. Not until 1894, at the age of twenty-seven, did he receive his first permanent appointment as a conductor, at the Regio in Turin. By 1898 he was becoming well known, and it was in that year he first went to conduct at the centre of Italian opera, La Scala Milan.

Fine conductor though he then already was, his volatile temperament and his insistent demands for nothing less than perfection of performance made him a difficult—and at times almost impossible—man to work for. There were endless quarrels and arguments with musicians, with singers and with theatre managers.

It was not until three years later, in 1891, when he was engaged by the principal opera house in Genoa and given a completely free hand to produce and conduct operas as he thought they should be presented, that he was able at last to settle down. He was in Genoa for five seasons, occasionally visiting Turin with his company in between, and these were the years in which he reached maturity as a conductor. He gave the first Italian performance of Wagner's *Die Götterdämmerung*, and the world première of Puccini's *La Bohème*; and began too his lifelong admiration for the music of his compatriot, Verdi.

During this period, as well as developing and perfecting his technique as a conductor, he set new standards of interpretation in his rigorous insistence that music should be played exactly as the composer had written it. On one famous occasion—repeated similarly literally hundreds of times afterwards throughout his life—Toscanini stopped a rehearsal because the timpanist failed to give an accent to a particular note. "There is no accent marked here on my copy of the score, maestro," he said. "Then put it in," said Toscanini. "It should be there, because that is how it was originally written." Some time afterwards the timpanist went to a library where the original of the composer's score was kept, and asked to see it. He turned through the pages until he came to the passage in question: the accent was there.

In 1896 Toscanini had his first opportunity of conducting a symphony concert. Prior to this he had been known only as a conductor of opera. He asked for three rehearsals before the concert in Turin, but the management would allow him only two because they were trying to keep down the expenses. On the day of the performance the public had been admitted to the theatre and the orchestra was ready on the stage. But Toscanini did not appear. The concert had to be postponed until the following evening—after another rehearsal in the afternoon.

By this insistence on high standards, and his absolute refusal ever to compromise, Toscanini began gradually to gain for himself the reputation he sought. Any impresario or manager who engaged him knew that despite all the quarrels and difficulties which would certainly occur, the finished performance would never be less than truly memorable, and any orchestra under his direction would attain heights which even the players themselves never imagined they could achieve. Every musician who ever played under him said the same thing: he got from them something extra and above their usual standard, which beforehand they had never known they could give.

"I don't know how and I don't know why," one player wrote, "but somehow you just knew how he wanted you to go."

In 1898 he was back at La Scala Milan for four seasons, and between them he toured both Italy and America with the orchestra. By 1908 his fame was world-wide, and he was invited to the Metropolitan Opera House, New York, for a season. As usual he was bitingly critical during rehearsals: he was so rude, in fact, that after a few days the players walked out. Toscanini would not change his attitude, his demands for perfection; he could not change his temperament or restrain the violence of his abuse. He was a perfectionist absorbed in the music, who felt sincerely—as he once said witheringly to a player at rehearsal who failed to please him—"Only you are standing between me and the composer's intention!" Toscanini stayed at the Metropolitan for seven seasons, and he made its orchestra into the finest in the world.

There were moments of humour, too, for the orchestra once they understood and allowed for his temper. When he was really angry, he would pour out a stream of curses in a mixture of English and Italian, and once when he did this a member of the orchestra replied suddenly, "Oh, nuts to you!" "It is no use to apologize!" Toscanini yelled back at him.

At the outbreak of the First World War he returned to Italy, conducting concerts in nearly all the principal cities. Despite pressure from government officials and other unintelligent people, he refused to exclude from his programmes music by Beethoven, Wagner and other German composers. To Toscanini all that mattered was their music, not their nationality.

In 1920 he was offered and accepted the post of Artistic Director at La Scala, with complete freedom to do as he wished, and for the next five years he concentrated on making that theatre into what it has remained ever since, the centre of opera for the world.

During these years other significant things were also happening in Italy. The Fascist dictator Benito Mussolini came to power, destroying all opposition and making himself the country's supreme and only ruler. He issued an edict that every public building including theatres must prominently display his picture, and all concerts must commence with the playing of *Giovinezza*, the Fascist martial hymn. The order was obeyed throughout the whole of Italy—except at La Scala Milan. Toscanini would not have Mussolini's portrait in the theatre, or play *Giovinezza*. By now he was too celebrated a world figure for Mussolini to do much about his defiance except refuse ever to attend any of the performances there.

On one occasion young Fascist hooligans attacked Toscanini in the street: Mussolini, though he fumed at the conductor's failure to pay him homage, knew this could only bring discredit to him in the eyes of the rest of the world. He ordered that Toscanini should be left alone.

In 1929 Toscanini went back to New York to conduct the Philharmonic Symphony Orchestra. With radio broadcasts and gramophone records spreading his music among millions, his name became even more widely known throughout America and the world. When he toured Europe with his orchestra he was given all the adulation of a "star". Paris, Vienna, Budapest, Brussels, London —he was received like a triumphant conqueror by them all. In one month alone, he and his orchestra gave twenty-three concerts in sixteen cities in nine different countries.

He had no strong political beliefs: he simply felt that Fascism and all it represented was a negation of artistic creativeness. When Hitler came to power in Germany, he said he would never conduct again in that country, and he became an exile from his own country too, saying he would not return until Fascism was destroyed. He spent the next ten years continuously on the move, until in 1938 he settled to live in New York. But he was not forgotten by the Italian people. The day after Mussolini was deposed in 1943, two huge banners appeared across the front of La Scala Milan—"Long Live Toscanini" and "Toscanini Come Back".

So he did. Damaged in air-raids, the opera house was rebuilt, and reopened with an inaugural concert on 11 May, 1946. In front of a packed audience, Toscanini conducted the orchestra in a programme which consisted entirely of music by Italian composers, and was given a riotous reception. Afterwards there was a huge banquet to welcome him, attended by all the élite of Milan. Toscanini did not appear: something in the performance had dissatisfied him. He returned to his hotel and went to bed.

In 1949 under the new constitution, the Italian President was given the right to appoint to the Senate for life five citizens who had rendered exceptionally distinguished service to their country. One of the five he nominated was Toscanini, who declined the honour in a telegram which began:

"It is an old Italian artist who addresses himself to you, and begs you to understand that this appointment is in profound contrast with his feelings and his way of life. . . ."

He was now over eighty, and he wanted before he died to leave a legacy to the world—not as a senator or a politician, but as a musician. His doctors had told him that he could not expect to continue indefinitely, energetic and fiery though he still was, in his devotion to the search for perfection. So in America he began the task of trying to establish, on gramophone records, a canon of performances of music which he himself might regard as worthy. To attain this he disciplined himself, for the first time in his life, to take orders and instructions from others—from the recording engineers in the gramophone company's studios, the men on whose skill he relied for the permanent reproduction of his art. He was so docile, so mild and anxious to please that none of them could believe this was the terrifying maestro known throughout the world for his temper.

He gave his farewell concert in 1954. From then until he died in 1957 he supervised the production of the recordings. He has left behind him, on these records, a living expression of his genius that others, born long after his death, will always be able to hear and recognize. For Toscanini was not *a* conductor: he was *the* conductor, not only of his own but probably of all time.

Yet there was one critic who heard the recordings and pronounced them totally inadequate and unsatisfactory, and groaned in agony whenever he heard them played. He was—of course—Toscanini himself.

He lived for ninety years. During his lifetime he was the subject of eight biographies, and in a few years after his death there were five more. No doubt there are many others still to come. Yet his life had no great personal tragedy, no scandal, few dramas. His marriage to Carla de Martina, the ordinary daughter of a simple Milan baker, was uneventful and ordinary; none of their children achieved either eminence or notoriety. His whole long life as a story in fact offers nothing—nothing, that is, except a pure and unchanging relentless devotion to music, to interpreting the compositions of others exactly as they intended them, to trying to produce the sounds they heard in their imaginations.

To a friend who was once praising him, Toscanini replied simply:

"No, I am no genius. I play the music of other men. I have created nothing. I am just a musician."

Yet to every singer and player in the world, their proudest boast if they can truthfully say it is always the same: "I performed under Toscanini."

Robert Falcon Scott
1868-1912

"Had we lived, I should have had a tale to tell of the hardihood, endurance and courage of my companions which would have stirred the heart of every Englishman. These rough notes and our dead bodies must tell the tale, but surely, surely, a great rich country like ours will see that those who are dependent on us are properly provided for."

THESE words from his scribbled "Message to the Public", almost the last words Scott wrote as he lay dying of gangrene and starvation, trapped in a blizzard thirteen miles from the depot where food was waiting, are the words of a man who accomplished, in this final, agonizing journey to the Pole, very little that can be measured against the yardstick of practical achievement. He failed to reach it before his rival, Amundsen; was greeted there by a note from the Norwegian, "Dear Captain Scott, As you are probably the first to reach this area after us, I will ask you kindly to forward this letter to King Haakon VI . . ." and perished with his four companions on the way back—a futile loss, it could be said of five remarkable men.

Yet, though the world was thrown, only two years later, into a war in which lives were flung away at the rate of thousands a week, the tragedy of these five men lives more clearly in our minds than much that has followed—for the simple reason that Scott was one of the most remarkable characters of his time, or any other. The significance of his exploits lies in its proof that men will face hardship and death in pursuit, not of practical gain, but of an idea.

To put Scott's achievements, and they were many, in perspective, one must glance for a moment at the history of the Antarctic. The Greeks had christened it "Antarktos", the land opposite the north pole, "Arktos", the Land of the Bear, from the constellation which sailed above it. They were agreed that the place was unattainable because of the boiling Equator which lay in between. Later, when the Equator had been crossed by unboiled sailors, every southern landfall was mistaken for this unknown "Antarctic"—only to be revealed as Australia, New Zealand, or an island. Captain Cook was sent southward in 1772, drove his ships deep into ice south of the Antarctic Circle, reported that nobody lived in the region; nothing grew. At the International Geographical Congress in 1895 a resolution reminded that "Exploration of the Antarctic Regions is the greatest piece of geographical exploration still to be undertaken."

The British Antarctic Expedition (the *Discovery* Expedition, after its vessel) set sail in 1901. Its leader had been selected, unknown to himself, some thirteen years before, when Sir Clements Markham, soon to be President of the Royal Geographical Society, had spotted a young midshipman during his visit to the naval squadron commanded by a cousin. An Antarctic expedition had long been in his mind and for years he made a point of meeting any young man whose training, aptitude and inclination might lead him to become its leader. Such a young man, it seems, was Robert Falcon Scott. Markham met him several times in the next dozen years, and on each occasion his certainty mounted that this was the man. In June, 1899, he informed Lieut. Commander Scott that an expedition was in prospect, and as he had hoped, Scott applied to command it.

Things moved slowly; it was June, 1900, before the appointment was announced, and Scott was promoted Commander. He had just attained his 32nd birthday.

Robert Falcon Scott was born near Devonport on 6 June, 1868. His father had been the sickly member of an active family (one brother in the Navy, three in the Army), had stayed at home to work in the family brewery at Plymouth. Robert was his elder son, who entered the R.N. via the training ship, *Britannia*. On his appointment to command the expedition, he was released from routine Naval duty to devote the next year to selecting his companions and planning his task. The expedition sailed in the summer of 1901, surveyed much of the Antarctic continent, made soundings of the Ross Sea. It returned after an absence of three years, and was greeted with wild enthusiasm. Scott was promoted Captain, given countless awards, decorations, honours. *The Times* commented: "The expedition commanded by Commander Scott has been one of the most successful that ever entered into the polar regions, north or south." It had, indeed, done remarkable work, mapping large areas, charting the earth's magnetism, bringing back meteorological samples. Scott was given nine months' leave to write his account of the expedition, *The Voyage of the Discovery*, published in 1905. By this time he had been appointed to a staff post at the Admiralty; shortly afterward he received the first of his battleship commands. During one of these, he met his future wife, Kathleen Bruce, a young sculptor. He married her in September, 1908, and in this very month plans were announced for a new expedition to the southern lands. The British,

Australian, New Zealand and South African Governments made grants towards it, but the expedition was unofficial, a private scheme of Scott's, with two straightforward objects: to reach the South Pole and to further scientific exploration of the Ross Sea area.

While it was being prepared, Scott's only child was born, a son who later became the naturalist, Peter Scott. Eventually, *Terra Nova*, the 744-ton whaler which Scott had bought, sailed from England in June, 1910, and reached Melbourne on 12 October. There Scott received a disturbing telegram: "Madeira. Am going south. Amundsen." This was a frank statement from the famous Norwegian explorer that he planned to reach the South Pole first.

On 29 November, 1910, *Terra Nova* sailed south from Dunedin. The expedition chose a spot for landing on Cape Evans, eighteen miles north of Scott's former quarters at Hut Point, and within a fortnight they had built a hut and unloaded all stores. The next move was to leave a ton of stores in a depot on the ice barrier which lay between them and the Pole. This was done, the spot was named "One Ton Depot", 150 miles from Cape Evans, and the members of the team settled themselves down to scientific work at their base through the southern winter, from March until October. The ponies on which they were relying for much of their load hauling had not taken well to Antarctic conditions, many died. It was judged unwise to attempt a start using them before the end of October.

The distance from Cape Evans to the Pole was 922 miles: they set off on 24 October, 1911, and took three days to reach Hut Point, a distance of eighteen miles—not a very encouraging start to a journey of 1,800. To their relief, the untried motor sledges which they hoped would take them some distance before being jettisoned, managed the slope up to the great Ice Barrier and gave good service until three days later when they broke down and had to be left, having covered fifty-one miles.

The pony party, under Scott himself, ten animals each drawing a sledge, had started after them, on 31 October, accompanied by two dog-teams drawing other sledges. The ponies were directly in the charge of Captain "Titus" Oates of the Inniskilling Dragoons, who failed to share Scott's faith in the animals, though he did everything in his power to make them give of their best. The pony and dog-parties reached the motorless motor party on 21 November, and someone facetiously remarked, "Haven't seen anything of Amundsen"—little realizing that the Norwegian was four hundred miles ahead of them, having begun his overland trip to the east of their own starting-point. They camped happily together, sixteen men, ten ponies, twenty-two dogs. The plan was for ponies and dogs to go to the foot of the Beardmore Glacier where the former would be killed for food and the latter would go home. From the foot of the Glacier, three man-hauled teams would go forward, two ultimately to turn back, leaving one to go on to the Pole.

Almost from the start the ponies, as Oates had warned, were a disappointment: walls of snow had to be built round them when they stood still, to protect them from the wind; they weakened rapidly. Yet morale of the men remained high: after twenty-nine days' march they camped four miles beyond the point where Scott had turned back in 1902. On that previous occasion he had taken fifty-eight days to reach it.

A day's march short of the Beardmore Glacier, they were caught in a four-day blizzard which kept them stationary, eating up precious rations, while the ponies grew weaker. When the blizzard dropped, they made a short march onward, then slaughtered the surviving ponies, cut up the meat for food. So far, they were keeping to schedule, but it was obvious to Scott that they had lost a great deal of their vigour after 400 miles and he kept the dog teams for 160 miles farther than had been intended before sending them back.

Scott and his companions reached the top of the Beardmore Glacier on midsummer's day, 21 December, and built the Upper Glacier Depot. One of the remaining, man-hauled, sledges now left for home.

The other two sledges went on and it was not until 3 January that Scott made his decision that the final assault party would consist of Wilson, Oates, Edgar Evans and Bowers. This decision, so crisply set out in the diary that was found eight months after his death, gives no hint of its difficulty. Scott was a sensitive man (once, when told his sister had been delivered of a child after a difficult confinement, he fainted). Now he decided that gallant little Bowers deserved of all people to take his place in the Polar party. As the other, picked, members of his team had at least an equal right, he was forced, in order to implement his decision, to take four men instead of three with him: Wilson (39), Evans (37), Oates (32) and Bowers (28). The sledges were in every way designed for a four-man unit, and the decision could be justified only on moral grounds, because, as Scott implied in his diary, Bowers' addition brought down the average age. Subsequently he found, "Cooking for five takes a seriously longer time than cooking for four—an item I had not considered when reorganizing."

On 16 January, 1912, they had "a very terrible disappointment, and I am very sorry for my loyal companions . . .", they found traces of Amundsen's party. They reached the Pole, slept there the night of the 17th and next morning found Amundsen's tent and his note to Scott. Near to it the British party built a cairn, hung a Union Jack and took a photograph.

The return journey was worse than a nightmare. Because they were brave men, they confined their bitterness to the weather. This was worse, far worse, than could have been anticipated and one by one they fell victim to frostbite, then gradual starvation as they were delayed and had to reduce rations. Edgar Evans carried on with immense courage, but on 16 February he was crawling on hands and knees, pulling his share of the sledge, and that night he died. A few days later, another cruel blow: all stores were in order at Lower Barrier Depot, except fuel, which had leaked away. Without fuel, in that temperature, food was almost useless.

On 15 March, Oates could go no farther, asked to be left behind. The others refused. He walked out into the blizzard and was never seen again.

"We knew that Oates was walking to his death, but though we tried to dissuade him, we knew it was the act of a brave man and an Englishman. We all hope to meet the end with similar spirit, and assuredly the end is not far.

"Monday, 19 March—17.8 miles from (One Ton Depot)—ought to get there in three days—have two days food but barely a day's fuel—feet are getting bad—amputation is the least I can hope for now—weather doesn't give us a chance—minus forty degrees today . . .

"Wednesday, 21 March—got within 13 miles of depot on Monday night, had to lay up all yesterday in severe blizzard . . .

"Thursday, 29 March—since the 21st we have had a continuous gale —every day we have been ready to start for our depot, 13 *miles away* —do not think we can hope for any better things now. We can stick it out to the end but we are getting weaker and the end cannot be far. It seems a pity, but I do not think I can write more. R. Scott. Last Entry: For God's sake, look after our people."

So died a man whose name will never be forgotten, a name synonymous with bravery. When the rescue party found him, eight months later, his arm over his dearest friend, Wilson, the body of Bowers beside, they read a burial service and built a cairn, sur-mounted by a cross, and left them there, to stay, without bodily decay, frozen in their greatness.

Mohandas Karamchand Gandhi
1869-1948

MOHANDAS KARAMCHAND GANDHI, whom the world called "Mahatma" or "Great Soul", was the only political leader of our times to achieve a major revolution by means of a policy of non-violence. As the architect of the most effective civil disobedience movement in history, he could be called the forerunner of all our modern sit-down protests, whether by strikers or ban-the-bomb demonstrators.

Yet this walking skeleton of a man—he had a frail and puny body which he trained to extraordinary vigour by his faithfulness to dietetic precepts and personal hygiene—could mould heroes out of common clay. Although afflicted by a shyness so great in his early career that he could not bear to make a public speech, such was the force of his personal integrity that he persuaded hundreds of thousands of his fellow countrymen to risk their lives, their families and their fortunes to follow his cause and to endure prison and poverty because of their devotion to him and his principles.

He was born at Porbandar, on India's north-west coast, on 2 October, 1869, being the youngest son of Kaba Gandhi, Dewan of Rajkot, by his fourth wife. He was married at thirteen to Kasturbai, by whom he had four sons.

In September, 1887, at the age of eighteen, having given his mother a solemn vow to observe strict vegetarianism, he was sent to London to study law. On the voyage and in his first London hotel he almost starved to death because of this vegetarian vow. Seldom can a visitor to Britain have been more wretched. His shyness cut him off from all normal contacts and his bewilderment at English habits was so intense that he decided to train himself for polite society by "becoming a gentleman". He bought stylish Western clothes—even a silk hat—spent hours arranging his tie and hair. He took lessons in dancing and music, but Western rhythms proved quite beyond him. Suddenly he came to his senses and decided that "if my character makes a gentleman of me, so much the better—otherwise I should forgo the ambition".

In time Gandhi settled down and became an active member of

the Vegetarian Society. He remained in England for three years and was called to the Bar in 1891. He returned to India but made little headway as a lawyer until he was summoned to South Africa by an Indian firm there. It was in that country that his social conscience was thoroughly aroused. He saw his fellow Indians treated as coloured trash and within a few years he was drawn into their struggle for elementary political rights.

His own early experiences in South Africa helped to show him the enormity of the Indian problem there. He took train from Durban to Pretoria and, although holding a first-class ticket, he was physically thrown out of the compartment. All his protests were met by railway officials with jeers and shouts of "Sammy" —the contemptuous nickname given by Europeans to all Indians (presumably because so many Indian names end in "sami" or "swami"). He had to complete his journey by coach—and was beaten up by the conductor because he refused to move to an inferior seat.

Gandhi quickly realized that South Africa was no place for a self-respecting Indian and his mind was increasingly occupied with methods of reducing the appalling discrimination. In May, 1894, he and some Indian friends founded the Natal Indian Congress and launched a campaign to raise the standards of cleanliness, sanitation, housing and education among the Indians of Natal. By this time Gandhi had convinced himself that the Good Life was lived near the soil, with a minimum of dependence on machinery. He himself learned the arts of farming, cooking, nursing and teaching.

In 1906 came the Zulu Rebellion. Gandhi regarded himself as a citizen of Natal with duties to that State and he wrote to the Governor offering to recruit a volunteer company of Indian stretcher-bearers for the Natal forces. His offer was accepted and Gandhi's company took on the task of nursing the wounded Zulus, royalists and rebels alike, back to health. His experiences in the field led him towards a decision to "purify himself" and he took, with his wife Kasturbai's consent, a solemn vow of celibacy (*brahmacharya*). He wrote:

> "It was borne in upon me that I should have more and more occasions for service of the kind I was rendering, and that I should find myself unequal to the task if I were engaged in the pleasures of family life. In a word, I could not live after both the flesh and the spirit. . . ."

Meanwhile, in the Transvaal, he found crisis rapidly approaching for his community. The hostile leaders of the Europeans juggled statistics to prove that there was an organized conspiracy by the Indian leaders to flood the Transvaal with illegal Indian immigrants without residential rights. This led to the drafting of harsh anti-Asiatic laws, including even the fingerprinting of women and children over eight, as though they were criminals.

It became a historic situation because, to combat the savage legislation, Gandhi organized his first civil disobedience campaign, built at first on a policy of passive resistance and later developing into a conception new to the world of international politics—*satyagraha* or soul-force as a weapon for the masses of under-privileged people in their struggle for justice.

This is how Gandhi himself defined *satyagraha*:

"It is soul-force pure and simple, and whenever and to whatever extent there is room for the use of arms or physical force or brute force. . . . I had full realization of this antagonism at the time of the advent of *satyagraha* (in South Africa).

"There is a great and fundamental difference between passive resistance and *satyagraha*. If we continue to believe ourselves, and let others believe, that we are weak and helpless and therefore offer passive resistance, our resistance will never make us strong, and at the earliest opportunity we would give up passive resistance as a weapon of the weak. On the other hand, if we are *satyagrahis* and offer *satyagraha* believing ourselves to be strong, two clear consequences result from it. Fostering the idea of strength, we grow stronger and stronger every day. With the increase in our strength our *satyagraha*, too, becomes more effective, and we would never be casting about for an opportunity to give it up.

"Again, while there is no scope for love in passive resistance, on the other hand, not only has hatred no place in *satyagraha* but it is a positive breach of its ruling principle. Whilst in passive resistance there is a scope for the use of arms when a suitable occasion arrives, in *satyagraha* physical force is forbidden even in the most favourable circumstances.

"In passive resistance there is always present an idea of harassing the other party, and there is a simultaneous readiness to undergo any hardships entailed upon us by such activity, while in *satyagraha* there is not the remotest idea of injuring the opponent.

"*Satyagraha* postulates the conquest of the by adversary suffering in one's own person . . . Jesus Christ has been acclaimed as the Prince of Passive Resisters but I submit that in His case passive resistance must mean *satyagraha* and *satyagraha* alone . . . the phrase passive resistance was not employed to denote the patient suffering of oppression by thousands of devout Christians in the early days of Christianity—if their conduct be described as passive resistance, passive resistance becomes synonymous with *satyagraha*."

While Gandhi was pondering on the practical application of *satyagraha*, the Transvaal further increased the restrictions on Asiatic immigrants and a trial of strength against the Black Act (officially known as the Asiatic Law Amendment Act) was on. This brought Gandhi his first taste of imprisonment—two months in Johannesburg gaol. It was during this period that he first wore the "Gandhi cap"—later one of the great symbols of Indian loyalty to the cause of self-rule—which was in fact the headgear he wore as a coloured prisoner in South Africa.

The imprisonment of so many Indian leaders brought Gandhi his first, limited victory for the *satyagraha* principle. A compromise was worked out under which, on 30 January, 1908, he was taken to see General Jan Smuts—the first meeting between these two great figures. Following this interview Gandhi and his compatriots were immediately freed from prison. However, General Smuts failed to carry out his side of the compromise and a new Act was passed prohibiting Asiatics from entering the Transvaal. Then an even greater insult was inflicted on the Indian community when a judgment in the South African Supreme Court ruled that only Christian marriages recorded by the registrar would be legally valid in South Africa. Under Gandhi's leadership, Indians got themselves arrested by the score as a protest.

The climax of the struggle came in 1913 when a further series of repressive measures aimed at keeping Indians out forced Gandhi to organize a march of his countrymen across the frontier. He was followed by a crowd of 2,000, many of them coolie labourers. The forbearance, courtesy and restraint under provocation of Gandhi and his ragged band of marchers impressed public opinion. A commission reported in favour of repealing the anti-Indian Acts.

His campaigning successful, Gandhi returned to India, having made an admirer of General Smuts. At home he soon flung himself into the growing agitation for *swaraj*, or self-rule, and became an activist in the Indian National Congress Party. And his first significant contribution to this campaign was an appeal to his countrymen to organize corporate *satyagraha*.

The first victory in the second phase of his *satyagraha* policy was among the peasants of Champaran who were oppressed by the Government system of indigo-growing. "*Satyagraha* brought this age-long abuse to an end in a few months," said Gandhi who moved on to support victimized peasantry in other provinces.

Already Gandhi was a force in India and he was invited by the Viceroy to attend the War Conference at Delhi in the hope of gaining his support for the recruitment of Indian volunteers for service overseas. Throughout his South African experiences he held staunchly to the belief that it was his duty to help the British Empire in its times of stress and again he was faithful to that view.

With the First World War over, Gandhi turned once more to civil disobedience as a campaigning weapon—this time (in 1919) against the Rowlatt Acts which gave the Government extraordinary powers to suppress unrest in the Punjab. The mood of the people was ugly and, in flat contradiction of the *satyagraha* principles, there were many outbreaks of violence. Martial law was declared and this led to an appalling massacre at Amritsar. Gandhi astonished many of his friends by calling off the campaign.

He later confessed to a "Himalayan blunder" in failing to understand that his people were not yet sufficiently disciplined to remain non-violent in face of severe provocations. Three times he was to call off his campaigns because they had erupted in violence.

During the years 1918–22 he worked steadily for an accord between the Hindu and Moslem communities and in 1924 he undertook a three-week fast in Delhi hoping to induce these traditional antagonists to reach better understanding. The following year he announced his intention of observing "a year of political silence" because he opposed the wish of Congress leaders to take part in new legislature set up under the Montagu-Chelmsford Reforms. In fact he spent four years in the political wilderness campaigning in Indian villages against the "evil" of Untouchability. At every village meeting he sat among Untouchables and he welcomed them to his Ashram, or settlement. He also fought against drink- and drug-taking habits, urged the villagers to tend their cattle well, and preached goodwill between clashing religious communities.

In 1927 Sir John Simon's Commission considered whether India was ready for another instalment of self-government. Congress resolved that, as the Government would give no pledge of immediate Dominion status to India, Gandhi must lead a new campaign of civil disobedience. He decided to single out the Government's salt monopoly for a dramatic demonstration and with his followers, joined by thousands en route, marched to the sea at Dandi. The march created widespread interest in Britain and America. It took Gandhi's band of *satyagrahis* a month to reach the sea. There, on 6 April, 1930, Gandhi ceremoniously picked up a piece of salt from the beach and thus, by a symbolic breach of the law, inaugurated the new disobedience campaign.

He was arrested a month later under a regulation whereby persons could be imprisoned indefinitely without trial. This action of the authorities was followed by a *hartal*, a day of political mourning, in all the chief towns of India. A truce was negotiated between Gandhi and Lord Irwin, under which the Viceroy withdrew repressive measures and Congress suspended direct action. Six months later the truce was broken and the repressive measures were reinforced under a new Viceroy, Lord Willingdon. Once more Gandhi was gaoled and kept in custody without trial.

Gandhi in gaol was as great a propaganda force as Gandhi at liberty. Indeed in that year (1932) almost all the Congress leaders were behind bars.

Before that year's end Gandhi started a "fast unto death" on behalf of the Untouchables. This was conspicuously successful. The Hindu and Untouchable leaders gathered around his bed and hammered out a compromise. In 1933 he was freed and for the next few years devoted himself to the cause of the Untouchables.

By 1938 he was back in the centre of the political stage, trying to bridge the ever-widening gulf between Hindu and Muslim and preaching his policy of non-violence right up to the outbreak of the Second World War. He was arrested again in 1942 after Congress had passed a "Britain Must Quit India" resolution. India was convulsed by a mass movement against the Government because of this arrest and it seriously interfered with the war effort.

Gandhi's wife, Kasturbai, who for many years had been sharing his vicissitudes, died in prison in 1944. The following year the Labour Party came to power in Britain and sent a Cabinet mission of three to frame a Constitution for India. Gandhi hailed the Mission's efforts as "sincere and honest". On 27 February, 1947, the British Government announced their decision to leave India.

During the transfer of power Gandhi toured riot areas and preached the need for peace and goodwill. He lived to see his great ambition for a free India recognized but he grieved at the mounting strife between Hindus and Muslims. In a further effort to bring about peace in his seventy-ninth year he fasted for five days. The rejoicing of his people at the fast's end turned to horror when, on 30 January, 1948, on his way to a prayer-meeting Gandhi was shot dead by a fanatical young Hindu.

Thus blind and unreasoning violence ended a life dedicated to denouncing its use in the affairs of mankind, and the world lost the counsel of a wise and selfless being whose deeds and words still guide the destinies of his vast nation and will continue so to do long after those who live by the sword have perished by the sword.

Frank Lloyd Wright
1869-1959

WHEN the most appalling earthquake in recorded history shattered the Tokyo and Yokohama areas of Japan in 1923, killing 250,000 people and destroying over 500,000 houses, one of the very few large buildings that stood intact amid the desolation was the Imperial Hotel at Tokyo. As the city toppled in ruins, the hotel rocked, but the walls and ceilings held firm. A few days after the disaster a cable arrived at Taliesin, Spring Green, Wisconsin, home of an American architect then aged fifty-four and named Frank Lloyd Wright. It was from an official of the Japanese Government, and read: *Hotel stands undamaged as monument of your genius. Congratulations.*

The building had stood safely through the tremendous upheaval simply because it had been designed by a great architect who was as brilliant an engineer as he was an artist. At his death in 1959 the *Journal of the American Institute of Architects* was to say, "This century's architectural achievements would be unthinkable without him"; yet he had no smooth path to the universal recognition which came only late in life. Like all great innovators he frequently met with opposition and active hostility among his professional colleagues.

Before we consider the life of this great man, it will be helpful to examine briefly of what his contribution to the modern movement in architecture consisted.

Architects of the nineteenth century both in Europe and America were almost totally lacking in originality. They preferred to follow traditional styles, particularly the so-called classical and Gothic revivals, which were modelled on the architecture of ancient Greece and medieval Europe. This often led to the most absurd results, as for instance when architects tried to make municipal buildings look like Greek or Roman temples, and ordinary dwellings like Gothic cathedrals. Although in America the nineteenth century saw the birth of the steel skeleton, it was almost barren of any real progress in architectural design. Minds absorbed with the forms of Greek and Gothic architecture were hardly capable of designing for the steel skeleton, an architectural innovation so great in its implications that it might well be called the cause of a revolution.

In all man's building before the development of steel, walls took the weight of the upper storeys and of the roof, so they had to be strong, which in turn meant that the walls of a large building usually had to be massive. The development, in the middle of the nineteenth century, of the form of construction using a steel skeleton enabled the weight of the building to be carried on the steel frame so that walls needed to be no stronger than was necessary merely to keep out the weather. The adaptation to the steel frame of the cantilever principle meant that each upright of the steel frame was supported on a huge footing (caisson) which virtually "floated" in the earth and could, within certain limits, move without wrecking the steel frame, which thus was accorded a measure of flexibility utterly impossible in a building where the walls took the weight.

Frank Lloyd Wright was one of the very few to grasp the significance and possibilities of the revolution in building technique and, by the close of the century he had developed his philosophy of "organic architecture". He argued that architecture should evolve quite naturally, from the character of its age, and its local surroundings, and that, in particular, buildings should appear as an integral part of their setting. He was to revolutionize the patterns of domestic architecture, for to him a house should appear to grow out of its natural surroundings. As he himself said on one occasion: "A house should never be *on* a hill, but always *of* a hill." Thus it was that many of his most famous private commissions, often executed for wealthy Americans, were conceived as a continuation of nature itself. Nowhere was this principle better demonstrated than in Wright's design for one of the most famous modern houses in the world; Falling Water, the week-end retreat at Bear Run, Pennsylvania, which he built for the Pittsburgh Department Store owner, Edgar J. Kaufmann in 1936. The house was cantilevered over a mountain stream, from which its name derived. Surrounded by trees and dense vegetation that was always clearly visible from the great window spaces of this astonishing house, it was possible for the occupants to identify themselves closely with the wonder and beauty of nature while at the same time enjoying all the comforts and amenities of a superb modern home.

The principle had been displayed, even earlier, in Wright's design of the Imperial Hotel at Tokyo, where trees, and plants, and pools of water were all introduced as integral elements in the conception of the building. Today Wright's principle of "organic architecture" is widely applied by architects throughout the world.

Wherever a house or a block of flats or a public building is primarily conceived in relation to its natural surroundings; wherever the architect strives to relate his conception to the immediate setting of trees, hills, water, etc., as is the case with the design of a great many modern school buildings; where the long simple lines of modern architectural design offer a complementary foil for the turbulences of a natural setting (Wright believed that buildings whose main lines lay along the surface of the earth would best display a sense of belonging to it) you may be sure that the influence of Frank Lloyd Wright's genius is at work.

In the summer of 1869 Anna, the young second wife of William Wright, a Wisconsin preacher and music master, waiting for the moment when her child would be born, studied books on English cathedrals and dreamed that her baby would be a boy and that he would grow up to be a great and famous architect. Anna, seventeen years younger than her husband William, was the daughter of Richard Lloyd Jones, one of a clan of Welsh preachers, teachers and farmers, who had migrated from their native land to live and work amid the hills of Southern Wisconsin. The future grandfather of Frank Lloyd Wright was a hatter, farmer and lay minister, who led his family to a homestead in the New World. It was here that Anna, one of a large family of brothers and sisters, met the forty-seven-year-old widower William Wright. At the time she was a schoolteacher, and it seems doubtless that Frank Lloyd Wright inherited from his mother and his Welsh ancestry the love of learning, the passion for teaching, the fervour of temperament, and the imaginative power which were to form the substance of his personality and his genius.

Soon after Frank's birth in Richland Center, Spring Green, Wright accepted a call to the Baptist Ministry, and left Wisconsin with his family, the three children of his first wife, Anna and the new baby, to take charge of a church in Weymouth, Massachusetts. Here little Frank attended a private school, collected stones of interesting shapes, and drew with gaily coloured pencils. About this time also Mrs Wright was responsible for creating in her young son the passion for building that was later to be translated into such wonderful reality. She bought him in these early days a set of wooden building blocks of the kind used for the advanced kindergartens of the day. Cubes, spheres and cylinders of smooth maple. As young Frank arranged the blocks in patterns and structures they fired in him a sense of architecture. As he said in later life, "Those blocks stayed in my fingers all my life."

But clouds were on the way for the Wright family. William had never found it easy to settle at any employment. He turned from preaching to music teaching, and shortly after the family move to Weymouth, Mr Wright dragged them to Madison, the capital of Wisconsin, where he set up a conservatoire of music. This failed. Relations between Anna and her husband grew ever more strained and gloomy and eventually Mrs Wright begged her husband to leave them. "I will manage the children," she said. Whereupon Mr Wright, taking only his violin, walked out on his family, who never saw him again. All the time Frank and his two sisters were at a public school. Mrs Wright was forced to return to her teaching to help to support her family.

The years passed happily enough, and in 1885 Frank entered the University of Madison to study among other things, architecture. The young man was restive at University. He dreamed of Chicago, and told his mother:

"There are great buildings in Chicago. But they need great architects. I am going to be a great architect, and Chicago needs me. I must go there, Mother. There is nothing for me here."

So, in 1887, when he was barely nineteen years old, Frank Lloyd Wright bundled up a few precious books, and with a borrowed seven dollars, boarded a train for Chicago. When he arrived in the great city, he had even less than the seven dollars he set out with for some of this had gone to pay his fare. He had to get a job, and quickly. He was lucky; a few days after he arrived in the city he was given a job as a tracer on an architect's staff. His salary—eight dollars a week. Less than twenty years before Frank came to Chicago it had been laid waste by the great fire of 1871, and there was tremendous scope for architects. Fate was kind, both to Chicago and to Frank Lloyd Wright, for it was in the burned out western suburbs of the city that eventually he distinguished himself—and the city. Elsewhere, throughout America, the pseudo-Classical and fake Gothic styles were in evidence, but Chicago, with its ever-increasing new class of millionaires, was hungry for architects to build vast dwellings and massive commercial houses. Self-made men the vast majority of them, these tycoons wanted buildings that would glorify and display their wealth. The city was not short of good architects, but only one at that time impressed young Frank. This was the famous Louis Henri Sullivan, who was then planning a gigantic block of business and entertainment buildings for Congress Street and Michigan Avenue.

Sullivan needed a draughtsman to assist with his preliminary drawings for this huge enterprise. Wright applied for the appointment. Looking over the young man's drawings Sullivan remarked, "Traced, I expect?" "No, sir," replied the applicant, "free-hand." He was engaged on the spot and for the next six years worked in Sullivan's office. During this fruitful period he married a Miss Catherine Toblin, a beautiful girl, in spite of family opposition on both sides.

Then in 1893 Wright broke with Louis Sullivan to set up his own offices, and began designing houses for his own clients. He was passionately fond of domestic architecture and this facet of his work was to become his crowning glory. He had already built his own home and now he built himself a studio, which was connected to the house by a corridor built around a willow tree whose trunk rose through its roof. As Frank's reputation and prosperity increased, so did his family. In all, Catherine was to bear him six children. Later he was to desert her for a certain Mrs Cheyney who eventually was installed as the lady of his house at Taliesin.

In 1914, tragedy struck. One day while Frank and his son John were in Chicago, a Negro servant, Julian Carleton, went berserk with an axe, slaughtering Mrs Cheyney and six employees of the Taliesin household before setting the establishment ablaze with gasoline, and then killing himself. This terrible tragedy left a wound in Frank Lloyd Wright's mind that never really healed. The tragedy gave rise to a great public scandal, and the Church in particular saw it as a visitation of the wages of sin, for although Mrs Cheyney was divorced from her husband, she was not married to Wright.

Despite many personal difficulties, Frank's fame grew, and the envy and enmity of his less-gifted colleagues grew also.

In 1915 he was commissioned to design the Imperial Hotel in Tokyo. Since his first visit to Japan in 1905 he had been intensely interested in Japanese art and architecture, and in their sense of relating buildings to nature. The Oriental feeling which Wright had by that time developed in his sketch drawings was immensely pleasing to the Japanese, and his plans for the new hotel were readily accepted. By now, Wright was again entangled with a lady; a Mrs Miriam Noel, and she went with him to Tokyo when he started work on the building. For seven years he travelled between America and Japan. Soon after his divorce from Catherine, and a year after the hotel was completed in 1922, he married Mrs Noel. The wedding ceremony held on a bleak, wind-swept day in November, 1923, was a curious one; Frank Lloyd Wright and his bride were joined in matrimony while standing at the centre of the bridge spanning the Wisconsin river. The ritual was meant to symbolize the bridging of all the difficulties that had hitherto stood between them. But the marriage was to prove a tragic failure. The man who had become one of the most famous architects in the world could find no real success or lasting happiness in his marriages. A few months after she had married Wright, Miriam left her husband to live in Los Angeles.

Worn and exhausted, Wright sought solace at the drawing board. During the years that followed he was constantly hounded by Miriam for money, possessions, and of his new liason with a divorced lady of Montenegrin extraction, named Olgivanna. Court orders and summonses continuously harassed Wright who became poverty stricken. In the late twenties, when he had at last won his freedom from Miriam, Wright married Olgivanna. This time, the marriage was to be a happy one. Work poured in, and money began to arrive. In Taliesin, now rebuilt, Frank and Olgivanna were ecstatically happy.

In 1932 Wright founded the famous Taliesin Fellowship which provided for a number of brilliant young architects to benefit from a year's study with the master. Years passed in hard work, ever-increasing success, and most blissful of all, in true conjugal happiness.

Some of Wright's most famous buildings were erected in the next few years, including the Administration Building at Racine, Wisconsin, for the Johnson Wax Co. This has since become one of America's most conspicuous architectural sights. Even in 1939, the building was visited by no fewer than 30,000 people on the two days following its completion.

Wright was always a man of imagination and generosity. When Dr Spivey, the President of the obscure Southern College at Florida appeared on Wright's doorstep one day and said: "Mr Wright, I have no money but if you'll design a new college building for me, we'll pay you when we can," Wright unhesitatingly put the plans in hand. In time the job earned Wright 100,000 dollars and put Florida's Southern College securely on the map as one of the greatest pieces of modern collegiate architecture in the United States. In 1951 Wright designed another project for S. C. Johnson & Son; a research tower at Racine. The last, and perhaps the most famous and controversial of his buildings was the Solomon R. Guggenheim Museum on Fifth Avenue, New York, erected in 1959. It was completed shortly before his death, and was the 700th structure designed by the great, and by then, grand old man. The building, circular in design, and clean in its long sweeping lines, is a worthy monument to the man who changed the face of architecture.

Much has been recorded of Wright's brilliant, often withering wit. On one occasion when he was asked what might be done to improve the city of Pittsburgh, he barked, "Destroy it and start again from scratch!" On another occasion, when a leak occurred in the roof of a house built by Wright the distraught owner called the great man on the telephone for his advice, Wright said: "Think nothing of it—rise above it!" "But the rain is falling into a lady guest's soup-plate," pleaded the owner. "Tell her to move her chair," retorted Wright and banged down the receiver. Whenever he was asked which of his buildings he considered the best, Wright would always reply with a chuckle: "The next one—always the next one. . . ."

On Saturday 4 April, 1959, Frank Lloyd Wright was operated on for an intestinal stoppage. He was in his ninetieth year. After the operation he appeared to rally, but on the Thursday, at dawn, he died. He was buried in the Lloyd Jones family churchyard at Spring Green, on 12 April, close to Anna, the mother who had dreamed her son would become a great architect, and whose dream had come true.

Lenin
1870-1924

BEYOND question the most significant of the twentieth-century revolutionaries—and perhaps the most astonishing in all history—was Vladimir Ilyich Ulyanov. Not the least remarkable feature of his most improbable success story is that his baptismal names are recognized only by students of history and international politics whereas his *nom de guerre* is known in every corner of the globe and, indeed, mentioned with awe or contempt in every spoken language.

This extraordinary man was born on 10 April, 1870, at Simbirsk on the Volga, but it was not until February, 1900, that he adopted the name by which he is remembered—Lenin.

Consider the odds against his success. His eldest brother, Alexandre, was hanged in 1887 for taking part in a plot to assassinate the Tsar. Ilyich Ulyanov was therefore a marked man from the age of seventeen; his whole family—he had two brothers and three sisters—came under the suspicion of the Tsarist police, with some reason, for each one in his or her way was engaged in revolutionary activities. There is, however, no valid evidence that this personal tragedy turned him into an embittered rebel, dedicated to the overthrow of the Tsarist régime to avenge his family's dishonour.

Lenin's father, who held a responsible position in the education service of the Province of Simbirsk, died one year before his eldest son's death on the scaffold. His mother, whose family owned a small estate in the Province of Kazan, never wavered in her loyal support of her revolutionary-minded children.

His brother's execution left a lasting mark on Lenin. It impressed him strongly with the futility of acts of terrorism by individuals as a policy for bring about fundamental changes in the social order. It helped to convince him that in any social system the class, caste or bloc with the economic strength wields the real power in the land and that any genuine movement towards a revolution of the working class cannot hope to succeed by attacking individual tyrants but by creating an organization with the aim of seizing economic power. With that extraordinary objectivity which was to prove of tremendous advantage to him in later life, he studied

the aims of his ill-fated brother and he came to the conclusion that
they could not be achieved by Alexandre's method (of assassination),
however wicked the tyrant or however heroic the revolutionary.

Six months after his brother's execution Lenin enrolled in the
University of Kazan to study law, but his career there lasted barely
a month. He was made the scapegoat of a student "rag" and banished
to the home of his mother's family in the country. He made repeated
applications to other universities but all were rejected until, in 1890,
he was permitted to sit the law examinations at St Petersburg
University as an external student. He passed and was admitted to a
law degree.

Alongside his law studies he became absorbed in the works of
Karl Marx and other revolutionary writers. He emerged from St
Petersburg in 1891 with a law degree and a profound understanding
of Marxist economics. At the age of twenty-three he abandoned all
thoughts of a career at the Bar and gave himself unreservedly to
what Marxists call "the working-class struggle". He had already
written one or two pamphlets on the subject and he linked up with
what Socialist groups were then in existence in St Petersburg.
Among his earliest contacts there was Nadezhda Konstantinova
Krupskaya, who later became his wife, co-worker and patient ally
through all his vicissitudes.

Lenin faced the choice of lining up with the old terrorist movement, now called the Social Revolutionaries, or one of the small
groups of Social Democrats—and without hesitation he attached
himself to the Social Democrats. Although he soon became one of
their leading controversialists, the eyes of the police and their
informers were almost always on him because of his family history.
Krupskaya, whose book *Memories* supplies a valuable record of
Lenin's activities, describes many of the devices they were forced
to adopt to keep their meetings secret—Socialist discussion groups
would be called under the innocuous title of "Pancake Teas";
routes to the meeting-places had to be varied each time to dodge
police spies; codes and invisible ink were in frequent use. In this
way Lenin tried to educate bodies of workers on the meanings of
Socialism and tried to elucidate Marx's *Das Kapital* for them. That
was how he spent most of his time until the year 1895 when he
suffered a serious illness and obtained permission to go abroad to
recover his health. He went to Berlin where he attended workers'
meetings and to Geneva where he met the recognized leaders-in-
exile of Russian Social Democracy.

He returned to Russia from Geneva with a trunkful of illegal literature, plans for a Socialist newspaper and even the printing press to produce it. The ever-vigilant Russian police swooped on his hide-out on the eve of publication and for the first time Lenin had a taste of prison life. That was in December, 1895. He served his sentence in solitary but, helped by books smuggled in from outside, confine-ment proved no disadvantage to a man whose mental discipline made him independent of rich food or furnishings. He was still working on his book, *The Development of Capitalism in Russia*, when his year's sentence ended. The Tsar then announced his banishment to Siberia for a further three years.

When Lenin heard this decision he jested: "Pity they let me out so soon. I would have liked to do a little more work on the book. It will be difficult to obtain reading matter in Siberia." Before he got out of prison, Krupskaya was thrown in and she therefore got no opportunity to see him before he left for Siberia in January, 1897. Later Krupskaya joined him in banishment and together they trans-lated from English into Russian *The History of Trade Unionism*, by Sidney and Beatrice Webb—although at that time Lenin could not understand a word of spoken English!

In February, 1900, his banishment ended and, now aged thirty, he decided to use the name N. Lenin as a *nom de guerre*. Soon after his return a conference of the revolutionary wing of the Social Democrats decided that Lenin should go abroad to re-establish contacts with their comrades in exile with the particular purpose of reviving the project for a Socialist newspaper. This idea had been nipped in the bud four years earlier. He went to Munich by way of Prague and Krupskaya followed him four months later. She found it remarkably difficult to trace him because of the ingenious way in which he had covered his track to throw off less-welcome pursuers.

By the time he reached Munich Lenin had a clear-cut idea of his plans and policies for the future. His immediate objective was to get the Socialist newspaper going, but his long-term aim was to weld an all-Russian Social Democrat organization with a common centre and a recognized leadership. It is a remarkable fact that Lenin had to wait until 1917 before he could freely make contact with the workers in Russia. Yet this one man, studying, writing, debating and plotting beyond the frontiers of his homeland, succeeded in changing its destiny fundamentally and with it, perhaps, the destiny of all mankind.

During his long absence from Russia he forged the conviction that the Tsarist régime must be overthrown by armed force and supreme power must be seized and used—ruthlessly, if need be—by the workers supported by the soldiers and the peasants. The party polarized into the Bolsheviks, of which Lenin was the leader and chief spokesman, and the Mensheviks. The Bolsheviks stood for an uncompromising, revolutionary approach based on the proletariat and peasantry; the Mensheviks were in favour of defeating capitalism by working with the liberal burgeoisie. Out of the struggle with the Mensheviks emerged the policy which was eventually to lead to the October Revolution and to the change in the party's name from Social Democrat to Communist.

Of their hardships together at this time Krupskaya has written:

> "Our door was never bolted; a jug of milk and a loaf were left in the dining-room overnight, and bedding spread on the divan so that, in the event of anyone coming on the night train" (from Russia to Finland, in this case) "they could enter without waking us, have some refreshment and lie down to sleep. In the morning we often found comrades in the dining-room who had come during the night."

At last the long-awaited Socialist newspaper came out in Munich. It was titled *Iskra* (The Spark) and a companion publication, dealing more profoundly with the theory of Socialism, was produced by the same editorial board—this was named *Zarya* (Dawn). At the centre of this journalistic activity was, of course, Lenin, with Krupskaya as editorial secretary doubling as circulation manager and Party secretary as well.

Early in 1902 it became impossible to continue printing *Iskra* in Munich as the printer was afraid of the risks involved in publishing a clandestine paper. It was decided to move to London. That is where the Lenins set themselves up in April, 1902. Lenin's life in London did not differ in essentials from his life in prison, in Siberia, Switzerland, or Germany. His concentration on his revolutionary goals was so all-absorbing that he needed only a chair to sit on, a desk to write at, and a room to pace. Krupskaya handled all the details of their domestic life and feeding arrangements. About this period she comments:

> "We found that the Russian stomach is not easily adaptable to the ox-tails, skate fried in fat, cake and other mysteries of English fare. We had to look after every penny and live as cheaply as possible."

Lenin's salary ran to about £6 a month (when Party funds permitted). The house they occupied was at 30 Holford Square in the area lying north of Euston Road. It was situated between the British Museum and Highgate Cemetery, where Karl Marx was

Above: Kitty Hawk, North Carolina: 17 December, 1903. Orville Wright at the controls of the first machine to make a powered flight. After he and his brother, Wilbur, had their plane ready on the launching track, Orville arranged the camera on a tripod and focused it. He asked John T. Daniels, one of those present, to snap the shutter as the plane cleared the starting rail. Daniels did as he was told; hence this historic picture. Owing to delays in the taking-up of the invention, the Wrights later found that there were those who contested their originality. One interesting claim made on behalf of a Dr Samuel Langley (whose plane is shown, *below*, in 1903 mounted on a houseboat) was that he had invented the "first man-carrying machine capable of powered flight". Not until 1942 was it conceded that the plane could never have flown.

Above: This 1958 addition to the Hotel Imperial, Tokyo, is of steel and concrete like the original 1922 structure. The magnificence of the hotel may be judged from the entrance (*inset*). Frank Lloyd Wright's building withstood the disastrous 1923 earthquake which killed 250,000 Japanese.

Right: The millions John D. Rockefeller made out of Standard Oil were by many regarded as "tainted". So he set up the Rockefeller Foundation to administer his charities. To-day in New York City the Rockefeller Centre, a group of fifteen stone and steel buildings, stands as his monument.

buried. In London the Lenins assumed the name Richter—a concealment necessary for the safety of his lieutenants and followers in Russia. Inevitably the reading-room of the British Museum became Lenin's favourite haunt, as it had been that of Karl Marx, so that august edifice has the distinction of having fed the minds of the two pioneers of Communism.

Lenin and Krupskaya also set to work to acquire a working knowledge of the English language. Regularly they listened to the open-air speakers in Hyde Park to improve their vernacular English. Krupskaya refers in her *Memories* to the deep impression made on her husband by the evidence of great wealth and great poverty existing side by side in London.

It was in London, too, that he had his first meeting with his great fellow revolutionary, Leon Trotsky. Immediately they were immersed in discussion of their ideas for the progress of Socialism in Russia. Although these two were often in opposition on major issues, in the truly critical period in 1917 they worked hand in hand and Lenin entrusted Trotsky with tasks vital to the success of the Revolution. In the first period of their association, Trotsky stayed on in London and became one of *Iskra*'s contributors.

The conditions of their life in England damaged Lenin's nervous health and the group moved back to Geneva in April, 1903.

Meanwhile events in Russia were making the ground fertile for the revolutionary seeds being prepared in exile. In January, 1904, Tsar Nicholas plunged his nation into an unpopular war with Japan over Korea which brought decisive defeats on land at Mukden and at sea at Shushima, forcing Russia to sue for the peace which was concluded in September, 1905.

At the beginning of that year (22 January, 1905) there had occurred an outrage which had, perhaps, done just as much as the disastrous war to stir up revolutionary ferment. This came to be known as the Massacre of Red Sunday. On that day a peaceful and unarmed demonstration of the poorest citizens, headed by a priest, Father Gapon, and carrying religious emblems, marched to the Winter Palace in St Petersburg (present-day Leningrad) to present a humble petition to the Tsar to take pity on their sufferings. The Tsar's troops were drawn up in readiness and, when the procession was within range, the order to fire was given. Two hundred of these poverty-stricken people were slaughtered where they stood.

In October, after the peace treaty had been signed with Japan, a general strike was declared in Moscow. It met with unanimous response, even the soldiery siding with the workers. The Moscow

Workers' Soviet (then an innocuous word meaning "council") issued an order that the strike was to be converted into an armed rising which raged for five days but was finally shelled into submission by reinforcements from St Petersburg, the then capital of Russia. This defeat spelled the end of the sporadic 1905 Revolution.

These dramatic events convinced Lenin that the time had come for his return to Russia. Father Gapon, leader of the Red Sunday procession, had fled to Geneva to meet Lenin. Although Lenin's group of exiles distrusted Gapon as a suspected catspaw of the Tsar and a priest, Lenin seized the advantage of having with him the central figure of such a notorious outrage and, with Gapon, busied himself organizing a supply of arms from Britain to the Fighting Committee of the Bolsheviks. By November of that eventful year Lenin was back in St Petersburg, working now in the open.

The crushing of the Moscow rising forced him back underground and, although he moved around addressing secret meetings of his followers, the police gave him no peace until once more he reluctantly decided to seek refuge in Switzerland. In the events of 1905, however, Lenin discerned several salient factors. The people had seized real, if only temporary, freedom; the Soviets of workers and peasants were the vehicles of potential revolutionary power; and for the first time on a wide scale the people had used force against their oppressors. These facts were to serve Lenin as guiding principles in 1917 in setting up the dictatorship of the proletariat as the new Soviet state.

When the great day came, the day for which Lenin had studied, planned and plotted for so long—he was still out of the country.

On 3 March, 1917, a strike of metal workers in St Petersburg spread to a general strike throughout the city. The Workers' Soviet got busy and the soldiers came over to the side of the strikers. Ten days after the St Petersburg strike Moscow, too, was in the throes of a general strike.

The Tsar, finding himself bereft of almost all support and being made the scapegoat for all the country's ills, abdicated in favour of his brother, the Grand Duke Michael. But Russia wanted no more of the Romanovs and Michael, too, abdicated after only twenty-four hours on the throne. State power was now firmly in the hands of Parliament (the Duma).

The revolutionary leaders in exile fretted to return to the scene of the action. Lenin was in Switzerland and therefore would have to pass through the territory of one or other of the belligerent countries —and he was not *persona grata* with the Allied governments. He therefore asked his Swiss Socialist friends to negotiate a passage for him through Germany. He appreciated that this might lay him open to a charge of being pro-German, so he took every precaution to safeguard his reputation in that respect. He wrote a detailed account for *Pravda* of the conditions under which he and his fellow Socialists were permitted to travel through Germany.

Lenin arrived at St Petersburg station on 16 April—and was taken aback by the great reception awaiting him.

On 7 November, 1917, Lenin became president of the world's first Soviet Government and faced a task of greater dimensions and complexity than any statesman, ruler, or tyrant in history. He had to spread his power over the largest land surface enclosed by any nation. He had to bend to his will a population of 150,000,000 people. He had to improvise a new machinery of legislation and administration. He had to persuade that vast population to break with the traditions of centuries and become builders of a new society—and ninety cent per of that population were still illiterate. He had to bring all this about by the force of his own will and intellect. His supporters were in the main raw recruits to the Bolshevik Party, utterly untrained in the use of power.

What manner of man was this Lenin who accomplished such staggering tasks? He was a short, stocky figure with a big head set down on his shoulders, bald and bulging. Little eyes, a snub nose, wide, generous mouth and heavy chin. The entire civilized world came to recognize his beard at a glance. Usually dressed in shabby clothes, with trousers too long for his legs. Unimpressive in appearance, a leader purely by virtue of intellect—colourless, humourless, uncompromising and detached, without picturesque idiosyncrasies, but with the power of explaining profound ideas in simple terms and combining shrewdness with the greatest audacity.

By 1922 Lenin's overworked body began to rebel—his night-and-day dedication to his gigantic tasks played havoc with his arteries. He was only fifty-two and, after a few months of rest, he insisted on returning to his .thousand duties. In March, 1923, he suffered a stroke which brought him to death on 21 January, 1924: his age—fifty-four. He had only five years of free activity in Russia before illness struck him down—five years in which he had controlled and directed a revolution vaster in extent and more lasting in significance than any known to history.

Few will now dispute that the structure he gave to his primitive, illiterate, feudal country made it possible for his successors to create the nation which today has emerged as one of the two greatest powers of the twentieth century.

Jan Christiaan Smuts
1870-1950

In the spring of 1917 Winston Churchill, as he then was, wrote of General Jan Christiaan Smuts:

"There arrives in England from the outer marches of the Empire a new and altogether extraordinary man. The stormy and hazardous roads he has travelled by would fill all the acts and scenes of a drama. He has warred against us—well we know it. He has quelled rebellion against our own flag with unswerving loyalty and unfailing shrewdness. He has led raids at desperate odds and conquered provinces by scientific strategy. . . . His astonishing career and versatile achievements are only the index of a profound sagacity and a cool, far-reaching comprehension."

Smuts was a hero to the British public as the rebel general who had during the Boer War in 1901 fought a successful guerilla war against the British troops under Kitchener, and it added to the romance of the story that he carried a Greek testament and Kant's *Critique of Pure Reason* in his saddlebag; he was a hero because, as a general in the British army in 1916, he had begun the conquest of German East Africa and the year before had taken some part in the conquest of West Africa with General Louis Botha, the South African Prime Minister.

In March, 1917, the war against Germany was being fought with great bitterness, and the arrival in England of an enemy-turned-friend gave the British a new faith and hope in their aims. His intelligence and sound judgment made a big impression at the meetings of the Imperial War Conference and Lloyd George, the Prime Minister, took the unprecedented step of inviting Smuts, who was then Minister of Defence in the South African Government, to be a member of the British War Cabinet. His service proved most valuable, for he was a tremendous worker, had no ties in England and could look at the war situation objectively with an exceptionally clear mind.

"We shall win this war but lose the peace," he said in 1917; he planned a future for the "British Commonwealth of Nations" and for a League of Nations.

He had also a great deal of practical work to do on various committees. One of the most important jobs he did was to organize an Air Ministry after the bombing of the East End of London by twenty-two Gotha planes in July, 1917. Previous attempts to co-ordinate the separate Air Forces of the Army and Navy had failed, but Smuts had special qualifications which enabled him to succeed. He was tireless, ruthless and prepared to override objections raised by generals and admirals. In a little over a week he had produced a plan for the co-ordinated defence of London and Great Britain, and a scheme for an independent Air Force under an Air Ministry, which were accepted by the Cabinet and by Parliament. He settled a strike of engineers at Coventry and of coal miners in South Wales at a time when the Navy had only one week's supply of coal in reserve.

Smuts could do useful things in England which he could not do so effectively in South Africa. He was impatient, arrogant and a hustler, which the Boers disliked; they expected courtesy and long discussions for which the quick and clever Smuts had no time or inclination. Delegates to Smuts's office in Pretoria used to come away fuming at the way they had been treated and would then be calmed down by General Botha, who was prepared to smoke and talk with them.

Smuts led two lives. He wrote:

"There were times when I could not help contrasting my circumstances in England with the distrust and hatred and revilings I had to strive against in my own country."

To find the reason for this remarkable contrast it is necessary to look back to his childhood and political life.

Jan Christiaan Smuts, known as Jannie, was born a British subject on 24 May, 1870, at Bovenplatz in Cape Colony. His mother was of French Huguenot descent and his father had Dutch parentage. Jannie Smuts was weakly, studious, reserved and complex in character. He studied the Bible and thought of going into the Church, but Shelley's *Prometheus Unbound* gave him other ideas. At Victoria College, Stellenbosch, he learned a Greek grammar by heart in a week. At twenty-two he went to Cambridge, came out first in both parts of the Law Tripos, read Law in Chambers in London and returned to South Africa in 1895 where he was admitted to the Bar in Capetown.

He became interested in politics and joined the *Afrikander Bond* which was working for a united South Africa inspired by the Dutchman J. H. Hofmeyr. At that time Cape Colony and Natal were controlled by the British Government; the Transvaal and the Orange River Colony were Dutch Republics. Hofmeyr worked for union with Cecil Rhodes, Prime Minister of Cape Colony, who had arrived from England in 1881 and had amassed a large fortune from the diamonds of Kimberley and from the gold of the Rand.

Jan Smuts had a great admiration for Rhodes and his large ideas which included a united Africa northwards to the Mediterranean. He spoke publicly in favour of Rhodes in Stellenbosch and attracted the great man's favourable attention, but earned the dislike of the influential Olive Schreiner and other Dutch who distrusted Rhodes. Rhodes wanted to get rid of seventy-three-year-old Paul Kruger, President and dictator of the Transvaal who stood in the way of reform, union and expansion northwards. Kruger also controlled the gold of Johannesburg and was friendly with the Germans who had colonies across the border in West and East Africa. In 1895 Rhodes was forty-two and knew that illness would shorten his life; he was in too much of a hurry and all his plans were destroyed by the hasty and mismanaged Jameson Raid, of which the plan had been that the Transvaal capital of Pretoria should be captured from Johannesburg, thirty miles away, and Kruger overthrown. The Dutch rallied round Kruger; Rhodes's political career was ruined and there was nearly war.

For Jan Smuts the raid was a turning point in his life; he had been betrayed by his hero Cecil Rhodes and he had made a fool of himself by praising Rhodes in a public speech. His own great ambitions in politics seemed to be ruined for he was distrusted by the Dutch and he had become fiercely anti-British. In newspaper articles he denounced as traitors the Dutch of the Cape who still supported Rhodes. He moved to Johannesburg to practise Law and became involved in a dramatic legal battle. The only limitation on Kruger's powers came from the Judiciary and Chief Justice Kotze fought hard to maintain its independence from the Executive. With his election as President for the fourth time Kruger felt confident enough to dismiss Kotze. There was an outcry from the lawyers, but one supported Kruger and that was Jan Smuts, who was then violently attacked as a traitor to his own profession. Kruger made him State Attorney at the age of twenty-eight. It was a wise decision, for Smuts could help him to combat the British in their plans to interfere in the Transvaal.

Smuts had been recommended to Kruger by Hofmeyr and, in spite of his poor physique, he was an impressive young man with his angry eyes "steely to hardness, brilliant, almost dazzling, almost affrighting". His enemies tried to unseat him but he was too smart for them and earned the name of *slim*, or crafty, Jannie.

Kruger regarded Sir Alfred Milner, who had arrived as High Commissioner of the Cape, as his main antagonist and as the protector of the Uitlanders of Johannesburg—the foreign capitalists and workers who had flocked there because of gold. An attempt to avert war between Dutch and English was made at a Conference on 29 May, 1899, at Bloemfontein between Milner and Kruger, who was accompanied by Smuts. "It is our country you want," muttered the angry Kruger. When he tired Smuts took over the argument with Milner, whom he disliked from the first, considering his haughty manner insuiting. There was no compromise; the Dutch prepared for war.

Smuts continued to display a fanatical energy. He wrote a violent attack on the English in a pamphlet called *A Century of Wrongs*, schemed to blow up the Rand gold mines and to raise revolt in India and Ireland. Kruger had a military agreement with Stayn, President of the Dutch Republic of the Orange Free State, and believed he could defeat the British as he had at Majuba. Joseph Chamberlain, the Prime Minister, sent ten thousand troops to South Africa and the Boers declared war in October, 1899.

Smuts took a leading part in the war, which lasted until 1902, as an administrator, as a commando leader and as a statesman. At the great Boer assembly at Vereeniging in May, 1902, he helped Botha and other leaders to persuade angry and sullen Boers that they must seek peace, though it would not mean the independence for which they had fought. He spoke of the concentration camps where, he said, twenty-three thousand women and children had died and he argued that the English would devastate the country: "We must not sacrifice the nation on the altar of independence."

The Transvaal and the Orange River Colony became Crown Colonies administered by Milner, now Viscount, as Governor. The Boers had had to accept but Botha and Smuts were considered as traitors by many of the Boers who clung to their independence. Smuts's wife was very bitter and refused to have any English spoken in the house.

After the return to power of the Liberal Party in England Smuts was sent to London to try to persuade the Liberal leaders to grant responsible government to the Boer states. When Smuts wished, he could exert great charm and had a persuasive manner. At an historic meeting with Campbell-Bannerman he persuaded the Liberal Prime Minister to agree and he in turn persuaded the

Cabinet. It was a remarkable decision for the British Government to take only three years after a bitter war. Had it not been taken the Boers would have been on the side of the Germans when the First World War broke out in 1914.

At the ensuing elections Louis Botha became Prime Minister of the Transvaal; Smuts was his Colonial Secretary and Minister of Education, acting as Premier when Botha went to London for an Imperial Conference. It was soon realized that the Transvaal could not stand alone and that there must be union between the four colonies.

After many difficulties union was achieved in December, 1909, after agreement with London. Botha and Smuts then ruled a united South Africa with the English and Dutch as equal partners of the one community. Smuts's dream, which had been also the aim of Rhodes and of Milner, was at last realized.

There was, however, growing discontent, which was exploited by those who continued to work for Dutch control of the country, and as war approached in Europe there was a rebellion in South Africa. Botha and Smuts had to fight their old comrades. They were victorious but the fighting left a trail of bitterness which followed Smuts throughout his political life. The older generation of Boers had turned in on themselves, distrusting and resenting Smuts's plans to make South Africa count in world affairs. Smuts was disliked more than Botha, who had a big following in the country and had the patience to talk and calm the Boer leaders. When there was a meeting of the Imperial War Conference in London in the spring of 1917, it was decided that Botha must stay to control the situation while Smuts went to England; there he remained for twenty-nine months.

The valuable service Smuts did in England for the war effort did not please many of the Boers at home, who considered that Smuts was interfering in matters which were not his concern nor the concern of South Africa. He was involved in the decision to carry out the disastrous Passchendaele offensive in the summer of 1917, and he was offered command of the British Army in Egypt to throw the Turks out of Palestine, but Smuts was a guerilla raider and not a good general. He refused on the advice of Botha who telegraphed: "We both know you are no general."

At the Peace Treaty discussions in Paris Smuts was joined by Botha. Out of the many plans it was Smuts's which appealed to Woodrow Wilson; he repeatedly consulted Smuts and used his memorandum as a basis for the final draft of the Covenant of the

League. As he told Lloyd George in a number of memoranda, Smuts considered that the terms of the Peace Treaty breathed "a poisonous spirit of revenge" which would lead to retaliation by Germany.

What exactly did he recommend, asked Lloyd George in a rather malicious reply—did Smuts wish to give back German West Africa? That was impossible. There were already mutterings from South Africa because the former German colony was not to be part of the Union but put under a mandate of the League of Nations. It had been Smuts's idea that the former German colonies should be put under "mandate". Smuts was persuaded by Botha to sign the Treaty but he issued a long protest which was widely published.

Botha died soon after his return to South Africa and Smuts became Prime Minister. He told his Cabinet:

"I have neither tact nor patience and you must take me for what I am worth."

It was a flash of humility which did not last long; without Botha to calm him Smuts became more arrogant and more disliked than before. In 1922 there was the Rand Labour revolution which, taking over command himself, he suppressed ruthlessly and courageously. It ruined his political career as he expected it would.

James Hertzog, his despised opponent, became Prime Minister and Smuts retired to his farm and family, writing his book *Holism and Evolution* in praise of freedom and the development of the personality. Smuts was a philosopher but also a very practical man. He realized that his thesis, which was most carefully developed, applied only to the white races. He had no solution as to how the black African was to develop and evaded the issue. "White and black are different," he said in another context, "not only in colour but also in mind." His aim was "a grand racial aristocracy" and he considered it would be debased by any mixture of coloured races. Apartheid was the only solution—large areas in South Africa "inhabited entirely by blacks, looking after themselves according to their own ways of life and forms of government". At times, however, he referred to Africa as "the Negro home" and wondered whether it might not become one day a Negro Empire. It would make a very bad impression in South Africa, he said at Oxford in 1929 when giving the Rhodes Memorial Lecture, if at any time "the British Government were to take the side of the native against the population generally".

In 1933, taking a courageous and wise decision, he returned to politics. He agreed to co-operate with his old enemy James Hertzog and to serve under him in the Government, in order to prevent further division in the country between Dutch and English. On the eve of the Second World War Hertzog resigned and Smuts became Prime Minister once more. He brought South Africa into the war on the side of the Allies, though the Opposition in Parliament bitterly opposed war against Germany. Smuts paid a number of visits to London and his services were used by Churchill as they had been by Lloyd George in the First World War, though not so extensively, yet he helped to create the United Nations at San Francisco. When the Opposition in South Africa won the general election in 1948 Smuts retired again to his farm and died on 11 September, 1950, a short time after the public celebration of his eightieth birthday. His statue by Sir Jacob Epstein stands today in London's Parliament Square—a spare, tense figure, alert as if about to leave on a long journey.

Ernest Rutherford
1871-1937

THEY had been cruising at thirty thousand. The morning sun behind them flung the silhouette of the giant bomber down on a white bed of cloud, a layer of stratus resembling a roll of cotton wool, stretched and spread flat. One moment the shadow would be hundreds of feet below, a midget aeroplane skating like a water beetle over the surface of the cloud, then, as they reached a higher formation, the silhouette would jump up at them, cruise just underneath, with bow and rear cannons clearly visible and the four engine nacelles jutting out in front of the huge wing. There was a break in the clouds; the sea, six miles below, came into view, like the green felt of a billiard table. A second later it had vanished and there was only their own reflection on the cloud. Then, without warning, the cloud ended, nipped off as with a pair of scissors. In front there was nothing but sea and, farther away, the light-brown fringe of coastline. A few minutes later the sea was behind them and there was nothing beneath but land.

The navigator ordered a turn to starboard and they flew a minute along the new bearing. Then, crackling, over the intercom, the crew heard him shout, "Steady on course—hold it—hold it . . ." and they strained for a sight of the target. A squat brown huddle of houses came into view. It looked like a village, but that was because it was so far away. Another adjustment and they were coming in on target. It was a quarter past eight, local time.

"She's away!"

The pilot pulled her into a steep climbing turn to port, threw open the four throttles and headed south-west. There was silence on board, absolute silence on the intercom, save only for the drone of the engines.

Suddenly the sky all round them seemed to explode with light. They had instructions not to look back, not to try to see what their strange new, cumbersome weapon was doing to the town behind. Now they knew why. If the light from the explosion were as brilliant as this, ten miles away, six miles up, and facing in the wrong direction, heaven alone would know how bright it was at the point of impact. Heaven and the inhabitants of Hiroshima.

They droned on back to base and it was a fortnight before they learnt what the first atomic bomb had done to Japan. The war was over.

If, in the blinding light, the roar and the million-degree heat of the explosion in the early Monday morning of 6 August, 1945, that caused 60,000 deaths and the almost total destruction of a great seaport, there had been any other sound discernible it might have been the rumble of big Ernest Rutherford turning over in his grave. It had been his most fervent prayer that no one would be able to make practical use of the atomic energy he had discovered and unleashed until the world was—for ever—at peace. The prayer had not been granted.

Ernest Rutherford had been born in Spring Grove (later called Brightwater), New Zealand, on 30 August, 1871. His father, James Rutherford, had been brought from Perth, Scotland, as a child by his parents, at a time when New Zealand had a population of only 2,000 white people. James had done his best for that problem: young Ernest had eleven brothers and sisters.

The boy was fond of games and practical jokes and at the same time a voracious reader, but it was some years before he showed the interest in physics and chemistry which was to make him famous. These subjects were hardly taught at the time in small country schools and it is perhaps a stroke of good fortune that while he was impressing his teachers with an all-round ability in Latin, French, history, English literature and mathematics, one of them was subtly influencing the boy in the wonder and excitement of physics, as an out-of-school hobby. The master—a classics master—was W. S. Littlejohn, a Scot from Aberdeen who later went on to become the Principal of one of the most famous schools in Australia.

In 1890, when he was nineteen, Ernest won a scholarship from his little school in the town of Nelson to Canterbury College in Christchurch. He was soon a respected member of the football team (and the largest man in it). Here, too, physics was not encouraged and it was not until he was nearly twenty-one that Rutherford was able to start Advanced Physics. Despite this, he graduated a year later with First Class Honours and within a month was doing experiments as a postgraduate in the damp cellar of the students' quarters. Shortly afterward he published his first scientific paper, "The Magnetization of Iron by High Frequency Discharges", a work which showed clearly his remarkable ability to make accurate observations with primitive equipment.

In 1894, after a short spell as master in a Christchurch High School—he was not a success, had no idea of keeping order and was puzzled that his class was always in a state of roaring pandemonium—he was awarded an "Exhibition Scholarship" to Cambridge. These "Exhibition Scholarships" had been founded to commemorate the great Exhibition of 1851 and it was with mixed feelings that Ernest learnt he had been selected for one: he had, in the intervals of trying to teach schoolboys, fallen in love with a girl. They agreed, in 1895, to a long engagement and young Rutherford set sail for England.

On arrival in Cambridge he was put to work under Professor J. J. Thomson in the new and splendid Cavendish Laboratory. It was an exciting time to start: a month after he put on his white overall for the first time, W. K. Röntgen discovered X-rays—a first breath of air into the closed room which physics seemed to have occupied since the time of Newton. A few months later A. H. Becquerel showed that uranium compounds produced radiation like X-rays, and a year later, Thomson himself proved the existence of the long-suspected electron. Now the theory which men like Thomson and Rutherford had nursed for years, that all matter had a common origin, had been built, as it were, from the same tiny bricks, became a probability. Rutherford began to experiment with the new "wireless waves" and succeeded in detecting them at a range of half a mile, which was at the time a world record. He caused a stir at the age of twenty-five by demonstrating them during the Liverpool meeting of the British Association. Then, because they seemed worthy only of commercial development, he deserted them for more fundamental matters. He turned his attention first to the problem of conducting electricity through gases, and found that by "ionizing" his gas with a stream of the new X-rays he could pass a sizable current through it. Uranium radiation, he discovered, had quite a different effect and eventually he found that it consisted of at least two different types, which he styled alpha and beta. Alpha rays caused heavy ionization of the gas but hardly penetrated a solid, and beta rays penetrated deeply and ionized less thoroughly.

In 1898, when he was twenty-seven, Rutherford accepted the Macdonald Research Professorship at McGill University in Montreal. He had enjoyed his work at the Cavendish, he had already achieved a great deal, but the chance of a Professorship, his friends told him, should not be lost. He thought briefly of his failure as a teacher in the Christchurch High School and booked his passage to Canada.

He fitted easily into the life of the young university, found his teaching pleasant and not too demanding and continued with his experiments. As a Professor, he could afford a wife, and in 1900 he went back to New Zealand, married his Mary, and brought her halfway up the world to settle in Montreal. They were happy in their new home, even though Ernest spent all day and half the night out of it, in his "wonderful laboratory, the best in the world" as he wrote his mother. It had been handsomely endowed by the Scottish millionaire Sir William Macdonald (who had founded the Professorship Rutherford held). Indeed Scotland can take much credit for Rutherford's work: an Aberdonian introduced him to science in New Zealand, another Scot, McGill, provided him with a university to work in, and a third provided him with a job in it and a fine laboratory.

Soon Rutherford's fame spread beyond Canada and he was approached with offers of appointments in London, Edinburgh, Chicago; but he loved Canada, his wife was happy there, and he could wish for no finer place to work than Macdonald's lab. Young men began to travel to Canada to work with him. One of these was Frederick Soddy; with his help Rutherford in 1902 put forward the revolutionary theory that "radio-activity is a phenomenon accompanying the spontaneous transformation of atoms of radio-active elements into a *different kind of matter*". It was not, as had generally been believed, a chemical reaction. He based his theory on the observation that radio-activity was quite unaffected by heat, cold or chemicals and the vastly more important one, which ultimately produced an atomic bomb, that

"radio-active change is accompanied by an emission of heat of a *quite different order of magnitude* from that accompanying chemical reactions."

(In fact, as was later proved, each atom produced three million times the energy it might have yielded in a chemical reaction like burning.)

The new theory was treated with scepticism, it cut right across the long-held theory that all matter was indestructible. Nevertheless, Rutherford was elected a Fellow of the Royal Society in 1903.

By 1907 he had decided to return to England and work in the new laboratory at Manchester University. There had been great strides in technology during the nine years he had been in Canada and now much of the equipment at McGill was obsolescent. In Manchester he formed the opinion that his "alpha rays" were in fact particles. With the help of Hans Geiger's new counting machine, he was able to complete a remarkable *tour de force*, proving not only that they were particlesof matter, but that they were positively charged atoms of helium and that 136,000 of them were ejected every second from one-thousandth of a gramme of radium. In a startling experiment with a piece of radium sealed into a thick glass tube, he was able to show the helium gas arriving as if by magic on the outside of it.

In 1908, a year after his arrival in Manchester, he was awarded the Nobel Prize for Chemistry. As probably the most famous physicist in the world—he was still under forty—he may have been surprised at receiving the award for Chemistry, but certainly his work held implications for both sciences.

As in Canada, he attracted the best men to him. Several left Canada to follow him and other front rank men came from the United States, Australia, New Zealand and Germany. In 1910 he was able to propound his new Nuclear Theory, that nearly all the mass of an atom is in the nucleus, positively charged. This is balanced by a quantity of electrons, negatively charged, at a relatively long distance away.

War in 1914 found him lecturing in Australia. He hurried back to the Manchester lab. to find, as he had feared, all the younger members of his staff gone. He offered himself to the Government and was put in charge of investigation into Underwater Acoustics, where he was instrumental, by devising methods of listening underwater, in controlling the menace of German U-Boats. By 1917 he felt he could safely go back to fundamentals in his Manchester lab. Not long afterwards he was able to prove that alpha particles bombarding the nucleus of a nitrogen atom liberate the nucleus of a hydrogen atom. In his earlier work with radium he had proved that helium is formed by the *natural* breaking down of that element: now he had achieved an *artificial* transmutation of matter, a thing which alchemists and others had been trying to do for a thousand years.

In 1919 he was elected Cavendish Professor of Physics at Cambridge, in succession to his old superior, J. J. Thomson. He and his wife moved again, and for the last time. His work in this last—but long and fruitful—period of his life was largely devoted to the study of "isotopes". He proved that the different elements might exist in stable forms, with the same chemical properties and nuclear charge, but differing in atomic mass. He reasoned also that in addition to negatively charged electrons and a positively charged nucleus in an atom, then there must be, to maintain equilibrium, a particle with no charge, a neutron. This he found. Bombardment of various elements with neutrons gave rise to numbers of other radio-active substances and it was this development and its pointer to the release of huge energy, that started investigation, using the "235", highly radio-active, isotope of uranium, into the possibility of a bomb and, subsequently, into the use of atomically generated heat for power.

In the last years of his life, which were saddened by the tragic death of his daughter and only child, Eileen, he began a campaign to get for the Cavendish the world's best equipment. Nuclear physics, as this branch of research was now known, could no longer be handled with the primitive tools he had once used. Only the best would do, and this Rutherford got, so that the Cavendish Laboratory, under his direction, became the finest in the world. He became the force behind the Cavendish, doing less research himself, guiding the hands of younger men—and then finding time, each evening, to continue his made-up serial story-reading to his bereaved grandchildren.

In 1931 he was created a Baron. He decided not to change his name but to commemorate the small town where he had first been to school, and became Lord Rutherford of Nelson. He cabled his mother in New Zealand, "Now Lord Rutherford more your honour than mine Ernest".

Before he died, in Cambridge in 1937, laden with almost every academic honour his country could give him, he had been awarded degrees by no fewer than twenty-five universities in various parts of the world. He remained to the end the big, modest man who wrote superbly well and spoke—in public—so poorly; the man who, as a colleague said of him on his death: "never made an enemy and never lost a friend"; the man with the resonant, frightening, laugh, who could drop asleep suddenly at a dull patch in the conversation and wake up ten minutes later to resume it. Once when a visitor had been invited to dinner at Trinity College, Cambridge, he had been disappointed not to see the great Lord Rutherford but had enjoyed discussing his favourite topic of farming with a man who had a surprising knowledge of it. The two of them talked till late and then, when they had parted and the visitor was being shown out by his host, turned to shake the proffered hand and said: "Thank you for a most pleasant evening; and just *who* was that fascinating Australian farmer?"

"That," said his host, "was Lord Rutherford."

Bertrand Russell
1872-1970

A SLIGHT, pencil-straight figure with a gnome-like face topped by bunchy white hair stood on the plinth in the centre of Trafalgar Square speaking in a squeaky, gritty voice to 30,000 eager followers, the great majority under twenty-five years of age, who listened in respectful, almost awed, silence to his impassioned words hurling down before all mankind an inescapable choice—mass extermination or an earthly paradise. The year was 1959, the occasion the arrival from Aldermaston of the marchers associated with the Campaign for Nuclear Disarmament, of which the compelling speaker was the leader.

The man was full of years (eighty-six of them) and honours (the Order of Merit, a Nobel Prize). He was certainly one of the greatest thinkers of his age and almost certainly the greatest philosopher. He was a peer of the realm and he had spent six months in prison for his principles. An agnostic, he was seeking with all the power of his considerable mind to demand that the young men and women before him in Trafalgar Square—and young ones like them in every country of the world—would not be denied their heritage and their right—a future. The man's name was Bertrand Russell, the third Earl Russell, grandson of one of Great Britain's most distinguished Prime Ministers.

He was born a top-drawer aristocrat, on 18 May, 1872, to Viscount Amberley and Lady Kate Stanley, daughter of Lord Stanley of Alderley. His grandfather was the celebrated Lord John Russell, who later became the first Earl Russell, and his grandmother, Lady Russell, suggested that the boy should be named "Galahad". His other grandmother removed that danger by saying to her daughter: "Pray do not inflict such punishment on your child." So he was named Bertrand Russell and insisted on using that style even after he had inherited his title. A remark passed by an aunt after a visit by Queen Victoria to his grandparents when Bertrand was three is worth recording: "Bertie made such a nice little bow—but was much subdued and did not treat Her Majesty with the utter disrespect I expected."

As his father died a year after Bertrand's birth, the boy was brought up at Pembroke Lodge, Richmond Park, a royal gift to Lord John Russell. There he came under the stern eye of his paternal grandmother (usually called "Lady John"—behind her back). Political tradition was, of course, strong in such a household and Bertrand was soon made aware that his family had a duty of public service. He grew up a boy apart, silent and shy. His elder brother, Frank, wrote of him: "Until he went to Cambridge, he was an unendurable young prig."

It is recorded that the author of that monumental classic, *Principia Mathematica*, wept over his first efforts to learn the multiplication table and began with a hearty dislike of algebra. At eleven he was given his first geometry lesson and was disappointed to discover that the subject proceeded from axioms which had to be accepted without proof. The incipient philosopher dared to question Euclid and demanded to be convinced that two things which are equal to the same thing are equal to one another.

He read hungrily in his grandfather's copious library and laid the foundation for that vast store of knowledge which was later to earn him the reputation of "the wisest man in Britain". At sixteen he strained his eyes and was forbidden to read or write, so he filled this gap by learning poetry by heart. John Stuart Mill had the greatest influence on his developing mind—Russell had an immediate affinity for empirical philosophy: the common-sense belief that all knowledge comes from experience. It was one of Russell's great achievements that he extended empirical philosophy by adding his theory of mathematical knowledge reinforced with a new logical discipline.

When the time came for Cambridge, he was sent to a crammer to bring his Latin and Greek up to matriculation standard because his grandmother, "Lady John," had a poor opinion of public schools. By that time Bertrand was fluent in German, French and Italian because of the background of European culture in which he was reared. At eighteen he entered Trinity College—and "a new world of infinite delight". He was to add to that extraordinary period of Cambridge history which produced such men as McTaggart, Moore, Whitehead, Eddington, Rutherford, Marshall and Keynes. Russell was particularly influenced by the friendship of McTaggart, the Hegelian philosopher, and G. E. Moore, who took the university by storm.

As Russell's lonely upbringing deprived him of any contact with girls, when he did fall in love it was for him an overwhelming experience. The object of his affection was Alys Pearsall Smith, a sister of Logan Pearsall Smith, the writer—their family were Pennsylvanian Quakers who had settled in England. "Lady John" was against the romance and got Bertrand a post as an honorary Attaché in the British Embassy in Paris, hoping that the pleasures of Paris would make him change his mind but he returned home as soon as he could and married Alys at the Friends' House in London in December, 1894.

Although his genius was many-sided, the foundations of mathematics were his prevailing interest until he reached the age of thirty-eight. His great work in that field was, of course, the three-volume *Principia Mathematica*, compiled in collaboration with A. N. Whitehead. Probably not more than a score of people have read the work in its entirety, yet it is regarded as a classic—and like so many other classics, it is taken for granted rather than studied. Its preparation took nearly seven years—"I got stuck for two years," Russell once remarked of it, "and, when I got unstuck, it took five years to write it down."

Despite his tremendous intellectual efforts during that period he found time, in 1907, to stand for Parliament—as a candidate of the National Union of Women's Suffrage Societies. At his first meeting some opponent of votes for women freed two rats among the ladies of the audience intending to panic them but in fact they ran among the men in front of the platform and the attempt at ridicule misfired. Russell lost the by-election by 7,000 votes. He made a more serious bid to enter the House of Commons in 1910 when he had ended his mathematical labours, seeking adoption as a Liberal candidate. When the local constituency association found he was an agnostic who refused to make even token church appearances, they would not have him. Later he became a convinced Socialist. To those who criticize his apparent change of view in politics and, indeed, in certain aspects of philosophy, it is important to answer that his approach to both was empirical, based on the evidence available at the moment and not on a set of fixed principles.

His views about marriage changed, too, and led him to a belief in free love, with children as the one limitation. He married four times. He separated from his first wife, Alys, in 1911, but it was 1921 before there was a divorce. With the break-up of his marriage and his opposition to—and Pacifist propaganda against—the First World War, he was cut off from people of his own class and outlook and he increasingly turned to men and women of unconventional ideas for his friendships, including Sidney and Beatrice Webb, Bernard Shaw, Charles Trevelyan and Herbert Samuel.

The war forced a radical change in Russell's thinking and way of life. After an initial shock of horror and despair, he turned to active agitation against the war which, for the first time, made him a notorious public figure. He joined the committee of the No-Conscription Fellowship and became the inspiration of conscientious objectors, pouring out articles for the anti-war publication, *Labour Leader*. Soon he incurred the hostility of the Government. He was arrested as the author of a N.C.F. leaflet, tried before the Lord Mayor of London at the Mansion House on 15 June, 1916, for statements likely to prejudice the recruiting and discipline of His Majesty's Forces, found guilty and fined £100.

The Trinity College Council promptly sacked him as a lecturer. Undaunted, he carried on with his propaganda for pacifism. He was invited to lecture at Harvard, but the Foreign Office refused him a passport for America.

Towards the end of 1917 an article which he wrote for the N.C.F. weekly, *The Tribunal*, landed him in Brixton Prison for six months in the Second Division. Thanks to his distinguished friends he was transferred to the First Division where he could get on with his reading and writing—but he had to pay rent of 2s. 6d. a week for his cell. He was visited by many celebrities and men-of-letters, including T. S. Eliot and Desmond McCarthy. His prison output consisted of the *Introduction to Mathematical Philosophy*, a review of Dewey's *Essays in Experimental Logic* and foundation work for his later *Analysis of Mind*.

The war precipitated Russell's conversion to Socialism, but he favoured a syndicalist re-organization of industry—that is, industries would be run by the men working in them and not by the Government. The Russian Revolution had excited him and in the summer of 1920 he was invited to visit the Soviet Union as an unofficial Labour delegate. He came to the conclusion that the Bolsheviks were remarkably similar to the Puritans. He wrote:

"Their form of government is almost exactly the same as the form of government established in England by Cromwell in the seventeenth century."

He had a talk with Lenin but when Russell said it might be possible to achieve Socialism in England without bloodshed, the Russian dictator "waved the suggestion aside as fantastic". The result of the experience was a critical analysis, *The Practice and Theory of Bolshevism*, which he summed up later by saying: "When I went there in 1920 I found nothing I could like or admire."

Later the same year (1920) Russell went to China where he found an enthusiastic welcome awaiting him—his views were already known there and they were impatient to hear an English aristocrat castigating British imperialism. They found, too, a lordly one who was prepared to consider China's problems from the viewpoint of the Chinese. Peking University students launched a special *Russell Magazine* and Sun Yat-sen called him the only Englishman ever to understand China. On his return he published *The Problem of China* —a remarkable forecast of the future trends in the Far East.

While in China he exhausted himself lecturing in cold and draughty halls and fell desperately ill. His life was despaired of and certain Chinese dignitaries had decided to accord him the honour of burial in a shrine by the Western Lake. Scholars crowded the German Hospital in Peking "to hear the dying words of the great English philosopher". Reports of his death were, in fact, circulated and Russell had the wry pleasure of reading his own obituary notices. He was nursed back to health by his devoted companion, Dora Black, who became his second wife on their return to England.

Russell stood again for Parliament as Labour candidate for Chelsea in the General Elections of 1922 and 1923. His house at 31 Sydney Street was used as the Labour Party committee rooms and his opponent in a safe Tory seat was the redoubtable Sir Samuel Hoare, who later became Lord Templewood. Russell was soundly defeated on both occasions. There was another General Election in 1924 and this time Dora Russell was Chelsea's Labour candidate but met inevitable defeat.

During his second marriage Russell's abiding interest was education and, with Dora, he set up in 1927 what would now be called a "progressive school". It was known as "Beacon Hill School" and was run at Telegraph House, owned by Russell's elder brother, Frank, near Harting. Its policy was to offer maximum freedom to the children in behaviour and self-expression. "We allow them to be rude," said Russell at that time, "and use any language they like . . . otherwise the things they cannot say fester inside them." His chief aim was to avoid repressions and disorders in his pupils.

The school, however, was a failure. It was always in financial difficulties, there were frequent staff troubles. It tended to become a haven for the problem children who had been expelled from the conventional schools. It was also over-run by visitors, sightseers and inquisitive busybodies. Russell severed his connexion with it on the dissolution of his marriage with Dora but she carried it on until the beginning of the Second World War. This second marriage ended in the Divorce Court in 1935 and Russell married Patricia Spence the following year.

During the 1930s he earned his living by writing and his output was prodigious, including *The Conquest of Happiness, In Praise of Idleness, Religion and Science*. A year before the outbreak of war he took his wife and three children to the United States, where he lived for six years, afterwards offering a mock epitaph for himself: "He lived in America six years, and did NOT write a book about it." The war years there were the unhappiest of his life. "Sometimes the longing for home is almost unbearable," he wrote.

In 1940, when he was at the University of California, he was given the appointment of Professor of Philosophy at the College of New York City to run from February, 1941, until June, 1942, by which time Russell would have reached the retiring age of seventy. A bishop of the Anglican Church protested against the appointment on the ground that Russell was a recognized propagandist against religion and morality. A suit to annul the appointment was heard and on 30 March, 1940, Roman Catholic Judge John McGeehan upheld the suit on three grounds; First, Russell was not an American; second, he had not sat a competitive examination for the post; third his books advocated "immoral and salacious doctrines".

Harvard University, however, stood firmly by an invitation to Russell to give the William James lectures there that same autumn. After these lectures he was rescued from unemployment by an eccentric millionaire who hired him to lecture on philosophy in Pennsylvania. In 1943 his millionaire became disenchanted with him and fired him at three days' notice. So, at seventy with a wife and three children to support, he found himself hard up and isolated in a foreign country. Out of this turbulence came one of his finest achievements, *A History of Western Philosophy*, regarded as the most illuminating history of philosophy ever put together in one volume.

Early in 1944 his old college, Trinity, invited him to return to Cambridge, an invitation he accepted with alacrity. He received a hero's welcome and his lecture-rooms were always packed. From that point his stock steadily rose in British public life—until his association with the Campaign for Nuclear Disarmament. In the winter of 1948 he was invited to give the first Reith Lectures for the B.B.C. on "Authority and the Individual" and in June, 1949, came the Order of Merit, the most exclusive honour in the awards of the Crown. Russell, however, refused to be put out to grass and, that same year—at the age of seventy-eight—he took on a strenuous lecture tour of Australia which lasted two months and was a triumphant success. Shortly after his return to England he was awarded a Nobel Prize.

In 1952 Russell was married for the fourth time—to Miss Edith Finch, from a long-established New England family, herself a writer and teacher.

At the age of eighty, he turned to a field new to him—fiction, announcing, "I have devoted the first eighty years of my life to philosophy. I propose to devote the next eighty years to another branch of fiction." His first stories appeared as the collection, *Satan in the Suburbs*. His new career was interrupted by the perfection of a weapon which narrowed international power politics down to a stark choice between mankind's survival and extermination—the hydrogen bomb. At once he became the standard bearer for the host of people in every country who suddenly found themselves living under the bomb's sinister shadow. In December, 1954, he wound up one of his most passionate broadcasts by saying:

"I appeal as a human being to human beings: remember your humanity and forget the rest. If you can do so, the way lies open to a new paradise; if you cannot, nothing lies before you but universal death."

The Campaign for Nuclear Disarmament was launched in February, 1958, with Russell as its first president and Canon L. J. Collins, of St Paul's Cathedral, as chairman of its executive committee to "demand a British initiative to reduce the nuclear peril and to stop the armaments race, if need be by unilateral action by Great Britain". In April came the first Aldermaston March—and its repercussions caused a major split in the Labour Party. C.N.D.'s first European Congress was held in January, 1959, at the Central Hall, Westminster, and was attended by 250 delegates from nine Western European countries.

Bertrand Russell, as British president, urged a stage-by-stage approach to world disarmament. Although in his eighties, he carried on his greatest crusade—to rally mankind against the madness of a nuclear war—as though *his* future depended on it. Indeed he left the Campaign for Nuclear Disarmament in 1960 because he was impatient with its progress. His long life of controversy ended on 2 February, 1970, at the age of ninety-seven—in the middle of another campaign. Two months before his death he protested to Mr Kosygin, the Russian Prime Minister, over the expulsion of Mr Alexander Solzhenitsyn from the Soviet Writers' Union.

It was his last plea for tolerance in an intolerant world.

Guglielmo Marconi
1874-1937

Marconi wrote:

> "My chief trouble was that the idea was so elementary, so simple in logic, that it seemed difficult to believe no one else had thought of putting it into practice. The idea was so real to me that I did not realize that to others the theory might appear quite fantastic."

In the attic of the Villa Grifone, the big family house outside Bologna, he experimented. He found that he could, with his elementary spark-gap transmitter, deflect a compass needle at the other end of the attic. This fact had indeed been prophesied and on at least one occasion, verified, by others, but that was the extent of it: it was a good trick for a lecture on the new Hertzian waves, and nothing more. But it soon became obvious to the young Guglielmo Marconi that if the needle could be made to respond to the distant impulses of the transmitter, controlled by an ordinary telegraphist's key, a message in Morse code could be transmitted and read off the fluctuating needle.

In order to do this, Guglielmo needed to enlist the aid of another; his secret would have to be shared. So he invited his older brother Alfonso to share it. Guglielmo was just twenty and the gentle, kindly Alfonso, who doted on his younger brother, was twenty-nine. Their father deplored the time Guglielmo spent on his "childish experiments"; in fact he destroyed every bit of equipment he found in the house, so it was important that at all costs he be kept in the dark.

With Alfonso at the home-made receiver, Guglielmo operating the Morse key, they passed a message—very slowly, for the Morse code was new to them—from one end of the attic to the other. Wireless telegraphy had been born—even though the infant might yet be strangled at birth by an angry father bent on destruction entering inopportunely the attic of the Villa Grifone.

The brothers were excited by the discovery and Alfonso, bursting with pride for his pale, dark-eyed dreamer of a young brother, agreed to go on helping. Carefully, when their father had left the house the next day, they moved the receiving apparatus downstairs. By this time Guglielmo had attached a relay and bell to it so that the three dots of the Morse letter "S" (this they agreed, was simpler than sending real messages, the three dots were clear and unmistakable) clanged out on the ground floor at the bidding of a genie in the attic.

A few days later they were able to move the receiver out of the house and hide it at the far end of the garden. Once again, the sound of the letter "S" came through, and Alfonso, shaking with excitement, picked up the heavy apparatus and struggled with it across two fields. Here, with trembling fingers he set up the aerial on its long pole and again the three dots found their way to him and sounded the bell. He waved his handkerchief, there was an answering wave from the attic window and another success had been recorded.

To Guglielmo when he stopped to think of it, this was elementary. Obviously if the signal could be transmitted at all it could be made to travel farther by making the transmitter more powerful. But for the discovery to have much practical application, the waves from the transmitter would have to be able to go round or through buildings and hills. In fact—and here Marconi was looking, as he always did, into the future of his discovery—the waves would have to follow the curvature of the earth or they would go as far as the horizon and then disappear into space.

Alfonso had used a handkerchief on the end of a long pole as their return signal, but for the next experiment, handkerchiefs would be of no use. Solemnly, young Guglielmo gave his older brother a hunting rifle and told him to go with the receiving apparatus to the far side of the hill behind the house and signal back by firing it. It was a warm clear, autumn day at the end of September, 1895, and the vines round the Villa Grifone were heavy with grapes. The walk over the rim of the hill took twenty minutes with Alfonso in the lead, then a farmer, then the village carpenter, carrying their share of the load. Staring from his attic window, Guglielmo lost sight of the little procession as it dropped over the horizon.

"After some minutes," Marconi wrote later, "I started to send, manipulating the Morse key. Then, in the distance, a shot echoed down the valley."

Guglielmo Marconi was born on 25 April, 1874, in the Italian town of Bologna, to the prosperous Giuseppe Marconi and his beautiful Irish wife, Annie. Annie Jameson had been sent to Italy by her parents to study singing. She had wanted to be an opera singer, but this, to the staid Jamesons in their moated Irish castle, was quite unthinkable. If Annie would forget the idea, they would send her to Italy for a year to study *bel canto*. To this Annie agreed, but within months she had shocked her parents again by asking their permission to marry not only a foreigner, an Italian, but one who was a widower and seventeen years her senior. This, even more peremptorily than the career in opera, was refused. However, by this time Annie had made up her mind. She quietly disappeared from home, met Giuseppe in Boulogne, married him there and crossed the Alps to her new home in Bologna. Here, twelve months after this elopement, Alfonso was born, and nine years after that, Guglielmo.

Guglielmo developed an interest in electricity before he was ten years old, and his mother was always his chief supporter. She understood that he must have some sort of a laboratory, despite his father's disapproval, and she let him use the attic. Here, from childhood, he assembled, tested, rejected or improved vast quantities of equipment. Little of it, as Guglielmo was the first to admit, was entirely original. The brilliant German physicist Heinrich Hertz, had developed a primitive detector to record his newly discovered "waves in the ether", and his findings were published when Marconi was fifteen. The detector relied on the discovery by an Englishman, David Hughes, that zinc and silver filings could, by the discharge of a Leyden Jar condenser, be made to cling together and form a conductor for electricity. A Frenchman, Edouard Branly, put the filings into a glass tube and, because of their action, called his instrument, which would detect Hertz's waves, a "coherer". Somehow, among the trays of silkworms which his mother insisted must share the attic with him, Marconi was able to build a series of coherers with different proportions of different metal filings, was able to construct a series of progressively more powerful "transmitters", using Hertz's discovery that an electric spark would cause waves of energy in the ether. (This phenomenon, which Marconi later discarded, is still with us, but has only nuisance value, as when a bit of electrical equipment which emits sparks—and, in a far grander way, the lightning itself—interferes with our radio or television reception.)

Gradually, Marconi's signals were made to travel farther and be heard more clearly, and at last, when the shot from the rifle signalled victory from over the hill, even old Giuseppe Marconi realized the value of his son's discovery. The family turned for counsel, as village people do, to the most august men in their community, the parish priest and the doctor. They, after consideration, recommended that the invention be submitted to Italy's Minister of Post and Telegraph, and this unwise decision was to drive the young Marconi from his native land, so that almost all his later development of "wireless telegraphy" was done in England and America. The Minister regretted that he had no interest in the young man's discovery. In fact, had Guglielmo submitted it to the Minister of the Navy, it would have been taken up with enthusiasm. Italy was building up her fleet and a miracle like wireless communication from ship to shore or even from ship to ship would have given the Italian fleet an advantage over the rest of the world.

The Italian Navy was not to have the chance. Guglielmo and his parents decided that with England the greatest maritime nation in the world, he should take his invention there. In February of 1896 he set off from Bologna, with his mother. She, we learn, was suitably dressed as a Victorian matron, while Guglielmo, always something of a dandy, was wearing a tweed deerstalker hat which he hoped would be the height of fashion in England. Beside them on the seats and above their heads in the luggage rack were the wooden and metal boxes containing the secret of wireless communication.

These, when at last they had crossed a choppy, fog-bound Channel, were opened by horrified Customs Officials. They found wires and batteries, dials and condensers. This, surely, was some offensive weapon. Had not a man recently fired at the Queen? Had not the French President been assassinated only two years ago? In their search for the more lethal aspects of Marconi's machine, they damaged it extensively. Guglielmo and his mother arrived in London almost in tears.

Here Annie's cousin Henry took them in hand. He met them at Victoria Station, consoled them, arranged their accommodation, then busied himself with assembling from all over London the materials with which Guglielmo would be able to repair his smashed apparatus. Cheered by this kindness, Marconi began to reassemble it, and by the middle of the year, having carried out a few more experiments, he was able to deposit the provisional specification of his invention in the London Patent Office. On 2 July of the following year, 1897, after he had done a complete specification with drawings for Improvements in Transmitting Electrical Impulses and Signals and an Apparatus Therefor, a first patent, Number 12,039, was granted to "Guglielmo Marconi of 71 Hereford Road, Bayswater, in the County of Middlesex".

Marconi was able, through his cousin, to get an introduction to the Chief Engineer of the Post Office, William Preece, a gentle, bearded Welshman of sixty-three. Despite the discrepancy in their ages, they liked and trusted each other at once. Preece offered Marconi the use of his own laboratory where he had already been searching for the answer the younger man had found, and arranged for him to give demonstrations before other Post Office officials. Not only that, but he allowed the younger man to annex one of his most valuable assistants, George Kemp. Almost immediately Marconi arranged a demonstration of wireless telegraphy over a distance of half a mile, from the roof of the Post Office in St Martin's-Le-Grand to the Savings Bank Department on Queen Victoria Street, and the signal was in no way diminished by having to pass through masonry walls on its way. Marconi was asked to conduct more demonstrations, but on a far larger scale. On Salisbury Plain the transmitter was housed in a shed while the receiver was dragged off in a military handcart. The first signal came in from a distance of a hundred yards, the next from a mile and a quarter, the next from six miles, the next from ten. Even if wireless telegraphy made no further progress, it was already of practical application, it was useful. As Marconi told a friend, *"La calma della mia via ebba allora fine"*—the calm of my life ended at this moment.

Later in 1897 the first message was sent over water, across the Bristol Channel. At about this time Marconi was faced with the decision whether to return to Italy and do his compulsory military service or become a British subject. He turned to the Italian Ambassador in London for advice and was soon granted permission from the King of Italy to stay in England and do some "military service" attached to the Embassy. Delighted, Marconi stayed on and sent his monthly service pay cheque to the Italian Hospital in London. By now, as he admitted to his close friends, his life was hopelessly out of order. He was just twenty-three, he had made and patented his key discovery at an age when young men were just starting off their careers. From now it would be a question of developing, on the largest commercial scale, the potentialities of his invention, and to do this he would have to put himself in control of men twice his age, not a few of whom were extremely jealous of his success. No wonder that the calm of Marconi's life was ended.

Later that year he went back to Italy, by invitation. The Italians had learnt that British naval circles and British investors were paying serious attention to the results of the Bristol Channel experiment, and Marconi was invited to perform a number of experiments at the naval base of Spezia. He succeeded in establishing contact with ships across ten miles of water, and the Italian Government, deeply impressed, urged him to make his home again in Italy. But in England his own company was being formed, and the move would have been out of the question. The company began as the Wireless Telegraph and Signal Company, but when the Italian Government expressed a desire that, even if he would not come home, Marconi's idea should be developed under his own, unmistakably Italian, name, he changed the title to Marconi's Wireless Telegraph Company. By this time signals had been transmitted between France and England and wireless had been installed on the East Goodwin lightship. Almost immediately after its installation the value of the innovation was proved: the lightship was run down by a steamer and a wireless message from her got lifeboats there in time to save the crew.

In 1901 came the most impressive demonstration of all. It had taken over a year to prepare the massive aerials and the powerful equipment, and there were numerous setbacks: the two-hundred-foot masts were smashed to matchwood in a gale, shorter ones proved inadequate, kites seemed the answer until they too, blew away. Eventually, however, the massive aerial arrays were ready, in Cornwall. Then 2,100 miles away, in the middle of an icy night, Marconi in Newfoundland was able to hear, faint but unmistakable the three magic dots of the letter "S".

From now on the development of this proved method of world-wide communication went on at great speed. It became possible, as a result of Marconi's further experiments, to tune both transmitter and receiver to a certain wavelength, so that an almost infinite number of circuits could operate at the same time. Previous to this, a receiver would be forced to pick up messages from whatever transmitters were operating, with no means of excluding any, so that messages, even for a practised operator, were often impossible to decipher.

The invention of the thermionic valve revolutionized first the receiver, taking the place of the old "coherer", then the transmitter, substituting one or more valves for the cumbersome, dangerous, spark gap and vastly increasing the power. With the thermionic valve it became possible to send not only Morse code but speech.

For much of the First World War Marconi was in his native Italy, serving with both her Navy and her Army in his own specialized capacity. In 1919 his King appointed him plenipotentiary delegate to the Peace Conference and he signed several treaties on behalf of his government.

In 1919 his company set up, in Chelmsford, the first broadcasting station in the world. Amateur experimenters had proved the useful-ness of short waves for long-distance work and now Marconi began to develop this new technique commercially. It had been proved that short waves did not in fact follow the curvature of the earth, but shot out into space and were reflected off electrified layers just above the earth's atmosphere, from which they returned to earth many hundreds of miles from their source. By working out the angle of projection mathematically, it possible was to arrange that a short-wave beam returned to earth at a predestined point and then bounced off again, to return second, third, fourth and further times till eventually it had circled the earth. And by beaming the signal, rather than letting it scatter in all directions as with longer waves, there was a huge saving in the power required. One has only to consider how much light would be needed to bring the whole of the night sky to the brightness of a searchlight beam, to realize the saving in power from Marconi's "beam wireless".

In 1929 he was given the title of *Marchese*. This, as he was an ardent patriot all his life, probably meant more to him than his other honours, which had been coming for two decades, ever since his award of the Nobel Prize in 1909. His life had been a full one and although he worked hard at his inventions and their development, almost everything he put his hand to was a huge success: never was there a hint of financial struggle. As *Vanity Fair* put it in an article on the dapper little man who had shrunk the world to the size of an orange, Guglielmo Marconi "never starved for more than five hours at a time".

He had two wives, the first, like his father's, from Britain, the second from Italy, and was devoted, in his mercurial way, to each of them. The first marriage eventually failed and was annulled by the Catholic Church and the second, to an Italian girl many years his junior, was a happy one until his death in 1937.

On that day the air fell silent, as all over the world wireless stations went off the air as a mark of respect. In London at the international wireless telephone exchange the girls who operated it rose and stood with bowed heads beside their switchboards. All the stations of the B.B.C. went off the air.

The silence Guglielmo Marconi had broken forty-two years before was back—for just two minutes.

Winston Spencer Churchill
1874-1965

WINSTON CHURCHILL came of fighting stock. His paternal grand-father, the seventh Duke of Marlborough, was of the blood of the first Duke, Queen Anne's world-famous General. His maternal grandfather, a pugnacious American newspaper proprietor, Leonard Jerome, had armed his office staff with rifles and artillery against a hostile mob. Winston himself, impetuous by inheritance, was born at a dance as a seven months' child.

Red-haired, snub-nosed, he was a wayward, intractable urchin. "The naughtiest small boy in the world!" declared one distraught mistress. His father, who despaired of getting him into a learned profession, saw him playing with soldiers and asked: "Would you like to go into the Army." Would he? It was his one ambition. At Harrow he entered the army class. Still a wilful dunce, he was, after two failures, squeezed into Sandhurst with a low pass by a coach.

Here he suddenly matured. His Sandhurst career was brilliant. He began, too, to take a keen interest in his father's political affairs. Lord Randolph Churchill was the nationally beloved leader of the group of Tory Democrats; but his premature death robbed his son of any chance of establishing deep understanding with him. Many years later, Winston paid his father the tribute of a brilliant bio-graphy.

From Sandhurst Winston was gazetted to the 4th Hussars. He seemed destined to the relaxations and narrow equine interests of a cavalry officer. But he wanted to fight—and to write. The only war in progress was one between Spain and insurgents in Cuba. He devoted his army leave to going there to join in the fighting. He took with him, to help to pay his expenses, a contract to send at £5 each descriptive letters to the *Daily Graphic*.

In 1896 his regiment went to India, where he learned to play polo brilliantly. His leisure hours he spent, unlike his fellow subalterns, in determined study of the great English prose writers—historians, philosophers, scientists. A minor war broke out on the North-west Frontier, and he spent his leave going to it as a war correspondent for the *Daily Telegraph* and the *Allahabad Pioneer*. He managed to get well mixed up with the fighting, too, and wrote a book about the campaign which brought him reputation and the equivalent of two years' pay, but irritated the military authorities by its frank criticism of their blunders.

In 1898 Kitchener launched his Sudan campaign against rebel Dervishes. Churchill resolved to join it. Kitchener refused to have him. So Churchill coaxed from the Adjutant General a commission in the 21st Lancers, provided he paid his own expenses. These he covered by a contract with the *Morning Post* as its war correspondent. After picturesque adventures he reached the front, and was the first man to sight the Khalifa's army. In the battle of Omdurman, the 21st Lancers made the last classic cavalry charge in British warfare. It ended in a concealed nullah or dry water-course, packed with Dervishes. Nearly a quarter of the regiment were hacked down, but Winston shot his way through and rallied his men to enfilade the nullah with their carbines. As always he revelled in the fight. "Did you enjoy yourself?" he asked his sergeant. The man laughed and cheered up.

On his return, he wrote *The River War*, a masterly survey in two fat volumes of the campaign and of the Egyptian situation. It brought him fame and profit, and helped him to decide his future career. He would leave the army, live by his pen and enter politics. He made a first political speech at Bath, and found that he enjoyed it. In 1899 he fought and lost a by-election at Oldham.

Then came the interruption of the South African War. Winston dashed off at once to the front as chief war correspondent of the *Morning Post*. Outside Ladysmith, an armoured train in which he was travelling was ambushed and wrecked, and he was taken as a prisoner of war to Pretoria. One night he made his escape. The Boers scoured the country for him, offering a reward of £25 for his capture, alive or dead. He managed to elude recapture and after a succession of hair-raising perils arrived in Durban. Britain, gloomy at the black news of its army's failures, went wild with delight at his safe return.

The War Office had forbidden its officers to be war correspondents, so Churchill joined a South African troop of irregular horse, the "Cockyoli Birds". With them he shared gaily in the fighting, cycled through Johannesburg while it was still held by the Boers, and was the first to enter Pretoria. High on a pinnacle of popularity, he returned to Britain and a political career.

In the 1900 General Election he was elected as a member for Oldham. To provide himself with means of support, he then went

In 1902 Ernest Rutherford put forward the revolutionary theory that "radio-activity is a phenomenon accompanying the spontaneous transformation of atoms of radio-active elements into a different kind of matter". His research into the structure of the atom, and particularly of its nucleus, made it possible for others to develop the atomic bomb. More happily, however, his work opened up a whole new field of atomic energy for peaceful purposes. Both developments are here shown: (*above*) an atomic bomb exploding in typical mushroom pattern; (*below*) a general view of Dounreay atomic power-station at Caithness in Scotland.

Above: Guglielmo Marconi with the wireless apparatus which he brought in 1896 to England and which the attentions of Customs officials almost ruined.

Below: Winston S. Churchill (born in the same year as Marconi), Franklin D. Roosevelt and Joseph Stalin photographed together during their meeting at Yalta in the Crimea in February, 1945.

on extensive lecture tours in Britain and the U.S.A., describing his South African experiences. Early in 1901 he made his maiden speech in Parliament. It had marked success, but annoyed his Party Leader by its frankness. Though a Conservative, Winston was too original a thinker, too outspoken and warm-hearted, to be hobbled by any official party line. From the first he spoke as he thought and felt, whether it was orthodox or not.

Intent on reviving his father's plan for Tory Democracy, he rallied a rebel group nicknamed "The Hooligans", to battle for social reform against the die-hards. He became a close friend of Lloyd George, the rebel Radical.

Joseph Chamberlain preferred to rally the party's fortunes with a policy of "Tariff Reform". It split the ranks, and a minority stood out as Tory Free Traders, Winston among them. He was repelled by the calculating selfishness of Protectionists, who would seek speculative commercial profits at the cost of the food of the poor. He toured the country, battling for Free Trade. His constituents disowned him. The Tories got up and walked out when he rose in the Commons to speak. On 31 May, 1904, he crossed the floor of the House to the Liberal benches and sat beside Lloyd George.

At the General Election of January, 1906, the Liberals swept the country, and Churchill found himself Under-Secretary for the Colonies. Then, and on a later occasion, his enemies charged him with changing to the winning side through deep-laid cunning. But Churchill was never a plotter. He really belonged only to a party of one man—Winston Churchill. Ready to work with any party sharing his aims, he was their ally, not follower. Linked with Lloyd George in a zeal for social justice, he was through important years his disciple and colleague. Always they remained warm friends, even when politically opposed.

In the Liberal Cabinet he backed L.G.'s pressure for social reform legislation. When in 1908 Asquith became Prime Minister and reconstructed the Government, Churchill chose, instead of the Admiralty, to succeed Lloyd George at the Board of Trade. There in the following year he set up Labour Exchanges, carried the Trade Boards Act to stop sweated labour, and took charge of the Unemployment Insurance section of Lloyd George's National Insurance Act. Though a member of a great ducal land-owning family, he broke with it to plunge headlong into the bitter strife of the Land Campaign in support of Lloyd George's Land Taxation proposals in the 1909 Budget. Its outcome was the 1911 Parliament Act, which ended the veto of the House of Lords.

In 1910 Churchill moved to the Home Office, and there carried the Mines Accidents Act, 1910 and the Coal Mines Act, 1911, which improved safety in mines, provided pit-head baths, and stopped the employment underground of boys under fourteen years of age. For their improved conditions today, the workers owe a debt of gratitude to Winston Churchill.

In November, 1911, he became First Lord of the Admiralty. Here his warlike spirit was in its element. He expanded the Navy, and in the summer of 1914, scenting battle, carried out a trial mobilization of the fleet. When the First World War broke out on 4 August, the Navy was ready. The seas were promptly swept clear of German shipping. Enemy craft were sunk or bottled up in their harbours.

His activity was unquenchable. He organized the Royal Naval Air Service to protect our coasts. He dashed spectacularly to rally Antwerp's defence against the advancing Germans, and thereby delayed them and prevented capture of the Channel Ports. He proposed a combined assault by Navy and Army on Turkey, to crush this weak ally of Germany and open a warm-sea route to our Russian ally. Kitchener was then unready to supply troops, and an abortive attempt by the Navy alone to force the Dardanelles was prematurely abandoned against Churchill's advice. He was blamed for its failure. When, in May, 1915, the Government was re-formed as a Coalition, Churchill lost his office.

Returning to the Army, he served for a time at the front as Colonel of the 6th Royal Scots Fusiliers; but when the battalion was merged with another, he came back to the House of Commons. Lloyd George wanted to give him office, but at first the Tories in the Coalition would not hear of it. They detested him for his part in the Land Campaign and other Radical legislation. However, in July, 1917, Lloyd George made him Minister of Munitions. When the war ended he was at the War Office, carrying out the tricky task of demobilization. He dearly wished to carry on with war on the Russian Bolsheviks, but Lloyd George would not allow it.

In 1921 he shared with L.G. the task of concluding a Peace Treaty with the Irish Sinn Fein leaders—an act which so incensed right-wing Tories that in 1922 they broke up the Coalition. At the election Churchill lost his seat. When in 1923 the Liberals put Labour in office, his dislike of Socialism was so strong that he moved back to the Conservatives, and in the 1924 Election was returned to Parliament as Constitutionalist Member for Epping. Baldwin promptly made him Chancellor of the Exchequer.

National economic problems have repeatedly defeated the alleged experts. Churchill, no expert in this field, accepted the disastrous advice of the Bank of England to put Britain back on the Gold Standard, which during the war had been abandoned. The resultant rise of the exchange value of sterling priced British coal out of the world markets. The mine-owners decided to lower their costs by a drastic cut in miners' wages. In support of the miners, the T.U.C. called a General Strike. During the nine days it lasted, Churchill hugely enjoyed himself running a Government news-sheet, the *British Gazette*, from the office of the *Morning Post.*

After the 1929 Election, Labour attempted a minority Government, which collapsed in two years and was replaced by a "National" Government. The period from 1929 to the outbreak of the Second World War was a dismal decade of massive unemployment at home and feeble appeasement of Mussolini and Hitler in Europe. Churchill, denied any office in successive Cabinets, was a tireless critic of the mismanagement of affairs, and used his enforced leisure in writing such masterpieces as his biography of Marlborough, in painting pictures and building the walls of his garden.

Appeasement, as Churchill had vainly warned the Government, led in September, 1939, to the Second World War. He was promptly called to the Admiralty. During those futile opening months of "phoney" war, when the Air Force dropped pamphlets on the German lines and the troops of France and Britain sat idle in their positions, the Navy did the only real fighting, hunting down submarines, sinking the *Graf Spee*, rescuing British captive seamen from the German prison ship, the *Altmark*.

The Prime Minister, Neville Chamberlain, as a war leader was nerveless and impotent. The Germans occupied Denmark and Norway in April, 1940, and then in May invaded Holland and Belgium. Chamberlain resigned, to the nation's immense relief, and Churchill took his place, to face a disastrous situation. Holland collapsed in four days, Belgium a fortnight later, while a German column smashed its way across France, splitting the French and British forces apart and swinging north to capture Boulogne and Calais. The British Army, penned against the coast round Dunkirk, seemed doomed, but the small craft of England, 650 of them, smacks, barges, yachts, dinghies, protected by aircraft and naval vessels, brought home in one miraculous week 85 per cent of the troops.

Churchill, on taking office, had warned the nation that he had nothing to offer them but "blood, toil, tears and sweat!" Now, with France collapsing and all the continent of Europe falling into the clutches of Hitler, he declared that we should keep up the struggle against Nazi tyranny, if necessary, alone.

"We shall fight in France, we shall fight on the seas and oceans, we shall fight with growing confidence and growing strength in the air. We shall fight on the beaches, we shall fight on the landing grounds, we shall fight in the fields and in the streets, we shall fight in the hills, we shall never surrender!"

His speeches voiced the ultimate courage of Britain, and the nation rallied to his call. Hitler turned on his air force, the Luftwaffe, to smash the country before invading it. The slender British air force met and battered it, while the men of the bombed and blazing towns formed a volunteer army, the Home Guard, ready to fight to the death against any enemy force that might enter the country. The invasion date was postponed and ultimately abandoned.

On surrendering to Hitler, France had yielded him her battle fleet, stationed in the Mediterranean. Churchill had it sunk at its mooring by a British naval force. He poured tanks and guns from his slender stock into Egypt, to protect the Suez Canal from Hitler and his ally, Mussolini. When in June, 1941, Hitler turned on Russia, Churchill promised Stalin full support, despite his own well-known antipathy to Bolshevism. Everything must give way to defeat of the Nazi.

Churchill's greatest achievement was the bond of fellowship he established with the United States—aided no doubt by the fact that his mother had been American. Conferring with President Roosevelt at sea, he reached agreement on the Atlantic Charter, which pledged its signatories to resist aggression, build a system of international security and promote freedom, independence and social progress throughout the world. The U.S.A. started pouring munitions and supplies to Britain. Then Japan on 7 December, 1941, launched an attack on the American naval base at Pearl Harbour and the flame of war wrapped round the world.

Churchill became the living incarnation of the resistance to Nazi aggression. Back and forth he travelled, addressing the American Congress and the Canadian Parliament, visiting Moscow, Persia, Egypt; eloquent, indefatigable, directing the strategy of the vast conflict.

The tide turned in the autumn of 1942, with Montgomery's victory at El Alamein, followed by the Anglo-American landing in North Africa. Thenceforward the Axis forces were in retreat on every front. June, 1944, saw the launching of the long-prepared "Second Front" in Normandy by British and American troops.

Fighting savagely, the Germans were rolled back across France, Belgium, Holland and in Germany itself. One by one their armies surrendered and on 8 May the war in Europe was ended.

Churchill was wildly acclaimed as the hero of the Western World. But his personal popularity did not benefit the Tory Party, whose leader he had become. At the long overdue General Election, held in July, 1945, the Labour Opposition swept the country, gaining a majority of nearly 150.

Though no longer Britain's official spokesman, Churchill kept up his keen activity in international affairs. At Fulton, U.S.A., he made in March, 1946, a speech urging a special association of America and the British Commonwealth to guard the free world against Communism, and in September, at Zurich, he pleaded for a United States of Europe—a proposal which started the movement for the European Economic Community with its Common Market. Among books that flowed from his busy pen was his massive, six-volume history of the Second World War.

In October, 1951, the Labour Government fell, and in the General Election a Conservative victory established Churchill, at long last, Prime Minister by the nation's official vote. In the fifty years since he first took his seat in Parliament, he had held more ministerial offices than any other politician. He had been victim of most rancorous hostility and stood on a pinnacle of popularity. He was now permanently established in the loyal affection of the nation, and in the esteem of all the world.

Three months later, on 6 February, 1952, King George VI died, and to Churchill fell the task of counselling the young Queen, Elizabeth, in her new task. On 24 April, 1953, she conferred on him a knighthood of the Order of the Garter, and he became Sir Winston Churchill.

On 5 April, 1955, being now an octogenarian, he resigned office, to hold until his death the position of the world's most honoured Elder Statesman. In 1962 the American Congress conferred on him the unique dignity of honorary Citizen of the United States. It was a fitting tribute to his work in drawing together the English-speaking communities in closer fellowship. Soldier and statesman, artist and historian, he will be remembered best in history as the leader of free men in the fight against aggression and tyranny, and as an architect of the citadel of world peace. His passing, on 24 January, 1965, plunged the world into mourning, and brought grateful tributes from every land.

W. Somerset Maugham
1874-1965

It is a rare occurrence that a writer proves equally successful in two distinct branches of his art. Such writers can be counted, in the field of English literature, at all events, on the fingers of one hand. From the middle of the nineteenth century only Oscar Wilde, Somerset Maugham and J. B. Priestley come readily to mind as having equal reputations as writers of prose and as dramatists.

Somerset Maugham was one of the most distinguished writers of his generation. His sense of character was acute and his brilliant wit and narrative ability placed him above almost every novelist of his day, while his witty social comedies were as valuable as mirrors of his times as those of any other contemporary dramatist.

ON 25 January, 1874, the youngest of six sons was born to Robert Maugham, solicitor to the British Embassy in Paris. Eight years later the mother died, and this son, christened William Somerset, eighty years later was to confess that time never healed the wound caused by her death. Two years after the death of his wife, Robert Maugham died of cancer.

Two of the six boys had died in infancy, and of the four who remained, Charles the eldest was already in his father's firm; Frederick was at Cambridge—he was later to become Lord Chancellor and Viscount Maugham of Hartfield—while the third, Henry, was at Oxford. Only the ten-year-old William was left homeless, and he was taken into the guardianship of his father's brother, the Rev. Henry Maugham, Vicar of Whitstable in Kent.

The Reverend and Mrs Maugham were middle-aged and childless, and had no idea how a child should be brought up. Laughter was seldom heard in the vicarage, and the playing of games or reading any book except the Bible were regarded with disapproval. In these circumstances, William was lonely and unhappy. His uncle regarded him as obstinate and lazy, when in fact he was in poor health. A natural shyness was increased by an impediment in his speech, and this his uncle regarded as sullenness.

Life in the vicarage was very different from the gracious, happy life at home in Paris in which he had passed the first ten years of his life. Nor was his life brightened at all when he entered King's School, Canterbury. His school-fellows made fun of his stammer. This may be considered natural; but such an embarrassing defect should have evoked understanding and sympathetic treatment from adults, yet his masters baited and bullied him as much as the boys.

Had it not been for his stammer, Maugham might have followed his two older brothers into the law. The Vicar, his guardian, was determined that he should go to Oxford and so into the Church. For that, young Maugham had no inclination whatsoever; he was equally determined that he would defy his uncle's wishes.

At this time, it was customary for the boys of good, well-to-do families to continue their education abroad for a year after leaving school. Maugham decided to try to persuade his uncle to allow him to do so. Somewhat surprisingly, his uncle consented, and it was arranged that he should spend a year at Heidelberg University in Germany. Here at last, Maugham found happiness. He had a freedom which he had lacked entirely at Whitstable and Canterbury. His companions made no comment upon his stammer, and introduced him to art, poetry, the theatre and friendly argument.

Many people who stammer and are embarrassed by it, often turn in upon themselves. This had happened to Maugham, but his introspection had been accompanied by an enhancing of his powers of observation, a quality which is apparent in all his writing. His experiences in Heidelberg determined him to be a writer; and his brief visits to other parts of Germany, to Italy and Switzerland during the year, implanted in him a wanderlust which he never lost, and which had a great influence on his writing.

He knew that his uncle would never consent to his becoming a writer, so, while he firmly refused to enter the Church, he did agree to study medicine. At the age of eighteen he entered St Thomas's Medical School as a perpetual student, which meant that if he did not wish to qualify he need not do so. Writing of this period of his life, he said;

> "I lived nearly all my student years in a boarding-house for eighteen shillings a week. Indeed my weekly bill came to no more than thirty shillings, and with an allowance of fourteen pounds a month, I lived very comfortably."

While he studied medicine he prepared himself also for the career he was determined to make for himself as a writer. He spent much of his time reading English and European literature, filling notebooks with character sketches, anecdotes, epigrams and plots for stories.

At the end of his second year he became a clerk in the Out-Patients' Department of St Thomas's, and this seemed to have increased his interest in medicine. But it was really the novelist and dramatist in him that aroused this interest, for he saw suffering, fear and despair, hope and courage; in fact, life at first-hand. Whether he realized it or not, he was actually laying up for himself a store of experience on which he was to be able to draw for many years to come.

It was during this time that he began work on his first novel, *Liza of Lambeth*. The book was published in his final year at the hospital, when he was twenty-three. In the same year his name was entered in the registers of the Royal College of Surgeons and Royal College of Physicians as qualified to practise medicine.

Liza was not outstandingly successful, but sufficiently rewarding for him to decide to abandon all thought of setting up his plate, and devoting himself wholly to writing. His brothers and his friends considered him somewhat foolhardy, but he pointed out that he did not have to rely on writing for his living. He still had £150 a year from his father's estate.

His first thought was to travel, and he went wandering through Spain and Italy, observing everything about him, and laying up a store of memories on which to draw. When he came to Paris, he decided to stay there for a time. He lived with a group of artists and writers, sharing a flat for a time with Gerald Kelly, later to become President of the Royal Academy. He wrote steadily, but without much success from the financial point of view. During this period in Paris between 1897 and 1908, his income from his writing brought him in an average of £100 a year.

Suddenly, in 1908, all this changed. He had written his first play in 1892, when he was eighteen. Its theme, however, made it impossible for it to be staged in the prim late-Victorian theatre. Eleven years elapsed before he embarked on his second, *A Man of Honour*. It had been given two performances by the Stage Society in 1903. Another four years went by, and he finished *Lady Frederick* and sent it to the Court Theatre. To his delight, and relief, it was accepted, and was produced in October, 1907.

Critics and public alike greeted it with almost wild enthusiasm, and its writer became famous overnight. With this success, it was comparatively easy for other successes to follow. During the next year Maugham found himself in the remarkable position of having four plays running simultaneously in London. The other three were *Jack Straw*, *Mrs Dot* and *The Explorer*, but none of them had the merit of *Lady Frederick*. They did, however, give Maugham what he most desired—financial freedom which would make it possible for him to do what he liked, and to go where he liked.

Before the outbreak of the First World War Maugham wrote five other plays, all of which were popular successes, though the more serious playgoer found in them—and quite rightly—nothing to claim his attention. Nevertheless, despite their having no great merit, with them Maugham played a large part in reviving one of the great glories of the English stage, the comedy of manners.

In 1912 Maugham began writing *Of Human Bondage*, the first of three "autobiographical novels". He corrected the proofs in the autumn of 1914, in Belgium, within the sound of German guns. When it eventually appeared in 1915, it had only a modest success, and was only to become the great favourite it now is after the appearance of *The Moon and Sixpence*, an immediate best-seller.

Maugham was forty in 1914, and he joined a Red Cross Unit in France, serving for a time as an ambulance driver and a dresser. After a few months, however, he was asked by Intelligence if he would undertake work for them. He agreed, and went first as an agent to Switzerland (out of his experiences here was to come what many consider, though on somewhat doubtful grounds, to be among the best spy-stories in English, under the title *Ashenden*) which was followed by a mission of information to America, a mysterious mission to the South Pacific, and finally a truly fantastic mission to Russia with the aim of persuading the Russian Government to carry on the war against Germany.

This trip to Russia proved too great a strain, and he returned to England stricken with tuberculosis. Sent to Scotland to recuperate, in the austere sanatorium at Nordach he wrote his most amusing comedy, *Home and Beauty*, and planned *The Moon and Sixpence*, a story based on the strange life of the French artist Paul Gauguin.

In 1916 he had married Syrie, a daughter of the famous Dr Barnardo. Mrs Maugham was one of the leading interior decorators of her day on both sides of the Atlantic. The marriage was not a success, and eventually ended in divorce in 1927. There are some who would say that the break-up of his marriage was a boon to English literature, for to escape from the unhappiness of his domestic life, he took to travel.

On his discharge from Nordach he returned to the Pacific by way of America. The main purpose of the journey was to gather material for the Gauguin novel. This achieved, he wrote the story quickly and it appeared in 1919.

Between 1921 and 1931 he was almost continuously on the move, driven by the wanderlust which had first bitten him in Heidelberg. Yet this decade was the most productive period of his life. Between these years he wrote three sparkling comedies, *The Circle*, *The Constant Wife* and *The Breadwinner*, which placed him in the front rank of modern English dramatists; the best of his exotic short stories; a first-rate travel book, *The Gentleman in the Parlour;* a collection of sketches, *On a Chinese Screen*; and the most outstanding of all his novels, *Cakes and Ale*, based on his early life at Whitstable.

In 1928 he bought a Moorish-style villa near the point of Cap Ferrat, midway between Nice and Monte Carlo. This he then made his home. It was to become the treasure house of one of the finest private collections of paintings in the world, and the place of pilgrimage of writers and admirers. He did not live constantly at the Villa Mauresque. Every year or two he travelled to almost every part of the world. By this time his popularity was world-wide, and his literary earnings were immense.

When the Germans invaded France, Maugham, who was on Goebbels's black-list on account of the spy-stories (*Ashenden*), returned to England. There the Minister of Information, Duff Cooper, asked him to go to the United States, still neutral, on a mission of propaganda and good will. He had not been in America long when that country entered the war. Maugham was retained in the United States until hostilities ceased.

In 1946 he returned to the south of France and set about restoring his war-battered villa. Between that year and 1950 he wrote his last novels. Of the three, *The Razor's Edge* almost achieves the standard of his best work. For the next ten years he devoted himself to writing essays, most of which were concerned with literary criticism. In 1958 he produced his last book, *Points of View*, a collection of essays.

Early in the 1950s he founded a fund to provide an annual award of £500 to a British writer under thirty who had already published one book of outstanding promise. He stipulated that the money must be spent on travel, which he believed to be the best way in which a writer may broaden his experience.

During the last two decades of his life he himself continued to travel widely. But after he had passed his ninetieth birthday his physical and mental powers waned, and he died in France in December, 1965. His ashes were buried in the grounds of his old school at Canterbury.

Albert Schweitzer
1875-1965

There are few who look upon life in its more serious aspects, who have not heard of the life and work of Dr Albert Schweitzer of Lambaréné, in French Equatorial Africa; and of those who have heard of him there can be few who have not felt a twinge of inspiration when they have considered his example.

The story of this great man—musician, philosopher and doctor— who rejected a brilliant musical career at its height, to put into practice his philosophy of life, reminds one of the story of St Francis of Assisi, who turned his back on wealth and pleasure for a life of poverty devoted to helping others. For Albert Schweitzer was no less a saint, though he was not canonized, and in these days, when the complexity of modern life makes saintliness difficult to achieve, this man showed, probably more vividly than any other, that "No way of life makes more sense than the way taught by Jesus".

EVERYBODY in the little Alsatian village of Günsbach liked the family who lived in the parsonage, from Pastor Schweitzer down to the youngest child. They were a happy family, understanding and sympathetic, to whom a plea for help never went unanswered, even if it meant that they themselves must be deprived. Into this family there had been born on 14 January, 1875, a boy who was given the name of Albert. As he grew up, Albert attended, with his brothers and sisters, the village school from among whose pupils, the children of the villagers, they made their friends.

One of Albert's closest friends was George Nitschelm. They walked home together from school; they played together; they were involved in the same boyish pranks.

One day as they walked home from school George said to Albert, "You wouldn't dare to fight me. I'm too strong for you."

"That's what you think," retorted Albert.

"Right!" exclaimed George. "Come into the field, and I'll bet you I'll come out the winner."

For a time they sparred, and then all of a sudden the young Schweitzer knocked his opponent off his feet and straddled him across the chest.

"There you are!" he exclaimed. "What do you say now?"

"You win," George gasped. "But if I got good broth for supper twice a week like you do, I'll bet you wouldn't have won."

Albert did not reply. After a brief pause, he got off George, stood up, picked up his satchel, and without a word hurried home.

Wondering what on earth was the matter with his friend, George hurried after him, and called to him to wait. Without turning his head, Albert Schweitzer hurried on.

That evening there was broth for supper. Albert's keen appetite was almost a family joke, and as his mother ladled out the broth, she gave him an extra helping, making a mild joke as she did so.

As he took the plate from her and placed it before him, suddenly he felt sick. He heard George Nitschelm's voice saying again, "If I got good broth twice a week like you do, I'll bet you wouldn't have won."

He pushed back his plate. "I'm not hungry," he murmured. His mother looked at him anxiously. "Are you ill, son? What is it?"

"No, I'm not ill, Mother," he told her. "May I go to my room, please?"

Up in his room, he went over again the thoughts which had come to him so suddenly when George had first made his remark, and he came to a decision; he would not be different from the village boys any more, they must be real friends, and that meant that they must be the same in everything. With a determination strange in one so young, he kept his resolution. He refused to wear an overcoat when the weather grew cold, because the other boys did not possess overcoats; he would wear only clothes like his friends wore, clogs, mittens, a woollen cap. A seemingly unending battle developed between himself and the parents he loved. He could not tell them why he was behaving in this way; they could not understand him. But he would not give way before their pleas, their threats or their punishments.

At lessons he was not all that bright, and now he seemed to take a delight in being beaten in one subject or another by such and such a boy, even to boast about it. There was, however, one activity in which, despite all the other changes, he did not change. When he was only five his father had given him his first lesson on the piano. He proved an extraordinarily apt pupil. He could read music more easily than he could read a book, and playing came as easily as speaking. At eight, he asked if he might have lessons on the organ. Readily his parents agreed, and his mother was particularly delighted, for her father had been an accomplished organist. Within a year he could play well enough to accompany the services in church when the organist was absent.

The struggle with the parents over clothes and other activities continued, however, and were to continue until he left the village school to continue his education at the secondary school in nearby Colmar, and later in Mulhausen.

In Mulhausen he studied the piano with Eugène Munch, the organist of St Stephen's Church there, and when he was fifteen transferred to the organ. Munch was an organist of considerable ability himself, and under his guidance Albert made impressive progress until he had complete mastery over the instrument. The organ was to become almost an obsession with him, and he was encouraged in his ambition to become a great organist when on a visit to Paris in 1893—he was eighteen—his aunt, with whom he was staying, asked the great organist and composer Charles-Marie Widor to hear her nephew play. Widor had agreed to do so only out of kindness, but as soon as he heard the young Schweitzer perform he asked him in a voice quivering with excitement: "How soon can you come to me for lessons?"

At first Albert could not believe that he had heard the great teacher aright. Widor, he knew, taught only the very best of the pupils at the Conservatoire; but at last he was convinced that the famous man meant it. So during the next few years, whenever he could do so, he went to Paris and there took lessons on the organ of St Sulpice, and later of Notre Dame.

He returned from his first visit to Paris to become a student at Strasbourg University. At his own choice, he studied theology. He did not know then that Strasbourg would house him for the next twenty years. In his second year, he was called up for his military service, but the authorities made arrangements for him to continue to attend his lectures at the University.

In German universities, unlike the custom in English ones, a degree course had no set time limit. The student studied his subject, and when he and his professors thought he was ready to sit for his examinations, he wrote a thesis on some approved aspect of his subject which he then defended before a Board. Schweitzer received his doctorate when he was twenty-four.

Throughout these six years he went to Paris as often as possible, and continued his organ lessons under Widor, and by his friendship with Widor he met the musical world of Paris. A year after he had taken his degree he was ordained, like his father, into the Lutheran Church, and was appointed curate of St Nicholas's in Strasbourg.

Long before he had taken his doctorate Schweitzer had appreciated that there were many questions about Jesus he needed to have answered, questions which his teachers did not or could not answer, so he set about trying to find the answers himself. These answers he began to set down in a book which he called *The Quest of the Historical Jesus*. It was a study of the different modern attempts to write a life of Jesus. When it appeared in 1911—it took several years to write—many of his colleagues thought it was a dangerous book, because it might shake people's faith in the Gospels. Schweitzer could not agree with them. "Faith which refuses to face the facts, is no faith at all," he told them. Nevertheless, the book did give rise to much controversy.

By this time, he had become famous in another field. Widor had asked him to write an essay on J. S. Bach, the great composer for the organ, intending it for the use of church organists in Paris. The essay, in some strange way, developed into a masterly two-volume study of the great musician, a masterpiece which has never been surpassed.

Schweitzer had also become as expert an organist as the great Widor himself, an outstanding exponent of Bach's music, and in this field, too, he had won an international reputation.

As a theologian Schweitzer had won the respect and admiration of the Strasbourg University authorities. So, when the Principal of St Thomas's Theological College resigned, they offered the post to Schweitzer, though he was only twenty-eight.

Untouched by the fame which he had achieved at so early an age in his two main fields of endeavour, he lived a life of happiness which few rarely achieve. No one would have been surprised if he had decided to spend the rest of his life in Strasbourg, travelling in vacations to give recitals on the organ in all the capitals of Europe, looking after his students, helping them with their problems and sharing in their jokes.

When he had been at St Thomas's only a year, by chance he came upon a report of the Paris Missionary Society and his eye was caught by an article headed "The Needs of the Congo Mission". When he had read it through, he remembered the parable of Lazarus and Dives. "We here in Europe," he told himself, "are rich, because we know how to fight disease. We are Dives, but those poor natives in Africa are Lazarus, full of sores. We are sinning against them."

Of a sudden he knew what he must do. He must go to Africa to help the natives, and because they needed doctors, he would become a doctor.

So he resigned from St Thomas's and became a student at the Strasbourg medical school. He qualified six years later.

As soon as he could call himself "doctor" he presented himself to the Missionary Society and offered his services. The Society, however, though needing medical missionaries desperately, hesitated to take him. His book, *The Quest of the Historical Jesus*, had just been published, and they had doubts about sending out a man whose religious ideas were causing such comment. He persisted in his attempts to persuade them, and at last they gave way.

For the next year he studied in Paris a course in tropical medicine, and spent his spare time collecting money to build, equip and run his own hospital which he proposed setting up at Lambaréné, on the Ogowe River, in French Equatorial Africa. He gave concerts to raise funds, approached friends, and received assistance which surprised and encouraged him.

In 1912 he married Helen Bresslau, a friend of long standing, and on Good Friday, 1913, he set out for Africa, accompanied by his wife.

The mission station at Lambaréné was built on three small hills above the river, on a narrow strip of cleared land. Twenty yards from the houses the forest rose up in a thick, almost impenetrable barrier, so it seemed. The only building available for use as a hospital until the sectional building which was being sent from Paris, arrived, was a disused chicken house. Nothing daunted, he had it cleaned out and there he set out his medicines and his instruments.

Here every day, before he was up, thirty or forty natives would arrive and with infinite patience squat in silence waiting for him to come. The news of his arrival—that is to say, the arrival of a doctor— had spread like a forest fire, and sick people came many scores of miles in hopes of receiving the magic of his medicine. To them all his great compassion poured out.

His wife looked after his simple bodily needs and helped him in the dispensary. When darkness fell, and his patients had departed, he would sit down at the piano which had been presented to him by the Paris Bach Society as a parting gift, and into the thick forest and over the river would peal out the majestic sounds of a Bach fugue.

Quickly his fame spread. The natives were most impressed by his anaesthetics. "First he kills the sick people, then he cures them, and then he wakes them up." He was the greatest of all medicine-men. In nine months, he wrote to his friends, he had treated over two thousand men, women and children, and he had seen almost every tropical disease there was.

Because they were German citizens by birth, despite the fact that he was working for a French missionary society, when the First World War broke out, the French authorities in the area placed the Schweitzers under house arrest, even refusing to allow them to work in their nearby hospital. They did not complain, but obeyed quietly, and on the second morning Schweitzer sat down and began to write. For the last fourteen years a plan to write a book about the philosophy of civilization had been forming in his mind. When he would write it he did not know. Certainly since coming to Lambaréné he had had no time. Now he had time. After a day or two, however, the guard over the house was gradually relaxed. He was allowed to work again in the hospital. For three years the Schweitzers carried on as before, then the stupidity of bureaucracy bore down on them again. They were taken to internment in France. They remained prisoners-of-war until the Armistice.

By this time the first two volumes of his great work *The Philosophy of Civilization* were complete and were about to be published. For the time being, returning to Lambaréné did not seem possible to him; but after two years in Europe he knew he must go back. Before he could do so, however, money was needed, and for the next four years he toured Europe giving recitals and lecturing to raise the necessary funds.

In 1925 he had raised enough for his immediate needs, and the Schweitzers set out for Africa once more. There he took up his work of healing the sick natives again, the Lazaruses of Africa. On Sundays he preached to them in simple language the simplicity of his own faith and his philosophy of life.

Lambaréné grew, permanent buildings replaced the old shacks and hutments, the work increased. The little settlement in which this great and simple man practised, as very few other Christians practised, the way of life which Jesus taught, and the man himself, became famous throughout the world. In 1952 he was awarded the Nobel Peace Prize for his services to humanity, and no other recipient has been so entirely and utterly worthy of it.

His wife once asked him how long he intended to carry on with his work. "As long as I can draw breath," he answered.

"Come home!" pleaded his friends in Europe. "We need you here."

He returned them a simple answer. "They need me here."

And Albert Schweitzer remained at his task until his death on 4 September, 1965. He was buried at Lambaréné.

Lord Nuffield
1877-1963

IT was November, 1939—Poppy Day—and a chill wind swept down the Oxford street as a young girl stood with her tray of poppies. Conscious that this year there were men—sons, brothers, fathers—across the channel, that some of these might not return, the people were buying poppies with abandon and the sixpences, shillings, florins and half-crowns had been clanging cheerfully into her collecting box. Now there were only half a dozen left and she looked up the street to see who might come to buy them.

For a moment the street seemed deserted. Then, striding towards her, she saw a small, neat, wiry man—wiry even to the stiff grey hair which was brushed back, without a parting, like thick steel wire. He was walking briskly, looking neither to right nor left, and he almost collided with the young poppy seller as he came to the corner of the street.

"I'm.sorry," he said. He looked at her tray with its six poppies, at the collecting box hanging from her wrist. "It's Poppy Day?"

"Yes."

The man fumbled in his pocket and then, to her surprise, took out a cheque book. He opened it, brought out a pen from an inside pocket and carefully, supporting the corner of her poppy tray with one muscular hand, wrote out a cheque on it. She was amused. No one had done this before: now, perhaps, instead of the half-crown she might have hoped for, this strange man would be making out a cheque for a pound—perhaps even five pounds. She watched, fascinated, and then, as the man's hand moved across the little strip of paper, she felt the blood drain from her face. Could those be—yes, they were—one, two, three, four, *five* noughts . . . . The man signed his cheque, blew on it to dry the ink, and then with a smile folded it and stuffed the little lump of paper into her box. Open-mouthed, too startled to give him his poppy, she stared at him as he walked away.

The hundred thousand pounds Lord Nuffield had just given away was only one of the countless gifts he made during his lifetime—and it was by no means the largest. That was to follow, four years later, in 1943, when he handed over stock in Morris Motors to the value of ten million pounds to endow his new Nuffield Foundation.

Perhaps the smallest donation (and not many were small) was the order he telephoned through for "twelve pairs of football boots, twelve jerseys, twelve pairs of shorts and as many pairs of stockings" for a boys' club in Aberdeen. The secretary of the club had written him on an impulse: they were poor boys and they'd appreciate any help he might give them in starting up a football team. The request caught the rich man's imagination and he telephoned the order.

Not all those who applied for Lord Nuffield's charity were successful. Towards the end of his life he was receiving two thousand letters a week, all marked "Personal" or "Private" and all demanding money. As he remarked, "If I even *read* all of them I wouldn't have time do to anything else, not a thing . . ."

He was born William R. Morris—R. for Richard—on 10 October, 1877, in St John's, Worcester. His father, Frederick Morris, had been an independent, venturesome man whose love of excitement took him as a youth to Canada, where, for a time, he drove a mail coach across the plains. He returned to England to marry his childhood sweetheart, Emily, daughter of an Oxford farmer and to settle down—surprisingly—as an accountant. Frederick and Emily were not rich, but they had sufficient, and young William never wanted for food, clothes or the necessities of life. At first, as a young boy, he was anxious to become a surgeon; later, he changed his mind and decided to become an engineer. The reason for the change was that he had discovered it would cost his parents a lot of money to put him through the training and he, Billy Morris, decided they couldn't afford it. Instead, he asked his father to apprentice him to a cycle shop in Oxford.

The request was granted and soon he became proficient, not only at repairing cycles but at building them. He built a lightweight racing model of new design, decided that it was so good he'd take up cycle-racing himself, and went on to win a steady succession of cups and seven Midland championships. But cups weren't money—Billy Morris was strictly an amateur, "old-fashioned", his workmates called him, he wouldn't race for money—and he asked his employer for a rise of a shilling a week, from five shillings to six. This was refused. Immediately, in the impetuous way ("all my best decisions are quick ones") that was to characterize so much of what he did, Billy threw up the job. "From now on," he said, "I only work for W.R.M." He found premises at Cowley, two miles from Oxford, and there he set up "The Morris Cycle Shop".

Within a month he was making a good living from it. The fame of the young man who repaired and even built bicycles better than anyone else spread far beyond Cowley. Encouraged, he enlarged his premises, began making motor-cycles and taking in motor-cars for repair. He even persuaded his father to come in as the firm's accountant, a post Frederick Morris held until his death in 1917.

At the back of Billy Morris's mind was the urge to make a car, a British motor-car. Over in America, Henry Ford was turning out his "Tin Lizzies" by the thousand and these were beginning to come across the Atlantic, to be snapped up—at £135—by those members of the British public who summoned up the courage to learn to drive. In 1912, in the disused, empty buildings of the old Grammar School in Cowley which his father had attended, and the nearby, defunct Military College, Morris built his first car, the "Morris Oxford". It was a superb piece of engineering, but at £175 it was £49 dearer than the Ford. At first there were few buyers. Slowly, though, the merit of this British car became apparent, its sales and production began to go up, and "Morris Motors" were just beginning to do a brisk trade when war came and the factory was taken over for the making of munitions.

In 1919 Morris had to start all over again. By now he had thought out the problems of "mass production" and he had learnt what he could of Henry Ford's methods. He set to work with gusto and within a year he was turning out thousands of cars. 1921 brought a bad slump and many engineering firms failed. Friends advised him to dismiss part of his staff, cut overheads, mark time till the worst was over. Instead, Morris drastically cut the price of all his models. There was stunned amazement in the motor industry but the gamble paid off. Alone among British motor manufacturers—and there were now several—his sales and profits mounted.

In 1923 he bought his first outside firm, the Hotchkiss Company of Coventry, which made engines for his cars, and renamed it "Morris Motors—Engine Division". Two years later, as his methods of production improved, he set up a European manufacturing record of 53,000 cars in twelve months. His ambition was to market a car for £100, but this was harder than he'd expected and it was not until just before Christmas, 1930, that he was able to realize the ambition and put the car on the road.

At the age of fifty-three he was a rich man and at last was able to start doing the things he'd wanted to do, helping causes dear to him. He had just been on a visit to the Argentine, he felt that more people should speak Spanish, and accordingly his first gift was ten thousand pounds to set up a Chair of Spanish Studies at Oxford. He followed this up with another gift to the University, for medical research. The gifts increased in size and number, he began to give away so much money that in a year people were asking whether he would go bankrupt in the process. Morris's own tastes were so simple, he and his wife seldom entertained or went out, they drove an old, small car and lived in a small house near the factory, that he felt no need for the money he was giving away. He was glad to be able to repay the world in the only way he could for what it had done for him. He never made the mistake of giving too little to too many. If he gave, it was the exact sum he felt the recipient deserved, whether it was for setting up a Chair, doing research, putting up a building or sending young men to University—it was never a half-measure. One of his gifts to medicine revolutionized that science. Fleming had conceived penicillin in 1929 but had been unable to produce the substance and it was only the research of Sir Howard Florey—financed by Lord Nuffield, as he had become—which made this possible. On another occasion he backed an iron lung of revolutionary design and issued one free to every major hospital in Britain.

It was in 1934, for his contributions to the British motor industry as well as his unparalleled generosity, that he was raised to the Peerage as the first Viscount Nuffield. His empire was still expanding and in the twenty years from 1919 to 1939 his annual output rose from 300 vehicles a year to 150,000. The firms which had made component parts for Morris cars, or could be converted to so doing, were all gradually acquired. The decision to buy up each one—in fact every major decision—was invariably taken by Nuffield himself. From the day he severed connexion with his first and only employer, Billy Morris had always made up his own mind.

"My best decisions are made in a minute. When I have to sit around a board table and listen to what the majority decides, I'm finished."

Advice—cautious advice about money—was never well received. "All my life," he said, near the end of it, "I have listened to warnings from bankers, solicitors, auditors—and then I have gone my own way. The others," he added with a smile, "they simply don't see far enough."

Nuffield has been described as an exacting employer, but he was scrupulously fair with his staff. He would never, he maintained, get rid of a man just because he made a mistake.

"I go on the theory that if I've got a good man and the bloomer he makes costs me half a million, it would be silly to sack him. I'd probably

get someone not so good who'd repeat it. It's unlikely that the first
chap will be fool enough to lose another half-million in exactly the
same way . . ."

After many years of living extremely simply in a house near the
main factory at Cowley, Lord Nuffield and his wife decided to move
to a quieter spot; a place near Henley, on the banks of the Thames,
with a golf course, seemed the ideal choice. The golf club was short
of funds and the committee were only too glad to have Lord and
Lady Nuffield take over a part of the clubhouse as their residence.
Shortly afterwards there was a change of committee, the Nuffields
were unhappy about it, and for a moment it looked as if they would
have to move. At last Nuffield made his decision: he bought the club.
Then, as the members—not surprisingly—were nettled at having
their club taken from under their feet, he gave them permission to
play, whenever they wanted, on his private course.

One of the most dramatic gifts of Nuffield's career—and for a
quiet and unassuming man he made a number of his gifts, like the
one on Poppy Day, in a startling manner—was to Oxford University
for medical research. He had made many donations to the University
and the town, and he was about to be publicly thanked, in the
Sheldonian Theatre, for his huge gift of £1,250,000. The chairman
was rising to make his speech when Nuffield waved and made it plain
he would like to say something first. Getting to his feet, scratching
his head and studying two bits of paper in his hand, he announced
that he had just learnt the target figure which Oxford hoped ultimately to raise for medical research was two million.

"I see no reason why your work should be held up by lack of funds.
And so I hasten to give you this additional cheque, bringing your total
to the required figure of two million pounds."

There was a stunned silence for several seconds: then the audience
began to cheer and applaud so that the building shook. It was a
minute before the chairman was able to make himself heard: then
all he could say was, "There is nothing—nothing whatever—I can
say."

Although Nuffield's benefactions embraced almost every country
and practically every worthwhile cause, from mental health in
Britain to blindness in Central Africa, he directed much of it to
Oxford University. He had never attended it, but he respected it and
was anxious to make it a still greater force in the world. Among his
benefactions was a complete new college, bearing his name. He had
hoped to leave behind him an undergraduate college devoted to

engineering, but to his disappointment the University authorities persuaded him to endow Nuffield College as a post-graduate one specializing in the social sciences.

Although the huge number and size of his donations—they totalled at his death, £30,000,000—and the impish or unpredictable way he sometimes made them, led some people to dismiss him as a rich eccentric amusing himself by tossing away a lifetime's savings, every gift he made was thought out carefully, its pros and cons weighed in Nuffield's mind. To this end, when the problems of supervising his own munificence needed sharing, he set up the Nuffield Foundation with £10,000,000.

Thanks to Lord Nuffield, the town of Oxford has some of the best-run and best-equipped hospitals in Britain, and one of his few boasts was that every Oxford mother could have her first baby in hospital. Yet despite his prodigal generosity, there was an almost childish feud between Billy Morris and the Oxford Town Council which lasted forty years, from the day in 1913 they turned down his application to run a fleet of motor buses, to 1952, when, after twice refusing the honour, he consented to being given the Freedom of the city.

Nuffield will be best remembered as an individualist—a one-man band. He made his own decisions and stuck by them, whether the decision was to increase the capacity of the Morris engine, drop the price of a car or give a million pounds to research. With his passing, on 22 August, 1963, Britain lost one of the greatest individualists of all time.

Joseph Stalin
1879-1953

JOSEPH STALIN was among the Bolshevik leaders who seized power in St Petersburg and Moscow in 1917 and, after a bitter civil war against White Russian generals backed by France and Britain, established Communism throughout Russia. Vladimir Ilyich Lenin was the unquestioned chief of this group, which included Trotsky who commanded the armed forces of the revolution. Others who were prominent were Zinoviev, Kamenev and Bukharin, experienced revolutionaries and also intellectuals who had passed much of their lives in London, Paris or Vienna. These men had acquired great reputations in political circles. On the death of Lenin it was Stalin, much less well known than his rivals in the Politbureau, considered by them as a man of no strong personal views but a good organizer, who very quickly assumed leadership of the State and, from 1929, remained the real ruler of Russia until his death in 1953. If Lenin brought about the triumph of the Revolution, Stalin was the maker of Communist Russia. Even by the thirties this Communist Russia with its Party aristocracy, its highly differentiated wages and salaries, was very different from the State which Lenin or Trotsky or Zinoviev had envisaged.

Unlike his rivals, Stalin was first and foremost a professional revolutionary and man of action, whose life had been entirely spent in Russia except for short visits abroad to conferences. Unlike them too he was of poor parentage and an Asiatic. The name by which he is known in history was given him by Lenin in 1912 and it means man of steel.

Joseph Stalin was born in 1879 at Gory, a small town in Georgia, near the capital Tiflis. His father Vissarion Djugasvili was a cobbler who had been born a serf—a man tied to the land, the property of a landowner who could sell his "souls" with his acres. His mother Ekaterina, also a Georgian, bore Vissarion three children all of whom died very young. Joseph, the fourth, was a tough child who survived an acute attack of smallpox and a poisoned arm which remained stiff throughout his life. Vissarion was a drunkard and a man of violent temper; he died when Joseph was ten.

Like many great men Joseph owed much to his mother, who, out of her earnings as a domestic servant, sent him to school, from where he earned a scholarship to a seminary at Tiflis, a grim monastic institution but recognized as the best teaching establishment in Georgia. Ekaterina hoped Joseph would become the Patriarch of the Orthodox Georgian Church.

Joseph Djugasvili seemed as a boy to have been a natural leader as well as scholar. The tradition of Georgia was that of an oppressed people with their heroes, princes or popular bandits, taking refuge in the mountains to swoop down on Mongols, Russians or other oppressors. As a boy, Joseph saw himself as such a man and, as an adolescent, he saw himself as a socialist revolutionary. He was expelled from the seminary in 1899 not for political activities but for reading banned books.

For some time he had a job at the Tiflis Observatory as a clerk. He was elected to the Committee of the Social Democrat Party of Tiflis and from 1900 to 1917, under the name of Koba and many other pseudonyms, Joseph Stalin lived the hard and dangerous life of the revolutionary underground worker. When the Russian social Democrat Party split in 1903 between Mensheviks and Bolsheviks, he chose the latter.

In 1904 Stalin on return from Siberia had married his first wife, Catherine Svanidje, a deeply religious woman. When she died in 1907 he is reported to have said:

"She was the one creature who softened my stony heart. She is dead and with her have died any feelings I had for humanity."

In 1908 he served a long prison sentence and in 1912–13 he spent the only long period of his life abroad with Lenin in Cracow and Vienna. It was then that Lenin in a letter to his friend Maxim Gorky referred to Koba as "the wonderful Georgian". Back in Russia at the end of 1913 he lived in St Petersburg but was betrayed to the Tsarist police and again imprisoned. He was one of the first of the Bolsheviks leaders to reach St Petersburg in 1917 when the Tsar was overthrown and a Provisional Government, headed by Kerensky, took over power. After the October revolution, Lenin made him Peoples Commissar for Nationalities.

The next really important step in Stalin's career was to become Secretary-General of the Communist Party in 1922. It was through his hold on the organization of the Party that he was able, after Lenin's death, to defeat all those who like him aspired to leadership. He had to overcome one great obstacle before the struggle began.

Shortly before his death, Lenin, in a private document, reviewed the qualities of the Bolshevik leaders. Of Stalin, he wrote that he had become too rough and proposed that he should be succeeded as Secretary-General by "someone else more patient, loyal, polite, attentive to the comrades and less capricious".

Fortunately for Stalin, Lenin had also attacked most of the other leaders and in 1923 when Lenin was not yet dead but no longer able to exert power, Stalin allied himself with Zinoviev and Kamenev to form a tripartite direction of the Party. Trotsky was thrust on one side; in spite of his brilliance as a thinker and soldier, he was no good at political manoeuvring and was finally exiled from Russia in 1929, to meet his death by assassination by an agent of Stalin in Mexico in 1938.

By December 1929, and his fiftieth birthday, Stalin had disposed of all his rivals for power among the old Bolsheviks of the Polit-bureau. If he had been only a clever intriguer, he might at some time between 1922 and 1930 have found his match. But Stalin's great organizing ability was accompanied by hard common sense which put him on the winning side in the ideological controversies which agitated the Bolshevik leaders. Stalin triumphed over Trotsky because he stood for Socialism in one country as against Trotsky's idea that all energy should be put into fermenting world revolution. Stalin instinctively opposed this romantic view. Communism might be an ultimate solution for the world but he was concerned with Russia and that was his first and only really great concern.

Stalin began the rapid industrialization of the Soviet Union in 1928. The first Five Year Plan saw the beginning of the huge Dneprostroy Dam and the great steel works, some of them beyond the Urals. The phrase of Lenin that "Communism is Socialism plus electrification" was revived, and admirers of Russia were impressed by the streams of tractors pouring out of the factories.

The collectivization of agriculture was begun with the aims of putting an end to rural capitalism which, after the famines caused by the civil war, the Bolsheviks had allowed to flourish; of driving surplus peasants off the land and into the factories; and of increasing the supply of food for the industrial workers through large, efficient enterprises. Progress in the early stages was carried out with great speed and ruthlessness and a complete lack of elementary precautions. Millions died of famine and hundreds of thousands of *Kulaks* or rich peasants were transported to labour camps in Siberia. There was for a while complete pandemonium in the Russian countryside.

Gradually a more rational *tempo* was imposed on the collectivization policy and peasants were allowed to keep a small part of their land and livestock. Stalin very cleverly got the best of both worlds. He dictated the policy of collectivization as a member of the Polit-bureau: but, as Secretary-General of the Party, in a pamphlet called "Dizzy with Success" criticized the inhumanity with which the Plan had been carried out. Having executed officials who had been backward in enforcing collectivization, he proceeded to execute those who had taken their orders too literally.

Stalin's responsibility for the catastrophic first phase did not escape those who knew him. Stalin's second wife was an intellectual, Nadiedja Alliloueva, twenty years younger than he. One evening, in 1932, with her husband in the house of Voroshilov, she spoke bitterly about the famines in the country and the moral blow to the Party which this cruel policy had created. Stalin, in front of a large company, burst into vulgar abuse of his wife. She committed suicide that evening. Stalin's enemies accused him later of poisoning her: as about much of Stalin's private life, there are allegations which can neither be substantiated nor completely rebutted.

From 1933, with the arrival of Hitler to power in Germany, Stalin began to be mainly occupied with foreign affairs. At first, he worked for a common front with the West against the Nazis and Fascists and Mr Litvinov was sent to Geneva to the League of Nations to try to create a system of collective security. In 1939, the year following Munich, a sharp change took place in Soviet policy. The Nazi-Soviet Pact which made the Second World War a cer-tainty was signed in August, 1939.

Thanks to his Pact with Hitler, Stalin was able to extend the territorial security of the Soviet Union by seizing a great part of Poland, Bessarabia and the Baltic States and to defeat Finland and impose a peace which defended access to Leningrad. Stalin's change of policy was motivated by the weakness of Britain and France in face of Hitler and his belief that British policy was to avoid fighting Germany and to embroil the Soviet Union with the Fascist Powers.

The Western Powers showed certainly a great mistrust for co-operation with the Soviet Union. This mistrust was in part motivated by a long series of bloodthirsty purges carried out by Stalin from 1936 to 1938, purges in which practically all the old guard of Bolshevik leaders perished and with them large numbers of Russian army officers including Marshal Tukhachevsky. Hundreds of thous-ands of Russians were executed or imprisoned. Not surprisingly the Western Powers became increasingly sceptical about the value of a common front with the Soviet Union.

The purges were on too large a scale, were conducted on pretexts of sabotage or treachery or espionage of so general and often so extravagant a nature for the real explanation to be anything but a comparatively simple one. Stalin, by the middle thirties, was determined that no rival should be conceivable, that no political faction not totally subservient to him should exist. Murder made more murder necessary, until finally the Russian secret police, the Ogpu, was pursuing anyone, soldier, politician, industrialist or ordinary citizen, who was guilty of individual thought or who might be even suspected of criticizing the régime.

When in June, 1941, Hitler suddenly attacked the Soviet Union, Stalin's policy of appeasement appeared no wiser than that of Chamberlain and Daladier. The Russian armies crumpled up before the German offensive and thousands of Russian aircraft were destroyed on the ground in the early days. Stalin had refused to believe that Hitler would attack Russia so quickly, in spite of a direct private warning from Churchill. He was taken unprepared. By December, 1941, the Germans were outside Moscow and Leningrad and in possession of a large part of Southern Russia including the Crimea.

On 6 December, 1941, the value of the factories constructed at such cost beyond the Urals became evident. One hundred well-equipped fresh Russian divisions were thrown into the battle for Moscow and a turning point of the war was reached. The Germans were driven back.

Standing on the Lenin Mausoleum in the Red Square in Moscow, Stalin finished a speech, more dramatic than his usual not very eloquent and rather laborious utterances, with an unexpected invocation of the spirit of all the warriors of Holy Russia. The Revolution which had banished the Russian past, now recalled it from exile.

In 1942, Russia was to undergo a renewed test from Hitler's armies but neither victory nor Stalin's leadership was any longer in doubt. Stalin, like Hitler, assumed complete command of the Russian armies. Although he lacked Hitler's superb military intuition, he was a far abler generalissimo in the long run. As André Deutsch has written: "Stalin had a peculiar method of making his decisions, one which not only did not constrict his generals, but on the contrary, induced them to use their own judgment".

Stalin's relations during the war with the British and Americans were never smooth but there was hope that after the war there might be peaceful co-operation between the Russia of "Socialism in one country" and the Western world where feelings of admiration for Russia and for Stalin were in the ascendant. It is possible that, while Roosevelt was alive, and notably at Yalta when Roosevelt promised Russia the huge reparations that Stalin was demanding from Germany, Stalin was genuinely in favour of an understanding. Churchill, however, guessed at the forces with which Stalin had to reckon in his own country and among his own military and political leaders.

In September, 1946, Stalin declared his belief in peaceful co-existence even though by that time there were many signs that the mainspring of Russian policy was going to be different. In 1948 when the Communist *coup d'état* in Prague took place, there could be no more illusions. Russian policy was not so much world revolution as that of occupying as many countries by Communist divisions as possible. By 1949 a Communist empire was established from the Elbe to the Adriatic and it included what seemed like a Russian satellite state, Red China.

There seems little doubt that after the war Stalin exerted a much less absolute sway than before and was forced to share power with the Soviet Praesidium. In foreign policy he seemed to be trying to exert a moderating influence, that of an old man who desired to end his days in peace. He certainly used his influence against Russian extremists at the time of the Berlin air-lift in 1949. One of his last statements was to express his willingness to meet President Eisenhower to discuss Korea and outstanding problems.

If his power was less after the war, the Stalin cult was at its height. His speeches on any subject, from linguistics to biology, were treated as gospels, the mention of his name at a Party congress in the satellite countries of eastern Europe would bring the whole audience to its feet in a prolonged ovation; statues to him were erected on the thirty-eight highest peaks in the Soviet Union. In appearance, Stalin corresponded better to the Father figure than any other modern dictator. He never struck violent attitudes and rarely used violent language in public. Short of stature with, in old age, hard grey hair and a grizzled moustache, he moved slowly, spoke quietly and usually had a watchful quizzical look, that of a naturally kindly but also undoubtedly powerful man.

The end of his life was sombre. From 1950 onwards great popular discontent with the Communist régime made new purges necessary both in Russia and eastern Europe. Whilst executions of leaders were few or at least not publicized, again hundreds of thousands of people perished on accusations of treason or sabotage. A savage campaign against Jews in the Soviet Union was begun. With this drastic action, carried out by Beria, the chief of the Soviet secret police, Stalin wholly identified himself.

In March, 1953, it was announced that Stalin was gravely ill and had suffered a haemorrhage affecting vital parts of the brain. He died on 5 March but the announcement of his death was not made until the following day, when Moscow was filled with troops, police and artillery on the orders of Beria. There is circumstantial evidence to suggest that Stalin was poisoned by his intimate collaborators who wished to stop the spread of the purges and to begin a new era.

The reaction against Stalin in Russia began almost as soon as he was dead and Beria had been executed. In 1956 Mr Khrushchev made his exposure of the ills of Stalinism before the Communist Party Congress. It was publicly stated that the crimes and cruelties which darkened the last days of Stalin's life were unforgivable and gradually all aspects of Stalin's long reign were examined and criticized. In 1961 his body was removed from the Lenin Mausoleum in the Kremlin by order of the Communist Party Congress and all the wreaths laid there also disappeared, including one from Mr Chou en Lai inscribed: "To Stalin the great Marxist-Leninist".

It is very difficult to judge Stalin's career or his life impartially, and indeed many facts concerning his personal actions and motives are subject to controversy. Soviet history was rewritten by Stalin and his henchmen: it is being rewritten again. Stalin was guilty of crimes as great as any dictator of the ancient or modern world, except Adolf Hitler. He was at times inhumanity personified. Under his régime, philosophy and the arts were robbed of freedom. Yet it must be said that Stalin showed a great respect for the culture of the past.

Under Stalin's leadership of some twenty-nine years, Russia transformed herself from a backward country into one of the industrial giants of the age, from an illiterate country to one whose population had a passion for learning. She survived triumphantly the Second World War, in part because the policy of industrialization and education had been pushed forward so rapidly. It is idle to speculate as to whether, under more humane leadership, backward Holy Russia, riddled with superstition, torn with the strife of so many nationalities both European and Asiatic, could have become the powerful state she is today. The point is that Russia made this leap forward under Stalin, a man whose achievements were enormous even if his crimes were enormous too.

Albert Einstein
1879-1955

FOR the first week of November, 1919, England seemed to be settling down to observe the anniversary of the armistice. The bloodiest war in history had been over for a year, the world was back to normal, even if people felt things had changed: the cost of living, for example, the behaviour of young people (some critics even included the weather), all this might have changed for the worse, but there was much to give thanks for. The London Press rose to the occasion with special articles, editorials, sombre headlines. The momentous anniversary seemed to be occupying people's minds to the exclusion of all else.

November 7 brought a different headline. *The Times* printed, in huge letters, "Revolution in Science—Newtonian Ideas Overthrown" and went on to describe the previous evening's meeting of the Royal Society. In this, the results had been announced of the expedition to the Gulf of Guinea to view the solar eclipse. The observations of the expedition had been more than satisfactory: the paper quoted the Society's President:

"This is not the discovery of an outlying island but of a whole continent of new scientific ideas—it is the greatest discovery in connexion with gravitation since Newton enumerated his principles . . ."

In effect, the expedition's observations of stars during the period of the sun's total eclipse had verified the whole of Albert Einstein's theory of relativity, the astonishing theory of high-speed motion, the new, half-understood physics which seemed to unify all the branches of the subject. The old Newtonian theories were now proved inadequate when dealing with objects moving at tremendous speeds approaching that of light (186,000 miles a second), though they would remain accurate enough for the ordinary occurrences of life. As an example, Einstein had calculated that a clock, a timekeeping mechanism of whatever construction, which chanced to be travelling at 161,000 miles a second, would be registering time at exactly twice the rate of a clock which was—relative to it—stationary. It would register that speed simply because time itself had speeded up. Not only time altered at these speeds; so did mass and dimension: at the same speed, a man travelling head first through space would be exactly half his usual length. (But as any yardstick he might carry to check this alarming fact would have shrunk by the same amount, he would be unaware of the change.)

These phenomena, and many more besides, had been arrived at by Einstein through a process of reasoning and mathematics. None of them, apart from a peculiarity in the orbit of the planet Mercury, which his theories explained, had been observed or even suspected. There seemed little immediate chance of checking on the behaviour of objects at the speed of light, but it was generally conceded that if light could be observed to bend as it passed near the sun—a phenomenon predicted from the same calculation and one which most scientists considered ridiculous—then the whole theory could be taken as accurate. The 1919 eclipse of the sun provided just the opportunity. Two expeditions set sail for the latitude where the eclipse would be seen as total, one to the Gulf of Guinea, West Africa, the other to northern Brazil, each as an insurance against bad weather conditions which might affect the other. In this latitude the moon coming between earth and sun would, for a few minutes, completely hide the sun. At the same time the sun would be in the midst of a group of particularly bright stars and with its light temporarily blotted out, photographs could be taken of the stars as their light passed close to its surface. The apparent position of the stars could then be compared with pictures of the same stars taken by night in London, when they were far removed from the sun and therefore much less exposed to its gravity.

The pictures taken during the eclipse triumphantly proved Einstein's theory, the star-images on the photographic plates were deflected by exactly the amount he had calculated. There could no longer be any doubt about the theory of relativity—it worked. Yet, as the President of the Royal Society went on to say, "I have to confess that no one has yet succeeded in stating in clear language what the theory of Einstein really is."

No one could. A few scientists understood the consequences of this new, all-embracing theory within their own special fields: none could as yet grasp the meaning of the theory itself.

Yet a few years later the theory was the standard, essential tool of every physicist, the words "Einstein" and "Relativity" were being bandied about, with greater or less understanding, over half the world. At least one reason lay in the remarkable character of Albert Einstein himself, a strange blend of kindness, intelligence and *naïveté* which gave Relativity a publicity no other theory in physics had ever enjoyed.

He was born on 14 March, 1879, in the town of Ulm in Württemberg but left with his parents when he was a year old and moved to the large south German town of Munich. His father had started a small electro-chemical factory there with his brother, and the family settled into a cottage in the suburbs of the town while the father busied himself (not too successfully) with the commercial aspects of his business and the uncle took charge of the factory. It was from this uncle, a remarkable man by all accounts, that Albert got his interest in scientific and mathematical processes. From his mother, who was a musician, he inherited a deep love of music.

The family was Jewish and the boy was brought up in the faith, but as there was no convenient Jewish school, he was sent to a Catholic one and studied that faith as well. This peculiarity of upbringing may have accounted for the lifelong hatred of prejudice and bigotry which characterized him, the reluctance to become identified with any particular nation or group. He developed an interest in science, deplored "the time one wastes learning Latin and Greek", and became fascinated by mathematics, largely through his uncle, who delighted in working through algebraic problems with him in the evening, much as a more normal uncle might read a story out loud. "The animal we are hunting, he's hidden, and we'll call him 'x' for the moment. But we'll get him, all right . . ."

When the boy was fifteen his father lost money, closed the Munich factory and went south to try his luck in Milan. As it was taken for granted that every educated German had a "Gymnasium" diploma, Albert stayed behind at his school, the Luitbold Gymnasium. But somehow the thought of sunny Italy, not a bit like cold Munich, appealed so much that he left the school, despite his parents' protests, and joined them. He was just in time to find his father bankrupt, unable to support him further. Deprived, through his own impatience, of the advantages of a Gymnasium diploma, the boy looked for some technical institution that might train him for a scientific career. Eventually, after a second migration, to Switzerland, he found that the Polytechnic Institute in Zurich would have him.

The Polytechnic had an international reputation and students flocked to it from all over Europe. One of these was a young girl from Hungary, Mileva Maritsch, who seemed to share the young Einstein's passion for physics. They would work together in the laboratory long after other students had retired to their lodgings,

Above: The Morris Cycle Shop at Cowley, near Oxford, where William R. Morris set up in business for himself.

Below: The original 12-h.p., bull-nosed Morris Cowley (1919), first of a long line of successful cars.

A proud and passionate Spaniard, Picasso was the most revolutionary painter the twentieth century has known. The marvellously inventive picture *Les Demoiselles D'Avignon* (*below right*) was painted in 1907 and was the first clear indication of the coming of Cubism, which has proved the most widely influential of all the isms of modern art. He used the symbols of the bullfight (man and horse representing the good and the horse representing the good and the bull representing evil) in his art and never more effectively than in the mural *Guernica* (*above*), inspired by the bombing from the air of the town of that name during the Spanish Civil War and painted for the Spanish Pavilion at the Paris World Fair of 1937. Picasso was also a master of the line drawing, as the figures (*below left*) show.

they became inseparable and within weeks it became tacitly understood that, some day, they would marry.

On leaving the Polytechnic, Einstein discovered, to his dismay, that no one would offer him the sort of work he wanted; after much inquiry he found himself a post in the patent office in Berne. He had come to love the country so he renounced his German nationality and became a Swiss subject. To complete his readjustment, he married Mileva, only to find almost immediately that, outside the laboratory, they had nothing in common: the girl was an earnest, reserved, suspicious Slav; he was a vague, happy-go-lucky, Bohemian. Two sons were born to them in rapid succession and these, because both parents adored them, kept the marriage together.

Einstein's work at the patent office was well paid and interesting: it consisted of making an investigation of every invention and it required an ability to pick out basic ideas from descriptions which were usually inaccurate and badly written. It left plenty of time for other studies.

In 1905 Einstein published papers on the production and transformation of light and on the electro-dynamics of moving bodies. These caused a small stir in the academic world: how could such research come from an official in a patent office? Investigations were made and it was decided that the young man must be taken from his unsuitable post and given some junior professorship. Things moved slowly; four years later Albert Einstein was appointed to the University of Zurich.

Here, life was very different. The salary was no higher than what he had been getting but now he had to keep up a social standard, wear socks that matched and a well-pressed suit. His wife felt at home in the new atmosphere but they were suddenly very poor—clothes and furniture cost money. As Einstein was to remark later, recalling the Zurich days, "In my Relativity I set up a clock at every point in space—but in reality, I found it difficult to provide even one in my room."

In 1911 he was appointed to a better-paid professorship in Prague. Here, there was a large Jewish community, of which he became a member and for the first time, aware of its problems. The German attitude to his people was hardening, there were unpleasant incidents which in the light of history can be seen as tiny pointers to the nightmare which lay thirty years ahead for the Jews of Germany. Therefore when Einstein was offered a post in Switzerland, teaching at his old Polytechnic, he was glad to go—and Mileva, who had been miserable in Prague, made sure they left immediately.

Publication of the results of more of his research made Einstein an international figure. He worked for only two years at the "Poly" before he was made the sort of offer no scientist can refuse: membership of the Royal Prussian Academy of Science and directorship of the new Kaiser Wilhelm Institute in Berlin. This would give him a larger salary and much more time to devote to research. He accepted, but this time Mileva refused to go with him. She knew she would hate Berlin—and in any case they were both agreed that the marriage, at last had failed. She stayed behind with the two boys.

Fortunately for Einstein a distant cousin, Elsa Einstein, was living in Berlin. She was a young widow, and a friendly, happy, soul; she was amused by her eccentric relative and she took good care of him. He returned the compliment a year later, by marrying her.

He spent twenty years, from 1913 to 1933, in Berlin, working hard on his theory of Relativity, thinking it out stage by stage, overcoming its mathematical difficulties, gradually evolving the all-embracing theory which has affected the work ever since of all mathematicians and physicists. His simple-sounding formula, E equals mc^2, which proved the unsuspected equivalence of energy and mass has since been abundantly proved and is responsible, among other things, for the invention of the atomic bomb. The formula shows that a small mass can be converted into a huge amount of energy, where E is energy, m is mass and c is the speed of light. It also gives the secret of the sun. If it were really burning, as people thought, it should have been consumed long ago; in the atomic reaction which Einstein postulated huge quantities of light and heat could continue to be liberated with the loss of only a very small mass.

Despite his preoccupation with work, he was far from happy with the spirit of militarism which surged up during the war. He refused to sign the various manifestos which were put in front of him, alleging things like "German Culture and German Militarism are Indentical", he took little interest in the prosecution of the war, and it was only his Swiss citizenship that saved him from going to prison as a "traitor". After the war, when his theories were beginning to rock the world, there was haggling as to whose property he was. As he put it himself in a wry, very typical, letter to the Press,

". . . by an application of the theory of Relativity to the taste of the reader, today in Germany I am called a German man of science; in England I am represented as a Swiss Jew. If I come to be regarded as a *bête noire*, the description will be reversed and I shall become a Swiss Jew for the Germans, a German for the English . . ."

By 1922 Einstein's own deep conviction that science is a religion and philosophy was becoming more general. In that year he was appointed to the League of Nations Commission for Intellectual Co-operation. He resigned a year later because he felt the League had "neither the strength nor the good will to accomplish its task".

Slowly he began to realize that Germany, much as he enjoyed his work there, was no place for a Jew. Reluctantly, in 1933, he accepted one of the many offers which were coming his way and sailed with his wife to take up a post at the new Institute of Advanced Study in Princeton, New Jersey.

To his great sorrow, Elsa, who had been unable to make the adjustment to the new world from the Germany she loved, died in 1936. He stayed on in Princeton, a shambling, good-natured genius, prepared to talk to anyone at any time. ("Why should I mind that you are late meeting me? Am I less capable of reflecting on my problems here than at home? Here . . .", showing a much-chewed pencil, "here is my laboratory.")

He died in Princeton in 1955, universally mourned as the world's and the century's, greatest man of science.

Lord Beveridge
1879-1963

WHEN Lord Beveridge came to look back over his long life he remembered something that had been told him by Edward Caird, Master of Balliol College, Oxford, where he was an undergraduate, and remembering it he realized what a tremendous influence it had had on his career. Caird had said:

> "While you are at the University your first duty is self-culture, not politics or philanthropy. But when you have performed that duty and have learned all that Oxford can teach you, then one thing that needs doing is to go and discover why, with so much wealth in Britain, there continues to be so much poverty, and how poverty can be cured."

The remark stuck in his mind, probably because there was such a novel ring about it. He knew that there were lots of poor people about, of course, but was not this only to be expected? Some people were born rich and some were born poor; so it had been from time immemorial and so, he had supposed, it would continue to the end of the chapter: but if poverty were not inevitable, if its causes could be ascertained and a cure for it discovered, what a wonderful life work that might be!

William Henry Beveridge was born on 5 March, 1879, at Rangpur, India, where his father, Henry Beveridge, held a responsible post in the Indian Civil Service. He was given what his parents considered to be the best education available at the time—public school (Charterhouse) followed by the university. He did well, very well, in all his examinations, and was granted a fellowship of his college. After four years at Oxford, when he was twenty-two, he had no clear idea of what he should do next. His father wanted him to become a barrister, and he did in fact make a beginning at the Law. Soon he found that he was not interested in the ordinarily humdrum life of the courts, and the prospect of a judgeship at the end of many years of uncongenial labour did not appeal to him in the least. Politics? He could count on the support of some influential friends in both the great political parties, but in his heart of hearts he knew that he would never make a good party man, apart from the fact that in those days M.P.s were not paid even the smallest of salaries and he had to rely upon his own earnings for his livelihood. Journalism then? He liked using his pen and he had quite a gift for words—a gift which, as we shall see, he put to full advantage. However, he could not get out of his head those words of Edward Caird's: Study poverty . . . find out what causes it, . . . see if you can discover ways in which its effects may be ameliorated.

To the surprise, and no little concern, of his parents, who thought that he ought to be making a start in a profession with some definite prospects of ultimate success, he accepted the post of sub-warden of Toynbee Hall, in Whitechapel, in the heart of London's East End. This was a "settlement" of men of the University type that had been established in 1884 by Canon Barnett, vicar of the church of St Jude, Whitechapel, and was named after the brilliant young economic historian Arnold Toynbee, who had recently died. Barnett was warden, but for months at a time Beveridge was in full charge, at a salary of £200 per annum. He had no fixed hours, no fixed duties—in fact, he was always on duty, constantly engaged in directing the activities of the settlement in the spirit of human sympathy and brotherhood. And he was always learning. He got to know the poor as only those actually living among them can get to know them. He became one of the managers of a board school. He supported likely candidates in local council elections. He joined a working-men's club, and was cold-shouldered for his pains. He attended innumerable meetings of one kind and another, and spoke at many of them. He organized the distribution of charity, and in 1903 he helped to administer the Lord Mayor's Fund for the relief of the unemployed. In this way he was started on what was to be his chief interest for many years—the problem of unemployment.

He wrote in his autobiography:

"I was learning—finding out how to do without instruction things that I had never done before; finding out about human nature; discovering myself through the eyes of others."

Before long he was recognized as an authority on the problems of casual labour and unemployment in general, but even so he was greatly surprised when in 1906 he was offered a post as a leader-writer on the *Morning Post*, a strongly Conservative daily newspaper that happened to be edited by a man of wide human sympathies. Each night he presented himself in the editor's room at about 10 o'clock, to see if he was "wanted"; he was paid three guineas a column of 1,100 words, and this brought him in an income of

£600 a year earned by working 10 to 11 hours each week. It was good pay, equivalent (so he carefully worked out) to what $27\frac{1}{2}$ London bricklayers would receive in the same time at their then rate of $10\frac{1}{2}$d an hour. What was more important, although he was a Radical writing for a Tory newspaper he was allowed practically a free hand to write on the social problems of the day—such things as sweated labour, housing, town planning or the lack of it, trade union law, the liquor trade, London traffic, local government, the issue of free meals to school children, infant mortality, the proposals to establish labour exchanges and to grant old-age pensions, and unemployment. Always and above all there was unemployment; that he considered to be at the root of the most pressing evils. As he saw it, the great majority of workers were always on the edge of an abyss. Their wages were generally so pitifully small that they were quite unable to put something by for a rainy day. Some of the skilled artisans were entitled to receive a small benefit for a few weeks when they lost their jobs, but for the vast majority a spell of unemployment brought them and their families to destitution.

In the two and a half years that Beveridge was a leader-writer on the *Morning Post* he wrote some 600,000 words, and, he was able to boast, "on any subject of which I knew anything, I never wrote a word that I did not believe". Nor did he ever have a word struck out or a contribution rejected.

What was more important, his articles were *read*, and by none more carefully than by those up-and-coming men of the new Liberal government that had been swept into office on the electoral tide in 1905. Campbell-Bannerman, the Prime Minister, Asquith, Lloyd George, Winston Churchill—here was a team of social reformers such as had not been seen for generations. The air was full of new schemes for the remedying of this, that, and the other.

A man who knew the facts and how to present them intelligibly, accurately, and with complete impartiality was at a premium. Such a man was William Beveridge, and in 1908 his call came. Winston Churchill was President of the Board of Trade, and he had expressed his intention of "taking up labour exchanges seriously". He asked Sidney and Beatrice Webb, who knew everybody who was anybody in the reforming camp, to suggest someone who might be put in charge of the administrative details in drawing up a scheme, and they at once declared, "you must have the boy Beveridge".

Mr Churchill was quick to act on the suggestion, and Beveridge was offered a post at the Board of Trade at a salary of £600 a year. This was no more than he had been making at the *Morning Post* for a very few hours of work a day, but "the boy"—he was actually twenty-nine—did not hesitate. Other persons had tried to get him into the Government service, he revealed years afterwards, but;

"Mr Churchill was the only person able to invite me to do what I was set on doing—to organize the labour market by labour exchanges."

So he became a Civil Servant, and had the immense satisfaction of helping a Minister, "who was immense fun to work for", to establish the first national system of labour exchanges. In February, 1910, the first exchanges, sixty-one in number, opened their doors, and another eighty-seven followed by the end of the year.

As a young man just down from Oxford he had witnessed the daily struggle for jobs by hordes of unemployed men; he had seen them standing at street corners, queueing up to read the "jobs vacant" ads. in the newspapers at the public library, hanging round factory doors and dock gates and sometimes fighting frantically to catch the foreman's eye. He had shared the misery of their disappointment as they were rebuffed and shuffled away, with no prospect but the same demoralizing and dispiriting round in the morning. Now the state had assumed responsibility for putting the employer in touch with the man out of work—had taken a hand in the finding of jobs for men who were ready and willing to work. Not surprisingly, Beveridge was appointed in 1909 Director of the new Labour Exchanges and head of the department which eventually was expanded into the Ministry of Labour.

What Beveridge called the necessary sequel to labour exchanges was unemployment insurance. In conjunction with Llewellyn Smith, the Permanent Secretary of the Board of Trade, he set about the formulation of a practical scheme. The scheme that they prepared owed nothing to any model overseas, for no other country, not even Germany, had started such a thing. Beveridge put "terrific energy" into the work, and in 1911 the National Insurance Act made it compulsory for workers in certain selected industries to be insured through a contributory system.

When the First World War broke out in 1914, Beveridge was given rapid promotion and increased reponsibilities. In 1918 he was at the Ministry of Food, where he prepared the national food rationing scheme. At the end of the war he became the Permanent Secretary at the Ministry and was created a K.C.B. Then the Food Ministry was wound up, and Beveridge, although he could have stayed on in the Civil Service to earn a substantial pension, decided to quit.

From 1919 to 1937 Sir William Beveridge, as he now was, was Director of the London School of Economics and Political Science. When he accepted the appointment, it was a small institution with part-time teachers and a small body of adult students, but in the course of his eighteen years as its head it was transformed into one of the largest and most influential of the colleges of London University. On his retirement from the directorship of the "L.S.E." he was appointed Master of University College, Oxford, and he retained that office throughout most of the Second World War. As one of the "Old Dogs" (his term) he was ready and eager to be of use, and in 1940 he accepted an invitation from Mr Bevin, Minister of Labour, to make a survey of existing man-power and its use. Then he was commissioned to draw up a new schedule of reserved occupations, and he made many suggestions for the better use of the nation's man (and woman) power in what had become, as he was never tired of urging, a total war.

All this was but the prelude to what was to prove the work of his life, the thing by which he will be always remembered. In the summer of 1941 he was made chairman of an inter-departmental committee on Social Insurance and Allied Services. Not very much seems to have been expected from the committee, but Beveridge soon changed that. Under his direction it was transformed into a body of Civil Servants who were his advisers and he sat down to prepare a report that was not just a tidying-up analysis of existing social insurance schemes but the blue-print of a whole system of social security. The final version, the Beveridge Report, was published in December, 1942, and achieved an instant success. It became the best best-seller of Blue Books. It was read by everybody, and quoted everywhere, not least in enemy countries. It immensely encouraged the fighters at the front and the workers at home with its prospect of a land worth returning to after the war, a land from which the Five Giants—Beveridge's phrase—of Want, Sickness, Squalor, Ignorance, and Idleness through unemployment, should have been banished once and for all.

Briefly put, his plan proposed, firstly a unified social insurance system under which, by paying a single weekly insurance contribution, everyone would be able to insure against unemployment, sickness, accident, and old age. Secondly, it proposed a scheme of Children's Allowances; and third, a comprehensive health service, by means of which medical treatment of all kinds would be secured by all citizens, again in return for the insurance contribution.

Archbishop William Temple said of the plan that it was the first time anyone had set out to embody the whole spirit of the Christian ethic in an Act of Parliament.

Beveridge had hoped that his plan would be enacted by the Coalition Government headed by Mr Churchill, who thirty years before had as President of the Board of Trade made a beginning with unemployment insurance. The Government did indeed accept the plan in principle and adopted a number of the proposals, but in the event it was the Labour Government headed by Mr Attlee that provided Britain with a system of social insurance, or social security, which, though it differed in detail in some respects from what Beveridge had proposed, was in its essentials the Beveridge Plan.

Shortly after the publication of his Report, Beveridge married in December, 1942, Mrs Jessy Mair, widow of his cousin and lifelong friend David Mair. She had been his secretary at the Ministry of Munitions in the First World War and also when he was head of the London School of Economics. Two years later appeared his book *Full Employment in a Free Society*, in which (still on his old subject!) he stressed the vital importance of maintaining a high level of employment and indicated ways in which this most desirable end might be brought about.

For a few months at the end of the war he was Liberal M.P. for Berwick-on-Tweed, but he soon regretted his venture into the political arena. He made no great mark in the House of Commons, and he was defeated at the general election in 1945. In the following summer he was created Baron Beveridge, and over the next few years he was active in the establishment and running of new towns in Durham. His wife died in 1959, and on 16 March, 1963, the "Architect of Social Security" as he was well styled, died at his home in Oxford at the age of eighty-four.

When he came to write his autobiography—it was published in 1953—he gave it the title *Power and Influence*, and in its prologue explained why. *Power* he defined as "ability to give other men orders enforced by sanctions, by punishment or by control of rewards", and *Influence* as "changing the actions of others by persuasion, appeal to reason or to emotions other than fear or greed". Power he had seldom possessed, he went on to state, but "since I came to manhood I have seldom been without influence". And that is how he preferred it. "I have spent most of my life most happily in making plans for others to carry out." The Welfare State of today was very largely his creation, and it remains as his monument. The Master of Balliol who planted the seed that bore such a bountiful harvest would have had good reason to be pleased.

Lord Beaverbrook
1879-1964

Beaverbrook was the last of the Press "king-makers". His story is one of outstanding personal success and of equally outstanding personal failure. His failures, which cannot be measured materially, rose out of flaws in his own character, chiefly in his often faulty assessment of other men. In one field alone can he be said to have benefited others besides himself—in the Second World War he was Minister of Aircraft Production, and it was owing to his efforts that Britain won the Battle of Britain.

IN 1880 the Rev. William Aitken moved from Maple, Ontario, to Newcastle, Ontario, taking with him five children, the youngest of whom was a boy called Max, then not quite one year old. Five other children were to be born in Newcastle, one of whom died in infancy; but of the ten, Max was to be always the odd man out.

From his earliest years Max Aitken was a rebel. It was a feature of large Victorian families that all the children "pulled together"; it was the only way in which they could derive any benefits at all from a home whose executive head, the mother, had her attention constantly centred on organization and administration.

Max was quarrelsome; he would go off by himself and wander in solitude in the woods or by the river; he seldom confided in his brothers or sisters; his closest friends were outside his own family. For five years he attended the public school called Harkins Academy. The academic standards of the school were not outstanding, but such as they were, the boy took advantage of them, though he was a frequent truant. His headmaster was quite certain that he would never make any great success of his life, because he lacked powers of concentration.

At twelve he acquired a newspaper round, which was quite a common activity in those days for boys of even quite "good" families. He operated on a different basis from that of his colleagues in the business; instead of selling all his newspapers himself, he employed sub-agents, and thus extended the scope of his round. Even after he had paid his agents, his profits were larger than those of his closest competitor.

During his last two years at school, which he left when he was fourteen, besides organizing his paper round, he also worked in a drug-store. He collected the key from the chief assistant and opened the shop at 7 a.m., swept the floors and washed out bottles, and then went off to school. After school he served behind the counter, often until ten o'clock at night.

For both his jobs he needed a bicycle. Since his father would not buy him one, Max borrowed enough money to buy several cases of soap, the manufacturers of which were offering a bicycle free in exchange for wrappers from the soap. He then hawked the soap from door to door, offering it at a lower price than was usually charged, on condition that the customers would give him the wrappers. In this way he repaid his debt and got his bicycle.

When he left school, his parents sent him to be examined for a clerkship at a local bank. He had decided that this was not the job for him, but instead of arguing with his parents, he sat the examination and took good care to fail.

By this time he had obtained the sole agency in Newcastle of two St John newspapers, the *Sun* and the *Telegraph*, which he distributed to the newsagents on a commission basis. He also acted as correspondent for the *Sun*.

In 1896, when he was seventeen, he took his first settled job, as a student-clerk in a law office at Chatham, just across the river from Newcastle.

From his earliest teens, Max Aitken had always preferred the company of those older than himself. In the law firm of Tweedie and Bennett, his best friend did not come from among his fellow apprentices, but was the junior partner of the firm, Richard Bennett, later to become Prime Minister of Canada. A short time after Bennett left the firm to set up on his own in Calgary, Alberta, Aitken followed him, and made a bare subsistence by selling insurance. He also formed a partnership with another young man, in a bowling alley. This proved a moderate success, but he tired of it, and moved to Edmonton, where he set up in business on his own collecting and delivering cargoes of meat.

In 1898 he helped Bennett in his election campaign for membership of the Legislative Assembly of the North-West Territory. It was this which gave him his first glimpse of politics and political life which were later to play a great part in his own life.

On his twenty-first birthday, while on a fishing trip at Truro, Nova Scotia, he seems to have had a sudden moment of revelation and inspiration. His activities were leading him nowhere; and he must have some direction. He would, he decided, become a million-aire! For many this would have been merely wishful thinking; for Aitken it was a goal to be achieved at all costs—and as quickly as possible. In the event, few men have gained their first million in any currency so quickly as Aitken.

Moving to Halifax, he managed to attach himself to the leading industrialist and financier in eastern Canada, John F. Stairs. Here the young man became a diligent businessman, selling stocks and bonds in Stair's steel company, making money and saving it. Everywhere he went he attracted attention; older, staid business men of experience found his selling methods irresistible.

In 1902, when he was just twenty-two, he formed a finance company to promote mergers. His fellow-shareholders were the four leading financiers of Halifax. They provided the money; he did the business. Four years later the Montreal papers were referring to him as a "financial wizard", and encouraged by this he moved to Montreal which offered him greater scope.

In this year, at the age of twenty-six, he married Gladys Drury, the eighteen-year-old daughter of a well-known military family. Within a short time of marrying he had achieved his ambition; he was worth a million dollars. He now set himself the goal of five million dollars.

He stayed in Montreal for three years. In that short period he set up every trust which was created at that time in Canada. Banking, steel, coal, hydro-electric power, transport—he was engaged in them all. His greatest coup was to buy thirteen cement companies for sixteen and a half million dollars, which he then formed into one great company, the Canada Cement Company, and sold the C.C.C. for twenty-nine million dollars.

He decided that he must seek wider fields still, and that these could be found only in the commercial capital of the world, London. So in 1910 he moved with his wife into a flat in Cavendish Square. A year later, in King George V's Coronation Honours list, Aitken was awarded a knighthood.

On a previous visit he had made the acquaintance of another son of the Manse, also born in Canada and in the same province as himself, New Brunswick. His name was Arthur Bonar Law. He had come to England some years earlier, had entered politics, and was Conservative M.P. for Dulwich. A friendship developed between the two men which was as true a friendship as any can be; it was also to have a very great influence on Aitken's own life and career.

The Aitkens had not been in England long when a second General

Election within a year was held. Bonar Law gave up his safe seat at Dulwich to fight a much less safe one, North-west Manchester. He asked Aitken to help him with his campaign, and Aitken not only agreed to help his friend, but astonished everyone by announcing that he was himself going to contest a seat in Lancashire. Such were the qualifications for membership to the House of Commons that he could do this though he had not yet qualified by residence to vote. Ashton-under-Lyne was vacant; he presented himself; and was accepted. Though an unpractised speaker—he was never to excel in the art—he fought on a platform of Tariff Reform and Imperial Preference; and was elected, by a majority of 196, while the much more experienced Bonar Law was defeated. So he entered politics, and though he was to become famous as a Press Lord, it was politics which were to absorb most of his energies for the rest of his active life. His newspapers were to him merely the instruments for the propagation of his views.

It was about this time that he read Burke's *Appeal from the New to the Old Whigs*, in which he came across a passage which struck him with great force. It read:

"The world is governed by go-betweens. These go-betweens influence the persons with whom they carry on intercourse by stating their own sense to each of them as the sense of the other; and thus they reciprocally master both sides."

He was not a successful parliamentarian, and the activities of the House of Commons so far as back-benchers were concerned did not appeal to him. He decided instead that his contribution to politics should be in the rôle of go-between, the power in the shadows, the manipulator of those who seemed to be the wielders of power. Within six months of his own election, he was already playing himself into this rôle, and was deep in intrigue to replace the then Leader of the Conservative Party, A. J. Balfour, with his friend Bonar Law. Partly on account of Balfour's too-great self-confidence and partly owing to the skill with which Aitken organized the opposition, it proved a facile operation.

Law promised Asquith, the Prime Minister, that if war came he could reckon on the support of the Opposition, and when war did break out in 1914, this promise was honoured. Law himself became Colonial Secretary in a coalition Government. Within two years, the military situation and conduct of the war had led to dissension in the coalition, and a movement was set on foot to replace Asquith with Lloyd George. Once more Aitken was the prime intriguer and manipulator. Again the plot came to quick fruition. By December, 1916, Lloyd George was Prime Minister.

Aitken had asked as the price for assisting Lloyd George that he should be given the post of President of the Board of Trade when the new Prime Minister formed his Government, and he was convinced in his own mind that Lloyd George had agreed. Within a few hours, however, he learned that the new President of the Board was to be Albert Stanley. When he sought an explanation he was offered a minor post which he refused, but accepted a peerage instead, and became Lord Beaverbrook.

In February, 1918, Lloyd George offered him the post of Minister of Information. There had long been a general feeling that Britain's war propaganda was being incompetently handled, and that Beaverbrook, with his experience of the kind of propaganda, was the man to put matters right in this field. It must be explained that early in the war Beaverbrook had been made Canadian Record Officer, a post which required him to attach himself to the Canadian forces at the front and to observe and record all that went on in their sector. In this work he had shown himself to possess journalistic qualities of a high order. By 1916 he had also acquired a controlling interest in the *Daily Express*, and had many contacts in Fleet Street. So it was on these two grounds that Lloyd George made his offer.

Four days before the Armistice he resigned on account of bad health: but during his short term he had done what had been expected of him.

For some time he had been toying with the idea of owning a newspaper. He had almost bought the *Sunday Times*, but had been prevented by Lloyd George, who said that there had been enough trouble already over Ministers who owned newspapers, and he could not allow Beaverbrook to acquire the *Sunday Times*, because it would be bound to add more fuel to this particular fire.

On 28 December, 1918, however, Beaverbrook founded the *Sunday Express*.

With Beaverbrook's support, Lloyd George won the Khaki Election of 1919 with an overwhelming majority. Gradually, however, the two men drew apart, and Beaverbrook withdrew his support, so that within a couple of years he was repeating his manœuvring to oust Lloyd George and secure the premiership for his friend, Bonar Law. This time also he was successful.

Unhappily, Bonar Law had not been long in office before he was discovered to have cancer of the throat and was forced to resign. Once more the leadership of the Party was vacant. Bonar Law's mantle fell upon the Chancellor of the Exchequer, Stanley Baldwin.

It may seem strange that Beaverbrook did not use his power to block Baldwin's succession, for the two men had for some time been at loggerheads. Perhaps the explanation may be found in Beaverbrook's great affection for Bonar Law. After the resignation, when it was apparent that Law could not live long, Beaverbrook refused all political and social engagements so that he might be near his friend, day and night. Though Law's death when it came in October, 1923 was expected, it caused Beaverbrook a deep shock, and he was, for a time, it seemed, inconsolable.

Within a year of succeeding to the premiership, Baldwin decided that there must be a new election, so that the Conservative majority might be consolidated. Beaverbrook opposed this move, and drew to his side the other powerful leaders of the Party, Birkenhead, Churchill and Austen Chamberlain. Despite an outward show of support for Baldwin, Beaverbrook conducted his campaign in such a backhanded way that the dissension among the leaders could not fail to come to the notice of the electorate with the result that the first Labour Government was returned to power.

Beaverbrook's main political doctrine was Imperial Preference—it was a chief plank in his platform when he fought his first election—and it was to this that Baldwin was opposed. He felt so strongly about Imperial Preference—his newspapers made this their constant chief political theme—that he formed the idea of creating a centre party, a fusion of the Liberals and Conservative, to oust Baldwin from his leadership of the Party.

The climax of these efforts came in the Westminster Abbey Division by-election in 1924, when Churchill was put up by Beaverbrook and his supporters as an Independent Conservative against the official Conservative. Though Churchill did not win, he polled only 43 votes fewer than the official candidate. This action by Beaverbrook made impossible any thought of reconciliation between him and Baldwin.

Encouraged by the Westminster result, Beaverbrook continued to oppose Baldwin; but he gravely under-estimated his man. Baldwin gave the outward appearance of being a lazy man, always ready to adopt the easy solution. However, he suddenly revealed that he could plan as effectively as Beaverbrook, and be even more devastating in his verbal and practical attacks.

First he gave a "sensational interview" to the *People* in which he

declared that he was under no illusions about the loyalty of some of
the chief members of the Party, and then went on:

"At the same time I am attacked by the Trust Press, by Lord Beaverbrook and Lord Rothermere. For myself I do not mind. I care not what
they say or think. They are both men that I would not have in my
house. I do not respect them. Who are they? . . .

"(Beaverbrook) had contracted a curious friendship with Bonar and
had got his finger into the pie, where it had no business to be. . . .
When I came in I stopped all that. I know that I could get his support
if I were to send for him and talk things over with him. But I prefer
not. That sort of thing does not appeal to me. . . ."

Everyone agreed that it was the most savage attack by a leader on
members of his own party that had ever been made. His Party chiefs
felt that he had gone too far, and he issued a disclaimer to each of
the men he had named. All accepted the disclaimer but Beaverbrook,
who made no reply.

Because his idea of a centre party inevitably meant collaboration
with many who were Free Traders, that is, opposed to Imperial
Preference, by the end of 1924 he had dropped it.

Five months after the *People* article, the Labour Government fell
and the Conservatives were returned to power. Within a few months
Beaverbrook was beginning to attack Baldwin ferociously once
again. This was followed by a somewhat strange lull, only to break
out even more violently in 1929. This reached its climax in 1930,
when Beaverbrook declared: "If the Conservative Party does not
adopt Empire Free Trade, it is my purpose to break up the Party."

In this campaign he had the unwelcome support of Lord Rothermere, who was trying to form a new party, the United Empire
Party. It was Rothermere who assured Baldwin of success.

At a mass meeting at Caxton Hall, Baldwin, while making his
main speech, read a letter from Rothermere in which he said that
he would not support Baldwin unless he knew beforehand what his
policy was going to be, and the names of at "least eight or ten of his
most prominent colleagues in the next Ministry".

Baldwin commented: "A more preposterous and insolent demand
was never made on the leader of any political party. I repudiate it
with contempt, and I will fight that attempt at domination to the
end."

Though Beaverbrook tried to wipe out the effect of Rothermere's
rashness, he could not overcome the lead which Baldwin had
acquired over all his machinations.

There was to be one more clash between the two men. This was in the matter of the King's Abdication. Out of this, too, Baldwin emerged the victor.

As the war-clouds began to gather in the late 1930s Beaverbrook tried to keep up the morale of the people by having his newspapers proclaim daily: "There will be no war this year or next year either." Whether he believed this or not, is not quite clear, but the *Daily Express* carried the slogan until a few days before war was actually declared.

Immediately Churchill became Prime Minister in May, 1940, he invited Beaverbrook to be his Minister for Aircraft Production. He made his request because, as he has said: "I felt sure that our life depended on the flow of new aircraft." Beaverbrook was the one man he knew who had the vision and energy for this extremely difficult job. Though he made many new enemies, his term ot office was undoubtedly Beaverbrook's finest hour; the R.A.F.'s victory in the Battle of Britain was owing to two factors—the man who produced the aircraft and the courage of the Few who flew them.

He also undertook a mission to Russia, when the Germans attacked her. In 1943, he became Lord Privy Seal—having served, after his tenure of Aircraft Production, as Minister of Supply, and of War Production—and retained this office until the end of the war.

After the war he did not engage in active politics. He was a public benefactor on a large scale, chiefly to causes in Canada. Though he had not been in formal control of his newspapers for a number of years, his stamp was on every issue.

Helen Keller
1880-1968

"BUT surely, Doctor—she was such—such an *intelligent* baby . . ."

"I know, I know. I remember, Mrs Keller. A remarkable little child."

"I just can't believe it. It's fantastic and horrible and utterly, utterly, untrue. How could the Lord . . ."

"We are not to question His judgments, Mrs Keller. But of course, He that takes away may yet—who knows?—give back. There are miracles, Mrs Keller. But I would be failing in my duty as a physician if I encouraged you to rely on one."

None came. Helen Keller, the beautiful baby girl who had been taken ill at the age of nineteen months, had lingered for weeks near death, was left totally, permanently, blind and deaf.

To say no miracle came is to be strictly accurate—but Annie Sullivan, nearly blind herself, was the nearest thing to one. With her help, Helen Keller changed, miraculously, from a savage with a useless, wasted mind in a clumsy prison of a body, to an example, a comfort, to others far less tragically afflicted than herself. Handicapped people could envy, try to emulate this remarkable woman who lived, behaved, as if she were neither blind nor deaf; could talk intelligently, intelligibly—brilliantly, some said—without ever having heard the human voice.

Helen Keller was born in Tuscumbia, Alabama, on 27 June, 1880, a normal, healthy child, the pride of her parents, Captain Arthur Keller and his wife Katherine. Arthur Keller was of Swiss descent, had been a Confederate officer in the Civil War, was a stern, firm, upright man—but even he was appalled, incredulous, at the tragedy which struck his family. Eventually, while the child stayed in its own, dark, silent world, responding to nothing, the Kellers came to accept the truth, gave up hoping for a miracle. The child, if it lived, would grow up incapable of anything, unable to perform any of the ordinary everyday actions which normal children—and their parents —take for granted: there was no way of teaching her. She would see nothing, hear nothing, never learn to speak, she would be entirely alone, for ever.

The child was nearly seven when Mrs Keller, reading Charles Dickens's *American Notes*, learnt of Samuel Gridley Howe, the remarkable head of the Perkins Institute for the Blind, in Boston, who had succeeded in teaching a similar girl to read and write. Mrs Keller was interested, though such a miracle seemed unlikely in the case of her own daughter. She got in touch with the Perkins Institute. Howe was dead—Dickens's *American Notes* were history by 1886— but his successor, the Greek-born Michael Anagnos whom Howe had met on a visit to Athens and persuaded to come to America and help in his work, suggested that the Institute send one of its recent graduates, twenty-one-year-old Annie Sullivan, to stay with the Kellers and try to instruct their child—teach it something, anything, even if the goal of speech, total understanding was too remote to contemplate. Captain Keller readily accepted and Annie Sullivan set off for Alabama.

The story of Helen Keller is so much the story of her teacher that one must lightly sketch Annie's background. She was the child of poor Irish immigrants, her mother had died when she was eight, her father had deserted the three children. The other two had been taken to State Institutions but Annie, born nearly blind, had been sent to the Massachusetts State Infirmary. Here she learnt of the Perkins Institute and one day when the Infirmary Board of Governors was paying one of its infrequent visits she tore up to a tall man in the corridor and flung her arms round his waist. She was too blind to know as she cried, "Mr Sanborn, oh, please Mr Sanborn!" that this was not Mr Sanborn, the Chairman of the Board, at all; but she was allowed to blurt out her request to be transferred to the Perkins Institute and a few months later it was granted. When she was admitted, almost totally blind, in the autumn of 1880, her future pupil was three months old and in full possession of her faculties. By the time Annie left the Institute, six years and two operations later, she could see fairly well and was the top of her class: Helen Keller was blind, deaf and dumb. Laura Bridgman, the girl Howe had taught, was still in residence at the Institute, a living memorial to a great man, but unable to make the transition to normal life outside its walls. She was an old lady, an inspiration to the young Annie Sullivan as she set off on the long trip to Tuscumbia.

She arrived there 3 March, 1887, the date Helen Keller always referred to as "My Soul's Birthday", a few months before the child reached the age of seven. The first four weeks were worse than she had feared. The child was a savage to whom it seemed impossible to communicate any idea whatsoever: it screamed, wept, kicked and bit. But Annie was patient. On 5 April, Helen had a first firm contact with reality. Annie had been dipping the child's finger in water, but now she poured water over the whole hand, and suddenly the symbol she had been tapping on that hand in the finger alphabet, the word she had been repeating, again and again, meant something, meant "water".

Everything has a name. This discovery, so obvious to a normal child, is the key to all knowledge. Helen pointed to Annie and got the message back, in the palm of her hand: "Teacher".

From this day, the child made tremendous, incredible progress. She learnt to read Braille in English, then in Latin, Greek, French and German; she learnt to converse easily through her finger language, the remarkable alphabet which had originated in Spain with the Trappist monks; she began to follow what was going on around her, comment on it, be affected by it. By the time she was ten she had read of a deaf Norwegian child being taught to speak and she was demanding to be given the opportunity. It was given her. After the eleventh lesson, she said quite suddenly in a strange, half-human voice, "I am not dumb now."

She entered Radcliffe College in 1900, at the age of twenty, and emerged four years later with a B.A. degree and top honours against girls who could both see and hear. She was, of course, given every help that Annie and the College authorities could give; the textbooks were put into Braille for her, she wrote exams on a special type-writer, she had, instead of lectures, conferences with her teachers. She had learnt from Annie how to "hear" the human voice by resting fingertips on the speaker's throat, absorbing the vibrations. She was an attractive, popular, vivacious girl who took a full part in the social life of the College. Her classmates found, to their astonishment, that they had difficulty in remembering she was not entirely like themselves.

During her years at Radcliffe she wrote a small autobiographical volume called *Optimism* and on leaving College she produced *The Story of My Life*, followed shortly by *The World I Live In* and a long poem, *The Song of the Stone Wall*. Already she was a legend, a young girl, shockingly handicapped, who had been able to conquer her disabilities, lead a normal life: her books sold faster than they could be printed. Then, tiring of her own subject, she branched into more straightforward journalism, the articles any alert, inquiring, liberal mind might have written: on socialism, the problems of miners, an article demanding that silver nitrate be put, as a matter of course, into the eyes of every new-born child to prevent blindness from venereal infection. But by this time Annie Sullivan had married a man called Macy and people began to accuse Helen Keller of being a freak mouthpiece for the "radical" views of Mr Macy. Sadly, Helen gave up journalism: she had talent and a great deal to say; but she was a freak, and unless she wrote as a freak, no man would trust himself to read it.

Eventually Annie's marriage broke up and the two women, on their own again, decided to earn a living by giving lectures. They found audiences insatiable: people would flock in their hundreds from miles away, to attend any hall where Helen and her teacher were booked to appear. Helen's speech, though fluent, was hard to follow and, at the lectures, Annie would translate some of the more guttural noises, and demonstrate her methods of teaching. Then a sad complication arose: Annie's eyesight, never strong, began to fail. They were fortunate in enlisting the services of a Scots girl, Polly Thomson, as their companion.

In 1918 a Hollywood company urged Helen to make a film with them, under the awesome title, *Deliverance*. This, after some consideration, she agreed to do, but the film, using every dramatic cliché and ludicrous situation (Helen Keller flying to France to demand an end to war, Helen Keller as Joan of Arc) to replace the necessarily humdrum details of her real life, was an embarrassing failure—though some of the better scenes were retained for a successful film, nearly forty years later, *The Unconquered*.

Frightened by the imminence of poverty, Annie and Helen rushed into vaudeville, sandwiching their lecture-demonstration between acrobats and performing animals. There were enraged howls of "Exhibition for Profit" and soon after this Helen Keller, who had been supporting two other women as well as herself, had to give the work up. It seemed that society, which so applauded her efforts to lead a normal, self-supporting life, was determined not to let her. By now, though, she was such a world figure that there was no question of facing real poverty. Gifts poured in—to be poured out again on the needy while Helen made every effort to keep her self-respect by earning her own living.

One of her staunchest friends was the Scots-American Alexander Graham Bell, who in the course of being Professor of Vocal Physiology at Boston University, had invented the telephone. He helped her greatly and with him she and Annie visited many parts of the country, feeling the spray of Niagara Falls, meeting great men in Washington. Helen would "talk" happily—with her hand on their throats—to men like Woodrow Wilson, Andrew Carnegie, Sir

Henry Irving, and the man she so greatly admired, Samuel Clemens, "Mark Twain". She had refined Annie's tactile method of "hearing", so that by resting her fingers on a man's throat she could describe his accent. Her "net income of sensation", according to the medical profession was "far in excess of ordinary people's": although she could see, hear, nothing, she had a clearer idea of what was going on around her than most. She could detect the scent of a flower, the hint of smoke or damp, when to the ordinary person there was nothing. She could instantly recognize a city by its smell.

She had her enemies. Some suggested that she was far from blind and deaf, that she was absolutely normal, a charlatan making a living from the credulity of others. Others, accepting her disabilities, hinted that she was an idiot, Annie's puppet, Trilby to her Svengali. Both suggestions were false, but there had been one unfortunate, much-publicized, episode when Helen, still a young girl, had sent "an original story" to the Head of the Perkins Institute, Michael Anagnos. It was entitled *The Frost King*, it seemed familiar, and it turned out to be a fairly exact copy of someone else's, published, story. Anagnos, already bitter because both Helen and Annie had left an establishment they might have stayed behind to grace—like Laura Bridgman—accused her of deliberate plagiarism, but it seems fairly clear that with her incredible memory she had unintentionally stored the tale away, years previously, and brought it from her mind as an original. Anagnos ordered an "inquiry", she was "exonerated", but he had nothing further to do with her.

In 1923, a year after Bell's death, she joined the American Foundation for the Blind. She was already a pillar of strength to those who had lost eyesight during the war, and with her multiple affliction she managed to set an example of full and worthwhile living which others could but envy. In so many ways she behaved like a sighted person, talking of things she could "hear" and "see", of the pleasures of "looking". When asked how she knew what a red rose looked like, she explained that Annie had painted her a picture of red from all the things in life which held this colour. She knew all the colours, and more besides, and it was only necessary for someone to say blue, red, green, loud, soft or melodious, for her to understand.

By 1936 Annie was quite blind and her health had almost gone. Before she died in October someone said, "Teacher—get well. Without you, Helen Keller would be nothing."

"Then," said Annie Sullivan, "—then I have failed."

She had not failed. Although her death was a cruel blow, Helen was quite capable of looking after herself and others as well. Her energy was boundless. During the Second World War she made tours of the war theatres, talking to blinded soldiers, sailors and airmen, infusing them with her courage. When the war was over, she continued the work, visiting country after country, lecturing, giving strength by her example.

There was still work to be done and soon she was back at the Foundation for the Blind in New York, dealing with her world-wide correspondence, giving advice and encouragement to those who sought it.

By 1950 she was seventy and had been working continuously for the blind for half a century. It was a major anniversary and the world's press noted with delight that this extraordinary old lady would celebrate it by taking her first-ever holiday. Helen Keller went happily, eagerly, to France and probably got more out of the trip than other tourists less handicapped. But few of the journalists who noted that anniversary can have guessed that the old lady, as indomitable as ever, would go on working for the blind of the world for another eighteen years.

Helen Keller died on 1 June, 1968, just a few weeks before her eighty-eighth birthday.

Kemal Ataturk
1881-1938

IN a tumbledown house beside a cobbled alley in the town of Salonika lived a minor government clerk, Ali Riza, with his illiterate, sharp-tempered peasant wife, Zubeida. To them was born, in 1881, a son whom they named Mustafa. He grew into a spindly, sallow, morose urchin, aloof and unfriendly. His father died when he was seven years old, and an uncle took him to his farm in the country, where Mustafa cleaned out byres and tended sheep, growing wiry and tough but still solitary and enclosed in temperament.

His mother doted on her unresponsive son, and when he was eleven, persuaded his aunt to pay for him to go to school. His career there was stormy. Clever and capable, he was rebellious and quarrelsome. He fought with his fellow-pupils and, after a fierce battle with a master, left the school and refused to return. He resolved to be a soldier: applied secretly to the Military Cadet School in Salonika, passed its entrance examination and was accepted.

Here his real ability began to show itself. He absorbed the military studies, was brilliant in mathematics and always neat and faultless on parade. He was still unsociable, arrogant, brooking no rivals. "Kemal" was added to his name to distinguish him from a Captain Mustafa who patronized him, but initiated him into vicious habits. At the age of seventeen he passed out with distinction and went on to the Senior Military School at Monastir.

There the ambitious, pugnacious youth began to understand the condition of the Turkish nation of which he was a member. It was a deplorable picture. More than four centuries ago, the Ottoman Turks had subjugated Mesopotamia and Kurdistan, Syria and Asia Minor, the Crimea and southern Russia, Egypt and North Africa; had seized Constantinople, conquered the Balkans, overrun Hungary and battered at the gates of Vienna. The Ottoman Empire had become the greatest Power in the Western world. Since then it had crumbled, become weak, disorganized, torpid. By the middle of the nineteenth century the Russian Tsar was dubbing it "The Sick Man of Europe". Russia had taken the Crimea. Greece had won her freedom. Serbia, Rumania, Bulgaria, were gaining theirs. Algeria had been annexed by France. Egypt came under British control in 1881. Crete was captured by Greece in 1898. While his empire melted, the cruel and despotic Sultan, Abdul Hamid, maintained a corrupt, reactionary rule from Constantinople, stamping out all movements for reform, and hunting down, with his armies of spies, every stirring of discontent.

The spies were needed, for there was seething unrest among thinking Turks. At Monastir, Kemal breathed in the spirit of revolt. He learned French, read the forbidden books of European reformers and preached insurrection among his fellow-cadets.

His ability was impressive, and at the age of twenty he was promoted to the General Staff College in Constantinople. Lusty, vital, void of moral principles, he plunged into all the lewd dissipations of that unclean city. Soon he reverted with equal intensity to his studies, was selected for the special General Staff course, and at the age of twenty-four was gazetted a captain.

In the College a secret society, the *Vatan*, was plotting constitutional reforms of the obsolete laws and customs which imprisoned Turkey in stagnant medievalism. Kemal became its leading spirit. The Sultan's spies got on the society's tracks. Its members were arrested and Kemal thrown into solitary confinement. The evidence against him was damning and his life hung by a thread. But the Sultan was loath to waste so promising an officer, and he was posted to a regiment in Damascus, where he had his first taste of war in an inconclusive expedition against the Druses.

Among the officers in Syria Kemal started a new secret conclave called "The Fatherland and Freedom Society". The movement spread quickly; but to start a revolt in Syria was not practicable. The forces there were too insignificant. He learned that a more serious movement was afoot in Salonika, and resolved to go there and find out about it. Helped by officers who had joined his Society, he sailed from Jaffa via Egypt and Greece to Salonika. Hardly had he begun contact with the disaffected officers there when the Sultan's spies spotted him. An order came for his arrest. Warned by his friends, he fled to Greece and back to Jaffa. There the friendly Commandant smuggled his uniform to him, helped him to dodge the police and escape to Gaza, where the Commander, another Society member, assured Constantinople that he had been there all the time, and that their spies were mistaken. Kemal cautiously suspended for the moment his conspiratorial activities, and by some careful wire-pulling got himself presently transferred to Salonika.

Here he found a secret reform movement, parallel to his own, called the "Ottoman Freedom Society". He became an active member, though often at loggerheads with its leaders about their aims and methods. His character and life's purpose were by now hard set and definite. He was an exceptionally competent officer and military leader. He was fearless, steel-hard, unfriendly, ruthless, irreligious, amoral, a stranger to tenderness or affection; vicious, dissolute, unscrupulous. To one cause only he was completely loyal and devoted: Turkey; its defence, its restoration, reform, modernization and progress.

Round Turkey his own personal ambitions wrapped themselves— and he was intensely ambitious. He, Mustafa Kemal, would smash the tyranny, the obsolete customs, the illiteracy, the dead hand ot Muslim laws and traditions which choked and prisoned it. He, Mustafa Kemal, would be his nation's leader and deliverer, and make it an honoured, strong, modern State. To this purpose he would dedicate his skill to plan, his strength to drive.

Long years would pass before he could realize his vision. His fellow conspirators at Salonika saw less far, less clearly. Their main purpose was to re-establish the Constitution which had been framed and accepted in 1876 but abrogated next year by the new Sultan, Abdul Hamid. They were linked with the Young Turk movement, whose leaders were chiefly exiled Turks living in Paris. They dreamed vaguely of restoring the old Ottoman Empire. Kemal planned far deeper changes, but for Turkey only.

In 1908 spies warned Abdul Hamid of the unrest among the officers at Salonika, and he summoned their leader, Enver Bey, to Constantinople. Enver discreetly fled to the hills. Another of the revolutionary officers, Major Niyasi, issued a defiant manifesto and followed to the hills with a force of troops and arms. The general sent by the Sultan to suppress the mutineers was shot in Monastir by one of his own officers. One by one, the Turkish armies joined in the revolt. With their support the Young Turks compelled the Sultan to restore the constitution. Niyasi and Enver were the heroes of the hour. Kemal was, with the rest of the Salonika Committee, a silent onlooker at their triumph. His hour was not yet.

Abdul Hamid did not long accept defeat. In April, 1909, his supporters staged a counter-revolution, raising the cry that the Muslim faith was in danger. The troops in Constantinople mutinied. The inexpert Young Turk government tottered, but the Salonika army came to its rescue, with Enver leading the advance guard and Kemal as Chief-of-Staff. The old gang were crushed, court-martialled and hanged. Abdul Hamid was deposed.

During the next nine troubled years the Young Turks of the "Committee of Union and Progress" held rule; but Kemal, solitary, opinionated, quarrelsome, was excluded from their councils. He went back to the army, organizing the Officers' School at Salonika with great efficiency, and preaching discontent with the fumbling incompetence of the Government. The War Minister grew nervous, and brought him to the War Office in Constantinople, to keep him under control.

In October, 1911, Turkey became involved in the first of a succession of wars. Italy had invaded Tripoli. Kemal made his adventurous way to the front, and found himself serving under Enver, with whose flamboyant ideas on policy and strategy he had no sympathy. Their uneasy alliance was interrupted in October, 1912, by the Balkan War, in which Montenegro, Serbia, Greece and Bulgaria fell on Turkey, and bid fair to strip her of all her European territory. Kemal wormed his way back across Europe to Constantinople, and was given charge of the vital front holding back the Bulgars from Gallipoli and the Dardanelles. Enver too got back, leaving Tripoli to the Italians. He shot the Minister of War, chased out the other Ministers and set up a stronger Government. But Turkey had to accept defeat, surrendering Macedonia and most of Thrace. Next year, however, another Balkan war broke out between the victors, and while they quarrelled, Enver recovered Adrianople and Eastern Thrace.

Despite Kemal's violent disagreement, Enver now called in the Germans to re-organize the feeble Turkish Army. When, in 1914 the First World War broke out, the German warships, *Goeben* and *Breslau*, dodged the British fleet to enter the Sea of Marmora. Under cover of their guns the Germans forced Turkey to take their side in the struggle.

Kemal, who had been sent off as military attaché to the Embassy in Sofia, managed to get himself recalled to Turkey and was given command of the troops in the Gallipoli Peninsula by the German General von Sanders. Enver, returning from a badly mismanaged campaign against Russia in the Caucasus, cancelled the appointment, but von Sanders, recognizing his quality, kept Kemal in charge or the half-formed 19th Division.

As anticipated, the British attack came in April, 1915. Von Sanders had expected it to be launched against the neck of the Gallipoli Peninsula, at Bulair, where he held his main force. It fell in fact on the part held by Kemal. Without waiting for instructions, he flung every man he could into the defence of the line of hills. He knew that if the British established their position on the crest of the range, all the peninsula would be at their mercy. For weeks he fought frantically, rallying his men again and again, exposing himself recklessly in the forefront of the battle.

On 6 August came the second big attack, the Suvla Bay landing. This very nearly succeeded. The Turkish forces were thin and their reserves at a distance. Von Sanders told Kemal to take charge, and somehow he checked the first onslaught. Next day he dashed to another part of the front which was giving way. In a hail of bullets he led his forces to the attack and swept the British down the slope. For three more months he kept up the defence, fighting desperately with scanty forces, till in December the invaders withdrew. Kemal had won; but for his military skill, courage and inspiring leadership, the British would have mastered the Gallipoli Peninsula and captured Constantinople.

The Gallipoli campaign was a decisive episode in Kemal's career. He was the only Turkish General to achieve victory in the war, and his reputation as a soldier was nation-wide. But the politicians would have none of him. Enver was bitterly jealous and packed him off to the Caucasus front, to tidy up the mess left after Enver's own futile campaign against the Russians. Kemal established order with a ruthless hand, and in August, 1916, advanced against the disintegrating Russian Army, recapturing Bitlis and Mus.

Next spring he was transferred to command the 7th Army in Syria, where forces were assembling to resist Allenby's advance through Palestine. Kemal, no friend to the Germans, quarrelled with General von Falkenhayn, whom Enver had secured to command the Syrian front. In October, 1917, he resigned his command and went back to Constantinople. He visited Europe with the Sultan's heir, Vahideddin, and in July, 1918, went to Austria for medical treatment of a kidney trouble, the penalty of his vicious life.

Still sick, he was posted back to the 7th Army on the Syrian front. He found it little more than a shadow force through failure of supplies, disease and desertions. The British and their Arab allies smashed the Turkish front in mid-September, and Kemal gathered such troops as he could rally and retreated to Damascus. Thence he fell back to a final line north of Aleppo. Here he was still holding out when, on 30 October, Turkey signed an armistice with the victorious Allies.

Kemal returned to Constantinople on 13 November, to find that Enver and his Young Turks had fled. A new cabinet had been appointed by Vahideddin, now the Sultan. These were timid men, whose one concern was to avoid any friction with the victorious Allies, whose warships packed the Bosphorus. They were meekly obeying their conquerors' orders, disarming their remaining troops, submitting to Allied violations of the Armistice terms and the piecemeal break-up of their country.

The former Ottoman Empire was, of course, gone for good. Egypt, Syria, Mesopotamia, Arabia were independent of the Sublime Porte. Kemal shed no tears for their loss. His concern was, as it always had been, for the revival and uplift of his own nation, the Turkish people, in their homeland. Here the need for rescue was desperate. Government had collapsed. Famine and pestilence stalked abroad. Greeks and other foes were raiding across the Turkish coasts and frontiers.

Kemal realized that his hour had come to get control. His way was unexpectedly smoothed by the Sultan, who did not want this restless person in Constantinople and ordered him to take charge of the army stationed at Samsun on the Black Sea coast, to restore order and to supervise the disarming and demobilizing of the remaining Turkish forces. Kemal managed to get his orders so drafted as to give him dictatorial powers.

Arriving at Samsun on 19 May, 1919, Kemal got in touch with the various resistance groups which were springing up. Far from suppressing them, he set to work to organize them. He called on the local Governors to send protests to outside Powers against the treatment Turkey was suffering.

At a secret meeting with the heads of Army and Navy a Declaration was framed asserting that the Central Government at Constantinople was under foreign domination, and that a representative Congress must be called, independent of the nominal Government, at Sivas. A Proclamation was issued on 22 June, summoning representatives from every subdivision of the Turkish provinces to this Congress. Backing him, Kemal had Kara Bekir, commander of the one remaining intact Turkish army—that of the Caucasus. The Sultan ordered Kemal back to Constantinople and when he refused to come, dismissed him. Kemal resigned his commission, and as a civilian presided over the Sivas Congress, persuading it to set up a National Assembly.

A grim tug-of-war now took place between Kemal and the Sultan over the body of Turkey. Kemal told the Allies that the Constantinople Government was illegal, no longer representing the nation. The Allies sought to suppress this Nationalist movement. The British occupied Constantinople and the Sultan as supreme

Caliph called on Muslims to overthrow Kemal. A religious war blazed up—the most merciless of all kinds of war.

At Ankara the first session of the Turkish Grand National Assembly met on 23 April, 1920, and elected Kemal as its President. He declared the Sultan-Caliph to be a prisoner of the Allies. Till he was free, government must be carried on without him. Sovereign power rested with the Turkish nation!

On 10 August, 1920, the Sultan's envoys signed the Treaty of Sèvres with the Allies—a treaty which spelt the destruction of Turkey, its dismemberment and reduction to a small puppet state at the mercy of its neighbours. The Treaty was dead before it was signed. The whole mass of the nation rejected it and rallied behind Kemal and his National Assembly.

Anxious to wash their hands of the matter, the Allies were glad to accept an offer from Venizelos to deal with the Turkish nationalists. Venizelos dreamed of regaining Greece's long-lost possessions of Constantinople and Western Asia Minor. Lloyd George admired Venizelos, and detested the Turks for their record of Bulgarian atrocities and Armenian massacres. He wished them turned out of Europe, "bag and baggage".

In the summer of 1921 the Greeks advanced from Smyrna to invade Anatolia. Strongly armed, well equipped, they drove back the loosely organized Turks. Kemal strove furiously to rally his troops, and made a stand at a line along the Sakarya river, south of Ankara. Here battle was joined, and continued relentlessly for twenty-one days. Sleepless, suffering, Kemal still inspired his slender forces to hold on. At last the Greek attack ceased and the invaders withdrew. The Turks were powerless to pursue, but Kemal's Government was widely acknowledged to be the real ruler of Turkey. Russians, French, Italians made terms with it.

Next summer the reorganized Turkish Army fell on the Greeks and drove them in headlong rout back to Smyrna, where the survivors escaped by sea. Swinging round towards the Dardanelles, Kemal advanced to invade Thrace. A small British occupation force still guarded the eastern side of the Sea of Marmora. Kemal came on resolutely but pacifically. He wanted no war with Britain. An armistice was patched up. Its terms were ratified in the following June by the Treaty of Lausanne, which confirmed Turkey's full sovereignty within her natural frontiers. Kemal would never consider suggestions to attempt recovery of parts of the old Ottoman Empire beyond those borders. Turkey itself sufficed him.

In the next few years he cleared up the country's major political problems. Dominating the National Assembly, he drove it to abolish the Sultanate, to transfer the capital to Ankara, and, finally, in March 1924, to end the Caliphate and with it the archaic tyranny of the old Muslim legal system which had held back all efforts at reform.

Then he set himself to modernize the nation he had freed. In August, 1925, he abolished the fez, with its reactionary Muslim implications, and in November made its wearing a crime. Turkey, he declared, must be civilized in dress, laws, education and constitution, and resemble civilized Western countries. Polygamy was abolished, and women given equal rights with men. Religious freedom was proclaimed. Kemal even tried to set up a political opposition party, but the country was as yet too unsettled. Rebellion broke out and the attempt was abandoned. It was not resumed till 1945, and only in 1953 did an opposition Party replace the Government.

In 1928 Kemal introduced a Latin alphabet to replace the old Arabic script. He travelled round the country explaining its virtues and, like a schoolmaster, teaching the people to write it. In 1935, he made Sunday replace Friday as the weekly day of rest. Surnames also were made compulsory for everyone. Kemal himself took the surname "Ataturk"—Father of Turks—and dropped his original name of Mustafa.

On 10 November, 1938, Kemal died, lamented and honoured by the nation he had so mightily wrought to save and rebuild. "The Turkish fatherland", said the Government communiqué, "has lost its great builder, the Turkish nation its mighty leader, mankind a great son!" His spirit lived on to guide his people. Turkey's determination to remain, though non-belligerent, on Britain's side through the darkest hours of the Second World War was doubtless owing to his farewell advice: "Come what may, stay on England's side, because that side is certain to win in the long run!"

William Temple
1881-1944

AN aura of ecclesiastical purple surrounded William Temple from his earliest infancy. He was born, on 15 October, 1881, in the Palace of Exeter, where his father, Frederick Temple, was the Bishop. Within four years they moved to Fulham Palace, as Frederick Temple had become Bishop of London. Eleven years later, in 1896, he rose still further to be Archbishop of Canterbury and Primate of All England. All William Temple's youth, up to his twenty-first year, was spent in bishops' palaces.

With such a background, it was easy for him to set his heart on a career in the Church. As a child of three, he once declared his intention to become Archbishop of Canterbury, and a favourite amusement in his nursery was to don surplice and mitre and preach to his nursemaid. The sincere religious and erudite spirit of his father pervaded the home, and he grew up in an atmosphere of scholarship and unaffected devotion.

Early he began to show that unusual intellectual capacity which was later to distinguish him as a giant among his fellows. At his preparatory school he quickly rose to be head boy, and in September, 1894, went on to Rugby, where, before becoming a bishop, his father had for twelve years been the Headmaster. There his contemporaries remembered him as a plump and brilliant kind of Billy Bunter—he was always very stout—who was calmly self-confident and cheerfully untroubled by ragging. His weight made him a massive forward at football. He was a tireless student, and by swiftly dealing with his school work made time for wide reading in many fields of knowledge, particularly of philosophy. He won a scholarship after one year at Rugby, and was moved up, when only fifteen and a half, to the sixth form.

He was from early boyhood devoted to music and had a keen musical taste. He was a competent performer on the organ and the oboe—his oboe is still treasured as a museum piece by the Canterbury Choir School. He enjoyed choral singing, and at Oxford joined the Bach Choir. He became an expert in Church music, but disliked plainsong. He might have grown into a brilliant and cultured

Charles Spencer Chaplin, known to millions as Charlie Chaplin, is one of the very few geniuses that the films have produced. From the days of the Keystone Cops and the Mack Sennett comedies of 1914, his films have revealed a seemingly unlimited comic inventiveness, and have been enjoyed by the world. His strangely dignified little tramp gallantly challenging an impersonal and hostile world seemed symbolical of the lives of millions of people during the inter-war years, and was perfectly attuned to the mood of the times; most of the films for which he is remembered appeared during these years. *Above*, a scene from *City Lights*; and, *left*, from *The Gold Rush*.

Above: "Bill" Slim when in command of the Fourteenth Army, the "Forgotten Army" that broke the myth of Japanese invincibility on land.

Left: Lord Louis Mountbatten when Supreme Commander, South East Asia Command. His versatility is attested by his success as the last Viceroy of India, a task of stupendous difficulty.

intellectual, an outstanding scholar, and nothing more. He was saved from this by getting drawn into work at the Rugby Club in Notting Dale, where he came into contact with young fellows far removed in habits and conditions from the ways of Bishops' palaces. He became a great favourite with the London lads, alike at the club and at the New Romney Camp.

In 1900 he went from Rugby to Balliol College, Oxford, with a Major Leaving Exhibition. Here he continued his brilliant academic career, getting a First in Moderations in 1902, and a First in Greats in 1904. He also became President that year of the Oxford Union, where he was a frequent and popular speaker, broadminded, tolerant, always very self-confident, even cocksure, and exceptionally well-informed. After graduating, he became a Fellow of Queen's College.

The lessons learned at Notting Dale stuck. While at Balliol he spent much of his vacation time working in the University Settlements of Toynbee Hall, Bethnal Green and Bermondsey—where he had the hitherto unfamiliar experience of finding big brown bugs in his bed!

At Queen's, no longer engaged in working for examinations, he had time to spare to devote himself to other problems, and he turned to study the issue of education for those less favoured than himself, with whom he had begun to make contact. At the suggestion of R. H. Tawney, he attended in 1905 the first National Conference of the Workers' Educational Association, which was being held in Oxford. From that time on, he threw himself whole-heartedly into this Movement, and from 1908 to 1924 he served it as its President. When pressure of other important interests forced him to resign this office, he kept on for another five years as President of the North-western Section of the W.E.A.

In 1906, after much heart-searching, he decided to seek ordination, and approached Paget, the Bishop of Oxford, to offer himself as a candidate. He admitted some uncertainty of mind about the doctrines of the Virgin Birth of Jesus, and of His physical resurrection. He had for years been steeping himself in philosophical studies, which lead to intellectual questioning rather than religious certainty. Paget felt that Temple was too unsure in his beliefs to be a fit person for ordination. It was the first sharp set-back Temple had experienced in his conquering progress.

During the next two years he plunged into questions of national education, and also became an active supporter of the Student Christian Movement. His contacts with eager men who were not just debating religious problems but struggling to apply Christianity to national affairs and human lives brought him to a less academic, more positive religious attitude, and in 1908 he approached Randall Davidson, the Archbishop of Canterbury. They talked things over, and the Archbishop was satisfied that Temple was now sound enough theologically for ordination. With Paget's agreement, he was ordained at Canterbury in December, 1908.

His limitless capacity for hard work was well exhibited in a tour of the Australian Universities which he carried out in the summer of 1910. The temper of these universities had been definitely anti-religious, but a small Students' Christian Union had recently made some headway, and Dr J. R. Mott, the leader of the World Student Christian Federation, urged Temple to go and help it. He went: to Adelaide, Sydney, Melbourne and Brisbane, lecturing to the students and holding countless interviews with them. On Sundays he preached in cathedrals and churches. In under six weeks he delivered ninety-one lectures and addresses, and was everywhere received with eager enthusiasm.

His exceptional quality was already well recognized, and Queen's could not hope to hold him. While on his Australian tour he was elected to the headmastership of Repton, and somewhat unwillingly decided to accept the post, hoping he might be able there to do something to broaden the character of the English Public Schools' contribution to English education. In the event, he achieved no such revolution, but staff and pupils at Repton long remembered the buoyant sunshine and radiant vitality he diffused, the help he gave them in his divinity lectures, and the sermons which so held their attention that the boys even stopped coughing!

Repton nearly lost him in 1912. The Prime Minister offered him the Canonry of Westminster with the Rectorship of St Margaret's, the church of the Houses of Parliament. Then someone discovered that for this post he must have been six years a priest, so with apologies all round the offer was hurriedly withdrawn. Repton, however, could see the writing on the wall. In May, 1914, the Lord Chancellor offered him the Rectory of St James's, Piccadilly. (The living was in his gift every third time.) Temple accepted it. He mentioned it to his friend, Dick Sheppard, who was embarrassed at the news because, as he explained afterwards to Temple, the Bishop of London had just offered him the living! It was in fact this time the Lord Chancellor's turn.

The rectory of St James's gave Temple a very influential pulpit in the fashionable heart of London, and his congregation, drawn from a wide circle, included many outstanding personalities in politics, commerce and society. He faithfully carried out his parochial duties, but these formed only a minor share of the multiple tasks he was here well placed to undertake. His life became very full. He was in constant demand as a preacher and speaker on important issues all over the country. He was busily engaged on his work for the W.E.A., for university extension arrangements, the Y.M.C.A. and numbers of Church organizations and popular movements.

In May, 1914, he joined in promoting a new Christian weekly called the *Challenge* as a medium for dealing in modern fashion with questions of theology in relation to social life. In 1915 he became its editor. Its readers were too few; in 1918 it came to an end.

The First World War, which broke out in August, 1914, brought up many fresh problems. Temple, with others, worked hard to deal with them. In 1916 a National Mission of Repentance and Hope was proposed. Leaders of thought viewed it with mixed feelings, but Temple decided to back it and became one of the five secretaries organizing it—a task that kept him extremely busy for the rest of the year. He travelled widely to speak for the movement, but its national impact was disappointing. It reached few outside the ranks of church-goers.

A very important event for Temple in 1916 was his marriage to Frances Anson, who was working as secretary of the Westminster branch of the Christian Social Union, an organization of which he was Chairman. She shared his outlook and was an invaluable help to him in the years that followed.

In 1917 Dick Sheppard proposed to him the founding of a "Life and Liberty" movement to reform the legal position of the Church of England and secure freedom to it to run its own affairs without constant parliamentary control and interference. The idea was denounced by Hensley Henson, the controversial Dean of Durham, and was discouraged by the Archbishop of Canterbury, but in spite of this it was launched at a crowded conference in the Queen's Hall on 16 July, where it received a practically unanimous vote of support.

Temple realized that someone must devote himself to keeping the movement alive. Under pressure from his friends and supporters he took the sacrificial step of giving up his living at St James's with its large stipend, and devoting himself to running the campaign. He spent 1918 in holding meetings all over England, at which the Life and Liberty programme was enthusiastically supported. His reward came in the following year, when a Representative Church Council was held which formally adopted for the Church of England a reformed order, by which the National Assembly of the Church was set up, in which bishops, clergy and laity each had their place, and Parochial Church Councils were authorized in every parish, through which the laity could co-operate with their incumbents in maintaining local religious work.

Parliamentary sanction was needed to establish this reform, and with untiring efforts Temple rallied support for the Enabling Bill, which was successfully carried through Parliament before the year ended. Thus a new democratic element was inserted in the structure of the Church.

Meantime, Temple was being sought after by many would-be captors of so outstanding a figure. He turned down offers to become Principal of Durham University and to take the Chair of Philosophy at Balliol College; but he accepted the living of St Margaret's with the Canonry of Westminster, where he was most centrally posted for maintaining his manifold activities. With his aid, the Life and Liberty Movement was kept in being for two years more, to help and guide parishes in the setting up and working of their P.C.C.'s.

In 1918 Temple definitely accepted membership of the Labour Party under its new constitution. Ever since he had joined the W.E.A. in 1905, he had been a lively supporter of the Labour movement, and in Church conferences he had repeatedly urged that the Church should develop a deeper understanding of, and kindlier sympathy with the needs and aspirations of the workers. Of course this provoked no small hostility to him in some quarters—hostility which left him quite unmoved. He was loved and prized by the working classes, who felt that in him they had a real friend.

In 1920, at Longmans' invitation, he agreed to edit a new monthly, the *Pilgrim*, a Review of Christian Politics and Religion. Needless to say, the political outlook was progressive and the religion practical. For the next seven years, however crowded his days and nights, Temple always managed to complete his monthly article for *Pilgrim* on time.

In 1920 the See of Manchester fell vacant, and on 26 November the Prime Minister, Lloyd George, offered it to Temple. It presented an immense task. With a population of $3\frac{1}{2}$ million and over 600 benefices, Manchester Diocese was second only to London in size. Everyone appreciated that with his well-known sympathy for industrial workers and his long history of efforts on their behalf, Temple was God's good gift for this densely industrial diocese. At his enthronement, the Dean declared:

"Out of the whole orbit of the English Church, we would freely have chosen you first to guide the destinies of this great Diocese!"

One of his most delicate tasks was to carry through the already formed decision to divide the diocese. With great tact and patience he at length achieved this. In 1926 the new Diocese of Blackburn was constituted to take charge of the northern part of Lancashire.

He was determined to raise the status of women workers in the Church, and was successful in this and in improving the training and remuneration of Deaconesses. His lively part in the annual diocesan Mission to Blackpool will long be gladly remembered. The University, the Inter-denominational Council of Anglicans and Free Churchmen, the Student Christian Movement, W.E.A., Toc H., Industrial Works Committees—the list of organizations to which his help was lavishly given is a long one.

In 1924 a great inter-denominational Conference on Politics, Economics and Citizenship was held in Birmingham, presided over by Temple and attended by 1,500 delegates from the British Isles, the Continent, China and Japan. It was the outcome of many years' quiet organization by a group working under him to study Christianity and Social Problems. C.O.P.E.C. was very much the expression of Temple's special message to his age. It played an important part in advancing the Oecumenical movement which was very dear to his heart and remains his great legacy to world Christianity.

In 1927 he was appointed by the Archbishop as a delegate of the Anglican Church to the Lausanne World Conference on Faith and Order, where representatives of all non-Roman Churches—Anglican, Free Church, Lutheran, Orthodox, American and Continental Protestants—joined to discover how near they could come together in doctrine and practice. Temple was deputy chairman, and the Conference's only nominee as chairman of its Continuation Committee. In 1928 he was a delegate to the Jerusalem Conference of the International Missionary Council.

At home, in 1927-8, Temple was very active in seeking to get the approval of Parliament for the revised Prayer Book, which had after some years of careful work been produced as a comprehensive book in which both High and Low Churchmen might be able to find common ground. It failed to achieve this aim. Low Churchmen saw in it the spoor of the Scarlet Woman and the House of Commons rejected it twice. The Church authorities decided on compromise, neither meekly accepting the Parliamentary veto nor defiantly demanding freedom by disestablishment. Bishops were recommended at their episcopal discretion to permit as a concession the use by incumbents of such parts of the new Prayer Book as they might sanction.

In July, 1928, Davidson retired from the Primacy of Canterbury, to be succeeded by Lang, from York, and Temple almost inevitably became the new Archbishop of York, to the sorrow of the Mancunians, who had learned to love him and his wife. C. P. Scott of the Manchester *Guardian* described him as "a bishop of all denominations". It was well said, for in the following years Temple took the lead in the movements to draw together the Christian Churches throughout the world.

At the Lambeth Conference of 1930 he chaired the Committee on Unity. He attended the World Conference on Christian Life and Work at Oxford in the summer of 1937, and a fortnight later presided over the Edinburgh Conference on Faith and Order. These two movements agreed to unite, and at Utrecht in May, 1938, Temple presided over a meeting of the representatives of seventy Churches to frame a constitution for a World Council of Churches. Before the end of the year the Assembly of the Church of England adopted a resolution proposed by Temple to affiliate to the World Council. Four years later the British Council of Churches was inaugurated at a great service in St Paul's Cathedral. It is noteworthy that no one ever thought of nominating any other man than Temple as Chairman of these Councils.

At the beginning of 1942, Cosmo Lang resigned the Archbishopric of Canterbury. Temple was the only possible choice for his successor; for Temple stood far higher in ability, scholarship, character, national affection and world-wide reputation than any alternative figure. It was no easy honour that was imposed on him, for the country was passing through the darkest hours of the Second World War, and he, with his engagement diary already crammed tight with commitments to many different causes all over the country, had to add to them the duties of the Primacy of All England.

It was embarrassing for him that the Archbishop of Canterbury is commonly assumed in his public pronouncements to advance, not his personal opinions, but the attitude of the Church of which he is the spokesman. Temple held always to his own views, with the same bland certainty of their correctness as had marked him through life. He would not suppress them. At a great Albert Hall meeting on 26 September, 1942, about Christianity and Social and Economic Affairs he expressed notions about banking with which few experts would agree. But to the end he was an impenitent reformer, valuing human needs more than the laws of material gain.

He wore himself out. He had been a lifelong sufferer from gout— not because of any intemperate habits, for he was a teetotaller and non-smoker. He did his work often in defiance of acute pain. In September, 1944, the trouble worsened and quite crippled him. He had to be carried to and from the services he insisted on taking. By mid-October he had to cancel all engagements, and on 26 October he passed quietly to peace.

All the world mourned him. Outside the bounds of the Roman Church he was recognized as the greatest Christian leader of his time. He had carried through notable reforms, and had led his generation to a wider vision, greater freedom, deeper sympathy with the under-dog, and a clearer understanding of that human brotherhood which the Founder of the Church had commanded to His followers.

Ernest Bevin
1881-1951

No man before or since exercised such power over the lives of Britain's population as Ernest Bevin exercised throughout most of the Second World War. As Minister of Labour and National Service he could—and did—move men and women about like pieces on the industrial chessboard. Yet this man—who later was for years to speak for Britain in the council chambers of the world as Foreign Secretary—was born the son of a poor agricultural labourer and spent eleven years of his early manhood driving a van through the streets of Bristol.

Nothing is known of his ancestry, and there is probably very little to know. For generations they had been landless labourers, and for long before that serfs tied to the soil. He was born on 9 March, 1881, at Winsford, a little village in Somerset not far from Minehead. He never knew his father, for he died four months before Ernest was born.

His mother was left with six children to look after, and another on the way, but somehow, by acting as the village midwife and giving a hand in the domestic work at houses in the neighbourhood and at the "local", the Royal Oak, she managed to keep the home together. She was a woman of strong character and possessed of a deep religious faith, being a staunch, even a fanatical Methodist at a time when Church and Chapel were at daggers drawn. She took Ernest to Chapel with her and sent him off to Sunday school as soon as he could toddle. When he was six, she was taken seriously ill, but she used to call him into her room after the service and make him repeat the gist of the sermon he had heard. That at least taught him to concentrate and to remember, and it was by no means the only good thing she taught him. She died when he was only seven, and he was given a home by his sister, the wife of a railway worker, first at Bishops Morchard and then at Copplestone.

For some years he attended the village school, walking to it across two miles of fields, and as before he went to the Methodist Sunday school. He did not learn very much, little more than the three R's. When he was eleven his schooling, such as it was, came to an end.

The Popes, his sister and her husband, were kindly folk but poor; the few shillings he might earn would be welcome. So he was sent out to work, living in as a boy-hand on a farm in the district at a weekly wage of sixpence, payable quarterly in arrears. There he spent his days scaring birds, picking up stones from the fields, following the plough, cutting up turnips, and the like.

He did not grumble, he did not think himself particularly unfortunate or put upon. It was one of the bad patches in agricultural history; all around him were labourers out of work or trying to exist on a pittance. He at least had enough to eat. After a few months he was able to find a better position at another farm, where he had a bed in a loft reached by a ladder from the farmyard, plenty of food, and a wage of no less than a shilling a week, all of which he might call his own.

Fortunately for him he had learnt to read—and even to write, though he was always rather ham-fisted with a pen—and at nights he used to read out interesting bits from copies of the *Bristol Mercury* that had arrived at the farm. Thus he came to understand that there was a great world outside his narrow horizon. He resolved to make for it as soon as he could. At thirteen he took the venturesome step. Perhaps he was just "fed up", perhaps he was cheeky and his master (so one story runs) went for him with a pick-handle. Whatever the circumstances, he quitted the farm and farm-life for good. He made his way to Bristol: he was thirteen, with his own way to make in the world, unskilled, friendless, knowing nobody.

His first job in the strange city was as a kitchen boy in a restaurant; for a shilling a day he helped in the washing up, scrubbed the floors, ran errands, made himself generally useful. Again he didn't complain. Looking back on those days he used to say that his employers had been quite decent to him, but the hours were long and he couldn't stick the smell of cooking. He sought another job, an outdoor one if possible, and found it as a grocer's errand-boy. Then he tackled a variety of different jobs, all alike in that they were dead ends. He became a vanboy, and then a conductor on the city trams, at a wage of twelve shillings a week. He did not like clipping tickets all day long: the scenery was always the same.

When he was eighteen he got what he called his first man's job— as the driver of a two-horse van for a firm of mineral-water manufacturers. He stayed in that job for eleven years, clip-clopping over the cobbles, delivering crates of minerals to hotels and pubs and private houses. He was not unhappy, or discontented. After all, it was an open-air job; and once he had wrapped his leather apron about his middle and cracked his whip, he was virtually his own master for the rest of the day. The wages were not so bad, either— eighteen shillings a week to begin with, plus commission on sales; he got married on that, and took a small house, where his wife made a happy home and their one and only child, a daughter, was born. On Saturday nights Mr and Mrs Bevin went to the music-hall, and how they enjoyed it! To the end of his life this remained his principal amusement. On Sundays they went to Chapel, usually a Baptist one. Bevin attended the Bible classes conducted by a popular local minister, he joined the Church and was baptized, he even became a local preacher conducting services in Baptist and Methodist Chapels in Bristol and the surrounding villages.

Some time in his middle twenties his interest turned in the direction of Socialism. He became a member of the Bristol Socialist Party, which was associated with the Social Democratic Federation, a Marxist organization that had been one of the founding bodies of the Labour Representation Committee that developed into the Labour Party. Bevin listened to lectures about Marx and his theories, but a good deal of what he heard left him cold. Never to the end of his days could he have been styled a Socialist theorist; he was first and foremost and all the time a practical man. Socialism to him meant not abstruse theories but the prevention of unemployment, raising the standards of living of the working class, and providing for one and all the things that were necessary for health and happiness.

It was only natural that he should gravitate towards trade unionism, and in 1910 he joined the Bristol Carmen's Branch of the Dock, Wharf, Riverside and General Labourers Union, known as the Dockers' Union for short. The branch was a new one, only just formed in fact, and Bevin was elected its first chairman. He proved an excellent one, firm, impartial, a weighty speaker in more senses than one. His burly frame exuded confidence and ability. Six months later he was appointed to a full-time job with the union, as branch secretary, at a wage of £2 a week. It was less than he had been getting as a drayman but he felt that this was a job that he could do, and do well. So he came down from his driver's seat and folded up his leather apron for the last time.

The next few years were a stormy time in the history of organized labour. The dockers and their allies were in the thick of the troubles that attended their struggle for a living wage. At that time their wages seldom exceeded sixteen shillings a week, fines were imposed for trivial faults, and the employment was altogether casual. A man never knew if he would still be in a job in a few hours' time. It was impossible to save for a rainy day, and there was nothing in the nature of State unemployment insurance or social security benefits. All that stood between a man and destitution, for his family as for himself, was the tiny benefits paid out by the unions and friendly societies.

A strike was a desperate measure, but the dockers struck, time and again. Bevin as an organizer of the Bristol workers was always in the thick of the struggle. He knew his members as individuals, he was proud of them—he always talked of "*my* men", "*my* union", and none of them objected—he was one of their leaders, and he felt a most serious responsibility for their welfare. People in Bristol complained bitterly of "paid agitators", but Bevin was never an agitator for the sake of it: he was cool-headed, practical, down to earth. He never allowed himself to be led astray by pretty theories and fanciful notions, nor would he allow "his men" to be led away if he could help it. But as those on the opposite side of the table soon came to realize, he was a most dangerous opponent, a most powerful advocate, a master organizer.

Bevin's great moment came in 1920, by which time he had risen to become the assistant general secretary of the Union. A claim had been put before the shipowners on behalf of the dockers for a wage of 16s. a day. The claim was rejected, and there were many in the Union, and the Transport Workers Federation to which it belonged, who clamoured for strike action. Bevin stood out against the demand. He had had experience of strikes before the war, and little good had come of them; besides, the Union was not strong financially; a strike of more than a week or so might cripple them disastrously. Why not take advantage of a new procedure that was open to them as a result of a recent measure—ask for a Court of Inquiry into their claim under the auspices of the Ministry of Labour? This was something that had never been tried, but Bevin persuaded his colleagues to give it a trial. The application was made and the Court of Inquiry was appointed under a High Court judge, Lord Shaw, and opened its sessions at the Law Courts in London.

For the employers was briefed Sir Lynden Macassey, K.C., who was one of the greatest authorities on industrial law in the country. Bevin appeared for the dockers, and his opening speech took two and a half days to deliver. When he began to speak he was just a trade union official, one whose name was hardly known outside his immediate circle; when he at length concluded his speech and sat down, he had become a national figure—the newspapers had seen to that. He had shown himself to be a powerful advocate, a master of facts and figures; he had met in argument some of the keenest brains in the country, and he had certainly not had the worst of it.

Briefly, his case was that in the period of the war years the ship-owners had made enormous profits, and were still doing so, but the position of the docker had steadily worsened. True, since 1905 the docker's wage on the average had increased, been doubled in fact, but in the same period the cost of living had gone up four times. What did this mean? Simply this, that the docker's wife, "the greatest Chancellor of the Exchequer that ever lived", had now to keep her man and her family on half what she had been given in 1905. The present demand was for a wage of 16s. a day. Was that too much to pay to a man who might be required to work sixty hours a week, lumping great loads about in dirty and dangerous conditions, and at the end of it no guarantee of employment beyond today? What was the alternative? If you won't meet the dockers' demand, then go to the Prime Minister, the Minister of Education and the rest, and tell them to close the schools and all that made for a better life, and get the men down to a simple "fodder basis"!

Then Sir Lynden Macassey presented the employers' case. He made great show with a family budget that had been drawn up by an eminent Cambridge economist, Professor A. L. Bowley, which sought to demonstrate that a weekly wage of 77s. was sufficient to house, feed, and clothe a docker's family.

Bevin made a careful note of the budget, and when the hearing closed that day he and his secretary went down to a street market in Canning Town and spent the amount, just that, no more and no less, that Professor Bowley had given as sufficient to buy a docker's family dinner. Then they took their purchases back to the Union's offices, cooked the dinner, and divided it into five portions, since this was taken to be the size of an average docker's family. Each portion they then placed on two plates, one containing a tiny piece of meat with similarly tiny portions of potatoes and greens, and the other a morsel of cheese and a slice of bread. The next morning when the Court met Bevin asked permission to produce his collection of ten plates. Then he turned to the judge:

"I ask you, my Lord, to examine the dinner which counsel for the employers considers sufficient to sustain the strength of a docker who has to haul, say, seventy tons of wheat on his back in the course of the day."

The demonstration went home. The Commission recommended the grant of the Union's basic demands; while as for Bevin, henceforth he was known to everybody as "the dockers' K.C."

In the next year he played a prominent part in the creation of the Transport and General Workers Union, in which thirty-two separate unions came together to constitute the biggest trade union in the world. Bevin was the first General Secretary, and he held the job (at a top salary of £1,200 a year) until 1940, when Winston Churchill called him, as the outstanding and most generally trusted and respected trade unionist leader, to take office in his National Government as Minister of Labour and National Service. Bevin was not in Parliament—he had fought several contests in years gone by, but unsuccessfully—but a seat was found for him as Labour M.P. for Wandsworth Central.

As a Minister he was generally considered to have been strikingly successful, as under his direction the nation's man, and woman, power was mobilized as never before. When the Labour Government was formed by Mr Attlee in 1945 Bevin's appointment to one of the highest places in the administration was inevitable, but there was considerable surprise when it was found that he was to be the new Foreign Secretary. Here again, the choice was proved right. He brought a breath of fresh air into the musty corridors and conference rooms. He got on well with all save the stuffiest of diplomats, and never forgot, nor allowed others to forget, the human approach. When he was asked by a foreign diplomat to explain his policy in a few words he said,

"Just to be able to go down to Victoria Station and take a ticket to where the hell I like without a passport."

It was a most difficult time for British diplomacy. America and Russia were asserting their positions as the two really great World Powers, but Bevin performed manfully at the Potsdam Conference in 1945 and at the Big Four conference at Moscow two years later; he supported every move for the restoration and eventual unification of Europe, and regarded the North Atlantic Treaty of 1949 as his greatest triumph. Ill-health compelled his resignation in March, 1951, and on 14 April, he died of a heart attack. A few weeks before the staff at the Foreign Office had given him a party in honour of his seventieth birthday. He had been greatly moved. "I don't think such a thing has ever happened before," he remarked wonderingly. He might have said that such a career as his had never happened before either.

Alexander Fleming
1881-1955

THE laboratory was bursting with bits of equipment—bunsen burners, crucibles, pipettes, test tubes, Petri dishes full of colonies of bacteria ripening for examination under the microscope, rubber tubes and glass jars. During the day, the lids had been taken off some of the Petri dishes to enable them to be studied under the microscope and as the Scot Alexander Fleming chatted to his young Englishman assistant, he lifted the lids again and looked in. Several of the cultures of bacteria had been contaminated by mould; this was a fairly usual occurrence, the air was full of "spores"—most air is—and when the tiny organisms settled in a damp place, they would proliferate, put out shoots in every direction and become a fungus. It was tiresome, the older man said, but that was all. "As soon as you uncover one of these culture dishes, something tiresome happens, things just fall out of the air." Suddenly Fleming stopped talking and looked carefully into one of the dishes.

The young man with him looked too. On the surface of the culture of staphylococci which they were studying, there was a growth of mould. It seemed exactly like the mould on several other dishes, except that, all around the edges of the fungus the colonies of staphylococci had been dissolved. Instead of being an opaque mass, a yellow clump of bacteria, they had lost their colour, they were simply drops of dew.

Without saying a word, Fleming picked up a small piece of the mould with his spatula and put it in a test tube. To the younger doctor there was nothing surprising about the fungus and its effect on bacteria: the same thing would have happened, the bacteria would have been killed, if one had dropped some strong acid into the dish. Probably the fungus was exuding some acid. After all, it was easy enough to kill bacteria in a dish, the problem was· to kill them in the human body, without killing the body in the process.

"This is really quite interesting," said Fleming, scooping out the rest of the fungus, putting it carefully into another test tube and then corking it. Only after he had put the test tube in its rack did he turn round, smile and resume the conversation.

The young man wrote later:

"What struck me was that he didn't confine himself to observing, he took action at once. Lots of people observe a phenomenon, feeling it may be important, but they don't get beyond being surprised."

Next day Alexander Fleming began to cultivate his mould. He took it from the two test-tubes and spread it on a larger bowl of the nutritive broth the laboratory used for breeding bacteria. The fungus grew, incredibly slowly, pushing out tentacles across the surface of the broth, becoming, centimetre by centimetre, a thick, soft, pock-marked mass, of white and green and black. For several days Fleming watched its growth and made no attempt to drop in some bacteria to see the reaction. Then, quite suddenly, the broth itself, having been a clear liquid, went a vivid yellow. Now Fleming took a drop of the yellow liquid and placed it at the centre of a dish on which he had arranged, star-fashion, half a dozen different colonies of bacteria, all radiating from the middle—streptococci, staphy-lococci, gonococci—and waited. Would the yellow liquid have the bacteria-killing properties of the mould? At first, nothing happened. Then, slowly, the colonies of bacteria began to dissolve, leaving only the "dew" Fleming had already observed.

Now Fleming knew he had stumbled upon a discovery of very great importance. There had been no method of killing these bacteria before, except by acids and disinfectants which would kill the patient as well. This, he was sure, was harmless and to prove it to himself he drank half a glassful, with no harmful effect. He tried diluting the liquid, first to a half-and-half solution, and gradually to one part in five hundred and still—though less rapidly—it went on killing bacteria.

It was important to find out what the mould was. The slow breeding of the original spore which had landed on Fleming's bench could not produce any large quantity in a short enough time to be of real use. He knew very little of mycology, the science of fungi, but he studied it and enlisted the help of experts in that field; their efforts at last were successful; they were able to establish a "penicillium notatum"—a penicillium, or fungus, of the "notatum" variety. The problem—or the first problem—was to get more of it, because, although it had been catalogued, no one yet knew where to be certain of finding it. The second problem, and the more intractable one, was to get the yellow liquid into a form stable enough to be stored and used when necessary. In the form in which Fleming first produced it, the germ-killing quality lasted only a short time before the mould degenerated into an inert, useless liquid. These two problems held up the development of what Fleming knew was a wonder drug for over ten years. Because he was unable to produce it in stable form, some people scoffed at his "discovery".

Then, quite suddenly during the war, there was a breakthrough in research, accelerated by the larger sums the British and American governments were prepared to spend on anything which might be of use on the battlefield. First as a trickle, then as a flood, the wonder drug became available and countless thousands of war-wounded, and men and women who would have died of meningitis, pneumonia, septicaemia and a host of other deadly diseases were cured as if by magic. The greatest discovery in medicine for a hundred years had been turned to account.

Alexander Fleming was born, the son of a Scottish hill farmer, in Ayr in 1881. As soon as he was able to walk he showed the interest in sport which was to characterize him throughout life and which was to alter the course of that life, and of the world. He and his brothers, though they were unable between them to afford a gun, would go out on hunting expeditions through the heather, stalking rabbits and catching them in their bare hands. They swam, they ran, they played football and climbed trees. They were happy. But from time immemorial, Scots have tended to go south to make their reputations and their fortunes; the Fleming brothers were no exception. By 1895, when Alec was fourteen, there were four of them living in London in an old house in the Marylebone Road, being looked after by their sister Mary. Alec's first job was as clerk to a shipping firm, work which he found interesting and congenial, and it is probable that he would have remained, and prospered, in commerce all his life, had not a legacy from an uncle given him the chance of taking up his brother Tom's suggestion of medical school. Alec agreed, even though the "wasted years" as a clerk made him older than his fellow students. He never regretted those years.

"I gained much general knowledge and when I went to medical school I had a great advantage over my fellow students who were straight from school and had never got away from their books into the school of life."

No doubt much of this advantage stemmed not from the city office but from the fourteen earlier years in the country, learning to use his eyes.

After he had succeeded in passing the entrance exam (and he passed top of all United Kingdom candidates, in July, 1901) he was able to choose his medical school. He chose St Mary's Hospital in Paddington for the very simple reason that he had recently played water polo against them. This apparently fortuitous decision flung him up against the great bacteriologist, Almroth Wright, in whose laboratory he now found himself working. This chance, in turn, was brought about by a young doctor wanting Fleming—as good a rifle shot as a water polo player—in the St Mary's Rifle Club: if the great Wright would ask him to join his own lab., no doubt the young man would make his career there. After all, such an introduction was considered a great honour.

The old bacteriologist, for the sake of the hospital's Rifle Club, made his invitation, which was gratefully accepted. Fleming was able to do a great deal of valuable practical work in bacteriology in Wright's laboratory before passing his finals in 1908. The handpicked team he worked with were a brilliant, artistic, talkative lot, very different on the surface from the circumspect young Scot, but their influence on him was considerable. He joined the Chelsea Arts Club, of all improbable moves for a shy young man from a Scottish hill farm, and throughout his life this remained for him "The Club", where he was happiest and most relaxed. At the same time—this was entirely his own decision—he joined the London Scottish, the famous Territorial regiment which, while providing him with opportunities for sport and a fortnight's camp under canvas, was a rallying point for Scots in London. His colleagues were somewhat surprised when Fleming, a trained bacteriologist, elected to go into training as a private soldier, sharing a tent with six or seven other men, but Fleming served several happy years with the London Scottish before deciding to leave because the training periods didn't fit in with his work at the hospital. Only a few months after his resignation the first war broke out and he found himself in France as a lieutenant in the medical research centre at Boulogne. It was here that he made his first important experiments in bacteriology.

In the terrible butchery of 1914 many wounded men were coming in to hospital with their wounds crawling with bacteria, and Fleming soon saw that antiseptics were useless. Not only did they do nothing to prevent, for example, gangrene, they actually seemed to promote its development. For a surface wound the antiseptics had some value as they destroyed—if used in strong enough doses—the bacteria while destroying only cells of the body which, being on the surface, could be replaced. But most wounds were far from superficial and in these cases the antiseptics were either useless or seemed to destroy the body's power to resist infection. In fact, the only antiseptic which could be of positive value, Fleming realized, was one that would help the body's natural defences. Various solutions were able to do this for a few minutes, but soon their efficacy vanished. Fleming wrote:

"Surrounded by all those infected wounds by men who were suffering and dying without our being able to do anything to help them, I was consumed by a desire to discover, after all this struggling and waiting, something which would kill those microbes . . ."

The war ended in November, 1918, and two months later Fleming was demobilized, without having found the microbe-killing substance he sought.

He was thinking along the right lines—and one of the very few who was. He knew it would have to be something—perhaps from the body itself—which would encourage it to kill invaders, and in 1921 he made his first important stride forward. He had tried various human secretions and now he found that human tears, dropped into a culture of bacteria, dissolved them with startling speed. The substance in the tear drop which had this effect he named "lysozyme" and he soon discovered that it was contained in nail-parings, hair and skin, and even in certain leaves and stalks of plants. Unfortunately, lysozyme, which was so powerful against some bacteria had very little effect on the dangerous ones. Its immediate use was therefore limited, but it was an important step in bacteriology. Fleming read a paper on it to the august Medical Research Club in December, 1921, and was much distressed when it got a frigid reception. Eight years later, he was to get exactly the same reception for his first discovery of penicillin, though a few years after that the doubters and scoffers would be eating their words.

Between lysozyme in 1921 and penicillin in 1929, Fleming never stopped his research into his own pet theory—that something from the human body, something living, was the answer to bacteria. Lysozyme, while never becoming a practical proposition, proved him right and for Fleming penicillin was merely the logical next stage. But from the day that the "penicillium notatum" blew in through his Paddington laboratory window, though he was utterly convinced of its ultimate value, Fleming and his colleagues—and indeed scientists who had never met him, including one who thought he was dead but who had studied his 1929 paper, worked on the extraction and stabilization of the drug. Fleming was able to perform several minor but nonetheless remarkable cures with the small quantities he was able to prepare, but there just was not sufficient—

as the stuff had to be prepared from the mould for each treatment and was not yet in a form in which it could be injected into the body—to embark on a major test.

By the outbreak of the Second World War in 1939, ten years after its initial discovery, penicillin could still not be produced in large quantity or made stable. Then a team under the Australian Howard Florey, got together in Oxford determined to solve the problem. Gradually they found they were able to purify small quantities of the mould by a complicated method of evaporation—"freeze-drying"—and the time came to try this new drug on a patient. An Oxford policeman was dying of septicaemia from a small scratch at the corner of his mouth which had infected his blood stream. On 20 February, 1941, an intravenous injection of the purified penicillin was given to the dying man and thereafter every three hours. At the end of twenty-four hours the improvement was almost incredible, the patient was practically recovered. Then the penicillin which they had laboured so long to produce ran out. The patient hung on for a few days but the microbes, no longer being attacked by penicillin, got the upper hand and he died.

Even this was not enough to convince sceptics of the value of the drug, but Florey's team was completely convinced. The stuff just had to be made faster and in large quantities. To this end help was sought in America and at last the Northern Regional Research Laboratory of Peoria, Illinois, agreed to help. This laboratory had been working on the uses for the organic by-products of agriculture and when they started work on the new drug from England, it was discovered that corn-steep liquor, a by-product of maize, was an ideal medium for the growth of fungi. The laboratory staff became enthusiastic and in a short time Peoria was producing twenty times as much as Oxford. At the same time the research team was on the look-out for mould-strains which might give a larger yield of penicillin. So far every gram of the drug that had been made had descended from the spore that had landed on Fleming's bench in 1929. Many experiments were made with moulds, but it was not until 1943 that the young woman the laboratory employed in Peoria to go round the markets looking for rotten fruit (they called her "Mouldy Mary") brought back a canteloup melon. The mould from this, a "penicillium chrysogenum", provided a remarkably productive mould of the penicillin type, and nowadays almost all penicillin in use is descended from that one rotten melon bought in the market at Peoria, Illinois.

At last, the real value of Fleming's discovery became clear to everyone. Production, both in England and America, mounted, by leaps and bounds. At first all of it was earmarked for the Services. Thousand upon thousand of dying soldiers, sailors and airmen were saved by the new "wonder drug". It was not until late 1944 that the military authorities felt able to spare any of it for civilian patients.

Honours showered down on the shy and sensitive Alexander Fleming. In July, 1944, he was knighted—in the basement of Buckingham Palace. He was proud to receive in the same year the freedom of Paddington, where he had spent all his medical life and a little later, the freedom of Darvel, the small Scots town where he had been at school. In 1945 he was invited to tour the United States. Here, as well as being fêted, he was able to see how his discovery was being developed. He had refused—as had all the "Oxford Team"—to patent penicillin, a move which could have brought him hundreds of thousands of pounds in royalty payments. The American and British firms which were developing new industrial processes to speed production of penicillin followed suit, making no attempt to "collar the market". The manufacture of penicillin became public property and all firms shared what knowledge they picked up in the process.

At the end of 1945, while on a triumphal visit to France as a guest of the French Government, Fleming was told that he had been awarded the Nobel Prize for Medicine.

A few years later tragedy struck: his wife, Sareen, to whom he had been devoted and who had given him the support he so badly needed when the world laughed, died. Fleming was heartbroken. He devoted his entire life, day and night, to his research. In 1953 he married a Greek girl, Amalia Voureka, a brilliant biologist who had received a British Council bursary to work in England and had found herself, from 1946, in Fleming's laboratory. Their happiness was short-lived. He died in 1955 of an illness (coronary thrombosis) which his drug was powerless to control.

The discovery of penicillin has revolutionized the treatment of disease and the young doctor of today can hardly realize how helpless his predecessors felt against so many deadly infections. Penicillin and the whole group of "antibiotics" it triggered off have enabled surgeons to perform operations no one would have dared consider a few years ago, and the average expectation of life has increased so greatly that the whole structure of society is altering. All because a brilliant research worker "did not confine himself to observing, he took action at once".

Pope John
1881-1963

DR JOHN HEENAN, now Cardinal Archbishop of Westminster, but then Bishop of Liverpool remembers how, at the requiem mass for Pope John's predecessor, the Bishops placed next to the Cardinals in St Peter's, could not help studying the faces of the Princes of the Church and wondering whom among them would be chosen as Pope. To Cardinal Roncalli, the Patriarch of Venice, scarcely anyone gave a second glance. With his fat good-natured face, he looked like a wise peasant: also he was seventy-seven years old. He was certainly not among the *Papabili*. When elected Pope John XXIII, the two-hundredth and sixty-third Primate since St Peter was regarded as a Pope who would give the Church a breathing space in which to think out some of the problems of organization and political relationship in the outside world which wanted answering. He was regarded as an easy-going, likeable man, who had always taken his priestly duties seriously but not as a great mind.

Pope John held his sacred office only for four years and seven months. Yet in that time the Catholic Church itself underwent a profound change, and as a result of this change, by the time Pope John was dead, the Church, in the minds not only of non-Catholic Christians but of atheists and agnostics, had become a force which was clearly on the side of the "men of good will".

How could one man in so short a time have had so much effect? The answer is that this very simple man leant his whole weight on that section of the Church (which had been growing stronger throughout the post-war epoch) which desired the Church to be social, evangelical and universal in its attitudes. It is significant that the last of the Pope John's encyclicals *Pacem in Terris* (Peace on Earth) was addressed not as is usual to the faithful inside the Church but to all men.

Pope John had no mysterious methods. He surprised the world, and this included the Vatican, by the fact that he was much more determined and clearer in his views about the Papacy and the Church than anyone had supposed. Moreover, he was much more powerful than anyone had imagined because, in his exalted position, his total lack of pretence and his simplicity, humility and love of humanity were suddenly apparent to the whole world; it was difficult to gainsay or circumvent him.

He very nearly did not go into the Church. Born at Sotto il Monte near Bergamo in northern Italy in 1881 of a poor peasant family, Angelo Giuseppe Roncalli, the fourth son of a family of thirteen, was educated at a small seminary some six miles from his house, to which he had to walk and return each day. After a good start, he suffered from various illnesses and grew discouraged and over-tired. His parents decided he should give up his studies and work on the land. Angelo was given a letter to the Head of the Seminary announcing this. Angelo read the letter, tore it up and, with an effort of will, managed to get himself into the dioscesan seminary and was ordained in Rome in 1904.

His first appointment was as private secretary to the Bishop of Bergamo, Monseigneur Radini Tedeschi who was one of the pioneers of the Catholic Action movement, the aim of which was the promotion of Christian social principles and which worked at correcting the reactionary bias of so many Italian Church dignitaries. Called for military service in the First World War, Father Roncalli became first a sergeant in the medical corps and then a chaplain to military hospitals with the rank of lieutenant.

After the war, following some service in training colleges and schools, he was given the title of Bishop of Areopolis and made the Apostolic Vicar to Bulgaria. Until 1944 Bishop Angelo Roncalli lived and worked for the Church in Bulgaria, Turkey and Greece; acquiring there the knowledge and sympathy for the Eastern Church which made him so able and determined an advocate of union between all Christians. He became very popular in Constantinople and later in Greece. It was his good nature, lack of pretence and above all his childish enthusiasms which won men to him. In Greece during the years of the Second World War, nobody laboured harder than he did to succour the people during the terrible famine after the German invasion.

Bishop Roncalli did not really think much of himself as a Papal diplomat and hoped for a diocese where he could work as a priest. However the Papacy clearly thought very highly of him, for he was sent, in 1944, to Paris to take the place of the Papal Nuncio, who, from his collaboration with Pétain and the Germans, was not acceptable to the Provisional Government of General de Gaulle. His stay in France was of great importance in the development of his views for he came into contact with the liberal progressive

Catholicism of much of the French Church, including many of its Bishops. He was undoubtedly successful as Papal Nuncio and managed to create good relations between Rome and successive French governments. He spoke French from his youth and liked and was liked to a very great degree in this country.

So valuable did the Papacy consider his work, that it was not until 1953 that he was given his diocese, the splendid one of Venice.

On his arrival in Venice he said, "Please don't expect to find a diplomat in me. I am only a parish priest and wish to remain so." He made many innovations, among others that of having his Palace open to all his flock at all times of the day and night to visit him privately. He used his office to encourage everything in the Church that made religion more real in everyday life. He was a great lover of music and it was in the great Basilica of St Marks that Stravinsky's religious works were first performed.

Ambition was the last thing in his nature. Yet when, in 1958, Pope Pius XII died and someone remarked that, in 1903, the man who was to become Pope Pius XI had left Venice with a return ticket in his pocket, he smiled and made no reply. There is some evidence for thinking that the Patriarch knew instinctively that he might well be chosen. He was elected on the eleventh ballot, taking the name of John which was that of his father and of his patron saint.

Pope Pius XII, the former Cardinal Pacelli, had held office for nineteen years, during, of course, the war years. An austere, even saintly, figure, he had been responsible for a number of important changes such as the relaxation of the Eucharistic fast, the introduction of evening mass and many liturgical revisions including that of Holy Week.

Although he was by nature aloof, he, after the war, had enormously enlarged the direct contacts of the Pope with the outside world, receiving not only monarchs, but cinema stars, artists, businessmen and hundreds of thousands of soldiers and ordinary people on a scale far greater than that of any of his predecessors. He spent much of his energy and time on these extremely well-organized audiences and needed the solitude with which he surrounded himself in daily life. Of aristocratic birth, his temperament was autocratic and during his reign he had done away with the frequent consultations of cardinals and advisers. He had once been loath to create cardinals and the College was much reduced in number.

The first act of Pope John was to restore Curial meetings and to make contact with all the administrative services of the Vatican. Almost at once the new Pope began his frequent visits, almost of an informal character, to the streets of Rome as though with intent to emphasize first that he was no prisoner in the Vatican but, as well as Pope, the Bishop of Rome. He went to the great prison in the city, the Regina Coeli, because, as he said, prisoners unlike free men could not come to see him. He talked on purpose to those convicted of serious crimes.

Once in Regina Coeli he told a group of prisoners that as a young man he had had an uncle who was imprisoned for lawlessness. This interview was reported by the *Osservatore Romano*, but the editor altered the word uncle to some more distant connexion. In his Roman diocese it was noted that he spent a great deal of his time with any priest who had incurred disciplinary sanctions or who was in any kind of difficulty. All his acts of getting nearer to common humanity—such as inviting his gardeners to lunch with him or his forbidding people to kneel to him when they entered his room—were significant because it was at once felt that they were not acts of policy but reflections of his nature. He did not like eating by himself and he felt cut off from people who knelt to him.

His naturalness, humour and humility immediately created real relationships. To an Anglican Bishop his first question was, "Are you a theologian?" "No," was the reply. "I'm so glad for I'm not either," he said. He once told a visitor that, when he found it difficult to go to sleep on account of worry, he would let the Pope say to him, "Angelo, don't make yourself so important please." With his loud laughter and his bypassing of pomp and stuffiness, his often-repeated remark that he asked God "to have patience with us fat men", he still remained what he had always been, a remarkably skilful diplomat. The common touch in no way impaired his ability to talk with kings. He made a serious distinction as well as a jocular one between himself as Pope and as man; he said once to some Greek seminarists: "You know, I am not infallible." When they looked surprised, he went on with a smile, "No. The Pope is only that when he speaks *ex cathedra* and I will never speak *ex cathedra*."

Indeed Pope John created no new dogma nor revived old ones. He used his great prestige as Head of the Church in other directions and first of all to break down barriers between Christians. A few months after his election, he surprised his entourage and the whole world by the calling of the second Vatican Council, widely known as the Ecumenical Council, the purpose of which was to advance towards Christian union. When he decided on this, one of his advisers said to him that there was scarcely time to organize the

Council for 1963. "Ah," said the Pope, "I mean the Council to meet in 1962."

The first Vatican Council had been held in 1870 and it had resulted, among other things in the dogma of Papal infallibility. The aim of the 1963 Council was defined by the Pope as to assist the spread of Christianty by presenting the life and teaching of the Church in a positive form. The Church was to revive its doctrines and its practices so that anything inessential which differentiated Catholics from non-Catholics was to be changed and at the same time the Church's ritual was to be closely examined so that anything which made it difficult for men to understand and worship was to be modified. Thus from the beginning the question of the use of vernacular tongues instead of Latin for certain parts of the mass was discussed and agreed on.

The purpose of the Ecumenical Council is well expressed in the Italian word *aggiornamonto* which means the bringing up to date. It was an attempt to reform the Roman Church so as to achieve a unity of spirit between the Church and other Christian Churches.

The Pope long before summoning the Ecumenical Council had made plain his intention of seeking a common basis with all Christians. A particularly pressing invitation was extended to the Russian Orthodox Church and, to the general surprise, the Soviet Government gave permission for Russian representatives to attend.

In 1960, Dr Geoffrey Fisher, Primate of the Church of England and Archbishop of Canterbury paid a courtesy visit to Rome, the first of its kind for nearly four hundred years since Henry VIII repudiated Papal supremacy.

The attendance at the Ecumenical Council of representatives from nearly all the Christian Churches was what gave the Council so great an importance. In the future there might be checks to Papal policy but the broad movement to unity could hardly be reversed it seemed.

Pope John was responsible for eight encyclicals. He did not pretend to have been himself solely responsible for them and he once said to a friend, "You know I *read* them." But in the two most important, *Mater et Magistra* (1961) and *Pacem in Terris* (1963) he expressed the guiding principles of his life. The first of these encyclicals, with its emphasis on the duty of society to see to the well-being of man was not new to most of the countries of Europe; but it had a tremendous effect in Spain and in Latin America. The second, *Pacem in Terris*, had, for all the very carefully chosen expressions and even the deliberate ambiguities, a generally revolutionary effect. Appealing for peace on earth the holder of the office which had several times emphasized the gulf between Christians and Communists, reminded the faithful that "error is not to be confused with the errors of persons"; that false philosophies (i.e. Marxism) are not to be identified with their associated historical movements (i.e. Communism) in which there might be patches of good. In an appeal for co-operation between nations he clearly included Communist countries when he wrote:

"a drawing nearer together or a meeting for the attainment of some practical end, which was formerly deemed inopportune or unproductive, might now or in the future be considered opportune or useful."

The Pope was criticized in some reactionary Italian circles who believed that *Pacem in Terris* had sown confusion in the minds of the Italian electorate and had therefore contributed to the increase in the Communist vote in the Italian General Election of 1963. To the vast majority of thinking people throughout the world, the aged Pontiff with his Court and his string of high-sounding medieval titles was showing that he was as sensitive as President Kennedy to the currents of world history. Again, it is important to see that the Holy Father in the most politically important passages of *Pacem in Terris* observed that perfect caution which carried with him all in the Church but those who were completely out of touch with the times. The caution was perfect because it prevented disruption but not movement.

His boldness as a diplomat was shown by his reception of Mr Khrushchev's son-in-law, Mr Adjubei, and his wife. Asked by Mr Adjubei to suggest a way in which East and West might come together, the Pope replied:

"You are a journalist and you certainly know the Holy Bible. The Bible states that God created the world in six days: the days were epochs, an infinite space of time. The first day the Lord said let there be light. Today, we are at the first hour. It is God who is giving us light. He, do not doubt it, my son, will give us rest."

At the same time the Papal Secretary was careful to explain the reasons why the Pope had undertaken this interview. The first was because the Russian members of the jury which had awarded the Balzan International Peace Prize to the Pope were in favour of the awards going to him and he wished to express his thanks. The second was that many years ago when he was in Eastern Europe, he had said that if a Bulgarian, a Turk or a Slav knocked at his door, he could enter because it would always be open.

The Pope's death in June, 1963, was after a long and heroically endured agony. His last words before he became unconscious were "May they be one".

Pope John was neither a great theologian, nor intellectual. But the goodness of the dove was accompanied in him by the wisdom of a serpent. His wisdom was instinctive and immense because it was grounded in humility. "See everything; turn a blind eye to many things; correct a little," was his favourite motto.

Why was his first act to increase the authority of the College of Cardinals? Why, in the organization of the Church in Italy, and in the organization of the Ecumenical Council did he increase the authority and independence of Bishops? It was because he knew that the cause of progress, of liberalism, of evangelism was the growing force in men's minds and that the association of as many men as possible with Papal authority would lead most surely to the triumph of that cause. An effort by himself alone to impose these things would not last long after him. "Pope John reaches his goal like water," somebody said of him.

In the cause of evangelizing, of winning over men to union and Christianity, his wisdom cannot be separated from his personal virtue. Was it wisdom or goodness of heart which made him, when he received the representatives of certain non-Catholic Churches, avoid using his Papal seat and draw up a chair next to them saying, "For you I am not the successor of Peter"? No Pope since the Reformation has ever made so wide an appeal to the non-Catholic and to the non-Christian world. People outside the Church thought of Pope John no longer as the representative of a proud organization which challenged some of their deeply held beliefs, but as someone who sympathized with them in their difficulties and who was on their side.

Discussing the greatness of the man whom he calls "the servant of the servants of God" the young Swiss-German priest, Hans Kung, professor of Theology in the University of Tubingen, wrote of him:

"What makes a man great among men was to John XXIII a thing of total indifference. But what makes a man, in the spirit of the Gospel, great before God was to him all important. It was this evangelical quality which distinguished him from his predecessors."

Pablo Ruiz Picasso
1881-1973

Pablo Picasso lived in France. When the armies of Nazi Germany invaded that land in the Second World War Picasso already was an artist whose genius was recognized internationally. The great mural called "Guernica", inspired by the horrible scenes resulting from aerial bombardment of the town of that name by German aeroplanes during the Spanish Civil War, had not endeared Picasso to the German invaders; yet though they dominated France, the Germans hesitated to interfere with him. His world-wide reputation stood so high that persecution of him almost surely would have antagonized a multitude of intellectuals, and among those, particularly in France itself and in America, the rulers of Germany hoped to find support.

IT was almost midnight on 25 October, 1881, when the artist who was to alter the whole course of art history was born at Malaga, in Spain. The infant was called Pablo Ruiz Picasso, the middle name being derived from the family name of Ruiz on his father's side. Don José Ruiz Blasco, father of the artist, was a Professor of Fine Art and a Curator of the local museum. In 1880 he married Maria Picasso Lopez, and the following year their son Pablo was born. His entry into the world was marked by a dramatic, and nearly fatal misjudgment. The midwife who delivered the baby thought that he was stillborn, and abandoned him on a table. Only the fortunate presence of mind of an uncle, Don Salvador, who hurried for a doctor, prevented the baby from dying of asphyxia. Later, in equally dramatic circumstances, and immediately following an earthquake, Picasso's mother gave birth to her second child, a daughter called Lola.

There is no doubt that the young Picasso learned a great deal about painting, and about art in general from his father, who was also a painter, though not a notably gifted one. Even before he could speak Picasso had begun to express himself with a pencil, and, as a baby, would sit for hours contentedly drawing spirals on sheets of paper or pieces of cardboard. Later, he delighted to draw pictures in the sand of the Malaga beaches. By the time he was fourteen he was to be a master of classical drawing.

The traditional centre of popular entertainment in all Spanish cities is of course the bull-ring, and, like most Spanish children, Picasso was taken to the bullfight at an early age. It captured his imagination, and has often been featured in his art. Viewed as a symbolic ritual the bullfight represents the eternal struggle between good (man and horse) and evil (the bull; one of the powers of darkness). It was these symbols which Picasso was to employ in the great mural "Guernica", which he painted for the Spanish Pavilion at the Paris World Fair of 1937. Here the bull, representing the implacable powers of evil and darkness, towers over the dying horse, symbolic of the suffering of the Spanish people during the Civil War.

When Pablo was ten years old, Don José, whose teaching fortunes had long been in decline, was forced to move to Corunna and accept the post of art master at the secondary school in that town. During the next few years life for the family was not altogether happy. Don José grew difficult and morose. Delivery came when he obtained a good post at the Barcelona School of Fine Arts. In October, 1894, a happy family set out for the capital of the province of Catalonia.

Here Pablo Picasso began painting in earnest. He was influenced in these early days by reproductions of paintings by Daumier, van Gogh and Toulouse-Lautrec. In the summer of 1897 a group of the young man's pictures was exhibited in Barcelona, and soon afterwards Picasso entered the Royal Academy of San Fernando in Madrid. On entrance day he astonished the professors there by executing drawings of staggering brilliance for one so young. Two years later, after a somewhat erratic career at the Academy, he returned to Barcelona where he lived and worked spasmodically until moving to Paris in 1904. Here, on the south-western slopes of Montmartre he was to live for the next five years among artists and writers, enjoying to the full the gay life of the typical French Bohemian. Here he painted the wonderful pictures of his *Blue* and *Rose* periods, pictures populated with beggars and circus folk.

From 1904 until his death, France had been the home of this Spanish-born painter, although, much to the chagrin of the French Government, he had always resolutely refused to take up French citizenship. He remained fundamentally, and at heart, a proud and passionate Spaniard.

During his early formative years in Paris, Picasso became the intimate friend of many distinguished people, among them the writers Gertrude Stein and Apollinaire, and the painters, Derain and Braque. He learned early in life how to make, and keep, powerful friends, among them the dealer Paul Rosenberg, and the historian of Cubism, Henry Kahnweiler. During these early years in Paris he kept returning to Spain from time to time, but always, inevitably, he was drawn back to Paris; to the stimulating, cosmopolitan life of the French capital. Picasso was a frequent exhibitor. In 1912 a group of his Cubist drawings and paintings were shown at the Stafford Gallery in London. The prices—£2 to £20! Today a painting of the same period would cost around £75,000! He exhibited also in New York, and gradually his international reputation grew. During the later years of the First World War Picasso began to design costumes for Diaghileff's Russian Ballet, another manifestation of his amazing versatility. He was a sculptor and an etcher as well as a painter. The genius of the little Spaniard was boundless. When the Russian Ballet left Paris for a tour of Madrid and Barcelona, Picasso went with it, and in Spain in 1918 he married the Russian ballerina, Olga Koklova. Soon afterwards the newly married couple returned to Picasso's beloved Paris. The war was over, but not the aftermath of suffering. Picasso's great friend the poet Apollinaire had been severely wounded in the head, and although he returned to Paris and for a short while resumed his writing, he died not long after the end of hostilities. The blow to Picasso was great. The news of Apollinaire's death reached him at the moment he was drawing a self-portrait in the mirror, a portrait which marks the end of an epoch. A beloved friend was gone; from that moment, and in memory of Apollinaire, Picasso abandoned for ever his habit of making frequent self-portraits. Although he was never again to paint a portrait of himself, Picasso did immortalize many of his famous contemporaries, among them Diaghileff, Stravinsky, Cocteau, and the poets Louis Aragon and Paul Valery. Picasso's work shows infinate variety. One of the hall-marks of his genius is the fact that he himself covered every aspect of the visual arts of our time. Cubism, Expressionism, Surrealism; sculpture, ceramics, stage decor and costume design; the arts of collage and poster design; of etching and book illustrations; he was master of them all. Indeed it would be true to say that his work is the focal point and fountain head of all that is meant by the art of the twentieth century. Since Leonardo no artist displayed so rare and wide a range of talents.

Picasso was certainly the most revolutionary painter the twentieth century has known. The changes that he brought about are every bit as startling and influential as those wrought by the masters of the Italian Renaissance. Michelangelo, Raphael and Leonardo da Vinci transformed the flat, two-dimensional character of medieval painting into the concept of three-dimensional realism which, until the coming of Picasso, was to comprise the traditional form upon which the whole edifice of European art was based. Conventions grow stale and sterile; there comes a moment when they must receive fresh blood or wither and die. Such was the position during the second half of the nineteenth century, by which time the great traditions of realistic art had degenerated into a mere slavish attempt to copy the outward appearences of nature, in a manner that a relatively new invention called the camera could do better. It was in such an atmosphere that the young Picasso began work as an artist. In 1907 when he was twenty-six and was working in Paris—he had moved to the French capital from Barcelona in 1904—he painted a picture which was to be a turning point not only in his own career, but, as it turned out, a turning point for the whole future development of modern art. One might even say that modern art really begins at the point this picture was created. Although the Impressionist painter Paul Cézanne had earlier hinted at what was to come, "Les Demoiselles d'Avignon" was the first clear indication of the coming of Cubism. And Cubism has proved to be the most widely influential of all the isms of modern art. Its influence has been felt throughout the whole field of the applied arts, from architecture to furniture design. It is a process of simplification and invention. Cézanne had begun to reduce nature to its basic geometry at the close of the nineteenth century and Picasso soon realized that here was the new and vital direction which European art must take. So he turned his back on the moribund "photographic" type of art favoured by the academies and created the first Cubist style painting. Thereafter, in his work and in the paintings of his colleagues Georges Braque and Juan Gris, Cubism was consolidated into a virile movement in which everything was reduced to the simplest geometric elements. Later, in what was to be called Synthetic Cubism, new shapes and forms were invented; the whole field of the visual image was paraphrased, extended, modified, distorted, and subjected to all those changes of appearance that have led to so many of the things we now take for granted.

Modern poster design for instance is only one field in which we can witness the influence of late Cubism. Its influence upon the products of industrial design is continually in evidence. Think of G Plan furniture, or the design of television sets, or washing machines The simplification of form in each instance stems directly from Cubism, and indirectly, from that one, marvellously inventive picture which Picasso painted in 1907. Cubism and all that this entailed as an influence upon so many aspects of modern living, was Picasso's greatest contribution to the art and life of our times.

Much of Picasso's life in France was spent near the sea. From the localities of Cannes, Dinard and Antibes, he drew some of the most vital strands of his inspiration. But in spite of his increasing fame, and a considerable accumulation of wealth, by the year 1932 when he bought the seventeenth-century Chateau du Boisegeloup, near Paris, there were signs that the marriage between Pablo and Olga was running into difficulties. At this particular time he had found a new and beautiful model, Marie-Térèse Walter, who provided the inspiration for many of his works of the period. Picasso's relations with her not unnaturally complicated the relationship between Picasso and Olga. They parted.

Picasso threw himself harder than ever into his work. He painted, made sculpture, and even wrote poetry that won the acclaim of many distinguished French writers.

The outbreak of civil war in Spain in 1936 heralded three years of horrible bloodshed. The outcome, victory for General Franco and the Fascists, meant that Picasso, an ardent supporter of the defeated Republican left wing, was unable to return to his native land. In the early months of the fighting the Spanish Republican Government urged by a powerful group of intellectuals invited Picasso to accept the Directorship of the Prado Museum in Madrid. Picasso previously had shown no public interest in politics, but he accepted this invitation as a sign of his sympathy with the cause of the Spanish Republicans. It was an appointment he could never take up. Scarcely a year after the ending of the Spanish Civil War, Picasso was to witness the defeat of his adopted country, France. Shortly before the end of the Second World War Picasso joined the French Communist Party. In a statement published jointly in Paris and New York late in 1944 the artist said: "My adhesion to the Communist Party is the logical outcome of my whole life . . . I was so anxious to find a homeland again, I have always been an exile, now I am one no longer; until Spain can at last welcome me back, the French Communist Party has opened its arms to me." The news was received coldly in Moscow. As a painter Picasso had always refused to identify himself with the stilted type of "social realism" which forms the basis of official Soviet art. As an artist pure and simple he had nothing to offer Moscow. Nonetheless Picasso kept closely in touch with the activities of the Communist Party in the years following the war, and attended the Communist sponsored Peace Congresses at

Wroclaw in 1948, at Paris in 1949, and at Sheffield in 1950. For the second of these Congresses he designed the Peace Poster which has since become world famous. It took the form of a lithograph of a white dove, later to be used on the postage stamps of China, and to be accepted throughout the world as an enduring symbol of peace. At the time of Picasso's visit to Sheffield the Korean war had just begun, and members of the Communist Party were regarded with suspicion. At Dover many of Picasso's travelling companions were refused entry to England because of their political affiliations. Picasso himself was permitted to enter. "What can I have done that they should allow me through?" he asked an English friend ironically. At the conference he gave a short address, part of which included these words: "I stand for life against death; I stand for peace against war." Although seventy years of age the artist displayed all the vigour of a man half his age. He seemed to possess the secret of inexhaustible youth. Small, and sun-burned to a deep bronze, with compelling black eyes of startling depth and intensity of gaze, this was only Picasso's second brief visit to England. As a protest against the action of the British Government in refusing entry to his colleagues, he refused to attend an exhibition of his work which was being held in London.

In 1954 a new influence began to make itself felt in Picasso's work. He met a beautiful young girl, Jacqueline Roque, and began to paint and lithograph a series of portraits of her that were to become world famous. Later she was to become the artist's second wife.

In 1968, at the age of eighty-seven, he produced an astonishing *tour de force*. Over a period of only seven months—between March and October of that year—he made a series of 347 engravings, many of them frankly erotic; a magnificent testament to the sexual life of man.

In 1970 Picasso gave to the Museo in Barcelona a huge collection of his drawings and paintings covering a wide period in time. A gift of incalculable value, when one bears in mind that a few years ago a single blue-period painting made the sum of £190,000 at a Sotheby auction. But it was clear that the gift was made rather to the capital of Catalonia than to the Government of Generalissimo Franco.

Picasso died on 8 April, 1973. He was 92. His last years were embittered by a series of unsuccessful court actions to prevent publication of a scathingly critical autobiography by a former mistress, Francoise Gilot, mother of two of his children. At the time of his death the artist was reputed to be worth between five and six hundred million pounds. But the value of his genius will remain incalculable . . .

James Joyce
1882-1941

LITERATURE constantly renews itself; if it did not, it would not be literature. One such renewal in English literature began in the 1870s, when poets and novelists began to exhibit a certain restlessness, as if their geniuses needed fresh air. George Meredith, Thomas Hardy, Stevenson, Wilde, Manley Hopkins, Kipling, Henry James, George Moore, Wells, Bennett, E. M. Forster—poets, novelists and dramatists—all contributed to this renewal, the main flush of which was beginning to work itself out when the First World War erupted.

The cataclysmic nature of that upheaval, in which, on the battlefields of France and Flanders, men's bodies suffered a degradation not experienced to such a degree since the Black Death, could not fail to affect men's thoughts, and the effects became clearly observable in the literature which, as they say, "came out of the war".

It was first seen in the poetry, which gave a clear indication of a new orientation. To begin with, the war-poets started with an outburst of lyrical and patriotic fervour—as, for example, Julian Grenfell and Charles Sorley—but soon their tone changed to one of outspoken bitterness and disillusionment, feelings voiced most strongly by Siegfried Sassoon and Wilfred Owen. For the most part these poets wrote in the old manner but with a completely new freedom of speech; but there arose also a younger generation who felt that poetry should be a sheer effort of creative energy which fulfilled itself in the personal and spontaneous ardour of composition, wherein the words extemporized the thoughts. If the imagination were to enjoy the freedom of dreams—and this they believed it must—then the expression must not be confined to the discipline of metre. The spirit should find an outlet in cadences which rose and fell with the flow of words, as in emotional prose.

For many who wanted to leave the shattered world behind and start afresh, beginning with their experience of themselves, this became the recognized technique of which spontaneity was the keynote.

There was much to encourage them. The anthropological and folk-lore studies of the latter half of the nineteenth century had revealed that man cannot avoid the influences of a very ancient inheritance. In the twentieth century this was taken even further, and it was hinted that man resists the caprices of evolution. Freud developed the theory that a man lives two lives within himself, the one, intellectual, built on to and obscuring the other, which pervades his senses, expands into his dreams and affects his sexual relationships.

In considering this, the artist began to realize that if it was true, he could not portray human nature successfully until he had explored the effect that the influence of the one life has upon the other. It was an exciting idea, and a revelation to the restless and inquisitive spirits of the time, outstanding among whom was D. H. Lawrence.

Lawrence threw himself almost blatantly upon the mysteries of sex attraction and those relationships which a man acquires but which have an unsettling effect upon his existence. It seems that in *Sons and Lovers*, published in 1913, and in *The Rainbow*, which followed two years later, he had come to the conclusion that a man cannot be complete until he has sunk his spirit in the "mindless creative stir of universal nature".

Lawrence, of course, was not the only writer to whom these ideas were exciting, but others approached them from a different direction. James Joyce, for example, sought the same revelations which Lawrence believed he had found in the instincts, in the unspoken speech which expresses the germs of thought and feeling as inconsequentially as they enter the brain. In his interpretation, language was the one implement which the human mind could not do without, and he came to the conclusion that by its mere functioning it revealed the confused excitement which underlies the consciously spoken words. This was a general principle, true of everybody; and he believed that if *all* the thoughts of one man in the course of one day could be recorded just as they came into his mind, then the study of the result would reveal the secrets of the processes by which the human being operated. This he attempted to do in a unique book, *Ulysses*, which he published between 1918 and 1922.

Ulysses is one of the outstanding works not only of English literature, but of world literature. In one aspect of its achievement—the literary as conceived by Joyce—it is entirely successful; but opinion is divided as to whether it succeeded in what Joyce hoped and believed it would, namely, that it revealed the secrets of the human processes.

Though Joyce's reputation stands on the achievement of *Ulysses*, he was a considerable writer.

Born in Dublin on 2 February, 1882, he was the oldest of a family of ten, four boys and six girls, the children of John Joyce and Mary James Murray.

In the autobiographical novel, *A Portrait of the Artist as a Young Man*, the hero, Stephen Dedalus (Joyce) has described his father as "a medical student, an oarsman, a tenor, an amateur actor, a shouting politician, a small landlord, a small investor, a drinker, a good fellow, a story-teller, somebody's secretary, something in a distillery, a tax-gatherer, a bankrupt and at present a praiser of his own past". This description fairly fits John Joyce, who was a reckless, talented man, who begot children and debts with a surprising facility. (Besides the ten children who survived, there were three others who died at birth or in early infancy.)

The Joyces, who were constantly moving house, lived in Dublin or in one or other of its suburbs. At the age of what Joyce himself described to his fellow pupils as "half past six", the small boy became a boarder at Clongowes Wood College, a school run by Jesuits. After a difficult start, he made for himself a distinguished career at the College on the academic side, and while on the sports side he disliked football, he won several cups for hurdling and walking and took a keen interest in cricket.

In politics, John Joyce had been a fervent supporter of Parnell, and when Parnell was disgraced and driven from office in 1890, it seemed as though he carried John Joyce's fortunes with him. At the age of forty-two John Joyce was pensioned off by the Collector-General of Rates, and his financial troubles, which had always dogged him, increased so that in June, 1891, he had to take James away from Clongowes.

The family also moved nearer to Dublin, and through the good offices of an influential Jesuit, Father John Conmee, James was able to attend Belvedere College, a day-school, without fee. At Belvedere, the boy's early promise seemed to fade except that his skill in English composition, and his flair for foreign languages quickly attracted attention. In the examinations at the end of his final year, he did badly in all subjects but English, his composition brought him a prize of £4 and the comment of the examiner that "it was publishable".

From Belvedere Joyce passed to University College, Dublin. Here he read for a degree in English, and also studied French and Italian literature. In 1900 he wrote an article on Ibsen's *When We Dead Awaken*, which was accepted by the *Fortnightly Review*, and drew from the famous Norwegian playwright the acknowledgment:

"I have read the very kind review by Mr James Joyce for which I would like to thank the author if only I had a sufficient knowledge of English."

Returning from a visit to London on the proceeds from the Ibsen article, Joyce wrote a play called *A Brilliant Career*, which he sent to William Archer, editor of the *Fortnightly Review* for his opinion. Archer replied that while he did not think it was a success as a play, he believed that Joyce had "talent—possibly more than talent".

Joyce graduated from University College in 1902, and since he was toying with the idea of making medicine his career, he entered himself at St Cecilia's medical school.

Having done so, he decided to make himself known to Dublin's literary circles, which at this time embraced such considerable writers as Yeats and Moore, Lady Gregory and George Russell, Douglas Hyde, Synge and the young Padraic Colum. To launch himself, he called upon Russell, with whom he had long conversations, and in October, through Russell, he met Yeats, a meeting which ended with Joyce telling the famous poet, "We have met too late. You are too old for me to have any effect on you."

Not long after entering the medical school, Joyce found himself in financial difficulties which he could not resolve. Somewhat impetuously, he decided to leave the school and seek admission to the Faculté de Médecine in Paris, where he hoped to support himself by teaching English. He also arranged to be sent books for review from the editor of the *Daily Express*.

Joyce arrived in Paris early in December, 1902. His stay there was short, for in April, 1903, he was called home by the approaching death of his mother. He had experienced grave difficulties in Paris, and, in fact, had not the money for the fare back to France had he desired to go.

In Dublin he made the acquaintance of Oliver St John Gogarty, who befriended and helped him. For a time, in 1904, the two young men lived together in a martello tower.

During this year Joyce met a young girl, Nora Barnacle. Having, by September, 1904, decided that he wanted to be a writer and that he must escape from Ireland, he asked Nora to go away with him, and she agreed. He borrowed money from whoever would lend to him, and scraped enough together to get them both to Paris. In Paris he raised sufficient to take them on to Zurich, where he understood there to be a job waiting for him in the Berlitz School of

Languages. There was no job, however, in Zurich, but he was told there was one in Trieste.

Arrived in Trieste, he was greeted with the same news—no vacancy in Trieste, but there was one in a new school at Pola, in Istria. Here in Pola, the Joyces' first child was born.

In the spring of 1905 Joyce was invited to join the Trieste school, and for the next ten years he and Nora Barnacle—they had not married—made their home there.

During this time Joyce had been working on a collection of stories, given the title of *The Dubliners*, and a "novel of sixty-three chapters", *Stephen Hero*. By the end of 1905 he had completed *The Dubliners*, which he sent to Grant Richards, a London publisher, who accepted it. Richards' printers, however, made objections to certain passages as likely to cause trouble with the law, and since Richards could not afford to risk trouble he asked Joyce to make changes, which Joyce refused to do. After a long and acrimonious argument Richards finally decided he could not publish, and as other publishers took the same view, and Joyce refused to make changes, the book was shelved.

By 1914 Joyce had converted *Stephen Hero* into *A Portrait of the Artist as a Young Man*. In December, 1913, he had received a letter from an American friend of Yeats, called Ezra Pound. Pound explained that he was connected with two impecunious English reviews, of which the *Egoist* was one, and he wondered if Joyce had anything to send him.

Joyce sent him what he had completed of *A Portrait*; Pound recognized the quality of the novel; and from this moment established Joyce more or less as his protégé. He persuaded the *Egoist* to serialize *A Portrait*.

This was the first true break-through, and on its heels Grant Richards asked if he might reconsider *The Dubliners*. He undertook to publish, and the book appeared in June. It at once established Joyce's reputation, though strangely in its first year it sold only 259 copies. *A Portrait* was even more enthusiastically received, but it marked the end of Joyce's first phase.

Since 1907 he had been planning *Ulysses*, and in August, 1914, just as war was breaking out, he began work on the book, and upon a play entitled *Exiles*.

The outbreak of war did not cause the Joyces to leave Trieste, and they remained there until the Italians declared war on the Central Powers in May, 1915. The family then moved to Zurich, where they lived until 1920. Then after a final return to Trieste, where he had hoped to take up his old job and the threads of his old life but found he could not settle, in his restlessness he decided to visit Paris for a week. He remained there for twenty years.

Finding a publisher for *Ulysses* was even more difficult than finding one for *The Dubliners* and *A Portrait* had been, for according to the legal definition of the term, large parts of it were obscene. However, an American literary journal, *The Little Review*, under-took to bring it out in instalments, and these, beginning in March, 1918, continued to appear at fairly regular intervals until December, 1920, when the *Little Review* was prosecuted and suppressed on account of the *Ulysses* material. It was quite impossible for English publishers to produce the book, and eventually, in 1922, the complete work was published in Paris by Sylvia Beach, an American, whose famous bookshop there was the rendezvous of all the great literary figures of the time.

For some years, besides suffering from a chronic penury, Joyce had also been in very poor health. His eyes gave him great trouble, and early in the 1920s glaucoma and inevitable blindness threatened.

On 20 March, 1923, he began work on a new book, *Finnegan's Wake*, which was to take nine years to complete. It was published in sections under various titles while it was being written, but the whole text was not published until 1939.

This was to be Joyce's last work. Poverty, illness and the publishing conventions both in England and the United States had continued to mar his personal life and retard the recognition which he merited. By degrees, however, the superb self-confidence which he had in his work was justified by a steadily rising reputation, and before he died in January, 1941, after a very brief final illness resulting from a perforated duodenal ulcer, in Zurich, whither he had returned on the fall of France, he had had the satisfaction of finding himself the centre of a cult and of a controversy, both of which still exist.

T. S. Eliot once remarked that Joyce was the greatest master of the English language since Milton. It may not always be possible for the reader to agree with this redoubtable assessment. Nevertheless, it cannot be denied that with *The Dubliners* he established himself as a master of the short story and with *A Portrait* an equal master of the novel.

A Portrait paved the way for *Ulysses*. Written from the point of view of the central character, it is Joyce's first full-length essay in the stream-of-consciousness technique which he employed, as we indicated at the beginning of this account, to discover the secrets of the human process.

Ulysses is the story of a day in the lives of three Dubliners—Stephen Dedalus, Leopold Bloom and Bloom's wife, Molly. As the title implies, it has a parallel with Homer's *Odyssey*, though the parallel is at times somewhat obscure. Divided into eighteen episodes, each composed with a different and special technique, the book, however, is closely knit by a most elaborate network of motifs subtly recurring. The stream of fragmentary thoughts and feelings of each of the three main characters is vividly rendered by a device known as the "interior monologue" (though it is suggested that "silent monologue" would be a closer translation of the French term —*monologue intérieur*—from which it is taken, and would more closely indicate its nature).

Joyce's first interior monologue was inserted at the end of *A Portrait*, where, however, he makes it seem less extraordinary by having Dedalus write it in a diary. There it had a dramatic justification, for Dedalus could no longer communicate with anyone in Ireland but himself. By sentence fragments and ostensibly casual connexions among thoughts, it relaxed the more formal style of most of the rest of the narrative. In *Ulysses*, Joyce eliminated the diary, and allowed thoughts to hop, step, jump and glide, in their apparent disconnexion cumulatively revealing the innermost depths of experience.

Ulysses closes with Molly Bloom's famous "monologue between sleeping and walking". *Finnegan's Wake* was to treat of the sleeping mind, and was planned as a kind of sequel, a kind of extension of the experimentation of *Ulysses*. In it, however, Joyce carried his experiments to such extremes that to many, even among his most devout admirers, much of it was meaningless.

The theme is the death and resurrection, the fall and regeneration of man. The characters move about in a dream world in which any characters, events, times and places may dissolve into one another. The permutations of dream and myth give unity to all human experience, and Joyce's use of sound and rhythm, and his word-technique endlessly blending meaning with meaning and illusion with allusion in several languages, is apt to leave one floundering in a kaleidoscope of possible interpretations.

With Joyce's death following so closely upon the publication of *Finnegan's Wake*, it is not surprising that for many years his work should have stood for the ultimate in obscurity in modern literature. Maybe *Finnegan's Wake* will never be wholly understood, but it is now generally accepted that T. S. Eliot's assessment is not far wide of the mark.

Franklin Delano Roosevelt
1882-1945

MARCH the fourth, 1933, was a day of crisis: bankruptcy faced the people of the United States of America. All over the country, a rising flood of panic-stricken men and women crowded the bank counters demanding to withdraw savings. The banks' customers wanted to put their savings away under the mattress, in the jam jar, up the chimney, anywhere rather than have them engulfed, lost, in this disastrous "depression". In a last-ditch attempt to stem the panic, the banks in thirty-eight of the forty-eight States closed their doors. This augmented rather than allayed the malaise which was sweeping America.

In Washington a tall, square-jawed man stood, a little stiffly, at the front of the rostrum to take his oath of office as the nation's President. He was watched by hundreds around him in the grey winter drizzle, listened to by millions on their radios. Could this new President of the United States, this man returned by the largest number of votes ever cast for any President, justify this country's faith in him? A calm, deep voice said: "I, Franklin Delano Roosevelt, do solemnly swear that I will faithfully execute the office of President of the United States and will, to the best of my ability, preserve, protect and defend the Constitution of the United States. So help me God . . ."

The strong hand—for a dozen years his hands had served their owner well, doing much of the work of crippled legs—dropped from the huge Dutch Bible before him, open at the Thirteenth Chapter of the First Epistle to the Corinthians, "Though I speak with the tongues of men and of angels, and have not charity, I am become as sounding brass or a tinkling cymbal," to grasp his stick. Three hundred years ago his ancestor from the Dutch village of Roosenvelt had brought this Bible with him to the New World settlement of Amsterdam—the New Amsterdam on the Hudson.

With difficulty, with evident pain, the big man turned from the Chief Justice who had administered the oath, to face the crowd. There was no smile, no sign of the well-known Roosevelt grin, the face was stern. A deep silence of anticipation was broken; the voice was still calm, but punching home its points, "The only thing we have to fear—is fear itself . . ."

At the end of the speech, there was silence again, but only for a moment, then a burst of wild cheering. Was this new mood to be justified? Millions of people were unemployed, farms and businesses were bankrupt, in the streets were starving people. Surely this was no time to cheer?

March, 1933, was the second crisis in Franklin Roosevelt's life, the second of the three that tested him and which he overcame. The first was his sudden, crippling and permanent paralysis at the age of thirty-nine; the third was the Second World War, the war he helped so greatly to win, yet of which he never lived to see the end.

Roosevelt was of mixed Dutch, French and English descent. His ancestor, Claes van Roosenvelt, arrived in New Amsterdam from Zeeland in 1644 (at much the same time that his maternal ancestor, Philippe de la Noye, later Delano, arrived in Massachusetts from Leyden). Twenty years later New Amsterdam fell to the English and became New York. The Roosenvelts made one small concession and changed the family name to Roosevelt. From this first Roosevelt there descended both Franklin and his fifth cousin Theodore, who was President of the United States before him, from 1901 to 1908, and whose niece Eleanor became his wife.

Franklin Delano Roosevelt was born on 30 January, 1882, at Hyde Park, the family estate outside New York, with the proverbial silver spoon in his mouth. His parents were wealthy, aristocratic, intelligent and unconventional. He was sent, despite a passion for ships and the navy, to Groton School—the Eton of America. Almost immediately afterwards he became desperately ill with scarlet fever. His parents had to rush back from a European trip. By the time they got off the ship, he was out of danger but still in quarantine. Now at this most famous school, Franklin's mother made history. On being told that if she visited him she would have to be quarantined, she went off and came back in a carriage with a ladder. This she erected against the wall of the school infirmary. For the next fortnight at fixed times each day the young, aristocratic and beautiful Mrs Roosevelt could be seen seated precariously at the top of her ladder, talking and laughing with a young man inside in his pyjamas.

From Groton, at the turn of the century, Franklin Roosevelt went to Harvard. Here one of his achievements—he showed, to his parents' dismay, considerable resource but little scholastic ability—was a journalistic scoop which earned him a place on the staff of the Harvard newspaper, *The Crimson*. Hearing that his cousin Theodore,

Vice-President of the United States, was going to pay a visit to the University, he wrote and asked if he might see him. The great man's secretary wrote back that this could be arranged after the Vice-President's lecture to Professor Lowell's class on government. Lowell had been jealously guarding the secret of this treat for his class, in order to prevent gate-crashers, but to his horror, on the morning of the visit, *The Crimson* came out with a four-column headline announcing it. By the time Lowell and his famous guest arrived at the lecture room, there was standing room only, the great man had the utmost difficulty even in reaching the platform.

Up to and including this episode Franklin had shown no interest in politics, but a few weeks later President McKinley was assassinated at the Pan-American Exposition in Buffalo and Theodore Roosevelt, as Vice-President, found himself, on 6 September, 1901, the twenty-sixth President of the United States. Theodore was a Republican, a member of the party to which so many Roosevelts, originally Democrats to a man, had switched at the time of the Civil War, when the South was Democrat. Franklin Roosevelt's branch had remained true to the original party, but, though he and his now illustrious cousin differed in political belief, the mere fact of having him in the White House aroused in the younger man an interest, a curiosity, in the affairs of government—if only to question the more conservative views of the President.

In 1904 young Roosevelt graduated from Harvard and moved to Columbia Law School in New York for his post-graduate studies. For years his only feminine companion had been his shy, gawky cousin Eleanor, and now, a few weeks after his graduation from Harvard, they announced their engagement. The wedding, in New York in the spring of 1905, was on St Patrick's Day, to enable the bride's uncle and godfather to give her away. In his capacity as President of the United States, Theodore was coming to New York to inspect the St Patrick's Day parade and he had decreed that he would make the visit serve both purposes. Apart from the drowning of the parson's words by the singing of "The Wearing of the Green" in the street outside, the ceremony passed off without a hitch and the bride and groom settled in New York. Franklin Roosevelt quietly continued his law studies.

He was admitted to the Bar in 1907 and joined a firm of New York lawyers. At this stage of his life—he was twenty-five—he still had no intention of entering politics, a game regarded in the United States at that time as undignified, not quite honest. He was interested in it, but he had no intention of throwing his hat into the ring.

Suddenly, in 1910, the Democratic Party in New York State found themselves in difficulty. They needed a candidate for the State Senate and, for the first time ever, none was forthcoming. No Democrat had won the seat for twenty-eight years, it was a lost cause, but hitherto candidature had always appealed to someone. Yet for the prestige of the party, it was important that a candidate, young and respected if possible and sufficiently resilient not to mind losing—should contest the seat—and so they asked Franklin Roosevelt to stand. Laughing, he asked for twenty-four hours to think it over and then, deciding the campaign might prove valuable experience for a young lawyer, he accepted nomination.

As with everything he had ever done, he put his heart and soul into the contest, and on 8 November, 1910, a very surprised Franklin Roosevelt was elected to the State Senate in Albany.

By the Presidential election of 1912, politics had got into his blood. He had developed a respect for the quiet, idealistic Governor of New Jersey, Woodrow Wilson, and when Wilson chose to stand for nomination as President, Roosevelt went to the Democratic Convention in Baltimore to support him. Here he had one of his first experiences of the rough and tumble of American politics, and found he could be as tough as the next man. He learnt that the supporters of one of Wilson's opponents, "Champ" Clark, were proposing to sway the vote by storming the Convention with a hundred men wearing Clark badges, shouting "We want Clark!" and to this end they had bribed the doormen to let in anyone wearing a Clark badge. Roosevelt went out and rounded up two hundred opponents of Clark, armed them with buttons saying "Clark for President" and got them past the doormen. Once inside, their roars of "We want Wilson" completely drowned the outnumbered cries of "We want Clark!" Wilson received the nomination.

He was duly elected, and three days before his inauguration as President, the grateful Democratic leaders asked the young Roosevelt if he would like a post in the new Government. He refused, but when Josephus Daniels, the Secretary of the Navy, asked if he would care to be his Assistant, his love of the sea and ships overcame him and he agreed. On 17 March, 1913, the eighth anniversary of his wedding, he took the oath of office as Assistant Secretary of the Navy. He and Eleanor and the children moved to Washington.

Here, much as his contemporary, Churchill, was doing across the Atlantic, he threw himself into the business of making a modern navy out of an out-of-date, neglected one. He scrapped the ageing "battle wagons", built new ones, converted the navy yards from jack-of-all-trades repair shops into major industrial plants, each specializing in the manufacture of certain equipment: radio equipment from Brooklyn, chains and anchors from Boston, ton after ton of paint from Norfolk. One of the first things the young Assistant Secretary did was teach the Navy to swim. A large proportion of the personnel came from the interior of the country and had never seen the sea: alarming numbers of sailors were being drowned each year. Roosevelt issued an order that every recruit would be able to swim before being posted to a ship, and then donated a cup to be awarded annually to the ship with the highest score in the "Roosevelt Test"—an eighteen-foot dive from the deck, followed by a hundred yards in the sea. By this time the United States entered the war in 1917, the efficiency and modernity of its fleet—to say nothing of the buoyancy of its sailors—owed everything to Franklin Roosevelt.

In 1920 the Democrats nominated him as Vice-Presidential candidate to stand with Governor Cox of Ohio, whom they had nominated to succeed the now unpopular Wilson as President. But the tide had so turned against Wilson's party that, at the election, the Republicans romped home and Harding became President, with Coolidge, not Roosevelt, his Vice-President. Having resigned his post with the Navy in order to campaign, Roosevelt found himself, for the first time in ten years, entirely out of politics. He had few regrets: he was able to settle down at last as a lawyer, to his planned life's work.

Up to now his careers, both of them, had been a tale of almost unbroken success. He had worked hard, but as he cheerfully admitted, there had been luck in all his achievement. Now, disaster struck—the first of the three crises. In August, 1921, when he was on holiday with Eleanor and the five children on the island of Campobello, off the coast of Maine, he went swimming in the ice-cold water of the Bay of Fundy. The chill which followed lowered his resistance to poliomyelitis—which at that period was almost endemic in the hot summer months—and after a month of pain and critical illness he was left, undaunted and optimistic—but paralysed from the waist down. His mother, as devoted now as she had been all those years before on the top of her ladder at Groton, implored him to return to the family home at Hyde Park where she could look after him through the years of helplessness she was certain lay ahead. But Roosevelt refused to accept defeat; in this Eleanor backed him to the hilt. He returned to his office on crutches.

His political days were not over. When "Al" Smith, the Governor of New York and an old personal friend, asked him to be his campaign manager while he stood for the Democratic Presidential nomination, Roosevelt agreed. Despite a brilliant, wildly applauded nomination speech by Roosevelt, on crutches, Smith, on the 103rd ballot, just failed to get the nomination. He was re-elected, instead, Governor of New York—but by now Franklin Roosevelt knew that his own physical handicap could not, would not, stand in his way.

Immediately after the campaign, he received a note from an old, half-forgotten friend, the philanthropist George Peabody, telling him of a small place in Georgia called Warm Springs whose waters were rumoured to help paralysed people. He took a few days off from his work and went down there, to find a run-down holiday resort with decrepit cottages, a hotel and a swimming pool fed by warm springs. The pool, he was proudly told, stayed day and night, summer and winter, at "exactly eighty-nine degrees Fahrenheit".

To his delight, a swim in it, using his powerful arms to drag himself forward and keep himself afloat, made the legs feel stronger. He stayed as long as he could. A few months later, he came back. Yes, the magic worked, he was still, very gradually, improving, the legs were becoming a part of him again.

In 1927, full of enthusiasm to share his discovery with others, he organized the Warm Springs Foundation for the relief of polio and endowed it with his own money. It was not until he was convinced of the value of Warm Springs as a treatment that would work for others as well as for himself, that he enlisted aid from his friends and the general public. Then the money poured in, a million dollars and more, and the future of Warm Springs was assured.

By 1928 he was as well as ever he would be. He could drive his own car, with its hand-operated, motor-cycle-type controls, his crutches had been discarded for canes. "Al" Smith persuaded him to stand for the Governorship of New York while he, Smith tried again for the Presidency. Smith failed in his attempt, convinced now that his Roman Catholicism was against him (and indeed, until John Kennedy in 1960, no Catholic ever became President), but at the end of the year Roosevelt was elected Governor by a huge majority.

His four years as Governor of New York State covered the 1929 stock market crash and its immediate aftermath. His handling of the crisis within the State, his championing of the "forgotten man at the bottom of the economic pyramid", while it did much to incense the right wing of the Party, so moved the progressive elements in it that in 1932 he was nominated as Democratic candidate for the Presidency. In November he was elected by a landslide—his 22,813,786 popular votes were five million more than Herbert Hoover's—and in March of the next year, at the very pit of the depression, he was inaugurated.

Within twenty-four hours he had justified the country's faith in him. He surrounded himself with the best minds available and the term "Brains Trust" was coined. He declared a bank holiday from 6 March to allow panic to subside; then, in the next hundred days, with the banks on their feet, he lifted the nation out of its troubles, by its bootstraps; he took it off the gold standard; partially repealed the corrupting Eighteenth Amendment to the Constitution, which had forbidden the sale of alcohol (beer, for a start, became legal: the rest would follow in a year or two as public opinion came round); set thousands of jobless men working for the Government, making roads, planting trees; set up the Public Works Administration, the National Recovery Administration; set in train the vast, imaginative scheme of a Tennessee Valley Authority, with its huge programme of reclamation and development; in short he got the country moving as it had never moved before.

In none of this was he afraid of making mistakes, or of changing decisions once they had proved to be wrong. He made enemies, indeed, seemed to enjoy making them, but in 1936 he was returned for a second term by another huge majority. In foreign affairs he was trying, steadily and with some success, to drag the United States from its policy of isolation, the policy it had adopted after the First World War. "If war comes," he declared in 1937, "let no one imagine the United States will escape."

In September, 1939, the threatened war arrived. In November, against much opposition, Roosevelt recast the Neutrality Act so that France and Britain could buy arms on a "cash and carry" basis. In August, 1940, after Dunkirk, he gave Britain fifty destroyers in exchange for a lease of bases for his own navy's use. Despite the unpopularity of these moves with an isolationist, but steadily dwindling, core of the American public, Roosevelt was elected that year for a third term—the first President ever to embark on a ninth year in the White House. Thereupon he introduced his Lease-Lend Act. It was passed in March, 1941, and the trickle of food and munitions across the Atlantic became a flood.

In August, 1941, Roosevelt and Churchill met in mid-Atlantic to sign the Atlantic Charter, setting out their ideals of a world democracy. In all but name, the U.S.A. and Britain were allies, but it took the Japanese attack on Pearl Harbour in December to rationalize the situation. Then Roosevelt took the sweeping decision to finish off Germany before turning his country's attentions to the Japanese. On 7 November, 1942, the Americans landed in force in North Africa, and two months later Roosevelt—the first President to leave his country in time of war—flew to Casablanca to confer with Churchill and the Free French. Here, with a host of military and economic experts, they agreed to demand unconditional surrender from the Axis; there would be no inconclusive end to this fight. It was a fight, as Roosevelt put it, "between human slavery and human freedom".

The tide of war turned slowly, inexorably, in the Allies' favour, and in June, 1944, they invaded France. Roosevelt agreed to stand for yet a fourth term, and once again, in November, he was elected. One of his first acts thereafter was to outline the American plan for a world security organization, a "new and better League of Nations". By this time, with victory in sight, dangers apparently past, he had become the bogeyman of a legislature, which was hostile to his social policy. He found himself appealing over its head to the people, as in his description of the 1944 Tax Bill, which he vetoed, as relief "not for the needy, but for the greedy".

His fourth inaugural· message—delivered—on 20 January, 1945, was the first wartime one since the days of Abraham Lincoln. The strains of thirteen years in office had told on Roosevelt. He was by now a sick man. When he went, the next month, to Yalta for a final wartime conference with Churchill and Stalin, the Press photographs of the meeting showed suddenly and shockingly how spent and exhausted he was. A month after that, in March, 1945, Allied troops forced their way across the Rhine and the end of the war in Europe was near. Roosevelt never lived to see it. Desperately needing rest, he went to his beloved Warm Springs for a few days and there, on 12 April, 1945, he died of a cerebral haemhorrage.

As with Lincoln, who also died at the moment of victory, his task was complete. He had taken charge of the United States in its darkest hour, had pulled it back to self-respect and to prosperity. He had brought its vast strength, the strength of a New World which Claes Roosenvelt could never have imagined, to redress the balance of the Old, and had worn himself out in the effort.

In Britain, the Roosevelt Memorial Act empowered the Government to erect and maintain in perpetuity a statue of President Roosevelt in London. On the third anniversary of his death, on 12 April, 1948, Eleanor unveiled it in Grosvenor Square.

Clement Attlee
1883-1967

"THE great thing is never to give up." This stirring advice to the old folk of Britain by Lord Attlee when he himself was in his eightieth year, seems to sum up the character of the man. Small in stature, seemingly diffident in outward manner, modest, courteous and quiet in speech, Lord Attlee had the heart and spirit and tenacity of a British bulldog. Whatever he chose to tackle, and his achievements were formidable, he always pressed quietly onward, never faltering and never for an instant entertaining the slightest thought of giving up.

Putney, beside London's river, was his birthplace; his father a president of the Law Society; his mother an extremely active social worker. His mother, too, was young "Clem's" early teacher—at least until he was eight, when he continued his lessons under a governess before being sent to a prep school in Hertfordshire. A fellow pupil chanced to be a boy named Jowitt. Many, many years later the pair were to meet again—when Attlee had become Prime Minister and Jowitt was Lord High Chancellor in his government.

At thirteen, Attlee went to Haileybury, where he soon interested himself in the school debating and literary societies. Thence he went on to University College, Oxford, to gain a second-class honours degree in history before leaving for London to read Law.

He was called to the Bar at Inner Temple, but his interests changed suddenly when someone took him on a tour of London's dockland. He saw enough and heard enough of conditions in the East End to convince him that here was real challenge. He worked at the Haileybury Settlement in Stepney. His sense of mission was confirmed; his earlier conservative upbringing forgotten. In 1908 he joined the Fabian Society, the Independent Labour Party and the National Union of Clerks.

With Beatrice and Sidney Webb he worked vigorously for social insurance. In 1910 he became Secretary of Toynbee Hall, the social settlement in the East End run by university men. When twenty-seven he lectured on Trade Unions at Ruskin College and followed this up with a spell as lecturer and tutor in social science at the

London School of Economics. He also spoke earnestly on socialism at various gatherings and at street corners.

In spite of pacifist leanings he joined the South Lancashire Regiment in the First World War. He was a captain in 1916 and served in Gallipoli and Mesopotamia. He was wounded and on recovery transferred to the Tank Corps. His unit was among the first across the German lines in 1918. Back in the infantry he rose to be major, gained the D.S.O. and came home in 1919 to enter politics.

He became Mayor of Stepney, then chairman of the Lord Mayor's Association. Between 1919 and 1927 he was re-elected as Alderman of Stepney at every election.

He turned his thoughts towards a Parliamentary career and, in 1922, took the first step in what was to become a brilliant climb to eminence by becoming Labour M.P. for the Limehouse Division of Stepney.

Two years later he was Under Secretary for War in Ramsay MacDonald's Cabinet. In 1927, significantly in view of later developments, he went to India with the Indian Statutory Commission under the chairmanship of Sir John Simon, to investigate results of local self-government.

When a Coalition Government came into being in 1931, Attlee resigned. A tour of Spain during the civil war led him to denounce Franco and all fascists.

On the outbreak of the Second World War he declined to serve under Chamberlain, but when Winston Churchill came to power and formed a coalition, Attlee was the first Labour M.P. to be invited to join the Cabinet. The offer was accepted, Attlee becoming Lord Privy Seal, with the duty of co-ordinating departments, besides acting as Parliamentary Spokesman for the Government.

In 1942 he became Deputy Prime Minister, and in the following year Lord President of the Council and head of the Cabinet Home Affairs Committee. Towards the close of the war he was delegated by the Prime Minister to go with Anthony Eden to the San Francisco Conference. Churchill also invited Attlee to accompany him to Potsdam.

He served in the Coalition with loyalty and distinction during the difficult war years, being frequently left in sole charge of affairs while Churchill was absent on those vital missions which took him to so many parts of the world. When, in the political reversal of Parliamentary fortunes after the war, Attlee became Premier in his own right, he was able to claim an unrivalled grounding for the heavy tasks and responsibilities which lay before him. He had already proved himself to be a firm and alert chairman, a shrewd judge of people, quick to estimate character or to grasp the most intricate details in any problem. As Premier he kept his ministers perpetually on their toes, saw that no time was wasted and insisted that all must come to Cabinet meetings fully primed with all essential facts for discussion.

His Party was pledged to the nationalization of heavy industries and transport. But economic difficulties were pressing and in 1947 his Government passed the Supplies and Services (Transitional Powers) Act which authorized the control of movement of labour in addition to production and distribution. Some of his followers were impatient to press on with the Party programme, but, wisely, their leader refused to be hustled and won T.U.C. support for his postponement of the nationalization of steel.

All this time he was grappling with numerous complex overseas problems as well. It was Attlee who had to face up to the major decision regarding the future of India and her teeming millions. He did not flinch. India and Pakistan were established as independent States. Then Burma severed connexion with the Commonwealth, and franchise was granted to Malaya, Ceylon, East Africa and the Gold Coast (which changed its name to Ghana).

Attlee, indeed, had always thought in global terms, being strongly in favour of world federation with law and order being enforced where necessary by international police. He held that the hope of the world lay in making the United Nations a success. In 1945 he told the U.S. Congress: "We cannot make a heaven of our own country and have a hell outside."

Poverty, he declared, was really attributable to the failure of human beings to run their affairs for the well-being of every member of the human family. Where it seemed impractical to concede self-government, he argued, the interests of the people themselves should be paramount, and there should be equal access to markets and to raw materials for all nations.

It says a great deal for his determination and consistency that he was able to keep his Cabinet together for over six years while the socialistic programme was being actively put into execution at home. In spite of his deceptively quiet mannerisms he was able to lead even the most impetuous of his team on a steady march of progress in which a considerable proportion of industry was taken into public ownership and sweeping social service and health schemes were brought into being. Those who thought the pace was not fast enough were restrained; those who wanted to move more slowly were urged along at what Attlee deemed to be the right rate for sure progress.

He held his difficult post as Prime Minister in two successive Labour Governments between 1945 and 1951, though he changed his seat and represented West Walthamstow in his last five years in the House of Commons. High office did not change him. Throughout all his battles with national and international problems he was never seen to waver in his quiet dignity and courtesy. A discerning assessment of his great qualities was once made by the late Ellen Wilkinson who testified to his outstanding gift of clear thinking. This, she declared, enabled him to pacify an angry meeting by interposing a quietly voiced judgment on a situation.

Always shrewd and alert in council, he tended to advocate a slow but sure policy and to urge the wisdom of making headway by one step at a time. The massive volume of his positive achievements may now be recognized as full justification for the cautiousness and sense of compromise which often proved so irksome to the more impetuous and less clear-headed among his mixed political followers.

It may also be said of Attlee that he was equally capable of swift, positive action when a sudden situation demanded it. Mr John Dugdale, M.P. has told how at a few hours' notice Attlee flew to Washington for discussion with President Truman over Korea. His purpose was to dissuade the President from launching an all-out attack on China which, he argued, could have led to U.S. forces being tied down for at least ten years.

Some of Attlee's other long-distance missions have been mentioned. He went to Ottawa and to Washington for discussions on atomic energy with both Mr Mackenzie King and President Truman.

Even when he became an Earl on his retirement at the age of seventy-three, his interest in world affairs was in no way diminished. His zest was clearly evidenced by his regular attendances at the House of Lords and by his extensive travels and lecture tours.

With all these varied activities he somehow contrived to find time for authorship and published a number of books, including *The Social Worker* and *The Will and the Way of Socialism*. His autobiography appeared in the bookshops just one year before his retirement. Modestly entitled *As It Happened*, it was a straightforward record of his active public service, set forth in a matter-of-fact style which completely reflected his modest, retiring personality.

Though Attlee himself was never one to seek the limelight, or indeed, any kind of acclaim, honorary degrees were bestowed upon him by several Universities. He was an honorary D.C.L. (Oxon), and an honorary LL.D. of both Cambridge and London. He was also an Elder Brother of Trinity House. He was made a Freeman of London and the list of provincial cities which similarly honoured him grew longer and longer. It included Birmingham, Leeds, Manchester, Oxford and Aberdeen. It was unlikely that the earnest social worker who busied himself in London's East End in the early twenties ever imagined that the lowly path he had chosen for himself would one day lead to such high distinction.

When one reviews the crowded years of Attlee's long public service it is natural to ask whether he could possibly have had any home privacy. The answer is that he made a serene background for himself and his family and enjoyed the support it gave him whenever opportunity allowed. He married Violet Helen Millar when he was in his fortieth year and they had four children, Janet, Felicity, Martin and Alison. He was, indeed, a home-loving man with the simplest of tastes. He enjoyed working in his garden and also found pleasant recreation in golf and tennis. His special hobby, carpentry, was turned to practical use for he carried out repairs on well-loved favourite pipes. He described himself as an inveterate reader. He liked history and biography but could enjoy a good thriller as much as anyone.

Most people entertain some secret dream, and Lord Attlee, the self-confessed young undergraduate who forced himself to overcome his shyness and to become an active politician and twice Prime Minister of his country, was not without his. He confessed that he longed quite earnestly to become a poet, and he wrote a considerable amount of verse, including some jotted down when on active service in Gallipoli. His poetic efforts attracted little if any attention, though some of his lighter effusions were marked by flashes of incisive wit. Quite late in his life he admitted with characteristic humility that he would never realize this particular dream and that poetry writing for him could be nothing more than "just a pleasant entertainment".

This confession revealed that complete candour was among the many qualities which he has developed in his long experience of facing up to realities. If he abandoned poetic dreams he remained a man of action. In his eightieth year he cheerfully undertook an exhausting lecture tour in Japan; and he had barely returned to London before he plunged into preparations for a trip to Geneva. So he spoke with authority when he counselled those old folk never to give up!

Lord Attlee died on 8 October, 1967. His ashes are buried in Westminster Abbey, near the tomb of the Unknown Warrior.

Benito Mussolini
1883-1945

THE First World War had been fought to make the world safe for democracy, and at its end the two autocratically ruled empires in Europe—the Hapsburgs' of Austria and the Hohenzollerns' of Prussia—had disappeared. Except in Bolshevik Russia the twenties looked like being an era of constitutional monarchies, parliaments and frock-coated representative politicians. Yet by 1922, Mussolini's Blackshirts had marched on Rome and a few years later the face of the new Dictator with its huge jutting-out jaw hypnotized the Italian people. Buildings throughout Italy were covered with placards which said "Mussolini is always Right" and defined the duty of the Italian people in the words "Obey, Believe, Fight".

The man Benito Mussolini who had substituted himself and his movement for Italian democracy was born in 1883 near Predappio in the Romagna, a region in Italy known for the violent passions of its inhabitants. Mussolini's father was a blacksmith of extreme Socialist views, intelligent but lazy and incapable of supporting his family. His mother was a schoolmistress and on her meagre salary the young family of three children largely depended. The principal source of information about Mussolini's childhood and adolescence is his own autobiography, and this is without doubt too highly coloured. He was certainly a wild youth and is said to have stuck a dagger into the thigh of his first mistress in a moment of anger.

He went to Switzerland in 1902, experienced months of extreme poverty, sleeping under bridges and in public lavatories and doing a variety of ill-paid manual jobs; eventually he found worth-while employment as a trade-union organizer in Lausanne. He had read widely, hungrily almost—Marx, Schopenhauer, Nietzsche, Kropotkin, Lassalle, all the political theoreticians of the nineteenth century. He had a natural gift for writing. To an intelligent, beautiful, though humped-backed Russian exile, Angelica Balabanoff, his mind seemed confused and his philosophical views those of the last book he happened to have read. Indeed he seems to have remained consistently faithful to only one tenet—admiration for violence. Angelica Balabanoff gives a picture of him when they first met.

"In spite of his large jaw, the bitterness and restlessness in his black eyes, he gave an impression of extreme timidity. Even as he listened, his nervous hands clutching at his big black hat, he seemed more concerned with his own inner turmoil than with what I was saying."

He seemed to her, when they first met, the most wretched human being she had ever seen. He became known in Switzerland for his violent attacks on kings, priests, soldiers, bankers and the established order generally. When he came back to Italy he had the reputation of being a revolutionary who had made his mark in Switzerland and in Austria.

In Forli in the Romagna where his father and mother had an inn he became a leading Socialist, condemning above all wars and nationalism. He was elected a municipal councillor in Milan and played a prominent part in the social disturbances which took place all over northern Italy in early 1914. During this period he had several times a taste of Italian prisons.

Yet by 1915 Mussolini began to advocate the entry of Italy into the war on the side of the Allies. It was a sincerely held view and he believed that France, the home of the French Revolution, should not be allowed to be overwhelmed by German militarism. He broke with the majority of his Socialist friends and became editor and founder of the newspaper *Il Popolo d'Italia* and used to great advantage his considerable gifts as journalist. "I don't know where Mussolini is going", wrote a journalist of him at this time when he had lost his position in the Socialist Party, "but he is certainly going somewhere."

He served as a private soldier in the Bersaglieri and in 1917 was wounded badly—whilst watching a demonstration of a new mortar. Back in Milan after a long and painful convalescence he wrote: "I am proud to have reddened the road to Trieste with my blood". He is said to have used his crutches long after the need for them had gone.

In 1919 Mussolini founded his Blackshirt movement. It was fiercely nationalist, advocated workers' control of factories, an 80-per-cent capital levy and the abolition of the Stock Exchange. Joined by angry ex-soldiers and by adventurers, among them two ex-generals, De Bono and De Vecchi, Fascism had its reverses and seemed at first a movement of little substance.

The reasons for its triumph are not hard to understand. Although on the side of the victorious Powers, most Italians were shocked and angered by the Peace Treaty which deprived Italy of what she considered her rights. Italy was a poor country and had been able to stand the strain of war only thanks to loans from the Allies. These ceased. There was widespread unemployment, riots and strikes on such a scale that from 1919 to 1922, normal life seemed to have broken down. There were municipalities which sat under the Hammer and Sickle flag and, although there was never a real danger of a Communist revolution, the middle classes were terrified.

More and more Italians turned to Fascism and Mussolini was able to keep control of the various groups of people who joined. He ceased to attack the monarchy and the Church, concentrating his venom on Communists and Socialists. So great was the disorder in the country that the great liberal philosopher, Benedetto Croce, who was later to attack Fascism courageously when it was in power, believed at this time that Fascism was better than the prevailing anarchy. Arturo Toscanini stood in 1919 as a Blackshirt candidate.

There was in reality nothing so wrong with Italy that vigorous and representative governments could not have cured. But the liberals and right-wing politicians who held power were discredited and a succession of weak governments permitted the Blackshirts to terrorize their opponents and carry out all sorts of illegal activities.

Of course Fascism came undoubtedly to represent a larger part of the will of the nation than politicians such as the aged Giolitti, the man of political *combinazioni*, and his like.

King Victor Emmanuel III never liked Mussolini; but he and his advisers saw that Fascism would not only avert revolution and stop strikes but it would bring some necessary new blood into Italian politics. "He is brutal enough to restore order and intelligent enough to govern," said the King of Mussolini.

Mussolini formed at first a government which included ministers from all parties, except the Communists, though he himself was Prime Minister, Foreign Minister and Minister of the Interior. A new parliament was elected and Fascism received 62.5 per cent of all the votes cast, a respectable popular justification. Deputies asked questions about the beating up of opponents of Fascism, and the Duce and his lieutenants answered them, not satisfactorily it is true, but the decencies were preserved.

Suddenly, in 1924, a Socialist deputy, Matteotti, who was believed to have a dossier of Fascist malpractices, was murdered. Faced with the wave of indignation and disgust which swept through the nation, Mussolini talked of resigning but was dissuaded by Roberto Farinacci and his more resolute followers. It was the crisis of his career. Mussolini had almost certainly not given the order to kill Matteotti but he may have said in a moment of impatience he wished to be rid of him—as Henry II said of Thomas à Becket. He was generally considered the murderer. In fact, at the time, Mussolini was seriously considering a reconciliation with the Socialists and the murder made this impossible.

Fascism was doomed to go on without a social doctrine and taking its own slogans seriously. It was to become rapidly more of a dictatorship and more adventurous in foreign policy.

Until 1930, however, the good side of Fascism was, to the outside world at any rate, more apparent than the bad. Italy's economic difficulties grew less, the order established by the new régime encouraged industry and indeed much was done to modernize the country and improve the standard of living. Work was deified and the Duce was frequently photographed with a pick-axe or baring his hairy chest and wielding a sickle in the harvest field.

Mr Winston Churchill when he visited Rome in 1927 said if he was an Italian he would don a Blackshirt; Lloyd George thought that the Corporate State with its emphasis on the rights of labour was a promising development; and Lord Rothermere thought Mussolini the greatest statesman of our time. To foreign visitors Mussolini usually appeared sensible, even rather diffident, an excellent conversationalist with a flow of original metaphors, bounding with physical and mental energy.

How long Fascism would have lasted if Mussolini had not allowed Italy to be drawn into the Second World War is a question difficult to answer. Just before his death, Mussolini, in one of his grim monologues to which he was addicted, said there is only one definition of Fascism:

"It is Mussolini-ism. Let us not delude ourselves. As a doctrine, Fascism contains nothing new. It is a product of the modern crisis— the crisis of man who can no longer remain within the bounds of the existing laws. One could call it irrationalism."

The economy of Italy was mismanaged by Fascism, though not so grossly as to provoke a profound reaction among the people. The new men who held power, the hierarchs of the movement, were mostly corrupt; too many bureaucrats and their friends and clients took their share of the credits of the great schemes launched by the State for land reform or settlements in Africa. Mussolini built motor-roads, made the railways run to time and constructed great liners. The poor Italian people benefited little and could not afford to pay for the electricity so plentifully provided.

Mussolini never understood this and was in many ways the

victim of his entourage. He little knew that, when he had inspected squadrons of Savoia Machettis, the pride of his air force, in Naples, these squadrons hastily took off to put themselves on show again at the next airfield he was inspecting.

Mussolini, himself, was disinterested in money matters. He lived with his wife Rachele, like himself from the Romagna, and his children in a wing of the Villa Torlonia in Rome and in a most frugal manner, sending his children to state schools. He was a devoted family man, treated his wife with great kindness and sympathy and adored his children—Edda (who married Count Ciano who became his foreign minister), Vittorio, Bruno and Romano. With all that, he had innumerable mistresses whom on the whole he treated with a certain brutality. Until the war, and his liaison with Claretta Petacci, his love affairs were largely hidden from the general public. In the case of Claretta Petacci (the liaison lasted seven years until their death together) scandal rose because Mussolini allowed the Petacci family to profit from their connexion with him. But it was not he who paid for Claretta's luxurious dresses and scents—the Roman shop-keepers did that—nor for her luxurious bedroom lined with glass with its black marble bathroom. When he was shown this bedroom, he was asked if he liked it and answered "Not much".

If Fascism had been altogether Mussolini's it would have been a more spartan régime with a much better social conscience. But "Mussolini-ism" could not live in peace. The idea of war as the natural state of man was the corollary of Mussolini's glorification of violence. Italy had to conquer. Mussolini would have had to be a much wiser statesman, if, animated as he was by a desire for Italian greatness, he could have avoided the fatal alliance with Hitler.

Mussolini associated Italy with Britain and France in efforts to keep peace and at the same time, he attempted to urge on them the need for alleviating some of the unjust hardships imposed on the vanquished Powers. It was Mussolini's armies on the Austrian frontier which prevented Hitler interfering in Austria in February, 1934.

Mussolini's first impressions of Hitler were unfavourable; "he is just a garrulous monk", he stated. After the Ethiopian war and the institution against Italy by the League of Nations of sanctions (which in the event were supported only in a half-hearted manner by the British and French governments), Mussolini acquired three things— a conviction of his own military might, for the war had gone well, better than expected; a thorough-going contempt for the Western democracies whose opposition he regarded as treacherous and at the same time feeble, thus reinforcing his views about the non-virile nature of democratic countries; and a belief that Italy could gain great advantages from a German alliance.

When in 1938 Hitler invaded Austria, Mussolini acquiesced. Austria whom Mussolini had called in 1934 "a bastion of Mediterranean civilization to be saved at all costs from Pan-Germanism" had now become "an ambiguity to be removed from the map".

After the Anschluss and the alliance with Hitler, the alienation of the Italian people from the Fascist régime really began. Mussolini's popularity was at its height in 1936 when he announced the triumphant ending of the Ethiopian war. It began to wane when he became more Germanophile and introduced the goose-step into the Italian Army. The aid given to Franco was unpopular and indeed the 50,000 troops, including an armoured division, which Mussolini sent to Spain did not exactly cover themselves with glory. His popularity had a slight recovery in 1939 when he announced that Italy would not enter the war on the side of Germany.

When, in 1940, Italy entered the war disaster was ahead. Lack of serious preparation became apparent to everyone. The defeat of the huge Italian force in the African desert by Wavell's much smaller army in 1940 was matched by the humiliation of defeat by the Greeks in the rash invasion of their homeland which Mussolini mounted without consulting the Germans, largely because the Germans hadn't informed him about the Nazi take-over in Rumania.

Mussolini's health and vigour deteriorated in adversity. The German alliance had been hated not only by the people but by the King. In July, 1943, a meeting of the Fascist Grand Council passed a resolution demanding that Mussolini give up to the King the command of the armed forces which he had assumed at the beginning of the war. Mussolini, suffering from severe stomach trouble, made an ineffective showing at this meeting. However he believed he could overcome all opposition and he was comforted by this belief when, the next day, he went to acquaint the King with what had happened at the Grand Council. He was arrested. He was taken first to Sardinia and then to Elba and finally imprisoned in a small hotel on the peak of the Abruzzi Mountains—the Gran Sasso—which could only be reached by a funicular railway. There he learnt that Italy had asked for an armistice and accepted a condition that he was to be handed over to the Allies.

In one of the most dramatic events of the war, a German parachute captain, Skorzeny, landed an aeroplane on the Gran Sasso and rescued Mussolini, who was taken to Germany. Hitler, after an emotional welcome, made it clear to Mussolini that Italy was now a subject State and that at the end of the war would have to give up the German-speaking provinces of northern Italy to the Reich. A new Fascist government was set up in northern Italy and Mussolini was to head it. At first Mussolini refused but later accepted and came, as he said, "to take Hitler's instructions". One of these was the trial and execution of all the Fascist Grand Council traitors then in German hands—including Mussolini's son-in-law Count Ciano. These executions were carried out at Verona.

Mussolini's government was set up at Saló, a small town on Lake Garda. The slogans of this puppet administration marked a return to the old socialist ideals of Fascism, but the government had practically no effect and its only active branch was the repressive squads of Blackshirts who captured and tortured Italian partisans. At Saló Mussolini was joined by his family and also by Claretta Petacci. He had now lost his grip and spent much of his time theorizing and playing the violin.

Mussolini, when the Americans were fast coming near Milan, intended to try to come to terms with the Italian partisans, and even met the partisan commander, General Cadorna. Then he learnt that the German garrisons in northern Italy were going to surrender and decided on flight. He had thought of a last stand in the mountains to preserve his myth: unfortunately his ministers could not find two dozen Blackshirt troops to share in this heroic gesture. Mussolini joined a small German convoy together with a fleet of cars which contained his ministers and Claretta Petacci. This was stopped by partisans at a lonely defile called, strangely enough, Musso. The German commander was not anxious to fight; he wanted only to get his men and vehicles back to Germany. Mussolini, although disguised in a German greatcoat and travelling in a German lorry, was recognized and arrested.

The Italian partisan commander, Count Bellini Delle Stelle, was anxious to deliver him safe and sound to the National Liberation Committee in Milan. He feared German rescue parties or Americans might take charge of Mussolini. There was some confusion; Mussolini's place of captivity was twice changed and on the second night after his capture he was joined by Claretta Petacci at a mountain farm. Meanwhile a certain Colonel Valerio, a communist, came from Milan to see, on the order of the Communist Party, that Mussolini was killed as soon as possible.

With some difficulty Colonel Valerio convinced the partisan

commander at Dongo of his authority. He fetched Mussolini and Claretta Petacci from the house where they were staying on the pretence that he was rescuing them. Some few miles away from the house they were both shot. Their bodies, together with those of some sixteen other Fascist leaders, were taken to Milan in a removal van. There the bodies of Mussolini and Claretta together with a number of other Fascists were hung up feet first where a number of Italian partisans had recently been executed by the Germans. The bodies after being subjected to all sorts of indignities were buried with numbered stakes and identity marks in a cemetery called (again a strange coincidence) Musocco.

When looking, today, at photographs or old newsreels of Mussolini and seeing him in his super-man postures, it is difficult to imagine that he impressed and overawed a people as intelligent as the Italians. Hitler, ranting, is still sinister; Mussolini merely comic. Of course, the living Mussolini possessed that exceptional amount of vital energy and that instinctive cunning or perspicacity which all who excel in politics must possess. But he was overmuch a *Comediante*. Unlike Hitler, he was not a wholly detestable man and he had some good human qualities. He was an affectionate father and in many ways a good husband. He had generous instincts. He could see through himself but, unfortunately, he lacked the moral strength to allow his flashes of self-criticism to affect his conduct. At Saló he once said in a conversation about the merits of contemporary statesman, "I am not really a statesman at all; I am more like a mad poet." Even there, he was over-praising himself and should have said journalist instead of poet. He was the victim of his own defects—his histrionic vein, his superficiality and his vanity. Unfortunately these defects brought much destruction to his country and despair to his people.

Bernard Law Montgomery
1887-1976

"The battle which is about to begin will be one of the decisive battles of history. It will be the turning point of the war. The eyes of the world will be on us, watching anxiously which way the battle will swing. We can give them their answer at once. It will swing our way. We have first-class equipment; good tanks; good anti-tank guns; plenty of artillery and plenty of ammunition; and we are backed by the finest air striking force in the world. All that is necessary is that each one of us, every officer and man, should enter the battle with the determination to see it through—to fight and to kill—and, finally, to win.

"AND LET NO MAN SURRENDER SO LONG AS HE IS UNWOUNDED AND CAN FIGHT.

"Let us all pray that the Lord Mighty in Battle will give us the victory.

"B. L. Montgomery, Lieutenant-General, G.O.C.-in-C., Eighth Army."

THE Battle of El Alamein, for which this was "Monty's" Order of the Day, was fought according to his plan, and although it was fought more bitterly than he or anyone else had imagined, it was, as he had prophesied, the turning point of the war. The Lord gave him the victory. Outwardly, Monty remained unmoved, and his reputation for ruthlessness, which had preceded him from England, grew fast, but no one could deny that within a few weeks of his Alamein assault, the Axis Armies had collapsed. Thousands upon thousands of Italians, exhausted, uncomprehending, gave themselves up while the rest of their compatriots—preceded by the Germans, who had taken all the available transport—tore off in wild retreat across the desert.

Although there was much hard fighting ahead, two and a half years of it before the German nation surrendered, this *was* the turning point. Until October, 1942, the Allies had been on the retreat everywhere, scoring a tactical success here, a gallant defence there, but slipping back.

The man who is given most of the credit for El Alamein was born

Bernard Law Montgomery, the son of the vicar of St Mark's Church in Kennington, a poor parish in south London, on 17 November, 1887. His was a prosperous Anglo-Irish family from Donegal and Bernard's father, a younger son, had been ordained, as was so often the custom, into the Church of England.

In 1889, when Bernard was not quite two, the Reverend Henry Montgomery was consecrated Bishop of Tasmania—and set off for the remotest corner of the globe with his wife and five small children. They arrived at Hobart in October, just as the southern summer was beginning, and found a sleeping country town, as beautiful as anything they had seen—but their happiness was utterly destroyed within a month by the death of the oldest daughter, Queenie.

Mrs Montgomery was determined to retain the family's English culture; she decided that only a school run by herself would do for the children. Tutors and governesses were brought out from England to help her. A few carefully chosen children from Hobart were invited to attend the Montgomery school, but a strict watch was kept on the family to see it picked up no Colonial habits, no sloppy Colonial speech. In later years Lord Montgomery was to recall being made to stand in a corner and repeat, again and again, with its correct "English" intonation, any word he had mispronounced.

In 1901, when Bernard was thirteen, Henry Montgomery was asked to resign his Bishopric and take charge of the Society for Propagation of the Gospel, in London. They took a large house at Chiswick, on the Thames near London, and Bernard and his older brother entered St Paul's School in Hammersmith. The transition from Hobart to Hammersmith was not entirely happy, the boys had no knowledge of organized sport, they pined for the open air, the sunshine of Tasmania, and Bernard, at least, had less than a schoolboy's interest in reading or music or painting. Yet within a month they had settled into their new life. Soon Bernard distressed his mother by expressing a desire to go to Sandhurst and become an Army officer. Reluctantly, the family agreed.

Bernard passed into Sandhurst at eighteen. Here the quiet, reserved, determined boy seemed to develop a slightly immature attitude which he never lost. He was to write without shame, half a century later, of having joined a gang of cadets who went round bullying boys they didn't like: one of their victims, to whose shirt they gleefully set fire, had to be admitted to hospital. The same attitude reappears in Montgomery's desert campaign, much of the driving force of which was supplied by an active, personal desire to grind the German Rommel into the earth: Rommel's picture was always with him:

he would sit and stare at it, pondering his next move. When Rommel had been defeated his successor's picture went up on the wall of the Montgomery caravan.

Passing out of Sandhurst at the age of twenty-one Montgomery was commissioned into the Royal Warwickshire Regiment. His first posting was with the 1st Battalion to India. As he didn't dance, bet, smoke or drink—apart from an occasional glass of port—the relaxed life of peacetime soldiering in that land appealed very little to him. He had few regrets when the battalion was posted home.

In October, 1914, he was with his battalion in France and badly wounded in a charge. A bullet passed through his lung: as he lay gasping a soldier who ran to his rescue, was shot through the head and died instantly, falling on Montgomery and remaining there for three hours before a burial detail came to dig graves for them both. Montgomery managed to show himself to be alive and was removed on a stretcher. For his gallantry in the charge he received the D.S.O., for his wound he got a posting to England, but in 1917 he was back, on the Staff. A year later, at the end of the war, he had risen to Lieutenant-Colonel as General Staff Officer, Grade One.

Like every Regular officer, he was demoted in the peacetime army. He held a succession of junior posts and attended the Staff College in Camberley. At Camberley he did so well that, in 1926, after another spell of Regimental soldiering, he was made an instructor.

With the straightforward, unemotional approach that was to characterize almost everything he did in life, he decided to get married. To this end he planned a holiday in Switzerland, where, he felt, one would be likely to meet—and all in one place—suitable English girls who might be pleased, in a foreign land, at meeting a compatriot. The plan was successful; he met a young widow, Betty Carver, and despite the doubts of his friends and hers—the girl was artistic, she painted, she couldn't have been less like Bernard, and she had two small children—they married in the summer of 1927. A year later their only child was born, a son whom they christened David. They were extremely happy.

By 1930, twelve years after the end of the war, Lieut-Col. Montgomery had regained the rank he held at its close. As C.O. of a battalion of the Warwickshires he was sent to Palestine, to Egypt and to India. By 1937 he was home again, promoted to the command of a brigade.

Then came tragedy. His wife, after the three of them had spent a day bathing, was scratched by something in the water. The scratch was painful and by the time Montgomery and David got her to their house in Portsmouth, her leg had swollen badly. The pain was mounting steadily and the doctor who was summoned diagnosed the condition as septicaemia—for which, in the days before penicillin, there was no cure. There was nothing for it but to amputate. Though this was done, it could not prevent the infection spreading to the rest of her body. Montgomery was already planning ways in which Betty's life as a cripple could be made bearable, but even as he prepared to get her the finest wheelchair in Britain, she died.

During their short span of ten years together, they had been idyllically happy, and Montgomery took a long time to recover from the shock of his wife's death. There was no question of marrying again; such a happiness could not be repeated.

A month after the outbreak of the Second World War he was again promoted, given the command of the 3rd Division and sent to France as a Major-General. After Dunkirk he returned, to find his house had been bombed, every one of his possessions destroyed.

It was when Monty became a Corps Commander that his peculiar characteristics first became apparent. Laziness and inefficiency had always appalled him. Now many a junior commander found himself summoned before the presence to be told, "You're one hundred per cent useless to me—you'll have to go. I'm sorry." Those that remained were ordered out on cross-country runs to get fit. Thereafter, all over southern England, overweight and elderly officers could be seen panting across fields in running shorts and plimsolls. From time to time Monty would summon the officers under his command to an empty cinema in a country town and address them on the state of the war, two hours or more without notes, sometimes ending up with a few sharp words on venereal disease.

In the summer of 1942, his chance came. News from Egypt was bad, General Auchinleck's armies had been driven almost completely from the desert, they were holding a line at El Alamein, a last-ditch defence of the Suez Canal. Churchill decided to replace both Auchinleck as C.-in-C. Middle East and General Ritchie as commander of the 8th Army. General Alexander was ordered to the first job, General Gott to the second, but Gott's aircraft was shot down. Churchill sent for Montgomery.

Under his command the 8th Army, as we have seen, won a brilliant victory, first repelling the Germans at Alam Halfa in September and then, after a build-up of strength, attacking at El Alamein in November to drive the Germans and Italians from Egypt and, by the following spring, out of Africa.

Although Montgomery conducted the campaign in his own way, building his army up to a fever pitch of loyalty to himself before doing so, much of the plan had been thought out by Auchinleck. The 8th Army had—for the first time in any battle of the Second World War—a huge material advantage in manpower, tanks and artillery. Even so to Montgomery must go the credit for knitting a tired, defeated army into a weapon of great strength and precision, an army which, like its commander (who usually affected either a Tank Corps beret or an Australian slouch hat, to neither of which he was entitled) wore the clothes it liked. The suede shoes and coloured scarves may have been a sort of uniform for Monty's private club, but they contributed much to morale and so to the fighting efficiency of the 8th Army. Montgomery's own régime remained what it had been throughout his career. Tea was brought by his batman at 0600 hours; there followed an hour's thinking in bed; after breakfast a tour of his command started at 0830. He returned by tea-time and from then until dinner worked on his plans and gave his orders. By 2100 he was in bed.

After Alamein he was knighted, but the campaign went on, and in March, 1943, he defeated Rommel's reinforced army at the battle of the Mareth Line and shortly after this captured the Tunisian ports of Gabes, Sfax and Sousse. Here a characteristic action did much to ruffle Anglo-American relations. General Eisenhower's Chief-of-Staff had jokingly suggested that if Monty got to Sfax by a certain date he would give him a four-engined Flying Fortress with an eight-man American crew. Montgomery arrived before time and demanded his prize. In vain did the Americans protest that it had all been a joke: Monty demanded his Flying Fortress, and he got it.

After the Sicily landing in the summer of 1943, the Allies, with Montgomery still in command of his 8th Army, pressed on into the Italian mainland. Early in September the Italians signed an armistice, but the Germans continued to fight. At first the Allied campaign went well. The Germans were compelled to regroup and to prepare to hold a firm defensive line. If Montgomery can fairly be accused of having luck on his side, this is probably the occasion when it played its biggest part. He was in Italy while things were going well and then, just as they started to bog down, he was recalled to a special post in London, under General Eisenhower, planning the next year's assault on the Continent through Normandy. He left Italy, a few days after Christmas 1943, an acknowledged hero, having led his Army for a year in a lightning campaign across North Africa and halfway up Italy, without a single failure.

He set up H.Q. in his old school, St Paul's, and devoted himself to the plan. When it was ready he spent his days furiously visiting units in southern England. His eagerness to be recognized, his readiness to be photographed, made him a number of enemies among his contemporaries, but there is no doubt that Monty performed prodigies in building up the loyalty and enthusiasm of the units under his command.

In June, 1944, the Allied Armies landed in Normandy, led by Montgomery under the overall command of General Eisenhower. Almost immediately there were quarrels with American generals. These were patched up by the diplomacy of Eisenhower, to whom must go much of the credit for keeping American and British forces fighting side by side with so little friction, right across France, across the Rhine, to Lüneburg Heath, where, in May, 1945, Montgomery achieved a main ambition and accepted the unconditional surrender of the German Armies.

After the war—he was already a Field Marshal—he was appointed C.I.G.S. and raised to the peerage. From 1951 to 1957, when he gave up active soldiering (though a Field Marshal is said never to retire) he was Deputy Supreme Commander of S.H.A.P.E. Always, because of a great American preponderance of forces, he was under an American general, but for these years he was a loyal and brilliant subordinate.

Since turning his back on soldiering, Field Marshal Montgomery has remained a controversial figure. The publication of his own and other people's memoirs raised storms of controversy over the conduct of each campaign, over his treatment of others taking part and over his comments on their shortcomings. He has travelled to many parts of the world as an unofficial, unaccredited and often unwanted ambassador. Fêted, as in Communist China, he has returned to put his glowing observations into print, and these have not always been taken kindly by the Press of his own country. Basically a simple man whose war-time Press conferences, full of remarks like "the chaps are in cracking shape" and "we shall hit the enemy for six", were the despair of journalists who waited in vain for facts, he is that phenomenon so often thrown up by Britain in her hour of need, the man for the job. However much he may have irritated a few of his fellow-countrymen—while remaining beloved and a hero to the rest—his name remains a legend, if only on the strength of his African and Normandy campaigns. Churchill's joke about him—which Montgomery himself enjoyed—holds more than a shade of truth: "In defeat—unthinkable. In victory—insufferable."

Thomas Edward Lawrence
1888-1935

THOMAS EDWARD LAWRENCE was born on 16 August, 1888, in Tremadoc, Wales, the illegitimate son of Sir Thomas Chapman, 7th Baronet of Westmeath in Ireland. The Baronet had run away to Wales with the governess of his older children, and changed his name to Lawrence. Sara, though fate and the laws of divorce deprived her of the chance to be a wife, was a conscientious mother and bore Thomas five sons, of whom "Ned", T. E., was the second. Ned was ten years old when he learnt the details of his birth, and the frank dislike of young, attractive women which characterized him in adult life may date from this shattering discovery, the discovery that he—the product of a moment's passion between two people he had loved and respected—was forever illegitimate. It seems certain, from remarks he made to his brothers, that he resolved at this moment to prove himself better than his fellows.

The family moved from Wales to Scotland, to the Isle of Man, to Jersey, settling eventually in Oxford, where Ned was sent to the High School and on to University.

As a small boy he had been fascinated by toy soldiers, and this hobby led gradually to an interest in castles and medieval archaeology. He went up to Jesus College in 1906, a slender youth of only five foot six with the magnificent head of a much bigger man, deep set, piercing eyes, strong chin, wide, sensitive mouth. He was soon noticed as a courageous climber of college walls, a man who would hang a hat or a flag on the highest spire while everyone slept. For his B.A. degree, he elected to write a thesis on Crusader Castles, and for this he decided to travel, during the summer vacation of 1908, through Syria and Palestine. He did so, fell in love with the Middle East and its people, and set himself to learning Arabic. Remarkably soon he had a colloquial knowledge of it. (But despite the popular belief that he could pass anywhere as an Arab, he never mastered their language: to the end, he spoke it with an English pronunciation which paradoxically endeared him to them. A suspicious people, they could be sure the man was not—seriously—pretending to be one of them.)

516

He passed his finals and was then awarded a "Research Demyship" at Magdalen College. The celebrated archaeologist, D. G. Hogarth, who was to become almost a second father to him, urged him to accept it and to use the money to join his expedition to Carchemish, the ancient Hittite city on the Euphrates, which Hogarth was excavating.

Lawrence arrived at the "dig" in March, 1911, found the work fascinating and stayed there three years. He made one visit home during this period, arriving unexpectedly at his parents' Oxford home with two young Arabs, the waterboy and the foreman from the excavation. He hired bicycles for them and together the three, in flowing Arab robes, rode wildly about Oxford, startling and shocking the inhabitants.

Back in Syria, he flung himself into his work, at the same time digging deep into the political problems of the Middle East. Already, he was becoming steeped in the Arab dream of shaking off the grip of Turkey. He decided, as he studied the map, that Damascus should be the capital of this new free Arabia, that his own life would be devoted to that dream, to putting an Arab king on his rightful Arab throne.

Meanwhile, as war drew nearer during the spring and early summer of 1914, Lord Kitchener, British Resident in Egypt, pondered on the defences of the Suez Canal. The key, to Kitchener, seemed the Sinai peninsula, which was under Turkish control and quite unmapped. In order to map it, a British expedition was mounted for the avowed and slightly ridiculous purpose of seeking the "Itinerary of the Israelites During the Forty Years in the Desert". The Turks permitted them to enter the country and much of the information brought back by the team—which included Lawrence —was hastily assembled into an Army manual. While the supplementary maps were being copied, war broke out and Lawrence, back in England, spent the rest of the year working on them.

In December, 1914, he was posted, as a junior officer, to the Information Service in Cairo. His love of toy soldiers had deserted him: he took an immediate dislike to military life and to the "fat and lazy" Army officers who seemed to infest the city and in particular Shepheard's Hotel. They in turn were shocked by this scruffy subaltern who refused to wear proper uniform, who roared round Cairo on a vulgar, noisy, motor-cycle.

The idea of sponsoring an Arab revolt against the Turks had been considered, without enthusiasm, by the British Commander-in-Chief, but Lawrence seized upon it with fervour. He obtained permission to contact the Grand Sherif of Mecca and his five sons, all descendants of the Prophet, all of enormous influence throughout the Arab world. After being in contact with each in succession, he came to the conclusion that the best for his purpose would be the Emir Feisal. He arranged to visit him at the village of Hamra and immediately the two young men struck up a friendship. Here at last, Feisal seemed to think, is an Englishman one can trust: here, thought Lawrence, is an Arab with the spirit and intelligence to lead my revolt.

Inspired by this meeting, Lawrence returned to G.H.Q. and was responsible for persuading it to support the revolt and provide arms. By refusing a half-hearted offer of British troops, he endeared himself to Allenby, the new, hard-pressed, Commander-in-Chief, Middle East, and also ensured that his own rôle in the proposed rising would be a major one. There would be no British troops in his area. He adopted Arab dress, to the annoyance of his few British colleagues, who considered it an affectation.

The record of Lawrence's dealings with Army officers of his own seniority, the few with whom he came in actual contact, is often a story of bickering and petty jealousy. To Lieut. Vickery, a regular officer of orthodox views who had the misfortune to speak far better Arabic than Lawrence and at the same time be attached to his force by G.H.Q., he behaved so waspishly that the unfortunate man had to think of a valid reason for getting posted away from his tormentor.

Allenby was a man of imagination and he supported Lawrence's plan to the hilt. His thrust was rapid: the Arabs, urged on by Lawrence, rose and captured, one by one, the Red Sea ports, taking Akaba, the final and northernmost, in July, 1916. At Wadi-el-Hesa, Lawrence led the Arab troops himself and inflicted a heavy defeat on the Turks, but after this he turned his attention to train wrecking. He had found that the Arabs were unreliable in battle, brilliant in a war of stealth: train wrecking, he reasoned, would come naturally to them. So great was his success in leading these bands of marauders who blocked lines and blew up trains, that the Turks advertised a huge reward for "El Orens, Wrecker of Engines".

Early in 1918 the raids on the railway had almost succeeded in cutting the Turkish Palestine Army's communication with Damascus, so that later in the year Lawrence was able to capture the town with his Arab forces and have the sly pleasure of holding it until the arrival of the British force, which had planned to capture it alone.

At one stage during the advance, while conducting too close a reconnaissance of a Turk-held village, he was captured. The Turks never realized who he was and he managed, according to his own account of the affair, to persuade them his light skin was Circassian. Although hideously tortured, he prided himself on not "groaning in English", which would have given him away, and was released, hours later, a bleeding wreck, just able to steal a camel and get back to his own lines. It has been suggested that the Turks knew only too well who he was, that they tortured, humiliated and then released him as an object lesson to the Arabs, but this is unlikely. There were too many rewards on his head.

It was nearly the end of the war: an armistice was signed in November. In the spring of the following year, 1919, Lawrence was called to the Paris Peace Conference, where he insisted on wearing Arab robes. Notwithstanding the mystery with which he surrounded himself, he failed in his attempt to gain Arab freedom. Turkey had been driven out, but the Allies, and France in particular, were determined to keep a foothold in the Arab world. These weeks at the Peace Conference seem to have broken Lawrence's spirit completely. After it, he sat down sadly—an utter failure in his own eyes —to write his account of the campaign. After months of work he left the manuscript in a railway carriage while changing trains and never saw it again. Undaunted, he wrote it a second time and the huge work was eventually published as *Seven Pillars of Wisdom*.

In 1921, Winston Churchill made him Adviser on Arab Affairs, and in this capacity he had the satisfaction of seeing Feisal become, if not King of the Arabs, at least King of Iraq. Even so Lawrence was still disgusted and saddened by the failure of the Allies to honour wartime pledges, ashamed of his own rôle in urging the Arabs on with promises of freedom. A year later, he entered the Air Force, to become an engine artificer under the assumed name of Ross. The widespread fame of his achievements with the Arabs resulted in the British Press discovering his whereabouts and made his position in the R.A.F. untenable. His service was terminated in 1923. Thereupon he joined the Tank Corps, which he hated, and was eventually successful, after months of correspondence with the highest in the land, in gaining permission to rejoin the R.A.F., having changed his name legally, by deed poll, to T. E. Shaw.

He served ten years with the R.A.F., was reasonably content in what he cheerfully admitted—though not to his fellow Aircraftsmen —was a form of self-abasement. He never married, and his few female friendships were with women older than himself. One of these was Mrs George Bernard Shaw, with whom for years he carried on an intellectual flirtation. After her death G.B.S., on going through her letters said ruefully; "She told Lawrence many things she never told me . . . ."

On leaving the R.A.F. Shaw finished a book on his experience of it, *The Mint*. (The R.A.F., Lawrence maintained, stamped the same pattern on all those who entered it; they were coins in a mint.) The book, from one who had gone to vast trouble to stay in the Air Force, was surprisingly bitter and was not published for many years. It seems, today, to show its author as a vain, small-minded man with a hatred of authority and a love of self-advertisement, but the picture, to those who knew him, is false: he was an exceedingly complex character, capable of great friendship, even love; a generous character, twisted with its own ambition, its love of flamboyant gesture (such as the wearing of flowing Arab robes in a Paris street). This very flamboyance helped him to become the leader he was, the man who could weld the disparate tribes and jealousies of the Arab world into a unified fighting machine.

He was killed, shortly after leaving the R.A.F., in a motor-cycle accident on 13 May, 1935, while returning from the post office to his Dorset Cottage. Two children were playing in the road: he swerved to avoid them and crashed, at eighty miles an hour.

Adolf Hitler
1889-1945

OF the great men of our time, none affected world history more violently than did Adolf Hitler. Yet Hitler was born without any advantages of birth or education. He was a soldier in the First World War but never rose beyond the rank of corporal. He never studied anything for its own sake nor achieved any degree of intellectual excellence. But he learned how to gain power over other people. His was a political genius of the highest order; and it was formed in the gutter.

Of lower middle-class origin, Adolf Hitler was born in 1889 at Braunau in Austria. He quarrelled with his father, a minor State official, because he wanted to be a painter. Having failed to get admission to an art school, he spent his adolescence and early manhood in various doss-houses in Vienna living like a tramp, painting postcards for a living. He was lazy, feckless and moody. When he earned a few shillings, he would go off and eat cream cakes in a confectioner's and read newspapers for days on end. He had no interest in women, neither smoked nor drank. His passion was talking politics and he would hang around night shelters where free soup was being distributed, sometimes getting involved in brawls.

His appearance was insignificant. He wore his hair long with the well-known lock that straggled over his forehead. He was also unforgettable to some who knew him well. His eyes had not merely the glint of fanaticism but a hypnotic power which fascinated and also made people afraid. He left Vienna for Munich in 1913, where in very slightly better circumstances he lived by peddling and painting cards. This part of his life ended in August, 1914, when he wrote a petition to King Ludwig III of Bavaria asking permission, as an Austrian to join the German Army. It was granted.

For all its triviality and sordidness, the early period of Hitler's life was of fundamental importance. Here among the *lumpen proletariat* he learnt his hates; and above all his hatred of the Jews. After the Jews he hated the "lower" races, such as the Poles and the Czechs. He hated equality in order to buttress the superiority he had to feel to those who surrounded him—tramps and casual labourers.

The politics he picked up were those that fortified his hates: nationalism, which for him was a belief in the superiority of the German race; authority—he saw how unscrupulous Viennese politicians held their power, kept their hold on the masses. He saw how the leader must rule the mob of the aimless and the criminal.

His idle life gave him leisure to read as well—works of ancient history, particularly Roman history, books on occultism, yoga and astrology. Here too he developed his ability to argue and above all to argue so as to attract the lowest type of mind. This environment taught him his basic philosophy which he expounded at the beginning of *Mein Kampf*, the basic tenet of which is that whatever position man can win it is owing to natural genius plus brutality. Vienna, Hitler said later, taught him all the profound lessons he needed to learn about men.

He made a good soldier, winning the Iron Cross, first class, in 1918. Strangely enough no official record exists to say what he won it for. His fellow soldiers found him a strange fellow, far too keen on the war and far too serious. He would harangue them occasionally, saying that the invisible foes of the German people, the Jews and Marxists, were a greater threat to victory than the enemy's guns. He never rose beyond the rank of corporal, presumably because of his eccentricity.

After the war he was employed by the Political Department of the German Army in Munich. Here he founded the National Socialist Party from a combination of various patriotic groups of working men and ex-soldiers, one headed by Julius Streicher, all thriving in the atmosphere of revolutionary and counter-revolutionary plotting which characterized the early days of the German Republic.

The French occupation of the Ruhr in 1923 was an enormous fillip to the German nationalist extremists. By then, Hitler, whose supporters then included Rosenberg and Goering, was important enough to be the main mover, with Ludendorff, in an attempted *coup d'etat* which very nearly succeeded against the Bavarian Government. Hitler spent just over two years in prison at Landsberg. It was a comfortable prison and Hitler as the leader of a Party had a room to himself. He began the composition of *Mein Kampf* a work which with its turgid repetitions is clearly that of a semi-educated man but which supplied, to those who cared to wade through it, the key not only to his thoughts but to what he was going to do. His thirty-fifth birthday was spent in prison.

From 1924 until the end of the twenties, Hitler had a hard period in rebuilding the Nazi Party, fighting off or placating rivals, and getting money for his movement from industrialists and the propertied classes.

The German Republic was doing better. The Young Plan and the Dawes Plan permitted Germany's economic recovery and unemployment fell sharply. The French moved out of the Ruhr and Germany into the League of Nations. The dark forces of German nationalism of which Hitler's was the most powerful element had to bide their time. Then came the withdrawal of America's money from Europe, the great Wall Street crash of 1929 followed by a financially smaller, but, in social terms, far more important series of bank and stock failures in Germany.

Soon there were five million unemployed in the Reich. In 1931 Hitler's Brown House was set up in Munich and his movement was being supported by the leading industrialists of the Ruhr. A perspicacious observer could have perceived that Hitler's Nazis and the industrialists who wanted a huge armaments programme and a disciplined working class were going to triumph.

Nazis fought Socialists and Communists throughout Germany and even on occasions combined with Communists in strikes designed to produce a breakdown of public order. President Hindenburg and his advisers tried to keep a respectable conservative government going and Hitler out of power. But in 1932 the Nazis won 230 seats in the Reichstag and were stronger than the Socialists and Communists combined. In January, 1933, Hindenburg, unwillingly, made Hitler Chancellor of the Reich.

In 1934 Hindenburg died and Hitler secured his appointment not as President but as Führer of the German people and Reich Chancellor for life. Hitler's success was due above all to his power to appeal to the powerful irrational feelings of his audiences. The technique of Nazi crowd mastery has never since been matched—the massed bands, the drum beats, the huge slogans above the ceiling, the standard bearers, the stalwart bodyguards of splendid young men—then the speech of a Nazi leader who in a familiar, half-jocular, way dwells on the ills of the Fatherland, unemployment, poverty, starvation . . . suddenly as an American journalist has described it:

"he grows savage and turns to them with a question: 'What is responsible for our misery?' Five hundred instructed Party members reply in unison: 'The System!' (meaning the democratic Republic). 'Who is behind the System?' 'The Jews!' . . . And then: 'What is Adolf Hitler to us?' 'A faith!' 'What else?' 'A last hope!' 'What else?' 'Our Führer.'

"Military bands crash a gigantic salute. Then the Führer arises, stands silent for an impressive moment, and speaks ... One hour. Two hours. Four hours. The crowd hangs on his words ... He states the most astonishing and totally inaccurate things. He roars; he pleads; if need be, he can weep. But he never analyses, discusses or argues. He affirms, attacks, comforts."

Until 6 December, 1941, Hitler's career as a statesman and war leader was one of a long series of victories. The first victories on the internal front after 1933 were easily won, given the mood of acquiescence of the Germans. The Nazis set fire to the Reichstag building and the Communists, accused of this crime, were deprived of their seats. In May, trade unions were abolished and on 14 July, 1933, the Nazi Party was made the only legal party in the Reich.

In February, 1934, Hitler made the governments of the States of Germany completely subordinate to the Reich, thus completing the work of unification carried out by Bismarck. In the summer of 1934, Hitler carried out a purge of the Nazi Party in which hundreds of his followers were summarily shot. This was to get rid of certain elements in the Party whom the German Army leaders, not without reason, disliked and to ensure Hitler's complete domination. He now had at his back the Army, the powerful Gestapo of which Himmler was for a while the Chief, as well as the S.S., the élite force of young men recruited from the Nazi Party.

His triumphs abroad were owed to his acute sense of reality and his willingness to take risks. He re-occupied the Rhineland in March, 1936, when his new tank force was still largely on paper. His military chiefs protested. His triumph was complete. In 1938 he took over Austria. Mussolini, the Fascist Dictator of Italy, had made common cause with France and Britain in defending Austria when Germany had appeared to threaten that country's independence in 1935. But Mussolini thereafter became an ally of Hitler's, though rapidly his status dwindled to that of a client.

At Munich, in September, 1938, Hitler and Mussolini dictated terms for Germany's renunciation of war with Czechoslovakia to Chamberlain and Daladier. Appeasement was a German victory; Czechoslovakia lost much territory including her fortifications and the great arms factory of Skoda. In 1939, on another pretext, Hitler took over the whole country.

Poland was to be the next victim, and the German-Soviet Pact of the spring of 1939 meant that Germany could crush Poland without a major war in the East. The Polish campaign was a triumph of military organization and ruthless tactics. When in May, 1940, after the successful invasion of Denmark and Norway, Hitler attacked

Belgium, Holland and France, the Corporal of the First World War scored the most spectacular success of his life. The German Army in a little more than a month smashed the French and British Armies and forced France on 17 June, 1940, to ask for an armistice.

After this immense victory there were some setbacks. He had hoped that Britain would sue for peace. He lost the air battle of Britain and he had to renounce invasion. He failed to get France to come into the war on his side. His Italian allies were defeated by the British on the frontiers of Egypt and Mussolini upset his Balkan policy by invading Greece and being defeated.

Hitler had to conquer Yugoslavia and then Greece. This threw out the time-table for his great enterprise, Operation Barbarossa, the smashing of the Soviet Union. Nevertheless, until 6 December, what a record of success: the whole continent of Europe under the Swastika, and the greatest Army the world had ever seen biting deep into south Russia and advancing near to Leningrad and Moscow. But this Army by winter had not taken either of the two great cities and was bogged down.

On 6 December—shortly after an official German spokesman had said the war in the East was over—Russia, to the complete surprise of the German High Command, attacked with a hundred well-equipped fresh divisions on the central front. This attack drove back the Germans from Moscow. It was Hitler's first major defeat. His brilliant gamble had failed. From now on Hitler's road that had seemed to lead to world empire began to go downwards to defeat.

On 7 December, his Japanese ally sank a large part of the American Fleet in an attack on Pearl Harbour and the United States was in the war. Hitler and the Japanese were still to gain some striking successes, Hitler in Russia, Japan in the Far East and in Burma. But early in 1944, the British and American forces were in Italy and in June the Anglo-American landings in France—the prospect of which Hitler had described as "military amateurism"—were consolidated. Germany was invaded from the west. From mid-January, 1945, after the failure of his Christmas offensive in the west—for which he had weakened fatally his Eastern Front—Hitler returned to Berlin and from then on rarely left the Chancellery building.

Hitler's health had deteriorated rapidly in 1942, owing to the long periods in his underground headquarters in East Prussia and to a generally unhealthy mode of life. He lived on drugs. An attempted assassination mounted by a group of high-ranking officers led to a bomb explosion in his headquarters in which his arm and eardrums were injured. Thereafter Hitler suffered from a nervous twitch and his violent temper and his habit of foaming at the mouth with rage were more frequently apparent. Yet such was his strange hypnotic power that even during those last few months when he was powerless to affect events, the German Nazi leaders and generals dared not oppose him, and carried out his orders when they could. Some perhaps even believed that the maniacal confidence he still expressed in his and Germany's destiny would turn out not to be an illusion.

The last month of his life was entirely spent in the deep bunker in the Chancellery garden. On the morning of 30 April, Hitler was informed that Russian troops were only a block or two away from the building. That afternoon he and his wife, Eva Braun—he had married his former mistress the day before—committed suicide together. Their bodies were burnt in the garden. It was a few days after Hitler's fifty-seventh birthday. A last propaganda lie went out on the radio stations still under Nazi control in northern Germany— "The Führer has died in battle at the head of his troops."

Hitler, throughout his life, was a vegetarian as well as a teetotaller and a non-smoker. He was inclined to hypochondria, suffered with his stomach which the taking of drugs and medicines had exaggerated. The woman who most deeply affected his life was Geli Raubal, his sister's daughter, who, with her mother, lived in his house at Munich in 1925. She was twenty years younger than him. He was intensely jealous of her and tried to keep her away from all male contacts: whether or not she was his mistress is uncertain. In 1931 she was found shot dead in Hitler's Munich flat and suicide was considered likely. Hitler was never, for the rest of his life, without her photograph.

Eva Braun was a flaxen-haired, unintelligent girl with whom Hitler had a liaison dating from some years before the war. It was a well-kept secret. Hitler made it clear that he had no intention or marrying her as it would destroy his prestige. She suffered greatly from the isolation which this liaison entailed. However she loved Adolf Hitler and willingly, it seemed, accepted her fate.

In private life Hitler behaved like an unpleasant type of semi-educated proletarian. He was dogmatic, repetitive, pretentious, particularly in his views about art on which he loved to expatiate. No ray of wit enlivened his conversation. He had no sense of humour. His laughter was most frequently aroused by other people's misfortunes and he used to split his sides when Goebbels recounted to him instances of the misfortunes and humiliations inflicted on Jews.

No statesman has ever been so closely in touch with the irrational forces of human nature as was Adolf Hitler. He understood mass emotion and knew how to utilize it to an extraordinary degree. He identified himself with the savage passions he aroused and yet could control them. He was a consummate actor, able to change from rage to quiet at a moment's notice, and as Alan Bullock[1] has written, the swiftness of transition from one mood to another was startling; one moment his eyes would be filled with tears, with pleading, the next blazing with fury, or glazed with the faraway look of the visionary. He was convincing when he said, "I go the way that Providence dictates with the assurance of a sleepwalker".

The Nazi régime could have been established only in Germany, whose men loved authority more than liberty. Even so, it is astonishing that the insistence of one man could induce a nation to carry out a policy which involved not only the enslavement of many thousands and their use merely as expendable material, but which also involved the degradation, torture and mass-murder of six million Jews.

Hitler's career left behind no legend—only a sense of horror. It was great, but revolting. For other political leaders whose crimes were on the scale of their qualities, men can find some redeeming features. But Hitler was wholly evil, like Attila, a scourge. Judgments are fallible in the light of posterity. This judgment is not likely to prove so.

[1] *Hitler: A Study in Tyranny.* Odhams, 1952.

Charles Chaplin
1889-

A SHABBY, strangely dignified little tramp—he is wearing, apart
from the baggy trousers and the immense shoes, a tightly buttoned
jacket and a too-small bowler hat—is escaping from a policeman in
the middle of a city street. Dodging through the traffic, he manages
to get clear by slipping through an expensive car parked at the side
of the road and arriving, undetected, on the pavement. A pretty
flower girl, hearing the door open and imagining a millionaire to
have stepped out, tries to sell him a flower. The tramp, as she gropes
for the flower he accidentally knocks from her hand, sees she is blind.
Smiling sadly, raising his hat an inch even though she cannot see the
gesture, he gives her his last coin and shuffles off.

The memory of the girl haunts him and the next day he comes
back and buys another flower. He realizes that she thinks him a
millionaire and although this worries him, he hasn't the heart to tell
her the truth. Each day he comes back, talks with her for a few
moments and buys one of the flowers; and one day, having been
befriended the night before by a real millionaire, a drunk one, he is
able to buy all her day's stock and drive her home in a borrowed car.
Now, of course, there is no point trying to explain: she is utterly
convinced of his riches.

The next day the girl is missing from her street corner and the
little tramp hurries to her home: peering through the window he
sees her in bed. The doctor is with her and he just manages to hear
the man announce that she is in need of special, nourishing food.
The tramp is no longer on speaking terms with the millionaire—
who is friendly only when drunk—but he resolves to get out and
earn the money to give the girl the food she needs. He undertakes
a variety of distasteful jobs including street-cleaner—after a herd of
circus elephants has passed—and sparring partner to a boxer (in
which rôle he nearly gets killed) before he is able to earn sufficient
to bring her the food. She is touchingly grateful when he arrives
with it and while she eats he reads her the newspaper. In it is an
article about a doctor who has discovered a cure for blindness: he
can perform a new operation which will restore sight. "How

wonderful!" says the girl. "If only that could happen to me! Then I'd be able to see you."

The tramp makes up his mind to get more money, somehow, enough money to make this operation possible. He is musing over his chances of doing this when a frown comes over his face: what will she thinks when she sees him?

He tries many ways, comic and pathetic, to make money and then, when he has almost given up hope, again meets his millionaire friend. It is evening, the millionaire is drunk and friendly: he welcomes the tramp with open arms. He takes him home and, when he hears the story of the flower girl, hands over enough money for the operation. Unfortunately, burglars are there before them and at this point they materialize from behind a curtain, cosh the millionaire and set off in pursuit of the tramp and the money. The chase ends with the tramp in the hands of the police, clutching the money, swearing he was given it. The millionaire on recovering consciousness, is sober and denies knowing the tramp. Terrified, the tramp breaks free, switches off a light and escapes in the confusion. He gets to the girl's house, breathlessly hands her the money for her operation, and tells her he must go away, that he will come back and see her again—but that she must have the operation. He goes out into the street and is arrested by the police . . .

Months pass, it is autumn and the leaves are swirling down the city street. The girl, now cured, is working in an expensive flower shop and whenever a handsome, rich man comes in, her heart leaps with the hope that he may be her benefactor—but each hope is dashed.

Meanwhile the tramp, released from gaol, wanders the streets, ragged, cold, unhappy. The girl has left her street corner, left her home, he has no idea where she is; he is utterly miserable.

He wanders, quite unknowingly, near her shop and here he is jeered at by a paper-boy. The shouting makes the girl look out through her shop window and see the comic little man trying to maintain his dignity. As she looks at him he turns, sees her and is transfixed. The girl, not knowing who he is, giggles to another in the shop, "I've made a conquest!" She holds out a flower and the tramp, frightened, starts to move away, but she runs out of the shop and calls after him. Shyly, he hesitates but she presses the flower and some money into his hand and now the touch of that hand tells her who he is.

"You?" she asks, looking into his eyes.

The tramp, embarrassed, nods. "You can see now?" he asks.

"Yes," she says and presses his hand. They stand looking into each other's eyes, as Charlie, finger in mouth, still holding his flower, smiles at her in a mixture of hope and terror. The scene fades.

At the time of this film, *City Lights* (of which this closing scene is considered one of the most moving ever screened) the little tramp was probably the best-known creature in the world. He was Charlie, he was Charlot, Carlino, Carlos, Carlistos and a host of other names in every country: everyone knew the little fellow with the shabby clothes and black toothbrush moustache. He had been born, on 16 April, 1889, in London and christened Charles Spencer Chaplin. His parents who were music-hall artistes, came, on the father's side, of French-Jewish stock, and on the mother's, of Spanish and Irish. They were always poor: whenever they had money the father spent it on drink and as a result, young Charlie had to be taught to dance and sing almost before he could walk. He was two when his mother began to boast of his acting ability and five when he made his professional début: his mother was taken suddenly ill and the father pushed him on stage in her place. He sang a song, the only one he could remember in his alarm, and he sang it again and again and again, until they dragged him off.

The parents drifted apart, the father to die of his weakness, the mother forced by constant ill health to give up both stage and children. Charlie and his elder brother Sid were sent to an orphanage until she was well enough to take them back and keep them; which, bravely, she did by sewing blouses.

When he was seven Charlie joined a touring music hall act, "The Eight Lancashire Lads", which survived one year, after which he was sent to school for two—the only schooling he ever had—and Sid went off to sea. His mother's mind was failing, and one day he returned from school to an empty home and was told she had been "taken away". From that moment he was completely on his own. Before he could get himself a job he lived for months as a waif—straight from the pages of Dickens—on the streets of London, an experience which coloured his life and his character and a part of which Chaplin has preserved in his film, *The Kid*. In this the tramp befriends a waif in the street, played by five-year-old Jackie Coogan, who is in roughly the same circumstances as the ten-year-old Chaplin of twenty years before. The film, a milestone in Chaplin's career, was the starting point of Coogan's.

Born trouper that Chaplin was, the wandering waif slowly worked his way back "on stage" beginning with tiny parts in the music hall and progressing through bigger ones to parts in real plays like *Peter Pan*—for which he played a wolf in the first production—*Sherlock Holmes, Jim, the Romance of a Cockney* and other popular dramas of the time. At last he was offered the chance of joining the famous Fred Karno company, of which his elder brother Sid—who had given up the sea—was already a member. In 1913, when Charlie was twenty-four and the company were nearing the end of a successful American tour, he was signed up by the expanding American film industry. By that time he was the leading comedian of the Fred Karno company and on 20 November, 1913, he played, with it, his last stage rôle, at the Empress Theatre, in Kansas City. The next day he left for California and "the movies".

December, 1913, when Chaplin entered films, was a period of chaos in the industry, much like the shift to sound, which was to come fifteen years later. It was marked in America by sudden, alarming competition from abroad and the springing up of new companies to meet it with "feature-length" films in place of the short two-reelers. There was a rush of screen adaptations of plays and of actors from Broadway. Many of the pioneer companies like Edison, Biograph, Vitagraph, Kalem, Selig, Essanay, Lubin, and Universal, the founders of the industry, slid into the shadows, most of them to vanish completely.

One company which had prosperous years ahead of it was Keystone—largely because they had been astute enough to offer Chaplin his contract. Their studio was a vast open platform with the sun diffused on to it by muslin sheets, and as all the films of the day were silent, there were usually several being made on it at the same time in an atmosphere of bedlam. Much of the Keystone output was slapstick comedy—and the "Keystone Cops", the helmeted incompetents who never got their man, have gone down into history. Chaplin had difficulty fitting into the school, its speed and violence upset him; he had been used to a more subtle performance, where the raising of an eyebrow, the flick of a wrist, the twirl of a cane, were important. For their part, the actors on the Keystone lot thought little of Chaplin: some were jealous of the new English actor, most were contemptuous. He was lucky enough to share a dressing-room with two very large, quite friendly, comedians, Arbuckle and Swain, to whom he could be no threat, and who took a liking to the little man. In his first film, *Making a Living*—which took a week to produce—he wore a frock-coat, top hat, walrus moustache and eyeglass. The film, released early in 1914, was a minor success and Chaplin got favourable comment. He hit upon the screen character and costume which were to make him world famous by accident. Mack Sennett, the Keystone producer, liked to put any of his actors and actresses who could be spared into the foreground of public gatherings, race meetings and parades, partly for the publicity and sometimes in order to shoot a film, using the crowd background and saving the expense of "extras". On this particular day a few of the Keystone comedians were sent to a children's auto race at the seaside resort of Venice, outside Los Angeles, and told to improvise a film, any film, that would make people laugh for a quarter of an hour. Chaplin decided to assemble a funny costume, taking huge trousers from Fatty Arbuckle, size fourteen shoes from Ford Sterling (worn right on left, so they would stay on his own small feet), a tight-fitting coat, bowler hat that was too small, bamboo cane and a toothbrush moustache cut down from the much bigger one sported by the "villain" Mack Swain. In this outfit he spent his afternoon dashing out on to the racetrack, getting in the way of the dummy camera which was supposed to be filming the races, while the real one was in fact filming him. He used, for the first time, the splay-footed, shuffling walk which broke into a dignified sprint only when pursued by the Keystone "police" and the "camera-men".

By this film, *Kid Auto Races at Venice*, which took forty-five minutes to produce, Chaplin's reputation was as good as established. Delighted, he wore the same improvised garb and make-up in every film for the next twenty-five years. It was a costume personifying shabby gentility, the fallen aristocrat at grips with poverty, and this was the character he presented to the world, with outstanding success through many hundreds of films. Many of the films were undistinguished—which is hardly surprising considering the speed at which they were made: Chaplin made one a week plus one long film, *Tillie's Punctured Romance*, a total of thirty-five, in his first year. But in almost every one the scenes in which he appears demand to be spooled back and shown again.

Chaplin's first year in films was a Keystone contract at a hundred and fifty dollars a week (three times his stage salary), but twelve months later his fame was such that Essanay Films took him over at twelve hundred and fifty a week. In February, 1916, when the Essanay contract expired, he was signed up by Mutual for ten thousand dollars a week, shortly before his twenty-seventh birthday. His great and sudden wealth had curiously little effect on him as a person and none at all on him as an artiste. Although not a facsimile of his real self, the earnest little baggy-trousered man he played on the screen, subject, despite his dignity, to sudden passions of love, hatred and vanity, was not too far off the real Chaplin, and that image has remained the same through his lifetime.

In the summer of 1918 when he was starting *Shoulder Arms*, his satire on army life, he met at a party the sixteen-year-old actress Mildred Harris. She had already been acting a year longer in films than he, in the studio where her mother was wardrobe mistress. Charlie, as he was to do subsequently with other young girls, fell hopelessly in love. They married in October and Charlie installed his bride in a Hollywood house described by one reporter as "a symphony in lavender and ivory, exquisite in every detail". The next summer a son—their "Little Mouse"—was born, but died three days later. Mildred complained later that Charlie's love for her died with the baby, but it seems likely that it had died even before the marriage. They had little in common: the child-bride was unable to understand the older, complex, husband. From now on, the collapse of the marriage was public property, with Press and public taking sides and much bickering over money, until the divorce was made final at the end of 1920. The unpleasantness of the affair was to a small extent offset for Chaplin by the phenomenal popularity of *Shoulder Arms*. Until *The Gold Rush*, this was generally accepted as his masterpiece. Although he was idiosyncratic in his films, for all of which he now wrote the scripts, directed and produced, he was eager for knowledge, his mind was receptive to other men's ideas. When D. W. Griffith's *Birth of a Nation* came to Los Angeles, Chaplin made a point of going to see it each week throughout its run.

The Kid, released in 1921, was Chaplin's first full-length production. As we have seen, it dealt poignantly with Chaplin's own early life, and for the first time he was more or less—though still in tramp's clothing—a dramatic actor. Chaplin made a personal profit of a million dollars out of it.

In 1921, after eight years in America, he paid a sentimental visit to London and found, to his delight, that he was a very familiar figure indeed, not only in London, but all over Europe. Crowds poured out in their thousands to see him and his reactions to this have been movingly set out in his book *My Trip Abroad*.

The Gold Rush, released in 1925, is probably Chaplin's most celebrated picture, and he has said himself that it is "the picture I want to be remembered by". In it, he plays a simple prospector chasing rainbows in the midst of frenzied Klondike gold hunters. Incongruously, he is still in his tramp outfit with bowler hat. From this one, Chaplin personally made two million dollars.

Shortly after this, he married—again disastrously—for a second time. Again, the bride was sixteen and an actress, but this time Lita Grey's parents and a lawyer uncle ganged up on the comedian and demanded an immediate marriage. Lita became the second Mrs Chaplin in November, 1924, and Charlie has been quoted by Lita herself—as saying, "Well, boys, this is better than the penitentiary, but it won't last." A son, Charles Spencer Chaplin, Jr., was born at the end of the following June and nine months after that, a second, Sydney Earl Chaplin, but the marriage was, from the start, a failure. This time the charges and counter-charges when the failure was made public far exceeded anything from the Mildred Harris affair and were sensational enough to drive much of the world's more factual news from its papers. Lita, who was suing for a large sum of money in settlement, had her supporters: Hollywood and Los Angeles clubwomen got together to raise funds for Chaplin's "penniless wife and children". Eventually, in 1927, the divorce was granted and Lita got six hundred thousand dollars and a trust fund for the boys.

City Lights was Chaplin's greatest film. During its filming he suffered the loss of his mother, whom he had brought over from London but who shortly afterward had to go to a sanatorium because of her failing mental powers. After visits to her, Chaplin would sink into melancholy for days and when she died he had a long and, to his friends, alarming bout of depression. Old Mrs Chaplin was buried beside the "Little Mouse" and Chaplin recovered sufficiently to finish *City Lights*. There had been speculation as to whether it could compete in 1928 with the new "talkies," but Chaplin was adamant: apart from a musical accompaniment, which he would write himself, the film would be silent. It was a huge success and he received much adulation as an intellectual giant who not only produced, directed and starred in his films, but also wrote—and conducted—the music. Critics have said that this at last went to Chaplin's head and that no film since *City Lights* displayed his old creative magic. He made one more, *Modern Times*, in the familiar costume, but since then the few he has made portray him in unfamiliar rôles.

He married and was divorced from the actress Paulette Goddard, but as the marriage was ostensibly secret the exact dates are not generally known. In 1943, he married, at the age of fifty-four, the daughter of the American playwright, Eugene O'Neill, who was then eighteen. It has been a happy marriage, blessed with numerous children.

Ever since his first arrival in America, Chaplin has been accused of

Communist leanings, and indeed he has never made the slightest effort to disguise his left-wing sentiments—sentiments which, in view of his slum childhood, are hardly surprising—but it seems that much of the clamour against his "anti-Americanism" has been caused by his steady refusal over the years to take out American citizenship. He is still a British subject. In 1956 he produced his first film in England, *A King in New York*, which had considerable success, but seemed utterly remote from the twenty-five years—from 1914 to 1939—of the little man with the smudge moustache. The little fellow who was once the best-known figure in the world, whose name is still a legend, now lives happily with his family in Switzerland.

Dwight D. Eisenhower
1890-1969

"THE heritage of America and the strength of America are expressed in three fundamental principles: First, individual freedom is our most precious possession: Second, all our freedoms are a single bundle, all must be secure if any is to be preserved: Third, freedom to compete and readiness to co-operate make our system the most productive on earth.

"The best foreign policy is to live our daily lives in honesty, decency and integrity; at home, making our own land a more fitting habitation for free men; and abroad, joining with those of like mind and heart, to make of the world a place where all men can dwell in peace."

This extract from a 1950 speech by Dwight Eisenhower, President of Columbia University, is perhaps the clearest statement on record of the beliefs of this great, yet simple, man—beliefs which had already sustained him as Supreme Commander of the greatest war-machine in the history of the world and would sustain him as thirty-fourth President of the United States.

He was born and brought up almost exactly at the geographical centre of his country. His father, David Eisenhower, was of Swiss stock which had come to America before the Revolution and had moved west from Pennsylvania to found a sect known as the River Brethren, dedicated to piety and pacifism. They founded their community at Abilene in Kansas to be "in closer touch with God", away from busy Eastern life. The young Eisenhower, born in Denison, Texas, was brought back to Abilene when he was a few months old. Here he grew up, accepting the strict principles of the sect, but being remembered later as a fun-loving boy, above average at lessons and sport. In some ways, Abilene was a microcosm of America, a parched town of four thousand inhabitants, split across the middle by the tracks of the Union Pacific and Santa Fé Railroad. The prosperous folk lived north of the tracks; the Eisenhowers lived south, but, being Americans, refused to consider themselves under-privileged: young Dwight went to school north of the tracks. He earned his pocket money by helping with the harvest and, in the few months between graduating from High School and going, as he had planned, to Kansas University, he took a job with a creamery. Here "Ike" did so well that he became, at the age of nineteen, night foreman, in sole charge from six in the evening until the next morning, and it was here that his good friend Swede Hazlett would come, during the evening, to chat and play cards. By Hazlett's account, "Being more or less kids, we weren't above raiding the company's refrigerating room occasionally for ice-cream, and for eggs which we cooked on a well-scrubbed shovel in the boiler room."

Swede was going to the Naval Academy at Annapolis and suddenly the idea struck Ike that this was exactly what he wanted to do, too. Swede, delighted, showed him how to apply. Ike took the exam and came out first—only to learn that he was already a year too old to be admitted to the Naval Academy. He would have to go to West Point, which allowed an older entry, and become a soldier. For the boy who subsequently went on to become almost the most famous soldier of his generation, this was a cruel blow. In the few months since he had considered it, he had set his heart on the sea, he wanted to be with his friend: he nearly refused the West Point vacancy. In the end, at the last moment, he took it.

He was not a particularly good cadet. The rigid disciplines of West Point could hardly have been more foreign to the carefree youth from Kansas, and he fell foul of the authorities in a hundred different ways. Yet his football, which was brilliant, his knowledge of history, his ability with the English language, kept him on the books, and, though he dropped a few places each year, he graduated.

His first posting, in 1915, was to San Antonio in Texas. As a good-looking young officer, he was invited to the various social functions and at one of these he met his future wife, Mamie, on holiday from Colorado with her parents. A few months later, they married. From now on, with the European war threatening to involve the United States at any minute, he found himself with a problem: if his country entered the war he was determined to go abroad and fight for it—and he knew in his heart that his country should and would enter—but at the same time the thought of leaving Mamie, so soon after their marriage, distressed him more than he had thought possible. As it happened, there were many months of waiting before President Wilson at last declared war on Germany and then many more before the War Department listened to his request to be posted abroad with the A.E.F. From Texas he was sent to Georgia, from Georgia to Maryland and thence to Camp Colt in Pennsylvania. Here, as a very junior officer, he was given the flattering and challenging job of commanding the only Tank Corps training unit in the United States. Unfortunately, not much training was possible: there was one tank, a French Renault, on which to instruct six thousand men. Eisenhower worked hard drilling his men, hammering in the theories of the new armoured warfare as they were evolved, but he was overjoyed when his posting abroad at last came through. Then, a week before he was due to embark, the war ended: Lieutenant-Colonel Eisenhower stayed at home.

Like most regular officers, he had slow promotion between wars. In 1935 he went to the Philippines. These were scheduled, by Act of Congress, to become a Commonwealth the next year and independent after that. Eisenhower was assistant military adviser under the flamboyant, gifted, General MacArthur. The political atmosphere, profoundly complicated by the many cliques and factions, made progress almost impossible. So four years later, in December, 1939, when Lieut.-Col. Eisenhower embarked from Manila with Mamie and son John (an earlier son had died in childhood) to return to his own army, he had achieved far less than his hopes. He had, however, won the respect of the Filipinos. Some of the credit for the gallant struggle which the Filipinos were to put up, two years later, against the Japanese, must certainly go to Eisenhower. As President Manuel Quezon put it, when awarding him the Distinguished Service Star of the Philippines, "—through his breadth of understanding, his zeal and his magnetic leadership, he has been responsible for notable progress in the Philippines Army—he has earned the gratitude and esteem of the Filipino people".

Even as a young man Eisenhower had an ability to make people under him work well as a team without too much trouble from conflicting jealousies and ambitions. His experience in the Philippines undoubtedly refined and improved his ability in this direction, and this was recognized by General Marshall. By 1942 Eisenhower had become one of his country's seventeen Lieutenant-Generals. In February of that year, two months after America had entered the war, he became Chief of Plans Division, War Department General Staff. The following June he achieved his long-held ambition of being a commander in a theatre of war: he was appointed Commanding General, European Theatre of Operations. This was not at first a big job and he soon went on from it to North Africa.

In many ways he seemed to his colleagues to have few of the external characteristics of the professional soldier; there seemed no desire for personal advancement, only a firm determination to get peace. If he had to win a war to get it, win it he would. But to those close to him it was very obvious that here was a man who knew everything about his own job as well as most about other people's, a man who had sharpened his military skills to perfection and at the same time had retained warmth and good humour. He had found that tact· and compromise achieved in most cases far more than direct assertion. Of the senior Allied commanders in the war, he was the one most able by charm and force of personality to get things done; he was probably the only General officer who could weld British, Commonwealth and American forces in Europe into one force. Through it all he remained a humble, approachable, deeply religious man who could get a sly pleasure out of some of his more bizarre assignments. In his 1942 notes, "Inconsequential Thoughts of a Commander", he wrote: "War brings about strange, sometimes ridiculous situations.—I have operational command of Gibraltar! The symbol of the solidity of the British Empire—an American is in charge and I am he—I simply must have a grand-child or I'll never have the fun of telling this—"

At the beginning of 1944 he was ordered from the Mediterranean to become, in England, Supreme Commander of the Allied Expeditionary Force with the British General Montgomery commanding the land forces. After many months of planning and preparation the invasion began, at 2 a.m. on 6 June, 1944, with mass air-borne landings behind the German positions in Normandy, followed by sea-borne landings on the coast. Five days later a beach-head had been secured, fifty miles wide and ten to fifteen deep. In this, the greatest amphibious operation in history, the combined British and American losses were remarkably small—thanks to meticulous planning and execution. Eisenhower moved his H.Q. to France on 1 September, and took direct command of all land forces, Montgomery remaining in command of the Northern Army Group, the American General Bradley taking over a Central Army Group, while forces which had just landed in the south of France became a Southern Army Group.

Victory came on 8 May, 1945, and the full story is told by Eisenhower in his *Report by the Supreme Commander to the Combined Chiefs-of-Staff*, published by H.M.S.O. King George VI conferred the Order of Merit upon him in June. By now Ike had begun to look forward to withdrawal from public life and retirement from the Army. In November, realizing that the end of actual fighting had not ended military commitments in Europe, he agreed to become Chief-of-Staff, a post he retained until February, 1948. Throughout his tenure there was continuous American agitation for him to enter politics. Not all of this was disinterested: leaders of both parties realized that this loved and widely respected man could be elected to the Presidency or any lesser office he chose, whichever party he espoused, and the whole of that party's bosses and Party Politicians would ride to power on his coat-tails. On countless occasions Eisenhower denied interest in politics, but the demand for his participation grew more insistent. Even the statement put out by the Army's Public Information Division that: "General Eisenhower is not in politics and would refuse nomination even if offered" had little effect apart from inspiring a famous cartoon in the *Washington Post*, which showed a disconsolate little "Mr American Public" sitting on a kerbstone, staring through his tears at the headline lying in the street before him.

As his appointment as Chief-of-Staff drew to an end, Eisenhower began to consider the many tempting offers from industry. He had never been a wealthy man and indeed the car he bought reduced his bank balance to such a tiny figure that he showed the gleaming vehicle to Mamie and said, "That's the entire result of thirty-seven years' work since I caught the train out of Abilene." Of the many jobs open to him the one he accepted offered far, far less than he could have obtained elsewhere. He agreed to become President of Columbia University in New York. He found the work immensely satisfying but after two years of it he again responded to the call of military duty and became Supreme Commander Allied Powers in Europe with the task of setting up the North Atlantic Treaty Organization. Two years later, in 1952, the renewed clamour for his participation in politics became so great that he allowed his name to be put forward for Republican Party nomination as President. He took office in January, 1953.

There were major problems during his term of office, problems which included the Korean War and the question which arose urgently after it, of the control of nuclear weapons. Had these been used in Korea, as they nearly were, the resulting all-out nuclear war might have destroyed civilization. Little progress was made (indeed the treaty for stopping nuclear tests, a first move in controlling the weapons, was not achieved until the term of his successor, John Kennedy) but proposals Eisenhower put forward led to the first International Conference on the Peaceful Uses of Atomic Energy in 1955. In the same year he suffered a severe heart attack. Despite that in the following year he allowed his nomination again on the grounds that without him the Republican Party, the Party he felt most fitted to run the country, would lose. He won, but, with his wartime reputation slipping farther into the past, his critics multiplied accused him of indecision, of being content to be carried along by events, rather than seeking to shape them. Some of this criticism was justified; it has been generally agreed that he was a better General than a President. Yet there can be no case of a President more reluctant to assume office: his critics for the most part were the very people who had demanded he assume it.

He did not contest a third term (custom has decreed that no man shall serve more than two, though this was upset by Franklin Roosevelt, elected four times), and in 1960 he retired into private life. He survived a further nine years, until the progressive heart deterioration which had plagued him even as President at last struck him down on 28 March, 1969. He was seventy-eight. The official announcement stated that the 34th President of the United States had died "after a long and heroic battle against overwhelming illness".

He was buried on 2 April in the chapel of the Eisenhower Museum and Library in Abilene.

Charles De Gaulle
1890-1970

DE GAULLE'S career falls naturally into four main parts. Born in 1890 he was the second son—he had three brothers and a sister—of a professor of history and philosophy at the fashionable Catholic college in Paris, the Ecole Stanislas. Jean de Gaulle, his father, was a man of deep and fervent religious and political convictions and his wife, a cousin by marriage, was also an intense and emotional influence in family life. The children were brought up with "an anxious concern" (de Gaulle's words) about their country and Charles de Gaulle's childhood seems to have been marked too— and this was not uncommon in Victorian times—by childish dreams of being a great soldier and saving France. In adolescence, he was a good classical scholar, studied philosophy with enthusiasm and read widely the *avant-garde* as well as the classical authors. He had a passion for history.

Jacques Soustelle, who joined him in London at the end of 1940, wrote of him:

"His thought directs itself naturally to great masses in space and time, to currents of opinion, to the tendencies of an epoch or of a country. He is capable for a long period of bringing everything back to one central idea, of turning and re-turning all the implications over in his mind. He is a meditative man moved to act only by deductions drawn from his meditations. When he acts as a soldier he is strictly military, but, outside of that, he is a philosopher of history who applied his philosophy to reality—a little like a physicist who is at the same time an engineer."

His father, who had wanted to be a soldier himself, was delighted when Charles decided to be one. No obstacles or checks were put in the way of Charles de Gaulle developing as he wished to form his inner nature. His parents encouraged him to grow up believing in himself, in the importance of his thoughts and perhaps even of his mission. No wonder he seemed set apart from his fellows and, consequently, had few friends. His first platoon commander, under whom he served as a private soldier before going to St Cyr, was asked why he had not given this promising recruit a stripe. He replied: "What would be the use of giving a stripe to a young man who already thinks he is the Constable of France?"

De Gaulle did reasonably but not exceptionally well at St Cyr, joined the Thirty-Third Infantry Regiment, then commanded by a Colonel Pétain, who was about to be retired at the age of sixty. In 1914, de Gaulle showed himself an officer of extraordinary courage; he was twice wounded, in 1914 and again in 1915, mentioned in despatches and wounded a third time at Verdun and taken prisoner. He spent the rest of the war in captivity and after trying to escape three times was treated with great rigour.

When the war was over de Gaulle went with a French military mission to Poland to fight the Bolsheviks. From 1922 onwards the fighting soldier became a brilliant staff officer. His career was helped by Marshal Pétain, and from 1932 to 1937 he held the important post of Secretary to the National Defence Council which advised Prime Ministers on military policy. Here he learnt much about the way public affairs were conducted and realized the grave disadvantages to the nation of the multi-party system with its constant changes of government—in his own experience there were fourteen different Prime Ministers in five years.

The outbreak of the Second World War found him a colonel in charge of a brigade of tanks behind the Maginot Line. His military career had been slightly injured by his advocacy of a French armoured force, in conjunction with Paul Reynaud, a very independent Right-wing politician who, in April, 1940, had become Prime Minister. De Gaulle as early as 1932 had seen what the Germans were planning and had hoped that France would have formations similar to the Panzer divisions. The military hierarchy however had rejected the de Gaulle-Reynaud proposals.

De Gaulle, was esteemed, if not liked, by his superiors, and on 15 May, when the German tanks had crossed the Marne in several places near Sedan, were streaking towards the coast, and about to cut the Allied armies in two, he was placed in charge of a very incompletely equipped armoured division. He mounted two counter-attacks against the Germans: both, after some initial success, failed for lack of resources. They were the only offensives carried out by the French Army during the battle of France, and de Gaulle had been able to show on the battlefield what could have been done. On 6 June he was called by Paul Reynaud to Paris to become Under Secretary of State for War. The first phase of his life, the first fifty years, was over.

He was a Minister for the eleven days which witnessed the total collapse of the French Army, the retreat of the government first to Tours and then to Bordeaux, the resignation of the Reynaud cabinet, and Marshal Pétain's request for an armistice. In those eleven days de Gaulle stepped into the world of high politics. Churchill had recognized him as a fighter and, when he met de Gaulle in the courtyard of the Prefecture of Tours after the last Franco-British war conference, had murmured to him "L'homme du destin". Before this at an Anglo-French cabinet meeting held at a château called The Lily of the Valley near Tours, Churchill's liaison officer General Sir Edward Spears, noticed, in a slightly caricatured portrait:

"De Gaulle, whose bearing alone among his compatriots matched the calm healthy phlegm of the British. A strange-looking man, enormously tall; sitting at the table he dominated everyone else by his height as he had done when walking into the room. No chin, a long drooping elephantine nose over a closely cut moustache, a shadow over a small mouth whose thick lips tended to protrude as if in a pout before speaking. A high receding forehead and pointed head surmounted by sparse black hair lying flat and neatly parted. His heavily hooded eyes were very shrewd. When about to speak he oscillated his head slightly, like a pendulum, while searching for words. It was easy to imagine that head on a ruff, that secret face at Catherine de' Medici's Council Chamber."

More important perhaps than the British view of de Gaulle was the first impressions de Gaulle had obtained during his two visits to London on Reynaud's behalf; he realized that Churchill would never give way and also that the morale of the British people was sound.

On 16 June, de Gaulle flew from Bordeaux to London, met Churchill, who was sitting in the garden of No. 10 Downing Street in the sun, and agreed that as soon as Marshal Pétain had asked for an armistice, he would make a call to arms from London. Pétain asked for an armistice on the afternoon of the 17th. On 18 June de Gaulle made his historic, though little-heard broadcast. In succeeding broadcasts he openly rebelled against his own government and plunged into treason. He was condemned to death *in absentia* by a French military court.

As history records, de Gaulle's venture did not go well at first. No French generals or important civilians on war-time missions in London joined him, and he recruited a bare 7,000 men in the first few months. Though French Equatorial Africa joined Free France

in the autumn, this was offset by the failure of a British-Gaullist
expedition to capture Dakar.

In 1942 British and Free French troops captured Syria from
Vichy; but after the surrender of the Vichy troops hardly any
joined Free France and it was noted how unhesitatingly de Gaulle's
supporters had been fired on by their compatriots.

President Roosevelt mistrusted de Gaulle and thought him a
narrow-minded nationalist, anxious to thrust himself on the French
people. De Gaulle and the Free French were excluded from the
North Africa landings in January, 1943, and General Giraud, a conservative fire-eater who had escaped from German captivity and from
Vichy, was put in command of the French troops and Administration. Gaullist supporters in Algeria were sent to concentration camps.

Yet Roosevelt's policy proved impossible because it was increasingly clear that the French people had rallied to de Gaulle. Leon
Blum, the well-known French Socialist leader, wrote from captivity
to Churchill and Roosevelt to say that only de Gaulle would be
acceptable as Prime Minister of France after liberation.

The French Resistance, after some hesitation, backed de Gaulle
wholeheartedly and so did the newly re-formed political parties,
which grew up clandestinely in France. In London and Algiers,
Communists, Socialists, Radicals, Catholics and representatives of
the Right sat together as part of the French National Committee of
Liberation.

De Gaulle continued to quarrel with Roosevelt and Churchill
who, somewhat against his own judgment, backed Roosevelt
consistently in attempting to hamstring de Gaulle. De Gaulle's
quarrels with Roosevelt were courteous but deadly: those with
Churchill rough, but a basis of understanding always remained. As
de Gaulle said in his memoirs, he and Churchill "navigated under
the same stars".

At the time of the landings in France—June, 1944—de Gaulle and
Churchill had their most violent quarrel; it was owing to Roosevelt's
shilly-shallying about recognizing de Gaulle's committee as being
entitled to govern liberated France. In his own mind, however, de
Gaulle knew that, whatever happened, the National Council of
Resistance and his own direct representatives would control liberated
France. What de Gaulle was worried about was that the Communists
would in fact gain control of the French cities and that he and his
provisional government would either become temporary Communist figureheads or that he would have—and this would have
been disastrous—to call on American or British bayonets. He in-

tended above everything else that France would emerge from the war as an independent nation able to make its voice heard in Europe. He succeeded.

When he entered Paris in August, 1944, General de Gaulle was greeted with overwhelming enthusiasm. As head of the provisional government he ruled France until the October elections. He received Churchill in Paris in November, 1944. He visited Stalin in Moscow. After the elections, de Gaulle was unanimously elected President of the Constituent Assembly, but throughout 1945 he had greater and greater difficulties with the new political parties—Socialists, Communists and the Catholic M.R.P. elected under the banner of Free France and the Resistance. Without warning, on a Sunday in July, 1946, he summoned his Ministers and announced his resignation.

That was the end of the second phase of his life—1940 to 1946.

From 1946 until 1958 de Gaulle lived in retirement although, from 1947 to 1951, he founded and led a movement called the *Rassemblement du Peuple Français* to fight the constitution of the Fourth Republic, which he believed to be unworkable. His movement had a great initial success but those who joined it were out of sympathy with de Gaulle's motives and represented, on the whole, French conservative opinion.

From 1952 to 1958, de Gaulle took virtually no part in politics. When, after 1955, the Algerian struggle became more and more deadly, the old man of Colombey les Deux Eglises, in the modest manor house in eastern France where he lived with his wife and sometimes his two children and their grandchildren, became interesting as a last recourse in time of stress. The Left looked to him as a refuge from a military-fascist coup, the Right hoped he would restore authority to government. De Gaulle did not believe that he would be called on to save France again. But he was very careful to do nothing which would spoil his chances. It was during this period that he wrote his war memoirs which, with their sometimes brilliant and often sombre portraits of contemporaries, their biting wit, their sparse, quick-moving narrative have been compared with the writings of Tacitus or Caesar.

As a result of a revolt by the settlers and the army in Algeria against the Pflimlin government in May, 1958, and of the consequent paralysis of that government, de Gaulle was asked by the President of the Republic and the leaders of the political parties to form a government. He agreed on condition that he would be given permission to draw up a constitution and submit it to the nation in a referendum. The nation accepted the constitution and de

Gaulle became President of the Fifth Republic in January, 1958.

One of his first acts was to offer freedom to all French colonies in Africa, including Madagascar.

De Gaulle may well have hoped that in the case of Algeria some form of association could be found, so close were economic and cultural links between the two countries. But the temper of the French Army and of a large part of French opinion obliged him to move too slowly, to negotiate too cautiously, with the rebels.

The Army revolt of April, 1961 when, as in 1958, parachute troops from Algeria might have descended as invaders on Paris, showed the F.L.N. that de Gaulle was playing from a weak hand. Reviled increasingly by Right-wing extremists as the betrayer of French Algeria and by the Left as a secret imperialist spinning out the war for his own ends, de Gaulle seemed at times to have failed. The logic of history and the will of the majority of the French people were, however, with him. The Evian Treaty of 1962 put an end to the Algerian problem, though the desperate conflict with the O.A.S. continued for some months.

Eisenhower said to him during the Algerian conflict that his policy deserved the sympathy of every democratic nation. However, between 1962 and today French policy was often and bitterly criticized by the West. General de Gaulle withdrew France from N.A.T.O. although, after the Russian invasion of Czechoslovakia, it was clear that France still remained inside the Atlantic Alliance.

In 1967 de Gaulle's attitude towards Israel pleased the Arab States and the Communists but alarmed France's nominal allies and shocked a large section of Gaullist as well as opposition opinion in France. Prior to Czechoslovakia, France's *rapprochement* with Russia was part of a general *détente* between East and West. De Gaulle's spectacular visits to Moscow in 1964 and to Poland in 1967 emphasized France's independence from any concerted Western policy. His attitude to Vietnam and Latin American crises won him popularity with the Third World, the uncommitted nations; it also showed how far off France was from the Anglo-Saxon powers.

Until the end of 1962, Europeans believed that de Gaulle was working for the political unity of Europe. This became increasingly doubtful. He blocked Britain's entry into the European Economic Community in 1963 and again in 1967 when all France's partners were convinced that only with Britain in could steps be taken towards the political integration of Western Europe.

In 1965 he stood for a second term as President and was elected, but not by a large majority. The prestige of his government, and his own, was damaged by the student revolt in May and June, 1968; for a moment he thought of retiring. He mastered the situation and, not for the first time, the world admired his courage in the face of adversity.

After the student revolt de Gaulle, fully supported by some, but not by a majority, of Gaullist leaders, decided that his task was the drastic reform of society on the basis of worker participation, decentralization and the creation of semi-autonomous regions. In April, 1970, he was narrowly defeated on a referendum on regionalization, mainly because the plan he put forward included the abolition of the Senate. This gave great offence to moderate opinion. Immediately the result was known he retired. He went for a holiday to Ireland to emphasize that he would play no rôle in the election of the new President. In November, 1970, a month after the first volume of his new memoirs—called *The Memoirs of Hope*—had appeared, he died suddenly.

The world paid a spontaneous tribute to his great qualities, nowhere more so than in Britain. Although he may have delayed the creation of a united Europe, it was his refusal at any time to accept the domination of the United States which had fostered the growth of a European spirit. He was, to many people, at once an anachronism and a statesman who held more intelligent views about the future than any of his contemporaries. There was something of the hero in the de Gaulle of the 1940 period, and this emerged again in his conduct of Algerian affairs after 1958.

His life had been dominated by a passion to serve France. In private life he was a highly civilized, well-educated, upper-class Frenchman; in conversation reticent, but often witty; fond to an extreme degree of literature; accustomed to living frugally; rather pessimistic in disposition and absolutely devoid of the vanity of a Mussolini or the mania of a Hitler.

It is in part because he represented no political party that he was capable of representing France. Long before he had his triumph in France in 1944, Churchill, with his peculiar insight, wrote of him:

"I had continuous difficulties with de Gaulle . . . But I always recognized in him the spirit and conception which across the pages of history the word France would ever proclaim. I understood and admired while I resented his arrogant demeanour. Always even when he was behaving worst he seemed to express the personality of France, a great nation with its pride, authority and ambition."

William Slim
1891-1970

"I have a theory that while the battles the British fight may differ in the widest possible way, they have invariably two common characteristics—they are always fought uphill and always at the junction of two or more map sheets . . ."

THIS very typical quotation from the writings of Field-Marshal Slim gives an insight into the mind of the man—as great an insight as the famous Alamein Order (quoted in the article on Lord Montgomery) gives into that other famous soldier.

Bill Slim, the dry, humorous, "Temporary Gentleman" who got a temporary, war-time, commission in the Warwickshire Regiment in 1914, was rather a different sort of senior officer to the type usually turned out by Sandhurst and Camberley. First a clerk, then Birmingham school-teacher, then foreman in an engineering works, he brought to his first war a variety of experience which served him and his infantry battalion well. He fought at Gallipoli, was severely wounded while leading an attack with his company, and was discharged from the Army as unfit for further service. By some undivulged method he reappeared in the battle line in Mesopotamia and was awarded his first decoration, the Military Cross. Deciding he liked soldiering, he applied for a regular commission and got it, in the Indian Army, with the 6th Gurkha Rifles. Immediately he hit it off with the little brown men—and they with him. He spent his inter-war years, for the most part, with them.

At the start of the Second World War he was given command of the 10th Infantry Brigade in Africa, and fought with it in Eritrea where he was again wounded. This was followed by the command of the 10th Indian Division in Syria, Persia, and Iraq, where he added a D.S.O. to his M.C., then the 1st Burma Corps and subsequently Fifteen Corps in India, before he received the command on which his fame rests, that of Fourteenth Army.

Bill Slim was born on 6 August, 1891, in Bristol and probably never unburdened his heart to any man, so details of his early life are sketchy. He attended King Edward's School in Birmingham and then held a variety of jobs before the first war broke out.

His first notable appearance, nearly thirty years later, in the theatre where he made his name, was as Commander of the 1st Burma Corps, hastily set up by the Commander-in-Chief, General Alexander, to create a unity of command between the 17th British Division and 1st Burma Division during the retreat of 1942. The Corps fought gallantly, but by the end of May the British Army in Burma had ceased to exist: Slim's units came out in rags but still with their arms. He was immediately given command of Fifteen Corps in India, to prepare it for the next move, the return to Burma.

At first, with British, Indian and Chinese Armies exhausted and disorganized on the eastern border of India, there was the blessing of five months' monsoon rain, a downpour which would stop the Japanese onslaught until reinforcements and desperately needed equipment could be brought in.

There was, immediately, no further Japanese offensive and the first British moves, after the retreat, were two small-scale, local invasions. One was an attempt to retake the Mayu Peninsula and the port of Akyab on the Arakan coast of Burma; the other was General Wingate's march with a brigade of men, deep into the heart of the country. Each was an experiment, each provided valuable experience, and little else. Wingate was accused, with some justification, of having led the Burmese to believe he was being immediately followed by the whole of the British Army, so that those loyal to Britain rose in his support and were subsequently punished by the Japanese. Slim and the units under his command learnt much, perhaps the most valuable lesson being that the Japanese were not as invincible as they had appeared during the retreat. Wingate came back with remnants of his force to report that the Japanese soldier "has carefully worked out the answer to all ordinary problems— but he hates a leap in the dark to such an extent that he'll do anything rather than make it." This was much the experience of Slim's Fifteenth Corps, pressing down the narrow Arakan strip between hills and sea, being held at bay by fanatical defenders fighting from bunkers set deep in every bit of high ground and joined by intricate honeycombs of connecting passages, in the early months of 1943. The Army, though, had high morale, found no difficulty in swallowing its pride, learning the lesson and regrouping for the final assault. A new Allied Command had been set up in South-east Asia, under Admiral Lord Louis Mountbatten, with the intention of carrying out large-scale combined operations and retaking Burma from the sea. These plans were rudely swept aside after the Teheran Conference, when all S.E.A.C.'s available landing craft, which Mountbatten had struggled to obtain, were allocated to European waters for the coming invasion of the Continent. Without assault craft, it was impossible to launch serious invasion the obvious way, from the south: it would have to be overland, from the north, where the American General Stilwell's Chinese and U.S. forces and British-led Burmese guerrillas from the Kachin Hills were moving south on Myitkyina; and from the west, where Slim's Fourteenth Army (he had handed over his Fifteenth Corps to General Christison) was waiting on the India-Burma border.

Slim's orders from Mountbatten were to sit tight but upset the enemy's plans by pushing Fifteen Corps (which was still under his overall command) forward in the Arakan. This he did, but once again the coastal campaign misfired and once again it would have been a near-disaster had it not been for the new technique of air supply, which kept the surrounded British and Indian troops going, enabled them to hold firm and later take up the offensive. Slim had anticipated the problem: ten days' rations for 40,000 men had been packed and dumped on forward airstrips. When the need arose, rations and ammunition tumbled like manna from the air upon the incredulous British and in full view of the equally incredulous Japanese.

Further, to distract the Japanese, Wingate went in again; this time by air, in troop-carrying gliders. It was a brilliantly conceived and executed move, the largest of its kind ever attempted, for which Slim was largely responsible. The Special Force ("Chindits" from the legendary Burmese Chinthay, half lion, half eagle) landed at night behind the Japs who were facing the bulk of Fourteenth Army in the west and Stilwell's troops approaching from the north, down the Hukawng and Irrawaddy valleys. The Japanese now took a major and ultimately disastrous decision: instead of retreating and trying to cover their rear, they advanced over the Chindwin River towards Imphal in Manipur; their objective Dimapur, Slim's railhead and an important link on the Bengal-Assam Railway which was the lifeline of Stilwell's forces.

Faced with this attack Slim had to make his first major decision since moving cautiously over to the offensive. He took it characteristically. He ordered a worried Stilwell to continue his advance, radioed the Chindits to carry on with their task. The big fighting, when the bulk of his Fourteenth Army would be engaged, was to come later.

The Japanese plan, "Operation U", had been shaped as early as 1943, and the descent of the Chindits merely triggered it off. It had a three-fold purpose, not only the cutting off of Stilwell's and Slim's supplies, but the capture of the main Fourteenth Army base at Imphal, and of the Assam airfields whence airborne reinforcements left for China. On the night of 16 March, 1944, the Japs crossed the Chindwin River in strength, and five days later they were at the frontiers of India. At Slim's request, twenty-four American air transports were ordered off the China supply run by the Theatre Commander, Mountbatten, to carry troops from the Arakan to besieged Imphal while Slim dispensed with unnecessary charges on his ration strength by flying and marching out 52,000 non-combatants and deploying the rest into "box" defences.

The forty days' hard fighting around Imphal and Kohima may be regarded as the turning point of the war in Burma. The enemy's attack was held everywhere. When the relieving battalions from the Arakan attacked the Japanese 33rd Division surrounding Imphal the Japs met disaster. Their attacks were broken off and they withdrew to regroup and refit during the monsoon weather. Neither Army previously had attempted active campaigning in the thick mud which the rains brought. One might move men on the ground, but effective supply was another matter. However, as Slim put it:

"the advantages of pressing a beaten enemy were so immense that I called on the troops and the air forces supporting them for the impossible, and I got it."

Under his leadership the troops poured—immediately—back into Burma, back into the country they had fled two years before. Bridges were built at incredible speed, bridges of every size and capacity, from simple wooden crossings to the 1,100 feet of Bailey bridges across the Chindwin. Despite the Herculean efforts on the ground the British, Indian and Gurkha troops would have been bogged down as the Japanese expected had it not been for Slim's resort to supply by air-drop. This utterly confounded the Japanese commanders, giving them no time in which to reorganize their battered forces.

The road to Mandalay was open and Slim was determined to keep moving down it, chasing his beaten enemy. He would bring the main body of Japanese into a "stand-up battle" and there he knew he would beat them. The battle took place, much as he had planned it, and Mandalay fell. Still there was no resting on laurels, he pressed south, and by the end of March the battle of the plains was over.

Meanwhile, as Stilwell's Chinese and Americans, with the help of Fourteenth Army Gurkhas and Kachins, captured Myitkyina and

Bhamo, Slim's old Fifteenth Corps was detached from him for the amphibious drive into the Arakan. This was entirely successful. Meantime the rest of his Army rolled on south to Rangoon and the Burma war was over.

The bulk of the Allied troops in Burma had been part of Bill Slim's Fourteenth Army and most of the fighting was done by it. A "Forgotten Army" for much of the war, its exploits overshadowed by the geographically more interesting campaign in the Pacific and the politically, strategically, more important one in Europe, it was the largest single Army of the war: when the Burma war ended, it numbered just over one million. It had held the longest battle-line of any British Army, from the Bay of Bengal to where India and Burma bordered on China, and it was the force which finally broke the myth of Japanese invincibility on land. The Americans, with their superbly executed seaborne landings in the Pacific, had thrown them off islands, but it remained for Fourteenth Army to prove that in a land-locked war, deep in mud and disease, the Japanese soldier could be utterly defeated.

Slim's Army was the first to plan and execute the movement of whole infantry divisions by air, was the only Army to develop air supply to the extent of maintaining its front-line troops with it. From the crossing of the Chindwin to the fall of Rangoon, his whole brilliantly conceived campaign was based on air supply at the prodigious rate of three thousand tons a day.

Slim commanded the Army from its inception to the end of the war, when he was briefly Commander of Allied Land Forces, Southeast Asia, before becoming Commandant of the Imperial Defence College. He was made Chief of the Imperial General Staff in succession to Field-Marshal Montgomery from 1948 and became a Field-Marshal in 1949. From 1953 to 1960 he was Governor-General of Australia and in this latter year he was raised to the peerage as a Viscount. After 1960 he slipped away quietly into an almost private life, though he became a director of several commercial firms. Despite the vastness of his Army and the prodigies it performed under his command, he remained after the war a relatively unknown figure compared with other commanders in other theatres. Quiet, humorous and unassuming, he had always written prolifically and well, maintaining that he did it "for the money, of course", but with a twinkle in the shrewd, narrowed eyes. He spoke vigorously and well, and his broadcasts over the B.B.C. which have been collected and published in book form under the title *Courage, and Other Broadcasts* are little masterpieces. One of his most passionate beliefs had

553

always been that the fighting capacity of a unit—any unit—depends on men's faith in their leaders, that discipline can start only with the leader and spread down to the led: comradeship in arms is achieved only when all ranks do more than is asked of them. It was this belief, which Slim transmitted through his personal example, which made the Fourteenth Army possible.

From 1964 to June 1970 he was Governor and Constable of Windsor Castle. But his health was failing and a few months after giving up the post Bill Slim died, on 14 December, 1970. He was mourned in many parts of the world, but most of all by the survivors of that Forgotten Army he had led.

Francisco Franco
1892-1975

GENERAL Francisco Franco, who ruled Spain for more than a third of a century, was born in 1892. He was the son of a naval paymaster at El Ferrol in Galicia, a province of north-western Spain where the soil is poor and the rainfall heavy. The inhabitants have the reputation of being dour, close-fisted and lacking the impetuous and attractive characteristics of most Spaniards. The boy was christened Francisco Paulino Hermenegildo Teodulo and, as is usual in Spain, his full surname included his mother's family name Bahamonde.

Franco benefited from no influence either of birth or fortune and at the age of fourteen failed to find a place in the Naval Academy for which he was destined. A very small, rather frail-looking boy, he was sent to the military school at Toledo, from which he passed out as an infantry officer to serve almost at once in the long, dreary and rather inglorious series of military campaigns in Morocco which occupied the Spanish Army from 1912 to 1927.

There exists no adequately impartial biography of General Franco, only a number of ecstatic works which sing his praises. It is difficult, therefore, to form an idea of his character at this period. His abilities were certainly considerable, for he became the youngest captain, the youngest major, and in 1927, when the Moroccan wars were over, the youngest general in the Spanish Army. He was certainly a brave officer in the field and, what is also important, a lucky one. He had the reputation of being a strict disciplinarian.

When he became second-in-command of the newly formed Foreign Legion, it is said that on his first tour of inspection a huge, bearded legionary threw a saucepan full of stew at him. He wiped himself down and proceeded slowly with the rest of the long inspection. At the end, he placed the commanding officer under arrest, gave orders for an enquiry into the feeding of the battalion and ordered the legionary to be taken out from the ranks and shot at once.

In 1923 he was decorated with the Order of San Fernando, the highest military decoration. In that year, when he married Maria di

Carmen Polo de Martinez Valdes, the daughter of a rich Oviedo businessman, the King of Spain was represented at his wedding.

So in the early thirties Franco was one of the most successful as well as the youngest of Spanish generals and one with an unrivalled hold over the Spanish and Moorish forces in Morocco.

He added to his reputation for efficiency in 1934 when the second government of the Republic called on him to deal with rioting in Madrid and Barcelona and an armed insurrection by the coal-miners of the Asturias in northern Spain. He brought over Moorish and Foreign Legion troops to suppress the miners, which they did with maximum speed and inhumanity. Franco was for a while Chief of the General Staff. In July, 1935, when a Popular Front government came to power, he at once lost this post.

As a public personality, Franco seemed not of the first rank. He was, with his slight corpulence noticeable in middle age and his rather high-pitched voice, not a very commanding figure. He was also a very cautious, almost timorous, man at a time when Spaniards of all classes were rapidly taking sides and exaggerating their animosities.

After 1931 when King Alfonso XIII had resigned—to avoid the shedding of blood, in his own words—Spain was rapidly moving towards the greatest blood-bath in its history.

The Spanish Civil War was brought about by a whole number of unresolved conflicts on not one of which was a solution easily to be found. There was the conflict between Monarchists and Republicans; that between the provinces, such as Catalonia and the Basque country, which desired autonomy, and the central government which refused it; that between the Church and the liberals which was of a bitterness unknown outside Spain. Underlying all was the conflict between the possessing classes, particularly the landowners, uncommonly unprogressive, selfish and ostentatiously wealthy, and an urban and agricultural proletariat whose economic conditions were worse than that of any West European country.

Not for nothing had Lenin considered that Spain would be the next Communist country after Russia. Had the Republic from 1931 onwards found leaders who were at once intent on righting economic grievances and yet, at the same time, gifted with the power of being moderate, of appealing at once to the idealism, the patriotism and the good sense of all the Spanish community, the story might have been different. But the leaders of the Republic were not men of great calibre. The 1935 election of the Popular Front brought into power a combination of Socialists and Liberals, supported by the

Communists and Anarchists. A Spaniard who looked at the events of his country impartially could have arrived at the conclusion that the nationalist revolt was an answer to a revolutionary movement based, finally, on international Communism which had as its aim the destruction both of the liberal Republic and the Church.

The Spanish Civil War quickly became the great international issue of Europe in the thirties. The cause of the Republic evoked the enthusiasm of the young and the timorous support of the progressive political classes in France and England; the cause of the Spanish Nationalists was solidly backed by Italy and Germany.

Just before war broke out, General Franco, whom the Republican government had sent into virtual exile as military governor of the Canary Islands, flew incognito, in a plane chartered in England, to Casablanca, and thence to Tetuan, with his uniform in a brown paper parcel on his lap. He halted at Casablanca on 18 July presumably to be quite certain that the army revolt had succeeded in Spanish Morocco.

In Tetuan he assumed command of the revolt. He managed to get numbers of his troops into southern Spain and, after a few weeks, aided by reinforcements brought over from Morocco by planes put at his disposal by Mussolini, was the undisputed master of a large portion of that region.

General Sanjurjo, an aged Monarchist, was to have led the Nationalist revolt; but the aeroplane bringing him from Portugal to Spain crashed, killing the general though not the pilot. The pilot stated that the crash was owing to the general's insistence on bringing too many suitcases.

When, in the autumn of 1936, Franco's nationalist forces had joined those in the north, the second obstacle to Franco was removed. General Mola, commander of the Nationalists in the north, was killed in a motor accident. So it was General Franco who in Burgos in October, 1936, was proclaimed Head of the State and Generalissimo. He adopted the title of El Caudillo, the leader, matching that of the Duce and the Führer.

The war dragged on through 1937 and 1938, the Republic holding most of eastern Spain, the capital Madrid, which was heroically defended, the industrial region of Catalonia and, for some time, the industrial and mining regions of the Basque country. In spite of winning help from Italy and Germany for the Nationalist cause, as compared with the International Brigades and Russian help for the Republic, there was still a stalemate at the end of 1938. Spaniard fought Spaniard with uncommon heroism and ruthlessness.

Finally the Nationalists received, in return for extensive mining concessions throughout Spain, enough additional arms and aeroplanes from Hitler to outmatch their increasingly disunited opponents. It was not only superior armaments which gave victory to the Nationalist cause. Throughout the Civil War the Republic was torn by dissension between Communists and Anarchists in Catalonia, between Communists, Liberals and Socialists in Castile. On the Nationalist side there was perhaps a greater class realization of the horror of defeat, although they too were divided between rival monarchist sects, the Falange, the Church, and the overbearing Italian allies (the Germans conducted themselves with more discretion).

Franco emerged as the undisputed leader because he belonged to no faction. He used the Falange to supply a political programme which was not purely reactionary. He was known to support the monarchical cause, but without fanaticism, and he was known of course to be a practising and even fervent Catholic without being inclined to tolerate interference from ecclesiastics. Indeed he tolerated no interference with the conduct of the war. Politics to him was a department of military science.

As Generalissimo he was not in charge of field operations. To German and Italian military advisers he seemed slow to grasp opportunities, an old-fashioned strategist in fact. His answer was that he was a Spaniard, anxious to spare Spanish lives, and greater haste would cause greater suffering. This attitude was not backed up by his behaviour and Franco, if not actively bloodthirsty, showed in the treatment of his opponents few signs of compassion.

The Civil War ended in March, 1939, and in September the Second World War began. After the defeat of France in 1940, Hitler and Franco met at Hendaye and the world presumed that Franco would pay his debt to Fascism. Hitler wanted to send two German divisions into Spain to take Gibraltar and close the Mediterranean to the British. The meeting did not go as the victorious Führer expected. To begin with Franco was half an hour late—he was finishing his siesta. Whilst the Caudillo expressed admiration for Hitler's achievements, nine hours of argument failed to get him to agree to Spanish intervention against Britain. Hitler said later:

"I would rather have three or four teeth pulled out than another interview with Franco."

Other Germans present at Hendaye remarked that the Spanish soldiers were badly turned out, with dirty rifles; that Franco himself looked like a pip-squeak. Thereafter Hitler never let slip an opportunity of sneering at Franco and his Foreign Minister for subservience to the Church. Franco, in Hitler's opinion, lacked the personality to face up to the political problems of his country and the Franco régime could not be put on the same level as National Socialism or Fascism.

This last was perfectly true. Fascism and National Socialism were in intention and, to some extent, in fact social revolutionary movements; both were anti-capitalist even though both made concessions to the bankers and industrialists in order to build up a war economy. National Socialism was fundamentally anti-Christian. Hitler and Mussolini were visionaries, demagogues, men dangerously animated by ideas. The Spanish Nationalist Movement, for all that the Falange supplied its slogans, was and is today fundamentally conservative and Catholic.

Franco was a professional soldier and what he made was not revolution but counter-revolution. He had no spiritual debt to pay to Hitler. Moreover, before the world war started Spanish opinion had been shocked by the German pact with the Soviet Union. In refusing to enter the war against Britain, Franco was, of course, following purely Spanish interests. It was certainly a proof of far-sightedness and ability to read the world situation in 1940.

After the war, Franco's régime had to face a difficult period. Public opinion in Western Europe identified the Spanish régime with those of Italy and Germany. President Truman stated that no one liked Franco's Spain. At one period both Britain and the U.S.A. withdrew their Ambassadors. The Pretender to the Spanish throne, Don Juan, received much support abroad, including that of many of the Republican exiles from the civil war, when he pledged himself, if returned, to restore normal political life in Spain, a rather unrealistic promise. Foreign pressures tended to unite Spaniards around Franco. Outside difficulties were greatly diminished by the outbreak of the Cold War, though Spain remained for long a sort of pariah-nation, excluded from most of the new international organizations.

Franco's role now was not so much that of Generalissimo as of Managing Director of a State monopoly, which possessed an army to protect its interest. These interests were those of the possessing classes. He had a Council of Ministers, to whom he listened and to whom he delegated power. He changed the composition of this Council fairly often, increasing the weight given to this or that political faction—in fact Spanish governments changed quite frequently but at Franco's wishes, not as a result of a democratic election.

Around 1958, for example, Franco was forced to realize that a huge American loan had disappeared without any tangible good whatever coming from it. It was then that he appointed a new Finance Minister and a new Minister of Commerce both belonging to the Catholic Lay Movement *Opus Dei* to clean up the financial administration of the country. The Spanish economy, substantially helped by this operation as well as by the growth of tourism, grew more vigorous. Money was found for social services including land improvements and progress towards modernization.

Modernization of the economy continued and, in October, 1969, the Cabinet was drastically re-shuffled to get rid of a number of die-hards and include a majority of young technocratic Ministers. Material progress was accelerated and a fairly large part of the workers began to enjoy a standard of living undreamed of in Spain a few years before. One of the aims of the government was for Spain to get association with the European Common Market and later, membership. The technical difficulties were not great, so rapid had been Spain's economic re-adaptation.

The major obstacle to Spain being accepted in the European Community was the failure, most marked during these years of economic progress, to adapt her political and social ideas and institutions to those of Western Europe. Some progress had been made in the early sixties when the censorship of the press had been relaxed. But this process had not been maintained. The trade-unions remained "vertical"—that is to say, with unions and management grouped together. Elementary human rights such as freedom from arbitrary arrest were anything but guaranteed. No political parties other than the official National Movement were allowed.

By the end of 1971 Spain was more prosperous and better administered; also more divided than at any time since the end of the Civil War, and the régime had a smaller consensus behind it. This was the time that General Franco stated at a Madrid rally—which was called to offset some harsh criticism from the Church—that so long as he was in power there would be no basic reforms, no change in the trade-union structure and no political parties.

In the course of this speech Franco told the crowd that there would be no fundamental changes under his designated successor, Prince Juan Carlos—who stood by his side on the rostrum. Spain had officially remained a monarchy, according to a law passed in 1947 and approved by a referendum. After Franco, many monarchists would have preferred the throne to go to the legitimate heir, Don Juan de Bourbon, the father of the Prince, who had long been a critic of the Franco régime. Under him, there could have been a fresh start and a constitutional monarchy. Prince Juan Carlos, taken away from his family in early youth, had been educated by the régime.

In June, 1973, Franco took the important step of separating the functions of head of state and head of government. This was the first time since Burgos in 1936 that he had shed part of his absolute power. The Prime Minister was Admiral Carrero Blanco, the Caudillo's closest political associate, who could be guaranteed to keep "Francoism" going. In December the Admiral was killed by an explosion engineered by Basque separatists and was replaced as Prime Minister by Carlos Arias Navarro.

Franco died in November, 1975. One of his final acts of state was to reject Arias's proposals for a liberal statute of political association.

Franco's private life was neither particularly simple nor was it ostentatious. From 1945 he lived in what was a royal hunting lodge called El Pardo some eight miles outside Madrid. The interior was as luxurious as many royal palaces, the guards were superbly equipped and the servants numerous. Franco lived there the strictest of bourgeois family lives. He worked all the morning and spent the afternoon with his family. Franco was very fond of his grandchildren; he enjoyed carpentry and was a landscape painter. He normally worked all the evening and went to bed around ten o'clock, a strange hour for a Spaniard: but he invariably read State papers until the gilded clock by his bedside chimed three. He ate and drank sparingly. In the winter, he spent much time boar shooting in the mountains outside Madrid and in the summer he went on his yacht tunny fishing.

Pessimism was the key-note of the character of a man whom Hugh Thomas summed up as "this clever, harsh, patient, unimaginative general". Stability and public order were undoubtedly Franco's achievement. From 1836 to 1936 Spain had three kings dethroned, two regents exiled, four attempts to assassinate the sovereign, two republics, two dictatorships, three civil wars, four prime ministers assassinated, twenty major army revolts and, in brief, a change of government on an average of every eleven months. In terms of the purely Spanish past, his achievement was a considerable one: yet the future will not necessarily be grateful to him.

Mao Tse-tung
1893-1976

"A revolution is not the same thing as asking people to dinner or writing an essay or painting a picture or doing fancy needlework; a revolution is . . . an act of violence whereby one class overthrows another."

So wrote Mao Tse-tung, peasant, poet, philosopher, guerrilla leader, visionary and statesman, after twenty-five years of bitter struggle. His revolution succeeded and he became ruler of a nation of seven hundred million Chinese in October, 1949. Having united China at the age of fifty-five, he challenged Khrushchev's orthodoxy and claimed leadership of the Communist world.

Born on 26 December, 1893, at Shao-shan in the province of Hunan of peasant parents, he came to the conclusion in his student days that the hard life of the peasant could be improved only by revolution, and that the peasants represented a tremendous source of energy which could be mobilized.

Instead of carrying manure for his father's rice-fields Mao used to read about China's history and the romances of heroes and brigands. He learned that the cause of the peasants had been taken up by the leaders of the great Taiping rebellion who had tried to set up a primitive Communism among the peasantry, inspired by Christianity, from about 1850 to 1865, but had eventually been ruthlessly suppressed by the Manchus. He learned of Sun Yat-sen, also influenced by the Taipings, who had organized his first insurrection against the Manchus in 1895, the year that Japan defeated China, siezed Formosa and ended China's control over Korea. By 1911 Dr Sun Yat-sen was President of the new republic and the Manchu Dynasty fell the following year. When Mao Tse-tung came to power in 1949 he spoke of China's debt to the Taiping rebellion and to Sun Yat-sen.

Mao was the eldest of three brothers and a sister—both younger brothers became Communists and were killed. He wanted to become a student and had many quarrels with his father who did not want to release him, but he managed to borrow money from friends and get to school; he spent many months in the Hunan provincial library at

Changsha from the moment it opened to closing time reading books and newspapers. He made friends with the peasants, corresponded with students, worked in the library at Peking where he met the scholar Chen Tu-hsiu, who was to found the Chinese Communist Party in 1921.

By 1919, at the age of twenty-six, Mao Tse-tung had travelled over many parts of China and had arrived in Shanghai. He joined students in angry demonstrations of protest because China, which had been an ally of Britain and France in the First World War, had been "betrayed" in secret agreements giving the German concessions in China to Japan.

What became known as the Fourth of May Movement was formed to rouse the Chinese to resist Japanese encroachments. Sun Yat-sen having failed to get help from the Western Powers, appealed to Lenin, who early realized the importance of Sun Yat-sen's revoluionary movement and sent money, arms and advisers to Sun Yat-sen's Kuomintang base in Canton. Mao Tse-tung was much interested in these developments and had decided to devote himself entirely to politics; he returned to Changsha in Hunan and edited the *Hsiang Chiang Review*, which had a great influence on the students' movement in south China. He read *The Communist Manifesto* as soon as it was translated into Chinese in 1920. "By the summer of 1920," said Mao, "I had become in theory and to some extent in action a Marxist." In the same year he married the daughter of his old tutor, Yang Kai-hui; she was a student of Peking University, was an active Communist and was executed in Shanghai in 1930. In May, 1921, Mao Tse-tung went to Shanghai to attend the foundation meeting of the Chinese Communist Party.

As a result of the agreement between the Russian Bolsheviks and Sun Yat-sen's Kuomintang, a combined front was formed with the Communists. Chiang Kai-shek was sent to Moscow; he impressed the Russians and they decided that he should be trained as successor to Sun Yat-sen, who was ailing; he died in 1925. Sun Yat-sen's Three Principles became the platform for both Bolsheviks and Kuomintang; they were peoples' sovereignty, peoples' rights and peoples' livelihood.

Mao Tse-tung was by now highly regarded for his ability and in 1926, aged thirty-three, he was acting Director of the Kuomintang Propaganda Department and also Director of the National Peasant Movement Institute which was the chief centre for training cadres of peasants. The next year, 1927, was disastrous for Mao and for the Chinese Communist Party. Chen Tu-hsiu, Secretary of the Chinese

Communist Party, was giving no direction and was secretive about the directives from the Communist International in Moscow. These were confusing; one directed that they should maintain the united front with the Kuomintang and another that they should carry out the peasants' demands for land confiscation. Friction was increasing between the Communists and the right wing of the Kuomintang backed by landlords, who were suspicious of Communist plans for land reform and especially of Mao Tse-tung who was spokesman for the peasants.

Mao had no doubt what ought to be done. In February, 1927, he presented his *Report on an Investigation into the Peasant Movement in Hunan*, urging that the Politburo of the United Front should organize a peasant revolt. Critics were numerous, describing it as a "movement of riff-raff" and Mao failed to get his report accepted.

Chiang Kai-shek, who was in command of the Kuomintang forces, revealed himself as violently anti-Communist and ordered the destruction of the peasants' and workers' unions; there were massacres of Communists in various parts of China and the Party went underground.

Mao Tse-tung returned to Hunan in August, 1927, and organized a peasant insurrection known as the "Autumn Crop Uprising". It was ruthlessly put down; Mao himself was captured and was to be beheaded but managed to escape. The uprising had not been sanctioned by the Central Committee of the Communist Party and Mao was dismissed from the Politburo and the Party Front Committee.

With about a thousand peasants in their cotton clothes he retired into the snow-covered mountain stronghold of Chingkangshan on the borders of Hunan and Kiangsi, the sea-board province to the west. About three-quarters of the Communists had been destroyed and the situation was desperate. Mao revealed great talent, determination and powers of endurance. He set up a soviet government and mobilized the First Red Army equipped with arms captured from Kuomintang troops sent against them. In May, 1928, he was encouraged and aided by the arrival of Chu Teh with troops from Nanchang. The only hope for the Communists was to adopt Mao's policy and rely on the peasants; Chingkangshan became a haven and a rallying ground for them. The Communist International under Stalin recognized the importance of what Mao had achieved and reinstated him in the Central Committee and in the Politburo at the Sixth Congress of the Communist Party held in Moscow.

Chiang Kai-shek, in command of the Kuomintang armies, was determined to mop up this small centre of Communist resistance before considering plans to counter the growing threat of a Japanese invasion. Between December, 1930, and October, 1933, he sent four large and well-equipped military expeditions against the Communist stronghold but suffered severe defeats. These were owing to the discipline of the men under Mao Tse-tung and Chu Teh, to the support they obtained from the local peasantry, and above all because of the ingenuity and carefully planned guerrilla tactics employed. These were described in Mao's *Strategic Problems* and became a textbook for the French in Algeria and the Vietcong in Vietnam.

Chiang Kai-shek's fifth campaign was most carefully planned with German military advisers, and nearly one million soldiers were mobilized. The campaign did not annihilate the Communists but it forced them to break out of the Kiangsi mountains and to find an area where there was room to manoeuvre. They chose the north-west provinces of Shensi and Kansu near the great wall of China. From there they could deal with Kuomintang troops coming from the south and the Japanese threat from Manchukuo and Hopei in the north-east. First they had to get there. They could not march with a whole army directly north-west across China for they were barred by the Kuomintang armies and they were not strong enough to fight pitched battles. They had to try to avoid the main forces of the Kuomintang by striking west beyond Kunming towards the Burma border and then northwards, a distance of about six thousand miles.

In October, 1934, began one of the greatest marches of an army and of a people in all history. They were constantly harried by local troops, by the Kuomintang armies and by native tribes. Against such opposition they crossed flooded rivers, jungle, swampy grassland and mountains covered with snow. The terrible journey lasted a year; they were nearly annihilated on many occasions, but their morale was high and they still had some fighting strength when they reached northern Shensi in October, 1935. There they settled, trained new recruits, taught the local peasants, set up soviets, collected information on Japanese movements and on the intentions of Chiang Kai-shek, now Generalissimo of the Kuomintang armies and Chairman of the Executive Yuan.

The reports about the character of Mao Tse-tung and of what the Communists had done had filtered through to the West largely from biased Kuomintang sources. In 1936 Edgar Snow, the American journalist, managed to get through the Kuomintang forces and visit the Communist area centred on Pao An in northern Shensi. In *Red Star over China* he gave the first coherent account of the Red

Armies' adventures and the part played by Mao Tse-tung and of his early life, which was dictated by Mao. Snow described him as:

"a very interesting and complex man. . . . . He combined curious qualities of naïveté with the most incisive wit and worldly sophistication. . . . Careless in his personal habits and appearance but astonishingly meticulous about details of duty, a man of tireless energy and a military and political strategist of considerable genius."

Agnes Smedley, who wrote *Battle Hymn of China*, saw him in 1937 in Yenan, which was then the capital; she was struck by a "feminine quality" in him but at the same time considered:

"he was as stubborn as a mule and a steel rod of pride and determination ran through his nature. I had the impression that he would wait and watch for years but eventually have his way."

Mao was then living close to the people and was in touch with reality; he had to persuade the peasants that it was to their interest to fight. He also understood better than did Chiang Kai-shek the dangers of Japanese invasion and he had, as early as 1932, offered to make a truce with the Kuomintang so that they could combine forces against the Japanese.

When the extraordinary event occurred of the arrest at Sian in Shensi Province of Generalissimo Chiang Kai-shek and his staff, Mao Tse-tung withstood the clamour from the troops of Marshal Chang Hsueh-liang and of the Communists to have Chiang Kai-shek tried and executed. He used his power instead to force the Generalissimo to agree to co-operate against the Japanese; he arranged that the Generalissimo should be freed in such a way that he retained sufficient prestige to be able to lead forces against the Japanese enemy.

With the defeat of the Japanese the United States Government tried in vain to prevent the resumption of the Chinese civil war. In spite of strong protests from the Communists the United States continued to arm the Kuomintang forces, but they were defeated and surrendered with their new American equipment. Chiang Kai-shek eventually retired to Formosa where, with American support, he continued to maintain a Chinese "national government" with the aim—despite the remoteness of the possibility—of retaking the mainland. On 1 October, 1949, the Communist leaders moved to Peking and the Central People's Government was established with Mao Tse-tung, aged fifty-five, as Chairman and ruler of the most populous Communist country in the world.

Mao Tse-tung had no intention of allowing China to settle down to rehabilitate in a slow and peaceful manner. Anti-Communists were killed in a series of reprisals; China took part in the Korean war; there was a drastically accelerated economic drive—the Great Leap Forward of 1958; an invasion of Tibet; crises over Formosa; invasion of India; and the quarrel with Russia. Remembering what loyalty and suffering he had been able to demand from the peasants during the civil war, Mao seemed to think that he could call on the same powers in peace-time from the whole country and that China could become great quickly through the energy of the peasants.

"The liberated, united and organized 600 million people, constitute the greatest creative force in the world, and in comparison the United States and Britain are but dwarfs."

It was also a challenge to Russia with its two hundred million people.

He was out of touch with reality and he tried to drive the people too hard; "stubborn as a mule" he would not listen to the advice of leaders of the Communist Party and acted as a dictator. Khrushchev's attack on Stalin and his demand for collective leadership seemed to Mao to be an attack on his own position; but he confidently accepted the idea of a "thaw" and announced his slogan, "let a hundred flowers bloom, let diverse schools of thought contend." The result of lifting the censorship was a series of bitter attacks on the Communist leadership from all parts of the country, especially from the students. The experiment was ended; many had to confess their errors or be executed for their criticisms.

Mao sought to turn this mounting social discontent to his own advantage by encouraging the non-Party intelligentsia to criticize bureaucratic systems and individuals suspected of anti-progressive views. Students were exhorted to be revisionist and to attack cultural decay and back-sliding: the result was the Great Proletarian Cultural Revolution, which began in the universities in May, 1966, and was carried into the streets by student members of the Red Guard. *The Thoughts of Mao Tse-tung*, expressing the purpose and ideals of Chinese Communism, was their guide in the violent purges of anti-revisionist elements and the public ridiculing of government officials and university professors which took place during the following three years of revolution. Mao's fourth wife, the ex-film star Chiang Ching, played an influential part during these events.

The years following the Chinese Communist Party Congress in 1969 were devoted to restoring normal conditions after the upheaval of the cultural revolution. Signs of return to normality were the reappearance in Europe of Chinese trade missions, the re-admission of journalists and officially approved tourists into China, and the release of foreign political prisoners. China's admission to membership of the United Nations in 1971 increased her status as a world nuclear power and served as recognition of her rising impor-tance in international politics.

But beneath the surface rival forces were contending for power and leadership. In April, 1976, there was a massive demonstration in Peking in memory of Chou En-lai, China's late Prime Minister, and there is little doubt that many important figures in public life regarded it as a vote for the China which Chou had envisaged and against Mao's concept of an endless revolutionary struggle.

Mao died on 9 September, 1976. It soon seemed clear with the arrest of the "gang of four", of which Mao's widow was one, that the radical faction had been defeated by the "moderates". But it was also apparent that unresolved tensions remained.

To the end Mao Tse-tung remained an untiring revolutionary, though the success he had as a revolutionary would have been beyond his reach had he not first won the loyalty of his countrymen as a nationalist. To Mao revolutionary struggle was to most im-portant thing in life, raising men's potentialities to their highest level and providing the testing ground for their ideals and tenacity of purpose. All else was subservient.

This belief was the driving force of his achievements; it was also the price his country had to pay for them.

Nikita Sergeyevich Khrushchev
1894-1971

JOSEPH STALIN died from a haemorrhage of the brain at ten o'clock on the evening of 5 March, 1953, and his heirs-apparent within the Kremlin were faced with their biggest problem. Hours went by and still the news was kept a secret. Midnight—2 a.m.—4 a.m.—it was not until six on the morning of the sixth that it was released. Beria, Malenkov, Molotov, Khrushchev and the rest had been in continuous conference inside the Kremlin, discussing the imminence of death ever since the morning of 4 March, when the first haemorrhage had taken place—but only now could the news be released.

By the time the announcement was made, Moscow had been sealed off by the M.V.D., the secret police. A detachment of them with tanks and flame-throwers was drawn up at almost every street corner. Few of the police knew why they had been called out, but the reason was crystal-clear in the minds of the men in the Kremlin. Now that Stalin, the "Iron Man", had gone, with no successor yet appointed, the question arose: just *whose* secret police were they? Now, if ever, was the opportunity for the relatives of those millions imprisoned and executed by the M.V.D., to rise in their hordes and destroy this apparatus of government—and with it, the government. So Stalin's illness, the details of it, its gravity—were kept a secret until the M.V.D. was in a position to defend itself, defend the party apparatus for which it stood.

Before a successor could be announced, it was essential to get rid of Stalin's private secretary and the head of his own, private police force. General Poskreyshev was taken out and shot. Only after this was the official announcement of Stalin's death made, at six in the morning:

> "The heart of Lenin's comrade-in-arms, inspired continuer of Lenin's cause, the wise teacher and leader of the Party and the people, has stopped beating."

The announcement went on to warn against "disorder and panic". By the 7th, the "wise teacher's" heirs had got together to announce that his mantle had fallen upon Malenkov. No one outside the

Kremlin knew why or how he was chosen, but the Party newspaper *Pravda* took him up, featured him, printed pictures. One of these, intended to prove how close he had been to the dead dictator, showed Malenkov, Stalin and Mao Tse-tung standing together after the signing of the Sino-Soviet Treaty of Friendship three years before. It had been dramatically altered in the darkroom. When it had first appeared on 15 February, 1950, it had shown Stalin and Mao together with—away to the right of the picture, among a host of minor Chinese and Russian officials—Malenkov. In the picture now presented the officials had been eliminated and Malenkov moved closer to the two principal figures. The Soviet Union has often been accused of falsifying history. For any citizen who had a long enough memory, here was the evidence, pictorially: the evidence was duly noted, duly committed to memory, in many quarters.

From this midnight reshuffle, Nikita Khrushchev became Second Secretary of the Central Committee of the Communist Party (Malenkov, as well as being Premier, was First Secretary). Among other things, he was appointed chairman of the commission organizing the funeral, and duly requested that Malenkov, Molotov and Beria speak at it. They did so, describing the dead man as "the great genius of mankind", yet subtly conveying the relief they felt at his disappearance. Though Malenkov was presented to the world as the Soviet Union's new leader, there was general agreement within the Kremlin that never again would any man have Stalin's absolute power—and Malenkov himself was only too well aware that he was being watched by the others, just as they were watching each other. It was agreed that Beria, in control of State security, had acted suspiciously fast in occupying Moscow by the M.V.D. on the night of Stalin's death: probably, the others reasoned, Beria himself had wanted to take over from Stalin.

A fortnight later, it was announced that Malenkov had given up his First Secretaryship of the Party to devote all his energies to being Premier. To those who understood Communist Party organization, this was a reduction in power if not in status. Six days later a great amnesty was announced, an amnesty which released thousands upon thousands of prisoners. It was announced, not by Malenkov, but by a new figurehead, the "Head of State", Voroshilov. As Beria had in fact imprisoned a great many of those being released, it seemed that he, too, was being discredited. Not to be outdone, Beria announced further amnesties of his own: the "Jewish Doctors" who had been under arrest for "prescribing incorrect treatment" to the ailing Stalin, were freed, with many others. Now the M.V.D. itself was being accused of criminal actions. Beria was playing with fire. Some time in June or July, Beria was tried by his colleagues, found guilty and shot: the news was released in December.

With Beria out of the way, the apparent order of importance was, Premier Malenkov first, then Molotov, then Khrushchev. Khrushchev was Second Secretary of the Party, but as no first secretary had been elected to replace Malenkov, he held the post, to all intents and purposes, himself. On 13 September, Khrushchev was granted the title of first secretary. Though still nominally third in order of precedence, he was now the strongest man in the Soviet Union and he hastened to put his own supporters in key positions. Within a year the Party secretaries of eight regions, from Leningrad to Armenia, had been replaced by Khrushchev's appointees. He began to travel extensively. As top man in the Party, he began to be represented in the Party Press as Soviet spokesman on every topic, from foreign affairs to agriculture.

In February, 1955, Malenkov resigned as Premier: Khrushchev's good friend Bulganin was elected in his place. A year later, Khrushchev startled the world and the Soviet Union with his outright condemnation of Stalin as military bungler, mass-murderer, falsifier of history. Opinions were divided as to his reasons, but it seemed likely that the anti-Stalin movement, which had been growing since the dictator's death, had got out of hand so that if Khrushchev, linked closely with Stalin for so many years, were to survive, he must leap to the front, be the most anti-Stalin of all.

Thereafter, Nikita Khrushchev was in control. Molotov, while not being forced to publish a letter of "confession" as was Malenkov, was banished to the Republic of Outer Mongolia as Ambassador. Malenkov had become "director of an electrical plant". Beria was dead. Voroshilov and Bulganin were amiable figureheads: Khrushchev was on his own—though even now he could take no action without looking over his shoulder. Stalin's days of absolute power were over.

Not very much is known of the early life of Nikita Sergeyevich Khrushchev, and his own good-natured reminiscences have tended to vary. He was born on 17 April, 1894, in the village of Kalinovka in the Ukraine, and probably he was a herdsman before becoming a metal worker. (To Polish, Danish, American audiences, he has said: "I remember my youth when I worked in a mine," "I worked in chemical factories owned by British, French and Belgian concerns;" "I herded cows for a capitalist.")

He had left Kalinovka by fifteen or sixteen and gone to the Ukrainian Don Basin where there was plenty of work. By the time he joined the Communist Party in 1918 he had a wife and child. He was jack of all trades, and this no doubt helped him to survive after the revolution, when the whole country was in turmoil, with bands of deserters, robbers, whole armies, looting and terrorizing the countryside. He joined the Red Guards, a regiment formed to defend the Ukraine against the Germans, served well and was made its "Party secretary". After two years he returned to mine-work and became Party secretary there. In the two years between 1918 and 1920, the Communist Party had changed. He found, as a civilian, that one had to be extremely careful not to get into trouble, there were informers everywhere. It was no longer a political party—it was "The Party", it was in many ways more powerful than the State. Khrushchev's shrewdness, loyalty and impeccably peasant origins continued to advance him. The secret police had just issued a directive on how to tell a man's loyalty:

"Ask him what class he belongs to, what were his origins, education and occupation—it is these questions which should decide the fate of the accused."

In 1922, when he was twenty-eight, he was selected for a three-year Party course at a workers' faculty in Yuzovka. It seems likely that he was already a widower and probable that he left his two children with his parents when he went there. In a short time he had risen again to be a Party secretary, this time, secretary of the whole school. He was its actual head, while still a pupil. He was noted as cheerful, a good dancer, fond of the occasional drink, and at the same time a shrewd organizer, the man who read his *Pravda* from cover to cover, kept abreast of the shifts and changes in Party policy.

Two years later, Lenin, father of the revolution, was dead. One of his last moves had been a futile attempt to democratize the upper levels of the Party.

("I suggest that the size of the Central Committee membership be enlarged to several dozen, possibly even to one hundred members—Comrade Stalin has concentrated enormous power in his hand and I am not sure that he always knows how to use that power with sufficient caution—Stalin is excessively rude . . .")

Despite his efforts, absolute power went to Stalin. Purges followed, hundreds of thousands, possibly millions, of people were executed; but Khrushchev remained above suspicion, a good Party member, loyal subordinate of Stalin. He remarried—his second wife, Nina, was a teacher of political science—and went on to become a leading Party official in Kiev.

In 1929 Stalin ordered the liquidation of prosperous farmers, the "kulaks" who were resistant to Communism. Years later he told Churchill that in this expropriation of land, nearly ten million families were dispossessed. Naturally they resisted, set fire to their crops, slaughtered cattle and horses—and in turn were bombed from the air, attacked by Red Army artillery, mowed down by machine-guns. At the same time, the cult of Stalin-worship, which Khrushchev was later to criticize so strongly, was earnestly fostered; huge posters and statues of him began to appear all over the country —while people continued to starve.

It required a great deal of fanaticism to continue with the liquidations, the collectivization of land: even Stalin's wife, the young Nadiedja Stalina, leapt to her feet in the middle of a party given by Voroshilov and spoke her mind about terrorism and imposed famine. A few minutes later, she went home alone and shot herself. Through all this, Khrushchev continued to rise: he had a flat in Moscow and a motor-car; he was Second Secretary of the Moscow City Party. In 1932 and 1933 he supervised, on orders from Stalin, the purge of the Moscow Party. He was a big man in the Soviet Union, he already outranked his later rivals, Malenkov and Bulganin. The American historian William K. Medlin has noted that in 1936 the Moscow evening paper, *Vechernyaya Moskva*, had pictures of Khrushchev in thirty per cent of their issues; he appeared supervising the building of the new Underground, visiting factories and construction sites all over the Soviet Union. It is hardly surprising that, on Stalin's death, he should have been well-placed for succession.

As leader of the Soviet Union after Stalin's death, his actions were carried out with one eye on world opinion, particularly that of the "uncommitted nations", the other on his own people and his post-war empire. There were big risings in East Germany, Hungary, Poland and elsewhere and a continuous conflict of opinion with Communist China. He tried to make life a little bit pleasanter for the ordinary Soviet citizen, focused more attention on the production of consumer goods, relaxed a considerable amount of control and from time to time tried to ease tension in the world outside. He could, however, never resist the urge to fish in troubled waters, to interfere in the affairs of other countries when it seemed profitable to do so, either to win them to Communism or use them as a weapon against countries like the United States who seemed to stand in the way of his professed goal of world Communism. The battle of nerves in which Khrushchev, having taken the world to the brink of war by installing missile bases in Cuba, agreed to remove them again, marked a turning point in the "cold war" and was followed a few months later by the signing of a treaty banning nuclear tests—the first step in the control of these total weapons.

But shortly after Khrushchev's seventieth birthday, in 1970, his star began to wane. He was relieved ostensibly on the grounds of age and failing health of his posts as Prime Minister and First Secretary of the Soviet Communist Party. After some criticism of his "subjectivist and personality-cult leanings" he retired still further from the public view. By 1971, when a British journalist tracked the old man down to his secluded country house, Nikita Sergeyevich could grin, shrug his shoulders and say, "What am I doing now? I am just a pensioner."

In fact, these last months of his life, as they proved to be, were worried ones. In December of the previous year a 639-page book had been published in the United States, and serialized elsewhere, entitled *Khrushchev Remembers*. What Khrushchev seemed to remember did him little good with his party leadership. He issued a statement dissociating himself from the reminiscences, stating: "This is a fabrication and I am indignant".

He died on 11 September, 1971, of a heart attack. Since then it has remained impossible to establish how authentic his book was. But the weight of expert opinion has been that most of it was compiled from "authentic sources".

Robert Menzies
1894-

In a little country school, in the dusty hamlet of Jeparit, in Australia, one day in 1904 the teacher announced to her pupils that on the following day a phrenologist was coming to visit them. Anyone who wanted his bumps read, must bring sixpence with him. There must have been quite a few sceptics in Jeparit, because on the next day, out of the two or three score pupils, only about a dozen came armed with sixpence. Among them, however, was a ten-year-old called Robert Gordon Menzies.

When the phrenologist arrived, he set a chair beside the teacher's desk. On his left he had a pad of forms and, as he felt the bumps of those who presented themselves, he would place a tick against a word or phrase on the sheet. Finally he would write across the bottom of the form the trade or profession in which the bumps indicated the child would be most successful.

Across the bottom of Robert Menzies' form, he wrote: "This boy will make a most successful barrister."

When school was dismissed at mid-day, on his way home young Menzies studied the form. There were many long words on it, some of which he could not understand. One of them was *barrister*.

His mother was busy in the kitchen when he burst in on her, calling out: "Mam, mam! What's a barrister?"

"A barrister," replied Mrs Menzies, "is a man who knows all about the law, and who speaks to the judges in the courts for people who don't know the law."

"That's what I'm going to be!" Robert exclaimed.

His mother smiled at him. "To be a lawyer, you have to study hard, go to a good school and the university, and all that costs money. Far more money than we have."

"I'll work hard and win scholarships," the boy told her.

A pot boiled over on the stove, and Mrs Menzies told Robert to call his two brothers to dinner. While he was gone she told herself that he would forget soon about being a barrister.

Probably no mother was ever more wrong about her son. Robert did not forget. Twelve years later he passed out of Melbourne

University with First Class Honours in Law, winner of the Dwight Prize for Constitutional History, winner of the Bowen Essay Prize, winner of the Supreme Court Judges' Prize and several exhibitions and scholarships, and accounted by all to be the outstanding Law student of his year, not only in his own State of Victoria, but in all the Commonwealth of Australia.

Robert Menzies' grandfather had emigrated from Scotland to Australia in the late 1850s, and settled in Ballarat, in the extreme west of Victoria. He had not been married long, and within a year of his arrival his first son James was born. James grew up and became a coach-painter, who, in the course of his work painted the first Australian locomotive built by the Phoenix Works.

In 1889 he visited Creswick, a town some eleven miles from Ballarat, to carry out a job, and while he was there, he met and married Kate Sampson, also a Scot. He took her back to Ballarat and by 1893 they had two boys, James and Frank, and a girl, Isabelle. To support his family, James Menzies worked hard. In 1894 his health broke down. He decided to move to the tiny wheat town of Jeparit, about 250 miles north-west of Melbourne and to set up there a small general store.

They had scarcely settled there when Kate Menzies knew that soon there would be another child. On 20 December, 1894, Robert Gordon Menzies was born.

James Menzies was a staunch "pillar of the Presbyterian Church". For a man of his rough-and-ready education he had a great gift of speaking, and it was more or less inevitable that from his work for the Church he should progress to become a leader of the local Jeparit community. From this he went on to become a member of the county council, then its president. In 1909 he was elected a Liberal Member of the House of Representatives of the State Parliament of Victoria, and served in this capacity until 1919, when he was defeated by the candidate of the new Country Party.

Mrs Menzies, too, was a highly intelligent woman, and with two such parents it was not surprising that the Menzies children should be similarly gifted. The little school could give them the rudiments of knowledge, but no more. Somehow these bright children had to be given the opportunity of a wider education, but money was short and the problem was how?

Grandmother Menzies came to their aid. She still lived in Ballarat and there was the larger State school, the Humphries Street School. So James and Frank were sent to live with their grandmother and attend the school. Robert followed them when he was old enough.

George Gershwin's transmutation of Negro musical idioms and style was a landmark in modern music. *Porgy and Bess*, his opera based on a story of Negro life in America, has won world-wide praise both on the stage and as a film. The film, from which the pictures on this page are taken, was directed by Otto Preminger and the principal rôles were played by Sidney Poitier, Dorothy Dandridge and Sammy Davis Jr.

The man and the machine at the centre of the world's attention and the focus of its admiration in 1927; Charles Lindbergh (*below*) stands in front of his aeroplane, the *Spirit of St Louis*, shortly before the flight which placed him firmly among the legends of flying. In this little aircraft with its radial engine Lindbergh became the first man to fly a heavier-than-air machine across the Atlantic from New York to Paris, accomplishing the flight in thirty-three and a half hours. The journey was nearly twice as long as that of Alcock and Brown eight years earlier. (*Above*) The *Spirit of St Louis* in flight; (*right*) Lindbergh in flying helmet.

On leaving school James and Frank entered the Victorian Civil Service. Later James became secretary to the Australian High Commissioner in New York and then Trade Commissioner in New Zealand. Frank, who decided to study Law, after a time became a prominent member of the legal profession and Crown Solicitor to the State of Victoria. In 1960 he sat as a member of the Monckton Commission to inquire into the problems of Central Africa in its progress towards independence.

John Sampson, Robert Menzies' maternal grandfather, a staunch Labour man, a miner, had been one of the founder members of the first Miners' Union in Victoria. He, too, was a great talker, who would take his small grandson on one side and talk to him about politics, little of which the boy understood. The influence of father, grandfather and his uncle Sydney Sampson who was also involved in politics, was to have a great effect on Robert's future.

From the day on which the phrenologist had made his prediction about his future career, Robert Menzies never faltered in his determination to be a lawyer, and he studied always to fulfil his ambition. This, as we have seen, he achieved in 1916, when he not only obtained a First Class Honours degree in Law, but was adjudged the most promising law student in the whole of Australia.

The organization of the legal machine in Victoria is somewhat different from the British system. In England a would-be lawyer on qualifying must decide whether he is to be a solicitor or a barrister; in Victoria, both branches are, in theory, one, though in actual practice the lawyer specializes either as barrister or solicitor. If he chooses to be a barrister, when he begins to serve his articles, he goes to the Secretary of the Bar Council, asks for his name to be put on the roll, and gives an undertaking to work only as a barrister. This is what Robert Menzies did.

As a pupil of Owen Dixon, one of Victoria's leading barristers, Robert Menzies soon began to make a name for himself and to attract a good deal of attention. He achieved nation-wide fame, however, rather in the way that an actor sometimes rises from obscurity to stardom overnight.

He specialized in Constitutional Law and in Property Law—today he is considered one of the greatest Constitutional Law experts in the world. One day as he was studying a brief in his chambers a solicitor arrived. He said:

"I'm in a fix, Menzies, I've a case coming on in the High Court in a couple of days' time. I had briefed X, but he's been taken ill, and won't be better in time. The case turns on a point of Constitutional

Law, and I'm told that you're pretty good at that sort of thing. Can you possibly help me out and take the brief? I shall be very grateful."

"May I see the brief?" Menzies asked.

The solicitor handed it across the desk, and Menzies glanced through it quickly. He saw at once that the solicitor was right, but that the point was also a very tricky one. He was unperturbed by this, however, and said he would take the brief.

When the day came, Menzies presented his case, and was about to sit down when the judge began to ask questions. Many of them had not occurred to him, others seemed to him to have no bearing on the case. At last the judge finished, saying:

"Mr Menzies, before you sit down, I want to tell you that a great deal of this argument has been forced on you by my questions, and I must congratulate you on the great ability with which you have conducted your case."

Only in very rare cases do judges congratulate young barristers in open court. The newspapers seized on it, and in no time at all the name of Robert Menzies was known throughout Australia. This fame was considerably increased two or three years later when he won a case of great importance against practically all the leading legal brains of Victoria.

In 1920 he was invited one evening to a party and there he met Pattie Maie Leckie. He fell in love with her on the spot, and asked her to marry him. She consented, and they were married on 27 September, 1920. On 14 January, 1922, their first child, a son, Kenneth, was born; on 11 October, 1923, a second son, Robert; and in 1928, their youngest child, a daughter, Margery, arrived in the family circle.

By the time that Robert Menzies had been ten years a barrister, the work he was asked to undertake became too much. When a barrister becomes a King's Counsel he is offered only very important briefs, and to try to cut down his work Menzies applied to take silk. His application was granted, and in 1929, at the age of only thirty-four, he became the youngest K.C. ever to be appointed in Victoria.

At the same time he decided to enter politics. His first attempt to be elected to the Victorian Upper House as a Liberal failed miserably, but at a second attempt a short time later he was successful. Within a few months he had been appointed a Junior Minister. He found the work of the Upper House dull. The Liberal Party was, as he put it, "suffering a bit from old age". The elderly leaders had lost the punch and drive in debate that a good Government party should have, so Menzies decided to resign from the Upper House and try for election to the Lower House.

Once again he was successful. In the Lower House he quickly won a great reputation as a witty, hard-thrusting debater and soon attracted the younger members round him, whom he formed into an organization within the Liberal Party, called the Young Nationalists. At the next General Election, the Young Nationalists won the majority of seats, but Menzies realized that he had not yet sufficient experience to be Prime Minister and made way for the leader of the Liberals. Nevertheless, in the new Government Menzies was appointed to three departments—Attorney General, Solicitor General and Minister of Railways.

The new Government had not been long in power when the Prime Minister became ill, and Robert Menzies became acting Prime Minister. In this position, he proved himself so able that he was made deputy leader of the Liberal Party. His rapid rise in State politics was noted by the Federal politicians, and one day in 1934, he received an invitation from the Federal Prime Minister to succeed the Federal Attorney General who was retiring through ill-health. In the Australian Parliamentary system the Attorney General is the third most important Minister after the Prime Minister and his Deputy. The offer was, therefore, a handsome one to a man just forty years of age. He hesitated, however, for it would mean parting from his family. When Mrs Menzies heard his reason, she made him telephone the Prime Minister to tell him that he would accept.

His rise in the Federal Parliament was as meteoric as his progress in State politics had been. Not only that, the United Australia Party, as the Federal Liberals called themselves, chose him to be their deputy leader.

In 1935 he was sent to England to plead a case on behalf of the Australian Government before the Judicial Committee of the Privy Council. His conduct of this case drew the attention of the greatest legal brains in England, and in the following year, he was appointed a Privy Councillor; moreover the members of Gray's Inn made him an Honorary Bencher, an honour they bestowed only on the most distinguished lawyers who were not members of their Inn.

Despite his great ability, or perhaps because of it, and certainly on account of his caustic tongue, he was not at all popular in Australia and even in his own Party he had many critics. Whatever he was accused of, and there were many terrible accusations, he was never accused of being crooked. He has always been a man who has adhered to what he believed to be right, no matter what the consequences might be. It was this in 1939 brought about his first great political personal crisis.

The Government had been preparing a scheme of National Insurance, in the framing of which Menzies, as Attorney General, had played a leading rôle. When the moment came for the measure to be presented to Parliament alterations were made, with none of which Menzies could agree. Rather than put forward something to which he was opposed, he resigned his office and became an ordinary Member of Parliament.

He was not to remain out of the picture for long. Within a short time the Prime Minister and leader of the Party died suddenly. The Deputy Prime Minister became Prime Minister. It was, however, Menzies who was elected leader of the Party. Everyone thought that the Prime Minister would make way for Menzies, but he refused. Not long afterwards he lost the support of his followers and had to resign. In April, 1939, Robert Menzies became Prime Minister of Australia for the first time. He was forty-five.

As Prime Minister during the war, he stood up to Sir Winston Churchill, who criticized the efforts which the Australians were making. No one else had dared so to take Sir Winston to task. Often when two men of very strong character find themselves in opposition, a mutual admiration seems to spring up between them. This happened in the case of Churchill and Menzies. They became firm friends.

Menzies, however, lost the confidence of his own Party and resigned both as Prime Minister and as leader of the Party. As a result, the Labour Party took over the Government, and remained in power until the General Election of 1943, when they again inflicted a crushing defeat on the Country Party.

The Country Party came to Menzies and asked him to lead them again. He agreed on one condition—that he could have an absolutely free hand in reorganizing the Party. Although he did his best, three years was not long enough to restore the Party's fortunes: in 1946, Labour were again returned to power.

In 1949 the tide turned. In the General Elections of that year the great efforts of Menzies to restore his Party to strength bore fruit. The U.A.P. and Country Party were returned to power, and Menzies was Prime Minister once more. For sixteen years Robert Menzies remained in power. Sometimes it was with very small majorities, which produced conditions of government which would have daunted many another man. Menzies fought off all opposition:

not only did he steer his own country through many severe crises, which made him the most outstanding Australian political leader in that country's history, but he gained a world-wide reputation as a statesman.

While on her tour of Australia and New Zealand in 1962, Queen Elizabeth marked his great services to his own country and to the Commonwealth by conferring on him the Knighthood of the Thistle. Sir Robert Menzies had come a long way from the little weather-board general store in Jeparit, as the phrenologist foretold he would.

In 1965, at the age of seventy-one, Menzies decided that the time had come for him to make way for a younger man. In an age in which political leaders show a distinct reluctance to surrender their positions of power this was a refreshing decision and at the same time a surprising one. It was surprising because many, even among his ardent supporters, had come to accept the idea that Menzies had grown accustomed to power. At the same time, however, it was typical of the man who, despite all the claims of his critics and opponents, had used his vast talents for nearly forty years sincerely in the service of his country.

The admiration and affection in which Menzies was held in Great Britain was practically demonstrated a year later when the death of Sir Winston Churchill, having left vacant the wardenship of the Cinque Ports, he was offered and accepted this ancient office.

George Gershwin
1898-1937

DURING the summer of 1937 a young composer was admitted to the Cedars of Lebanon Hospital in Hollywood. For a few months he had been suffering from severe headaches. On 10 July, he was operated on for a brain tumour, and died the following morning without recovering consciousness. He was thirty-eight years old, and celebrated throughout the world as the composer of *Rhapsody in Blue*. George Gershwin, although primarily a writer of popular music, made a unique and widely influential contribution to the history of modern music. Yet his music was always fundamentally American in spirit. Its basis was jazz—the traditional music of the American Negro. He once wrote:

> "I regard jazz as an American folk music, a very powerful one which is probably in the blood of the American people more than any other style of folk music. I believe that it can be made the basis of serious symphonic work of lasting nature."

On another occasion he wrote:

> "Jazz is music; it uses the same notes as Bach used. Jazz is the result of the energy stored in America. . . . It is an original American achievement that will endure, not as jazz perhaps, but which will leave its mark on future music in one way or another."

Of course he was right. Gershwin absorbed into the pattern of his own music the basic harmonies and rhythms of Negro jazz. *Swanee*, his best-known song is a clear case in point. In the wider sense of the word, he cut new paths which many others were to follow. His significance as a creative pioneer must not be underestimated. He was one of the few genuine shapers of musical trends in the modern age. In this sense he ranks with Debussy and Stravinsky. It was Gershwin who convinced musicians throughout the world that American popular idioms could be used as the basis of serious music. Although both Debussy and Stravinsky had made tentative efforts to incorporate the popular idioms of American musical style in experimental compositions, it was the inventive and daring genius of George Gershwin which brought a full recognition and acceptance of these traditional sources.

Some indication of the significance of Gershwin's influence can be gathered from the fact that his *Rhapsody in Blue* was followed by such compositions as Hindemith's *Neues vom Tage*, Kurt Weill's *Mahoganny*, Ravel's "Blues" Sonata, Constant Lambert's *Rio Grande* and Aaron Copland's *Concerto for Piano and Orchestra*. Gershwin helped to create and establish an American musical idiom which was indigenous in spirit and in technical style; yet an idiom that was gradually to influence the whole course of international music.

George Gershwin was born in the Williamsburg district of Brooklyn on 26 September, 1898. His brother Ira who was to be closely associated with him in later life, was born two years earlier when the Gershwins were living in a small apartment on the corner of Hester and Eldridge streets above a pawn shop.

His parents were Russian Jews who fled to America along with thousands of their co-religionists in the last quarter of the nineteenth century. They fled from St Petersburg and the pogroms to begin a fresh life in the new world. Moshe Gershovitz, Gershwin's father, changed his name to Morris Gershvin (and later to Gershwin), and, when George was born he was a leather worker in New York. He was a man of no particular ability or calling, and was continually changing his employment. At various times he was a bookie, a restaurant owner, the manager of a Turkish bath, and the landlord of a boarding house. He also liked moving about and, in the twenty-two years following his marriage in 1895, he moved his family more than thirty times! George's mother, Rose, was the daughter of a furrier whom Morris had known in St Petersburg. The family was never poor, but their early years in New York were spent in poor and poverty-stricken surroundings. There were four children of the marriage. Ira (whose real name was Israel), George, Arthur, who was born in 1900, and a sister, Frances, who was born in 1906.

As a boy, George was indistinguishable from the thousands of boys, Jewish and Gentile, who lived, played and fought one another on the tough East Side of New York. At this time there was no sign of the passion and creative genius for music which was to be the dominant factor in his life. The love of music gradually began to make itself felt. One day, when he was about six years old, he stood outside a penny arcade listening to the automatic piano playing Rubinstein's *Melody in F*. "The peculiar jumps in the music held me entranced and rooted to the spot," he recalled.

The East Side was a tough training ground in those days. Kids literally fought for survival. Instinctively they developed a savagely competitive spirit, and George Gershwin learned at a tender age that he would have to fight to survive. In later life he was continually trying to prove himself better than the next fellow.

His first real encounter with music came at the age of ten, when he was attending the public school on Fifth Street and Second Avenue. One day while playing ball in the school yard he chanced to hear the sound of Dvořák's *Humoresque* drifting from an open window. The violinist was little Maxie Rosenzweig, the son of a local barber. So impressed was young George that he called at the lad's house to tell him how much he liked his playing. The two boys became firm friends, and it was now that George decided he would become a musician. He began to take piano lessons at fifty cents a time.

Soon afterwards he acquired a piano of his own and, although he played with little subtlety or finesse, he soon learned to play his favourite pieces, *Humoresque* and the overture to *William Tell*. He was about fourteen when he met Charles Hambitzer, who realized instantly that George's pianoforte playing was really not very good. Himself a Russian emigrant, Hambitzer was a composer and instrumentalist of considerable reputation. He was also a skilled teacher of the piano, violin and cello. After hearing young George play the overture to *William Tell*, he remarked: "Who on earth taught you to play like that? Let's hunt out the guy and shoot him—and not with an apple on his head either!"

George became the pupil of Hambitzer, and although he was to have other teachers, it was Hambitzer who taught him most and provided the influences of lasting importance. He introduced Gershwin to Chopin, Liszt and Debussy, and these were the sources of influence that remained.

The Gershwin family were unconvinced that George's musical gifts were sufficient to provide him with a livelihood, and accordingly, at fourteen, he was sent to a commercial college to learn typewriting, shorthand and double-entry book-keeping. George had other ideas. He hated his work at the commercial school and soon began to wonder if he might try his hand as a professional pianist and song writer. After a year at the college he became a song-plugger in Tin Pan Alley, the youngest song-plugger in the business. He was then only fifteen.

Every day a deafening orgy of sound rose from the Alley, where more than a hundred pluggers pounded away in their little cubicles.

It was to Tin Pan Alley that the streams of producers, singers actors, orchestra-leaders and publishers came in their search for talent and musical merchandise. George was a good, hard-working song-plugger, and he made a success of the job. Still he was only a hired hack, plugging other people's songs. He began to grow restless for his own share of recognition. In 1917 he left the Alley and spent the summer in a variety of aimless jobs. Then his big chance came. He met Max Dreyfus, the man who had first spotted the promise of Jerome Kern, and who was head of the Harms publishing house. He offered Gershwin thirty-five dollars a week, so long as he turned over all his compositions to the Harms Company. There were no fixed hours, or specific duties; he was free to work and compose as he pleased, and provided with a little room and a piano.

For the next twelve years all George Gershwin's music was published by Dreyfus. His first full-scale musical, *Half-past Eight*, which he wrote in 1918 was unsuccessful; his next *La La Lucille* which appeared in 1919 was only a moderate hit. Yet in the same year Gershwin wrote the song that was his first real musical success, and which brought his name before millions of people. *Swanee* was composed during an evening bus ride after he had been dining with Irving Caesar at Dinty Moore's restaurant. By the time Gershwin and Caesar reached the Washington Heights district of New York where George was then living, the song was already almost complete in his mind. He rushed to his piano and played the tune while his friends and family gathered around him admiringly.

It was a song destined to sweep the world, and, when it was written, its composer was barely twenty-one years of age. Gershwin belonged to the age of jazz; to the era of the Charleston and the Black Bottom. But the haunting and plaintive element in his music stemmed directly from the nostalgic yearnings of his Jewish blood. Like the American Negro, the Jew also yearned for a lost homeland.

In 1922 Gershwin wrote a short opera called *Blue Monday* which described the love affair of Vi, Joe and Tom, all Negro characters. It was a landmark in Gershwin's career, both as a forerunner of *Porgy and Bess*, and technically, because he demonstrated here how jazz music could be openly applied to operatic themes.

Paul Whiteman was among those who saw *Blue Monday* and he was deeply impressed. In those days Whiteman was the undisputed "king of jazz", whose great belief it was that jazz deserved to be elevated to the status of great music. He declared: "Jazz is the music of our time. Jazz is the voice of our age."

So it was only natural that the two men should team up, and it was for a Paul Whiteman concert that Gershwin composed perhaps his most celebrated piece of music—*Rhapsody in Blue*. He wanted to write a "blues" concerto for Whiteman and the inspiration came during a train journey to Boston for the première of his musical *Sweet Little Devil*. The main theme of *Rhapsody in Blue* is the description of a train journey; this particular train journey, and indeed all such journeys. The whistles, the rattle and clatter of the wheels, and the exciting confusion of symphonic sounds which any of us can hear as we sit and listen to the natural music of a speeding train, all these George Gershwin took and blended into the wonderful, immortal rhythms and melodies of *Rhapsody in Blue*.

By the time he arrived at Boston Gershwin had worked out in his mind the main construction of the rhapsody. That train journey had given him the beginning and the end of that piece of music. The middle came suddenly, and in a characteristically inspirational fashion. A few days after the Boston train journey, Gershwin found himself called on to improvise at a party. As he once said: "When I'm in the right mood, music drips from my fingers." It certainly dripped that night. As he played, a "blues" theme that had long haunted his mind suddenly took shape and spilled over into his playing. This brief, melancholy snatch was to provide exactly what he needed as the middle section of *Rhapsody in Blue*. Gershwin completed the composition in January, 1924, and after a rehearsal at the Palace Royal Night Club before a specially invited audience, Paul Whiteman presented it at a concert which took place at the Aeolian Hall, New York, on 12 February that year.

The programme was a curious mixture, ranging from Berlin to Schoenberg, from Elgar to Gershwin. Among the celebrities who attended that night were Rachmaninoff, Stokowski, Mischa Elman, John McCormack and Stravinsky. Gershwin himself was at the piano for the *Rhapsody*. Although there were certain criticisms, *Rhapsody in Blue* was virtually a smash-hit from the night of the first public performance. It was to make Gershwin a very rich man. In the ten years following its first performance it netted its composer more than a quarter of a million dollars.

Rhapsody in Blue turned Gershwin into one of the most famous persons in New York. Thereafter he was lionized by wealthy hostesses, who competed to get him to play the piano at their lush parties. The time was the gay twenties and Gershwin lived at a furious pace. A killing pace as it was to turn out. All the outward signs of material success were now his to command; beautiful women, fantastic cars, lavish parties, expensive clothes. Everywhere he travelled he was fêted and reported like a king. He was the owner of a magnificent penthouse on Riverside Drive. Millionaires clamoured to introduce their daughters to the great man—a king or the jazz age. In his spare moments he indulged his favourite hobby; painting. Although he possessed little real talent in this direction the practice of painting brought him very real pleasure. He collected paintings as well; good paintings; by Picasso, Chagall, Modigliani, Gauguin and many more of the great names of modern art.

His appreciation of painting was immensely sensitive and penetrating. Once when he was shown a Picasso side by side with a Paul Klee, he remarked after a moment's reflection: "I can see it now: Picasso is the full orchestra and Klee is the string quartet . . ."

1928 was an exciting year for George Gershwin. He made his fifth visit to Europe. He came to London, and attended a George Gershwin evening at the Kit-Kat Club, then the city's leading night club. He renewed his friendship with the Mountbatten family and the Duke of Kent. He was tailored at Savile Row, and sported a bowler; even so far as he could an English accent! In Paris, in May, his *Concerto in F* was greeted triumphantly at the Paris Opéra.

He was working on the preliminary drafts for a new composition called *An American in Paris*. In December, 1924, the New York Philharmonic gave the first public performance of this work at Carnegie Hall. It was a ballet in the modern style intended to suggest a young American wandering through the streets of Paris. Gershwin himself described *An American in Paris* as a "rhapsodic ballet". It had a mixed reception. *The New York Evening Post* criticized Gershwin for his curious assortment of instruments, and went on to wonder whether anyone would remember it in twenty years' time. Another critic described it as "dull, patchy, thin, vulgar, long-winded and inane". Yet *An American in Paris* remains one of Gershwin's most characteristic works.

Soon after completing this latter work, Gershwin began writing songs for a Ziegfeld musical comedy called *Show Girl*, and the next step was inevitably a move to Hollywood. Late in October, 1930 he was on his way to California to write a score for a Fox musical comedy film called *Delicious*.

The tempo of life in Hollywood, its ceaseless round of gaiety and night life, of fast and flashy living, seriously interfered with his work as a serious composer. He was rich and famous, but his work was suffering. Yet his last, and perhaps his greatest, contribution to music was still to be written. Certainly it was his most serious operatic composition. *Porgy and Bess*, a story of Negro life in America opened at the Colonial Theatre in Boston, on 30 September, 1935, and was acclaimed at once both as a masterpiece, and as a near miss. "It should be played in every country of the world—except Hitler's Germany—it doesn't deserve it", said one wildly enthusiastic critic. Other, less enthusiastic critics described it as "fake folklore music" . . . "a strong but crippled opera" . . . "an aggrandized musical show. . . ."

The half-hearted response of New York critics did not shake Gershwin's own faith and enthusiasm. *Porgy and Bess* was based on the novel *Porgy*, written by DuBose and Dorothy Heyward. In transforming the play into an opera, Gershwin brilliantly assimilated the elements of Negro song and dance into his own unique writing. His transmutation of Negro musical idioms and styles was a landmark in the history of modern music.

As one critic has said: "writing Negro music so strongly flavoured with folk ingredients was certainly the logical goal for Gershwin. The man who wrote *Porgy and Bess* grew out of the boy who had acquired a vivid and unforgettable musical experience from hearing a Negro band in Harlem. . . . ." Alas, Gershwin was not to see his faith in *Porgy* vindicated. He died two years after the première and it is only since his death that the opera has taken its place as one of the unquestionable masterpieces of the music of our time.

Meanwhile his work in Hollywood continued at a hot, and exhausting pace. He wrote the songs and music for the Fred Astaire-Ginger Rogers musical *Shall we Dance?* and was planning to return to New York to write the music for *The Goldwyn Follies* when he was struck down with the series of appalling headaches that were to lead, and so swiftly, to the Cedars of Lebanon Hospital.

The shock of his death, and at such an early stage in his glittering career, threw a pall of grief over the nation. He was, after all, the spirit of the youth and gaiety of the twenties; and a genuine creator of music and songs that will last for ever.

Ernest Hemingway
1898-1961

IT was a tremendous chance for the cub reporter—the biggest fire in Kansas City for years—and he tore to it as fast as his legs would carry him. From a dozen blocks away the smoke was visible, a cloud curling up into the evening sky. As he got nearer there was the sound of burning, the crack of flames, the quick explosion as dried wood caught fire. Were there—or did he imagine it?—were there shrieks of people trapped in the blaze?

There was a cordon round the area and he waited till the nearest policeman was looking away before he hopped over the barrier. The heat was immense, but he was determined to get a story, a better story than anyone else. At least he was nearer the fire.

A reporter on a rival paper caught sight of him, grabbed a policeman by the shoulder. The man turned. "Hey you!" he roared, "come outta that fire—"

He pretended not to hear and in fact the roar of flames, the singing jets from a dozen firehoses, had drowned all other noise. The heat was unpleasant, almost painful, and he wondered fleetingly whether one really got a better story by getting nearer, whether it would be the old, old business of missing the wood for the trees. At least—and he started to write in his notebook—at least one could give a description of what it felt like, burning to death. He noted with interest that sparks had burnt holes in his new brown suit—but of course that was part of the game, one didn't count the cost. In any case the paper would pay compensation, would have to, after his story. He would have a new suit, a better suit, tomorrow —on the Kansas City *Star*.

He evaded the police a second time, tore up the street to the *Star* offices, composing a story to end all fire stories as he ran. Several people had been lowered to the ground while he was watching, one of them was screaming, all of them must have been burnt. It would be a story all right.

In twenty minutes it was on the Night Editor's desk, an hour later it was the front page of the morning edition, much as he had written it. There could be no argument, the story was superb, the Editor sent for him to say so. It was a proud moment.

"Thank you, sir. I'm glad you liked the story. And—and, sir?"
"Yes, Hemingway?"
"I'd like to claim for a new suit."
"A *new suit*? Are you mad, boy?"
"No, sir. I burnt mine, getting that story."
The Editor looked at him for a moment and smiled. "I'm afraid, Hemingway, that's a risk we have to take in life."

The incident never left Ernest Hemingway's mind. "It taught me," he said years later, "it taught me never, never to risk anything until I was prepared to lose it completely."

Ernest Miller Hemingway was born on 21 July, 1898, in Oak Park, a suburb of Chicago, the elder son of Dr and Mrs Clarence Hemingway. His father was highly regarded in the community, a gifted, widely travelled man who had studied medicine in Edinburgh. His wife, Grace, had been a professional singer before the marriage, and, although she was a good mother to Ernest, his brother and his sister, she never quite forgave the marriage for ending her career. Ernest grew up outdoors, loving birds, yet at the same time loving to hunt with his brother, go shooting rooks and rabbits. He wrote prolifically for his High School paper. To his parents' dismay he refused to go on to college and study medicine and moved instead to Kansas City to work on the Kansas City *Star*. Here one of his first assignments was to cover the fire which cost him his suit.

A few months later the United States entered the First World War and Hemingway, keen to fight, was refused entry into the Army because of his eyesight, but managed to get into the American Red Cross. In April, 1918, he was sent abroad to the Italian sector as an ambulance driver and stretcher bearer. Three months later he was severely wounded, by the Piave River. At first it was just a scratch, a graze from a mortar bomb, it was nothing: but then he picked up the companion who had fared less well and tried to run with him to shelter. He got him there, but was hit twice by bursts of machine-gun fire.

He spent the next three months in hospital, fell deeply in love—as he was to do, again and again, through life—and was refused by the girl. A few years later he made her a central character in his war novel, *A Farewell to Arms*, under the—false—name of Catherine Barkley.

War over, he returned home, but again he refused to stay. He managed to get himself a job in Toronto, tutoring the son of Ralph Connable, the new Canadian head of Woolworth's. Connable introduced him to the editor of the Toronto *Star*, for whom he was able to do some freelance work. It satisfied his urge to write, but it was scarcely profitable: the first fifteen articles, painstakingly wrought, sold for a total of a hundred and fifty dollars. Soon the wanderlust came back and to the great distress of his parents who had just convinced themselves that Ernest, though far away, was doing well for himself, he threw the job up, in the spring of 1920, to visit Michigan and "go fishing". There may have been other considerations. He married his first wife, Hadley, a few months later, in Michigan.

He had kept up his freelance connexion with the Toronto paper and in December, 1921, he was able to go back to Europe as their Paris correspondent, on a piecework and expenses basis. He had confidence in his ability, he was certain that the piecework would support himself and Hadley in a life of comfort. If at first he failed to achieve it, he had soon impressed the *Star* sufficiently for them to put him on the enhanced rate of seventy-five dollars a week, plus expenses. Things were moving in the right direction and he began to indulge a long-felt ambition to write fiction. He knew many expatriates in Paris and one of them, Sylvia Beach, who ran the quaintly named "Shakespeare & Co." bookshop, set out to help him. With her encouragement and that of other friends, Ezra Pound, Gertrude Stein, he brought out, in a small, French edition, *Three Stories and Ten Poems*, followed a little later by a collection of short stories, *In Our Time*.

The Hemingways had gone home for the birth of their first child and during the visit Ernest had precipitated one of the quarrels which, with love of adventure and susceptibility to women, were so strongly characteristic of him. It was a violent quarrel with his editor and it ended a career with the Toronto *Star*: but soon he was back in Paris, with wife and son, determined to succeed as a writer of fiction. In 1924 he paid a visit to Pamplona and was gored by a bull—getting his material as he always did, the hard way. Towards the end of 1925 he published his first novel, *The Sun Also Rises* (published in England as *Fiesta*). By this time his work was becoming known throughout the English-speaking world: the novel was an immediate success.

By 1927 he had published more short stories under the title *Men Without Women*, and by the end of that year he was divorced from Hadley and married to a second wife, Pauline. Once again he took his wife home for the birth of a child, but this time, after a second son had been born in Kansas City he decided to settle in Florida and work on his novel of the World War, *A Farewell to Arms*.

It was while Hemingway, his wife and two children were living in Key West that his father, troubled by illness and debt, shot himself with a revolver. Hemingway was appalled by this: the causes of his father's suicide and the old man's method of taking his life were to stay with him until the end of his own.

A third son was born in 1931 and he decided to settle in Cuba. Once again he refused to stay still: almost immediately he embarked for Africa and safari. He had developed a lean, spare, masculine and unique prose which was already producing its legion of imitators, and quite probably he had begun to see himself, as a man, in terms of his writing—the lean, spare, one-hundred-per-cent masculine man, who wrote of nothing until he had experienced it. This image of himself sparked off a number of vicious quarrels with people who questioned it. In particular, the self-styled adventurer, Richard Halliburton who had, among other exploits, swum the Hellespont and crossed the Alps on an elephant and written books about it, enraged Hemingway and was cruelly and publicly humiliated by him in Havana during the course of what he had hoped was a friendly call on a fellow writer. Shortly afterwards, the American critic Max Eastman was indiscreet enough to suggest that some of Hemingway's writing conveyed an air of "fake hair on the chest". Versions of their encounter are many and hilarious, but although there is doubt as to who won and by what margin, there is little doubt that the episode ended in a hand-to-hand fight.

In 1936 the Spanish Civil War began and Hemingway, now a world-famous author, had no trouble in arranging to be sent as correspondent for the North American Newspaper Alliance. Here, as in his first fire story, he was absolutely fearless, sending back a stream of live, action-packed despatches in an inimitable style, but within weeks of his arrival he had objected to the presence in Spain of the actor Errol Flynn, screen specialist in the swashbuckling rôle Hemingway played in real life, and he gleefully quoted examples of the man's "cowardice".

The issues of the Spanish Civil War really engaged his heart and mind and the Spanish novel *For Whom the Bell Tolls* is deeply moving. By 1938 he was back in New York giving his "first and last" political speech to the League of American Writers in Carnegie Hall, an impassioned attack on Fascism. On his return to Spain he handed over 40,000 dollars in royalties to the Government.

It was in Spain that he met again the writer Martha Gellhorn, then a newspaper correspondent like himself: she became his third wife.

When America entered the Second World War at the end of

1941, he was invited by the Government to take part in secret work in the Caribbean, concerned with the tracking of enemy submarines. This he did with his customary disregard of danger, earning a Presidential citation, a document which he carried with him everywhere and of which he was extremely proud. The work, in blinding tropical sunlight, in an open boat, gave him a skin cancer which prevented him from shaving—and the beard which characterized him in later life dated from this experience.

By 1944 he was chief of Collier's European Bureau. At the height of the "buzz bomb" campaign on London he was involved in a car accident and the story swelled into one of violent death at the hand of the enemy, culminating in handsome obituaries which, like the Presidential citation, he collected and cherished. On D-Day Hemingway crossed the Channel with the Allied invading forces and later undertook a series of hazardous flights with bombing missions against sites from which the buzz bombs were being launched. There was little time for imaginative writing and by March, 1945, he felt he had done his duty for his country: he flew home to Havana.

More domestic upheaval followed; he was divorced and married his fourth wife, Mary. His war novel, *Across the River and Into the Trees*, did not appear until 1950, when it had a mixed reception, but by 1952 he had left the war behind and published *The Old Man and the Sea* which, two years later, was to win him the Nobel Prize.

By 1960 Hemingway's strength was failing. He left Cuba and settled with his wife Mary in Sun Valley, Idaho. Early on the morning of 2 July, 1961, Mary Hemingway heard a shot, ran down the stairs and found him dead, with a shotgun beside him.

At first it was insisted that death was the result of an accident; but by August, 1966, his widow could reveal to a magazine: "He shot himself... I soon realized it was stupid to go on pretending, believing in an accident..." He went on writing to the end, even while being treated for diabetes and the acute depression and persecution complex which had already driven him twice to attempted suicide.

Hemingway had a profound effect on twentieth-century writing, not only in America, but throughout the world. The cub reporter from the Kansas City *Star*, product of the twentieth century, left his indelible mark upon it.

Louis Mountbatten
1900-

"Well, you've read your papers; you know Ribbentrop signed a non-aggression pact with Stalin yesterday. As I see it, that means war —next week. So I give you, not three weeks, but three days to get this ship ready to sail. None of us will take off our clothes or sling our hammocks or turn in for the next three days and nights, until the job is finished. And then we'll send Hitler a telegram saying, 'The *Kelly*'s ready—you can start your war!' "

IT was August, 1939; three thousand men had volunteered to serve under Lord Louis Mountbatten in the newly commissioned destroyer *Kelly*—from those three thousand a ship's company of two hundred and forty had been selected. Now the two hundred and forty were being told that the commissioning programme laid down by the Royal Naval Dockyard, Chatham, was a lot of nonsense. The customary three weeks for learning stations and duties, for getting cordite, shells, fuel oil and stores on board—three weeks that had always been sacrosanct—would because her commander said so, become three days.

The job was done by a devoted ship's company—and none of them could have guessed the trials that lay ahead, before the *Kelly*, two furious years later, found a final resting place on the bottom of the Mediterranean.

Their first, pleasant, task—carried out at dead of night—was bringing the Duke and Duchess of Windsor back from France to Britain, for the first time since the abdication three years before. Little else happened to break the routine of coastal patrols until December when *Kelly* struck one of the new German magnetic mines and had half her stern blown away. Mountbatten and his crew got her to port. In May of the following year she was again out of action, this time for eight months, by a torpedo off the Dutch coast. It was a clear spring night and the watch on duty stood helpless, fascinated, watching the boiling track approach. Later, Mountbatten described it. " 'That's going to kill an awful lot of chaps,' I thought. Curious, isn't it, one's instinctive belief in personal immortality?" When the torpedo struck, there was a tremendous yellow flash,

594

then orange flames that leapt higher than the bridge from the hole, fifty feet across, which had been torn in the destroyer's hull. A large part of the ship's company was killed and wounded and many of these were trapped in the twisted, scorching metal.

This second return to port, towed by the destroyer *Bulldog* while German bombers and fighters dived on them, was one of the worst experiences of Mountbatten's career. Common sense—and the admiral—dictated that the ship be abandoned—a sitting, leaking target but Mountbatten and his skeleton crew clung to it like barnacles, supervising the rescue of wounded from the holds, helping in the all-pervading darkness as the ship's surgeon worked on the casualties. After ninety-one hours on tow or hove-to, most of it under heavy bombing attack, *Kelly* got back to Newcastle. Here, thousands of spectators who had heard of her exploit gathered on both banks of the River Tyne, cheering wildly, hysterically, as she limped her way to the shipyard with a filthy, oil-soaked, unshaven Mountbatten on the bridge.

Repairs took eight months, during which period the officers and men were parcelled out to other ships, but in December, 1940, *Kelly* was ready for action. Her recommissioning was a proud moment—even though Mountbatten found a hundred and seventy among his crew who had never yet been to sea.

From that time she was in almost continuous action, yet the ship survived until May, 1941. Then, despatched in a heroic attempt to stop German reinforcements reaching the island of Crete, she was bombed again and again till finally, still under full steam at thirty-two knots, she turned turtle. Half an hour later she sank, with two-thirds of her crew.

Three days later, when the survivors had been assembled at Alexandria, Mountbatten said his last sad words to them:

"We've had so many talks, but this is the last. I've always tried to crack a joke or two, but today I feel I've run out of jokes—and I don't suppose any of us feel much like laughing. The *Kelly*'s been in one scrap after another—but even when we had men killed, the majority survived, brought the old ship back. Now she lies in fifteen hundred fathoms and with her more than half our shipmates. There may be less than half the *Kelly* left, but I feel that each one of us will take up the battle with even stronger heart. The next time you're in action, remember the *Kelly*. As you ram each shell home, shout *Kelly!* and so her spirit will go on inspiring us . . ."

He flew home, with a heavy heart, to take command of the aircraft-carrier *Illustrious*, but before he could assume the appointment it was cancelled on Churchill's personal instruction. A week later the letter "M" appeared after his name in the Admiralty lists: "Nature of Appointment Secret".

Louis Francis Albert Victor Nicholas of Battenberg, younger son of Prince Louis and his wife, Princess Victoria, granddaughter of Queen Victoria, was born on 25 June, 1900, at Frogmore Lodge, Windsor. His father, disinherited by his own father's morganatic marriage from the House of Hesse, had left his native Germany as Prince of Battenberg to become a British subject and a naval officer of distinction. His younger son, known from his fifth name, "Nicky," became "Dickie" to avoid confusion with his cousin Nicholas, Tsar of Russia, and the name has stuck among Mountbatten's close friends.

Like his father, he joined the Royal Navy, and four years later in 1917, when anti-German feeling was at its height, the family changed its name to the transliteration Mountbatten and Prince Louis was raised to the United Kingdom peerage as Marquess of Milford Haven. This title passed, on his death, to Lord Louis's elder brother.

From the beginning Lord Louis seemed to have been born with the proverbial silver spoon in his mouth. The blood of most European royal houses ran through his veins; he was unusually handsome and remarkably gifted. Perhaps his greatest gift was that of sheer dogged determination. Having married a beautiful heiress, Edwina Ashley, and found himself wealthy overnight, he decided to take up polo. His friends, seeing him on a horse, roared with laughter and agreed that he looked like a sack of potatoes. He had always been poor at games and at this one he looked like being ludicrous—but he went to great lengths to master it. Carefully he made slow-motion films of the best players, studied them at length, then went out and practised. At length, when he was ready, he organized a team of naval officers, "The Bluejackets", which made naval—and military —history by defeating all the best army teams, losing in the final of the Inter-Regimental Championship only when one of the team broke a leg. Shortly afterward Mountbatten published his *An Introduction to Polo*, by "Marco". It is still the standard textbook.

Above all he was a professional sailor. He wrote a manual of wireless telegraphy which became a standard instruction work; his dictionaries of French and German naval terms are still the best available. He was appointed Commander at the early age of thirty-two, the first indication that the Admiralty had begun to regard him as exceptional. His devotion to his career did not save him from the attentions of the Press. His looks, his wealth, his royal connexions, his love of fast cars and motor-boats (for which the Royal Yacht Club blackballed him) all painted a picture of a playboy, and the Press underlined it. It took a war to rub out the picture and raise him to his full stature as an ice-cold professional in a fighting Service. His service with *Kelly* earned Mountbatten the D.S.O. and was immortalized in the film *In Which We Serve*.

After *Kelly*, things were very different. The appointment which followed the cancellation of his posting to *Illustrious* was that of Head of Combined Operations Command, with the unprecedented acting ranks of Vice Admiral, Lieutenant General and Air Marshal. Many of his contemporaries were enraged, but Churchill had not been wrong in his choice. During the two years of his appointment Mountbatten presided over the development of weapons and tactics which made ultimate victory possible. Before he left the Command he had planned, with his staff, the amphibious operations against North Africa and Sicily; the lessons learnt from these were used in the vital invasion across the English Channel.

By 1943 Churchill had decided fresh blood was needed in the war against Japan. He set up a new, independent, South-east Asia Command. At the Quebec Conference Lord Louis Mountbatten was chosen to head it.

Once again—he was only a substantive Captain, the ranks he had enjoyed in Combined Ops were only acting—the appointment caused a sensation, but he paid no attention, his new task was too daunting. The Army in his new Command had been starved of vital equipment and Churchill explained to him that even when the war in Europe ended he would have lower priority than American forces in the Pacific. Apart from this, his American bombers and transports would get their orders direct from Washington—and he would have as his deputy the touchy and suspicious American General Stilwell, who owed allegiance to both his own Chiefs-of-Staff and General Chiang Kai-shek. It was a situation without precedent, but Mountbatten surmounted it by diplomacy and improvisation. He made two great and much criticized decisions, both of which proved right. He made use for the first time anywhere of bulk supply from the air to enable his troops to overcome the difficulty of moving supplies through thick mud and thus to campaign through the five months of monsoon rain, so catching the enemy by surprise; and he forced the Japanese to fight in the worst disease-ridden areas where he knew his superior medical arrangements (in particular the use of Mepacrine, a malaria suppressive) could keep his own men going. In all this he worked closely with the indomitable General Slim, Commander of the British Fourteenth Army, and the campaign, despite shortage of equipment and last-minute changes of plan (as when all his landing craft were removed to Europe before his planned amphibious invasion of Burma), was a brilliant success. Not the least contribution to it was Mountbatten's personal effect on morale: he made a point of speaking to every unit under his command.

As usual, his decisions were taken with complete disregard of his own future. When Slim required troops in a hurry from the Arakan to the threatened Imphal area, Mountbatten took the necessary aircraft from the American supply route to China, having been expressly forbidden by President Roosevelt to do this. He did it, saved Imphal—and got away with it.

With the war in Europe over, he was given back the landing craft he had so urgently needed, but by then most of Burma had been retaken over the hardest overland route and he planned a major amphibious assault on Malaya. The atom bomb fell on Japan before he could carry it out.

The job for which Mountbatten will be most remembered is the granting of independence to India. He had become respected during his Combined Ops days in London by the leaders of the Labour Party and, with a postwar Labour Government in power under Mr Attlee, he was persuaded to go out to India as Viceroy—the last Viceroy. Still in his forties, he accepted the post.

In India he was able to win the absolute confidence of everyone with whom he came in contact. The British Government was sincere in its intention of granting independence, but the problems seemed insuperable and Mountbatten's personal contribution to what many regard as a miracle was quite incalculable. He had been instructed to hand over power to the Indians by June, 1948. Within a week of his arrival he "realized the date was too late rather than too early", that something had to be done immediately if there were not to be a general conflagration. He did it, after non-stop consultations with Nehru and the Muslim leader Jinnah and achieved partition, with independence by August, 1947. There was bloodshed, but the necessary deed was done, and with superb skill. In India there is still undying devotion to his name, though in Pakistan there is less gratitude since he is blamed for the disadvantages of the partition on which Jinnah insisted. (In fact, in 1971 the stresses inherent in a divided Pakistan eventually reached a critical point and then burst the social fabric. With the support of the Indian Army the new state of Bangla Desh was set up in December, replacing what had formerly been East Pakistan.)

At the request of the new Government of India, Mountbatten became the first Governor General, holding office until June, 1948. He had been made a Viscount in 1946 and an Earl in 1947. Then, determined to go back to his peacetime job, "the one profession I know something about and the one profession I enjoy", he went back to his naval duties. He became Commander-in-Chief, Mediterranean, in 1952, Commander-in-Chief Allied Forces, Mediterranean, in 1953, and in 1955, First Sea Lord. He was made Chief of United Kingdom Defence Staff and Chairman of the Chiefs-of-Staff Committee in 1959, retaining the post until 1965. Having been Personal Naval A.D.C. to both Edward VIII and George VI, he was made A.D.C. to the present Queen in 1953.

Countess Mountbatten, the wife who did so much to further his work in South-east Asia immediately after the war and in the last days of British India, died suddenly in 1960, in North Borneo, during a tour as Superintendent in Chief of St John's Ambulance Brigade.

His life has remained an extremely busy one. In 1966 he was designated by the Home Secretary to examine prison security and report on it. He became President of the International Council of World Colleges and it was in this capacity that he met Emperor Hirohito of Japan when the latter paid a state visit to England in October, 1971.

In 1969 a television series, "The Life and Times of Lord Mountbatten", was screened: it had taken three years to make. When the series was sold to West German Television, Mountbatten, who had narrated the English version, dubbed his own voice into German.

Charles A. Lindbergh
1902-1974

THE book had been fourteen years in the making—from its beginning in 1938 to its end in 1952, it had occupied much of the author's thought and time. It had been rewritten eight times. *The Spirit of St Louis* was a good book; it was enthusiastically received by the critics. In 1954, it was awarded the Pulitzer Prize for biography. The film—Warner Brothers had paid a large sum for the rights—was eagerly awaited. The star would be James Stewart, at the very zenith of his popularity: the film seemed assured of success. It lost money. The dismayed producers conducted an audience poll and found the reason: nobody under thirty—people who were born the year Lindbergh made his famous flight and later—had ever heard of him. Very few people under forty—though they must have been affected at the time by the "Lindbergh Miracle"—had heard of him. Those that had, didn't care. The *New Yorker* magazine touched the heart of the matter with a cartoon of a puzzled boy walking out of a cinema with his father, looking up at the older man, with the caption: "If everyone thought what he did was so marvellous—how come he never got famous?"

Lindbergh's lone flight across the Atlantic, in 1927, had indeed been marvellous—but the scenes which immediately followed were incredible. A nation went mad, and half the world followed suit. President Coolidge sent a cruiser of the United States Navy to bring this young private citizen back from France. A single Sunday paper contained a hundred columns about him. Of the 55,000 telegrams he received, one was signed with 17,500 names, had to be delivered in a scroll 520 feet long, by ten messenger boys. After his triumphal welcome in New York, in which, by tradition, the public tore up paper, threw it out of windows to make a snowstorm of greeting, the Street Cleaning Department picked up 1,800 tons— twelve times as much as after the Armistice celebrations, nine years before.

The fervour mounted, the outpouring of love—the word is scarcely too strong—dropping at times to a trickle, surging again to a flood, continued until September, 1941, when Lindbergh took the step which destroyed him as a "hero". He remained, though, a great man. His achievement was history, whatever happened that could never be undone.

Charles A. Lindbergh was born in Little Falls, Minnesota, the son of an energetic high-principled, lawyer of Swedish descent, who became a man of affairs, buying farms, becoming bank director as well as prosecuting attorney, known far and wide as "C.A.", the man who cared more for principle than profit. His first wife died young, leaving him with three daughters, and shortly afterward he married the science teacher of the Little Falls High School, Evangeline Land. On 4 February, 1902, their only son, Charles A. Lindbergh, Junior, was born, and as soon as the child could crawl, was subjected to "tests" to develop his qualities of endurance and character. By the time he reached his teens, he was his father's chauffeur on many of C.A.'s speaking trips: the older man had plunged into politics, become a Congressman, was scourging "big business", advocating Prohibition. On one occasion they descended a steep hill, son driving, father beside, when the brakes failed. The car plunged downhill towards the railway where a train was passing, while horrified on-lookers saw the older man sitting erect, making no effort to help his son. Just in time the boy swerved the car into a ditch.

"Yes," said C.A., later. "It was a good chance to see what sort of stuff the boy was made of."

C.A. retired from politics shortly before his country went to war in 1917 and then published, at his own expense, a book with the impressive title *Why is Your Country at War and What Happens to You after the War? and Related Subjects*. In it he claimed that the war was caused by an industrial clique, and while local businessmen bought up all available copies to prevent this disgraceful document circulating in Little Falls, its author loudly and publicly reiterated his views.

This strong-willed, incorruptible man was the main influence in young Charles's life, at its most sensitive and formative period. Charles loved his father, admired C.A.'s contempt for popular opinion. At the same time, he loved his mother, who had begun to find C.A. a bit of a strain for twelve months of every year, and he spent happy weeks, sometimes months, staying with her at her parents' home in Detroit. From his maternal grandfather, a dentist who also made household gadgets—baby-rockers, air conditioners, oil burners—he acquired a love of machinery.

By the time he left the Little Falls High School, Charles was a shy, slim, blue-eyed youth of six-foot-three who seemed to have no time for girls, didn't smoke or drink. He was, according to the local people, totally unmemorable, apart from the speed at which he rode his motor-bike, and the fact that he was C.A.'s son. From the University of Wisconsin—selected because its mechanical engineering was reputedly better than that in Minnesota—and which he left before completing his course—he hitch-hiked to Lincoln, Nebraska. Here the Nebraska Aircraft Corporation maintained, as well as a factory, a flying school—which turned out to have one plane, one instructor, and—now—one pupil. After eight hours of instruction, it was announced that the school, having got a good offer for its plane, was closing down. Lindbergh was still owed another two hours' instruction, but there was nothing he could do but attach himself and his still modest flying experience to someone with an aeroplane. He was accepted by a stunt pilot, H. J. Lynch, and succeeded in trading in his two hours of instruction, plus twenty-five dollars in cash, for a parachute.

The nation, in 1922, was looking for excitement—any sort of excitement; bootleg whisky, flagpole sitting, marathon dancing—and when "Daredevil Lindbergh" offered to perform "Death-defying Stunts" with Lynch, the crowds poured in. They gasped as he scrambled out on the plane's wing and plunged off, to be saved from a messy death by his parachute. They screamed as he stood on the top wing while Lynch looped the loop.

A year later he was twenty-one and had saved the five hundred dollars to buy a 90 h.p. Curtis "Jennie". He omitted to mention, as he handed over the money, that he had never soloed (licences were still not required) and nearly killed himself in his first landing. Surviving it, he was soon making good money as a "barnstormer", the man who landed in any field that took his fancy, then took the locals up for joyrides. A year after this he had decided to enlist at San Antonio, Texas, as a Flying Cadet on the Reserve. This would give him an opportunity, at the Army's expense, of learning the niceties of navigation, and getting a lot of free flying. He finished the course with distinction (only 18 out of 104 got through) and was then saddened by the death of his father, still battling hopelessly against big business, the Church and politicians, when a brain tumour killed him.

The end of the course coincided with the passage through Congress of a Bill transferring the carriage of air mail from the Post Office (which hired Army planes and pilots) into private hands. (Ironically, the Bill was carried by railway interests who resented Government competition with their carrying of the mail: within a few years it was to destroy their own passenger business.) Lindbergh joined a syndicate which was awarded the route between Chicago and St Louis. The work was satisfying but left time for contemplation. He found himself considering the prize of 25,000 dollars offered by hotel owner Raymond Orteig for the first man to cross the Atlantic in a heavier-than-air machine, from Paris to New York or vice versa.

The offer had stood since the end of the war, it was still unwon. True, there had been the famous Alcock and Brown flight from Newfoundland to Ireland in 1919, but that had covered only 1,960 miles, whereas the distance from New York to Paris was 3,610. By early 1927 enthusiasm and confidence had grown, there were several contenders, and one of these was Lindbergh. His first problem was to get hold of a suitable plane, and at least one company refused him: even if the young man could pay for it, the firm's reputation would be flying with him, and this gangling youth was not the man for them. Eventually an unknown company, Ryan Airlines, agreed to redesign one of their models to give a range of 4,000 miles. It would carry no radio, have a minimum of instruments, and only one engine.

Shortly after the entry was listed, from "C. A. Lindbergh, Air Mail pilot from St Louis," Commander Byrd and two companions crashed their contender for the prize on its first test landing. A few days later, Davis and Wooster, in a critically overloaded plane, crashed and were killed outside New York. A week later the Frenchman Nungesser took off with his co-pilot, from Paris, was never seen again. Opposition began to mount. France's expert, General Duval announced that the competition was "barbarian", took him back to "the days of gladiators".

Interest was beginning to focus on this "boy with pink cheeks, dancing eyes and a merry grin", a youth, alone and with the minimum of apparatus, who would challenge the rest of the world. At 0752 on the morning of 20 May, 1927, his *Spirit of St Louis* took off on its flight. The whole of the country was emotionally involved as never before: people bought each newspaper edition as it came out, huddled round the radio, learnt that he had headed out over open sea beyond Newfoundland. At the Yankee Stadium, with the Sharkey-Maloney fight about to begin, 40,000 boxing fans rose to "pray for Lindbergh". The next day, when he was reported over Ireland, England, the Channel, tension mounted unbearably. When America learnt that Lindbergh had landed at Le Bourget at 1024 p.m. on the 21st, had been mobbed by cheering Frenchmen, rescued by the American Ambassador, it went mad.

As we have seen, a cruiser was despatched to bring him and his plane back. His modesty, courtesy, good looks and youth had captured all hearts in France and England. On his return to the States, he was commissioned Colonel, given the Congressional Medal of Honour. He was persuaded to send messages to companies, assuring the public that his Wright engine, his A.C. sparkplugs, his Waterman pen, all functioned superbly, a commercialism of which he was scarcely aware and which the public demanded. He was also encouraged to serve his country in the best possible way by making personal appearances outside it with *The Spirit of St Louis*. In particular the American Ambassador to Mexico, Dwight Morrow, was convinced—and rightly—that the appearance of this brave young aviator would serve the cause of diplomacy. Lindbergh cheerfully agreed and landed at Valbuena Field on 14 December before a wildly cheering crowd of 150,000 Mexicans. The incident has its greatest significance in the fact that Lindbergh met and later married Morrow's daughter, Anne.

Their married life began typically at the Morrows' family home in Englewood, New Jersey, with an unheralded wedding ceremony during a "bridge afternoon". Suddenly a door opened, Anne appeared on the arm of her father, the pastor got up from his table, Charles appeared, and the ceremony was over before the wildly speculating Press knew it had begun. Life continued as a game of hide and seek with Press and public, and Anne's flying lessons, their flights together, their home life, all were minutely examined. Charles Lindbergh showed signs of ambivalence in his attitude to publicity: on more than one occasion, during a much-publicized flight, he would land at an intermediate airfield and urge the staff to secrecy. When he became overdue at his destination, the Press went mad with conjecture, and a few hours later he would reappear, refuse to comment on his change of plan.

The year 1932 brought tragedy—the Lindberghs' infant son was kidnapped. The whole apparatus of Press and radio was used, horrifyingly, to impede not only the apprehension of the criminals but the safe return of the child. An army of reporters, photographers, broadcasters, moved in on the household, obliterating all footprints, all clues, stayed there, churning out thousands of words a day.

The child was found, dead; and four years later, after one of the most sensational manhunts in history, the murderer, still denying his guilt, was executed.

The Lindberghs made a number of important research flights in the years preceding the war, during which they lived for some time in England. Charles began to take an interest in Nazi Germany and by the time he returned to the U.S.A. in 1939 he had paid it several visits. He reported that the Germans were invincible. When war broke out he spoke passionately against Lend-Lease, urged America not to support Britain: his popularity, such was the mood of the country, dwindled fast.

In September, 1941, in a widely reported speech, he declared that "pressing this country towards war are the British, the Jewish and the Roosevelt administration—" By this sudden injection of a race issue into the debate he revealed to a horrified public that he supported the Nazis in all their aims. The columnist Dorothy Thompson wrote in a memorable article:

"We may learn . . . that only the British Fleet has stood between us and Lindbergh . . ."

When America at last entered the war, Lindbergh served his country well. He had renounced his colonelcy; now he went out to the Pacific as a civilian representative of an aircraft firm to study "combat performance". This meant that, unprotected by the Geneva Convention, he would fly fighters against the Japanese. He did this with gallantry and skill, devising new tactics and techniques which, among other things, added 500 miles to the range of a fighter without reducing its performance.

Lindbergh spent his later years quietly and outside the glare of publicity, though he became interested in conservation and active in conservation organizations following a trip to Africa in 1964.

He died in 1974 on the small Hawaiin island of Mauii, which had been his home since 1971.

Lindbergh was an enigma. Strongly criticized for his Hitlerian sympathies during the Second World War, and for his apparent anti-Semitism, blind to the villainies of Naziism, stubborn and proud, he was nevertheless a considerate, delightful, sensitive and helpful friend and an unpretentious man. He undoubtedly kept more for himself, and his wife and children, than he ever gave to his public who demanded so much.

Dag Hammarskjöld
1905-1961

"HE died as he had lived—gallantly, unselfishly—in the service of the highest ideals of humanity." That tribute was paid by Dag Hammarskjöld to a fellow Swede Count Folke Bernadotte, the United Nations mediator in Palestine who was assassinated by Stern gang terrorists on 17 September, 1948. On that same day thirteen years later Hammarskjöld himself was killed in a plane crash near Ndola in Zambia on his way to try to arrange a cease-fire in Katanga. Those words described Hammarskjöld and many touching tributes were paid at his funeral on 29 September, 1961, at the ancient town of Uppsala in Sweden; the rulers of the world were represented there to mourn the loss of a great man who had worked for peace so courageously and untiringly.

In the eight and a half years that Dag Hammarskjöld was Secretary-General of the United Nations he vitalized the organization by his own ascendancy—his "moral magistracy"—combined with an humility which inspired trust and affection, especially from the new, emerging nations of Africa and Asia. He wrote:

"From generations of soldiers and government officials on my father's side I inherited a belief that no life was more satisfactory than one of selfless service to your country—or humanity. . . . From scholars and clergymen on my mother's side I inherited a belief that, in the very radical sense of the Gospels, all men were equals as children of God."

When he was elected Secretary-General in April, 1953, he defined the duties of an international civil servant, which were at that time "not yet fully understood and accepted". In September, 1957, when he was elected to a second five-year term he was described by the President of the Assembly as "our supreme international Civil Servant". He left behind him an important body of doctrine and a philosophy contained in statements and reports, published as a selection under the title of *The Servant of Peace*, which should continue to be a guide and inspiration for the future work of the United Nations.

Dag Hammarskjöld was born in Sweden on 29 July, 1905, of a

distinguished and stern father, who was Prime Minister of Sweden during the First World War, and of a charming mother who had "a radically democratic view of fellow human beings". He was the youngest of three brothers and devoted to his mother. This may have kept him from marriage in early life and later he was so busy with government work that he did not want anyone, he said, to suffer as his mother had from the long absences of her husband on public business. When Dag Hammarskjöld was having an argument with Ben Gurion, Prime Minister of Israel, during his first tour of the Middle East in 1956, Mrs Ben Gurion rounded on him, saying, "Why don't you get married? Then you would have to worry about your wife and would leave us alone." He considered he had enough to worry about in trying to keep pace with the problems of the world.

At school and at Uppsala University he was a brilliant student, outstanding in gymnastics, a good mountain climber and a fair skier; he used to go for long expeditions in Sweden and Lapland. His father was then Governor of Uppland and the family lived in the castle looking over the town of Uppsala. "If I were as gifted as Dag and had his talent for dealing with people," said the elderly Hjalmar Hammarskjöld, "I would have gone far". The son drew strength from his upbringing and from his love of Sweden. He said later, having travelled round the world for the United Nations:

> "Faced with the world of others one learns that he who has fully absorbed what his own world has to offer is best equipped to profit by what exists beyond its frontiers. . . . The road inwards can become a road outwards."

In 1930, when he was twenty-five years old, the family moved to Stockholm and he went into government service in the capital. He joined the group of brilliant young Swedish economists, known as the "Stockholm School", who were studying the crisis of the 1930s; he was made secretary of the Royal Commission on Unemployment and later worked for the Riksbank of which he became Chairman. He was not quite thirty when Ernst Wigforss, Social Democrat Minister of Finance, made him his Under-Secretary, regarded as the most important civil service post. One of his brothers was Under-Secretary in the Ministry of Social Welfare and together they drew up the laws which turned Sweden into a model Welfare State. During the war he had many dealings with Norway and London, and afterwards became one of the key figures in the Organization for European Economic Co-operation meeting a wide circle of European and American statesmen. Because of the impression he made at that time, said Ernst Wigforss, "for his acute intelligence, good judgment and ability to find ways out of bothersome situations" it became possible to launch him successfully later as a candidate for the important post of Secretary-General of the United Nations.

When Dag Hammarskjöld arrived at the United Nations in April, 1953, to take over from Mr Trygve Lie he showed himself to be a modest, gentle, rather silent and aloof, fair-haired Swede of forty-eight. Officials wondered whether he would have enough character to deal effectively with all the pressures exercised in that maelstrom of intrigue. His first action was a bold and determined one showing that he did not intend to allow any interference with the international staff of the Secretariat which numbered about 3,500. At that time some sections of the American public were violently anti-Communist, partly as a result of the activities of the notorious Senator McCarthy; Mr Trygve Lie had felt obliged to accede to the pressure of the U.S. State Department and allow F.B.I. Security agents to visit the offices of the United Nations and investigate members of the Secretariat. Hammarskjöld ordered all of them off the premises, and yet managed to keep on good terms with the American Government.

With the help of his staff he set about methodically reorganizing and building up the authority of the United Nations, which was being ignored by the more powerful nations on important matters.

His first really critical task came in December, 1954, when a resolution was passed asking him to try to bring about the release of United States' airmen who had been shot down in the Korean War and imprisoned by the People's Government of China; the Peking Government had sentenced eleven airmen as spies. He realized that there was little object in sending notes of protest to Peking when the People's Government was not a member of the United Nations. "You either condemn or you negotiate; you can't do both", was his argument; but he was not sure that the Government would negotiate with a representative of the United Nations. He took a decision which he knew would infuriate the China Lobby and other groups in America—he would go himself. He knew that a rebuff would lead to an increase in the violence of American feeling which had already been roused by the Communist bombardment in September of the islands of Matsu and Quemoy held by Chiang Kai-shek's troops backed by the United States.

After careful planning Hammarskjöld succeeded in obtaining an

The photograph *below* was taken in September, 1960, when, in the Assembly, Dag Hammarskjöld, Secretary-General of the United Nations Organization, was defending the operations in the Congo and refuting Krushchev's demand for his replacement by a "troika".

The picture *above* was taken almost exactly a year later near Ndola in Zambia after a plane in which Hammarskjöld was travelling to meet African leaders had crashed and killed its occupants. During his tenure of office Hammarskjöld through his great industry and moral stature helped incalculably to vitalize the United Nations Organization.

Right: Major Yuri Gagarin, the Soviet cosmonaut who on 12 February, 1961, became the first man to be launched into orbit around the world.

Below: On 21 July, 1969, Neil A. Armstrong became the first man to set foot on the moon. A short time later he took this photograph of colleague Edwin E. Aldrin deploying scientific equipment on the lunar surface. In the background stands the lunar module.

invitation to Peking. By his tact and ingenuity he was able to discuss with the Foreign Minister, Chou En-lai, the question of the airmen. This was regarded by the Communist as a purely internal matter. Commenting on the meetings which lasted four days Hammarskjöld said: "If I express myself in circuitous terms it is nothing compared to Chou." The one man descended from Chinese mandarins and the other from Swedish aristocrats got on well together. No conclusion was reached, but Hammarskjöld believed that he had succeeded. Six months later it was revealed that he had, for he received a message from Peking congratulating him on his birthday and saying that the airmen were being released for his sake. Officials at the United Nations heaved a sigh of relief and realized that in Hammarskjöld they had a diplomat of ingenuity and resource.

During these early years Hammarskjöld had to keep himself up to date about the complicated politics of the Middle East where there was growing tension. From July, 1956, when Colonel Gamal Nasser nationalized the Suez Canal one crisis followed another up to the climax of Israel's invasion of Sinai and the Anglo-French military landing on 31 October at Port Said. Then came the ruthless Russian Suppression of the Hungarian revolt. The Secretary-General was asked to report on the situation in Hungary at the same time as he was to collect a United Nations Emergency Force to deal with the Suez situation. Another major problem was the collection of a salvage fleet to clear the Suez Canal. Speaking of Hammarskjöld at this time General Eisenhower, President of the United States, said:

"He has a physical stamina almost unique in the world . . . night after night he has gone with one or two hours' sleep and worked all day intelligently and devotedly."

As a result of his handling of the Suez crisis Hammarskjöld's authority was still further increased, though he was bitterly attacked by some.

When a year later he was elected to a second term of five years he outlined what he considered were the duties of a Secretary-General. These gave the post a great deal more authority than his predecessor had assumed; it was an expression of his belief in the need for preventive diplomacy. Again he emphasized the importance of the Charter; the Secretary-General should act under guidance of resolutions passed by the Security Council or the Assembly:

"On the other hand I believe that it is in keeping with the philosophy of the Charter that the Secretary-General should be expected to act also without such guidance, should this appear to him necessary in order to help in filling any vacuum that may appear in the systems which the Charter and traditional diplomacy provide for the safeguarding of peace and security."

So great was his prestige that this interpretation was accepted, in spite of the fears so often expressed about the great influence exercised by any permanent body such as a Secretariat run by a determined Executive. When, during the Lebanese civil war of 1958 Soviet Russia vetoed a Japanese resolution to give the Secretary-General powers to try to improve the situation, the Secretary-General carried out the terms of the resolution despite the veto. The Russians had noted the growing authority of Hammarskjöld: they tried later to force his resignation and abolish the post suggesting in its stead a triumvirate or "troika" as it was called.

Africa became the next great test for Hammarskjöld and the United Nations. When he took up his post in 1953 there were four African members of the United Nations; by 1960 there were twenty-six members. The growing voting influence of the Afro-Asian group caused apprehension at times to the Great Powers who had originally drawn up the regulations of the United Nations with the idea that they would remain in control. When their views were at variance with those of the Afro-Asian group it did not always seem right to them that the vote of a small African or Asian country without much experience or money should equal the vote of a great Power. That was not Hammarskjöld's view:

"Neither size, nor wealth, nor age is historically to be regarded as a guarantee for the quality of the international policy pursued by any nation."

He had already seen what he considered to be "sterile self-assertion" displayed by some European Powers and he disliked the platform of the United Nations being used to propagate the cold war when it should be "primarily a centre of reconciliation". He was pleased when King Hussein of Jordan toasted the United Nations in April, 1959, as "the summit meeting of small nations". When later Khrushchev demanded Hammarskjöld's resignation the Secretary-General replied:

"It is not the Soviet Union or, indeed, any other big Power who need the United Nations for their protection; it is all the others. In this sense the Organization is *their* Organization, and I deeply believe in the wisdom with which they will be able to use it and guide it. . . . I shall remain in my post as long as *they* wish me to do so."

It was a point of view which made him popular with the majority but not with all the larger Powers. Throughout the last six months of 1960 he was bitterly attacked and became a scapegoat for confusion in the Congo.

His visit to twenty-four African countries at the beginning of 1960 made him appreciate how watchful the Governments were lest the United Nations should try to impose a political solution on the Congo or on any other part of Africa as the instrument of the larger Powers. Following the celebrations in Leopoldville of the Congo's independence from Belgium in July, the United States and Soviet Russia backed different African politicians and each endeavoured to influence the United Nations in this cold war. There was a time when the United States, as well as Russia, but for different reasons, objected to the conciliatory line adopted by the United Nations and wished to act independently of it. Hammarskjöld insisted:

"The only way to keep the cold war out of the Congo is to keep the U.N. in the Congo."

The British Government was fearful that the confusion generated from Leopoldville would spread to Elizabethville and Katanga and for a period strongly supported Tshombe's government in Katanga. Hammarskjöld saw that with such disorder as there was in the Congo it might be necessary to force acceptance of the basic constitutional law of the country, but pointed out that he had not been given authority to do this. It had been laid down by the Security Council that members of the military force that had been raised, known as O.N.U.C., should not fire except in self-defence and were not to become involved in internal conflicts.

On 13 December, 1961, Hammarskjöld arrived at Leopoldville, capital of the Congo, for four days of consultation before returning to New York. It was a most critical time. The United Nations forces in Katanga were engaged in severe fighting against the Katanga gendarmeries controlled by Belgian and French officers from Algeria; the U.N. forces had no air protection and were attacked by a French Fouga jet plane flown by a settler, Joseph Delin known as the "Lone Ranger". Violent articles were published in the British and European Press attacking the United Nations troops for using force in Katanga. Hammarskjöld was hard pressed by the Leopold Government and by other governments to crush Tshombe; the British Government sent a special envoy, Lord Lansdowne, to argue the opposite point of view.

The pressures were so constant and considerable that Hammarskjöld seems to have lost some of his usual *sang-froid*. He took a decision which was hasty and unwisely planned. On Saturday, 16 December, he decided that he would try to arrange a meeting with Tshombe at Ndola in Zambia. He did not summon Conor Cruise O'Brien, the U.N. representative in Elizabethville, to report in Leopoldville with the latest information and also to explain why a more forceful military policy was being carried out in Elizabethville than Hammarskjöld had authorized. In spite of the fact that Tshombe on Saturday threatened "total war" if the United Nations did not quit Katanga and that he made conditions about meeting Hammarskjöld although the latter had said he would not accept any conditions, the Secretary-General insisted on going even though he was not certain that Tshombe would be there, though in fact Tshombe did go to Ndola. Hammarskjöld knew that the flight would be dangerous; the greatest secrecy was maintained about the route of the flight and there was no wireless contact in flight for fear of an attack by the "Lone Ranger".

With sixteen others Hammarskjöld left Leopold airport on the afternoon of Sunday, 17 September; the plane crashed and burst into flames that night, nine and a half miles from Ndola airport. One passenger lived for a few days and the others were dead when the rescue teams arrived rather belatedly the next morning. Two separate inquiries were held but nothing was proven as to the cause of the accident.

The confusion in the Congo had spread intense partisanship among the Powers, some of whom did not support the United Nations at a time when it most needed it; Dag Hammarskjöld was overwhelmed and engulfed, but his high reputation remained. He had said:

"Working at the edge of the development of human society is to work at the brink of the unknown."

Douglas Bader
1910-

Of all the stories of personal bravery that came out of the Second World War, none so caught the popular imagination as that of the young legless man who in 1939 persuaded the Royal Air Force to take him back into the Service, who subsequently led a Fighter Squadron with great success, and who for four years after he was shot down in 1941, led the Germans such a dance that on occasions in their exasperation they almost shot him. Douglas Bader's story is a supreme example of the persistence and determination not to admit defeat that go, with many other qualities, to make up courage.

DOUGLAS BADER's father was a civil engineer working in India, where, in 1907, he met and married, when he was thirty-seven, Jessie McKenzie, aged seventeen, the daughter of another British engineer. In the following year his wife presented him with a son, Frederick, and in 1910 with a second son, Douglas.

Because the doctors had told Mrs Bader that she might have difficulty in bearing her second child, her husband sent her home to England to have the baby. When all went well, she returned to India, leaving Douglas with relatives to escape the rigours of the Indian climate until he should be stronger. He stayed with the relatives for two years, and then joined the family in Sukkur.

In 1913, Frederick Bader, the father, resigned his post in India and brought his family home to England. When war broke out he received a commission in the Royal Engineers and went to France, where in 1917 he was severely wounded by shrapnel. He died from the effects of these wounds in 1922. Since the time that he had joined the Army, Bader had been almost constantly away from home. It was left to Mrs Bader, therefore, to bring up her two high-spirited sons, who, as they grew older, lost their enmity towards one another and became friends.

Mrs Bader's sister Hazel had married an officer in the Royal Flying Corps, and it was Cyril Burge's stories of the war, his uniform and his ribbons which seem to have inspired in Douglas the ambition to join the Royal Air Force when he grew up.

Both boys started school at a day prep-school in Kew. Then

Frederick was sent to board at Temple Grove, Eastbourne, where after a short time he was followed by Douglas. At Temple Grove, Douglas proved to be more outstanding at games than in the classroom, and had not been there long when he was playing in the senior rugby XV.

From Temple Grove, Frederick went on to King's School, Canterbury, but on the death of their father, Mrs Bader found that she would not be able to send her younger son to a public school unless he won a scholarship. Though loath to become a swot he settled down to work, but he did not slacken off his games, and in his final year, at the end of which he gained a scholarship to St Edward's, Oxford, he was captain of rugby football, of soccer and of cricket, and in the school sports won every senior event, besides setting up a new record for throwing the cricket ball.

By this time, Cyril Burge had become adjutant of the Royal Air Force College at Cranwell, and it was with the Burges that the two Bader boys spent part of their summer holidays this year. Here Douglas saw, and examined, his first aircraft on the ground, and made up his mind that he would return to Cranwell as a cadet.

Throughout a distinguished sporting career and an undistinguished academic career at St Edward's, he did not lose sight of this ambition, but when the time came for him to think about entering for Cranwell his mother, who had remarried, opposed the idea, first, because she did not like flying, and secondly, because she could not afford the £150 fees that would have to be paid. Douglas was undaunted. He consulted his schoolmasters and asked them if they thought he might have a chance of winning a scholarship to Cranwell. They replied that if he really set himself to do so they thought he could succeed.

In June, 1928, he sat the examination and found the papers not too difficult. He still had to face an interview and a medical test. At the interview he gave the right answers, and passed on to the doctors. Here he met with a slight setback. A couple of years before he had had an attack of rheumatic fever, which had left him with a slightly abnormally high blood pressure. However, the doctor was sympathetic and sent him away for a few weeks, telling him to rest as much as he could. When he reported back, though the blood pressure was still up a little, it was not sufficient to bar him from the Service. Some time later he learned that he had passed fifth in the examination and had won a prize cadetship.

After only six hours' dual instruction, on an October day in 1928, Douglas Bader flew solo for the first time. From that moment he used to insist, "You cannot be in the R.A.F., you must be of it; and you cannot be of it unless you fly."

Besides flying and studying, at Cranwell he added to his laurels on the sports field and in the boxing ring, and the rugger men in the R.A.F. already had their eye on him. He was full of boisterous spirits which Service discipline did little to control. His exploits became so outrageous that he was eventually summoned before his Air Officer Commanding who told him grimly that if he did not change he would have him removed. The shock of the thought that he might be expelled from the Service and not be able to fly again, wrought a remarkable transformation in Bader. He applied himself to his studies and his flying duties with an intensity that made his instructors suspicious at first, and then proud.

He continued his sporting activities and in both his years at Cranwell he gained the College's equivalent of a Blue for cricket, rugby, hockey and boxing. At the passing out, he was beaten to the Sword of Honour by a really outstanding man called Patrick Coote, and his assessment was "Plucky, capable, headstrong; flying rating, above average." He was posted to R.A.F. Kenley as a pilot officer, to No. 23 Squadron.

At Kenley he made rapid progress as a fighter pilot. There were occasions, however, when his high spirits brought official displeasure. He was also invited to play rugger for the R.A.F., and proved one of the star attractions of the team. In November, he was selected to play fly-half for the Combined Services.

Three weeks later, on 14 December, 1931, he flew over with some friends to Woodley Aerodrome, a civilian flying club. While in the clubhouse drinking a cup of coffee, some young pilots asked Bader questions about aerobatics, and presently someone suggested that he should give a practical demonstration. Bader said no, and one of the men made a comment that suggested that he did not dare. He said nothing, but inside he was furiously angry.

As he and his companions took off to return, the young men came to watch them. Still angry, Bader, when his turn came, banked steeply almost as soon as he was off the ground. Something went wrong, and the aircraft began rolling to the right. As he tried to bring her out of the roll the left wing-tip touched the ground and jerked the nose down. Propeller and cowling exploded into the ground; the engine tore out; the aircraft collapsed in a mass of tangled metal.

Bader felt nothing; heard only a terrible noise, then a sudden silence.

An ambulance took Bader, still conscious, to the Royal Berkshire Hospital. Those accompanying him did not think he would reach there alive, for his state of shock was great, though he did not realize how badly he was hurt.

At the hospital he was put to bed. Surgeons looked at him, and decided that they could not operate until and if he came out of the state of shock. As the hours passed and he did not die, Mr Leonard Joyce, the surgeon, decided that he would remove the right leg. He hoped he might be able to save the left leg, though hope was faint. On the second day the faint hope faded, and the other leg was removed, too.

Strangely, it seems, it did not occur to Bader that without his legs he would not fly again. As soon as he had recovered his strength and had been fitted with a wooden limb on his left leg, which had been removed below the knee, he was planning how to drive a motor-car again, and bullied his mother into letting him experiment. The experiments were successful enough for him to arrange for the foot controls on his own sports MG to be changed round, and since he would not have to use his legs like this for flying, he convinced himself that he would soon be in the air once more.

The R.A.F. had him fitted with two artificial legs. These were difficult to get used to. Day after day, in the process of trying to walk with them, he stumbled and fell. He refused to give up and eventually could walk on them without the aid of sticks, indeed people who did not know he had no legs at all, believed that he had only a bad limp.

The moment came when it was to be decided whether he could return to the R.A.F. To him this meant only one thing—flying duties. Before going for his medical he was sent to the Central Flying School to see if he could handle an aircraft safely. He passed the test, and was confident, when he went to Air Ministry for the interview, that he would be told that all was well.

He received a shock.

"I've just been reading what they say about you at the C.F.S. They say you can fly pretty well. Unfortunately, we can't pass you to fly because there's nothing in King's Regulations which covers your case."

Bader tried to argue: it was no good, and a couple of months later he was put on the retired list with a disability pension of £100 a year, which with his retirement pay, brought his total income to just under £4 a week.

He had to a have job, so he applied to the Officer's Employment Bureau and was put in touch with the Asiatic Petroleum Co. who offered him the job of selling aviation spirit to airlines and governments, for £200 a year.

For some months he had been in love with Thelma Edwards. Though they had very little money between them they decided that there was no point in their waiting to get married, and did so in secret at Hampstead Registery Office on 5 October, 1932.

For the next seven years Bader worked for Shell, which took over the Asiatic Petroleum Co. shortly after he joined it, giving satisfaction to the extent of earning himself an annual rise.

Then came the war. On 4 September, 1939, he applied to the Air Ministry to be returned to the active list. This time the situation made it possible for King's Regulations to be bent. If he could pass a flying test, he would be acceptable.

On 8 December, he was back in the R.A.F. A refresher course followed, and on 7 February, 1940, he was posted to No. 19 Squadron, Duxford, to fly Spitfires. Within a short time he was promoted to flight commander with No. 222 Squadron, and in June he was given his first command of a squadron, No. 242, stationed at Coltishall.

No. 242 Squadron was the only Canadian squadron in the R.A.F. at this time. It flew Hurricanes; and its members were a tough bunch, with that easy discipline of Dominions warriors which, in the Mother country, appears very like indiscipline. Bader took their measure quickly, and within a few days had transformed No. 242 Squadron both in their own and their commander's opinion into the best squadron in Fighter Command.

As with the other squadrons of Fighter Command the testing time came during the Battle of Britain. They acquitted themselves better than most, and Bader himself claimed fifteen victims.

In March, 1941, Bader, now a D.S.O. and a D.F.C., was promoted Wing Commander to command a wing which was to carry out' fighter sweeps from Tangmere, on the south coast.

It was while he was flying with this wing on 9 August, that he was shot down. He was taken prisoner almost immediately, and there followed one of those rare acts of chivalry which very occasionally brightened up the hideousness of the conflict. On landing, one of Bader's artificial limbs had been damaged. Bader's prowess had already come to the knowledge of the Luftwaffe, just as his invincibility had become a legend in the R.A.F. The Luftwaffe signalled the R.A.F. what had happened to the leg, and said that if the R.A.F. would care to send an aircraft with a replacement, it would be given a safe conduct. And so it was.

Bader was to remain a prisoner for the remainder of the war, and was to prove one of the most obstreperous officers in captivity. He was always planning to escape—he made one attempt when he was in hospital at St Omer, actually getting out of the building by a rope of sheets—and was constantly on the look-out for opportunities to bait his captors. After another escape from Stalag VII B, on being recaptured he was sent to Kolditz where the Germans held their most difficult prisoners.

On his release in 1945 he was asked to stand for Parliament but refused. For a time he commanded North Weald Fighter Section. In the victory celebrations he led the fly-past of Spitfires.

Late in 1945 Shell wrote to him offering him a job. He could have his own aircraft and fly all round the world doing business for them. He accepted, after a few months' thought, and left the R.A.F.

His own persistence and courage have been an inspiration to hundreds of other disabled men, many of whom he has visited and cheered with his encouragement during the difficult period of their readjustment. He is, indeed, a supreme example of what a man may accomplish who refuses to accept defeat; an embodiment of the nation which displays the same quality in the darkest hours of its history.

John Fitzgerald Kennedy
1917-1963

ON 30 October, 1962, the United States lifted its naval blockade of Cuba and halted its surveillance flights over the island. The Secretary-General of the United Nations flew in: the crisis was over. For the first time in history, the world had stood on the actual brink of nuclear war, a war which would mean, if not the end of civilization, a catastrophe beside which the Black Death, the biblical flood, would seem trivial.

John Kennedy, 35th President of the United States, had won a bloodless, immensely important victory; had, by his resourcefulness, his courage, forced the Soviet Union to retreat for the first time in sixteen years.

It had been known since July that the Soviet Union had increased its military aid to Cuba, but the evidence until mid-October was that the equipment was defensive. The Russians, when pressed, had assured the Americans that this build-up, so close to American shores, was all part of Cuba's defence. Mr Gromyko had given the latest assurance as recently as 18 October, in Mr Kennedy's office in the White House. Then a United States reconnaissance aircraft brought back a picture which told a different story. Bases for a type of missile which could be only offensive, and could penetrate deep into the North American continent, had been newly built, more were being completed. They showed clearly on the aerial photograph.

From that moment the fate of civilization rested on the wisdom and courage of a small group of Americans. President Kennedy consulted his advisers and decided that those bases had got to be dismantled or destroyed. A mere promise from the Russians to stop shipping offensive weapons to Cuba would not be enough. The island would be blockaded by the United States Navy, ceaselessly observed from the air, until bases and their missiles were removed.

The world held its breath: would Mr Khrushchev, the Russian leader, back down, or would one or other of the antagonists fire the first and fatal shot? There were cries from America's allies that

President Kennedy had been taking altogether too much on his own shoulders, had not consulted them: the United Nations should decide these matters—in any case, what did it matter that Russian missiles were in Cuba? American ones were in Turkey and these could easily reach Russia. But John Kennedy knew that with this first entry of Russian nuclear power into Latin America (an incursion which made useless the United States Early Warning System, which was designed to deal with attack from the north, over Canada) the United States had to act, act fast. He imposed his blockade, despite Russian threats of instant, devastating, retaliation—and he won. Mr Khrushchev agreed to remove his missiles, and John Kennedy wisely resisted the temptation to gloat. He imposed no time limit for the removal of the weapons, demanded only assurances that they were, in fact, going to be removed, assurances which he could verify by aerial reconnaissance.

Within a month the bases had been dismantled; Soviet troops and technicians were on their way home. For the first time, a part of the Western World had effectively resisted a major threat from the Soviet Union. Paradoxically, United States–Soviet relations thereafter were better than they had been since the war. Carefully, President Kennedy left the way open for discussions not only on Cuba, but on disarmament, on Berlin, on every other source of friction—and his olive branch was accepted.

John Fitzgerald Kennedy was born in Brookline, a suburb of Boston, Massachusetts, on 29 May, 1917, grandson of an Irish immigrant who had left his old country during the mid-nineteenth-century potato famine and made a fortune in his new one. John Kennedy's father went on to make a bigger fortune, then instituted for each of his nine children a trust fund which would give each one on reaching maturity a million dollars. The oldest, Joseph Kennedy, Jr., would go into politics—that was the family plan—with the frank intention of reaching the ultimate goal of the Presidency of the United States. The rest of the family had clear-cut rôles; but for Joe, Junior, it could only be politics.

War intervened and young Joseph Kennedy was killed. The next brother, John, had distinguished himself in the Navy in many ways, the most notable being the occasion when his torpedo-boat was rammed by a Japanese destroyer in the Pacific Ocean off the Solomon Islands. He rallied his crew on a few pieces of wreckage and got them to safety, himself towing a badly wounded sailor for three miles through shark-infested water with the man's lifebelt strap gripped in his teeth.

With the war over, John Kennedy began to consider the political career which had been intended for his older brother. He had studied political science in England, under the famous Professor Laski at the London School of Economics. His father was American Ambassador to the United Kingdom before and during the first months of the Second World War; and had written a thesis about Britain's unpreparedness which was considered so remarkable that it was later published as a book under the title *Why England Slept*. In many ways John Kennedy was well equipped to enter the political arena. Then an old back injury, dating originally from school football in Massachusetts, much aggravated during his service in the American Navy, flared up, and for much of 1945 John was in hospital. He used the enforced leisure to write *Profiles in Courage*, studies of politicians and statesmen faced with agonizing decisions. He came out of hospital, had a short spell as a newspaper reporter, then entered politics and was elected Congressman for Massachusetts at the age of twenty-nine. With his father's enthusiastic support, financial as well as moral, he went on to become, at thirty-five, the junior U.S. Senator from the State. His own and his family's wealth and ambition, coupled with his Roman Catholic faith, hindered him as much as it helped.

Congress soon found that "Jack" Kennedy had a mind of his own. He firmly refused to belong to any faction within his own Democratic Party, he made every decision on its own merits, and the respect he gained resulted in his being returned as Senator in 1954, '56 and '58, with handsome majorities. In 1956 he ran for the Vice-Presidency, unsuccessfully, but made a mark for himself in national politics: he was still under forty. Now the Democratic Party began to consider him a possibility, a dark horse but possible, for the Presidential election of 1960. This hope brightened in November, 1958, when he was returned to the Senate by a record-breaking majority.

In July, 1960, Kennedy was nominated Democratic Presidential candidate with Senator Lyndon B. Johnson of Texas as his "running-mate", the candidate for the Vice-Presidency. At first, Johnson, an older, more experienced politician, refused to be second to the young Senator from Massachusetts; then he changed his mind. The decision was to have consequences not only for Senator Johnson but for the United States and the world.

The Republican candidate was Richard Nixon, Vice-President to Eisenhower. During the campaign Kennedy urged repeatedly that the choice lay between "contented" Republicans and "concerned"

Democrats; he urged voters not to be complacent about the country's future as it was developing under the Republicans, not only at home, but abroad. For the first time in a Presidential campaign there were nation-wide televised debates between the two candidates. These were an important factor in Kennedy's ultimate success; partly because he produced better arguments than his Republican opponent; partly because the broadcasts made an almost unknown Senator from Massachusetts as well known to the general public as the Vice-President.

There had never been a Roman Catholic President of the United States and, although Kennedy's religion was not a recognized issue between the candidates, he was repeatedly obliged to affirm his belief in the separation of Church and State, to assure voters that his faith, if he were elected, would have no effect on his duties. On 8 November, 1960 after a hotly contested election campaign, he defeated Nixon by a small margin; but as the University of Michigan Research Centre showed later, Kennedy's faith had cost him a million and a half votes. We may take it that on the real issues involved, he was elected by a very adequate majority.

President Kennedy's major government appointments, largely of intellectuals, who included Adlai Stevenson as Representative to the United Nations and Dean Rusk as Secretary of State, were well received at home and abroad. His choice of his brother, Robert Kennedy, as United States Attorney General was open to a certain amount of political sniping, suggestions of a "royal family", but this appointment was soon justified on its own merits.

His young and attractive wife, Jacqueline, whom he had married when he was junior Senator and she a cub reporter sent to interview him, won an immediate success as "First Lady" of the United States. White House entertainments ceased being "folksy" affairs and an invitation to dinner usually included a concert or a recital by an international artist. Jacqueline Kennedy made extensive changes to White House décor, exhibiting great taste and originality, and her televised tour of the building, showing what she was doing to it, was a success not only in America, but in many other countries.

The Kennedys had two young children who caught the imagination of the American public: Caroline, born in 1957 and therefore three years old when her father was inaugurated President, and John, Jr., the only child ever to be born to a President-elect, who arrived three weeks after his father's defeat of Nixon. Subsequently they lost a second son, born prematurely, a personal tragedy which was shared by the nation.

It is more than probable that John Kennedy would have offered himself for a second term, and probably that he would have been re-elected, to serve a total of eight years. Fate ruled otherwise and he served only thirty-four months, but they were momentous. Within three months of his inauguration in 1961, Cuba was invaded by a small band of nationals who opposed Dr Castro and his régime. The invaders landed at the Bay of Pigs counting on support from America and a rising within the island of Cuba. The rising did not take place and Castro's troops swiftly overcame the tiny force which landed. Kennedy, who had nothing do to with either the invasion or the expected rising, was castigated on the one hand for having made a mess of a legitimate "defence of democracy"; on the other for having been an "aggressor". At the same time the Russians sent a first astronaut into orbit, in April, 1961, a slap in the face for American technologists, who had been believed the finest in the world. This was followed by Kennedy's first face-to-face meeting with Khrushchev at Vienna, the "summit" meeting, which achieved nothing and left him, according to White House sources, "terribly terribly disheartened". In August, the East Germans defiantly built their wall across the middle of Berlin: the Americans felt themselves powerless to intervene.

In the light of all these setbacks Kennedy's resolute stand over the Cuban missile bases is seen to have been even bolder than it at first appeared.

At home, he pressed hard for a Civil Rights Bill which would guarantee equal status for the American Negro. By this he alienated the South which normally voted solidly Democrat, and it was partly with a view to setting this situation right that, in November, 1963, he set off on a tour of Southern States. His life had been threatened many times during his brief career (860 times during the first year in the White House) and there were renewed threats when it was announced that he would visit Dallas, Texas. However, his arrival at Dallas Airport on 22 November was a friendly affair with welcoming crowds and a band. After inspecting a guard of honour, he and his wife prepared to drive with Governor Connally into the city centre. Theirs was the first car in a twelve-car "motorcade".

As the procession drove slowly down Dallas's main street, three shots were heard. There were screams; a Secret Service man ran forward from his car and leapt on to that of the President. John Kennedy had been hit, no one knew how badly. The driver of the Presidential car broke convoy and roared through the centre of Dallas towards the hospital, three miles off.

The President's head was cradled in his wife's lap his blood staining her dress. He had been hit by two bullets; the third had hit Governor Connally though his injury was not serious. The President's wounds were mortal. Even before the nation had quite realized the shock of Kennedy's death, Lyndon B. Johnson, who had been travelling two cars behind the Kennedys in the procession, was sworn in as 36th President of the United States.

Shortly afterwards a suspect Lee Harvey Oswald was arrested: he was seen leaving the building from which the shots had been fired and had recently purchased a rifle similar to that found by the window. He, however, was murdered by a member of the public, while under escort, so that no formal presentation of the evidence against him could be made.

In an unprecedented display of genuine sorrow, Heads of State, or their representatives, from all the major countries of the world flew to Washington for the funeral, joining the Kennedy family and the thousands who knelt in the street in tribute to the youngest elected President the United States of America had had.

But tragedy was not at an end for the Kennedy family. Just as John Kennedy had taken over the political career intended by his older brother Joseph, his younger brother Robert ended speculation by putting himself into the race for Democratic nomination for the Presidency in March, 1968. His political career had naturally been overshadowed by that of his brother, but it had been successful, taking him to United States Attorney-General and then Senator. On 5 June, 1968, he was making a speech celebrating his victory in the California primary election, leading towards Democratic nomination, when he was shot, in the Ambassador Hotel in Los Angeles.

Robert Kennedy died a day later. His murderer was an Arab, originally from Jerusalem, Sirhan Sirhan, who claimed "I did it for my country", because Kennedy had expressed his support for Israel. Sirhan was convicted, sentenced to death, but never executed.

There was one brother left to step into the Kennedy shoes. Edward Kennedy was already in politics and he, too, soon became Senator.

Edmund Hillary
1919-

Even the men who climb mountains cannot explain to their own or anyone else's entire satisfaction, why they accept the hardships and the risks of death in which their activities always involve them, when what they are doing has no useful end-product.

In fact, it is personal courage which provokes climbers to accept the challenge which the great mountains of the world, from Mont Blanc to Everest, evince; and anything which helps in any way to develop this characteristic, which is among the greatest of all human qualities, cannot be said to be useless. For not only the individual benefits; by his example the rest of mankind is fortified.

The snow-capped summit of Everest is, therefore, not merely a beauty and a wonder of nature. By its challenge to the élite of mountaineers it has been a source of inspiration to many who have never seen a mountain.

The men who strove over the years to conquer it and those who eventually succeeded—Sir Edmund Hillary and Sherpa Tenzing—did more than climb the most difficult mountain in the world. They showed their fellows that in effect there are no limits to human courage and endurance.

On 2 June, 1953, the eyes of the world were turned on London, for there on this day was to be crowned, with all the ancient splendour of long tradition, the young Queen Elizabeth II of Great Britain. For several days, London had been filling up with visitors from all over the world who had come to witness the most splendid pageantry which can be seen anywhere in the twentieth century. Since the afternoon of the day before, crowds had been assembling on the route which the processions would take; good-humoured crowds who sang and and chatted and dozed the night away on the pavements and in the parks in the drizzling rain.

Though none of them knew it yet, shortly before midnight a small red despatch-box had been delivered to Her Majesty. It contained one short document, but that document held the news of one of the most exciting achievements performed by man in this age of nuclear arms and rockets. Yet it had nothing to do with science, nor with war; it belonged exclusively to human activity.

After the failure of five expeditions, all of which had caused loss of life, the summit of Mount Everest, the world's highest mountain, had been reached—and by a citizen of the British Commonwealth, a New Zealander, Edmund Hillary, with whom had been the Sherpa leader, Tenzing.

No more exciting gift could have been offered to Sovereign or people on this great day; and when the news was broadcast in the early hours of Coronation Day it was greeted with cheering as loud as that which was later to greet the young Queen as she passed by.

Edmund Hillary had been born in 1919 on a bee-farm on the North Island, New Zealand, not far from the city of Auckland. At the week-ends and during the holidays from Auckland Grammar School, he helped his father and his brother Rex to tend the bees. By the age of sixteen, he had been no farther afield than Auckland, and had seen no mountain.

In his sixteenth year, 1935, the school had arranged a skiing party to Mount Ruapehu, the 9,000-foot volcano in the centre of the North Island, and Hillary had joined the expedition. For ten days the boys skied on the lower slopes of Ruapehu, and Hillary returned home full of enthusiasm for the snow and the cold and the sport. Despite his enthusiasm, however, he returned to the mountains at very infrequent intervals, and it was not until he was twenty that he made his first climb, on Mount Cook, the 12,000-foot-high mountain in the South Island. By this time, he had left school, spent two years at the university, and joined his father and brother as a partner in the bee-farm.

He had not gone to Mount Cook with the idea of climbing it. For the first two days of their visit, he and his companion had been content to scramble up towards the snow-line and back again. One evening, as he was sitting in the hotel lounge at the foot of the mountain, two men entered, and a moment or two later someone near him muttered that they had just climbed to the summit of Mount Cook. As he watched the men, and saw the quiet excitement of their achievement reflected in their faces and their voices, he decided on the spur of the moment that next day he would go out and follow their example. So, next morning, hiring a guide, he and his friend started off on their first mountaineering expedition—and reached the top of Mount Cook. From this time, Hillary spent two holidays every year climbing mountains all over New Zealand.

When the Second World War broke out, he joined the R.N.Z. Air Force, and on his posting to a Catalina Squadron stationed at New Plymouth, not far from the foot of Mount Egmont, he made the summit of this mountain a place of weekly pilgrimage. In his leisure moments, Hillary, who had become completely enslaved by the sport, read all he could about mountains and mountaineering. Already he was falling under the spell of Everest.

In his practical exercise of his sport he was taught much by the ace of New Zealand climbers, Harry Ayres, with whom he climbed a number of the higher and most difficult mountains and in 1948, with Ayres, he became the first to reach the South Ridge of Mount Cook, a particularly steep and difficult climb, which has been repeated only four times since.

His most frequent companion on his climbing expeditions was another enthusiast, George Lowe. When they were not climbing mountains, they dreamed and talked of Everest, and from dreams came the decision to work for the organization of a New Zealand Everest expedition, and initial plans were laid.

In 1950, Hillary came to England to meet and climb with English mountaineers in order to gain more experience and, at the same time, to obtain information about the equipment which would be needed on a Himalayan expedition. On his arrival, however, he discovered that almost all the leading British climbers were at that moment disporting themselves in the European Alps. So with two New Zealand friends, he hurried to Austria, where, after the New Zealand peaks, he found the mountains too easy. He then moved on to Switzerland, and found the Alps there not much more difficult. In five days he climbed the peaks of five mountains over 12,000 feet high.

While he was in Switzerland, he received a letter from George Lowe, telling him that another group of New Zealand climbers were planning an Everest expedition, and that he and Hillary had been invited to join them. Hillary agreed, but on his return to New Zealand, found that the group were running into difficulties with finance and in obtaining permission from the Nepalese authorities for the expedition. In the face of these difficulties, many members of the group withdrew. Soon only Hillary, Lowe and two others remained.

Weeks went by, and they were making little headway, when news reached them that a British reconnaissance expedition was going to the Himalayas in the near future. This seemed to put paid to their plans for an all-New Zealand expedition, since they appreciated that the Nepalese authorities would not give permission to two expeditions at the same time.

While they were still nursing their disappointment a cable reached them with exciting news. Eric Shipton, already famous as an Everest climber, and who was leading the reconnaissance expedition, had heard of their plans. He invited two of them to join his expedition. Since there were four of them, they eventually decided to draw lots, and the two lucky men were Hillary and Earle Riddiford. So on 28 August, 1951, these two set out to join Shipton in Jogbani.

There had been five previous Everest expeditions—in 1922, 1924, 1933, 1936, and 1938—all of them British. On the 1924 expedition the climbers had reached 26,800 feet, and then two of them—A. C. Irvine and Leigh Mallory—set off to scale the remaining 2,202 feet. Both men disappeared. On the 1933 expedition, a height of 28,100 feet was reached, but the attempt on the summit had to be abandoned. The 1936 and 1938 expeditions also had to abandon their attempts when still some way from the summit.

As a result of Shipton's reconnaissance in 1951, tentative plans were made by the Royal Geographical Society and the Alpine Club to mount a full-scale expedition in 1953. The excitement which this news caused among the climbers was somewhat reduced, however, when it was learned that an extremely well-mounted Swiss expedition was to make an attempt in 1952. If the Swiss succeeded, there would be little point, if any, in the British plan being developed.

The Swiss failed, and the British expedition became a certainty. To his great delight, Hillary and George Lowe were invited by Shipton to join a training party in the late summer of 1952, in preparation for the grand attempt in the following year.

Again there was to be a period of depression. The Swiss announced plans for a second expedition, and not until this, too, failed did the British party go all out on their plans.

The 1953 expedition was led by John Hunt, and the climbers were George Band, Michael Westmacott, Thomas Bourdillon, George Lowe, Evans and Hillary, the rest of the party comprising scientists, doctors, experts in the use of oxygen equipment, Sherpas and porters. The equipment was the very latest that had been devised. All went well up to the setting up of Camp 4, at about 26,000 feet. From there, Hunt and a Sherpa transported supplies to 27,350 feet, above the South Col, and from here the final assualt was to be attempted.

Hunt had chosen Evans and Bourdillon to make the first attempt, Hillary and the Sherpa Tenzing to make the second assault if the first failed. On 24 May, Evans and Bourdillon set out. At half-past three in the afternoon, they came staggering back into camp, covered from head to foot in ice, at the end of their strength and with the sad news that they had failed.

The weather had taken a turn for the worse, and Hunt decided that the second assault should not be made until it had improved. Four days went by before this happened, and on the morning of 28 May, 1953, Hillary and Tenzing, preceded by Lowe, Gregory and a Sherpa, set off, the last three to carry supplies to 28,000 feet from where Hillary and Tenzing were to make the attempt on the last 1,002 feet to the summit.

At 28,000 feet they camped for the night. The wind had dropped. and the next morning dawned sunny and calm. After a breakfast of sardines on biscuits and sweet hot lemon water, Hillary and Tenzing set off.

By nine o'clock the two men were on the south summit, with a few hundred feet still to go. Those few hundred feet were the steepest of all and covered with ice.

After a short rest, during which Hillary worked out the route which seemed to him to give the greatest safety, they went on. Roped together, they took it in turns to cut steps in the ice. Once ice blocked the exhaust tube of Tenzing's oxygen bottle, but Hillary spotted it in time and cleared it before the Sherpa passed out.

After some progress, they found their way blocked by a rock cliff about forty feet high. It had no climbing holds and would have to be skirted. To do so on the west side would mean descending a hundred feet or more. In their state of weariness, they could not afford to do this. The east route was a vertical split between the cliff and a cornice leaning out over the valley. The cornice was already beginning to break away from the cliff and might at any time go crashing down into the valley ten thousand feet below: but there was no other way. Slowly, Hillary leading, they made their way to the top of the split. Still the summit was hidden by what seemed an endless procession of ice-humps. They thought they would never come to the end of them; but presently their path was no longer going up but sloping away, and they knew they had done it! They were on the summit!

They stayed on the summit a quarter of an hour, and then began the climb down.

Describing his sensations during these moments, Hillary has said:

"My first sensation was one of relief. But mixed with the relief was a vague sensation of astonishment that I should have been the lucky one to attain the ambition of so many brave and determined climbers."

In her Coronation Honours List, the Queen included Hillary. Hunt and Tenzing, honouring the first two with knighthoods.

When the expedition returned to England, Sir Edmund spent several weeks lecturing, and then returned to New Zealand, where he married Miss Louise Rose. The following day he set off on another lecture tour, that took him and his bride to almost every country in the world. Later in the year he returned to Nepal to lead the New Zealand Barun Expedition. He then settled down to write accounts of his various experiences; but not for long.

In 1953, Dr Vivian Fuchs, the geologist and explorer, already well known for his work in Greenland, conceived the idea of organizing an expedition to make a crossing of the Antarctic continent on foot, which had never yet been achieved. He invited Hillary to join him, and Hillary accepted.

Two years were to pass before the expedition was ready to set off, and in December, 1956, sailed from New Zealand, in the *Endeavour*, seen off by the Duke of Edinburgh. The expedition was a great success, but unhappily it was somewhat marred by a disagreement between Fuchs and Hillary over the plan of campaign for the crossing. Sharp words may have been spoken on both sides, but it was merely a difference of opinion which might never have reached the public had the Press not got wind of it and blown it up into "a serious row".

"Conquistadors of the Useless" someone has recently dubbed mountaineers. Perhaps it may seem to be a true description at first sight, but anyone who has read the story of Sir Edmund Hillary's single-mindedness, of his courage and of his utter disregard of danger cannot fail to be impressed by the quality of his character. In the final ascent to the summit of Everest he displayed man's supremacy over nature, and in a world where science is now the idol most generally worshipped it will not come amiss to remind oneself of men like Hillary, who, by their actions enhance the qualities of the spirit.

MEN IN SPACE

Yuri Alekseyevitch Gagarin
1934-1968

John Herschel Glenn, Jr.   Neil A. Armstrong
1921-   1930-

ALL over the world, men were listening. Scientists from Vladivostok to Jodrell Bank were tracking and listening for signals from a body in space which was of interest both to science and to the man in the street. The body with which they hoped to establish contact was a perfectly normal human being, floating, if not serenely, at least calmly, outside the earth's atmosphere, a man in space.

Fifteen minutes after the astronaut had begun his journey into the unknown, the listeners heard words in Russian, faint but intelligible, "Flight proceeding normally. *Kharasho, kharasho*—I am well—"

The message came from somewhere over South America, a message from a young man who, a quarter of an hour earlier, had been lying down in Eastern Russia, in the nose of a rocket waiting to be propelled beyond reach of gravity, of human aid. He left Russia in the early morning of 12 April: when his words were heard on the radio he was above Argentina, on the late evening of 11 April.

An hour and forty-eight minutes after he had been thrown into space, Yuri Gagarin landed at a prearranged site in the Soviet Union. In Moscow the time was 10.55 a.m.—the date, 12 April, 1961. The first man in space (the first man, at least, to be put into orbit around the earth and brought back alive)—was in good health and good spirits. He was fine, it had all been wonderful fun. "One's legs, one's arms, they weigh nothing. Objects just float in the cabin, and I didn't just sit in my chair, I hung in space—"

The man who had just accomplished this feat on behalf of the Soviet Union was round-faced, snub-nosed, five feet two inches, smiling, blue-eyed and aged twenty-seven.

Ten months after Gagarin's flight, on 20 February, 1962, an American, John Glenn, followed that single orbit with three. In between had come the Russian Titov with his seventeen and a half orbits in August, 1961. But it is with the first men in orbit from each of these two Powers that we are concerned in this article—to compare, as best one can, their backgrounds and their achievement.

We know little of Gagarin's last hours before blast off, but we do know that in John Glenn's case, the delay, the postponements, of the flight were enough to have shattered confidence in a lesser man. He had been chosen in April, 1959, as one of the seven astronauts-in-training for the United States, had undergone rigorous training—as had Gagarin—and had been disappointed at being selected Number 3 in the launching series. His colleagues Alan Shepard and Virgil Grissom made sub-orbital flights into space in May and July, 1961, and John Glenn was not named to attempt orbital flight until November that year. The flight was scheduled for 20 December: it was postponed no fewer than ten times over a period of months as weather conditions and technical hitches altered plans. On several occasions Glenn lay strapped into his capsule for hours before learning the launch had been cancelled. Eventually—three hours after he had been closed into his capsule on 20 February, seven hours after he had been woken—he was blasted off. Twelve hours, almost to the minute, after he had started breakfast, he was back on earth, having circled it three times, seen three sunsets, three dawns.

John Glenn's capsule, to the television audience which was watching, a tiny pimple on the nose of the huge Atlas-D rocket, was blasted into space at 09.47 a.m. At first, through clouds of smoke and vapour, it seemed not to be moving, merely to be wobbling precariously on its launch pad. Its name *Friendship 7*, was clearly visible, painted in large letters round the side. Then slowly, that name, centre of a million television screens, wobbled away to the top-right-hand corner, obscured by clouds of what seemed steam. There was a mounting whine from the rocket and it began to crawl into a clear blue sky. Its speed rose as it cleared the tower, but still, to viewers, it seemed too slow to be true, it was like some slow-motion film. Then it moved faster, rose rapidly and disappeared. Moments later it was visible again, a white-hot flare in the sky, growing smaller and fainter.

At an altitude of a hundred miles, an electrical mechanism tilted Glenn's rocket and capsule, separated them so the capsule was free to travel alone on its orbit of the earth. From now on, Glenn was in continuous contact with the ground, reporting what he saw, how he felt, how *Friendship* 7 was behaving. (The number 7 had been adopted by all seven astronauts chosen for training: already Shepard and Grissom had done their sub-orbital flights in *Freedom* 7 and *Liberty Bell* 7.) Glenn's flight lasted four hours fifty-six minutes, covered 81,000 miles at altitudes between ninety-nine and a hundred and sixty-two miles. It ended at 2.43 p.m. when *Friendship* 7 dropped into the ocean off Puerto Rico and was picked up by a destroyer.

The trip had been successful. Two things went wrong and were rectified: the hydrogen peroxide jets for controlling the capsule's balance behaved erratically and Glenn took over manual control to let *Friendship* 7 complete its third and final orbit; and a faulty mechanism signalled that the heat shield, designed to prevent the capsule overheating during its descent into the earth's atmosphere, had become detached. In reality the descent worked smoothly.

The fact that an American had achieved orbital flight was of immense importance to American (and indeed, Western) morale, which had suffered since the launching of the first, unmanned Russian satellite in 1957. It seems likely that though the Russian capsules were heavier, their rockets more powerful, the American control and reporting devices on *Friendship* 7 were considerably more sophisticated. Certainly the Russians had not used research satellites on the lines of those which the United States began to put into orbit; immensely complicated bundles of equipment varying in size and shape from a football to a sailing boat, with functions as various as the measurement of cosmic radiation, function as "communications satellites" designed to relay television signals around the earth and as means of obtaining data to assist in the forecasting of weather.

Like Gagarin, Glenn was fêted on his return to earth. He spent two days of examination and rest in the Bahamas, near where he had "ditched", then joined his wife Anna and their two children in Florida. From here he was taken in procession to Cape Canaveral (now called Cape Kennedy, in honour of the late President) where he was greeted by the President himself before being sent on to Washington and New York for parades in his honour.

In a variety of ways, the two astronauts were very different. Perhaps the most notable was the disparity in their ages: John Glenn was forty when he went into orbit; Yuri Gagarin twenty-seven. John Glenn was born in an American town, surrounded by the technology of the twentieth century: Gagarin was born in a remote Russian village, with nothing as far as the eye could see but rolling fields of grain. Both had manifested an intention to fly at an early age, had managed to join the Services and fly there, but when Glenn was serving as a wartime fighter pilot in the Pacific, earning his first and second Distinguished Service Crosses, his Russian rival was a ten-year-old refugee from the invading German armies, hiding with his mother in the hinterland of Russia, while his father fought the Germans. After the war Yuri was eleven before he got back to school; developed a marked interest in technology, study of which could be pursued only at a technical school. The nearest and best for his purpose was in Lyubertsy, the industrial suburb of Moscow, and here, to Yuri's delight, there was a large aircraft factory. Day after day, as he sat by his desk or worked in the laboratories, he could see through the window new aircraft being wheeled from their hangars, taxied to the runways, flown off by test pilots. Soon his ambition was to become a test pilot; these were the men he admired, wanted to emulate—but there were plenty of other students with the same idea and only a very limited number of vacancies. Yuri took a job as moulder of engine parts in a factory, but continued his studies at night and before long won a vacancy to the Industrial College of Saratov. Here, to his delight, there was an aerodrome and a flying club. He joined, found he had a real aptitude and resolved that this would in future be his life's work. In 1955, when he was twenty-one, he enrolled as student pilot in the Air Force Training Centre at Orenburg. The course lasted two years, he passed out with the highest honours, and was accepted as pilot in the Russian Air Force. Towards the end of his training he met and married a young medical student, Valentina Ivanovna.

John Glenn was born in Cambridge, Ohio, on 18 July, 1921, the son of a railwayman who went on to become the owner of a motor business. He was brought up a few miles away in New Concord, where he was an honour student in high school and a leading member of the football, basketball and tennis teams. Like Gagarin, he had soon wanted to fly, and in 1942, at the age of twenty-one, he was able to take a Naval course in flying for civilians. He went on, in wartime, to join the United States Marines with a temporary, wartime, commission.

During the war he served in the Pacific, was awarded his first two D.S.C.s (there have been more since), was promoted to Captain and accepted for the regular Marine Corps, which he entered in March, 1946. After another spell abroad, including service in Korea, he became a flying instructor in Texas, thence a test pilot. He made the first nonstop supersonic flight scross the United States in 1957, and in April, 1959, a few days after his promotion to Lieutenant Colonel, was selected from over a hundred volunteers to become one of the seven astronauts for training under "Project Mercury". From that time he and the other six U.S. astronauts were (like Gagarin) exposed to extremes of heat and cold, strong forces of gravity, complete weightlessness, and the various other conditions it was anticipated they would meet in space. They learned and practised to survive in both desert and water; they studied astronomy, astronautics, meteorology, aviation biology and geography.

These, then, were the first men in space. Much has happened since their exploits, though even with men landing on the moon and, in 1971, American and Russian spacecraft studying Mars, the forward strides may not have been much greater than those of Glenn and Gagarin. Future space research is more likely to involve the construction of space stations, and for this work the problems of blast-off, weightlessness and re-entry are paramount, as they were for the first astronauts.

Nevertheless, Commander Neil A. Armstrong's arrival on the moon was one of the most thrilling events in history. His mission, which has been repeated and improved on since, was more sophisticated than the first flights in space. He and "Buzz" Aldrin landed on the lunar surface in their small "lunar module" *Eagle*, which detached itself from the larger "command module", *Columbia*, blasted from Cape Kennedy. The 38-year-old Armstrong climbed down *Eagle*'s ladder and was on the moon at 0256 GMT 21 July, 1969. Minutes later, he and Aldrin were standing on the lunar surface talking by telephone with the President of the United States.

While this went on, Michael Collins continued orbiting the moon in *Columbia* before his colleagues re-entered their lunar module, blasted it from the lunar surface and with perfect precision joined him to go back to earth.

Armstrong, like Glenn, was born in Ohio, and like him is a tall man, very unlike the diminutive Gagarin. He flew with great distinction in the U.S. Navy before joining the National Aeronautics and Space Administration. Both Glenn and Armstrong have now left NASA, and while remaining as consultants to it have settled into civilian life, Glenn into commerce, Armstrong as Professor of Engineering at the University of Cincinnati.

The first man in space did not live to see men on the moon. A year before that event, Yuri Gagarin crashed his jet trainer, on 27 March, 1968, and was killed, with Colonel Seryogin who was flying with him. After a state funeral procession watched by half a million Russians, their bodies were immured in the Kremlin wall.

Index